The Marsco Sustainability Project

Book Three of

The Marsco Saga

By James A. Zarzana

ISBN-13: 978-0-578-57354-0

Library of Congress Control Number: 2019914108

For the SMSU Lunch Bunch—all the usual suspects—
with gratitude for your steadfast support.
And in special remembrance of Don Plefka, a devoted reader.

ACKNOWLEDGEMENTS AND THANKS

Many thanks to the members of the English Program at Southwest Minnesota State University. Thanks to Dr. Paul Derwent of the Fermi Lab for his scientific assistance. With appreciation to the late Walt Collins, *emeritus* editor of *Notre Dame Magazine*, who many years ago told me, "Go ahead—write a sci-fi series." To Dr. Vincent LaPorte, MD, who provided valuable medical information. Also, thanks to Bruce and Shannen Louwagie for information about dairy husbandry and farming. Once again, I offer my appreciation to Cathy Bernardy Jones, my editor, for her continuing and outstanding work. Finally, to all those who have helped me persevere, my deepest gratitude.

AUTHOR'S NOTE AND DISCLAIMER

This work is entirely a piece of fiction. "Marsco" is a completely invented entity, created solely for the purposes of this fictional work. It is not to be mistaken for any past or currently existing corporation or business. Any similarity of name or of characteristics to existing corporations or businesses in the use of the name "Marsco" is purely coincidental. Similarly, all characters in this work, except known historical figures, are fictional and created solely by the author.

The Six Accords Notes and Fifty-Year Timeline, followed by a glossary of terms specific to Book III, may be found at the end of this novel. Terms related to the Marsco world are provided in a glossary at the end of Book I and Book II of *The Marsco Saga*.

The Marsco Sustainability Project

The only hope, or else despair
Lies in the choice of pyre or pyre—
To be redeemed from fire by fire.
—T. S. Eliot, "Little Gidding"

———— • ————

"I have one great fear in my heart,
that one day when they are turned to loving,
they will find that we are turned to hating."
—Alan Paton, *Cry, the Beloved Country*

———— • ————

I am compelled to fear that science
will be used to promote the power of dominant groups,
rather than to make men happy.
—Bertrand Russell, 1924

———— • ————

Marsco sustainability shall renew all.
—Marsco Internal Medical Research Report #216 from Doctor Johns, 2151

PROLOGUE

(On the *Sirius Odyssey II* beyond the Oort Cloud, 2124)

This must be what the Piazzi *looked like*, Mei-Ling Shanghai thought as she viewed the digital recording for the fifth time. Tessa and Zot sat on each side of the pilot. Walter Miller, the fourth member of the crew, remained in cryo. Zot had checked his father-in-law, making sure he was comfortable and safely iced. No need to wake him, especially because the three members of the crew were all going back under soon. Their *Sirius* was running perfectly.

On a projection screen, a two-minute replay condensed the last forty-eight hours of Dr. Martin Herriff on board the escaping ship. The old engineer entered a cargo bay that he'd converted into his quarters for this event. His movements were slow, heavy. He coughed, clearly having trouble breathing. The screen displayed his last hours from more than twenty-two years before Shanghai repeatedly viewed them.

The pilot hadn't been awake at the time of Herriff's final recording. She was motionless, in cryogenic stasis, as were Miller, Tessa, and Zot. Near his end, the old engineer was the sole crewmember awake. And clearly, he knew he was dying. In the cargo bay, he laid down on a cot, drew up his blankets, adjusted an oxygen mask over his nose, and fell asleep. *Must have been doing that ritual for months*, Shanghai conjectured, *anticipating his natural end.*

The monitors at the side of Herriff's bay glowed green; Zot pointed that out the first time they viewed this scene. In the sped-up action of the recording, next to the reclining Herriff, over a ten-second interval, that set of green monitors went to amber then to red, as the last of Herriff's life slipped away. After twenty more seconds of no movement in the bay by the reclining figure, the system shut itself down. The recording had run for less than a minute, but the timeframe was over twenty-four hours. The engineer was clearly dead. And the computer knew Herriff was gone.

At that point, the bay doors opened to space, and the old engineer's remains—his bunk and blanket, everything not locked down in the cargo area—were sucked into space.

This was the part of the recording that reminded Shanghai of the *Piazzi*. While she had been under hibernation on that Marsco Asteroid Service shuttle so many years ago, the passenger module had ruptured and sucked the hiberman, Jamie Maissey, into space. Back then, the iceman was awake and trying to save a family of iced passengers. They were all alive when pulled into space. Herriff was dead. So the circumstances weren't really all that alike. Maissey and that family had been murdered; Shanghai was convinced of that. Herriff went naturally before space would have him.

"He'd planned it that way," Zot explained during their repeated viewing of Herriff's last hours. "Once dead, his remains would be taken into space. That's why he slept in the bay for months."

"Godspeed, Uncle Martin," Tessa whispered.

Four days before, as preprogrammed, Zot had been brought out of cryo after twenty-five years. He was to come out of ice every quarter century to check all systems, especially his iced charges, then return to his own suspended animation. On his first routine reawakening, he found Herriff gone and two recordings waiting for him, this one and a second to the crew.

The three awake crewmembers didn't need to watch the first recording a sixth time. It wouldn't change. Miller would have to watch later; best to keep him safely iced, Zot explained. Herriff had passed, and the preset controls sucked him into space to save the iced crew the trouble of finding his decomposing remains when they awoke. *Thoughtful as always*, the pilot noted of the engineer who, like Walter Miller, had put so much trust in her.

Apparently, however, in the end he hadn't put so much trust in her guidance system. Before his death but while he was of sound mind—or so the second recording to the entire crew stated—he had reprogramed their course.

"You've confirmed everything?" Tessa asked.

"Yes," Shanghai replied. "I've rechecked Herriff's calculations and followed his logic. He was spot-on."

"So, we're heading—"

"Back to Earth. No doubt."

"ETA?"

"Here's the hitch. The computer gives a spread of several months depending on how much speed we pick up by flyby. We'll fling around two gas giants once back in our solar system. The main computer puts us home sometime between early summer and mid-autumn of 2154. That's the best I can give you at the moment."

"Pretty much thirty more years and we're home," Tessa remarked.

"Affirmative. Within a five- or six-month spread." The pilot paused. "About fifty-five years after our initial escape."

"Any chance of reversing Herriff's alterations?" Zot asked.

"Zero to none," Shanghai replied. "We're mostly reoriented toward Earth at this point anyway."

The three sat silently for several minutes, taking in the fact that their escape was lost.

"Earth," Tessa finally ventured. "Marsco. Mid-twenty-second century. What's that going to be like?"

"Well, won't be that long 'til we know," Zot assured the two women.

"Another thirty years. Good chunk of a lifetime," the pilot added.

"But on ice," Zot reminded them. "We'll all have to go back under. Won't seem that long."

Tessa and Shanghai made sure they had some time alone before they went back into cryo for what would be the last time before the *Sirius*'s new course brought them well into their own solar system. Each woman had something to ask the other.

"At the risk of sounding like a tween," the pilot confided, "what do you think Walter thinks of me?"

Tessa wished she hadn't asked. Gingerly, she began, "You know, he loved Bethany, my mother, deeply. They were a pair. And, I've seen him with other women, like Allison, whom he admired and worked with but never felt anything," she hesitated, "anything—"

"*Romantic*. I get it. That's hardly encouraging if he only thinks of me like that, as a colleague."

"It's more than that, really." Tessa once more danced around her answer.

"A *daughter*, right? Is that your word?"

"Well, speaking as his only child, yes, but really, it's not so terrible after all."

"Unless, well, one of us wants more. I do… I do love him, Tes." Shanghai didn't tear up or go on in a hurt way, she just frankly admitted how she felt, deeply.

Tessa laid her hand around the woman's shoulder as a sister might.

Shanghai looked out a view panel. Amid the range of stars by the thousands, around one star—the Sun—their home orbited. What awaited them there? What was it going to be like arriving back after fifty-five years away? What had happened during their hiatus? She'd be home soon enough to find out. With or without Walter, she'd be home.

Before their talk, the engineer had been sick once more. She cleaned up after each episode over the past five days while the crew was awake; no one had much privacy. The pilot and Zot had to know Tessa was often sick.

"Mei-Ling, you don't have to give away anything," the engineer began tentatively. They both knew the pilot had a hidden life, a pre-Von-Braun-Center life. She needn't go there. "But, as a shuttle pilot, when you hibered—you must have often—did you know any woman, any passenger or crewmember, who went under while pregnant?"

"Knew of a few, and yes, icemen read you the riot act about being pregnant and not reporting it. But actually, mother and child were quite safe. Especially with a top iceman."

"That would be Zot, certainly."

"But, no one asks *that* question," the pilot smiled, "without some suspicion." She noticed how drawn Tessa looked, tired even though she seemed to sleep a good deal these past few days. And her intermittent vomiting; that had Zot and Shanghai worried. Some type of hibersickness, Zot'd imagined. Shanghai had suspected this—a woman would—but Tessa's husband was too preoccupied to.

"Are you sure?"

14

"I can't be. Not definitely. No way to check. Who thought to bring anything like a test kit for *that* on an interstellar escape?"

Shanghai reached out to hug Tessa. "If Walter treats me like a daughter, then we're sisters, right?"

Tessa began sobbing quietly. "I know I'm not myself. I bark at Zot, then coo to him. I want to tell him, but I'm so afraid he'll be furious or he'll do something while I'm iced, thinking I'd be better without a stowaway."

"My God, Tes, that's total asinine bullshit. He loves you. He'd never do anything like that. Never hurt his own child or you. When do you plan to tell him?"

"Not sure. I'm afraid he won't let me ice if I do." She whimpered, uncharacteristic of her usual confident self, "And then he'll ice and leave me awake. And I'll be old when he reawakens and I'll have this twenty-something stranger, his child—"

"Well, let's see, vomiting, sleeping beyond normal parameters, and raging hormones making you utter completely irrational statements. Don't think we need a medical test, do we?"

As Tessa wept, Mei-Ling rocked her. "Tes, I promise, you'll be fine. It's natural. You'll be fine." The two suffering women held each other, their black and auburn hair tumbling down over their shoulders. Shanghai whispered, "Zot'll be beside himself with joy. And, he's the tops. You'll be fine under his ice, the both of you, I promise."

ONE

THE REGENERATION OF CHESNEY

(Marsco's Seattle, April 2153)

"**S**uch a beautiful day," the vice-chair of the Marsco board, Raymond Jon Chesney, told his attending medical staff as soon as they released him from their care. "I'll take a scooter to my Bunker," he insisted. With that, he was off on a commandeered upright two-wheeler with only a small entourage of six guards trailing behind. The doctors, nurses, and med technicians who'd spent two months treating him watched the VC zip away.

Unlike the past several years when he had looked sickly and pallid, Chesney appeared robust in the morning light. His blue eyes shone; the redness and droopiness under them was totally gone. He had a wholesome tone in his cheeks. Having been sequestered in the med center for cutting-edge treatments, this astonishing renewed vigor to Chesney's movements shouldn't have surprised anyone. He felt years younger, no doubt.

Moving along a tree-lined walkway at the head of his guards, the VC took deep breaths that filled his newly strong chest. Between gulps of fresh air, he ran his right hand up over his high forehead until he reached the hairline, then brushed his thinning, gray hair aside.

His thin hair made his head seem all the smaller, as though set on the wrong set of shoulders. Since his early teens fifty-plus years ago, he had been embarrassed by the size of his head. Today, he merely shrugged. *Perhaps that too can be altered*, he concluded, *but even so, continuing on indefinitely as the second most powerful associate in Marsco, going on forever as such, was worth a few drawbacks in my appearance.*

Marsco's main medical center stood adjacent to the sprawling Academy and the Marsco Institute of Technology. In turn, east of these two campuses lay a complex of offices set amid the remnants of a former nature center whose pines and scrubby dunes screened the most surreptitious aspects of Marsco. Chesney gained speed on his zipping trip as he crossed the open and public parts of the campuses, heading toward what seemed to be the emptiest space around.

"Good morning, good morning," the vice-chair called to the first associates he scattered near the Academy. The startled pedestrians had to jump off the walkway to let his standup scooter past without collision.

"Sixty-seven and inexplicably acting like a kid again," Lieutenant Colonel Devon Chavez-Sherman noted half aloud but only to himself as he stepped aside to let the dignitary and his entourage whiz by. Like most of the Marsco world, the Academy prof recognized the VC immediately. "Well, if the rumors are true, he has a new heart. Explains a great deal," the officer added under his breath.

Behind the vice-chair, the phalanx of Security bodyguards followed. None were ahead; the VC was in the lead, always. The six guards stood as straight and tall as possible on their own gliding machines, each wearing a twentieth century-style dark grey suit, almost a uniform among twenty-second-century associates, with dark glasses to block any evidence of their darting, probing eyes.

Like the very heart of Marsco itself, Chesney was circumspect. Had he just walked down to old Pike's for a cup of coffee—and not for heart treatment—he wouldn't have said where he'd been. And coming from the wing of the med center expressly reserved for Marsco's elite made it absolutely clear that Chesney was not about to disclose where he had been in the last twenty-four hours or days or weeks—let alone two months. He smirked with the thought that his whereabouts were so private. Even though he'd been ministered to at the med center near where he tirelessly worked, no one knew where he'd been or why. Hidden in plain sight. He liked that.

"Good morning, beautiful day, what?" Chesney called to a collection of pedestrians scurrying across the upper Marsco campus that sunny April morning. Even a few sids were among these students and professors traversing campus.

During the past week, a freak storm had driven sheets of rain across quads and greenswards, leaving limbs down and large pools of standing water. But today was absolutely perfect. The sun and light breeze. Fresh verdant lawns. What a day to realize how magnificent it was to be alive, to feel young again, to dash about without a care in the solar system. Not a branch, not a leaf, not a blade of grass was out of place this morning. Chesney and Marsco liked it that way.

The rejuvenated VC breathed in deeply, his strong heart pounding. Previously, regeneration treatments had regrown his heart's weakened tissues, renewed them into a new, vigorous organ. But these past two months, he was in the hands of Doctor Johns. Just as the campus had weathered an unusual lashing storm, so too had he come through his darkest times via a routine procedure—regeneration—and then an experimental procedure administered by Johns. But now, with Marsco medical science enabling all his renewed, vibrant life, his time ahead was composed of continuous, unbroken sunny days.

The vice-chair came upon gaggles of associates so quickly that few had a good look at him. Those who did swore he was smiling or at least wearing something approaching a real, happy smile, that showed something like a promise of renewed joy for life, probably brought on by an imminent opportunity to squelch hapless opponents.

Chesney *smiling*. Even with all the weight of being second in command to the world's largest power during its most significant transition, the associates jumping out of the way didn't know what to think. Chesney with a smile? Had the VC a reason to smile, especially during this time of transition?

When it happened, Chesney's rare smile was a slanted thin mouth that ran the gamut of dour emotions. The upper right corner of his mouth, hooking up toward an often purposely deaf ear, began his approximate pleasant expression, even if everyone doubted something pleasing ever lurked behind it. His lips slanted the whole way downward, from almost glib, to neutrally unimpressed, to sardonic, to scheming, to absolutely vindictive. His single expression carried all these connotations.

Prior to today, that visage had made Chesney famous, caricatured in postings on the Marsco Net, postings that Internal Security promptly removed. Well away from Seattle, on a lunar colony or at the Von Braun

Center tucked into the *Valles Marineris* along the Martian equator, daring associates often poked fun at that slanted, ominous glare-smile-grimace expression. Everyone got that chance once, once only, in their careers.

"Good morning, Jennifer!" The VC slowed and called out to a solitary associate on a bicycle. "How's that finger disk upgradability schematics project?" Chesney had personally given the designer this project.

"Fine, sir. Report comes out in a fortnight!" the disk engineer managed to reply after steering off the macadam onto the grass to avoid a bike-to-scooter collision.

"Get it to me this evening?"

"Of course, sir, absolutely," the researcher acquiesced, dreading the need to crack the whip over her staff and rush through a report two weeks sooner than expected.

Although his eyes were generally fixed on a point immediately in front of him, for a moment the vice-chair glanced around. Because he was on a rising part of the undulating pathway, he caught a glimpse of snow-capped Mount Rainier standing above the far horizon.

Chesney was heading southeast to the point where his own HQ fiefdom left the Academy campus behind. Few associates crossed these grounds with their widely separated and cleverly concealed buildings. The grounds looked more like an arboretum than the 24/7 headquarters of the organization that guided the whole solar system. Beyond the Academy and the Institute of Technology campuses, Chesney's domain, his secret complex, spread out farther on toward the lake. Scattered, partially buried compounds lay hidden in groves of evergreens and wetlands.

Lieutenant Elkton, who had been commissioned only a year before, crossed the VC's path on his own scooter and stopped for an impromptu briefing. Chesney's guards hung back as though admiring the lush scenery. Their posturing gave the appearance that the VC had total isolation, although they were recording the whole exchange.

"Been to our training facility?" Chesney asked, motioning with his head toward the snowy peak visible in the distant south.

"Affirmative, sir."

"All well there?"

"Exceptionally fine, sir. Things moving apace."

"And your friends, willing and eager?"

"Yes, sir. Cassy, that's Catherine Tomas-Higgens, sir, and Arthur Wicks, they're definite. Others as well. More all the time. I'll have a full detailed report soon. Mia Wang, Harold Crosley—"

"Is he the one called 'Hap'?"

"Yes, sir. Mia and Hap were once on the fence but are now definitely leaning our way. No hesitation now. And, sir, Mia thinks she can convince Roncalli."

Wrinkles filled the elongated brow of Chesney. "Roncalli? Was he originally on your list?"

"No, sir, but he'd be an excellent choice. He scored tops on the leadership quotient exam last winter." Elkton hid his own embarrassment about placing lower than average. "Kyle Truman Roncalli—his Truman family line, sir—they were in Security during the Great PRIM Mutiny. Distinguished service. His Truman grandfather is apparently still alive, living in retirement on the Serengeti."

"Parents?"

"Both dead. He has a brother and sister settled in colonies, Indie colonies."

Each man knew that was a black mark against the associate in question.

"So, high leadership potential, you say."

"Yes, I'll get you his scores. He tied an Academy grad from the last century, one Anthony Grizotti, who had held that record alone for over seventy years." Elkton thought a moment, "Well, I guess they share it now."

"What happened to this Grizotti?"

"Shattered his career, sir. Flushed it! Joined the Ice Service back when hibernation was the most necessary part of shuttle travel."

"So, an iceman? That wasted his career, what?" Chesney paused then picked up their string. "So, you think this Roncalli has potential with us?"

"Yes, sir. He'll fit in fine. Mia's convinced."

"If you say so, and if she says so, and he's not a risk to the initial group of you," Chesney laughed as though he had just invented this nickname on the spot, "of you 'Young Turks.'"

"Oh, I forgot to mention, sir, Roncalli's had Security experience. Fourteen months in the regulars between his first and second years at the Academy. And a recent lunar posting, actually, technically, with West Con Security. Gives him a bit of an edge, all that Security work."

"That certainly provides him with an advantage, yes," Chesney noted, thinking more of the Security experience than the fact that part of it was with West Con and not Marsco. "I'll look at his service file when I have time," he added, opening the pad he kept close at hand. Roncalli's digital popped to a screen, a headshot. "Must take after his Truman side." Roncalli had sandy hair and hazel eyes, neither feature suggesting a Med ancestry that his name implied.

"We're all just busting with pride at being asked to join in, sir. The thought of sustain—"

Chesney's constant frown turned to a distinct scowl. Even here in this arboretum setting and alone with the vice-chair, uttering the word *sustainability* was verboten.

"Yes, sir, you've caught my drift. I'll have Mia work on Roncalli; she'll not over-explain until he's on board and totally committed."

But who wouldn't be? Elkton smirked mentally. *Immortality and total control of Marsco! You'd be a fool to pass that up?* Emperors, monarchs, potentates, dictators: they all had once dreamed of the absolute power that was within the grasp of these Young Turks. Well within their finger disks, their twitch potential. And lives extended long enough to be able to enjoy this control indefinitely.

"Thank you, Lieutenant, for this impromptu briefing. Full report in thirty-six hours," the senior associate ordered.

Chesney drew in a deep breath but withstood the impulse to touch his chest at the heart. *Regeneration had been only the first step. Who would be idiotic enough to stop at renewed health when a totally perfect, potentially endless, life awaits those daring enough to step fully into the arms of Marsco med-sci?*

Chesney crossed an internal stopline well below the MIT/Academy junction, the only one in the entire complex. Two of his six guards dropped away. At last, he entered the center of his domain proper. What looked benign and deserted actually thrummed behind and under the shore dunes and low bluffs.

As the VC and his remaining guards moved deeper into the former arboretum, only hints of the inner sanctum of Marsco were visible. Security and its dark twin Internal Security each had its own separate annex to ensure discrete work with Chesney from here. The Finger Disk Control, Research, and Distribution Center lay farther north, completely out of view. The MAS Liaison Building gave hints of its existence because of the dish farm adjacent to its buried warren. All these annexes aided in controlling Marsco's entire domain; these warrens kept a direct and continuous link to the ceaseless heart of Marsco's headquarters. Its skyscraper rose gleaming on the far side of the Academy campus.

But here minions acted under the unrelenting auspices of Chesney. Marsco HQ received all the intel it needed from here. But only after it was refined, rarified, and filtered by Chesney through this shadow ops he'd built and expanded over the years.

That morning, the vice-chair did not stop at any of these hidden burrows but headed to his own Bunker, the last lair, where expansive wetlands met the lakefront. The chair of the board, Barston Oakes, had a huge office complex in the center of the former financial district of the old city of Seattle, the visible and easily accessed skyscraper where lefter associates, invited subsidiary dignitaries, and even those few PRIMS who occasionally visited, mingled. All the while, it was Chesney who labored down here, buried as he was, far from the open and obvious thrum of power, safe from distractions, safe from other associates who might dare to push their noses or twitch their finger disks into his furtive business. Here, even Chair Oakes rarely visited.

From the north side, the Bunker was invisible because it lay under a small hillside like a partially buried Martian colony. Its few windows all faced south, overlooking the expanse of lake and away from any activity behind. Farther east stood a dish farm linked directly to the entire Marsco's domain. Should anything happen "up top" where Chair Oakes ran Marsco's vast ops, Chesney was fully capable to run everything from down here.

Yes, Chesney always noted with satisfaction, *so much like a colony; detached from the rest of Marsco yet performing such imperative duties.* And like a Martian colony, buried, hidden, remote.

The first item on the VC's morning agenda was a meeting with Oakes. They did this by tele-link even though Chesney was just minutes away by hover from the towering central HQ complex. For years before Marsco took power, it ran its global operations for this skyscraper.

As the chair's morning staff meeting began, the vice-chair appeared as a hologram sitting with the dozen other members of the Marsco board. "Shows solidarity this way," the luminous projection assured the chair.

"You're looking fine," was Mr. Oakes first comment. Even as a projection, Chesney appeared healthy.

"Thank you, Mr. Chair. Never felt better."

"Good to hear."

"Anything I should know, Mr. Chair?"

Oakes let out a laugh. "Isn't it *you* that usually tells *us* what's up?"

"Once I'm up to speed, I'll have a report on how the Accords transitions are doing, Mr. Chair. I presume they are going as well as we wish at this point." The chair was adamant that he be kept fully abreast of the Six Accords because so much of the Marsco world—and thus so much of the whole world—was now dependent upon those settlements.

Their meeting ran smoothly and ended quickly.

<hr />

Immediately after closing the hologram system, Chesney met with his in-house subcommittee for its weekly briefing on the worldwide transition taking place because of the Six Accords. He'd rarely missed a briefing during the past eight meetings, even with his intense post-regeneration treatments. Regardless, he knew he'd left the Bunker in exceptional disks in the persons of Jason Rhores and Robert-Timothy "Bobby-Tim" Liddle.

Rhores, who theoretically answered directly to Chair Oakes, looked humorless and steely. His manifest cold, reptilian exterior never totally hid his predatory nature. Liddle had a rodent mouth and nose that joined to give an impression of a ferret. He had much more warmth than Rhores, especially since his principle duty was to keep Chesney out of danger by casting the VP in as warm a glow as possible.

If a stinger in the heel of Marsco existed, it was the Six Accords. These agreements irritated with each step as though a burr tangled in a sock of the chair or vice-chair. Under their leadership, every step the pair took forward was a step to keep Marsco a permanent fixture on Earth, a daunting task given the very purpose of the Accords.

Yet now, every step felt the nettlesome effects of the Six Accords, which were having the opposite effect. And as with Achilles, this heel spelled vulnerability to all of Marsco. Relinquishing its power was inevitable, imminent. If not attended to, protracted, delayed, whipped away, altered, or blotted out entirely so no record of these resolutions remained, then Marsco would cease to exist as soon as the last three of the six Accords went into effect. In less than a dozen years.

And the clock was ticking.

Chesney was committed to derailing the whole Six Accords process. Marsco would remain with him holding the reins of power.

"Any emerging problems?" the vice-chair began the morning's subcommittee meetings. No minutes were kept, but foggers came forward immediately to ensure nothing was ever heard of this meeting—nothing, ever.

"No, sir. All's going too damned well."

"Damn," repeated the vice-chair. He was hoping with every fiber of his Marsco being for a pretext to stop the Six Accords, even though half were successfully in place.

After the Six Accords were finally signed in 2141, one Accord came online every four years so that the massive changes these six agreements brought about could be digested in an orderly fashion. The First Accord, the Power Sharing Accord, began as midnight ended 2144 and gave way to the new morning of 2145, 1/1/45.

One-One-Forty-Five! How the celebrations ran as the subsidiaries of the world became federations. One hundred fifty-eight of them at a single go. Each brand new. Never seen before. All these federations instantly became members of the new UIF, the Union of Independent Federations. All were allowed to have free and democratic elections along timeframes they individually saw fit, a point Marsco had promised as far back as 2070, when it initially seized world power.

At present, in April 2153, most feds had provisional and transitional governments in place. But in the western Euro sids, in parts of NoAm with long traditions of democracy, elections were coming on more quickly. At that very moment, elected legislative bodies sat, debated, passed laws, rewrote constitutions, even talked with Marsco as an equal. *An equal!* Elected groups of sids and even former PRIMS sat in legal sessions debating their future, a future without Marsco's benevolent guidance.

It all made Chesney simmer with disgust.

Marsco was forced to sign them, the VC groused silently, then let fly. "Forced," he exploded, slamming his desk with his disk-laden right hand. Rhores and Liddle watched without a concern for their boss's heart. Regeneration was that efficacious.

The initial and seemingly innocuous meetings between Marsco and a few subsidiary delegates had begun innocently enough in 2108.

"Just an Academy plebe then," his memory ran with his outburst, "but still, Marsco was fine." His own steely eyes, showing their renewed vigor, looked at his two listeners. "Remember that adage, 'If it ain't broke, don't fix it'? Well, was Marsco ever broken down?"

"Never, sir," Liddle whispered.

Rhores nodded his agreement and mumbled, "Not broken."

2108 was only four years after Security finally put down the Great PRIM Mutiny, a series of uprisings that had lasted four years. But, in reality, elements of this mutiny had begun in the previous century, in the late '90s.

"All this Accords nonsense started *after* the PRIM Mutiny, really, to satisfy the leaders of *the subsidiaries*, not PRIMS at all," Chesney spoke softly now. It wasn't the first time he had made such an assertion. "After all, if not for Mandela Transkie-man and his henchman, Javâher Panditji, PRIMS would never have been seated at the table with Marsco's representatives and the leaders of the subsidiaries."

The two PRIM leaders, Transkie-man and Panditji, were simultaneously praised in some circles and condemned in others. As new talks began, the pair seated at the table held together a tenuous collation of PRIMS, the PFM—the PRIM Freedom Movement—dozens of ragged and dubious groups that stretched from nonviolent to militaristic but now forged into an unyielding alliance. This ascetic pair held all these bickering factions together, and once unified, these two moved the PRIM bloc forward relentlessly but with realistic promises for a lasting peace. Without that pair, a bloodbath was all too possible if Marsco loosened its grip. With these two at the table, the Six Accords were finally, slowly, inevitably, delicately ironed out.

Drawing a deep breath, the vice-chair let out his assessment of those times, "Better to have kept that pair in jail!"

"Well, they're both dead now," Liddle tried to placate.

"Impossible, sir, keeping them penned up," Rhores attempted to explain political necessities. "The pressure brought by the PFM was too great. But your disks are clean of that. The worst Marsco promises were given years before you and Oakes rose to power. You inherited that weak hand and were forced to play it."

"Yes, but the very thought of it!" Chesney pointed out hotly. "Once the leaders of this PRIM Freedom Movement were released, Marsco was forced to, *one*, recognize PRIMS as never before, and *two*, grant that disgusting PFM seats at the ten-year-old Accords summit."

Nods of agreement from the listening pair were meant to soothe their boss. renewed organ or no, he needed to remain calm. The reddening of his neck suggested that was imperative.

"And still they weren't satisfied, those PRIMS," Chesney went on grousing but under some self-control.

After the addition of the PFM to the negotiations table, these talks dragged on for another twenty-three years. Two-way, face-to-face negotiations between subsidiary leaders and Marsco were difficult enough, but a three-way go-round with the newly seated PRIM leaders added wariness on all sides and complicated matters beyond measure, or so Chesney felt.

"Those talks got out of control," Chesney gave his take on the history of those protracted discussions. "They commenced from a nebulous desire by a few selected subsidiaries for more control of their own territories. Clearly, Sid leaders at first only wanted more autonomy. They weren't looking to convene legitimate and sanctioned assemblies."

"But they let the genie out of the bottle," Liddle groused.

"Certainly, the sids didn't want assemblies with duly elected PRIMS sitting there," Rhores noted.

"But over those dragging thirty-three years of talks, throw PRIMS into the mix, and—" the VC added an air-twitch for emphasis, "—they morph into the full-blown Six Accords we despise so much!"

"But are obliged to accept," Liddle noted with remorse.

"And even so, the PRIMS went wild again for three years," Rhores moaned. "And allowing the protracted negotiations to end and the Accords to be signed was the only way to have PRIMS accept any terms for a cease-fire."

"A shit storm, for sure," Liddle hoarsely whispered.

"It looks like a payoff," Chesney shot. "It looks like we caved under pressure, Oakes and I." By this time, they were the two chief board members, leaders sworn to protect and sustain Marsco's influence throughout the entire solar system. "We looked like craven cowards," the VC added, with a table slap for clear emphasis.

Liddle answered softly, trying to keep the vice-chair from exploding, "Yes, sir, you are so right. Marsco conceded to those final demands under pressure. Full freedom for PRIMS under the Second Accord." He shrugged then added, "But let's watch the future. Someone may slip."

The vice-chair shook his head in disgust.

Chesney and Oakes had taken control of the board while the stalled Accords talks were dragging on with no end in sight. Only in the midst of fresh PRIM upheavals did the talks move ahead swiftly. Transkie-man and Panditji's PFM saw to it that all PRIM violence ceased, Security eased off, and the Accords, all six of them, were signed.

"Looks like bookends!" the fuming vice-chair noted. "PRIM Mutiny starts the Accords talks—"

"—without any damn PRIMS present," Rhores added.

"Thirty-three years later, the loathsome Accords are signed only after the next PRIM rebellion *ends* and thus allows for the signing to take place in relative peace."

"Does look like a sellout," Liddle agreed while trying to control the soaring blood pressure of his chief.

"Damn! We should have never signed! Never signed!"

"You're so right, sir," the reptile answered in complying subservience.

"Yet, signed they were," the vice-chair barked then added softly in revulsion, "as though they held an Enfield to our heads."

"And half in place as we speak," the rodent replied, "the first three already fully implemented."

Chesney turned over his disk-laden right hand to look at all the blue-green implants. He had the one exceptional disk as well, a red command-and-control disk at the tip of his right index finger. With that hand, even though prepared to twitch-endorse any Marsco screen, he and Oakes had been forced to actually hold pens and sign every single one of the 160 copies of the Accords *in ink*. One hundred sixty times on parchment. One copy for each of the 158 new federations that rose up to replace the existing subsidiaries. One additional copy for the new oversight and high-level congress of this created-anew world, the Union of Independent Federations housed in old Geneva. And one final copy for Marsco itself as it shrank in size, in importance, and in world domination.

"How humiliating that we, the guardians of Marsco, should be forced, coerced, driven to splitting apart such a powerful, perfectly sound, and reasonable apparatus for governing the Earth." On his left hand, Chesney sported his second set of disks, all blue-green except for the recently added jet-black disk.

Calming himself, the vice-chair asked softly, "So, nothing on the horizon that might signal a collapse of the Accords so we can go ahead and reapply lawful Marsco authority everywhere?"

"Correct," replied Bobby-Tim Liddle like a boy before a mentor who had a feared and dark leadership style. "We're waiting for the right kind of trouble, but nothing's surfaced thus far."

"Give it time, sir," Rhores suggested. "Meanwhile, we're preparing. We'll have plenty of Security battalions in the wings."

"Well, I hope we're not training new Security units just to turn them over to feds later." The vice-chair gave a stern look. "When does that happen?"

"Technically, with the Second Accord, four years ago," Rhores explained without a care about this breech of principles. "But it's a complicated matter, sir. Some former subsidiaries simply aren't ready administratively to take over a police force of this scope and strength. And thus far the UIF isn't looking particularly hard for evidence of noncompliance. So, well, we're arming, training, prepositioning at an ever-increasing rate." He snapped his fingers, made louder by his implants. "We're in place and ready to re-secure any area."

"And, sir," Liddle pointed out, "that black disk. You'll need to cover it before meeting your next appointment."

"What? Oh, yes, disks are going the way of Marsco, too," he groused.

"Well, again," Rhores twisted his head, "not really, not so technically, as our people unilaterally read the supporting documents. While the Third Accord opens the Net, it does not specifically outlaw disks."

The Finger Mouse and Finger Disk Accord, which had taken effect this past January, eradicated the distinction between the functionality of an implanted finger disk and a slipped-on finger mouse thimble. In effect, any user with either method had total and complete access to the newly reopened Net.

The separate and secure Marsco Net had ended.

Theoretically.

The vice-chair looked down at his left-hand implant and his recently added black disk. Nothing was mentioned in the Accord about Marsco creating and utilizing a supernumerary disk implantation system. "Right you are," he complied. "I'll cover it with a small bandage; it'll look like I burned myself or something."

—————•—————

Lunch that day was with Lieutenant Colonel Devon Chavez-Sherman, professor of astrophysics at the Academy, a researcher who had been on board the *Armstrong-Aldrin-Collins* exploration craft, which had made only the second Marsco journey beyond the Asteroid Belt to Jupiter's orbit.

At more than 184 centimeters in height, the lieutenant colonel stood taller than Chesney. Even though tied to a desk at present, he remained trim at around eighty kilos. Vigorous and fit, he looked younger than he was; hibernation flights helped there. When his journey to Jupiter ended, he'd joined the Academy's science faculty. He kept his dark hair short, and whenever out of uniform, he was natty. Both his left and right disk arrays were impressive. Decades prior, his acceptance to the Academy as a plebe brought him to Earth more or less permanently. He'd been born on the Moon of longstanding associates.

The VC liked working lunches, and so his Bunker had two artfully appointed dining rooms for such events. The larger one gave only half the diners a view of the lake because the long table ran parallel to the view panels overlooking the gleaming waters below. A smaller one had a V-shaped table pointing into the room so that eight diners might each sit comfortably without having to put a back to the window.

Chesney loved this knotty pine room; he often brought work here to luxuriate in the view. On a clear day like today, the snow-capped Mount Rainier stood in the distance. Marsco's ace in the hole was there, training, toughening up for the months, years ahead. One such locale of many.

Today, the lieutenant colonel and the vice-chair sat alone, one on each side of the table's apex, each eating heartily from the finest and freshest food Marsco could provide.

"Cera Langley still your chef?" Devon asked to make small talk.

"Yes, a Euro-trained culinary specialist is difficult to come by, but yes, she's here, distinct accent and all." He added a cynical laugh. "Even Oakes is jealous. Always hints we should meet down here when our schedules call for a working lunch."

Devon thought, *If Moses won't come to the mountain*, then added, "I can see why. Great food. And the view, spectacular!"

"Eaten yet at the chair's residence?"

"Not since we returned, were feted, and given our commendations. That was January '51. I left the VBC then and started up at the Academy that spring term."

"And you like it here? I mean all of here, the Academy, Seattle?"

"Yes, of course, but I miss space. Strangely, I found a sort of peace out there. Can't really explain it."

"Peaceful amid all that danger?"

"Very. I'm sure you've experienced it, too." Devon then remembered that both Oakes and Chesney had never been part of the Marsco Asteroid Service or served under the auspices of the Von Braun Center on Mars. All their years ascending up the ladder of leadership had been totally in Security and Hygiene or Internal Security. They'd done nothing exploratory or even extraordinary, like piloting a shuttle beyond Mars. He wondered if either had ever been in space, deep space, beyond the Moon's orbit.

Coffee and dessert awaited them on the terrace just outside the polymer panels that lined the small dining room. In the afternoon, the sun warmed the terrace; the rest of the Bunker blocked any wind.

"Well, let's have you earn this lunch, professor," Chesney finally said after a sip of coffee. "What about your Rascal report?"

"I gather you've seen my preliminary findings?"

"Bobby-Tim got the full text; I got his précis."

Devon looked puzzled, not being part of the inner sanctum.

"Liddle, *Robert-Timothy* Liddle." Chesney gave a knowing laugh. "He keeps me pretty damn apprised of what I need to know."

"Well then, sir, you know our preliminary data show that this Rascal was in the Kuiper Belt when detected, and all indications are it is heading toward Earth."

"And all indications at this point are this is not an issue, right?"

"Yes, sir. If a large comet or asteroid, it has hundreds of AUs yet to travel. We've about a year before it reaches anything of interest, anything that might need protecting. The MAS has ample resources available to push it aside, change its direction if it proves to be a comet or an asteroid on a collision course."

"Now, you say you found it when it was still in the Kuiper Belt, but that was, when? 2048?"

"Actually, '47, once we cleared the asteroid belt and had less clutter on our scopes and sensors. Rascal's half again as big as our largest shuttle but in space a minuscule object."

"So what's so bothersome?" Chesney then added, "And why so insistent that *I* know of it? I'm rarely directly involved with MAS activities."

"The object is displaying totally unusual characteristics; I felt you needed to know. Don't want you blindsided later on."

"No, can't have that."

"When internal rumblings of my findings surfaced, Liddle asked for a full report. He then thought you should hear it all directly from me."

"Makes perfect sense. Please continue."

"Rascal may—underscore, this is a hypothesis—it *may* be trailing plutonium ions. Still unclear if it is or if our sensors are just picking up traces of something else."

His whole career spent based on Earth, Chesney looked perplexed. The former explorer needed to give him a quick history of space flight. "Upscaled and massive plutonium ion propulsion was toyed with last century. We know for sure that the *Sirius Odyssey II* was the first craft to fully utilize such ion engines for power. And incredible power it was, years ahead of its time. I've seen the specs for such a ship. I'm not an engineer, but I could tell the propulsion system was quite a triumph of design; her engine bells are massive."

The vice-chair laughed contemptuously but not at himself, more at Devon for going so tech-wonk on him. "You'll have to connect the dots, colonel."

"Easy, sir. Here's the significant point. So far as we know, plutonium-239 does not exist in nature; it's an isotope that needs to be refined. At this point we think the ion trail we're tracking is just that, the remains of *processed* fuel. So, whatever is coming toward Earth at an ever-increasing speed is not natural but designed and built, especially if trailing the remnants of that particular radioactive isotope in its wake."

"And you've confirmed this?"

"Not yet. Again, a true, positive reading is just beyond our sensor range. But, as it approaches, it's only a matter of time."

"What was the phrase two centuries ago, 'Take me to your Leader'?"

Devon let out a laugh, a deep bellow with just the right touch of humor. What surprised the explorer most was that Chesney had made the joke. *Had he showed me his butterfly collection or explained his album of baseball cards from that long-lost game, I'd be more shocked.* "Something like that, sir," he replied, finishing his laughter.

"Is it from Earth? A ship coming home?"

"Records are sketchy from before the Wars, the Continental Wars, onwards. But, historically, nothing could have launched such a ship back then but us—"

"—*us?*"

"Us—Marsco, the Von Braun Center with the cooperation the Marsco Asteroid Service, maybe."

"Not NASA?"

"Definitely not. That would go back before Divestiture and the rise of Marsco, sir. Almost impossible to believe that scenario. It's conceivably possible and can't be discounted until evidence points to another conclusion, but probability and possibility are against it."

"Other guesses?"

"We know that the *Sirius Odyssey II* was ion-powered. The *Sirius Odyssey I*, her immediate predecessor, was a top-notch shuttle of her day but merely a reconfigured standard shuttle used as a test ship. That particular craft was a mule, a dog ship. Its ion system—only one ion engine actually—was merely affixed to her as a test bed, not really an integral part of her schematics. She never went far before being abandoned. She remained a derelict in Mars orbit until nearly twenty years ago. I actually got a look at her on a plebe's flight to Mars in '30 or '31. It was dismantled soon after that time."

"So?"

"The VBC keeps good records, sir. Nothing was ever built there that ran on plutonium except the *Sirius* line, numbers I and II. And we know number II was destroyed. It's fairly safe to say Rascal was not built there; thus, it was not built via Marsco or for all practical purposes, not built in this solar system."

"Are you suggesting?"

"The big divide is natural or manufactured. Is it a probe of unknown origins? Or is it a rock or block of ice, a natural object somehow trailing an isotope? Big universe, myriad possibilities of it being a natural phenomenon. But, what if it's a ship or a probe?"

Devon drew a breath, his dark eyes focusing on the renewed eyes of the vice-chair. "I don't want to speculate, but I can lay out four scenarios. Number one, some Independent colony had more flight and propulsion technology than we ever imagined. It sent a ship out. That ship is returning."

The VC understood, so Devon continued. "Number two, the VBC on Mars made another ship like the *Sirius II*, a sister ship, and somehow got that twin out of the solar system without leaving any records of the voyage. If so, she is returning."

Another nod, then Chesney added, "The Center always did have a trace of Indie colony about it." He grimaced, "Still does."

"Yes, sir," Devon replied, but mentally added, *more than you know.*

In a moment, the explorer went on, "Number three, the *Sirius II* did in fact *survive* that final battle. For whatever reason, Internal Security hid that fact or never knew that fact, but here she is coming back home."

"So, you are suggesting this is the *Sirius Odyssey II*?"

"Only suggesting it as one of four possibilities."

"And your fourth is?"

"That Rascal is extraterrestrial."

"My 'little green men' scenario?"

"Still, it can't be ruled out at this point."

Both associates sat silently contemplating the ramifications of such a visit to Earth.

Finally, Devon remarked, "For lack of a better description about little green men visiting, yes, we're looking at this possibility but actually as a low one. That is a huge universe out there, and our Earth is just a dot, a speck of sand on the infinite ocean's beach. How could intelligent life just find us?"

"Well, maybe if crossing the void of space has become easy, finding us has, too?"

"Certainly, and Rascal's course is definitely towards Earth. At least the preliminary data consistently suggests that. But the gas giants Neptune and Uranus will pull it off course. We'll know conclusively if it adjusts its trajectory by using Saturn then Jupiter to alter its course back toward Earth." Chesney looked puzzled so the explorer explained. "Those gas giants will pull it off course; they have that much g-force. If it's coming home, it has to adjust its trajectory. And all that will happen in the next twelve to fifteen months. Difficult at present to determine when exactly."

"What's the best course of action, from HQ's point of view?"

Devon instinctively wanted to say, *Well, let the VBC handle this and keep Seattle's finger disks off it*, but decided to placate the vice-chair. "I'm keeping track from here, and so are the arrays at Resnik, a far-side lunar colony. The MAS, the VBC—we're all watching. I've been tagged as a consultant to all their studies. We'll know in time. She's increasing speed, but it's still at least a year away from Earth orbit as I said."

Chesney blew a breath. "You'll keep this office informed of any changes, of course. Provide regular updates to Rhores."

"If you wish." The two men paused to contemplate the ramifications of all this information.

Finally, the VC went on, "You requested this meeting. Is this it?" He then gave his guest a look that suggested "next item."

"My last set of business has to do with rumors."

"So, our green men are out?"

"No, sir, I meant more immediate rumors."

"Ask away. You're a lefter and a trusted associate. If I can cut off rumors, so much the better." His shrug suggested the contrary, that he wasn't going anywhere black.

"The Sustainability Project, sir?"

Chesney whipped his face and glared directly at the explorer-turned-professor. "Yes, what about that closed-down research track?"

"Is it? That's my question. Is it closed down?"

Devon knew he was asking a man who may have recently benefited from a Marsco regeneration team. In the 2130s, researchers had perfected a regeneration protocol, one that used someone's own DNA in a recombinant procedure to regenerate tissue growth, renew an organ, repair an injury, replace a lost eye. A heart? And, although the vice-chair hadn't said it directly, Devon was fairly sure the rumors were true and that Chesney actually had undergone treatments that allowed him to regrow his diseased and weakened heart into a healthy, thriving, much-younger organ.

All this was merely unsubstantiated buzz, of course, but the scientist side of Devon, versus the more adventurous explorer side, did see a pattern.

It would be natural for the second most powerful associate on Earth to undergo this proven method.

But it was not just the immediate medical application of regeneration that bothered Devon. Regrowing organs inside a living body was science. Proper and ethical science. And preferable to harvesting PRIM organs— eyes, lungs, hearts, kidneys—for implants. Regeneration used a patient's own DNA to revitalize living, healthy tissue. Marsco med science mastered that for the better for humanity.

But, sustainability? Here Devon drew a line. Although the lieutenant colonel had been three years in Security, faced battle and death, he drew an anxious breath before asking his next explosive question. "Sir, rumors, mind you, I've heard rumors that Marsco medical boffins are once more experimenting with sustainability?"

Chesney shot an I-don't-know glance at the officer.

"Sir, the euphemism seems benign, as all euphemisms are, but the implication is mind-boggling. And downright despicable. I have to ask directly, sir; it is imperative I ask you directly. Are our medical wonks at this moment trying to use regeneration as a lead-up to sustainability, the pair of techniques used in tandem to create *immortality?*"

The vice-chair gave one of his cynical laughs that sounded nothing like the entertained laughter from Devon earlier. "That's impossible, for one," the VC began, "and second, unethical. I think even some sub-para in some Accord must outlaw it as well."

That's not an answer, Devon concluded. Instead of pushing, the professor went a different track. "One last rumor, sir, then, office hours for me back at the Academy."

"Yes, you must be busy with exams coming down in only a few weeks."

"Yes, sir, I am, but here's another rumor I'm hearing. That Security is dragging its feet on handing trooper battalions and Auxiliary units over to subsidiaries. I mean, over to the auspices of the new *federation* officials."

"Easy to get caught up in the changed terminology, isn't it?" the VP laughed once again, another one far from a hearty, sincere laugh.

"The Second Accord took effect in '49. This Accord was to start the process. But I hear Security is training *new* battalions and increasing their firepower."

"Well, robotic knights aren't really in Security's inventory, colonel."

"Yes," the professor replied, his knowledge of Security coming through, "the C-Powers tried bots to boost patrols back in the 2050s, over one hundred years ago. Well before Marsco. Dismal failure."

This robotic weapon, tried by the Powers, had the same faults that their drone Lightnings had. Vulnerable to interference by other operators. Marsco quickly learned to co-opt this weapon system years before the C-Wars, rendering them inoperative every time these bots tried patrolling too close to Marsco areas.

Devon laughed. "I understand 'bot tipping' became quite a prank, too. The weapon wouldn't attack unarmed children, and I gather that mobs of kids would surround one and tip it."

Chesney grew serious. "By this time in the twenty-second century, robotic knights are all but forgotten. Although they must have been magnificent. Over 250 centimeters tall, their skin metallic black and gleaming. Besides, a Bradley vehicle with adequate firepower offers enough protection for our forces. Marsco depends mostly on crowd-control vehicles via our heavily armed Brads and our counterinsurgency tactics. At present, the largest weapon on a Brad is a 30 mm repeating cannon, a super-sized Enfield of sorts. Who needs robotic knights now?"

"I've heard they moved quickly and can be used to disrupt anything *ahead* of Brads and troopers."

"That might be the case, Devon, but let me assure you, Marsco has no need for bot knights. Look at how our Security boffins defeated the Powers and their robotic Lightnings. Why set up the same scenario again? The bot knight in combat is vulnerable since its operators—its crew—are well to the rear behind the lines. Disrupt the com-links, and a bot is useless even while its command crew remains safe and secure at some remote bunker.

And a robotic knight always has the potential for someone else taking away total e-control of the very weapons we are fielding."

"Yes, sir, Marsco proved that in the C-Wars."

"There you have it. Why invest in an already compromised weapon system?"

Devon rose and gave a slight formal bow. Shaking hands was out of the question; disk-shock between the two well-disked associates made such a quaint courtesy unwanted. "Thank you, sir. That's how I see it. Especially with the Second Accord. You've been more than kind with your time, more than frank with your answers, as always," the professor noted.

Devon turned and headed toward the closed door to the dining room. It opened as he approached, and Liddle came forward with a forced smile. He'd been watching and probably recording this whole private exchange.

It was for that reason that Devon did not mouth his thoughts; a digitalized lip-reader might catch his response. Instead, he mentally noted, *I never mentioned the term "robotic knights."*

TWO

AT NEW GRANGE

(South of Sac City, May 2154)

"**N**o, Father," Chase Brunel explained, "Columbus is not *a firebrand*." He stretched his voice low to mimic his father's. "He's all about peace and reconciliation and returning to the old ways *he* knows are true."

"That's brazen," sneered Sarah, serving her brother his lunch. Her mother, Celine, patted her arm to keep the younger sister from interrupting so brusquely, especially when Roxanne had just brought out a carafe of water. Speaking rudely in front of PRIMS was never tolerated in the Sherman or Darrow household.

"I am sure you'll be interested in hearing him. I've invited him and several supporters to visit New Grange." Sensing reluctance on his parents' part, Chase kept up the pressure. "They will be out of the way in the largest guesthouse."

Chase was a younger image of his father, Trent, without his thickening chest and thinning hair. Both were strong, hardy men with penetrating brown eyes, although Trent's were kinder than Chase's.

In a verbal fight, neither held back, even though the father, a trained engineer who became a farmer, tended toward reticence. Chase argued more, sometimes over incidentals and moot points. And even given the fact that he would inherit New Grange one day, no one was quick to call him a farmer. The son of a farmer and descendant of a farming family—his mother's—he let his father and mother tend the land. At twenty-five, his direction was away from farming but not toward any profession that would occupy the remainder of his life.

Sarah could not restrain herself. She considered that particular guesthouse her domain; it had their only pool. "I swim there every day!" she insisted, pointing from the main house where the four sat at a long table in the flower garden. The largest guesthouse perched on a low rise in the distance. "Oh, Mother, it's so lovely being there and using the house to change and dry my hair."

"You fuss too much with your hair!" Chase shot back. "Columbus says a girl's head should be respectfully covered. Then she won't be so clearly, clearly, well, *a girl.*"

Sarah pouted, looking at her father and then her mother for support. "In case you haven't noticed, I'm not *a girl.*"

"You're not?" her older brother scoffed.

"You know what I mean! I'll be twenty-two in August."

"Well, it's May now, and you're still twenty-one. Besides, *a young woman—*" he stretched out the words, "—should modestly cover her head around others, especially grown men."

Chase, as usual, wasn't checked by either parent, an older brother's prerogative.

Finally, Celine did speak. "I hope you are not in the water alone, dear. New Grange has had one drowning of a girl; that was enough." Her head moved toward the garden's corner where the guilty pool in question had once cut into the ground.

Leave it to her to bring up that again, Chase thought, mentally retelling his mother's story of a visiting Darrow cousin, dead and distant, going down for the third time just outside the main house. *Give it a rest. Sarah and me weren't even born yet when that happened.*

"That was the last time my Darrow cousins ever again came here in such numbers for a summer holiday." Those visits had made Celine Darrow happy as a girl. The death changed so much of her girlhood. While the extended family stayed away from summer visits, the Chavez-Sherman side of the family still came almost every winter. And of course, Devon came intermittently, as often as such an important associate could.

"Oh, Mother," Sarah tried cheering her up, "some'll be here—"

"—in force," blurted out Chase.

"—here this Christmas."

"And Devon's coming soon," Trent noted, one of the few times he spoke up the whole meal. His morning work on the farm made him too hungry to say much until he had cleaned his first plate. He went down to the far end of the long table and selected a leg and wing of a hen that once roamed his garden. After he grabbed another warm dinner roll, he returned to his seat.

He was anxious to speak with Devon, a Marsco explorer and close connection to his entire family. Maybe he would have some reassurance about what Marsco was up to with its Six Accords and this new Union of Independent Federations. Trent's own new federation, the Western Constitutional Federation, West Con, was just beginning to find its depth. But, any talk of massive change was unsettling to the granger who, like most farmers, longed for a consistency of all good things. The seasons changed; that was enough change for anyone.

Celine threw up her hands. "I can't keep all your remarks straight!" Everyone enjoyed her antics even while she sorted out the threads. "Chase, yes, your friends may have the largest guesthouse as long as they know that Sarah will swim there every afternoon."

"And I rarely go alone, Mother," Sarah defended. "I taught La'Shay to swim last summer, remember? She often comes with." Although Sarah often studied and swam with the second oldest Richardson daughter, Hyacinth, the Brunel daughter was never as close to Hy as she had been to Patrice. Or even as she'd grown to La'Shay.

Celine smiled. Patrice and Hyacinth were Richardsons, daughters of a neighbor with a spread less than a quarter the size of New Grange but good people. Sid background, no PRIM blood. *Not like they're Shermans or Darrows or Brunels, but not many people are.* Pride in her background spread across her face in a pleasant smile. She shook her head having made that point solely to herself. "Is that fine with you, Trent?"

Having finished half his second plate, the granger looked up distracted, smiled, and agreed. "Yes, rather have people here. So much work, I can't be away longer than I already have to." As an appointed member of the new fed's provisional Assembly, Trent had been in Sac City a good deal over the winter. That body met to write a new constitution (a necessity for a federation named after one), conduct elections, and set a legislative agenda for complete independence as the Six Accords came online.

"When's Devon coming?" Sarah asked.

"Two weeks, I believe." Trent's answer betrayed none of his desperation to speak with his wife's cousin. The associate and Celine shared Grandfather Sherman. It was her Darrow grandfather, not her Sherman one, who had restarted New Grange forty-seven years before, a few years after the Great PRIM Mutiny had devastated all the successful granges in this area. Fighting had even flattened much of Sac City to the north.

 "Well, he'll get the smallest guesthouse," Celine went on. "He likes it there."

"Good viewing, he says," Sarah added. That house, set on a low rise away from the other houses, stood where most ambient light from the grange was blocked.

Devon knew the heavens, the stars, the planets. The explorer loved New Grange, too, even if his older cousin had drowned here. He was only a year old at the time, and the dead girl was ten or eleven; Sarah couldn't remember which. Either way, the accident left little impression on him. Unlike her mother, who was probably eight then. Devon was born and raised on the Moon in a Marsco colony; all his family were associates, as were many Shermans. Often coming to visit directly from space, he loved the irrigated greenery, the bounty, the openness of New Grange.

During those winter visits when Devon had come regularly with his father—Chavez-Sherman senior, a long-retired shuttle commander—and one or two siblings and their growing families, New Grange was alive with Shermans and Brunels. Trent truly loved those times. In the great room before a roaring hearth, he sat at the head of a large table, its linen tablecloth decorated by Celine and Sarah. His daughter was happy to see how contented he looked at those times. Like a *patriarch*, a word her tutor had taught her before he had been dismissed seven years ago.

Mother was still on her list. "Yes, and he's promised to come next Christmas, as well."

"Good," Trent responded pleasantly. His smile, Sarah noted, showed he meant it.

"Now, what else?" Celine asked herself aloud. She had these three only for the afternoon meal before everyone scattered: Trent to take a short siesta then return to the fields. Chase to disappear and maybe reappear when his father headed out. And Sarah to attend to her studies because her mother wanted her to complete her last semester before the summer. *Her last year of schooling*, her mother knew, *since she'll probably be marrying soon.*

Under the trellis that shaded the garden, each Brunel fell into separate thoughts. Celine looked deeply at her daughter. *Nearly twenty-two!* She tried not to let anyone see tears welling in her eyes. Had she not lost a series of pregnancies after her only daughter's birth, perhaps others would be at table. But such losses were common for women living outside the direct auspices of Marsco. Or so the Marsco-trained doctor up in Sac City had explained.

Sarah finished her meal and rose to serve everyone fruit for dessert. Mother and daughter both had deep blue eyes and long dark hair, just as father and son had similar hair and brown eyes. Sarah's hair, parted simply in the middle, hung down over her shoulders. Celine always tucked hers up in a tight bun. When Sarah wore hers up, she looked older, mature, sophisticated. Celine had seen associates and shuttle pilots who might visit with Devon admiring her daughter when it was up like that. And, of course, that tutor had, too.

Sarah turning twenty-two in August. Celine had married Trent at only twenty, even though he was nine years older. Chase came when she was just twenty-one. *Will she marry soon? Not to just anyone,* she insisted with motherly protection. *When the time came for me, a Brunel happened into my life.* Brunels didn't own land, but they still were prosperous. Before marriage, Trent owned nothing. A trained engineer, his family made water pumps and superior irrigation equipment. Not a single grange within two hundred kilometers of Sac City, Celine knew, was without some Brunel pump or other. Even the Food Consortium bought them by the dozens. *And I'd love that brick Brunel house up north in Sac City even if cheek-by-jowl with other houses and hardly room for a decent garden,* Celine admitted, a wish that often crossed her mind.

<hr>

From the garden after everyone went inside after lunch, Trent watched the land around him. As far as he could see were tender grain shoots growing taller in the sun and wind. And as far as he could see, the land was his. Or more accurately, his wife's before they married. Brunels made their share of MMUs, but they never had land, *terra firma*, soil. Trent did.

New Grange itself had four houses. Their own—the largest—and three they called "guesthouses," once the main houses of three smaller places

New Grange had bought out over the years. Two were acquired by Old Man Darrow, Celine's grandfather and founder of the estate; the other— the one with the pool—by Trent himself. He kept each house up and functioning, because his large spread brought visitors by the score to it. He would have it no other way.

Such thoughts, he knew, were wasting his time—and time, like water, was something a granger never squandered—so he turned to enter the great room. The grange's main house was large, built in a piazza style that afforded many suites and ample space for the four of them and their domestic PRIMS.

Coming out of bright sun and heat, he found the interior cool and dark. Slipping off his work boots, he crossed the great room with its massive stone fireplace, where their Christmas feasts were held. He heard Celine and Sarah in the kitchen, laughing along with the soft voice of Roxanne. *Celine does too much that the PRIMS should do*, he thought when he reached his recliner in his vacant office. That conclusion kept him from noticing that he had not seen or heard Chase after lunch.

Loosening his belt, he sat down in a leather recliner made exclusively in Sac City using specs that dated from the twentieth century. He cranked the seat back, planning to rest for ten minutes before rejoining his PRIM gang in the fields. He had a sid manager, but Trent never missed time with his laborers. He loved it all too much: the sun, the sound of the wind through the fields, birds on the wing above, the cheerful chatter of his workers. He loved the tangible nature of his land, with crops thriving from planting to harvest. The Sac City Assembly was slower, less tactile, but Trent—surprisingly—loved that too. His labor there was rebuilding a country.

Eyes closed, his mind raced. Devon would be able to explain everything about the world in flux beyond the boundaries of New Grange and the swath of independent granges around it. But enough of that. Trent had much to do later this afternoon, making sure his condensers provided all the water his greening fields needed in this heat and dusty wind. And then he thought: *I hope Chase comes to help this afternoon.*

His mind was alive, too jumbled for dozing. *Chase may not want New Grange. He certainly wants the prosperity it brings, but he isn't eager to put the work into it to profit from it. Well,* Trent mentally ran over the spread's history, *it passed from a Darrow to a Brunel, the result of a generation without a son and heir. I married New Grange, after all.* But, he honestly admitted, he really loved Celine Darrow from the start. And he had enough Brunel wherewithal to make a living without her acres.

But would Chase? New Grange had gone to a son-in-law once already. *The next generation, what will it bring?*

The Third Accord, like the first two, had come and gone with hardly a noticeable change at New Grange or the Richardson place down the road. The Net had once been strictly controlled by Marsco via its finger disks, most of it off-limits to those without implants. But last year, in theory at least, the Net was flung open to anyone using even an old-fashioned finger mouse. Open Net created limitless possibilities for most former sids, even a few former PRIMS daring enough to take up a thimble and twitch a pad.

The Six Accords troubled Trent. He shared his deep concerns with Sarah often. Father and daughter were alike in their love of history and politics. Readers and deep thinkers. He'd love to explore his ideas with Chase as well, but he never seemed around. Yet speak of them or no, the Third happened last year, in 2153, and three more were coming like the last, each four years apart. When the final, Sixth Accord inevitably arrived, "the New Marsco Accord" eleven years away, the Marsco everyone knew, dreaded, feared, revered, shunned, or aspired to would cease to exist. Marsco—which had ruled since 2070, since last century—was going to content itself with outer space exclusively from 2165 on. Ruling Earth was going to be up to this new UIF, the Union of Independent Federations, that theoretically had come into being with the First Accord nine years ago.

———•———

"I'm glad you napped, Trent," Celine whispered, her gentle kiss waking him. "I could tell you were tired earlier."

"Was I out long?"

"Forty-five minutes."

He pulled the recliner upright, fastening his belt. He didn't want to be any later, although his PRIM gang knew what to do without him. He paid them well and they worked hard for him. That aspect of PRIMS wasn't his concern. He mentally caught himself. Technically, they weren't PRIMS anymore. They were, like himself and his family, free citizens of a federation.

"I'm glad Devon's coming soon," Trent said softly to his wife. "He's intelligent. Generous." Celine smiled as she thought of all the platinum asteroid jewelry he had brought her and Sarah over the years. "But, this Marsco stuff, these Six Accords—"

"Are you that worried about them, dear?"

"Who can't be worried? I'm a farmer. Farmers like changes as in 'the seasons change dry to wet' and 'our green corn ripens to golden yellow.' But we are like soil: some changes are too much. I like my soil fertile and in one place. Preferably a place I own and my son will own."

She glanced at him to agree. "I'm a farmer's daughter, remember. I totally understand."

"Well, I'm an Indie, and this's what I don't understand: 'Marsco Power Sharing Accord' nine years ago. Just what the hell *is* democracy? And will it work or bring on anarchy like the old days? 'Subsidiary Parity Accord' five years ago. PRIMS essentially no longer exist!" He gave a laugh and motioned his head to signify his fields beyond the house. "Well, there are two dozen of those *nonexistent* PRIMS working our land right now. Working damn hard. And they live in a PRIM village not seven kilometers from our south forty. A damn fine tidy little village, too."

"I know, Trent, great concerns."

"I haven't the foggiest what has changed with the 'Finger Mouse and Finger Disk Accord.' Mine still work." He held up his right hand to form a V with his index and middle finger; each held a blue-green implant at the tip. They were daily reminders of his youthful dream to be an associate, not an Indie. He was the only granger he knew who sported disks.

Trent drew a breath. "I think we, the provisional Assembly, have things under control. At least when we adjourned last month it seemed so. But I think we're all waiting for Marsco to do something else unexpected."

"Devon will know, dear, believe me."

"I know, hon," he replied, kissing her lightly. Devon knew a great deal of what was stirring in Marsco, in the subsidiary to the north, roiling up there because Marsco was churning.

Between Trent and Celine, nothing had been said about Chase, yet they both knew they should have been speaking about their son.

While her parents talked, Sarah slipped out of the kitchen after chores and headed up toward the largest guesthouse. It was just 2:00, but a swim later this afternoon would clear her mind. Lunch today was a swirl: Devon coming, Chase acting worse than usual, this Columbus character honing in on her guesthouse, her mother bringing up the drowning at New Grange. *Again.* Sarah wasn't sure, but she thought it was *not* the only accidental death here. Others had occurred on this land, and the grange's cemetery proved it, but no heartrending losses like the young Darrow's, as far as she knew.

She frowned when thinking of Devon's young and dead cousin but then smiled about Devon himself. He was her absolute favorite. And Sarah, although long past her girlhood and closely related to him, still harbored an innocent crush toward the man. It wasn't something he would ever know, but in her heart if she ever married (a distant possibility for the stubbornly independent farmer's daughter) her future mate would have to have all of Devon's looks, knowledge, and courage.

As an associate, an explorer, he'd gone all the way to Jupiter. He'd used that trek to research the Kuiper Belt. She'd used her school computer programs to look it up, that ring of comets and space debris floating at the farthest edge of the solar system, beyond Saturn, Uranus, and Neptune. It made her dizzy just thinking of all that. Her prince would have to be loved like a son by Devon.

At the low whine of an electric motor, Sarah faced toward the gravel trail alongside one planted field fifty meters off. *Well, there goes my not-so-princely bro.* Leaving a tan, swirling cloud behind, Chase rode his ATV without a helmet as fast as he could in the opposite direction of a knot of PRIMS who were setting up field sprinklers. She knew these wouldn't start until after the heat of the day, when the winds died, so the jets of water could settle without the dusty gusts evaporating their spray. All night long, the robotic irrigation system would creep across the fields watering her family's livelihood with a slow, steady sweep. Without that system and the PRIMS to set it up, New Grange would be a parched dust bowl.

Water, she'd heard her father explain more than once, *New Grange is all about gathering water and utilizing it for maximum good.* Hence, nearly three acres devoted to Marsco-standard condensers, plus solar panels and windmills to run them, four gigantic buried cisterns, numberless links of piping, and dozens of Brunel pumps to move the liquid miracle that made her life possible.

You Brunels are so rich! She remembered Patrice Richardson teasing her. The Richardson spread was smaller, devoted mostly to orchards (apples, pears, nuts) with some livestock fed on Brunel grain. A small dairy herd. Although hardworking, the Richardsons—as her mother constantly pointed out with sharp derision—were *not* Darrows or Brunels.

Walking toward her guesthouse to study then swim, the young granger remembered the Patrice of her girlhood and how she and her neighbor had spent many afternoons together talking.

"This is *so* nice," Patrice would often remark.

"Chase says a pool had been on this very spot a century ago," Sarah remembered telling her once. "When this area had closer connections to Sac City. Associates may have lived out here, or at least, he says, important sids. Imagine, working in Sac City, or over as far as Silicon, then coming home in a hovercraft to swim in your own pool."

Dig anywhere on the Brunel or Richardson land and you'd find evidence of that pre-Marsco world.

"It's a wonder we have one—a working pool, I mean. Dad's brother has been restoring pools in Sac City, an extension of Brunel pumps, after all. My cousin comes to service it. Says all the schools and parks up there have pools once more."

The guest smiled. "Don't you think it's a gift from your dad to you?" The over-abundance of Richardsons, who came along as regular as Christmas, made spoiling one child impossible.

Blushing, Sarah had to admit, that yes, it probably had a great deal to do with her. "I guess the water could be used for irrigation, in a pinch." Sarah sighed, knowing chlorine made that impracticable. She defended this luxury nonetheless. "It's probably the only thing at New Grange that seems more Brunel than Darrow," she admitted.

"That may be true," Patrice grinned, "but you seem to have a bit of Sherman in you, frankly."

"How do you mean?" Sarah shot back that long-ago day, caught off guard by the remark and not sure if it were meant nicely or cruelly.

"I mean, you love Devon—"

"—he's my *cousin*!"

"I know, but you'll run off with some associate one day, just you wait." She grinned all the more, then twisted a smile. "Are they born with finger disks?"

At first, Sarah didn't respond but then realized Patrice wasn't suggesting the birth of the associate *himself*; this birth was to be from *her*, after her union with this mythical associate. When this all dawned, she blushed deeply once more.

Her friend, blaming herself for this embarrassment, reached out and took her wrist. "I'm sorry, Sarah. I'm joking pretty roughly." She sighed. "Too many brothers."

"It's okay."

Patrice was so pretty; young Sarah would heave her then-flat chest in envy, having no concept of her own looks. Her friend was taller, with long, tanned legs and blond hair. *Blond!* She waved her head to throw her own dark brown hair behind her, out of sight. *And green eyes!* Sarah turned nearly green herself with envy. *And yet*, she thought as her jealousy subsided, *what a sister she shall be, if Chase ever grows up!* It was clearly understood that Mr. Richardson expected Patrice to marry Chase, for Brunel land if nothing else.

This was before, when she was younger and before Patrice essentially left her father's spread for good. Perhaps that was why she left. Chase and she did not work out, but the pressure from her father didn't cease—marry, have children, bring more land under his control.

As these memories subsided, Sarah put on a PRIM-made straw hat. It was hot; the afternoon temp was close to 38°C. Come mid-summer, the afternoons would top the 40s without any problem. Might stay close to 32°C overnight. Marsco's Vanovara bombardment in the C-Wars decades before still affected the weather. Long, hot summers. The distant mountains devoid of snow even after winter. The wind whistled around her, buffeting the few intrepid birds that dared to call to each other in the growing heat. Come dusk, the air would be alive with them but not so now.

Still a hundred meters away from the guesthouse and caught in a dusty gust, Sarah looked forward to her swim. She had one assignment to finish first, and with it she would complete her last term of biology. Calc and history were already done. Completing this degree was more for her mother than it was for herself. She was never leaving New Grange. Never.

Years ago, Devon had wanted her to go to a boarding Marsco Prep, to eventually join Marsco itself, but her mother was against it. She didn't want her daughter to move that far away while still so young. A farmer's daughter's response: life revolved around the land your family owned, so you stayed close and tied to it, as deeply rooted as the trees in the windbreaks.

If she even lets me marry someone from as far away as PRIM-Lodi or New Stockton, I'll drop dead on my wedding day, she had smirked at her cousin. Growing up on a farm, that part of married life wasn't a shock. The shock was thinking her mother would ever let her go.

Her father, from Sac City, was more open but deferred to Celine. Even now, as he read up on how to make this new fed a real democracy, he shared his books with her, texts she eagerly took to, almost as eagerly as she took to this land.

But over the years, Devon was not deterred. He gently urged her to seek a Marsco education. As the Sac City university grew, he encouraged her to go there and take some classes, as Patrice was doing now.

Marsco Prep, the Academy, being an associate, these were notions that ran counter to her self-concept. Smart enough? Strong enough mentally, physically?

You are! Devon had insisted, trying to persuade her. *Look, it can be yours!* This was when Sarah was thirteen. That summer Devon was preparing for his five-year trip to Jupiter. Now he had an Academy post and a research position on the Moon studying Kuiper anomalies. Twice a month he landered up to his lab and dish array on the far side of the Moon. And now, another, much-delayed trip out past Jupiter was in the works.

That particular night, they talked like father and daughter while he set up a twenty-centimeter telescope and showed her Mars, Jupiter and its Galilean moons, and an asteroid. Chase didn't bother to come out and look.

"I can never do it. Leave mother and father. Leave my home," she often recalled saying, that night, that talk always in the back of her mind.

"Yes, you can, leave both New Grange and your folks."

Sarah had never thought of herself in that category, as someone able to pass a Marsco entrance exam. Today, however, she smiled. Once again, Devon was right. She knew she'd have aced it.

In her cohort of online students around the planet and throughout the solar system, she was seventh of two-fifty. Her rank was surprising to her and all the more impressive considering she often rushed through her calculus even as she read her pre-Marsco history carefully, a new federation requirement. Those old republics and democracies held her attention. She took all her studies seriously, but she knew some in her group *wanted* to join Marsco. They needed an 82% to do so. She worked hard enough to stay at 98.5% without finding the limits of what she might do if she really pushed herself. She had opted out of the physics elective, for instance, choosing soils instead. Hardly a challenge to her, studying her natural habitat and comparing a few soil samples sent from greenhouses on the Moon and Mars.

But why leave New Grange?

She stopped just outside the ring of trees and hedges around her guesthouse. It sat perched on a low rise, almost like a battlement in some ancient scene. She'd come one and a half klicks across the lowest part of New Grange with a fallow clover field on the left side of the path and a plowed grain field on the right. Down the way stood the grange's main house, also surrounded by a hedge and trees, with a large vegetable garden just beyond the kitchen and a small orchard out of sight from her vantage point.

Taking time to walk around the periphery of the hedge, she surveyed the physical limits of her life. The east border of New Grange showed where Tillson's land started. Her family's land was well-tended and rich, filled with signs of state-of-the-art irrigation. Tillson land was rocky, desiccated. Yellow grass sprouted just beyond Brunel cultivation. A dozen mangy head of Tillson steers grazed on dry tuffs that sprang up from his dead land. Even a drifting tawny hawk seemed lifeless. The few valley oaks there wilted in the heat as though threatening to burn up right before her eyes.

When that PRIM-son Tillson dies, if the bastard can actually die, Chase once speculated, *every granger in the whole area will scramble for his crappy land.* Trent would more than likely put up the highest bid. Sarah sensed that the land in question would come with her hand.

To the south, Brunel property gave way to more prosperity and the signs of a sizeable PRIM village. They had plentiful work these days and good wages. West, both the main house, and well beyond, the Richardsons' orchards were visible. It was as though the wind carried the sounds of bees amid the rows of pink, white, and cream blossoms. North faced a thriving track of land, hundreds of times bigger than New Grange, of acres cultivated under Food Consortium sponsorship. Nearby, another neat, trim PRIM village sat in a grove. Even farther northward but seen only as lights along the horizon at night, was Sac City, an emerald city Sarah had visited only a few dozen times in the whole of her life. And never alone. Also, a stopline separating Marsco from the valley. The Six Accords was changing all that, but she knew the line, a shadow of its former self, had essentially been abandoned for years.

Rather than nestling down in the shade near the faux waterfall at one end of the inviting pool, Sarah walked around the hedge one more time, straining to see as far as possible beyond the perimeters of her limited world. She was living where she meant something. She and her future soul mate were going to live here; they were going to give the plain vanilla "guesthouse" a real name. Those parched Tillson acres, when they were theirs—her soul mate and hers—that land would flourish with Brunel pumps and their hard work.

Chase and either Patrice or Hyacinth—Sarah still held onto both those unlikely dreams equally—would end up with most of New Grange, but she would have her slice and would only need to move a few kilometers from her father and mother. Roxanne's oldest daughter, La'Shay, would be her main domestic PRIM, or whatever the technical term for them would be at that time. Devon would set up his telescope below the eastern hillside, which blocked any ground light, so he might show her children the four bright moons of Jupiter and the rings of Saturn.

Children! The very thought sent conflicting emotions throughout her slender body.

Years ago, once the twelve-year-old Sarah had defended PRIMS as being just like herself. The older, wiser Patrice had explained that PRIM girls were sold by their fathers to strange men like calves from breeders. Sarah had never heard any of these disgusting concepts; they had to be explained to the naive girl. Sarah's head swirled at the very thought. As Patrice explained each scabrous detail, the breathless girl became so nauseated and dizzy she almost fell over. Even today, Richardsons think little of PRIMS.

"Imagine letting disgusting creatures, them PRIMS, have equal status with us? With us Indies?" Patrice had maintained at the time.

"But not *all* PRIMS are like that," the girl Sarah had insisted. She wanted to point out that both Roxanne and La'Shay were ever so gentle.

"But where's her father? And if he was here, wouldn't he just up and sell that girl any time he wanted? She's just the right age, about your age!"

Sarah had wanted to ask, *but to whom? Who would buy her? What kind of man would?* She was afraid to ask, afraid to hear Patrice's answer.

And then a few years later, that kiss from her tutor when she was only fifteen. He was at least ten years older. It was a strong memory and not sweet. Her innards churned; she did not want *that* at all.

Then few years later still, when Sarah was sure she had figured it all out, she'd had her one-time experience with Nate Richardson, Patrice's older brother. It still pained her, that she once thought she was actually in love with him. Given it happened as it did, with her willingly accepting him, she knew she was lucky she didn't carry the consequences. She lived on a grange, surrounded by livestock. She knew what might have been.

I'll be twenty-two in three months, but I sometimes want to be twelve all over again, before Patrice's talk of PRIMS for sale and that tutor's unexpected kiss and believing she loved Nate.

Sarah backed up against the branches around the guesthouse, her future home, and let the greenery surround her.

Patrice was there for a good deal of Sarah's life, even though over the past three years, Sarah had seen her only a few times. If she came home for the holidays, they'd squeeze in a long walk and talk together. She might be here soon for the Brunel solstice party and her sister's birthday the next day.

Last Christmas, Patrice had asked, "Has Chase taken up with Hy, do you think?"

"Can't say." Sarah spoke with a note of disappointment. She realized Patrice wanted to see her face, read her answer. Turning, she said again, "I really can't say, because I truly don't know."

"He used to talk to me all the time when we went swimming as teens. Before I moved away. Sometimes he'd just sit and watch me."

"He called it *lifeguarding*."

The pair laughed and fell silent. They were walking toward the guesthouse and its pool, but it had been a foggy December day, raw and still.

"I sometimes thought," Patrice confided, "that he *was* going to lifeguard me forever."

That damp afternoon, Sarah took her friend's hand but could tell it remained distant, not at all like that of a future sister. "What happened?"

Patrice deflected her question. "Have you ever kissed anyone? I mean anyone you loved?"

Sarah didn't quite know what to say, so she admitted little and hid her true story about Nate. "Not many chances. Nate grew interested in others girls and married even before you left. Tillson's boys ran off years ago, and they were all way older. I think father's Enfield would come out in principle if any of them even stepped on our land, let alone came to kiss me!"

Patrice didn't give her any more time for reflection. "Chase always wanted to kiss me—behind your back," she added seriously. "At least he did years ago," she laughed admitting that. Serious again, she went on. "I didn't mind. But he always seemed to be moving his hands, well, along me. You know." Sarah blushed. "And he always asked me things—to do things."

Sarah wasn't sure she wanted to hear all this about her brother but didn't know what to say to stop Patrice from revealing so much.

"He *is* a kind man," the Richardson daughter went on. "And so much better than he appears to be. Or knows he is. But I think—I know—he wanted to have me do things that he might ask others to do as well, if you're following me."

Trying not to believe what she knew instinctively to be true of her brother, Sarah nodded to keep Patrice comfortable and speaking. She must listen to her closest friend, even if what she heard wasn't the best of her brother.

Patrice gave another laugh. "Don't get me wrong—*I* enjoyed myself; *he* enjoyed himself. And we didn't get *that* far, so there won't be a basket on your folks' door one night or a bundle left to be a PRIM at some Marsco orphanage. But, oh, I thought after a while, I am more serious than he is. One time, I had a very heavy period and still he wanted something, wanted me to do something. I was *not* able, all that cramping tying me up. That day, I realized I was *his* only when I was pleasing *him*, if you catch. I wasn't that important to him when I wasn't that pleasing."

Sarah saw her friend's face contort as never before. The dark misty evening light hid her tears. "Oh, Patrice it's okay. We'll always be close friends—"

"Please *don't* say that—it's probably not true." Seeing the unexpected pain in her friend's face, she quickly added. "It's *me*. I've changed. And I'm gone from here, really. No more pretending I'm ever coming back after years in Sac City. I'm not."

"What? Where? Leaving here? New Grange?"

"Oh, *that's sweet*!" Patrice smirked cynically. "New Grange? I'm a Richardson, remember? I live on a small spread with no name except 'the Richardson place.' I'm not *a Darrow* or *a Brunel*—I've heard your mother say that often enough." Fighting back her anger, she breathed out, "I thought I'd be part of New Grange once, but not now."

Sarah was now the one contorted with uncontrollable tears. She turned her back on Patrice to hide them.

Patrice moved closer to Sarah and whispered, "Hey, I'm the one who's changing. Who's leaving. *I'm* the one who wants to change and wants to go away. Stay away."

"But I don't understand," Sarah sobbed.

"Look, father is still after me to marry. Marry soon. Any man. Just as with Chase, marry land. Have kids like Mom on a yearly basis." She shook her head in exasperation. "I went away to find out what *I* wanted, if that's possible."

After a few moments, Patrice asked her friend, "If you could live anywhere, where would it be?"

"Right here! This very house!" They walked up to the well-lit guest-house with its rows of windows overlooking the pool. Roxanne and La'Shay were making it ready for Brunel guests at Christmas. "And you'll be a New Grange with Chase."

"No, dear Sarah, no. That's not possible anymore. Can't you understand? And if these Accords create changes, as things are opening up, then I'll make a life in Sac City."

"What? Are you joining Marsco?"

"No, but I'm nearly a nurse. One more year of study. The fed is bringing back hospitals for everyone. I'll have plenty of opportunities."

Sarah remembered that December afternoon like it was this morning. But, today, in the hot wind of May, a day flooded with memories of her childhood and teen years, she felt bewildered by all the changes roiling around her.

Devon had been warning them for years, warning her father, warning her as she looked toward her future, that New Grange was in a bubble, as he called it, a bubble about to burst. "There's pressure mounting; more from outside than in. Ignored by Marsco, existing fully independent of the subsidiary, a speck of something so rare over the past few centuries." He hadn't said it aloud, but Sarah knew he wanted to add, *But this Indie area around New Grange can't go on like this, not forever, not indefinitely*. He did say this out loud, "Your Indie status no longer exists because you're part of a federation. The Western Constitutional Federation is bursting to life all around you. And you *are* part of it."

She shuddered. Regardless, *here* was her home. "It's the only one I've ever known," she sighed defiantly at the gusts of wind picking up dust around her. "And come what may, I aim to continue living here, all alone if need be. Devon may come to visit, Patrice too, but I'm safe at New Grange. So safe. And I never want to leave it. *Never ever.*"

THREE

THE YOUNG TURKS

(Marsco Academy, Seattle, May 2154)

"I can't imagine living where I couldn't swim," Cadet Mia Wang declared, short of breath but ready for more laps. She pulled off her goggles to talk in an easy manner, face-to-face. Her dark eyes focused on her swimming partner, Cadet Kyle Roncalli.

Time was, Kyle thought, *I swam in your eyes.* With each lap the pair completed, he realized exactly what was slipping away. They were opposites in many ways, dark hair and eyes, sandy and hazel. But somehow, to him, once a fit.

The Academy natatorium was thinning out of other cadets, but Mia and Kyle still had forty-five minutes before it closed.

Kyle was enjoying the water, and surprisingly, because the pent-up tension between them hadn't eased, Mia's company. A life without swimming, however, *that* he could imagine. Early last term he would have been reluctant to disagree because he was in that trying-to-impress-her stage of their relationship. Tonight, not so. He was in a worse state now, in that raw are-we-or-aren't-we stage.

"Oh, I don't know," he began, moving closer to her lane but purposely not catching her intriguing eyes. Only the lane floats separated them at the shallow end. Mia reached for him under the water with her legs and locked him in a tight grip. He hadn't expected that.

"Mars won't have much in the way of swimming, water being an issue, the lack of gravity making it evaporate so quickly." He threw an arm skyward to point out the massive space that the Olympic-sized pool took up. "Pressurize all this on Mars, just for swimming? Not likely."

His fellow cadet shot him a glance to remind him that she had taken those planetary geography classes as well. Besides, neither had ever been to Mars. In no mood for such a conversation, Mia let go of him, adjusted her goggles, and swam off.

Kyle stayed at the edge of the pool and watched her graceful strokes. With her hair pulled back out of her face, her porcelain cheeks were more prominent than when she was in uniform. That and her sleek swimsuit made her all the more hot, although her body was distorted under the water and moving swiftly away. Even so, from what Kyle could tell, she was nearly perfect. Her body seemed to glow, to radiate health and purpose.

Two lifeguards walked along the pool's edge above Kyle. Like all cadets, they were trim and robust. The pair was flirting with each other; only Mia and he remained in the water. They seemed in love with no reluctance or barrier between them. "Some guys have all the luck," Kyle groused, not knowing if he spoke loud enough to be heard.

"Go ahead, get in some laps," the young man, a second-year student, encouraged his partner. Without hesitation she dove into the water.

From what Kyle could tell, both guards were devoted swimmers with chests and arms that showed they worked at the sport. Kyle was tall at 187 cm but sinewy, much slimmer than the second-year standing there. He had long ago grown out of his gangly, uncoordinated stage. At twenty-four, Kyle had already served one fourteen-month hitch in Security, between his plebe and second years, that toughened him. His tour was supposed to be a routine two-month summer training exercise. Hastily but thoroughly trained, he saw more than enough Security action during those months for any career.

The guard in the water quickly caught up to Mia. Even from here, it was obvious the Mia was more petite.

But arm in arm, we fit together well once, Kyle remembered the past autumn walking with her before his lunar semester, arranged via a federation university linked to an Indie colony. He let out a frustrated sigh. *Once!* He cupped his hands and pumped water jets. *Had all that! Sucks*, he continued firing aimless streams of water, *she's graduating and I'm not*. His academic life had proceeded much differently than her straight four-year course.

Kyle had just come back from a semester on the Moon, returning to campus two weeks before graduation. Mia was done, hence her wish to swim on a Thursday night when normally she would be studying. Kyle had finished with his spring term on the Moon and one class through the Academy online. The admin here managed to find ways to keep him busy.

More to the point, which made the night so tense at times, at the end of last term in December, they had parted roughly. It was a nebulous exchange of remarks, a date that had started romantically with a dinner atop the new Marsco Space Needle in City Center but ended with a fight. Other names of cadets came into play, notably Arthur Wicks.

When Kyle was lunar-side, he and Mia had exchanged a few voice messages and holographic projections until the end of February, then little more, the slow death of a once-intense relationship.

Kyle was under the impression that at spring break Mia had gone to a Banff resort in a new fed for skiing with her tight circle of friends, Roland Elkton and Cassy Tomas-Higgens, Alexis Peterson, Jon Darby, and of course, so he heard, Wicks. Except for Elkton and Wicks, from last year's class, all were then still cadets.

As Mia finished her solo lap, she slid to a stop next to him. He half expected her to rise up from the water and declare, *So, you don't like snow skiing*.

"I was surprised when earlier this evening you messaged me about swimming," he remarked casually. They were next to each other again as close as before, but she didn't reach for him this time. He avoided her eyes, not sure what was there. *Renewed love? Tolerance? Just an old friend? I'm just here to be kind*, or more accurately, *total indifference?*

"Why?"

"I don't know. We left things so vague. Just hanging."

"Actually, in December, I should have said this. Things were getting too—" she searched for the right word, "too involved."

Kyle gave a burst of laughter. "That's one way to say it."

"I don't mean just *that*! I mean, where was it taking us?"

"Now, I am confused."

"Well, you're pretty certain to leave Marsco—"

"*What?* And just what gives you *that* idea?"

"Your interest in Indie colony work for starters. And you were under the auspices of a fed while on the Moon. The Six Accords are changing everything, and so, if you're a supporter of them, you're getting out."

Kyle gave another laugh. "I like your logic. What a syllogism. Have you read the Six Accords?" Her dark eyes focused at such an accusation. With the whole Marsco world shifting beneath their feet, of course, she had read them, even the fine print. "Okay, let me restate. I want to work on colonies, and Marsco *is* keeping the MAS, all its colonies."

"It's dropping Twelve Thrusters." Put in place even before the C-Wars, these Marsco regulations created its monopoly of space travel. Its grip remained strong until the Accords.

"But that's the only real change in space. Nothing else Marsco is doing off-planet will change. Lunar service. Hell, its current lunar colonies, those in the Asteroid Belt, the VBC." Both associates knew that half the lunar colonies and most of those on Mars were staying Marsco's.

"But colony work? Running greenhouses? Damn, Kyle, that's like being a farmer or something worse."

For protection, Kyle gave a laugh. "Hydroponics *is* a science. And on colonies, gardens and farming domes are vital. No one lives in a colony without them. But," he added, trying—and failing—not to sound defensive, "I also minored in extraterrestrial water science: finding, melting, pressuring, purifying water on colonies." He didn't add that his family had once been grangers—and Indies, although technically sids—down by Sac City. Leaving Marsco and joining West Con wasn't that far-fetched, either. And with the Accords, not that difficult. Almost expected.

"So, either a farmer in a dome or an ice miner," Mia sneered. When she dug with such barbed remarks, they cut deep and stayed hooked.

"'An associate in good standing' is how I'd characterize my ambitions," he shot.

"Sure you're not aiming to be a sid?"

"It would be a *fed* citizen, if anything." He let that remark slip too quickly, catching her using old, inaccurate terminology. Technically, subsidiaries along with their residents, or sids, no longer existed; neither did PRIMS. In theory at least. But his quip sounded like he was aiming to be *out* of Marsco and *into* a newly created federation.

"Let's just let it drop," she insisted.

Her sid remark hit a nerve. Even though his grandfather had been in Security for many years, Kyle was a sid by birth, born and raised in a mid-continent subsidiary. As such, he had needed to attend a Marsco prep for two years before matriculating at the Academy. Those years prepared him well for the rigors of the school but also made him older than his classmates. In August, he was turning twenty-five and still not commissioned.

From a longstanding associate family, Mia had started through an accelerated program and had turned twenty-one while Kyle worked at his lunar colony. She hadn't received flowers or even an e-greeting from him on the auspicious day.

"You done?" she asked.

"I'm ready if you want some more."

"I'm asking about swimming."

"I meant that to be just about swimming," he shot, once more sorry he spoke so soon. He easily could mean it any way she wanted.

"No, I'm done, let's bolt."

He let her swim by him to the ladder. Her trim form went up the steps with such grace that Kyle nearly reached to promise her anything so long as he was part of her life. This wasn't the only reason he had initially liked her and had fallen in love her, but her lithe form certainly was an added attraction.

"Look, I'm on duty at 2400 hours in my hall. Want a burger first?" he asked.

"Can't," she said, drying her hair poolside. She wore bangs, but down her back fell luminous jet-black hair. "How'd you get res hall duties?"

"Coming back for only two weeks, I got put into a plebe hall. The assistant res director had an appendectomy, and so I'm watching first years prepare for exams or sneak off to raise hell."

"Oh, joy."

"I'm tall, am older than them, and can shout like a Security sergeant. Probably know all their tricks, too. It's cake. Also, Chavez-Sherman wants to see me tomorrow about a summer lunar project."

"I hear he's up to something," she replied vaguely but not with assurances it was something he'd like.

"Hey, any guy who's been to Jupiter who's 'up to something,' well, sign me up."

"Then why didn't you take the pre-Flight track?" She sounded almost nagging. "Why not pilot a shuttle?"

"Why didn't you?"

"Security attracted my attention."

"I've had plenty of Security duty, thanks just the same," Kyle reminded her needlessly. Even though the Accords were lessening the chances of an Academy graduate being rostered permanently to Security, Marsco still shunted cadets to summer training. This two-month program accelerated the preparation of cadets for that now-rare eventuality. All Security battalions and Auxiliary units were supposedly moving under federation auspices. But Kyle knew firsthand that two months can easily grow into fourteen.

In Kyle's case, his first summer months of training became the actual thing, patrol duties with an Enfield and a platoon. He was lucky he was dismissed in time for fall semester after his tour. Apparently, Mia had loved her compulsory Security summers. While Kyle was on patrol, she had stayed at a training center her entire eight weeks.

Kyle thought it bitterly ironic that he'd had an intense tour but clearly wanted no more, and yet Mia, with what amounted to cushy internships, actually did.

"Give me domed gardens. What can I say?" He took her in his arms. She tensed a bit then relaxed. They were at the side of the pool, not in a private place. Looking deeply into her eyes, he whispered, "I fear we're destined for orbits that are mutually exclusive." He hadn't meant to, but his remark came out with unmistakable regret. When he reached down to kiss her, she turned away. *Air kiss.*

"Walk me home when I'm done?" she asked, working herself free of his embrace and stepping into the women's locker room.

———— •◦•═ ————

The campus near midnight was aglow with extra light from a Marsco Moon. Even though only at three-quarters full, the lunar surface and clouds drifting into space created more light than any twentieth-century Moon ever had.

The trees lining the greensward cut the light, but the pair still saw each other clearly. Without realizing it, Kyle slipped his arm around her waist.

She returned the gesture after shifting her tote. They kept a graceful pace, holding tight.

"I can't ask you up," she said as her res hall door came into view ahead. They were in a grove of pines with her dorm down a path off by itself, a quiet setting because its cadets were known for their serious academic habits. "It's study week. No visitors allowed."

"'So cadets have ample opportunity to fulfill their academic duties,'" he mimicked. "Yes, I know; lived here two and a half years under those regs, remember?"

Her hair shone in the light. Her eyes, too, had a radiance he had somehow forgotten on the Moon. "Mia," he began, stumbling, "look, I know *we* didn't, *I* didn't—"

She cut him off with a warm kiss, gently ending it by licking his lips teasingly. "It's okay, Kyle. I've so much to tell you." She kissed him deeply. "Look, I'm busy and away until Saturday afternoon. But some of us are going clubbing for dinner and dancing once back. Join us. We'll find time to talk. Promise."

Kyle stood there puzzled but ended his uncertainty by kissing her. Confused or not, he couldn't pass up such a woman in his arms. "Yes, Mia, yes," was all he whispered. It had been months since he had held her like this, but somehow, she seemed more solid, more substantial. He held on tightly, not knowing where the next few days or weeks were going to take them.

After their embrace, she pulled back. Knots of students were coming down the path.

"I'll message you," she whispered, breaking away and scurrying off toward the lit doorway.

———•———

"So, a solar system research project based at Resnik Colony, not something dealing with hydroponics," Devon Chavez-Sherman explained the next morning.

The professor-explorer sat at a desk in his faculty office speaking to one student, Kyle Roncalli. The prof kept his office neat and had bookcases deep with manuals and reports. Oddly, he even had several paperback novels and a few old textbooks on political theory. Kyle read their titles hastily whenever the colonel's eyes scoured a monitor to reread the cadet's application and academic record: *The Federalist Papers*, *The Assault on Reason*, *The End of the US Presidency*, the writings of Thomas Paine, whom Kyle had never heard of, and even two histories of constitutional governments. What made the cadet do a double take was a bound printout of *The Ascendancy of Marsco*, a suppressed text.

"Can you tell me," the officer went on, "why you signed up for this project? Your major doesn't suggest any interest in my research." Few cadets had asked to join Chavez-Sherman's summer project, but even so, the professor would rather have committed interns than those looking for a lunar lark or an excuse to bug out of summer Security training.

"To tell you the truth, sir," Kyle began with a calm voice.

No lying in that tone, Devon quickly sized up the cadet. "I would expect nothing less."

"I was on the Moon until last week, as my app clearly states."

"Yes, working lunar-side at three Indie colonies in their domed gardens."

"Correct, sir. Independent study on applied colony hydroponics. And for personal reasons, I wanted to hunker down, not even return to Earth. I had hoped to get your internship and just stay put until you arrived."

"I see," the officer stated. Grinning a bit, a gesture Kyle did not expect, the officer asked, "So, is your request related to avoiding summer Security?"

"I've had over a year already, sir. I doubt even Security HQ thinks training me any further is worthwhile. But, if Security wants me, I'll be gone in twenty-four hours, no question. But, I'm not volunteering."

"May I ask if this is related to a lunar significant?"

"Yes, sir, of course. But, no sir, it is not."

"Nursing a broken heart?"

"Not lunar-side, sir," Kyle shrugged.

"Just in case, Cadet Roncalli, let me remind you, the ratio of men to women on Resnik Colony is roughly 58.5 to 41.5. Not the best place to pick up babes, if you catch."

"Totally understand, sir."

"And I'll be working you pretty hard. I wanted three interns but will be taking only one."

"If I may ask why?"

"No, actually, no," Devon laughed out his answer. "Well," his voice lowered to a self-effacing tone, "you're my only viable applicant left. I thought I'd get six or eight apps, weed out the sightseers and malingerers, and have a remaining core of three or four to bring along. Evidently not!" His deep laugh encouraged Kyle to smile.

"Summer Security inexplicably that interesting?"

"Apparently."

The colonel twitched another set of files on the monitors before him. Kyle's records were striking. "Wow," the officer let out with a pleased tone. "Do you know your leadership score? You took the standard assessment inventory last November. Did you get the results?"

"Yes, I glanced at them once, sir."

"And you want to work *alone*, I mean with me and a small team at Resnik?"

"I don't understand the question, sir."

"Your score! It knocks the hell out of any score in years. Aren't you interested in pursuing that part of your associate's career? Something leadership?"

"Again, sir, I'm not sure I follow? Besides, leading a platoon under fire *is* leadership."

Devon gave another of his deep laughs. "That's just it. Your scores suggest if you lead, others will follow. You've got great potential, commanding a shuttle—"

"I hope not leading a battalion of troopers."

"I'm sure you'll have to start at platoon- or company-level first, young man, but leadership doesn't have to be just that."

"I understand that, sir. In fact, I know firsthand. And I did command a platoon of legionnaires, after their training but on their—well, *our*—first deployment."

"Well, I'd think about it, Cadet Roncalli, think about the MAS."

"I'll give it some thought, sir."

"Flight isn't out of the question with your academic record here. You'll have to bone up on pre-Flight classes from last year. Think of the opportunities for piloting a shuttle, possibly going beyond the belt."

"Well, in a way I have thought about it. My real goal is working at the Palmer Hydroponics Garden Domes at the Von Braun Center, sir, in the *Valles Marineris*."

Devon was impressed the cadet had all the Martian names correct.

"That's why I did colony hydro work, sir, all that resumé building, if you catch."

"Well, think about resumé building via the MAS and its exploration wing."

"Truly, sir, I'll give it some more thought," Kyle answered. "And, sir, may I ask, about 'beyond the belt'? Any plans for another run to Jupiter?"

"Interested?"

"Curious, sir."

"Well, that'll kill the cat. Why Marsco and the MAS puts everything into black, especially now after three Accords have begun opening issues up, I don't know. Force of habit, I guess." He laughed, but this time silently. "I'll only say at present, 'I cannot confirm or deny that curiosity of yours,' Cadet Roncalli."

"Good enough, sir. 'Wink's as good as a nod to a blind PRIM,' sir."

"Something like that."

The colonel rose, and the cadet snapped smartly to his feet. "I'll let you know officially tomorrow, but I am almost certain you'll be on board."

———— •◦———

Devon cared little about the private life of his new intern, but his scientific thoroughness pushed him into lefter territory. It was distasteful, all the personal intelligence Internal Security amassed on associates. Nonetheless, the officer needed to know several answers to unasked questions. Was Cadet Roncalli likely to come down with something—something HH GAS—while on the Moon? Was he likely to be off chasing ass when he should be working? Was he trustworthy around members of the Resnik staff or likely to make others, specifically any young women, uncomfortable? In all fairness to Roncalli's personal life, because the mission was black, the colonel felt he had to know.

Working alone in his office, Devon looked deeply into Kyle's career; lefter status opened dozens of windows of the cadet's e-history. He found strong grades. Always selected by peers for leadership roles. Always carried through on tasks. *Several res hall demerits, none serious; those're almost impossible to avoid*, Devon noted. *Means he is clever enough when making trouble to avoid being caught. Or that he never attempted anything really, seriously wrong. Not a fool but not a spineless associate either. He stayed on course and knew what he wanted. He was odd in that he declared his major as extraterrestrial agronomy from the get-go and never wavered.*

Kyle's Security record was spotless of command mistakes and included praising of his bravery and initiative. "When asked, he delivered," one reviewer noted. *Courageous and smart, two keys to a fine officer.*

His lunar semester remained a puzzle. While on the lunar surface, he was ostensibly in West Con Security. *A security unit on the Moon was a useless as teats on a bull*, Devon thought. *This cadet was sometimes neither fish nor fowl.* Technically, he was not actually an associate during his lunar stay. A red flag only a high wallah might object to, nothing Devon was worried about. *So, it was Sac City U.* Devon wondered about the coincidence of his own life tied in many ways to Sac City and New Grange near there. Probably nothing, he concluded.

Devon knew of Kyle's personal history, of his relationship with Cadet Mia Wang. In a week, she'd graduate and become Lieutenant Wang. Both were mature enough to handle such things, if staying together or not.

Devon twitched to her graduation portrait with her already bedecked in her officer's uniform. Dark eyes and jet hair, always neat in or out of uniform. Book smart, the professor knew from class, but a bit Marsco naive. Always with different students, never in a clique until lately. The kind of student and future officer you could trust with orders and your life.

"But over the past two semesters," he drew a breath while whispering to himself, "I don't know, she began displaying a sort of withdrawn behavior."

Unlike Kyle, she had changed her major, from pre-Flight to Security. *Damn*, the colonel mentally exploded, *why all this interest in Security in her class? And last year's too. With the whole damn solar system just begging to be explored.* "I swear," he mumbled to himself, "if I were asked to give an address to this class, I'd yell at them, 'Get your asses out into space!'"

Of Mia, he'd heard only one rumor. That she'd undergone regeneration. "Several treatments!" he stated loudly. He was in his private faculty office but was glad it was late Friday afternoon so he wasn't likely overheard. His ubiquitous fogger kept him from being recorded. "Why would a healthy woman need regeneration treatments? If she were sick—*that sick*—the Academy might ask her to resign or take a med leave." *Were these sanctioned by the Academy and Marsco? Performed right near here at our med center?* The Marsco Medical and Research Center was connected to the Academy and MIT.

All rumors, of course, and no way to find out without actually cooperating with the nefarious Internal Security by using their files to find an answer. He was high enough up the lefter-status chain to ask for such a report but didn't.

Even without going full Internal, Devon sensed something was up with part of that class. Since his return from Jupiter, he'd been here at the Academy. And he'd gotten to know a segment of each class well. It struck him as damn peculiar that a large circle wanted an Academy degree—which suggested space flight or science—but then selected Security permanently. Many current cadets remained loyal to Marsco, even as it shifted and evolved, but life in Security wasn't for them at all. Except this one particular knot. *There's something about that cohort*, he thought again, *Elkton, Tomas-Higgens, Wicks. A handful of others.* And, apparently, Wang had joined them.

"Mia's better off having a harmless fling with Kyle," he whispered, sounding too much like her father and not enough like a disinterested professor.

He would officially offer Cadet Roncalli the internship tomorrow morning. He hoped that the cadet would get things straightened out with Wang; she did seem like a fine, dedicated officer. *Perhaps they're well matched after all*, he concluded. He then added as though a command, *Break up now, make up a few years later*. That had worked for him once.

Devon opened a file and began working on one of the projects he needed to wrap up. But his mind kept returning to his students and the portion of them so interested in Security after graduation. Something was up with a collection of this year's and last year's class. He suspected that vice-chair Chesney's disks were guiding it but had no proof. He couldn't put his disks on it, but he knew something underhanded, perhaps dangerous, was pulsing just beneath the surface.

Like Kyle, Devon would be happy to be on the Moon for a summer and far away from the boiling caldron of HQ politics and the shifting landscapes brought on by the Accords.

Over the years, Marsco had allowed sids to open clubs and restaurants that clustered along a main thoroughfare not far from campus. Because thousands of cadets were living on campus, young-set establishments thrived there, with strict closing times and policies to conform to Academy regs. With HQ nearby as well, several apartment buildings rose here, residences for high wallahs and a sprinkling of sids. The area was crammed with liaison offices from former subsidiaries around the world. Each of these new federations all needed to speak with Marsco, now more than ever, as the Accords went active and as every aspect of the relationship between old subsidiaries and Marsco altered.

Mia's group started with sparkling wine at a rooftop club. They listened to a retro jazz band while waiting for their meals. Elkton and Cassy were an item, had been for years. Also, Altina Clarke and Harold Crosley were now engaged. Tina sported a large Martian diamond ring; such signs of commitment were coming back into fashion.

"We'll stay here for dancing after dinner," Elkton stated, almost as an order. "It's a great band." Cassy looked pleased; everyone knew she loved dancing.

Mia's glances asked Kyle if that was fine. He smiled back and reached for her hand under the table, giving a reassuring squeeze.

When Mia and Kyle had first met, she was not really part of this group. She had many friends, made others from across campus: cadets with associate, sid, and even PRIM backgrounds. Only recently did she seem to focus on this tight faction that was so deeply rooted in Marsco.

Cassy had on a long gown, shimmering and light-colored, prefect for a spring evening. Mia and Altina wore shorter dresses, especially so in the case of Mia. Her sophisticated sequined top plunged down her back, so she wore a shawl over her shoulders. The trio had selected elegant attire reminiscent of the early twenty-first century, the *de rigueur* style now. As the colorless Marsco world broke apart, that idealized, distant era became the one to imitate. Because Cassy and Mia had longer hair, they wore theirs up. The refined elegance of the three women turned heads.

Kyle felt proud to be part of the group.

Hap Crosley wore a suit, cut in late twentieth-century style; he might have passed for a new fed bureaucrat. A dress uniform seemed inappropriate to Kyle. He wore a blue shirt and tie with a linen jacket that accented his slim build.

Elkton sat at the table's head, wearing his dress uniform. No one else came Marsco-attired, but no one else was commissioned. And he had his Enfield.

It did strike Kyle as odd that Elkton had a weapon. But, the cadet figured, Hap might easily hide one under his jacket.

Hell, he reminded himself, *if I wasn't in the heart of Marsco, I'd be packing.* For all his sympathy for the new feds, he wasn't a fool. The lingering effects of Security duty. Marsco might be re-forming its old subsidiaries and UZs into self-governing federations, but it was still a troubled world. *Even so, here in Seattle, spitting distance from HQ, no one needs to be packing.*

The attentive staff dutifully hovered. Wine flowed; laughter filled the table. As the evening progressed, Kyle felt more at ease, certain that part of the reason was the sincere attempt by the others to make him feel welcome. And Mia's actions to make him feel loved.

"Is everything fine?" Mia leaned over to ask. He again noted that she'd donned that flattering outfit for him. Kyle sensed she was trying her best to let him know what she really felt. He appreciated that she was working so hard to make the long-simmering tension between them disappear.

"All's fine now," he confided, "but I'm not the best dancer."

"I like the way you dance," she replied, her shining dark eyes captivating him.

Dancing for Kyle just meant holding Mia tightly and letting her sway in his arms. He looked forward to that, already imaging the feel of his hands along her bare back.

Elkton rose to propose a toast. "Well," he began, "here's to a group of friends and classmates. The best I could ever imagine."

"Hear! Hear!" The group took a deep slip of wine.

"And to our newest real, *forever* couple, officially so, Tina and Hap."

The group burst out, "Hear! Hear!" before another taste of their wine.

"And, I wanted to say to Mia, how lovely you look and how lovely a couple you two make. To Mia and Kyle. Thanks, man, for joining us!"

"Hear! Hear!"

Kyle shot her a confused glance; it asked whether something was there she was telling *them* but wasn't telling *him*.

"When we have a chance," she answered in a whisper.

"So, this's where we're all off to," Arthur Wicks burst in on the three couples as they finished dinner. He looked smart in his uniform but approached them in a foul mood.

Grabbing a chair from another table, he swung it between Mia and Kyle. Seating himself with a thump, he scowled at her. "Thought you were my date?" he whispered hoarsely.

Elkton was the only one who had any control over Wicks. He spoke up before the intruder got very far.

"We missed you earlier, Arthur," Elkton began.

"Well," came the reply, "Chesney had me running errands down to Rainier."

The intruding lieutenant's presence instantly revived all sorts of suspicions in Kyle about Mia.

"We've eaten, Arthur, and we're staying to dance. Do you have a date?"

"Well, I thought Mia here was."

Kyle was ready to jump to his feet, but both common sense and discretion held him back. Wicks was thick-set, not as tall as Kyle, but well-built and much more aggressive. Kyle might outthink him, but few men could outfight him. Besides, striking an officer over a date was not a wise course of action. The cadet didn't need classes on Marsco protocol to understand that.

His rival was seething at Mia, at Kyle, at being cut out of their party. He worked to check his anger, but he did want everyone to know how important he ultimately was. "Yeah," he sneered, "Chesney called *me* to do *his* bidding down there."

Kyle wasn't sure if Wicks had been drinking or was intoxicated by the rush of authority vested in him by the world's second most powerful man.

"Is *he* one of us?" Wicks snidely shot, loudly, catching the attention of others seated near him, "or are you having your last little fling with a regular guy?" It was clear he was addressing these questions to Mia and was implying Kyle. If the table understood fully, the sole outside cadet didn't. Other diners seated at adjacent tables sensed the rising animosity in this party.

"You're going into black, Wicks," Elkton shot in an authoritative tone.

That was enough for Wicks. He rose, bowed gallantly to the women, and strutted out of the stunned and hushed restaurant.

———••———

Without a word about Wicks, the three couples danced to mournful tunes and halting rhythms. Kyle hardly moved but just held onto Mia as she swayed. Wicks aside, it all felt right.

When the combo took a break, the pair went up one floor to a viewing platform that showed the whole city below. Taking his hand, Mia led him into a secluded corner. Because few other couples were about, it was unlikely anyone would be barging in on them.

Kyle was giddy, not with wine, but with the ambiance, with Mia, with the lights and beauty of Marsco Seattle seen from this perch as its sky darkened. A new world was before them all with its renewed prosperity and freedoms and inviting promises.

"Not like the lunar surface," he told her. "It has a beauty, a stark and terrible beauty, but not like this."

"See," she smiled with her answer, "stay Earth-side, and all this belongs to you."

He had no doubt what was included in that *all*.

"I have to ask you, Kyle," Mia began in a low voice, "I have to ask you about something important."

Swept away by her appeal for him, her dress and her dancing, the evening, he was prepared to promise her anything.

"Have you noticed anything different about me?"

"Should I?"

"Yes, well, yes, but I guess it would be more noticeable in a year or so; it might take five years."

He had no idea where she was going with this. He was alone with her, feeling keener about her and more deeply toward her than ever before. He wanted just to hold her; talking could wait.

"Look," he tried to joke, "Wicks may bust in again any sec." He leaned down to kiss her.

"You're missing the essential point, *my* point," she replied, not cooperating with his romantic moves.

"Okay, I'll bite. What gives?"

"Kyle, we're changed. *We*, not *you*."

"I don't follow."

"Please realize, my darling, I'd love you in a minute—*if*—"

"If? If what?"

"Have you *ever* considered Security?"

"Other than my one ball-busting tour I've already spent at their beck and call, no, I don't think about them. But why?"

"Well, if you volunteer, think of the perks!"

"Are you one?" he asked, then concluded where she was going. "Is that it? This a recruitment drive?"

"We're in, all of us. Elkton, Cassy, Hap."

Kyle wanted to laugh. "How can a guy nicknamed 'Hap' want to be a Security goon rousting up former PRIMS?"

"Security will be doing more than controlling PRIMS," she shot. "Kyle, it's all changing, and we're on the ground floor."

"Mia, of course it's all changing. The Accords—"

"I wouldn't trust my disks on those damn Accords," she flared up, a new emotion in her voice.

"Look, Mia, I don't understand what this means, where you're going."

"Feel me," she whispered, "feel me anywhere."

Not sure what she was intending but not wanting to pass up the opportunity, Kyle ran his hand down her strong back. She cooed and kissed his neck, letting him know it was all okay. Because he was sure they were alone and not likely to be interrupted, he moved his hands lower along her firm, petite body.

"This will never change," she whispered.

He squeezed her inviting body, happy to be holding her so. She welcomed his embrace.

Kissing deeply, neither spoke until she added, "I won't ever change. Trust me."

"Look," he pulled back, "everyone changes." He grew completely serious. "Everyone switches careers and ambitions." *Even lovers*, he almost added.

"It doesn't have to be that way," she pleaded.

"I'm not sure I know what you mean."

"I am under orders not to reveal any more. All I can do is invite you *to want* to join me, *us*, and with your commitment, you'll enter a new world, a permanent world, one that ensures your status and Marsco's."

His head began to swim; if he fully understood what she was saying, he didn't let on. "Does this have anything to do with Wicks?"

"I have to say, indirectly, yes." Mia lowered her dark eyes. *Embarrassment? Shame? Need for secrecy?* Kyle could not tell.

In the distance, the music began once more, even more mournful than earlier. Other couples stirred from their shadowy haunts where flirting had given way to deeper feelings of true affection.

"C'mon," he said, walking her toward the crooning singer before his partner could change her mind. "One last dance before I get you home. I've plebes I have to tuck in."

"Come up and check on me in first," she whispered. "It'll be wonderful. I promise."

FOUR

TRACKING RASCAL

(Resnik Colony, the far side of the Moon, May, 2154)

Once established under Resnik's dome, Lieutenant Colonel Devon Chavez-Sherman opened a cyber doc he was preparing as his final report to HQ. He left-twitched with a finger mouse to open the program on a Security notebook. He then put the thimble in a pocket inside his tunic.

He's taking no chances with his data, Cadet Kyle Roncalli noted. He'd already read the prelims that gave a brief précis of Rascal's first discovery, its odd tracking and heading, its mysterious intent.

"This past week," Devon reminded him, "the VBC confirmed its size and relative shape. It is cylindrical, about half again as large as a standard Mars-Belt shuttle."

"So about as massive as the *Armstrong-Aldrin*, right?"

"Exactly. Pretty tangible proof it's constructed, not natural." The colonel flipped a slide. "Note also, it's not tumbling as most asteroids do. In the parlance of flight going back to the Wright brothers, it's 'straight and level.'"

"Suggesting its actions are purposeful, under control."

"Affirmative. It's being guided, steered, or so everything suggests. It may yet prove to be a natural phenomenon, but I doubt it."

The cadet added, "Its fuel trail of plutonium-239 nails it, doesn't it, sir?"

"Yes, that's really the clincher." The professor was pleased the student had paid attention to lectures on spaceflight. "The VBC confirmed that as well. But all this evidence still doesn't tell us who's the crew? Someone returning? Limited options on that. An Indie consortium with this much rocketry tech? Not likely but still possible. Alien? Least likely."

"So, this summer, we're here only to confirm what the VBC just reported."

"Affirmative."

Double-checking results in science was imperative; the cadet knew that, but some of this seemed superfluous.

"Here are the viewing specs for the next sixteen weeks," Kyle showed his superior. In less than twenty-four hours at the lunar colony, Kyle had the dark phase tests lined up and calibrated. While the Earth side of the Moon grew to full then began to fade, the far side's opposite phase would create optimal viewing.

Devon glanced at Kyle's file. "Very well, we start in ten hours and go until our light phase begins." Ten Earth days in duration, the dark phase provided 240 hours of unbroken blackness.

"I'm already working on a clarity report for our next phase. Marsco shipping manifests are accurate to a second. Nothing should interfere then, either." It'd be tedious, Kyle knew, to do the same thing three times over the next sixteen weeks to garner the same results as Von Braun. Mia in her narrow cadet's bunk crossed his mind.

Kyle twitched a pad to cross-reference several data files: the delivery dates of mining asteroids, their placement schedules and locations, and the predicted cloud intensity and range of the ashen trails of dust clouds such placements caused. He and Devon needed perfect viewing to verify the VBC data. Kyle hoped their fresh lunar observations would be the last before this intel went to Marsco HQ.

"Are Campbell and Planck online?" The explorer asked. At those other far-side colonies, arrays pointed outward into the silent abyss. "Of course," he groused, "if I really wanted exactness, I should have gone to Vesta. Her arrays would be aligned perfectly by the time I got there."

"Where, sir?"

"The Asteroid Belt. We'd be that much closer, about 1.8 AUs closer."

"Mars is about as far out as I want to go," Kyle confided.

"Why stop at Mars?" the colonel chided, "a whole solar system is just waiting for us—for *you*!"

"I joined Marsco, sir, to go to the *Mars* part of *Marsco*, if you catch, sir." His mind drifted to an imagined future at the VBC. Von Braun had magnificent greenhouses originally started nearly a century ago by Dr. Bethany Palmer. *Said to be the best example of colony hydroponics anywhere in the solar*, he reassured himself.

Kyle was so serious about Mars, he'd majored in extraterrestrial agronomy and minored in water recovery science. That's where his heart lay, in the garden domes of Mars. Not on hiber trips to and from the asteroid belt or years-long trips to Jupiter. The cadet could hear himself griping to classmates during his on-campus Academy days, "If Marsco thought going to Jupiter was such a fantastic idea, it would have sent more expeditions than the original *Gagarin* trek from last century and the single, relatively recent *Armstrong-Aldrin-Collins* mission."

Those gardens at the VBC remained as enticing as Mia. The cadet thought of his last nights on Earth entwined with her. Those Martian hydroponics pulled at him, but she had once been training to fly. He rationalized, *Plenty of pilots needed on Mars. We could make this happen yet.* His groundless belief lingered that Mars and he had a stronger pull on Mia than Security.

Devon gave a laugh as if reading his assistant's mind. "We've been here how long, and we're both acting space happy. I'm talking Asteroid Belt, you the Red Planet."

"Yes, sir, close enough." The cadet didn't let on that his lovemaking with Mia had been cut short by Chavez-Sherman dragging him away to the barren Moon days sooner than anticipated.

In all the time Kyle had known Chavez-Sherman at the Academy, the space-explorer-turned-professor was the consummate cool-headed officer. But since arriving at Resnik, Kyle noted an element of strain in his superior.

He wondered if it were the workload, except they'd only just arrived.

Something's haunting the colonel, Kyle concluded, *and it's not the task ahead.* The computers and the deep-space array's permanent staff would be doing the bulk of the tedious work. Neither lunar visitor needed to worry about liquid nitrogen for the spectrometers or dish array capacity or backup storage. The lunar crew had that well in disks.

No, something in the research itself weighed on Chavez-Sherman's mind, Kyle sensed. Something obsessed him, goaded him to angst over a seemingly small task: to trace rather needlessly, one—*and only one*—bogie for the next three dark phases.

Both researcher and assistant had been in Security, hot Security. This was cake.

———•———

"Roger that, we copy." Kyle switched channels to report, "Campbell, Planck, and Resnik arrays are in sync." Looking up from his monitor, he added, "All three sites are trained, sir. Ready to commence first sweep."

"Very well, Kyle," the officer replied informally.

To increase his chances of zeroing in on Rascal, Chavez-Sherman had arranged the use instrument dishes at three colonies spread out on the far side of the Moon. Each trained its spectrographic sensor on a quadrant of the solar system just within the orbit of Saturn.

Most of this data is already known and confirmed, Kyle knew. *Devon fears something else,* the cadet sensed, *something his data isn't telling him yet.* Although not in the Marsco Asteroid Service, he knew its old saw, *"There are millions of mysteries in space."*

While Chavez-Sherman had been on the *Armstrong-Aldrin-Collins* expedition in the '40s, instruments had picked up this anomaly in the Kuiper Belt. All preliminary calculations of the mystery object even then pointed to its heading being exactly to Earth. For months while cruising home from Jupiter to the belt, the *AAC* observed the enigma.

"Even with the background clutter in the Kuiper Belt, our rogue stood out," Devon explained to Kyle yet again. "Just think of all those comets and asteroids floating in Kuiper, massive objects our mysterious pongo needed to move around. And yet, once it altered direction to avoid a collision, it was right back to an Earthward bearing."

"Earth seems to be home. Are we sure?"

"That's exactly what I aim to confirm, Kyle," Devon concluded, treating his subordinate like a colleague, almost like an equal.

Kyle's monitor beeped a reminder. "All's set, and recording has commenced, sir."

"Very well. Time will tell now."

The cadet dutifully reported, "Observation duration 240 hours and counting."

Unbroken screen time became the norm, superfluous babysitting of the glowing computers. But, Devon left nothing to chance. The currently star-studded skies above the Resnik's dishes were free from ground-impact clouds. As per the colonel's request—and MAS orders—the immediate vicinity of the whole of the Apollo Crater, along with those areas around Campbell and Planck, remained free from lander and asteroid shard traffic. Nothing was allowed to disturb their work.

Even the colonists took note of that. *Boffins and spooks in our midst*, the gossip went around. *Taking up that much tech, that much dish time.*

"You should see their storage capacity," one two-disk programmer whispered.

"Have you ever seen the need to twitch to get *in* and *out* of our monitor rooms?"

Chavez-Sherman had a cot brought into the monitor station where he dozed in snatches during the first of those 240 hours of continuous, unbroken night. Only twice did he leave for a quick shower and shave and a hot meal. Kyle was released at more regular intervals for a proper nap in a bunk, if either man thought a bit about their now-disrupted circadian rhythm. Five hours was the most Kyle was ever away.

As the Campbell, Planck, and Resnik arrays kept their dishes focused and registering, Devon examined their preliminary readouts. Over time, his creased forehead went to a truly wrinkled brow. The freshly gathered intel was clear, yet Devon wanted more.

<hr>

"Confirm that, sir," Kyle responded, suppressing a yawn, "in less than fifteen minutes we'll have traffic closing in, sir. That ends our clear view."

"What? It's been less than 175 hours since we started?" Chavez-Sherman glared at the cadet. *How could you miscalculate this so badly? What a screwup.*

"Affirmative. Some sort of shipment's being parked above us. Geocentric."

"Shit. Geocentric? Then, indefinite. Indefinite duration."

"Yes, sir. Unscheduled. Unplanned," Kyle reported. "As far as I can tell, it's a surprise to even the colonists."

"Shit," Devon scowled again, his second unprofessional response.

"And, sir, it's black. Nothing in any databank. I can't find even a measly gig about this shipment anywhere. Something this large would have terabytes of info on several sites." *CYA. Not my fault.*

"So, end of our clear shot at Rascal."

"Affirm that, sir. And for the indefinite future."

Chavez-Sherman sat at a monitor without looking at its graphs and charts. The sine curves no longer meant anything to his blurry eyes anyway. Rising, he walked over to a small viewing portal. The bubble gave him a view of the horizon. A dark ashen lip of the surface gave way to a view of the uncountable stars above. This was the constant view above during this phase, ceaseless night with billions of stars.

The stars behind outlined unmistakable, arrow-headed shapes above Resnik. Dozens of them came into the star-filled sky in tight echelons, clearly, not an ordinary mining asteroid shipment.

Devon needed to check a computer, because what he was seeing were too small for mining shards and too regular for drifting asteroids. A few right-twitches magnified a view of the objects and confirmed their geocentric placement above Resnik. It took serious left-twitching, however, before he found an old file that gave the schematics of Vanovara weaponry. *How can I be looking at weapons from a century ago?*

"That's it then. We're out of business," he concluded. "Lock down everything at Campbell and Planck."

Kyle had a sense that *this* was what Devon was waiting for all along.

<hr />

After returning to his assigned bachelor quarters for a shower, Kyle walked through a linking tube alone. Since Rascal tracking began, he'd eaten mostly to-go packs at his monitor station. And when he messed, he sat alone. Resnik didn't house a large population; aside from its research dishes and limited greenhouses, little reason existed to live here permanently. Scientists and researchers came and went, like Devon and his one assistant.

As informal as the colonel was during their research, the rest of the colony hadn't overlooked that he was a dignitary. When free for a meal, the colonel was whisked off to the officers' mess. His lowly noncommissioned assistant ate with warrant officers and technicians. During his infrequent meals, Kyle found this mess only a quarter full. Along one wall, steam tables held ample food, which Kyle found well-prepared and tasty. It topped any Security mess.

Kyle looked forward to a hearty meal with no need to hurry.

Moving through the line, he grabbed eggs, hash browns, and a pile of bacon. "Love to see the gardens that grew these berries," he sighed under his breath, covering a pancake with warm fruit compote.

"It's a date," a voice from right next to him replied.

Intent on heaping his tray, Kyle hadn't noticed a string of techies behind. The closest to him smiled. Her uniform showed she was part of the colony's permanent crew, the agronomy section. In the dim lighting of the mess, her short hair looked dark. Because she was in work overalls, he couldn't tell her rank, but when she reached for eggs under the steam table hood, he clearly saw disks on her right hand.

"Greenhouse gang?" Kyle asked.

"Yeah, a misplaced farm girl from a Kansas Sid."

"I'd love to see your greenhouses," Kyle stated, rather too boldly and loudly.

"Yeah, bud, she's gotten that one before, and plenty," someone behind them jeered.

"Casey's heard 'em all, son," another voice down the line taunted.

The woman whirled around to silence her trailing coworkers. "Come along, too, if you want." Back to Kyle, she added with a smile, "They don't really want to go back to the greenhouses now because it cuts into their down time with Cyber-Sally and their lube."

"At least she puts out," a third voice added with a bitter tone.

"She does teasin'; you do squeezin'," she snapped back in a singsong voice. To Kyle, she whispered, "Come over here," and led him to an empty table off to the side.

The cadet started to apologize for creating such uncouth ridicule from her coworkers.

"Look," Casey cut him off, "don't bother with their crudeness or with them." She motioned to her work gang's crowded table out of earshot, "Lunar work for those dipshits is a three-month duty rotation, a two-week leave, three months of rotation, until a periodic two-month furlough with some randy HH GAS-free tarts, then maybe an adequate retirement. With only a few years of service left, these old has-beens're just putting in time."

"And you?" Retirement was not her agenda soon. She looked about his age, mid-twenties, unless she'd hibered a bit.

"Trying to get to Mars or an asteroid colony," she chirped with excitement. "Moon duty sucks."

"How so?"

"Well, for starters, it readily accepts handle jerks like them. Leftovers of real space careers. Old sweats who can't pass a physical for deep space, who no longer want to work hard, and for novices like me, ones who missed the shuttle-asteroid-Mars tour by a few points, a few twitches too slow." She wiggled her right fingers, showing more disks than Kyle would expect. "And with these new Accords going down, more coming along, I want to cement my chances with the MAS while the getting is good."

Casey was that rare associate who didn't hold back, who gave you her life on a platter without you asking for it. And yet, she smiled invitingly and did have access to those intriguing greenhouses.

Kyle finished his tray before Casey had hardly touched hers for all her amiable chatting. While he went for coffee, she wolfed down a portion of breakfast, preparing herself for another lecture. "Hot chow's hot chow," she replied, sounding too much like one of his legionnaires from a few summers back.

"Yeah, guess I learned that at the Academy and on my first tour."

"Oh, a cadet? Impressive!"

"Didn't drop *that* to be impressive, believe me."

"I was impressed that you cared about hydroponics." She smiled. In the light here, her hair was clearly a deep brown, as were her lively eyes. Finishing her food, she asked, "So, I've not seen you before. New here? Here long?"

Motioning with his head to have her look at the top rim of the visible Resnik dishes, Kyle let them indicate why he was here. A common-enough reason.

"So," she gave a wry glance, "you part of the über-secret, snooping-boffin team?"

Ice water shot down Kyle's back. He wasn't on a Security sweep now—

he'd developed a sixth sense with skinnies wanting to kill him—but knew enough to be guarded, evasive on that subject.

Hearing no answer, Casey resumed her questions. "I hear that this is it. *TBO: The Big One!* That there's a massive asteroid coming in, one mother-humper, Earth-banger that'll knock us back to the Stone Age."

Kyle sipped his coffee without emotion or answer. Security training.

"You know," Casey went on, speaking slyly under her bangs, "if I show you my gardens, maybe I could sneak a peek at your data. You know, *quid pro quo?*"

"Isn't really something I'm a liberty to discuss, Casey," the cadet replied. *You probably won't be able to understand our preliminary data anyway.*

While he was silent, something in her manner seemed changed. And her eyes, he began to notice, actually seemed older than a novice waiting for deep-space work. "Tell me, why didn't you elect the Academy to get into the MAS?"

It was her turn to be evasive. "A sid? Getting in?" She shrugged.

"There are *other* schools, *other* campuses. Scores have reopened in the past twenty years alone. Or a Marsco prep, that's what I had to do for two years prior to matriculation."

"You do look older than a typical cadet," she said. His insignia made this status clear, but it wasn't something a dome techie might recognize.

Besides the fact that her vocabulary didn't sound that sid (*quid pro quo*), something else caught Kyle's eye that convinced him to shut down totally: she was a lefter. He should have been suspicious when she reached for her food and later when she wriggled her disks, that her right hand was so fully loaded. Holding her tray left-handed had kept him from seeing anything else, but now at the table, she was not paying careful attention to her hand movements. On her left hand she clearly sported three blue-green implants. *Not a vast left array but large enough. Devon has five left disks, and imagine all his experience.*

Finally, he made up his mind. "Tell me, why are you so interested in my work, my alleged work?"

"Well, when a guy says he wants to see *gardens*!" Her smile came on thick.

"My major is ex-ag, after all." Her eyes showed the cadet's slang was new to her. It shouldn't be. *Ex-ag* was *ex*traterrestrial *ag*ronomy, her very occupation. Allegedly.

Kyle had seen enough. Casey's sham innocence had grown wearisome. He was glad he'd be moving onto real greenhouse work and saying goodbye to Devon's black ops.

"You done? Let me bus your tray," he said politely but with a tone that suggested a completed fact.

She locked her arm in his as he stepped away from the return line. They looked like an item for all to see, the fastest hookup he had ever had, and a cadet uniform was a magnet most places on Earth. Kyle had seen it used with success many times. But this topped anything he'd ever personally experienced.

"Why leave so soon?" she cooed. "You need to get back to your work on the double? Tell me some of what you do, anything. Must be *fascinating*," she stretched out the word for emphasis. "Really, truly, I *am* enthralled."

Kyle smiled down at her. She returned his gaze with a forced grin. "The gardens are off that way." She tugged him to the left.

"Well, I'm off this way." He gently let her arm fall.

Casey looked blank.

"You know I can't speak a word about my work. A *lefter* especially ought to know that."

"How was your meal?" Devon asked.

"Too eventful for words," Kyle replied vaguely.

"Do tell. People prying?"

"Well, one person."

"Was she cute?"

"Yes, and fast. If it had come to that," he bragged a bit, "I think Resnik's Edenic gardens may have seen another original sin if she had dragged me down there."

"Lucky you. I knew I picked the right guy for this."

Kyle wasn't sure he liked being characterized like that, in so loaded and vague a manner. Careful as he was, he wasn't frozen or unresponsive. He thought of Mia. He shook his head. "Should we report this?"

"Why? My meal was even more blatant. No subterfuge at all. Just several officers and lefters cornering me. A barrage of 'off-the-record' questions."

"Doesn't take much to kindle a rumor," the cadet smirked, glad he had let nothing slip. "But how do these colonists even know enough—*incorrectly*—to even begin a rumor circulating?"

"Easy—Rascal was first spotted by the *AAC* science team. Our prelim report was scientific so not restricted until Chesney got wind of it. Then, he labeled everything 'Top Secret.' That roused everyone's curiosity."

"My favorite 'true fact' thus far: this is a planet-killer asteroid coming in."

"Good luck on that. It's not that big as anomalies in space go. If it comes into the atmosphere, it'll probably burn up entirely. It's mostly metal; VBC confirmed that."

Finally, Devon said, "Look, I won't stay coy with you. You deserve to know what's up. But I have a call to make first; then we'll talk."

I don't need this to run a greenhouse of Mars, Kyle insisted to himself, the only one convinced his future was eventually on the Red Planet.

"I know I can trust you. So, go to your quarters and stay there. No walks down lovers' lane in the gardens."

"Roger."

———————⏺———————

Devon's call went directly to Seattle HQ. "Even though my research has been cut short," he reported dutifully, "I have enough data about Rascal to make my official report... *Come in person*, I understand, sir, HQ doesn't want anything over the air. We're closing down all our ops now. Take us about a week to tie everything up here, cleanse the local databanks. Cadet Roncalli can manage the Campbell and Planck sites for that. I'll dispatch him off to them first thing... Yes, sir, totally trustworthy, or else he wouldn't be here." He listened then confirmed, "Yes, sir, we'll definitely be done here in a week, so make it ten, eleven days from now until I'm in Seattle. See you then."

Something about all this didn't just seem right, didn't feel right. He didn't mention the Vanovara weapons floating above Resnik that abruptly ended his summer research.

⸻ ◦ ⸻

After only twenty minutes, Devon called Kyle back to his quarters. "Look," he began, "I'm telling you everything, but much is still uncertain." Devon was holding a data disk in his right hand, playing with it, tapping it on the desk before him as they spoke. "I want you to go directly to a new fed and," he stopped fidgeting with the disk to hold it up, "deliver this to someone who should be told *unofficially* about our discoveries." A data disk was the most secretive of methods. Devon would have it tagged so only the waiting recipient could open it. Kyle, the courier, wouldn't even have access.

"Don't mention those V-weapons or any suspicions we have. Let him read my documents and answer any questions but offer him no other intel until he reads it." He handed the disk over to Kyle.

"Too large to swallow if caught," Kyle kidded.

Devon shot him a stern look. "It isn't something to joke about, cadet." The lieutenant colonel caught him. "I'm sorry, on all accounts. I asked you to help me research and now this. But, I'm trusting that you aren't in with them." It was growing clearer to Kyle who *them* was.

"I'm in all this to get to Mars, sir," Kyle reminded his superior. "But, I trust you, too, sir."

"Once you've delivered it, get to these Sac City coordinates stat. But come with your Enfield."

"Yes, sir. Always wanted to see that grange," he caught himself, "that area."

Devon didn't miss his assistant's stumble. "Oh, that's right. You know quite a bit about my cousin's grange. Well, first this Earth-side task, then New Grange."

The ex-platoon leader nodded his compliance even though this lunar trip was taking on more and more cloak-and-dagger aspects. At least Security was up front about its tactics; pacification sweeps in hot zones are straightforward, uncomplicated. This was altogether like Internal Security, veiled and surreptitious.

⸻ ◦ ⸻

Down the corridor from Devon's on his way to his own quarters, Kyle met

Arthur Wicks. A lieutenant only weeks ago, Wicks was now a Security captain and standing in the narrow hallway as audacious as ever.

Kyle stiffened, saluted; in the confines of a passageway, it came off awkwardly.

"Cadet Roncalli, what brings you to the Moon?" the officer demanded.

"Summer internship, sir," Kyle replied, thankful that he was telling the truth while hiding the reason.

"Good for you, cadet," the captain spit with a condescending tone. "Glad to see you are adding something useful to your academic pursuits."

"Thank you, sir." Kyle reacted without emotion, beginning to move on.

"Stand at attention while I'm speaking to you, cadet." Kyle snapped back to a frozen stance. "Devon Sherman, he around here?"

"Does the captain mean Lieutenant Colonel Devon Chavez-Sherman, sir? I just left his quarters. May I show you the way, sir?"

"No need, cadet. Where is he?"

Kyle pointed out the colonel's quarters.

The officer left the cadet at attention and walked away. Over his shoulder, he glowered, "I've been swimming quite a bit lately to keep in shape." His words came out savagely. "Been doing laps with Lieutenant Wang. A fine swimmer, Wang. Born to the water. I believe you know her, cadet."

"The captain is entirely correct," Kyle responded to the broad back that disappeared down the passageway.

The cadet, now alone, watched the empty corridor in case the captain reappeared. Mia with Wicks, incomprehensible. It wasn't jealousy so much as rage that a man like that was with a woman like her.

Even more so, that Wicks was now a captain in Security. Kyle had led troopers through hot zones not so long ago. Taken fire. Been slightly wounded once. Taken serious casualties to his platoon. And yet, he remained without a commission. That duty had taken a year out of his life and given him nothing in return. But Wicks had a promotion and no history of action.

And seeing Chavez-Sherman? It was all too much for him to comprehend.

After Captain Wicks left, Devon looked at the wall chronometer, one of those units with several faces to show the times at various locales. It was 0315 local at New Grange, too early to call even farmers. No one at Seattle HQ seemed upset when he'd called; they were that anxious for word from him. The two conversations, first with Chesney's HQ and then Captain Wicks here at Resnik. Both seemed laden with hidden purposes. Wicks particularly seemed to be probing about Devon's final decision to join or not join Chesney's new cadre.

The captain hadn't brought up the V-weapons, but the researcher thought that the real purpose of the junior officer's trek to the Moon was to check them out.

Alone, the colonel sat and thought quietly. Studying Rascal was easy compared to all this.

Devon's next call an hour later was of a personal nature. "Sorry to wake you, Celine, but if I don't call now, I may not get another chance. Tell Trent that I won't be down until after a few more weeks, maybe longer."

"Well, you're welcome here any time, you know that," his cousin replied, suppressing a yawn.

"Yes, I do. Say, is Sarah there?"

"Oh, no, she's sound asleep."

"Well, tell her I have an associate here I want her to meet. He has some interesting tales to tell you all about New Grange."

"Our New Grange?"

"Of course, odd but true. I won't spoil his thunder, but I've collared him to come with me. He's quite the history buff, and now that records on the Net have opened, well, he has quite a tale to tell all of you. He knows about the early history of your spread."

"Really? Can't think of what I don't know already," Celine insisted.

"We'll just have to wait and see."

The woman's voice turned maternal. "Is he nice looking?"

"I'll let you—and Sarah—decide when we get there, but I'm bringing him because he's my aide."

"Well, you're always welcome here. Your friends anytime, too." Celine yawned again, trying to remember something important. "Oh, Devon, Trent is beside himself with questions about the Accords."

"You just tell him that the Accords are *the least* of his worries. Say it just like that: 'Devon says they are *the least* of his worries.'"

Not sure what to make of that, Celine went on. "We'll be having our solstice hog roast next month; try to make that."

Checking his planner, he confirmed. "I'm at the mercy of Seattle HQ, but I have it down. I ought to be able to wrangle leave that weekend."

———————

"Before we leave here, you scoot up to Campbell, then over to Planck. Nothing must remain in their databanks of our work. Close and cleanse everything."

"Can do, sir."

"They'll probe you like hell at those places, too."

"Swell, a girl in every colony."

"And you may as well know why. As much as I can tell."

"Thank you, sir, but I think I know." Devon looked quizzically at him. "My grandfather—he raised me—was part of the Security detail in SoAm in the '90s, sir. I've heard stories of Vanovaras all my life. They are unmistakable."

"Okay, then." Devon paused. They both understood that the Accords and V-weapons didn't square.

Kyle was quick and, trusting him, Devon added his growing suspicions about Chesney's HQ. The cadet had heard Wicks allude to such a connection with Chesney. Devon sighed. "Who else but Seattle could put these weapons up here?"

Had the good colonel suspected those Vanovaras were on their way all along? Kyle wondered but didn't ask. His summer research project was turning into a Centurion's nightmare.

Mars seemed light-years away. Mia even farther.

FIVE

THE OLD WAYS

(New Grange, late May 2154)

"I know all this to be true. The old ways are the best ways," Columbus stared, putting on an image of a solemn sage. "It goes without saying." Looking around at the four Brunels, the only ones at the outdoor table, Columbus thought with self-assured confidence that they were in agreement. *Why think otherwise?*

Reaching the top of its sweep across the night sky, the partial Marsco Moon shone with eerie brightness, like a dimmed sun in clouds. Shadows were stark, faces and expressions clearly visible as though under artificial light.

The moonlight added depth to Columbus's plump face. In this light, the scalp of his shaved head glistened. Drooping eyelids hid his pale blue bloodshot eyes. When he spoke, his bulging cheeks seemed disconnected from his neck, making his head appear to float. His movements were quick, unexpectedly so, because his bloated body seemed too swollen for normal movements.

After a pause, he continued, "My ancient people knew so much more of the wise ways when this was all our land, before Marsco. When honesty and kindness and love flowed from our capital, Columbus, for which I am named. All us virtuous folks and them marked by God for labor and servitude, we all knew our places."

In the gray light, the four Brunels listened to their guest. The evening was warm enough to sit in their garden long after a late meal and soak in the Moon's glimmering and these words of wisdom. "How we lived in harmony then, without war, without tears, without any questioning of our right to follow as our wisest leaders saw fit. Love was our rule. We all loved then."

Sitting nearest her mother, Sarah leaned toward the mystic as though he were sunlight itself and she a thriving plant. The Moon's radiance enhanced the young woman's face, giving her a lustrous hue. Her blue eyes deepened to nearly black, but at times they blazed with intensity.

She wore her "argument dress," as she called it. She had pleaded with Celine and wheedled Roxanne for weeks to have it made, fashioned after pictures Hy and she found in articles online about idle lovers vacationing during the early twenty-first century, beautiful women and buff men together on pristine beaches. It was white cotton and gathered across her chest and stretched down over her shoulders so that her strong upper body caught the moonlight glow—clearly not a fashion Dot Richardson approved of. Nor Celine, but she'd lost that argument, worn down by her insistent daughter.

Sarah kept her gaze fixed on the speaker. While she stared, the philosopher moved his eyes slowly from host to hostess to the devoted children, but his look kept returning to Sarah and locking on her eyes, shoulders, neck, until her innate modesty moved her to lower her view. She knew in that instant, captured by his smoldering regard, she shouldn't have worn this dress. The young woman, her skin radiant in the unnatural moonlight, started believing more in the vibrant world of those old websites than in the stale one Columbus was trying to resurrect.

When her face lowered, Columbus sighed and moved his dejected, penetrating eyes away.

Forcing himself to be polite, Trent sat still as though a child coerced by his parents to be there. While the mystic spoke, the granger's mind drifted onto tomorrow's work. A long day in the fields awaited. And he knew, given this visit, Chase would more than likely spend an inordinate amount of time making sure his guests were comfortable, thus spending less time in the fields.

"I don't believe in these imposed niceties of asking your forgiveness," Columbus went on. "When I speak, I know you should be listening."

Glances from Chase chided his family for failing to be totally attentive.

Where Chase had actually met his guest, Trent and Celine never heard. *Probably our own fault*, the granger concluded. *Should have been more aware of his actions. But with his own Darrow money he readily tapped.* He shrugged. *Probably up in Sac City.* That acknowledgement stung. They would never let Sarah go to the subsidiary alone and rarely let her accompany them when they needed to go. Yet, Chase was free to roam anywhere, ample tokens in his pocket, without their slightest concern.

When the sage sighed momentarily in preparation for another pronouncement, Trent rose. "I'm sorry, Mr. Columbus, but my fields will be wanting me very early tomorrow. I've got to go in." He offered his hand to his guest, an old-style gesture of shaking hands that had mostly gone by the wayside with pandemics and the division of PRIMS from the rest of society a century ago. Columbus hesitated at first, then offered his fleshy right hand. He couldn't help but notice Trent's two disks. The granger couldn't help but notice that the visitor had no calluses from hard work.

"Again," the sage proclaimed, "such niceties of which I am unaware. Our old ways had no forced politeness. We were all decent together. We were just ourselves."

When Trent rose, his dog, Shadow, rose as well. At thirty kilos, the black lab was instantly on guard. A low growl, hardly audible, came from him, his eyes focused on the mystical guest. Sarah came forward to pet the dog into obedience.

"See, once again, turning dogs into my enemy. Such a disruption of our old ways."

Shadow focused silently, guarding, as if to dispute those words.

"I must make my leave to speak to my own," the sage stated, rising with a grunt from his chair. Granger and visitor were about the same height, but the farmer was muscular. "Such a sense of duty warped by Marsco and others before it, making you a slave to their ideals of labor." He drew a knowing breath. "In the old days, the decent knew how to make 'the marked ones' labor, before all were mixed up to make PRIMS."

Trent chuckled silently at the suggestion while Chase bowed in acceptance of the devout proposition. The granger knew his own hard labor provided the meal this sage hadn't had trouble devouring. Even his six acolytes, who'd sat with them at table earlier, then left, showed no reluctance to lap up platefuls at another's board.

"I'll walk you to the guesthouse," Chase offered.

Sarah felt jealous. Not about being with the sage, but walking out in her fields in this glorious moonlight. To walk along silently, to have this aura around her; it portended peace, tranquility, connection to the very soil of this grange she loved so much. Chase had all the luck to bask in this fine evening that much longer.

Disappointed, Sarah turned from her mother to find Columbus standing right next to her. He took up her hands in a stylized gesture. He held them to his chest, smiled into her eyes, then moved their joined hands back to her bare shoulders. The young woman felt his hands against her; even their slight touch was instantly uncomfortable. "I sense your devotion, child." He grinned. "Keep that in you always."

In a moment, he was gone, with Chase following behind like the shadow of a gray cat moving off in ashen light.

———•———

Roxanne urged Sarah to be off to her room and let her finish the washing up. Celine had a way of coming into the kitchen to do PRIM work, no Darrow daughter was ever above that, but the young woman needn't be here any longer.

"Go, sleep," the PRIM whispered to Sarah as though her own daughter.

Celine rushed in. "I forgot to give our guest's friends some extra towels, afraid they'll be needing them. More came than I expected."

"I'll take them, Mother," Sarah offered before Roxanne ordered La'Shay to run them up to the guesthouse. She's be fine by herself on her father's land, under that magnificent Moon.

Celine and Roxanne both hesitated about her going, yet neither was prepared to name the reason for their reluctance. In the end, Sarah was through the garden, on the path between a sown field and a fallow one, pacing swiftly to the guesthouse. As Chase had followed Columbus, so Shadow went with the young woman.

———•———

The Moon, now behind Sarah, cast blue light before her. Her dog zipped in and out of the darkness, often invisible but close at hand. Striding up the last stretch of a rise, Sarah opened the gate of the pool's fence. She knew her way even without any other light. She made Shadow stay outside the gate.

He seemed distrustful of the sage. Sarah wanted no more embarrassment from the dog.

Walking beside the water, she noticed the Moon dancing on the ripples the warm breeze created. *What a time to swim*, she thought, *if only Patrice were here and Chase's guests not.*

Three bedrooms of the guesthouse fronted the pool. Each room had a door that went outside directly and one that opened inside the house. Only one low light glowed, so Sarah tapped softly on that door.

When the door cracked, one of Columbus's acolytes stood there bare-chested. Patchouli scented the air. His body glistened from some sort of greasy application or sweat; Sarah couldn't tell. Behind him was a second acolyte with the same sheen. Soft music was playing back in the cloud of incense. Neither young man, both very pale-skinned, smiled nor spoke, but the one closest to her grabbed for the towels.

Alone now, Sarah turned and walked halfway down the pool, heading for the gate. Shadow began to whimper, then stood silently and focused. The light on the water once more caught her eye. Only a hoot of an owl and the rustle of the breeze disturbed the scene. Standing there charmed by the lure of the reflected light, she felt as though she were standing under the gaze of the Moon next to an immense mountain lake or the ceaseless ocean, neither of which she had ever seen firsthand.

"Just imagine," she whispered, envisioning her ordinary pool as an enchanted cascading waterfall or a majestic fountain at some castle. Her simple dress, now a bejeweled gown, shimmered in the moonlight, gracing her form. She wished that an ardent gallant stood at her side, the finest gentleman she'd ever know. Hy and she had been reading too many once-difficult-to-download novels. Her heart pounded, her breath shortened, longing for her magnanimous squire to declare his love outright, to kiss her for the first time right there under the hallowed starlight.

When she whispered *yes* and her dream came true, all this would become her home. She wouldn't need a chateau. She'd have this place and pool with the Tillson acres added on, her valiant devoted paladin at her side.

Two hands fell on her shoulders, holding her roughly, tight enough that she wasn't able to bolt. A man's breath went down the back of her neck.

"We thank you for your kindness, young one," Columbus's hoarse voice stated. He was trying to draw her backward against him, as though he wanted to move her into an embrace, but she broke free, not caring if she seemed rude. Two acolytes hung back in the darkness, different ones than those who'd snatched the towels. Like them, they were Euro stock. In a passing thought, the woman realized the sage's acolytes were all Euro ancestry, an oddity in the Marsco world where so many had been shunted about from continent to continent for decades.

"I'm sorry! You startled me," Sarah breathed out in a rush, now facing him.

"Words of wisdom are often startling for their directness. We are straightforward people following our old ways, which were simplicity itself. Nothing sophisticated or deceitful in the old people, as with Marsco." He went on as though the long explanation erased his earlier actions, cast them in an acceptable light. "We virtuous ones know the responsibility of the old ways."

"I'm sorry, I must be going," was all she said.

He stretched for her again with one hand. His face in that light looked like a silvery skull. "Stay, child. We—my devoted followers and your brother—we are still speaking. Come, join." He motioned back to the dimly outlined window. "You'll find it enlightening."

Shadow was up with his front paws against the gate, his single bark sharp, this one deep report strong enough to catch their attention.

"No, Mother and Roxanne are still up and working." Sarah had stepped away from another attempt to clutch her and was speaking over her shoulder. The words, "I'm sorry, I have to help them," drifted back toward Columbus as the gate shut behind her. Shadow danced at her feet.

Pausing a moment before returning to the others, Columbus watched the slender, white-clad form and the swirling black dog fleeing down the path. *In time*, he knew instinctively, *in time. You'll come to me. I know you are calling me to you. And the brother will aid in this, for he perceives such lights as few in the now-darkened Marsco world comprehend. Your call for me is strong, young one. I cannot resist you long.*

Back inside his suite of rooms, Columbus found Chase and his six acolytes waiting in a haze of incense. Without speaking, he moved to cushions set in the corner where a comfortable chair had originally stood. Chase's revered guest preferred this pile of cushions. It kept him humble, he explained, and enabled his followers to be at his feet as he preached.

"Your sister is spirited," Columbus noted as he settled into his corner. "And yet sadly, I think she fears to let her spirits soar; thus she holds herself back. An eagle of old never held back, so she shouldn't. We must make her soar."

"As you wish," Chase acknowledged with a nod.

"Say not, 'as you wish,' for my wishes are not paltry things, expressions of a mere, humble man. No, say rather, 'as is best *for her*,' and know what a reward you give her when she feels comfortable, not fearful, in my presence."

Chase's forehead creased in a way that made him look very much like his father. He responded, "Yes, I think I see."

"No longer *think*! Just *see*. I show the light to see our ways and our will. Follow without question or not at all."

Humbled, Chase lowered his eyes, wishing he didn't stumble around so much when near his sage. Faltering as he often did, he dreaded committing other unintentional insults, an inadvertent mistake, a misspoken word, or an expression of a stray thought controlled by Marsco. He had found out through Columbus that Marsco *did* control many of his thoughts, even though he grew up well outside its direct influence, which was waning anyway.

You have breathed in its poison, child-son, Columbus had explained from the beginning before Chase had uttered a single word to him. *You have to think as a decent old one, as our forefathers did, taking what they wanted from this land and celebrating their freedoms without fear of Marsco. We must have our freedom to stop slander against us when they called us 'PRIMS' and mixed us in with peoples who were marked by God for servitude. We are truly, as our righteous name says, "a Free People." When Marsco made PRIMS, it then tried to destroy us by treating us the same as those marked ones. So now, our pure and decent forefathers wail and cry until we have our vengeance against Marsco in their name. We are not for servitude as the marked ones are.*

When Columbus settled down, Chase humbly asked, "May I speak of Hyacinth?"

"You must," the older man replied, his expression one of sheer delight at the reminder of that young woman.

Chase knew he would never have the courage to ask his own father about Hyacinth, about what Hy was doing to him, to his mind, even to his soul. He thought he'd loved Patrice once. But, really, it was Hy whom he desired now. He knew he had approached her roughly the last time they met at the pool right outside. He ought to speak differently next time, but how?

He had thought about asking his father but shrank from his stern answer. *Do you love the young woman, son? Enough to marry her?* His father gave the son questions and not answers. At first, Chase had liked that, but in time it grew tedious, not knowing and being left to ponder for himself. In a way, they were sound words, ones he wished he cherished. After all, he had to admit, New Grange was well run, its owner a solid provider and a kind overseer. Trent was respected, thorough, devoted. A generous man.

But the son was not interested in *forever*. It seemed every time he closed his eyes of late, where once he had imagined Patrice, he inexplicably saw Hyacinth. And, all this somehow meant, if he saw her as his parents did, this all meant hours sweating under the hot sun, bending and stretching to make equipment work, seeing PRIMS tended to and paid, seeds planted, grown, and harvested. He wasn't ready for all that, didn't want all that.

He only wanted Hy so badly he ached for her. He wished he had spoken plainly to her, spoken his soul. But then he rebelled and declared, *Why do I need to do all that to have her?*

Columbus was different. He had a direct answer that suited Chase's temperament. *Plant seeds in ground you don't own*, was one comforting dictate, *for certainly the soil does not give permission to the sower.* And, *Sow seeds you never intend to harvest because she is only there to bear without complaint.*

Waiting patiently, Columbus finally whispered, "So, my child-son, speak of your own girl."

"How do I proceed with her?" He was going to confide his torment, his internal conflict. Trent's vision for the pair might be worth the ongoing sacrifice, might be worth laying aside other walks with other girls. Richardsons were fine people, even if not Darrows or Brunels. Even so, Chase knew—as if siding with his own father—she might be worth the hot and dusty work of New Grange after all.

But before he stumbled forward with more of his confused inner thoughts, Columbus laughed to cut him off.

"I hear your anguish, my child-son." His eyes shimmered, knowing he was to save his newest follower much deep pain. "You must be a man now," he gently whispered. "Our old ways teach that a man must lead. Must take. What he wants, he grabs. He does as he knows is right and expects his own to follow without reservation. When today happens, regardless of tomorrow, a real man knows his actions on the third day will be *his* actions and unchanged. Unchanged!"

He drew a short breath. "She must know she is to bring you what is truly important to you, only you. Like those signed for servitude, she is a woman and is marked as well by God to labor for you, her man."

"You mean—"

"I mean it is our unshakeable truth we know and we follow without question, as I know truth and my acolytes follow me without question. She must know you and follow. Reluctance is weakness. In our old days, such a one as her knew to obey. Or she was made to. Let her know that."

<hr />

Trent was unable to sleep deeply. After the bright Moon fully set and before the coming dawn brightened his land, the granger was wide awake. No sounds came from outside. No animal stirred yet; no PRIMS came down from the village to begin their labors. Roxanne hadn't yet moved to the kitchen to prepare for feeding two dozen field hands, the rest of the grange, plus now his son's gaggle of visitors.

Chase is a worry, to be sure, the father painfully admitted. *Perhaps we've given in too much.*

Looking out his bedroom at the still-dark sky, the granger drew a deep breath. *And this Columbus character. World's full of them, spouting 'wisdom' and not knowing jack. Never lifting a finger to work.* But at issue was extricating his son without alienating him in the process. To expose a charlatan was easy but such exposure often made his followers even more devoted. Chase was on the edge, the tipping point.

Dressed and walking outside, Trent breathed in the life-filled air of New Grange. He smelled the earth, the abundance surrounding him. This spread had in a way fallen into his hands with no effort. He simply fell in love with a fine woman, and that was it. But he had worked ceaselessly on this boon, and his labors had paid off handsomely.

Glancing at the largest guesthouse and ignoring what stung about it at present, he acknowledged he had bought it for Sarah. He'd had her pool installed, which cost him more than a handful of tokens each month. But the house was solid with the potential for a fine garden and a large orchard on the east side overlooking Tillson's place. Trent intended to buy that spread at any cost as soon as it went up for sale. He had even placed his latest solars and buried a new cistern just inside his side of their property line near Tillson's in preparation. It was no secret: Chase would have the largest portion of New Grange, but that house plus sizable acreage to its east were Sarah's and her husband's when that time came.

"Well, not soon. Nate Richardson didn't measure up. At least he stood up to his old man's worst nonsense and married a girl he loves, but he never was for Sarah," he muttered as though judging a breeding bull.

Devon's visit had been postponed again. Trent wished he'd spoken with him the other day. Celine had let her husband sleep when she took her cousin's call. The granger wanted Devon here as soon as possible, but their Solstice celebration seemed the soonest, if then. "Perhaps," he whispered as though walking with the man, "I shouldn't have sided with Celine about Sarah and that prep school. God knows, she's smart enough."

As the first dawn rays brightened up the eastern horizon, he looked in every direction. His land, the Richardson spread, Tillson's. *What's to become of all this? Who's really going to end up with it? Any of it? Marsco's changing rapidly, at times unpredictably. What's coming next? Will West Con be ready? Are we up for this, we of the Provisional Assembly? Our forefathers failed. Not in the era of Columbus's bogus history but our own real history. Will we make the same mistakes?*

He had no answers, although Devon might.

— • —

Sarah woke with a start and rolled onto her right side. Her pillow was damp with tears. She'd been crying until nearly two hours ago. Shadow looked at her as if to say, *I already lost a night of sleep for you.*

When she had reached home from the guesthouse, she ran to her room, avoiding Roxanne and La'Shay, who were still up and anxious for her.

What had happened at her poolside, the young woman didn't fully understand.

At first, while Columbus spoke after dinner, she was spellbound. Sitting at the table, she was initially convinced that she was feeling the actual devotion Chase experienced—the warmth of the sage's profound wisdom, the thrill of sharing insights with such a perceptive mind. The mystic could show her that unknown world of which she knew so little, become her guide to the hidden wisdom she knew existed but had never tasted.

Or so she thought at first until his words drifted away from a clear path of enlightenment. As he droned on, the more his history grew fuzzy and confused. Her own reading and her discussions with her thoughtful father and her astute cousin, Devon, conflicted with the sage's version of reality.

And later that very evening, seeing his acolytes, then feeling his pursuing breath and sweaty hands on her shoulders—she shuddered at the memory—sorry, ashamed, tortured, but glad she had flown.

Running to her room, throwing herself onto her bed, she wept until exhaustion overtook her and she slept.

It never crossed her troubled mind to fear for Chase.

Her room sat at the side of the house that overlooked their animal pens down the way. Their small dairy herd must be stirring, she knew, waiting to be milked by two old PRIMS who doted on their few gentle cows. Amid all the muted voices and footsteps, she clearly heard her father's and mother's voices, hushed with concern.

"They're already worried about so much." She sighed. "I won't tell them about the guesthouse. About Columbus." It was her way to hide unpleasantness from them. "That'd only add another burden to them."

But, she drew a breath while scratching Shadow, *when Devon's here, I'll tell him.*

SIX

OPEN QUESTIONS

(The Marsco Academy, Seattle, early June 2154)

"That's one of several open questions, of course, Representative Bulawayo," Lieutenant Colonel Devon Chavez-Sherman politely responded, sure of his answer but not wanting his conviction to sound domineering.

The board representative walking beside the space explorer nodded, but she gave away nothing in the way of agreement. The pair, currently both professors at the Marsco Academy, stood nearly the same height. Bulawayo was at least twenty years older and had never been under hibernation.

"Marsco has always traveled in the solar system," Devon continued. "Humankind has always explored space simply by gazing at the heavens, but for nearly two hundred years, we have traveled *in* space." For emphasis, he added, "Humankind must *never* rest from such travels. To rest is to rust unused. We must shine in use."

Gwanda Bulawayo nodded once more, intent on listening but not one easily persuaded on this or any point. "Robert Browning, I believe," she noted softly, identifying his source.

They both laughed at his attempt to be inspirational.

They made an odd pair, deep in conversation, walking across the shaded edge of a quad, nearly empty with the summer recess. Devon tall and trim, obvious Euro ancestry, with his officer's mien and bearing clearly evident. As an explorer prior to his appointment to the faculty here, his rhythms and strides were conditioned well before taking up the mantle of professor.

Gwanda Bulawayo, also tall, walked with her own strong stride, demonstrating she'd overcome much growing up PRIM on the South African subcontinent so ravished by disease and poverty for the last several centuries. And yet, age had not diminished her powerful comportment.

Initial policies of the Continental Powers well over one hundred years ago were an attempt to control the outbreaks of disease that so devastated her homeland. Early in the last century, some of the initial unincorporated zones had been created there to cordon off streams of refugees and famine victims, the diseased and impoverish humanity that many countries at that time no longer wanted to help or support. Her heritage carried the scars of that pre-Marsco policy of Abandonment.

History had been cruelly grinding to those masses shunted off to zones, cut off from their homelands. The world was still paying the price for those misguided policies of neglect.

The representative's dark eyes were quick and intelligent. Her deep brown skin seemed ageless; the sprinkling of gray hair gave her gravitas. Although she preferred attire suggestive of her heritage, today she looked the part of a seasoned professor, wearing a navy blue skirt and cotton blouse.

At sixty-five, she had seen much turmoil firsthand: The Great PRIM Mutiny at the start of the century and the last PRIM uprising fifteen years ago—when Devon had served in Security. She had served as Mr. Mandela Transkie-man's personal assistant—one of two founders of the PFM, the PRIM Freedom Movement. As that inspirational leader aged and grew too weak to fulfill his role, she replaced him to become one of only two PRIMS at the Accords table during those final dozen years of arduous negotiations. She sat at these talks with Transkie-man's comrade, Javâher Panditji, who soldiered on for years but who also grew too frail to continue. He passed away just at the end, never seeing the Accords finally accepted and approved.

Signing the Accords in their stead, Bulawayo echoed her mentor by stating his belief: "We declare our right to be fully recognized as human beings—no longer just as mere PRIMS; to be respected as individuals; to be given the rights and the dignity of full citizens in society, on this Earth, in this solar system, on this very day when we bring into existence these Accords."

Soon after signing the Accords, she was granted a seat at on the Marsco board.

Devon continued speaking as the pair walked. "As a member of the board, Representative Bulawayo, I know you voted against a second *Armstrong-Aldrin-Collins* mission. No secret. But may I ask why?"

"The Accords are now finally coming into play," she answered in a calm tone, not seeking to justify but merely to explain her decision. "Many subsidiaries and zones, now free federations, are reeling from years of neglect. Not all are as wealthy as West Con seems to be. And Marsco merely waving its finger disks over these does not eliminate all our continuing problems. Can Marsco afford so much effort into that little jaunt of yours, to Jupiter? Should it?"

She gave a laugh, which showed the age lines of her mahogany face. "Most PRIMS don't know what Jupiter is!" She paused thoughtfully. "And of course, PRIMS no longer exist. They are all free citizens of our new federations."

"I understand that, Representative Bulawayo," Devon countered, still speaking formally, "but since Marsco is keeping its space ops, the only aspect of her former self, and since it is granting self-determination to federations, it makes sense that it will share what it learns. Who else is there to benefit from this science but the feds?"

"You've just returned from the Moon, have you not?"

"Yes, ma'am, I make no secret of that."

"Do you wish to tell me what you were doing there?"

He gave a stuttering laugh. "No, Representative Bulawayo, it's restricted. Top secret. I can't divulge my research."

"Research? So, was it scientific?"

"Of course."

"But you are not going to share it?" In the deepening silence between them, she added, "As my rival Patrick Mellon-Hart would often say, 'I rest my case.'"

Devon laughed in a self-effacing manner to hide his inherent embarrassment. "You know, Representative Bulawayo, you were *meant* to be a board member. I hope you use your shrewdness on Oakes and Chesney with as much aplomb."

Stopping him with a light touch on his arm, Bulawayo asked softly, "Should I call you Lieutenant Colonel or Professor Chavez-Sherman?"

"Well, actually, Devon's fine. Do you have a preference for your title?

You are a member of the board and a professor of political and economic theory here." He motioned to the large campus surrounding them.

It was the woman's time to give a heartfelt laugh. "Please, *Wandi* is the name my friends call me. And, I gather you haven't heard, *Representative* Bulawayo is *not* appropriate. The board in all its infinite wisdom stripped me of my seat last week. Nothing's been made public, no official statement. It's Chesney's way, *secretive*, thus I'm sure you are unaware."

"I wasn't aware. I'm shocked." He paused, taking it all in. "I truly had no idea. But you should've said so as soon as I called you by your title."

"Well, two shocked professors, then, are having a collegial chat this fine morning. I still don't know what to make of it myself."

The growing silence between them took a gloomy turn that contrasted with the lovely late spring morning on campus. Few others were about. They walked on, absorbed in isolated thought, along the central quad. Ahead was the main administration building, its dome gleaming in the morning light.

Reluctantly, Devon ventured to ask, "Any reasons given for your dismissal?"

It wasn't that he felt like he shouldn't ask; it was more that he was unsure of the trust that existed between them. His pretext for their walk, that they were both professors of the Academy and should know each other better, was finger-disk thin. If she didn't trust him, however, why had she consented to this walk where they could easily be digitized by Internal? He wore a fogger under his sweater; certainly, she did the same.

She knew exactly what his vague question was referring to.

"Does Chesney need a reason? Of course, it fell to his hatchet Madame Representative Anne Kelly to tell me. My term was up next December, so I'm told, but the whole board of directors is up for renewal then. Only I and four others got the axe early, thank you very much."

She paused a moment, sizing up Devon one last time before continuing. "It may be construed by some that the timing of the board changes coincided with a 'housecleaning' of those not totally loyal to Oakes. Five of the most vocal reps were gone at one stroke. That Mellon-Hart chap, whom I actually dislike, even though he and I always voted nearly the same. Maria de Janeiro, unlike me, a sid and not a PRIM; she's gone. We're alike in one aspect; we have PRIM names."

Devon didn't understand.

"We're named for *locations*, not family or heritage. Our names are drawn from where our families were at the time we needed a surname."

"PRIM-ification was that complete."

"Exactly so." Bulawayo gave a knowing shrug. "Two others as well," she continued explaining the housecleaning. "Silvia Taichung and Chrisni Melani from Sri Lanka."

Devon once more looked puzzled.

"I think *that* got her into trouble. She insisted on using the pre-Divesti-ture name for her new fed, not the name given to the area by the Continen-tal Powers. Marsco had insisted on keeping that old colonial name from centuries ago, *Ceylon*, while Chrisni wanted her new fed to recall a recent history steeped in democracy, Sri Lanka."

"Awesome being so brazen."

"Brazen, yes, even if not totally effective."

"So, all the real federalists are gone?"

"Totally. But worse yet, next onto the board comes an Academy grad of all things: Captain Elkton. Did you know him? A recent grad of the Acad-emy. Seems like I just taught him. And now a *captain* in Security? Now, that's a skyrocketing career."

"Actually, I did have the young man in class once."

"'Bloody conceited twit,' as my archrival Mellon-Hart might say." She gave another laugh. "I'll miss our go-rounds—Mellon-Hart and I—about Euro appointments versus non-Euro. I'll miss quibbling over his choice of words, just because I could. I think I scared him." She laughed and confided, "You know, actually once we argued over how best to make *tea* and *coffee*." She puffed herself up. "But, on real issues, we tended to agree. I grew up in a zone and took no prisoners protecting myself and my own. Won admittance to a PRIM school for girls, a leadership academy that had stayed open during Divestiture. I think my own strength blinded me from ever seeing him as an ally, not another enemy."

"He's an associate from way back," Devon admitted.

"Yes, I know, yet for all that baggage, he truly believes in the Accords. I should have been kinder to him over the years. It broke his heart when he was sacked. He took it so personally."

"How so, Wandi?"

"Convoluted Marsco pride. You associates can be an arrogant lot!"

"Don't need you to tell me that," Devon laughed, not ashamed of his status but well aware of its haughty pitfalls.

"Well, Mellon-Hart truly believed what Marsco was telling us, at least at first, before Chesney started in. That Marsco was telling us the truth when it signed the Accords. I think he took a large measure of pride in Marsco, its philanthropy, and its new beginnings through the Accords."

"And you don't believe it is still serious about moving that way?"

"*This* board? Oakes and Chesney? Look around, Devon. Do you think it'll just drop all this? Walk away from all this? I don't mean the Academy. I mean the power invested in its nearby HQ." She motioned toward the horizon. "Think of all its power. Power, raw power is an inducement few can just let go. Entrenched power. And really, do you think that *they* would simply let go of all that control and influence? Just let it slip through their finger disks without a fight?" She paused, "I'm sorry. I'm painting with too broad a brush. Many associates, like yourself, and even my archnemesis Mellon-Hart, believe in that old and longstanding Marsco promise of a new world order and a better world, post-Marsco."

"The promises of the Accords."

"Yes, truly." Once more she paused to make her words exact. "But clearly, the Chesney factor is strong on the board. And it's easy to tempt young men and women with so much new power. And power corrupts."

"'And absolute power—'" Devon let the rest of quote pass. "That's the story of history."

"What makes you think Marsco can live outside of history?"

Bulawayo's open questions went unanswered for several moments as the pair moved from the north quad to the south. Ahead lay the natatorium and sets of dorms. To the side stood a row of classroom buildings; in one, Devon had his office.

"I've sent my aide to speak with him," the explorer confided.

"My good old foe? Why?"

"Well, he's gone back to his home subsidiary, now a federation in the western Euro area. Out of Marsco altogether and a true federalist, so I understand. He's pushing for early elections in his former subsidiary so that, at least in his locale, the Accords will be implemented smoothly. His fed will be up and running soon."

"Is that what you wish to speak to him about?"

"I want to know all about his suspicions of Marsco."

She drew a deep breath. "How did he put it upon leaving Seattle? He wanted to return home 'to thrash out a new constitution based on democratic principles.'"

"Noble ambition, that."

"Yes, indeed, and Accords or no, a dangerous ambition at this time and place."

"Wandi," Devon stated, "you must have a great deal of confidence in me to share so much."

"I'm a good judge of character, Devon. Besides, if Chesney wanted the goods on me, Internal wouldn't have to listen to me today. I never held back on the board and never held back when home, either."

"I know. That's why I sought you out."

"Ah, now, I was waiting for this. Just why did you seek me out? If you wanted exercise, certainly you can find much better ways." She pointed to a pair of young cadets jogging by.

"While I won't tell you the nature of my visit to the Moon, I will tell you I saw some things there that surprised me. Startled and frightened me."

"For as much as I wanted you *not* to go to Jupiter again, it took courage to go that first time. For you to be frightened!"

"Physical courage is different from, shall we call it, *historical prescience*."

"I'm not sure I follow you: a simple PRIM by birth, after all."

"A sophisticated leader of a bloc of sids and PRIMS who's well-respected—"

"Ah, yes, by some associates, too; don't forget that nettlesome Mellon-Hart."

"A bloc of board members who were truly pushing that the Accords be fulfilled. Finalized. What I saw does not square with the Accords. I am sure I saw Marsco amassing Vanovaras above the far side of the Moon."

Devon's comment brought the former board member up short. She'd witnessed their use, knew their terrifying history. The V-1 comet head explodes as an airburst, creating a fireball equivalent of a small atomic bomb but without any residual radiation. The V-2, a metallic asteroid shard honed for a precise hit, is the more accurate of the two. Smaller, for pinpoint placement, it was in its own way equally devastating.

"Unconscionable to think about using such horrors," Wandi whispered, shocked.

"But if you look at our history, when has humankind ever backed away from horrific weaponry?" Devon responded.

"A philosophical question, I gather."

"Whether metaphysical or not, real V-weapons are being produced and stored above the Moon."

"That's a pretty intense claim. Any proof?"

"Besides some digitals I took, none."

"And they can be faked," Bulawayo noted.

"Yes, I'm open to the charge of fabricating my evidence, I know. But, if I lack incontrovertible proof, it's merely a matter of a delegation going to the Moon and looking. A V-weapon can hardly be hidden, even on the other side, the side that never sees Earth. They have to remain in space. They are space-launched after all."

The Bunker never seemed to sleep, so it didn't surprise Devon when he was asked to meet with Chesney there at 2000 hours the same day he had talked with Professor Bulawayo. The surprise came when President Oakes was with the vice-chair, seated in the corner of a reception room appointed in the high-style elegance of over-done eighteenth-century Euro trappings.

"My wife picked this out," Chesney explained, trying to look comfortable in an uncomfortable chair. "They called the age 'the Age of Enlightenment' once," he went on.

"Certainly, sir," Devon answered, hiding his discomfort at meeting the highest members of the Marsco board. He wanted to remind the two that during the Enlightenment, the theory of democratic rule started taking root. That age had seen the beginning of the end of autocratic rule, at least in Europe and this continent. But he let the history lesson pass.

When the pair focused on the scientist before them, Devon began. "I sent my report. I'm sure your science advisors have gone over it. My main point is that Rascal is definitely trailing plutonium isotope 239, an extremely rare material. It can be found in a natural environment periodically but only at minuscule trace levels. Nothing like this, a continuous vapor trail. From all appearances, I think I'm safe to conclude what we have observed is a fuel that had to be synthesized."

"And *what* are we to conclude from this?" Oakes asked.

The explorer answered, "It signifies that Rascal is being driven by a propulsion system, sir. It is conclusively a propelled object fueled by a processed isotope."

"A spaceship, then."

"In essence, yes."

"Manned or unmanned?"

"*Inhabited?* No evidence either way. It is not broadcasting *back* to any base, nor trying to communicate *forward* with us."

"So," Chesney jumped in, "it may be an unmanned probe."

"Yes, sir, that's a possibility. I know that in the NASA era, robotic craft were used to explore Mars and Venus long before astronauts traveled to those planets, before humans made those hazardous journeys." He drew a knowledgeable breath. "Seems like standard procedure for any space exploration. Let the bots go first, let them find something worth exploring. Marsco did that with the belt no so long ago. In the late '30s, that's the 2030s, it sent unmanned exploration craft out to the belt looking for the best asteroids to mine and colonize."

Chesney responded, "Last year when we first spoke of this, you listed two main possibilities about this craft: a natural object or a spaceship or probe."

"Yes, and if some sort of vessel, then was it an Earth ship returning or something from another solar system exploring ours? Few other possibilities exist."

"Your best assessment?" the vice-chair asked after Rhores came in with a list of calls he need to make in the next hour. Clearly, Chavez-Sherman was being urged to move things along.

"My best guess? Well, its fuel is not natural, so it's a ship of some kind. Other than that, I'd put my MMUs on it being from Earth and returning."

"Why? Any basis for that or just wishful thinking?"

"I think a probe from another solar system would have been preceded by years of sensor readings. Our deep-space arrays searched the heavens for decades before the Wars, before 2060s. Since then, of course, this isn't the case."

Chesney stated flatly, "Priorities shift."

"Yes, sir, but lately, last ten years or so, some deep-space listening has begun again. I gather some SoAm and Euro feds are back in the game big time. Traditionally, they always were. Also, a Hawaiian array is up and running. The dark-side lunar arrays are functioning as well. Those are all still Marsco's, of course."

"Your point is?" Oakes did everything but snap his fingers to get a speedy answer.

Not a scientific mind, Devon smirked. *Science doesn't give quick and clean answers to complicated and dirty problems.* "Well, even given the gap created by the period of no data, between the old data once compiled decades ago and the new data we're gathering now, essentially, no intel of anything probing us has ever been gathered. If *I* were going somewhere across the nearly endless void of space, *I'd* want constant data streams. That's my sense of how any ops of this kind would run. That alone makes me conclude that our mysterious Rascal is coming *home*, not looking for a *new* home."

That answer seemed to mollify the chair, who rose to leave. "Thank you again, colonel, for your insights. I'll leave you with Mr. Chesney to settle any odds and bits you missed."

As he left, Bobby-Tim Liddle entered, wearing his friendless grin.

"Chair of the board Oakes and I," Chesney began almost solemnly, "have need for devoted associates, as I'm sure you appreciate, colonel."

"Undoubtedly, as the Accords come online, Marsco still has vast ops it must run, upgrade, perpetuate."

"It's the *perpetuate* part we're interested in. Suppose something happens to derail the Accords?"

"I'm not sure I follow this hypothetical case. Three of six are in place right now. Quite peacefully and successfully, as far as I can tell."

"Yes, but if trouble started brewing, could we just allow Number Four to commence? As though nothing were wrong? Who can see into that crystal ball, but *what if*, say, freedom for PRIMS may just mean their hordes seeking retribution? PRIMS running riot?"

"I don't believe that, technically, any PRIMS exist at this time."

"Okay, point taken, but hypothetically—"

"In such a hypothetical possibility, I believe that then, sir, it would be the responsibility and duty of the new federations to restore law and order.

That's why Security battalions and Auxiliary units were placed under fed auspices early in the process."

"Ah, but that's just my point. What if feds are unable to act, because of all this destabilizing transition, what if they can't mobilize these forces that are being just handed to them? Shouldn't the board, shouldn't Marsco, be in a position to guarantee that the Accords *do* eventually come online but possibly in a safer future, not now during all this trouble?"

"Has there been much trouble?"

"As a matter of fact, no. A few isolated cases but nothing serious. Nothing widespread. And where trouble has regrettably hit, these new feds have handled it well. But that's the small-beer part. I'm looking big picture."

"I'm still not sure how this deals with me? When not in space, I am a prof here." He motioned toward the campus behind him.

"Ah, but here's why. The board is identifying officers, experienced officers like yourself—Security for three years in your case, I'm sure *you* know *we* know your record—experienced officers like yourself we can count on for loyalty and devotion to restoring Marsco's order."

"Yes, any officer can be compelled to join Security at any time. That, as you note, happened to me years and years ago. It's a longstanding Marsco tradition, 'best honored in the breach than in the application,' if I might paraphrase a line."

Chesney smirked with a slanted grimace. "The perks for those loyal enough to join up willingly, ahead of those ordered in, are indescribable. And we're establishing such a cadre so we might be fully prepared for the Accords trouble—" He saw Devon about to question this assumption, so he angled his answer, "we'd be derelict in our duty not to be prepared for that eventuality, however distantly remote these threats to Marsco's good order and safety are. And so, to those officers who step up now we're offering commissions with unimaginable rewards."

"I think I catch your drift, sir," Devon replied, confused all the more. "The first volunteers will get the best perks." He did not add that, rightfully, it would be the new federations' good order and safety, not Marsco's. As a world ruler, Marsco had technically and legally ceased being a player.

"Yes, and let me say, these perks are infinite, long-lasting, beyond belief as we understand it. Beyond regeneration."

"No hyperbole, then?"

Liddle spoke for the first time. "What we offer defies imagination. Defies science as understood for the past thousands of years."

"Some offer, if a bit vague."

"Consider it; get back to Bobby-Tim if you have an answer, an affirmative answer."

"Yes, sir, I will." He waited a moment then clarified, "I will think about it." Shifting his focus, he asked, "Oh, am I allowed to keep my intern for the summer? I've grown used to his assistance. He's been invaluable."

Liddle asked, "That would be Truman Roncalli, right? I believe it's Kyle?"

"Yes, Kyle Roncalli."

"I believe his offer has been made, and he's mulling it over. Encourage him, as he decides. Let him see how you stand, and that will sway him, we're sure. He seems devoted to you, colonel."

Devon nodded and rose to leave.

———•———

"Toland Hall," he ordered to the robotic four-seat HFC. Sitting alone in what would be the pilot's seat of a manned hovercraft, he was whisked away from the Bunker and toward the campus. The automated craft stayed perfectly level and ran smoothly. Devon was deep in his thoughts as the Bunker grew smaller behind. To his right, Chesney's separate Security and Internal HQs stood. Much of the essential—and shrouded—workings of Marsco passed through here, through Chesney's shadowy purview.

The explorer was unsure of what exactly that last exchange had actually meant, but he didn't like it one bit. Rumors of unrest. Suggestions of the Accords being suspended. He hadn't even mentioned Vanovaras hidden on the Moon.

And worse yet were those allusions of something beyond regeneration if he cooperated? The officer tried to get his mind around the meeting's inferences. *Am I being offered what science at one time could hardly imagine? Is this now a viable possibility?*

Ahead in the distance were the lights of the Academy with its lit dome visible through the trees.

Behind him, all visible traces of the Bunker faded into the night. Devon Chavez-Sherman was not totally sure, but he thought he had just been offered immortality.

SEVEN

STANHOPE FARM ON THE WOLD

(County Durham, June 2154)

"**W**ell, laddie, I got not *one*, but *a brace* of messages saying to expect you." Patrick Owen Mellon-Hart stood tall and lean. He was older than Kyle expected, over seventy, thin but wiry. No hiber had delayed his aging; even so he'd kept his vigor. "Not often I find a Marsco uniform looking for me," he bellowed.

The former board representative was not the sort Kyle was expecting, although the cadet didn't know what he should find after taking a lander halfway around the world.

As soon as he arrived back on Earth, Kyle had made his way on a Security lander to a field near the outskirts of the remains of London. Prior to the C-Wars, this capital city had taken an "inadvertent" hit from an "errant mining shard." Even well before those Wars, Marsco had mastered the art of asteroid shard placement. Converting the shards into a military weapon was an easy enough task for Marsco engineers more than a hundred years ago. *And today.* Kyle remembered Resnik.

From the lander field, Kyle took a restored HFC hauler north. As his hovercraft glided down well west of Old Durham, Kyle found Mellon-Hart with his walking stick, baggy corduroy trousers, and hiking boots there waiting. Three dogs followed in his wake. "You ready for a walk?" Kyle nodded. "We'll hoof it; good for the lungs and heart."

Outside the lander terminal, a woman waited in a rusty rover, one formerly used by Security. "Meet her later," Mellon-Hart stated, motioning to the driver and stowing Kyle's gear. The former representative eyed the lightweight summer uniform. He grabbed a thick sweater from the back of the rover. "Here, take this jumper; may need it."

The rover passed the two walkers and three dogs on a country lane a few minutes later. The driver tooted and waved before disappearing around a bend.

While the paved road went westerly and switchbacked along the rising and falling low hills, the walking trail stayed about fifty meters above a restored straight railroad cut. Both rose at a moderate pace.

"Years ago, scores of small farms prospered out this way. Now, mostly sheep out there grazing."

"You live here year-round?"

"Yes and no," the older walker replied. "Spent most of my year in Seattle until recently. And now that the federation is up and running, if selected during the early election, I'll be living in Oxford. That's our temporary capital while we finally rebuild London central. Marsco wasn't much interested in fixing the mess they made decades ago."

Even with a quick pace along the path, Mellon-Hart didn't lose his breath. He was evidently in fine shape for a man his age.

Kyle had no trouble keeping pace. Security duty and the Academy had prepared him well. *And, I'm probably fifty years younger*, he noted, determined not to fall even half a pace behind the energetic walker.

In due time, Mellon-Hart stopped them at the crest of a craggy hill. The dogs gathered at their feet as if taking in the view along with the pair.

To the west, the hill rose to a grove, then rose again to show a bare crest covered with green heather. To the east, lower rolling hills stretched out, covered with grazing sheep. Fog was moving in.

"Weather's changing, laddie. Let's get a move on; over two kilometers left before Stanhope and tea."

———————————•———————————

The hiking trail made several switchbacks plus had three sections of easy steps cut into the hillside. At one point, the pair came out of a grove where a low wall was situated right above the entrance of a reopened railroad tunnel. The wall protected walkers from the drop-off.

"This's a long tunnel, longest around for quite a spell. I like it here; hard to get to. Steep above—" he pointed to a sheer face behind them "—and no one can come up from the tunnel entrance." Besides that, the walking path was visible in both directions for nearly 150 meters.

Mellon-Hart pointed to a bench carved into the rock face. Motioning the cadet to sit down, the older man joined him and leaned slightly on his walking stick.

"You're here for a purpose. And where we sit and with my fogger, the echoes caused by these hills, and the noise of the cataracts—" farther ahead, the trail crossed a rushing stream that cascaded down the hill, "—we're safe from any, shall we say, Internal interference."

Kyle had worked up a sweat walking; he was happy for the heavy sweater even though it didn't fit him well.

"I've several others you can select from at Stanhope," Mellon-Hart stated, handing the cadet a sliver flask. "Meanwhile, this'll cut your chill."

On swallowing, Kyle coughed. "Stronger than I expected."

"That's good single-malt whisky," Mellon-Hart laughed loudly, throwing back his own deep drink. "Keeps the chill off, the howling fen sprites away, and it keeps everyone guessing what I'll say next."

When Kyle accepted a second round, he was surprised when Mellon-Hart seized his left hand before the cadet drank with his right. Kyle let him turn over his hand without resistance. The former board rep ran his fingernails along the palm and skin of the cadet's fingers. "No lefter disks." He looked closely a second time. "And no black disk; that's what I'm really looking for." The three dogs eyed Kyle as though they too were determining his trustworthiness.

Kyle caught it immediately. "You think I'm Security. You don't know me from Adam. And here I am." The cadet wanted to ask, *What's a black disk?* but didn't.

"So, you're a sharp one, that's for sure And cool as these stones in a hoarfrost. And not armed."

"Devon—Professor Chavez-Sherman—thought it best I come to you without an Enfield."

"Well, you're a damned fool to come all this way if you aren't from Internal. I haven't said anything here that I haven't already said back in Seattle when those bastards took over the board."

Kyle raised his right hand, one that did sport four implants but no red command-and-control disk. "I really don't understand what you're alluding to."

"Come to ask about sustainability or come to have a pleasant hike with me?"

"*Sustainability* to me," Kyle tried to explain as a future colony agronomist, "has more to do with the renewing quality of a colony's greenhouse environment."

Mellon-Hart looked deeply at the cadet. His piercing eyes reminded Kyle of his grandfather's searching look. "Truly?"

"Why speak of it any other way?"

The former representative's eyes bore in on the cadet. "Well, you aren't lying to me, I can tell that." His voice was the softest it had been all afternoon.

"Thank you."

"So, why are you here?"

"Frankly, I don't know. I started a summer internship on the Moon. The next thing I know, my advisor is having me lander out here to speak with you."

"What do you want me to speak about, dogs and sheep and fog banks?"

"Search me. Devon, just said, 'Go ask him what he knows. Rumor has it he'll have much to say.' And oh, he gave me this disk."

"And this," Mellon-Hart pointed to the disk he refused to take from Kyle, "more intel, no doubt. Or more questions. Only a fool, however, puts anything on a physical disk in these times." He pointed his bony finger to the cadet's forehead. "Rely on this, laddie, your own wits, or else you're leaving a trail for Chesney's hounds, like that Bobby-Tim, to come sniffing about."

"I'll remember that, sir."

"And so, this—" he waved at the memory disk, "this is supposed to explain it all?" The old man emphatically rejected the disk from the cadet a second time.

"I hope so; I haven't a clue why I'm here. I want to be on a space colony running their hydroponics domes."

"Aspirations to be a planetary farmer, then?"

"Yes, sir."

"Then why'd you come here?" He drew a breath; he knew the answer to his own question. "If I trusted you, I'd have plenty to say."

"Really?"

"Aye, laddie, that I would. If I thought you weren't going to blurt it all back to Chesney or his henchmen, his Immortals. It's him to fear, the smirking-smiling Chesney, not Oakes."

Immortals, thought Kyle, *that's something else I've never heard. Like black disks.*

After that vague reference, the older walker rose and stamped his feet, signifying he was raring to go. "Not far, and the kettle's on, I'm sure." The dogs started running ahead.

———— o ————

In four hundred meters, they crossed a stone arch bridge where the walking trail and road rejoined. Mist from the foaming water below kept the surface wet and slippery. Beyond the rushing stream, they passed through two small replanted groves above more segments of the cascading waters. After a turn away from the streambed, a stone farmhouse came into view. Above the lane leading to the house, a wrought-iron sign proclaimed: "Stanhope Farm on the Wold."

"Welcome, laddie, to my humble home."

Kyle saw little humility in Stanhope Farm. The house was large and rambling, two stories high and solidly built. It had a slate roof, green wooden shutters around a dozen windows, and a covered porch guarded by two stone lions. To the side was a long barn, the rover visible inside one stall. Behind the house was another larger barn, its roof rising above the house's gable. A hedge separated the house from the surrounding pasture where sheep grazed without a care.

As they crossed the cobblestones approaching the house, the dogs let out with baying. "Good laddies, good dogs," Mellon-Hart called out above their noise. "Harmless as they are boisterous, but they like home," he stated to Kyle ushering him into a side door. "Leave your muddy boots here. We'll find you dry socks and something warm for your feet."

It was clear to Kyle that such walks were common here. Cloaks hung from pegs, three pairs of leather boots and two of rubber wellies were tucked under a bench. Out of his heavy outdoor wear, Mellon-Hart opened a door at the top of three stone steps. "Diana?" he bellowed above the commotion of the dogs, "I'm here with our mysterious associate." He made no attempt to hide his lingering mistrust as he called out.

Diana, the driver of the rover, appeared from the back of the farmhouse. She was several years older than Kyle, about his older sister's age, he guessed. Her hair was light brown, her eyes hazel. Although she had no resemblance to Mellon-Hart, Kyle assumed she was his daughter.

When the visitor said as much, his host roared with laughter. "Did Internal tell you that? To cover your tracks after reading up on me? My dossier must be mega-gigs in length! Diana's my *wife*, my third wife! I'm sure Security knows Number One died and Number Two ran off with some hotshot lander pilot twenty-odd years back."

"Welcome," Diana said with a firm handshake. She obviously worked hard; her hands felt calloused, while her smile and demeanor were pleasant. "I'm Diana Williams," she continued softly, her gentle voice in stark contrast to Mellon-Hart's overbearing tone. "Please, come in." She motioned to a large fireplace and a table, which had been prepared for a meal.

After eating a hearty supper, Mellon-Hart asked Kyle to show Diana his memory disk. "Should I?" he asked.

Ever so slightly, the woman's head shook to signify no.

"Sorry, laddie, won't touch it. Others in Seattle might. Ones once on the board, like Wandi." Mellow-Hart drifted onto memories of his time with the board. "She and I go way back, an indifferent-but-tolerant relationship. Oh, she's honest and tells the truth but can be stubborn as any PRIM-born woman—"

Diana's arched eyebrow over her hazel eyes stopped him from his unrelated ramble. She brushed her light brown hair aside without taking her gaze off her husband. He wasn't so much humbled as reminded that their guest had not proven himself as yet.

"But this is from Lieutenant Colonel Chavez-Sherman," Kyle implored, the disk still offered to the former board member.

"Makes no difference." Looking at his wife, he laughed loudly to explain, "The cadet says he knows nothing of sustainability and black disks."

Diana looked at him, like her husband earlier, searching for signs of lying, her face gently shifting into a smile. "Better off without, Cadet Kyle," she spoke in a soft, considerate voice.

Diana rose to bring out a warm apple tart. "We have vanilla sauce with it," she explained.

"Ever had it?" Kyle shook his head no. "See, laddie, you've not traveled enough."

"Been to the Moon twice."

"Travel, man! I mean around our Earth. See our new world. You're tied to Marsco like a wee bairn tied to apron strings."

Kyle felt he had to defend himself or he would be bowled over verbally by his intense host. Thin he might be, but his bearing suggested he thought of himself barrel-chested, robust and unstoppable. "Actually, after the Academy and the Accords are settled, I see myself living on Mars working on colony greenhouses."

Mellon-Hart gave a smirk. "So, you think these Accords of yours *will* be settled? With the likes of Chesney's disks at the helm? His black disks and all those Immortals?"

Another arched look from Diana silenced the man.

<hr />

"Breakfast only after you've worked up a sweat," the farmer yelled to Kyle before any sign of morning light. All was black. And it was damp. Not a sound cut the thick fog lying around the house, barns, and yards. The farmer threw some work clothes onto the guest's bed. "These fit my youngest son when he was your age. Should do for you." Kyle was quick to get dressed. "You need to get a fire roaring if Diana's to cook," the farmer said.

Outside, Kyle found a pile of wood, the pieces too large to burn in a kitchen stove. In his kit he had work gloves that protected his finger disks. With an iron maul and wedge, a sharp double-headed axe, and a stump, nothing stopped the cadet from piling up enough dry oak and ash to blaze for several days.

Mellon-Hart passed a few times on his way to feed chickens and hogs. He stopped only once to size up the cadet, who by this time had stripped down to a T-shirt. His sinewy arms were strong; his axe swing showed he knew what he was doing. The pile grew faster than the farmer imagined. And he didn't have to tell Kyle anything about filling the box near the kitchen door and the bin next to the stove. Both were heaped with wood cut to just the right size. The young man had worked at this before.

As they washed up before their morning meal, Mellon-Hart reached for Kyle's hands as he stood drying them. "You've no sign of blisters. You know how to handle an axe, laddie, that's for sure."

"I said I wanted to farm on Mars, didn't I?"

"Aye, that you did," the old man answered still with a wary lilt.

"I won a place at the Academy," Kyle explained with no emotion. "I wasn't born an associate."

"Well, get out now, that's all I'll say. Get out of Marsco's clutches. Join a fed and stay a fed. If not—" This time he stopped without his wife glancing at him.

Still suspicious, Kyle concluded.

———————•———————

Six people sat around the table for a large breakfast. Mellon-Hart and his wife; his laborer, a former PRIM; his wife; and their small son—and Kyle.

After the meal, Kyle was prepared to help with the farm again when Mellon-Hart declared, "The south train comes in three hours; you should be on it. It'll get you to where you can catch a lander."

"Not going to look at the disk? Not even ask me anything?"

"You said you don't know why you're here."

"That's true, but there has to be a reason; at least listen to Devon's disk."

"We've already been through this, young man. Why should I say more than that I am a *fed* now? Not an associate. And that I believe in all the Six Accords, even if the board is trying to squelch them."

"How do you know that?" Kyle demanded, losing his temper for the first time at the old man's stonewalling. "You have to know something. You have to suspect something. I should hear it. Or give that intel to Chavez-Sherman."

"Get back in your uniform, laddie," Mellon-Hart simmered, but controlled himself. "I'll get you to that train."

———————•———————

Kyle reentered the kitchen, a cadet once more. Before Mellon-Hart could react one way or the other, the sounds of vectoring jets filled the tense silence. It was still too foggy to see skyward, but from its unmistakable sounds, an HFC was hovering and preparing to set down. The dogs were yelping, the others looking skyward, frightened.

"You bring them down on us, son?" Mellon-Hart shot him a look that accused him of betrayal.

"I didn't. I know less than you do."

"Son, there was no call for this. No cause. I'd have gone in if you wanted me. *Them?* What've *they* done?" He motioned to the startled people in the large kitchen.

Kyle was perplexed as well.

Diana ran to her husband. As he held her, possibly for the last time, he softly said, "We always expected this, my dear; it's just sooner than we thought. Once those bastards booted my arse off the board, we expected this."

Discharging jets allowed an eight-seat HFC to adjust its descent angle and correct its landing orientation. Its skids were down. A Security craft for sure, its onboard computer had no difficulty locating the Stanhope Farm and setting down on the cobblestones outside the kitchen.

"You're safe, too, mate," Mellon-Hart called to his worker. "You have the status of a fed citizen, not a PRIM. You've done nothing. It was appropriate to remove your disk. All three of you are safe, I promise."

The owner of Stanhope stood tall, but the others around him were not so sure of their protected status.

Kyle bolted toward the HFC as a hatch opened and a gangway lowered. He was about to demand that Security back off, as if a mere cadet had that kind of clout.

An officer, a woman, came down from the craft toward Kyle. He mentally smirked, *Holy hell, like I'll be able to counterman a Security captain.* Rank was what he first noticed, her bars of rank. Second, that she was in a black uniform he had never seen before. *Must be a new unit from this fed*, he surmised, grasping at straws; all the other markings were clearly Marsco.

It was only when she stood right before him in the still-shrouded light that Kyle recognized the Security captain as Mia Wang.

"Kyle," Mia announced bluntly, "you're coming with me."

Kyle found himself a passenger behind the flight deck of the eight-seater. Mia sat in the copilot seat in front of him ordering the pilot to set a course for base. When high above the Stanhope Farm, she joined Kyle. The HFC was empty except for the three of them.

Without an introduction, Mia took Kyle's hand. "It's the only way to talk with you alone," she insisted.

So much around Kyle was new that it took a moment for him to absorb it all. Her uniform and bars, a captain yet only weeks ago a second lieutenant graduating from the Academy. And that black uniform. Even the pilot, a Marsco warrant, wore a traditional ashen gray Security uniform. Both were armed; Kyle wasn't. Security was throwing around its authority in an independent federation where technically it had no right to do so.

Mia didn't allow Kyle much time to examine his situation before she explained, "We're heading to an abandoned base near Harrogate. Always was one there; Security's just reopened it for its current purposes," she glossed over, "but we're heading directly to York from there, you and I. It'll be lovely, really."

The HFC skimmed along, using lookdown scanners to hug the rugged landscape below. Mia needed to return to the flight deck and engage in communications to secure permission to land at the Security base. Alone, Kyle watched the blanket of fog. How could he be so important that the S & H was fetching him in this manner? He thought of that communication disk he still carried for Mellon-Hart, the one the former board member had refused to examine.

Is this all aimed at Devon?

"The south side landing bay has an HFC waiting for me," Mia told the pilot without any trace of military courtesy. Her voice carried more authority, and Kyle admitted, more Marsco arrogance.

Their HFC slowed as it passed the sprawling Harrogate base. To the east on a low, lonely hill stood a surveillance dish farm, its array clearly fully functional. But it was the activity at the field that caught Kyle's eye.

For an abandoned base, these landers are humping tons of tech, the cadet concluded. Cargo haulers were coming in, off-loading, then leaving by the minute. No wonder the HFC needed clearance to land. The sky was crowded with traffic.

On the ground, supplies were being disgorged from cargo bays with dispatch. The equipment being unloaded caught the cadet's attention. Brads and rovers by the dozens came off the endless stream of massive landers. Obviously, this was an ops in full swing, at red-alert status.

"Something's up, that's for sure," he mouthed with his face to a view panel, turned away from Mia.

He didn't receive a reply.

"Is this to turn over to the new fed?" Kyle wondered out loud. The Second Accords promised that Security would begin relinquishing its weaponry in order to arm the fledging services in each fed. Security battalions and Auxiliary units had technically already begun reverting to federations, thus local, control. Not Seattle control. The upcoming Fourth completed all command-and-control transfers.

"Stockpiling plenty of materiel, that's for damn sure," the pilot sighed, gracefully dodging a large lander to his starboard.

Mia snapped, "Just land us where I ordered; it's out of the way. And then forget whatever you see."

"Roger, captain," the warrant replied impassively. He wanted to see nothing. It was always safer that way with Security.

Before touching down, Kyle had several moments alone to contemplate: *What will Mellon-Hart think of me now?*

As the hovercraft settled on its skids, Mia barked at the warrant to hurry with the hatch so she could exit quickly. Leading Kyle by the hand, she guided him off the eight-seater and to her waiting two-seat runabout. She flew the smaller craft with dispatch.

When autopilot kicked in, she leaned back. They were alone at last. The sprawling base with all its frenetic resupply activity was behind them, out of sight. At once, she changed from the in-charge officer to a softer woman. Her passenger liked the change, no doubt.

Nonetheless, Kyle had to say something of the obvious difference in her uniform, those captain's bars. "Oh, by the way, congrats on these. Plebe-cadet-lewy-captain in only a few easy steps."

"I have reservations and plans for us," she answered with that inviting voice he remembered, laying her hand on his neck.

"With all your friends?"

"No, just us, so I can explain everything fully. I promise this time. Completely alone."

"So, no Wicks?"

She laughed, almost playfully. "Doubt he'll show up."

"Yeah, I know," Kyle answered with a critical edge to his voice. "I saw the good, new captain just last week, or maybe ten days ago. Lunar-side. Like you, what a promotion. And there he was, possibly the nursemaid to a gaggle of—"

"Of what?"

"He didn't say. Classified," Kyle replied, lying. He was only just now putting Wicks together with those lunar Vanovaras.

The autopilot beeped as it approached a landing pad. Mia took control, her finger disks twitching in the proper glide coordinates.

York was a completely different sight than the Harrogate base. By now, it was midday and the sun had burned off the ground haze. As they crossed the River Ouse, the water sparkled on its lazy way toward the waiting distant sea. The Minster stood proudly above the rest of the city. In the east and south, high-rise buildings stretched skyward. Built by the subsidiary after the accidental destruction of London's city center, much governmental infrastructure had been relocated here since the 2060s, nearly one hundred years ago. Although the parliament would eventually meet in Oxford, York would remain the financial and bureaucratic center of this new fed.

After the HFC settled on its skids and as the craft's engines shut down, Mia announced, "First thing, we have to get you out of your cadet gear."

"But I *am* a cadet."

"Kyle, just spend the day with me and maybe *that* won't be your only option."

Prosperity had returned to the former subsidiary as it turned itself into an independent federation. Shops and stores flourished in such an important hub city. The pair had no trouble finding something for Kyle.

"I like this," he announced. He changed into a pair of tan slacks and a light blue sweater, a bit old-fashioned and a bit too like cadet blue, but everything fit him well.

Mia had brought her own off-duty clothes and was out of her black uniform by then. She wore a top that flattered and a skirt that hugged her tightly as she walked. It had shimmering fine threads made with woven asteroid silver. Her attire graced her perfectly, made her glow with love and desire.

"What's next?" he asked.

"Hungry?"

After a lunch at a sun-drenched café, they strolled throughout the old quarter of the city, near the Minster, down through the curving streets. Mia was relaxed, always attentive, never evasive, although Kyle kept their conversation general. No mention of Elkton or Wickes, no mention of Mellon-Hart. Kyle basked in his renewed feelings for her as though the Marsco world were light-years away. The vibrant gardens where they walked, her relaxed air and outfit—to the cadet she seemed perfect. But perfection was illusionary, and Kyle wondered if the perfection before him might actually be slipping away.

To anyone watching them saunter by, they looked like a conventional couple rediscovering their love after a silly quarrel. Kyle had never felt happier. It seemed like old times with more great times still ahead; he sensed it.

Hand in hand, the pair sauntered alone all afternoon. Finally, Kyle had to ask. "How did you find me?"

"Easy. We traced your finger disks' twitches. Once you were on the lander to Durham, we knew where you'd end up. No one else worth seeing up there." She was vague, but her evasion was clear. Only Mellon-Hart made sense to Internal.

Their voices echoed in the narrow confines of the half-empty streets, so Kyle spoke more softly, "Internal Security's that good?"

"When it has to be," she whispered. "But its Black Brigades will be even better. But, I'll tell you all that later."

"Okay, I'll buy that for now. But can I ask *why* you found me?"

"It's cooling off without the afternoon sun," Mia purred at that point, so Kyle wrapped his arm over her shoulders. It didn't take long for her to guide him to the loneliest spot she could find.

Sure they were all alone, she whispered, "I've a room. We'll be together for a night, two if you like. Then you'll know why I'm here and why I love you so."

Mia set her HFC down atop one of several modern buildings on the fringe of old York. She had planned on this hotel rendezvous to give her uninterrupted time with Kyle. "Meet me upstairs in fifteen minutes," she whispered as they finished a candlelit dinner in a bistro off the lobby.

Fifteen minutes of confusion dragged for Kyle. Mia had said nothing of why he'd been whisked away, why he was so important to her, because clearly more than passion existed in her plans. Love might be there, but much more lurked underneath appearances. *And Harrogate? All that weaponry?*

No one was telling him anything, but on the far side of the Moon, he'd clearly seen Vanovaras. Devon hadn't mentioned them. Wicks had to know of them, Kyle conjectured, or why else was *he* there? The colonists weren't expecting the weapons; their ops had given Devon a schedule of clear signals for weeks. Coming over that base at Harrogate, he had seen scores of Brads being stockpiled. Just to be given away? All that didn't seem plausible either.

If the Accords are giving Security battalions and Auxiliary units to the feds, what gives? Marsco largesse? He had no answer.

He was sitting in a recently created federation, one now legally independent of Marsco. He concluded, *No wonder Mellon-Hart's guarded, convinced Marsco was coming for him. No wonder the man wouldn't touch Devon's memory disk, which probably laid out more questions about the murkier workings of Marsco these days.*

"No answers," he whispered to himself, "No answers, only a lady waiting."

The room was spartan, almost like a cadet's digs with a table and lamp but a larger bed. Mia had lit candles. Music played low in the background. As Kyle shut the door behind him, she stood before him, pristine in her beauty, her black hair down her back, her eyes inviting with love.

She was stunning, no doubt; Kyle had no hesitation admitting that. Her negligee was black and showed a black gown underneath. Her petite body curved flawlessly.

Approaching him, she whispered, "Kyle, I can offer all this and so much more, all of it endlessly." Her brown eyes were filled with longing but also with hope that he would have the will to join her forever. "Without change. Without blemish. I'm so yours, if you step over toward me."

"Let's talk later," he whispered. She complied, their love that burning. She knew she'd been ordered to speak first and let him taste his reward later, but her desire, her true yearning for him, was too ardent. The appeal of his deep love overwhelmed her sense of duty to Marsco.

In his arms, accepting his passion, she was fully in love and recklessly off the trajectory set for them by others. It didn't matter to her. He mattered. At this moment, his love for her mattered more.

———————————

And finally, in the afterglow, she did explain why she'd fetched him. "We'll both be perfect. Our plans are perfect. We have a chance never grasped by any humans ever before and never again, since we will retain power and remain unchallenged."

"I can't follow this, Mia, your logic. People fall in love, are in love. They grow madly in love—"

"As we are," she cooed.

"Yes, as we are. But, change and aging, that's part of the package."

"It no longer has to be for you."

"And not for you?"

She smiled and moved his hand to her breast. "I have been given this practically forever," she whispered. "My body is now ageless. Unchangeable. Sustainable." He tried pulling back his hand even as she explained, but she tightly pressed it to her. "I don't age. I can't age. Not any longer."

"And me?"

"Join us, please, and it's yours. I'm yours. Virtually forever."

Still not fully comprehending—but he'd heard her use that word, *sustainable*, that so frightened those at Stanhope—he did comprehend her caress, her movements, her yearning. In a heartbeat, they were entangled for another episode of breathtaking passion.

———————————

Kyle walked through York until nearly 0400 hours. By the light of a Marsco Moon, he had retraced their steps from that afternoon when so much between them seemed so right. His mind ran without stopping, yet he didn't know what to do or where to go. He looked at his disks; if he twitched anything, Security would find him at once.

When he left their bed two hours ago, Mia still slept.

"You must join us. Join me. Have me," she had implored repeatedly.

"You interested in a life on Mars?"

"Mars? I'm offering you a place in the new Security. Rank and power. Sustainability. Near immortality."

"If I understand you correctly," he began.

"I've made it perfectly clear," she replied, an edge coming into her voice.

"If I understand, you are not offering me a Marsco post-Accords—"

"Oh, the Accords, the Accords. They will destroy the most powerful force this world has ever known, a force now perfected." She rose to stand next to him. In the dim light of the last flickering candles, she glowed. "My God, perfection for me, for you, forever."

His head swam. "That much flawlessness must come with a cost."

"Yes, your loyalty. Your commitment to the new Marsco. Its Black Brigades of Security." Mia spoke quickly, hitting all the points she needed to say. Points she was ordered to say *before* she had let the man she loved express his keenest desire for her.

And yet, in the end, as she slept, he'd silently opened the door and slipped in to the night, the unknown. The room wasn't so dark that he hadn't seen a black disk on her left palm, a spot where ordinarily no disk would ever be implanted.

———— • ————

During his two hours walking around Old York, Kyle wondered what to do next. Where could he go? What she had spoken of was ambiguous and blurry, a dream of massive proportions that wouldn't end well. Couldn't end well. Her talk included distinct references to Black Brigades with Immortal Officers leading them. She spoke heatedly, not only of them as a couple but as future leaders of a never-fading elite, ceaselessly ruling Marsco, a new Marsco under Chesney.

"His vision of our future." She'd eagerly explained after their passion; her words ran ceaselessly through his mind. "It's dazzling! Awesome! The power, the ceaseless power we'll share via this man's new world vision."

He had *felt* more than understood what she was alluding to. And what he felt in the depth of his gut was not love or longing but disgust, even though she'd offered him immortality as an ever-satisfying angel offers paradise.

Walking alone, his unsettled mind raced. *Immortals. Black Brigades. The world vision of Chesney.* His mind grew more agitated as the full impact of these ideas came to him, as he grasped the sinister nature of her bargain.

If he understood her, his whole being, the fabric of every single one of his cells, was repulsed.

And if he understood her, he loved someone who was no longer fully human in the ordinary and commonly understood way. Earlier that evening, before him stood someone remodeled, augmented by recombinant DNA and egotism.

In a way, I was just offered all that. Totally mine for the taking, he smirked, half mouthing his words. He cut down a small street, doubled back, glanced again at the silent Minster towers, then walked on. He might be a marked man by now. Might be followed right now. And he was without an Enfield.

At least, he reasoned, Chesney's plans can't be totally ready. They were still looking for officers, ones who would take time to train and time to step beyond this mere mortal body. So, if he could get back to Devon, perhaps he could buy time and be temporarily safe.

Kyle walked on aimlessly for another forty minutes. Only when he saw the train station did he move in any purposeful way. A line of coaches waited at a platform. Ordinarily, a twitch bought him a ticket, but if he did so, he would be instantly identified and located.

Leaning over the entrance barrier, the cadet called to a conductor standing near an open carriage. "This going up to Durham?"

"Yes, sir. Leaves in five minutes, sir. Gets you there in less than two hours."

"Then let me on."

"Well, punch yourself in." He motioned good-naturedly to the screen and turnstile. "Easy as sin, mate."

Kyle threw out his chest in Marsco fashion, began using terms he'd heard from Mia but didn't fully understand. "I'm an officer within a Black Brigade. I hardly think I need twitch my way in." *A conductor out here can't be aware of the differences between Mia's uniform and my cadet's. And years of being cowed by associates helps. Old Marsco habits die glacially.*

When the conductor showed reluctance, Kyle added in a more forceful tone, "If you have any questions, contract Captain Wang up at our Harrogate base. She'll approve this for another Immortal like herself. But at this time of morning—"

Another rail official came forward. The pair looked at each other, then gave the associate a blank glance and mutually decided one ticket more or less was worth it to keep their hides out of something Marsco was cooking up. Rumors were too strong about what was out there at Harrogate. Neither knew anything for sure; neither wanted to find out. Not this way.

In time, Kyle reached a station outside Durham. A few other passengers left the coaches with him, and he purposely stayed with the pack until the exit turnstile. There, he walked without missing a stride and without twitching himself off the platform. No one bothered with him, his Marsco status obvious to all who witnessed his escape.

The cadet's train came in close to where HFCs glided down. The path to Stanhope Farm was easy enough to find and follow. "If I get there, will they help?" he asked himself over and over.

Was it only yesterday? Can some days pack in so much? He tried to clear his mind, because he had no distinct plans for when he reached the distant farmhouse.

The windows of the kitchen showed no light. At first, Kyle was afraid everyone had bolted as soon as Mia's Security HFC left yesterday. Or that they'd been caught up in a follow-up Security sweep. He knew S & H's methods too well.

He approached the side door, expecting an outburst of dogs or possibly an aimed Enfield confronting him.

Starting softly then growing more insistent, Kyle knocked. Nothing stirred. *Where are your dogs?* No noise inside answered. He rattled the handle. Locked. He thought of putting his shoulder to it, but its obvious thickness argued against any strong-arm tactic.

"Now what?" he asked himself, frustrated. "Have to get going, get to a lander field and head back to Seattle and Devon. How?"

As he turned away, a door cracked open at last. "You, laddie? You still alive?"

"Yes, also hungry, wet, and tired."

"And what do you want me to do about it? You got Security on your arse again?"

"I have tried not to leave a trail, but Internal's pretty persistent."

The door swung fully open, a welcome sight for the cadet.

<hr>

Stuffing a second bacon sandwich into his mouth, Kyle explained as best he could about what Mia had offered him, everything, even if he was unsure of the details. He withheld remarks about her nearly convincing methods.

"So, they *have* dangled sustainability in front of you," Mellon-Hart noted. "Like a charm but really a curse."

Kyle nodded. "But why didn't you warn me? Aside from the fact that you didn't trust me?"

"Would you have believed me? I don't know all the concrete science behind it, but I know it's real. Would you just accept that?" Mellon-Hart shook his head, knowing the cadet wouldn't have believed him. "And, besides, you're right. I didn't trust you."

"And now?"

"Have to, laddie. Have to. You're either with them or a fool on the run, sort of like me."

"You're quite courageous, Kyle," Diana added with a caring smile, "to refuse a Black commission, no doubt."

The cadet blushed, swallowing half a sandwich and washing it down with warm tea. "I don't understand *any* of these terms," he insisted, as perplexed as ever, or *any* of the reasons. I'm studying hydroponics to run a greenhouse on Mars or an asteroid colony."

"They need officers; that's my guess. *Loyal* officers. It'll put loyalty above training any day. And if it has battalions and units that it kept from being released back to feds and then these are led by trustworthy, devoted officers, imagine how easily it can disrupt the Accords and reestablish its iron-fist control."

"You serious?" Kyle asked. He hid the fact that he did have fourteen months' experience in Security already.

"Have you met Chesney? 'Power corrupts,' as the saying goes. Few among us will stand aside from such a temptation. But they're finding it hard, I think. The ideals, the promises and vision of our feds, are catching on. Marsco's ruled for so long, folks want their own ways now. Some are quite committed to the Accords and all they promise, so I think these Immortals will find a hot reception awaiting."

Diana spoke up. "Wasn't it a common expression from your continent centuries ago, 'Give me liberty or give me death'?"

"I believe so."

Mellon-Hart added, "Well, citizens of the new feds around the world are waking up to that, even as those hunkered down in Chesney's Bunker are trying to reel in the Accords. What's another line from your continent a ways back? 'For though the flames of liberty may sometimes cease to shine, the embers can never expire.' We almost forgot that, but not now. We've had a taste of our freedom here in this fed. Other feds have as well. And just a small taste of liberty is never enough."

"But Marsco signed the Accords—"

"Did they do so in the spirit intended? I think not!" He drew a deep breath. "You watch. If there's *any* trouble from some PRIM or sid hotheads, Marsco will step back in. It'll suspend the Accords on the least provocation. Chesney will. You mark my words."

"That's how it came to rule in the first place," Diana explained. "The world was chaos and anarchy. It *temporarily* came to power to end all that and then stayed in power."

"Aye, it's really waiting for another pretext. Mark me." Mellon-Hart drew a thoughtful breath. "Some group feels it can stand up with a few arms, outside of federation law, outside of the Accords, and you watch, Marsco will use their anger and misplaced violence to crash the whole of the Accords. We need to follow the law, follow the letter of the Accords, or we're handing Chesney and his shadow HQ the pretext they want to suspend everything and retake control."

"Or is Seattle setting up some incident? Getting ready to stage something?" Diana added.

"Yes, laddie, armed men outside the rule of law, who think they speak for the masses when they don't, can easily be swayed. It's happened before. History is a nasty reminder of how frail our egos are."

"That would explain Harrogate," Kyle added. "Security's there preparing for just such an eventuality. And yet, it's still unclear to me exactly what these *Immortals* are, these *Black Brigades*."

"Confusing, laddie, no doubt."

"Merely mentioning them to some sid rail workers—I mean, they're free fed workers now—and I put the fear of Security in them. So, someone's been using those terms to keep folks in line already."

"And since Seattle hasn't—*as promised*—released any Security and Auxiliary personnel back to this fed, or any other fed, we can't do anything about it. We haven't the strength or ability to totally stand up to Marsco."

Diana had left them for a few moments. When she returned, she carried a bundle of clothes and a small leather wallet. Giving them to her husband, he explained to Kyle. "They'll trace you back here easily enough."

"In a nano once I use my disks."

"Yes, you have to leave now. The sooner the better. I can get you near an Indie lander field. Catch a ride to Seattle from there. Back to Devon. May be roundabout like via Lisbon and the Azores or maybe Glasgow and Iceland." He handed over a few thousand MMUs in credit strips and tokens to Kyle. "Don't need to twitch with these. Let's get going."

"How?"

"I promised to buy a boar from a spread on Barrenshead Heath. You can catch a train there that'll get you to that lander field. It's only two kilometers from a platform to a small strip. Dangerous but worth a try."

In the cobblestone yard, Diana hugged the cadet goodbye. The last woman who had held him was no longer fully human. He was now absolutely sure of that. "Take care," she whispered. "Come back when it's safe."

Before they had driven too far, they came to a stone bridge crossing a cascading stream near where the pair, the fed farmer and Martian farmer-to-be, had talked just the other day. Kyle asked him to stop the truck mid-span.

"I know you won't want to see this now," the cadet explained, holding out Devon's memory disk one last time. "And I certainly don't want to be caught with anything like this, especially if it would incriminate Devon."

He tossed the disk into the torrent of rushing water underneath the stone span.

"Safest there," he smirked.

Before restarting the engine, Mellon-Hart advised the associate, "The moment you're able, become a fed, laddie, that may save your life. Become a fed."

EIGHT

THE MILLERSVILLE INCIDENT

(New Grange, June 2154)

"I'm sure Devon's cadet won't mind taking you. You'll be perfectly safe with him," Celine explained to the flustered Sarah.

"What? That space cadet?" Sarah shot. Celine missed her insult.

Mr. Watanabe had their pineapples ready, but his voice urged caution. He'd even added remarks like, "Send Sarah *with someone like her brother* to pick up the fruit." Celine missed any suggestion of trouble in his remarks. Millersville, close to New Grange, had always been safe. It wasn't as far as Sac City, after all. Chase was nowhere to be found, even in the frenzy to finish preparations for the solstice celebration that evening. He'd gotten a hog into the fire pit early in the morning, then disappeared. That hog, plus ample chickens, and two large turkeys were almost all ready, except for Trent's pineapple.

"You'll have to go with him, and that's it," Celine insisted to Sarah.

The young woman balked. Being alone with *that* stranger was not at all what she wanted to do. She bent over and hacked feverishly at several carrots. A dozen other helpers scurried around the house's stoves and under a tent in the garden that served as a temporary kitchen.

"No time to go all the way to Sac City," her mother stated firmly, "and I've checked; Watanabe has what I need." When the polite Mr. Watanabe had originally called at New Grange personally several weeks past to inform the Brunels of his expanding establishment in the thriving village, Celine never imagined she would ever be using his business at all, let alone this soon.

All around mother and daughter the kitchen was a whirl as the Brunel family prepared for the annual first day of summer hog roast—but without pineapple, which was unthinkable. "Where Trent ever tasted pineapple is beyond me," his wife groused, "but he won't have this meal without it."

Sarah smiled, remembering the sweet yellow wedges decoratively placed on each table. Without this finishing touch, she knew, her father would think the night a total loss.

Celine dragged her daughter away from the protective gaze of Roxanne. "Tell Mr. Watanabe who you are, dear. He sent off for two dozen especially. He's being extremely solicitous."

Preparing for this evening entailed Celine and Roxanne already making four tedious trips to their usual Sac City purveyors over the past week for everything, but in the gathering, storing, and preparing, somehow the pineapples had been overlooked. They were hard enough to find in Sac City at best. A delicacy for many PRIMS, she knew—even her own family ate them fresh only this one night—but Trent insisted that this special meal for his laborers be as fine as any offered to other guests at New Grange. Everyone who had done any work on his land in the past year was welcome.

Still, Sarah felt her place was here in the kitchen with all these scurrying helpers and La'Shay. "But, Mother, Roxanne wants—"

The old cook had followed the pair into the back garden near the tent kitchen. "No, you go, as your mother asks. She knows best." She untied her charge's apron and primed her like a doll, fussing with her hair.

Before Sarah had time to say another word, Celine had her by the hand, tugging her across a lawn under two oak trees to find the associate in question. At a table placed at the end of their shady garden, Kyle was focused on his tablet. The Brunels needed only so many chairs, tables, and tents set up. Kyle willingly pitched in. He had tried to get into the kitchen after he'd helped Chase place the hog in the roasting pit dug just beyond the garden, but Celine wouldn't hear of it.

Kyle's screen slowed a detailed map of New Grange and the surrounding area. For two entire days, he had been taking measurements here and at the Richardson place, walking the hedges around the largest guesthouse to get bearings. He transferred his observations to a large, hand-drawn paper map but had kept its meaning a secret.

Can't be planning on tossing us off our own land, Celine concluded, *not with Devon right here. Besides, this is Darrow land. Has been for over fifty years, no matter who says so.*

"Oh, Lieutenant Roncalli," the granger stated softly, knowing she was interrupting his deep concentration, "Sarah and I have a favor of you, if you wouldn't mind."

His smile erased any concern mother and daughter had. He raised his head, looked at women, then settled his gaze on the older one. "Yes, certainly, Mrs. Brunel, but I'm still a cadet thus not an officer yet, and I won't have you being so formal with me. Please, call me Kyle."

A bit flustered, she agreed in the familiar way grangers had. Living out here all her life, she had met only a handful of associates, usually those who came with Devon. It seemed right to give them such proper decorum, space explorers and professors from the Academy. And Major Cyndi Maricourt, a pilot, who had come with Devon before she'd died so tragically.

Hardly drawing a breath, as though speaking with another granger across their fields, she started in. "New Grange, well, Trent would never think of hosting our guests without a supply of fresh pineapple. It's a whim of my husband's." The spicy aroma of the hog cooking in the pit hung in the air. "Everyone will be here in about four hours. Can you escort, yes, *escort*," she shot her daughter a silencing glance, "our young Sarah here to a nearby PRIM village where there's a shop owned by a Mr. Watanabe?"

The cadet drew a breath as though calculating for an orbital burn on a lander. "That's in 'Millersville,' I believe, and Mr. Watanabe's father achieved sid status fifty-five or -six years ago."

Both women marveled at his knowledge of the locals and their area. Celine breathed out her reply. "Why, yes, I believe that Millersville is the PRIM village's official name."

In defiant prissiness, Sarah commented, "Mother, of course, they are feds now, not PRIMS."

Standing to the side sulking, Sarah looked at the cadet in disbelief. During the past two days, he'd shown such familiarity with a great deal of the history of her grange. Why and how, she didn't understand, but he added many details that even her mother hadn't previously known—like Tillson's had once been a dairy farm—and Celine had grown up here. *She was the repository of all their stories. Please don't mention anyone drowning,* the steaming young woman implored them both.

In spite of herself, Sarah took a good look at the associate. His sandy hair and hazel eyes seemed to suggest a different heritage than his Mediterranean last name implied, but Sarah was afraid to ask him anything about it. Devon assured her it was okay, that associates were much less skittish about that in 2154 than seventy years ago, when hiding PRIM ancestry was axiomatic. His tall body, taller than either Devon or her father, was muscular but agile and relaxed. He seemed to smile much more than an associate should, but truth be known, she didn't really know how much they were supposed to smile. Devon was the only one she really even knew; he smiled a great deal when here—and readily. But he was family.

Unaccountably embarrassed by this whole episode and wishing to avoid him totally, Sarah began offering excuses. "Oh, mother, Mr. Roncalli is—"

"*Kyle*, please, Miss Brunel."

"Mr. Kyle here is studying," Sarah went on without a pause, "a cadet *must be* studying all the time."

"Nonsense," he responded but not as admonishment. "This is family genealogy," he pointed to his tablet and a long scroll of paper with a branch scheme for working out ancestry.

"But our old rover," the young granger continued, throwing out any and every excuse she could grasp, "was bought at auction years ago, and we've nearly run it into the ground since, and it's all rust and duct tape, and anyone can see it was a Security vehicle because the post-auction paint has gotten so thin and peeling off, and what PRIM wants to see *that* in Millersville?"

In a deadpan, Kyle replied, "And, of course, those would all be fed citizens now, right? Not PRIMS."

Sarah scowled, but her mother was slightly amused. *Our Sarah's been gently taken down a peg and doesn't even know it.*

Kyle smiled and motioned to a six-seater rover. "Finest around, I'm sure. VIP model with no sign of Security near it," the cadet assured them against obvious indications of the opposite. It was weaponless but had a locked-down hatch above the two back seats for mounting leths or non-leths if called for. "Colonel Chavez-Sherman rates, but you know that. The Security wallahs up in the Sac City were beside themselves with helpfulness to lend us that machine."

He didn't mention the Enfields that the associates brought with them from Seattle as a matter of course.

———•———

From the first time she'd seen Kyle the day he arrived, Sarah vowed never to like him. As the cadet and Devon approached New Grange near the Richardson place, Kyle asked to be let off. He was reading his tablet and wanted to find out if his records corresponded with how the owners explained the history of their granges. It didn't hurt that he'd seen two Richardson sisters, Hy and her next sister, Emily, walking along toward their house.

Stepping out of the rover, the cadet called to the young women, hand out to shake theirs and motioning to their father's spread.

When Devon saw Sarah a short time later, he laughed when explaining the scene to his young cousin. "And I thought he had a girlfriend, another cadet like himself."

One hour later, Sarah's initial dislike for a man she had yet to meet solidified as Hy walked with the cadet in question over from the Richardson place to New Grange. The same extended hand and fake smile—Sarah was sure it was forced—greeted her. *Some people are good at expressing false sincerity. He's a master.* Yet, Hy seemed to enjoy hanging around him.

"See you soon," he said to Sarah's neighbor as Hy turned back toward her father's place. Her brown hair, in a curled ponytail, sashayed away, as if to make sure he remembered the sight.

Richardson women are like that, Sarah fumed, even though she still counted Patrice as her best friend. *They've got it; they show it.*

To Sarah's shocked face, he answered, "Miss Richardson told me of your family's party and how excited they were to come to it every year. Your reputation precedes you."

"What did they say about me?" Sarah asked sharply.

"That you were the smartest girl they knew."

"Girl? I'm nearly twenty-two," was her shrill reply.

Instructed to show him to the guesthouse, she marched him off without any Brunel courtesy.

"Since you're so smart," he tried teasing, "have you been at the Academy?"

"No!" her answer came over her shoulder, hardly looking back, three paces ahead. "What makes you ask *that*?"

"Your pace has that taking-a-plebe-to-a-discipline-hearing gait to it, that's all."

Sarah stomped on all the faster, not sure if she were being insulted or teased.

———•———

The Brunel daughter's peculiar attitude toward the cadet and her cold-shoulder voice was just another item on Kyle's list of curious and unusual events over the past few weeks, this one trivial. He still needed to speak with Devon about them all, but they hadn't had time yet. Stanhope Farm, Mellon-Hart, Mia and her offer. Those landers off-loading materiel at a supposedly closed-down Marsco base. His roundabout way across the Atlantic back to Seattle. Once there, off to here in a shot, now armed.

On a ranked and prioritized list, obnoxious Sarah hardly counted. The eager and sassy neighbor, Hy, seemed interested and interesting. But after the passion he'd spent with Mia, another woman didn't seem appealing, even one as attractive as that Richardson daughter.

Am I safe? he asked himself more than once. The answer seemed to be *yes*, so long as he was close to Chavez-Sherman. Or possibly both of them were under scrutiny and suspicion. Mia had come out of the blue to snatch him away, ostensibly to speak with him about the sustainability enigma but in reality, to exhaust him with her ardent desire. Marsco had demonstrated its omniscient eye and extended reach once again, even if Security couldn't stop that passion.

Mia gave him more headaches than the dismissive Sarah ever could.

———•———

When ready to leave, the only thing Sarah said was, "This *is* New Grange. You've no need for that!"

Although he hadn't mentioned the sidearm, Kyle's first stop away from the main house was the smallest guesthouse, which he shared with Devon. He had placed his tablet, genealogy chart, and map on a desk and quickly strapped on a holster before rejoining Sarah in his rover. Looking around the empty house set so far off by itself, the well-trained associate appropriately thought of Devon's weapon. He brought the second holster along and stored it in the rover's empty weapons locker.

The cadet felt the granger's seething glare. "There's just no call for wearing *that*," she fumed, not letting up. "There's been *no* trouble out here for years—"

"I know, since the PRIM uprising of '24, but I'm taking no chances," the associate answered with a bit too much bravado and knowledge of local history.

"Makes no sense," she added bitterly.

"Regs, Sarah, Marsco regs," he tried to say as kindly as possible. "'No associate shall leave a Sector or Cantonment without appropriate safeguards.'"

"Well, that's vague. They should be locked up in father's gun cabinet."

"He asked us to. Devon intervened."

"You know why? Father doesn't want an incident with some armed zealots, as he calls them, going off on their own and proclaiming a new fed within this fed. Anything that might make Marsco renounce the Accords."

"I *am* an Academy cadet."

"Yes, I know, space cadet."

He scowled.

"All the more reason to follow our new federation laws. Father wants this, our new fed, to be run on rules and laws, not armed groups randomly stating they're in control."

Kyle understood enough of the pre-history of Marsco to know that was part of what brought down the old democracies and brought about the Continental Powers, armed groups proclaiming secession and their own harsh laws. All that chaos in turn set up the rise of Marsco.

"To carry a weapon here and now, you have to be loyal to our fed and trained in safety. Even so, Father wants them locked under his control on his grange."

"Well, this's one that isn't going to be," he tapped the webbed belt. To Sarah, he came across as macho and insensitive, a mere boy needing to show off his prowess and masculine strength in the worst way, his adulthood a pretense.

Incensed, Sarah was about to give directions, but the rover was off as though Kyle knew the way instinctively. He had studied his maps. He knew the current road network, such as it was, and the plat of the area from before the Great PRIM Mutiny, more than fifty years ago.

The granger crossed her arms, brooding, sullen. Until the Enfield appeared, their outing had actually taken on a feeling of a lark, something reluctantly approaching an adventure. Not so now. And before she knew it, the rover was down from the guesthouse and onto a well-tended road heading northwest through the last parcels of Brunel land.

Off the compacted gravel road of New Grange, the rover bounced along dirt tracks that ran parallel to the surveyed roadway that the fed was soon to pave. "That'll be like the newly resurfaced road Devon and I used from Sac City until we got off onto paths like these," the associate finally stated, trying to smooth tensions over with Sarah.

"Father is pretty pleased with all the road construction around here," Sarah finally said, pride in her father's Provisional Assembly work making her speak up.

After a few icy minutes, the rover came to a fork in the road. There, the associate abruptly pulled off to the side even though it was clear he needed to continue down the left-hand trail.

Sarah's breath shortened. She was glad it was full daylight. He wouldn't dream of trying anything, to his host's daughter, to his superior's younger cousin. She gritted her teeth in anticipation of some sort of Marsco assault; she had heard of associates like him and how they take what they want.

"May I ask a gigantic favor?" Kyle softly said, his hand behind her seat.

If she bolted, just as with Columbus, she knew he would try to restrain her. Sarah tensed up and readied herself. The whole scene felt too much like the night when Chase's visitor had tried to pull her into his arms, an incident she had spoken about to no one. "Please, we're in a hurry, if father doesn't—" she squeaked out, visibly shaken and turning pale. This entire trip was a disaster from start to finish; she braced for serious trouble.

"I won't be a second, believe me," he responded, pulling away at her obvious discomfort. He had to remind himself that most sids, and certainly a larger majority of Indies like her, were still terrified by Marsco.

"I'm tracking down some old landmarks around here, even some long-standing families, if possible," he explained in a thoughtful voice, "some from outlying granges. I'd also like some intel about these unclaimed tracts of land." He motioned to the nearby thistle-filled fields, uncultivated for years. "I need a guide, someone who knows her way around and who won't draw Enfield fire." He laughed at what he thought was clearly a joke, "If you excuse the expression, I'd hate to have my ass shot off by one of these old-time Indies."

Behind what she clearly understood was his pathetic humor, his eyes held an honesty in his request, his voice sincerity. The young woman relaxed a bit, managed a grin. "I didn't know associates were afraid of Indies."

"I'm *afraid* of *how afraid* I make them feel. And I'm afraid of anyone who is trigger-happy."

"Oh," she replied flatly. "Then stay off Tillson's land." She motioned behind them in the general direction of his spread out of sight in the far distance. "Don't go onto his land with that holster; that'd be the best way I know to keep your scrawny hide intact," she shot more bitterly than she intended.

"I'll remember that," he replied, ignoring her antagonism.

Feeling a bit ashamed, she added, hoping he thought her tone a joke, "Although he uses rock salt more than Enfield shells."

"I'll remember that, too."

The rest of their ride was in uneasy silence.

Watanabe Supplies sat on one corner of two main cross streets in Millersville. One was paved coming into the village all the way from the larger road Kyle had used a few days before. The other road had mostly small houses, trailers, a stray tent or yurt made secure, more or less permanent on its small plot. Each dwelling, however modest, was clean and neat. All of them had a small vegetable garden, although a few residents had added rows of blooming flowers nearest the road. A plot to the north showed where the fed school would open next fall.

"Grew up less than ten kilometers from here," Sarah sighed, "yet have never set foot in this PRIM village alone before."

"Alone?"

"Without my mother or father. Or Roxanne."

"Do they shoot first and ask questions later?" the associate wondered, once more in a way that began seriously enough but ended with a wry twist.

In her own fearful confusion, she was reluctantly amused. "I think we're perfectly safe." She stifled a laugh, determined not to let him know she was almost beginning to enjoy herself.

When the pair entered Watanabe's, they found the proprietor setting up a display of bananas at one end of a long counter made of solid dark wood with the words "Doc Willy's Saloon" carved in front. Kyle laughed, knowing that the counter had once stood in a local tavern two centuries before.

"Oh, Miss Brunel, we've been expecting you." The gentle old Mr. Watanabe smiled. He called to the back of his establishment. A door in the rear opened and closed. The associate immediately recognized a familiar refrigeration unit slamming shut.

"Did that system come from a colony simulation display?" Kyle asked.

"You are quite knowledgeable, Cadet—?" he gave a polite cough to ask for a name.

"Kyle Truman Roncalli." The associate reached out and shook hands. His finger disks gave the proprietor a slight tingle. "Haven't been to a deep-space colony yet, but I know that unit from mock-ups. These units are often cannibalized for Earth-side reutilization. For my studies, I need to know about those systems, so if you want me to take a look at it, give it a once over and tweak, I'd be happy to."

"Yes, ours is quite old but still running well," Mr. Watanabe noted with satisfaction. "But, yes, if you have time, you can check it out. We'd be lost without it."

The proprietor's pride increased when two of his teenage sons appeared, each with two cartons of fresh pineapple. "Miss, when your mother contacted me, I sent my sons to Sac City especially," he began explaining more than he needed to. "We own an HFC, of course, for fetching supplies and making deliveries. We were quite willing to deliver, but she insisted we not bother. And here you are coming all this way. I know where to get all this fresh. And it's no trouble to deliver." He motioned to the sons, either one of whom would love to skim to New Grange.

Sarah forced a smile, wishing he had delivered and spared her this embarrassing time with the overbearing associate. And yet, even that wasn't how she totally felt. Kyle had that associate's confidence as she expected but also a respect for the locale and its inhabitants she hadn't anticipated. All with an air of naturalness she had suspected associates would never have.

Proudly, Watanabe flipped open the top box and urged the young woman to inspect a pineapple. "Beautiful looking fruit, Mr. Watanabe," she whispered, overtaken by the effort her father put into thanking his work gang. She knew no Richardson ever laid on a feast like this.

"I'm so pleased Mrs. Brunel trusted us at the last minute." The grocer took a moment to describe a growing market exchange that served scores of smaller stores like his. "A private lander brings in goods fresh five days a week, so we have access to the best, as you see."

"Who would have believed it?" Kyle whistled in disbelief. "As good as in Seattle itself."

"Been like this only in the past few years," Watanabe stated, "the way markets have opened up, distribution has streamlined." All three marveled, Sarah most of all. "Look," he went on, "the pick date on the box says June 16, only days ago, and here it is on the outskirts of Sac City, which a dozen years previous was a hinterland of the subsidiary."

"And fifty years ago, a wasteland," Kyle added.

"Precisely," Watanabe agreed.

Sarah realized they were chatting about Grandfather Darrow's time when he first came down from Sac City and founded New Grange. She wanted to hear more of that history, which Kyle seemed to know, when—hiding embarrassed panic—she realized that her mother had given her no MMUs. Turning to Kyle, she whispered in mortified tones, "Do you have any tokens?"

The associate answered, "Taken care of, Miss Brunel." He didn't mention these were left over from his recent trip across the Atlantic.

Walking to the rover where the sons carefully loaded their precious fruit, the proprietor and customers spoke a bit longer.

"Miss Brunel, please tell your mother not to be shy about asking me to find her anything. I can get wonderful fresh-roasted coffee. Have you ever tasted salmon before?"

"Wonderful," the cadet exclaimed; his years in Seattle explained his knowledge. Sarah was at a loss.

"And bananas."

The father ordered a son to run inside. In a moment, the young man returned with eight pieces of yellow fruit. Sarah had never seen the like. She'd had little access to any exotic food.

"You peel them; the fruit is soft and sweet," Kyle explained, handing Sarah one to taste.

The cadet assured the grocer he'd be back soon to examine that refrigeration unit.

———•———

Kyle guided his rover down the main street then back onto the rutted path they had used earlier. Gusts threw grit against the windshield. The associate knew they were pressed for time, but even the best Marsco rover couldn't smooth out the path.

"Get you back in a second," he finally said after a slow two kilometers.

On a long piece of road, Sarah watched the flawless sky. Out her window the land she loved stretched boundless to the horizon. Here, it was unplowed, unoccupied. Her father, through the federation, was working to open this to farming for former PRIMS. Give them land and a chance. New roads, new schools, new laws to make their West Con thrive. Get Marsco out, and her world was on the verge of blossoming. Sarah looked askance at Kyle, viewing him as part of the problem.

Within minutes, while Sarah grew as tense as earlier, they drove parallel to a thick grove for three hundred meters. Millersville was three klicks behind, New Grange several ahead.

Where the road dipped to cut through a grove and cross a streambed, something seemed odd, different, too quiet. Making a sharp turn to start down the last slope to a dry creek, they were stopped by a menacing stack of rocks and logs laid across their way.

"Has to be for us," the associate snapped. "Who else is out here?"

The pile totally blocked the road as it curved right to cross the summer-dry stream. On either side was a thicket close to the road with taller trees along the edge of the cutting. *Perfect place for an ambush*, Kyle thought, flicking his Enfield to charging.

"What are you doing?" Sarah shouted at him. "Don't arm that silly thing. There's nothing here but some rocks come down this creek because of a storm."

"When did it last rain here?"

"Last April, why?"

"We came this way, what, an hour ago? That's why."

It dawned on her at that second, a nano before six fist-sized stones hit the windshield. They bounced as harmlessly off the thick polymer in front of them as Enfield fire would. If either exited the rover, they'd be pelted.

No attackers showed themselves, but six more rocks slammed into the rover, three from each side. Fortunately, the thicket started several meters from the trail; otherwise, their attackers could get much closer undetected.

"What are you going to do?" Sarah yelled, "Don't go out there!" If she'd felt tense in the rover with an armed associate, she was frightened now. All her life, she'd lived peacefully in this area; this assault was totally new to her.

More rocks rained down. A large one, thrown two-handed, bounced along the roof.

"You stay here," Kyle ordered and threw open his door. Jumping on the hood, he looked right, spun left, holding out his Enfield to scare anyone who might see him. But with his back turned, rocks came at him but missed wildly. When he wheeled, more errant rocks came from the other side. "Glad baseball's dead," he said, smirking.

"Get in here," Sarah screamed.

"Hold tight." Even without a live bogie in sight, the associate aimed at a tree in the right-side grove, a target elevated about twenty degrees. His three-burst shattered the trunk halfway up. As the tree exploded, it fell to one side. He heard shouts and running.

Turning, he repeated the same tactic, blasting a second tree in half.

When the last echo of Enfield report died away, he jumped to the pile and pulled as much rubble aside as he could without damaging his finger disks.

When Sarah came to help, he warned her to get back in the rover. "Might be hiding an IED, dammit!"

"What?"

"Look, I've got this," he shouted, protecting her even if she didn't realize it.

Disregarding him, she bent to move a log. A rock hit the side of the pile harmlessly. She startled when he grabbed her, forced her down with him on top. The granger was stunned by his brazen act, not thinking of the rocks, only of him on her. He seemed to press down and grunt. A dozen rocks flew at them, fist-sized or larger. These had vicious intent. He grunted again. She pushed his shoulder, and he winced but then was up, waving his Enfield, first to one side, then the other.

She got up slowly, happy she'd hurt him after this failed attack, oblivious to all the rocks showering around them. "What the blazes are you doing?" she demanded.

"High clearance! We'll be fine," he ignored her then began dragging her away from the roadblock. "We're fine, honest! And they'll be bolder soon."

Praying that this was a low-tech attack and not one from some real sophisticated Luddite cell hiding a landmine, Kyle shifted to four-wheel and climbed over the remaining rocks and logs without much effort.

In a moment, they moved along a clear part of road quietly, tensely, Kyle watching for more trouble, Sarah seething at what he had brought upon them, all this violence to her peacefulness so close to her grange. And his grabbing her, pushing her down, falling on her. Inexcusable.

———◆———

At last on Brunel land, the associate pulled to the side of the road. The land wasn't fenced but wide open. The only sign that anyone was entering New Grange was the change in cultivation and the better condition of the road. But fence or no, Sarah felt safe here.

Kyle continued to watch for more trouble. He climbed on the rover's roof for a better view and studied the landscape they had passed through. In the distance, he made out where Millersville sat. Beyond it by at least two kilometers were some small granges recently founded by newly freed feds. From there, smoke was rising. Thick black smoke. As he watched, off to the left side of the village, still at quite a distance from New Grange, another fire started.

"Any idea what that might be?" the associate called down to her, pointing north.

Sarah stood below him, but the rising smoke was clear even from her angle. "Grangers wouldn't be burning anything at this time of year, when so dry," she stated knowledgably. She then concluded sharply, "It's the groves you started with your blasting of those trees!"

"*I did this?*" he shot at her, as though he hadn't just saved her from who knows what, "*I did this?*" He motioned to her. "Come up and have a look." He held out a hand to help her. She ignored the offer. Joining him, he pointed, "This is beyond Millersville, not on your side of it. How in the hell did I do that?"

Sarah, now next to him on the roof, shouted, "This wouldn't have happened if you weren't firing wildly."

She started to lose her balance and instinctively grabbed his shoulder to stay standing. Her hand felt something warm and wet. With that, the young woman whirled around, jumped down agilely, and set off on foot across the field toward the main house.

Twenty meters away from the rover and the space cadet, she realized her hand was covered with his blood.

———— • ————

"I send her off for a short trip and she takes all afternoon," her mother exclaimed.

"Now, Mrs. Brunel, it's all my fault," the associate went on.

Celine looked pensive. Had he done anything with her daughter, *no of course not, Devon wouldn't bring such a man.*

"Then where *is* Sarah?"

"She wanted to walk the rest of the way," Kyle lied, carrying in the last of the fruit boxes.

"Guests will arrive in an hour—and now where's Roxanne?" She dropped a pineapple. "What's wrong with your shoulder?"

He wanted to joke about one of Sarah's knives but thought better. "Not being careful, I guess."

Roxanne appeared. Seeing his blood, she tore away his tunic. "I think I can close them." Three wounds needed cleaning and tending. Celine and Roxanne were the very people to help him. Both had fixed up too many farming accidents to count. Each wound took three butterfly stitches caringly applied.

———— • ————

Alone at his guesthouse, Kyle had time to think of the attack. Was it merely a menacing attack or one intended to do serious harm? Was he a target of opportunity? A shakedown by a local gang gone wrong, the attackers not figuring on Enfield fire to disperse their brazen assault?

What if she'd been there entirely alone? Would they have let her pass? Collected a few tokens? Taken all her fruit? Even her rover? Gone after her snooty ass? Considering how she had reacted and had blamed him, he was surprised at his concern for her at all. He knew these three sharp blows could have seriously injured her if they'd not hit his shoulder.

That's gratitude for you, he mentally raged on. *Like the whole damned world, never stopping to think what Marsco has really given them: stability, a type of peace unheard of before. And these grangers, thinking their asses are really independent. Marsco steps back, and you watch how quickly their damned granges are plundered just like during the PRIM uprisings of 2099 and in '24 and again in the years just before the Accords were finalized.*

In his reaction at the attack, at Sarah, at these stiff-necked Indies with their self-righteous independent attitude, the cadet didn't readily notice anything different about his digs. Then in an instant, everything seemed in place but not exactly right. As he inspected closely, he noticed his clothes had been moved around, as if lifted up from the drawers to see if something were underneath.

No secret that associates carry Enfields. His ancestry chart and tablet still sat on the desk but now upside down, his map folded up incorrectly. Devon's room seemed undisturbed, but a drawer was cracked open by a few centimeters. No associate left his room like this, especially a prof at the Academy. *Never pass a surprise inspection they throw at plebes, that's for sure.*

"I think she's right," he whispered, confronted with the mounting evidence around him. "I *will* lock up our weapons in Mr. Brunel's cabinet."

Roxanne found Sarah in a fury. The former PRIM knew that the young woman wanted to cry, rage aloud, crumple onto her bed like a child.

Comforting her, Roxanne was met with resistance. "I *hate* that man! I *loathe* that man! I *despise* that space cadet!" Sarah thundered. "Thinks he's so damn rough, because—" But Sarah didn't know how to finish her outburst.

When the whole story tumbled out in broken bits, Roxanne held her as she had for her entire life. "He saved you, child," she crooned. "He did;

you must know that." Roxanne had been a girl in the riots of '24. Her own memory of those times remained vivid. Most PRIMS died at the hands of other raging PRIMS during the uprising, wanton violence flaring, as the stronger tried to grab power from the weaker, the vulnerable.

Sarah refused to listen. Instead she washed up, got ready, prepared to greet guests. "I hope he chokes on a wedge of pineapple!" she finally lashed out.

To calm her, Roxanne explained, "I can see it in his eyes."

"See what? Vile Marsco arrogance?"

"I can see his soul in his eyes. He has a great soul."

"Well, if he ever did have a soul, he sold it to Marsco long ago." She gulped breath and added, "Devon's not like that—"

"To save you, he would have been."

"Save me?" Roxanne stopped her with a penetrating look. "Oh—" The young woman had already washed her hands, but her shirt and pants tossed aside on her bed were stained with Kyle's blood.

NINE

THE SUMMER SOLSTICE

(New Grange, June 2154)

Whoever's *burning off fields picked a terrible time of year for it*, Trent Brunel thought, drawing a deep breath of evening air. A slight breeze heading down from the north brought a scent of burnt wood and tar, even a pungent flicker of fat blackened by all-consuming flames.

The rest of the evening seemed impeccable. The tables for his guests were bountiful. The air, except for that occasional pungent stench, was warm and languid, inviting everyone to relax, enjoy. Each aspect of his yearly party reassured Trent that the night would unfold as it should, perfectly.

In the garden behind the grange's main house, the head table stood perpendicular to seven long tables where one hundred guests ate. Lanterns strung from the surrounding trees and scores of candles on each table lit the scene, although the evening sky stayed bright this night, the shortest of the year. Those lights and a gibbous Marsco Moon provided enough illumination for all of Trent's guests to see the mounds of food before them: pork, chicken, and turkey, potatoes, early season green beans, end-of-season asparagus, and loaves of fresh bread with mounds of Richardson butter. And kegs of local beer brewed up in Sac City, kept cold in tubs of ice. And trays of pineapple trimmed and cut decoratively.

At the head table sat the Brunels; even Chase knew not to miss this. At the side of the son sat Columbus. Beside this visitor, Devon. The associate spoke with the granger's foreman to his right more than he did with the sage, but any tension between the associate and Columbus wasn't visible.

Next to Trent and Celine on the other side sat Lionel and Dot Richardson, seats for Nate, their oldest son and his wife—they hadn't yet arrived—then Sarah at the end seated next to another conspicuously vacant chair. She was supposed to sit between Nate's wife and the second Marsco visitor, Kyle. Because neither had appeared, she moved next to Dot, who chatted with Lionel the whole meal. The rest of the Richardson clan, all except Patrice, was scattered about amid the throng of guests. Sitting with PRIMS or no, the younger ones didn't refrain from filling and refilling their plates during the much-heralded annual feast, the likes of which they wouldn't see tomorrow night during Hyacinth's twenty-first birthday celebration.

Trent noted with a mix of pride and gratification that the once-budding romance between the eldest Richardson and his daughter had ended years ago. The Richardsons were fine people, hardworking and honest, and the granger's reluctance was more than "they aren't Darrows or Brunels." He left that excuse to his wife.

No, Trent thought while his mind should have been on his guests, *it's that the Richardsons haven't joined this new world.* What all that meant he wasn't sure himself. But walking among his laborers and joking with their children and laughing at old grannies with their broad smiles filled with gratitude, all that gave him a clear sense of what he meant but couldn't articulate.

"Did you get enough, young lady?" Trent asked a wrinkled crone who had stayed with moist chicken thighs and potatoes because her front teeth were missing.

"Oh, Mr. Brunel!" she laughed heartily, then drank down half a glass of beer.

To her blushing grandniece who was not yet seven, he inquired, "And you, young-lady-looking-so-grown-up tonight, did you get enough?" The shy child had no answer but grinned, showing the same gap in her mouth as her great-aunt's but this time a natural loss of teeth.

"Thank you so much, sir," the girl's father whispered in a husky voice, tipping his mug at the granger in salute.

"Tomas, is that roof fixed?"

"Yes, sir, all fixed."

"Good. When it rains next autumn, if it rains, I want you all dry."

Along with Sarah, Celine joined her husband. Such neighborly small talk continued as the Brunels went table to table. Trent knew most of the families down to the youngest, even if only the men and older sons came to work his land. He never allowed children to labor a full day until they were older than sixteen, even if Richardson employed some children as field hands as young as seven. Trent paid his well—better than any of his neighbors—but knew that younger siblings and even some mothers had to work on other fields to make a go of things.

Living out here in an Independent area, safe and immune from Security lander sweeps, many women had long ago let their birth control strips lapse. Most families had several children, something unheard of with PRIMS under the direct auspices of Marsco back in the last century.

Well, the old Marsco, the granger reminded himself. *The Second Accord five years ago ended all that officially.* In most locales, forced birth control of PRIMS had been virtually gone for more than twenty years. Another example of the world slipping off down unknown pathways.

"Why, Lieutenant Kyle," Celine said with a sly twist to her voice, the way a flirting, still-attractive older woman might speak to a striking younger man, "I won't have you back here in the dark."

In the partial light under a large oak, Celine and Sarah could pass for sisters. Sarah's thick brown hair was brushed to a shine and gathered to the side so it cascaded over one shoulder. Lantern light danced off both their sets of blue eyes, showing how much Celine was enjoying herself. Seeing so many children hovering around the associate, Sarah smiled. Many of them she had taught to read. But when her face caught Kyle's glance, her smile flattened.

Hyacinth had had no trouble finding the cadet earlier. She sat as adoring of the fascinating visitor as the children who had this Marsco demigod in their midst. She placed herself too close to him, guarding him, serving him. Her smile beamed. His too.

The associate was at the dead-last seat of the seventh table, out of sight from the head table. He wasn't discovered until the Brunels finished walking up and down the rows to speak with each guest individually. They had missed several of the younger Richardsons, who were running back and forth to the food tables, and missed Columbus's acolytes, who turned their heads away to speak among themselves when their hosts appeared. Celine had tried to seat Chase's friends throughout all her other guests so they'd mingle, but they had stayed together in a tight knot.

"Oh, Lieutenant Kyle," Celine went on playfully, "I *must* have you join us up front. Sarah's saved you a seat."

"Celine," the associate responded earnestly to her banter, "I came late and didn't want to disturb." He took a quick swallow of beer for strength. "At the Academy, that means demerits, showing up late. And with one of my profs up there—"

The woman scoffed at her all-so-important cousin. "I paddled his bottom a few times. So, when he's snooty, you keep that in mind if he plays god almighty." She then smiled with a twinkle in her eyes, "But he won't; he's such a dear."

"That he is," the cadet replied candidly. "But I'll remember that paddling tactic, your whacking-the-snooty rule, believe me."

Sarah wondered if the cadet's remark were aimed at her, not the professor. Either way, his voice was teasing and playful, unexpectedly so.

"You go right ahead," her mother replied, enjoying their banter. "I just hate people who are above themselves."

It was only then that Kyle turned to fully acknowledge Sarah. "Good evening, Miss Brunel," he said with restrained dignity, trying to hide the amount of beer he'd downed. Hy snickered at his formal, tipsy tone to her familiar neighbor. "Your family throws one hell of a party. Best I have ever, ever seen." He spoke in a forced way, but behind his slightly intoxicated nervousness, both Brunel women heard genuineness.

"C'mon, son," Trent insisted, delighted to see the stiff young guest enjoying himself. "I'll not have one of Sarah's friends back here out of sight. You, too, Hy, you c'mon to where we have plenty of room."

"It's okay, sir. I'm doing fine here," Kyle explained. Hyacinth's snickering gave the wrong impression of what he meant, so he added hastily, "I've been talking with about a dozen locals, two sets of Richardson twins—" he pointed to a set of toe-heads and two other fawn-haired children scooting about "— and a distant relation to the Truman clan, an interest of mine. Truly, I am well taken care of." He also motioned to the brunette at his side, who showed her ownership of the cadet once more.

Celine smiled. "Glad you've made our special guest so welcome, Hy," she remarked while wrapping a ladylike arm around the associate to usher him toward a vacant seat at the head table.

Trent brought along Hyacinth, so Sarah was left standing alone. She felt like taking Kyle's now-vacant seat in the dark and hiding. But, she couldn't let the scene of Hy hanging over Kyle become the centerpiece of the head table.

Plucking up her confused courage, Sarah caught up with her mother. She gracefully tugged Kyle away from Celine and took his other arm. Mother easily let daughter claim the young man. Sarah felt him wince—the injured shoulder.

"You don't have to hide from me," she whispered. "I don't hate all associates."

"Never imagined you would. You're more focused than that."

Once more, the young woman didn't know if she were being insulted or teased.

By the time the granger's daughter and the cadet reached the head table, the strained truce between Columbus and Devon was breaking down. For most of the meal, the associate had spoken pleasantly with the grange's foreman and ignored provocative remarks from Chase's guest. When the workman left to help Roxanne tap another keg, Columbus bore down on the associate: left-handed disks; a firm, poised attitude; the deference paid to him by others, especially PRIMS.

"You must be here to gloat of Marsco's crushing power," he began, "but here among these Indies, their self-sufficiency must stick in your throat."

Devon sipped from his mug—he was still on his first—and gave a pat reply. "I've visited here two or three times a year all my life. Celine, your host, is my cousin. We share Grandfather Sherman."

"But really, Marsco hates this place and such like it," the mystic goaded, "places that show autonomy from its sway." His face was covered with beads of sweat even though it wasn't unpleasantly warm. He kept a set jaw and a pair of blazing eyes, always searching for a return look to stare down, intimidate, force to lower. He was shorter than Devon but much heavier. Were it not for his glaring abhorrence of everyone he looked at, he would hardly be noticed at all. "Is it not so?" he went on, "that Marsco hates all these grangers?"

"Not so sure of that," the associate responded in a noncommittal tone.

He picked at a moist chicken thigh La'Shay slid onto his plate. "Great cooking! Roxanne's a chef supreme."

"You evade my question," he scowled.

The associate smirked. "You're basing your conclusion on partial evidence. Did you try this chicken? I love the lemon and dill she uses."

"Again you sidestep," Columbus replied, never failing to accuse everyone of insulting him by their every innocuous action.

"Have you even been on a sweep through a zone when it's hot? I mean buzzing with hostile skinnies just egging you on for a fight? Well, unless you *want* that fight—and there are times when you do—unless a commander wants that fight, he patrols well away from the hornet's nest."

"I gather nothing from your words," Columbus retorted, puffing up his chest a bit, "except fear."

"*Of you*, I presume?"

"Yes."

"I fear no one save the ignorant who spout 'wisdom' without any real knowledge to back it up, so possibly in that special sense, you're right." His snide remark hit home. But rather than revel or renew his attack, he took a slip from his mug and returned to his chicken.

Turning to Chase, Columbus informed him, "This one has no soul; his eyes show he has no soul."

Far from nodding in agreement, Chase worried about openly insulting his cousin in front of his parents. He had enough Sherman and Darrow blood to know this was not the time and place for picking a verbal quarrel.

"Have you had enough?" the young Brunel asked, playing the host if merely for this one guest. "Roxanne's chicken is excellent," he insisted. "She serves it often, but I never grow tired of it."

Columbus waved off his offer. "Do not hold onto that which is passing, young one," the knowing seer derided. "'All passes, nothing stays.'"

"Better have that last leg then." He grinned as half the meat disappeared in one bite. "Tastes great."

⸺ ◦ ⸺

"Can't imagine what's keeping our Nate," Lionel Richardson wondered as Sarah and the rest rejoined the table. The tallest man seated there, he had to unwind his long legs and shuffle as Kyle settled in. Leaning down toward

Sarah, making sure the young woman knew his oldest was to appear soon, he went on, "He's a hard worker, that's for sure. Wants to double his herd over the next two or three years; that's his plan, anyway, and he has the grit to do it, our boy." He was certain his words were salt to her wounds.

Looking at his wife, who didn't seem pleased with the term *boy*, Nate's father added hastily, "Course, he'll be twenty-six next September, not *a boy* no more, that's *fur sure*, and old enough to handle a spread of his own, that boy is."

Dot Richardson had grown used to these kinds of comments from her generally quiet husband. But Nate's life spoke for itself. He was tall like his father, strong, diligent, clever, without a drop of PRIM blood. *What young woman wouldn't want him? Well,* Dot had to admit, *I guess a young woman with a substantial slice of New Grange as part of her future can pick and choose. And so, our Nate had to make his own way as best he could.*

Without a piece of New Grange, he had to start from scratch, a demanding task for even the strongest young man. *No,* she smiled at the Brunel girl, *a quarter, a third, maybe half of New Grange—Trent dotes on his only daughter—that would've done well for our Nate.*

"Tell 'em," Hy motioned with her head at her parents, "tell 'em what you saw today in that dirty, old PRIM village."

Sarah had mentioned nothing to her parents and Devon about the attack at the dry stream. Roxanne would keep her peace. And she instinctively knew Kyle hadn't reported it; even though, she surmised, as a cadet, he should have. Even so, she knew what the Richardsons expected to hear, that her trip to Millersville had been a disgusting example of PRIMS living on their own, virtually in the midst of Indies. But it had been quite the contrary.

Diplomatically, the granger's daughter began, "I was surprised how many shops there were. Four or five. I mean shops stocked with goods, doing a brisk trade from all signs. PRIMS there are doing well. I'd say about one hundred live there, most in real houses, some in tents, but I saw gardens, signs of actually staying put, making a go of it. Was there only fifteen minutes—"

"That associate took her," Hyacinth interjected, eying Kyle. Her parents' frown cut that line of discussion off. PRIMS settling in permanently was disappointing enough; associates were clearly as unsatisfactory.

"My cousin brought him down," Sarah resumed. "He's, he's, well slightly inebriated at the moment but generally very proper and formal to the point of being obnoxious."

The older Richardson heard *inebriated* with a self-satisfied Indie smirk, Sarah—too good for his son—showing off while her associate showed his true colors. Lionel had sipped lemonade all evening. But Hy heard *proper and formal* as somehow belonging to a grand and elevated world they'd never be allowed to enter. She took a longer, more desiring look at the young man, whose animated, florid face lit up the far end of the table.

"'Millersville,' you called it?" Lionel rebuked Sarah. "Didn't know a rundown flea-trap PRIM village ever got a name."

"It's listed that way on one of Kyle's Marsco maps. And it wasn't so rundown, really rather the reverse, I'd say. And he's," she motioned with her head, "Kyle's surveying this whole area for some inexplicable reason. We should ask him now. Takes a few beers to get him chatty."

Marsco taking an undo interest in Lionel's small grange was more disturbing than a handful of damn PRIM squatters settling down indefinitely in his locale. "Maps? What's he up to? What's Marsco up to?"

Hy snickered, "Know *that* and you'll know everything."

Sarah shifted gears and dropped her voice to a soothing, lilting note. "Oh, Kyle," she intoned, as pleasing as she ever was when trying to coax Roxanne or La'Shay to fix her hair a different way or shorten a skirt's hem against her mother's wishes.

Taken up abruptly by the call, Kyle looked down the table at the two intriguing young women surrounded by Richardsons who didn't seem pleased with him. La'Shay, fussing with the table's ample platters, urged him, "Go on, move down, there's plenty of room near her. She won't bite."

Kyle reversed a chair to create a barrier between himself and the hostility Sarah usually displayed. She should have asked about his shoulder but didn't. "We've some questions for you," his host's daughter began all too politely.

"Yes?" he remarked slowly to suppress any giddiness from too much of Trent's fine beer and his daughter's unexpected attention.

"Tell Lionel and Dot why you're here and what you are doing with your maps," Sarah ordered. She put on airs around him after he was seated;

even Hyacinth hadn't done that. When he was closer, the women leaned into him and watched intensely.

"Well, I'm here at Devon's orders." He left that vague then stated proudly about his maps, "Those are my personal hobby." He sipped some beer. "I'm descended from a *Truman*—" Lionel recognized the name as local. "I'm Kyle *Truman* Roncalli, and I'm looking around for traces of where Trumans lived near here at one time. And died, some of them, near here."

Hy spit out, "Did they drown?"

Sarah shot her a look, but her neighbor ignored it.

"No, don't think so. Can't say."

The beer made the jovial-appearing young man grow lugubrious.

"There're Trumans right here tonight," Hyacinth answered him, to reassure her folks that this man was really one of them.

"Yes, met a few down the way, when I was first eating," he explained. *Wish I was surrounded by them now, those distant cousins of mine, and not so near Devon's cousin.*

The late evening glow and the rising Moon cast Sarah in perfect light. She seemed flawless, above reproach, as beautiful as the other woman near her, but somehow this vision was beyond his reach. Mia and sustainability. Sarah and New Grange. He longed for Martian gardens even more than before. The strong beer didn't help keep it all straight.

"Have you been to Mars," Hy asked, as if reading his mind, sweetening her voice, her brown eyes trained on his face. "Tell us about Mars," she whispered. Delicately, she placed her hand on his arm as though that motion were part of the earnestness of her question.

"Never been. Only to the Moon on training exercises and of course with Devon recently." He caught himself before confiding too much about something Marsco wanted kept black. "Moon's awesome, so silent, empty, lonely. Like no place on Earth." The associate made the obvious seem insightful to the young women hanging on his every word.

"Gee, ya think," Sarah stretched out her comment, dismissive.

"So, do you float way from it?" Hy asked, "the Moon, I mean."

"No, there's some gee on the Moon." She looked puzzled. "*Gee* is gravity; about one-sixth as much there," he pointed skyward, "as here." He grinned at the younger woman who soaked in his attention, although he enjoyed Sarah's patronizing attitude more.

He then abruptly hung his head, wishing he'd remained reticent, praying he hadn't made too much of an ass of himself already, especially in front of Sarah. *She'll never speak with me after this afternoon and now tonight.* He pushed his half-filled beer mug onto the table and out of his reach.

Hy imagined him flinging her skyward into the star-brimming night, so black against the silvery-gray moonscape around them. She saw how she would float above the rim of a crater and float tenderly into his waiting arms. She never stopped to think about surface suits, air tanks, and pressurized helmets.

None of those watching this exchange—not Lionel and Dot, not Sarah for some reason she didn't fully fathom—was pleased with the attention Hy was showering on Kyle. And now Kyle was returning it. And Sarah knew all about the lunar surface. She'd taken those classes and paid attention, even if Hy hadn't.

Chase observed all this from down the other end of the table. In that moment, he seated himself next to Hyacinth, nudging Sarah aside to do so, and waited like a brooding presence for the next exchange between the associate and his girl.

"Do finger disks hurt?" Hy asked, ignoring Chase and everyone around her but Kyle. She took his right hand and gently turned it over. His palm-side fingertips showed only four blue-green disks. "Are you what they call a *lefter?*"

"No," he tipsy-laughed, "that's rich." He held up his left hand, which showed no implants.

Still holding his hand, Hy asked, "Would Chase have his on his left hand? He's a lefty anyway."

"The old ways never had disks," the young granger spit, surprising everyone with his comment.

Hyacinth's flirtatious ways brought simmering tension to the fore between the two men. On principle, Chase didn't care one bit about the associate spending the whole afternoon with his sister; but him captivating Hy, that was too much like rustling his cattle.

Kyle smiled but removed his hand from hers. "No, he'd start with right handed disks. That's just Marsco's standard policy."

"You should know, space cadet," Sarah shot while Hy smiled, doting.

———⊷ ◦ ⊶———

"It was Marsco that created PRIMS by destroying our free peoples of old, making them suffer so," Columbus insisted, addressing Devon, who sat eating pineapple and melon and not responding.

When Chase went down to protect Hyacinth, the buffer between the young man's guest and his mother's cousin dissolved. Columbus's temper flared in just those few moments, even though it was clear that Devon was not taking the bait. He had been caught by Columbus, who wouldn't verbally let go, but the associate knew well enough not to engage. That might ruin Trent and Celine's party.

"These people," Columbus pointed to the former PRIMS sitting along the seven tables, "descended from our slaughtered peoples who once roamed here so free of Marsco. We free men once ruled here, knowing what was best for everyone—"

Cutting him off, Devon surveyed the laughing, well-fed crowd in front of the head table. "They look pretty damn content to me," he smirked. He lifted his mug to them, saluting their joie de vivre made possible in large part by the granger's generosity. "And it'll only get better with the Accords—"

Just then, the appearance of Nate Richardson, his pregnant wife in tow, brought the evening festivities to their abrupt close.

Out of the shadows, his rover skidded on the gravel road nearest the kitchen garden. He jumped out and once up at the head table, yelled, "Christ Almighty, what a goddamn mess, a bloody, goddamn mess! Fire. A huge fire."

Everyone shrieked, shouting questions of their neighbors along the tables, wondering what this roaring, bewildered man meant.

His face was smudged with soot. His greasy hair was pushed back, showing his mother he hadn't bothered to clean up after tending his herd.

Nate's outburst had everyone on their feet demanding to know what was happening when a second young man plunged into the circle of light around the tables. "Mr. Brunel, oh, help us! Mr. Brunel." Sarah recognized this new interruption as one of Watanabe's sons. "I didn't know where else to run, what to do." The young man collapsed at the feet of the granger, who like his guests, was shocked by what was happening.

One moment the crowd was eating, drinking, enjoying itself; the next it was confused, scattering, yelling questions and nonsense.

Trained to react in an emergency, Devon and Kyle found each other.

The lieutenant colonel ordered his subordinate, "You watch the Brunels; don't let anything happen to them in this confusion."

"Yes, sir." Kyle ducked back to find Sarah. In that second, he felt fully sober.

Devon jumped onto the head table and shouted for order. "Folks, everyone, NOW!" He gave a shrill whistle. "Hey, NOW!" he whistled a second time. "Settle down until we assess what's going on."

To the instantly silent faces, the associate looked powerful, commanding. They were mostly PRIM background, accustomed to Marsco taking control. The only ones not listening to Devon were the few bent over the collapsed Watanabe boy—Sarah included—and Columbus's six acolytes. They had stayed lockstep throughout the whole night. Now, they were off to the side and out of the umbrella of light.

Looking around until he spotted Nate, who was rambling unintelligibly, the officer barked, "You there! Come up here and explain yourself, *slowly, clearly*!"

Complying with his head down like a tardy schoolboy, Nate stood next to the imposing associate, then began. "I finished with my herd, but smelled sompin' odd on the wind. Sompin' burning. Been dry, always dry—fire *ain't* a good thing. I walked up our rise, and in the north, unmistakable, fires on the horizon." He pointed to assure them it was true. "I got the rover going and went for a look. Didn't need to go far, couple of minutes and it was clear that the PRIM village was burning."

Everyone in the crowded reacted at once: disbelief, confusion, panic. Millersville on fire. Devon silenced them.

"It's true," Nate went on. "But, I went on a few *more* minutes, to the last junction. Can't miss seeing the village from that vantage point. I seen half the place was gone up in flames by then, the other half sure to go. Saw men with buckets trying to confine the blaze, but they were being chased off by other men with rocks and sticks."

Sarah shot a look at Kyle. She'd made such a scene when they'd spotted some of this burning earlier. She was sure her antics stopped him from reporting what they'd witnessed.

"When he awakes," Kyle pointed to the collapsed Watanabe son, "we'll know more." His singed clothes weren't a good sign.

Devon asked his host, "Any chance to fight those fires?"

Nate explained hurriedly, "From what I saw, it's all too late. The village was all smoke and flames 'n gettin' worse."

Trent was now in charge. "Tomas, let's get everyone home, back to your village." Theirs was toward the south border of New Grange, the opposite direction of Millersville. Being that close to the largest grange gave it an aura of invulnerability. "No one must go alone. Tell me quick if you see any strangers," he ordered.

He ran back into the main house. He returned with an old, but still-serviceable Enfield sidearm and both holsters belonging to the associates.

"Devon, will you stay here?" The associate nodded to the request. "I'd like to take your assistant if you don't mind. We won't be long."

With increased independence, local authorities—in this case Trent—were authorized to organize small forces for emergencies like these. He had a group of trained and disciplined men at his disposal, ones not likely to go off half-cocked at the slightest provocation.

———◦———

Chase walked Columbus and his cohort up the low rise to the largest guesthouse. Looking north confirmed what Nate Richardson had reported. Two glowing patches on the farthest horizon showed the smoldering remains of a pair of granges burnt down earlier that day. Millersville was in bright flames still, the village burning itself out.

"Never seen anything—" Chase breathed out in frustration. His entire life here had been spent in total peace. "Looks like something from the PRIM Mutiny at the end of the last century," he commented to Columbus. Those real events were myth to the young Brunel, ancient history, past events he believed he would likely never witness in his lifetime. After those clashes ended, his Grandfather Darrow came out here and began New Grange from the burned-out waste of a previous spread. That was so distant in the past it seemed like fable. This was real. A part, only a fringe at this point, but a part of his world was now in flames.

"Those who want to cooperate, to collaborate with Marsco, are now playing with fire," Columbus stated in a vindictive tone. Even the young granger thought his comment callous.

The acolytes stood transfixed by the distant flames, savoring the yellow fingers that shot skyward periodically with each gust of wind.

———•◦•———

Using Devon's rover, Kyle drove Trent along the route he and Sarah'd taken that afternoon. They needn't go too far to see Millersville blazing on the horizon. Kyle listened in the silence of the darkening night. "I don't hear any Enfield fire. Or any other sound of fighting." Unlike while with Sarah, Kyle had two intruder scanners on. Neither detection device warned him of anything unusual near the vehicle.

"Whoever attacked seems to have slipped off."

Trent was relieved to find those granges between the village and Brunel land alert and safe.

No attacks were now happening in this immediate area.

———•◦•———

After returning to New Grange, both Devon and Trent pounced on the cadet. Obviously, he and Sarah should have seen or suspected something earlier that day.

"It wasn't something I *knew* was unusual," Kyle explained once more about seeing the strange fires. "I thought maybe some granger was burning off his fields."

Trent laughed bitterly, "You don't know much about farming, son. Burn off a field? *Before* harvest? In the middle of a dry spell?"

Devon cut the deepest. "And for all your training? You don't seem much of an officer, failing to report something like this, especially out here so far from Security."

Trent shot his cousin a knowing glance. "This is a fed issue now, not Marsco's."

If Kyle explained further, he'd have to explain Sarah bolting when they first saw the fires together and then explain *why* she had bolted, which meant disclosing the attack. That might look terrible for her, and so he kept silent about it. He didn't want her father and cousin viewing her as unobservant, unable to grasp a precarious situation, one he saved her from even if she'd never admit it. After all, she'd lived on this land all her life. She should have known that those fires weren't common. Too intent on loathing him, she'd denied those unusual fires were precursors of something far worse.

Kyle felt he had to protect her by keeping that fact from them, even if it made him look the fool.

Trent walked to a cabinet beside the largest window of the great room. The view faced south. All appeared peaceful. It was up north he was concerned with, even though their search showed all had settled down up there. He brought out three glasses and a bottle of brandy. "Vintners making this down the valley once more," he reported. "Well, what's done is done," he stated, handing around the drinks. He liked Kyle and didn't want him to be embarrassed or belittled. "No one's blaming you, son. Drink up."

— • —

Although under the watchful eye of Roxanne, Sarah managed to slip out and run off toward the largest guesthouse just after two that morning. A rover had returned forty-five minutes before. Her father, Devon, and Kyle were still down in the great room talking. The rest of the house was finally quiet. The household had been ordered to bed even with the kitchen still a mess.

Shadow went along with Sarah, his black coat making him disappear at times. She knew the way and got there quickly, fearful that Roxanne would discover her gone and track her down before she had a thorough look. Because the guesthouse stood on the highest ground around, it afforded her the best view.

With her back to the hedge and standing well away from the dwelling, she knew she was alone and unobserved. She scanned the northern horizon. Shadow nudged her then settled at her feet, ever alert. What she saw sickened her. From the safety of New Grange, she looked out at the embers of three distinct fires. Each still glowed, set for reasons unknown and unfathomable to her. They'd burned themselves out for lack of fuel, not from any effort to control them.

All my world's going up in smoke, she breathed, as though the main house and pool house were grey and black skeletons and already gone.

She studied the horrifying scene. The closest shimmering locale was once Millersville, now embers that momentarily flared up in the nighttime breeze. The two glowing spots at the greatest distance had to be the ones Kyle'd pointed out as black smoke late in the afternoon.

He's an associate. Why hadn't he raised an alarm? she demanded to know, blaming him totally. But she knew why he'd held his peace: he would have to explain away *her own* response to him at that roadblock. He would have to explain that he actually saved her in that dry streambed with someone bombarding them with rocks, with maybe worse than rocks yet to come. Anyone willing to burn down an entire innocent village, she realized, wouldn't respect a young woman whom they'd captured.

His Enfield didn't start any of these fires. He should have reported this. But I never gave him the chance. I didn't want to give him the satisfaction of knowing he'd saved me. That he was right.

"Damn it," she muttered softly to Shadow, "he's been protecting me all along." *Keeping me safe on the way home. Not saying a word even though we should have told father and reported it to Devon immediately.*

The last notion that came to Sarah was the hardest to admit, but she instantly knew it was true. That attack in the afternoon was serious and intentional—potentially life-threatening—but not about *her* at all. It had to be aimed at Kyle, a symbol of Marsco. And that rampaging mob would never have been content to take him down and then spare her. She knew enough about riots to picture the worst that might have happened.

As she walked around the hedge, putting her back to the fires, the night darkened. The Marsco Moon had set. The south sky brimmed with stars. The Milky Way stretched horizon to horizon. But the short summer night was nearly over. How often she'd seen this starlit sight, never the other. *What will my life be now?* Asking that, she gave herself no time to answer.

"Roxanne's right," she whispered to Shadow, "I owe him my life." With that, Sarah slipped down the hill and headed toward the center of New Grange, more confused and terrified than she'd ever been.

TEN

THE DAY AFTER

(New Grange, June 2154)

"**N**o sign of 'em, sir," a West Con officer reported to Trent and his two Marsco guests. "Not a trace." Captain Archer Andrews led a contingent down from Sac City to investigate the previous night's fires. The four sat in the shade of the main house's garden and sipped coffee. At midday, Trent, Kyle, and Devon got their first face-to-face report from Andrews' detachment.

Neither associate recognized the officer's uniform nor its insignia. The captain wore a khaki outfit not as well-made as anything issued by Marsco. Kyle knew the grays of Security well. And he'd recently seen a new black uniform on Mia. Never one like this.

The captain, born a PRIM with a removal scar to prove it, was determined to defend this fed. He would have a chance for a free life after the Accords were fully implemented. He wasn't letting that chance slip away without a struggle. He instinctively suspected but didn't say aloud that somehow Marsco was complicit in these attacks, either directly by organizing them or indirectly by letting them happen without its Security stepping in to prevent them.

Captain Andrews had no way to be sure of this theory. Nor any method to confirm his second suspicion that the associates at New Grange were thinking exactly the same.

"Any idea where they went?" Trent asked.

"Best guess, the skinnies made off to the river in the west and are hidden in the groves along there. Or had transport. Coulda gone east into the foothills with transport." He finished his coffee and accepted more from Trent.

"Actually, if they had a lander," the captain went on, "they could be on the Moon by now."

"Not a likely scenario," Devon replied.

"Certainly. I suspect they're locals, of sort," the captain insisted.

"Brazen locals," Trent noted. "Or pongos with local support. But who? Why?"

The four men stopped speaking a moment and looked north. In the cloudless noon sky, three distinct trails of gray smoke rose, two smaller ones and a larger one signifying the remains of Millersville.

"And did they ever burn everything at the two granges. I mean, houses and barns, everything in flames. Even slaughtered the herds. Damn shitstorm, if you catch."

Both Devon and Kyle assumed the captain was originally a Security centurion up through the ranks, his manners and expressions suggested it.

"Thanks for the assessment, captain," Trent replied. "I got near there last night but didn't want to proceed in the dark without backup. Too much of a risk being cut off. Anything left at the village?"

"All gone. Wasn't more than a few brick or wooden structures to begin with, at least that's what our ops computer reports."

"That's pretty accurate," Kyle stated. "Was there yesterday afternoon before this all started. It was mostly tents and temporary structures, though everyone seemed to be building permanent dwellings and businesses."

"And our school," Trent added.

"All gone now," the captain replied.

"Any idea of numbers for such an attack?" Devon asked.

"We estimate thirty, so platoon size at least."

Ever the scientist, Devon probed. "On what evidence?"

"Scope of their attack. They hit the village from three sides at once and thus kept residents from fighting the fires or defending themselves."

"Worst attack of this kind around here in years," Trent breathed out in frustration. The granger had grown used to stability.

"Casualties?" Devon asked the officer.

"At each grange, hard to tell. Did folks hightail their asses out into the dark somewhere? Are there bodies in the fields? In the rubble? My men are looking through the burnt-out buildings." Everyone knew that kind of detail that was slow; at each turn troopers dreaded what they might find. "Did find three bodies. Women. By all indications, they'd been raped then murdered. Two at the farthest grange, then a solitary one closest to the second. Ain't sure if others weren't thrown into the damn fires to destroy any evidence."

"They were all former PRIMS," Trent added. "Those granges only started 'bout two years ago. Hardest-working folks you'd ever want to meet. They would've made a go of it out there, too, no question, even without water like I get." He pointed to his own condensation units. "They've been hauling theirs for miles or dug ditches for irrigation. And that land out their way was actually a shopping mall and apartment complex over two hundred years ago. All that abandoned construction mucking up any cultivation. Imagine removing cement substructures *by hand* before you actually had a field to cultivate."

The captain went back to his report. "At the village, nine confirmed dead. No sign of raping this time. I gather the attackers knew the flames would attract attention. And as I said, the skinnies skedaddled pronto once they'd lit everything up."

"Nine bodies and the one boy here, possibly dying. So, we know of ten of about one hundred for sure. Likely some fled into the wilds."

"If they weren't hunted down," Kyle remarked. He knew the type of attackers they faced. They want blood; little satisfied them until they'd slaughtered their fill.

"What about tonight?" Trent asked, wanting to know what to tell his neighbors. Hyacinth had turned twenty-one yesterday, but the Brunel solstice gathering took preference over her celebrations, as it had for years. The Richardson daughter always held her party the next day, even if a much smaller one than his. "Any reason to suspect more trouble tonight?"

"Not around here, not with us patrolling."

"That's good to hear."

"I'm hoping one squad can remain on the grange due west—"

"That would be the Richardson spread."

"Well, their pop ain't happy about it." The captain smiled to himself. His daughters all seemed pleased. "I've also put a six-man detachment eastwards, out with the scraggly cattle that crazy old man grazes."

"Tillson. Don't get shot at. He's cantankerous enough to eat cactus."

"He wasn't all that bad. I guess he got wind of the burning and figured he'd pissed off enough pongos in his day to be the object of a planned attack or a spontaneous target of opportunity."

"That's the old man to a 'T,' I'm afraid," Trent added.

"Well," the captain went on, "we'll have our three HFCs doing over-flights and personnel in the area, alerted backup on standby up in Sac City should we need more muscle; yes, I say let them have their party. Richardson's determined to go on with it irregardless. Keep to the grange, of course, no joyriding out into the hinterland to hump in haystacks."

As their discussion ended, Captain Andrews motioned to Kyle. "I'd like to speak with the lieutenant, if I may."

Devon informed the officer that his aide was still a cadet.

"Haven't seen an Academy uniform in quite a while," the fed officer replied. "If I could just have you twitch your ID link, cadet." He held out a pad. "Have you reported to Security HQ about your whereabouts?"

"Marsco knows where I am."

"I meant *West Con* HQ," the captain responded briskly. "You're in West Con now, no longer technically in a jurisdiction of Marsco. Your host should have known that, certainly, a member of the Assembly and all."

"Why would I need to report, if I'm with—"

"The way *this* fed reads the Accords, you come here, you're subject to *our* decision of whether to place you in our forces or not."

"Am I being drafted, sir?"

"No, you just might be reassigned according to the Accords. You're a cadet, after all." The captain held up his pad. "It'll take me a while to examine your records." He looked at the name and rank, *Cadet Kyle Truman Roncalli*. He skimmed two screens. "And already served in *our* forces."

"That was a technicality, sir, to set up an independent study term on the Moon. In colony gardens."

Andrews remained unconvinced.

"You see, sir, I'm a cadet at the Academy, but I transferred to Sac City U, to their officer's training corps, once in, I took classes on the Moon, hardly need a Security detachment on the Moon, sir." Andrews nodded.

Kyle grinned, breaking the tension. "I did more *gardening* than *guarding*, sir, if you catch."

"That is all," the captain replied without smiling.

Thinking it best to remain silent, Kyle saluted, pivoted, and turned toward the guesthouse. His Martian greenhouses seemed light-years away.

———————⊰•⊱———————

As evening twilight deepened, Kyle drove Sarah down from New Grange to her neighbor's spread. If Sarah was to go to Hyacinth's party, she had to attend with an escort. Kyle was up for that duty. He went armed. Sarah wore her argument dress but didn't feel self-conscious about it. As conflicted as she felt toward the cadet, her white attire had caught his attention; she was secretly pleased by that.

It was the first time they had seen each other all day. For most of the day, after she saw Watanabe's son taken off to Sac City's best hospital, Sarah had been cleaning up with Roxanne and La'Shay from last night, even though she had spent the last hour getting ready for the party. She looked pretty in a graceful way that befitted her family's position and her Indie status. Kyle had been out with Trent and Devon most of that afternoon, checking the area south of the Brunels' lands where the West Con detachment hadn't patrolled. Everything was calm, quiet, and safe down there.

Still, the Richardson party and his attendance seemed surreal. But the granger was adamant on holding it. His daughter was twenty-one, and it was time she married and began her husband's family.

As the pair drove, Sarah said nothing. Kyle knew she was still uncomfortable with him. Tonight, however, it didn't matter. If Chase wasn't bothering to make an appearance—he had stayed overnight at the largest guesthouse and hadn't been seen the whole day—then Kyle figured he'd chat with that flirty Hy as much as possible.

He wore his light blue cadet uniform, a cap, and his Enfield. He might not have achieved officer status, but he was close enough, an obvious catch for any granger's daughter. Save one.

As they approached the Richardsons' property line, Kyle pulled to a stop. Trent had told them to walk the length of the drive to keep the dust down. The evening was lit the lingering setting Sun and a waxing Marsco Moon.

Sarah walked with Kyle but not really close to him, keeping a meter-wide gap between them. A few paces from the rover, out of the shadow of a large oak bordering the grange, a trooper rose up. His helmet and khaki flak jacket contrasted starkly with the bucolic scene. As the apparition appeared, Sarah moved in closer to Kyle, his presence reassuring her, even if he was of the same ilk as the specter.

"Good evening, sir!" The trooper acknowledged Kyle as though he were an officer, not a cadet. "Nice evening for a walk."

"Evening, trooper. All quiet?"

"Yes, sir." On the air was a hint of music and scent of meat on a spit. "Not a usual assignment, that's for sure, sir." The young man eyed Sarah the whole time, forcing her to stand even closer to Kyle, not as a declaration of her intent but of her unavailability, should this young legionnaire—he looked sixteen—think about hitting on her. As a defense, her face went blank to imply, *I'm with him.*

Kyle silently ushered her forward, and the pair walked on toward flickering decorative garden torches nearer the house. Unlike New Grange, whose border was a kilometer from the main house, the Richardson home stood a hundred meters down a shaded lane. On one side was a field with green feed corn almost two meters high. The other side was a small pasture. It stretched to a vegetable garden that Dot and her daughters hovered over all summer and finally to a mowed lawn where the party was underway.

"These trees were all replanted after the Great PRIM Mutiny ended," Kyle explained, his first words since the trooper. In the five decades since then, they had grown tall and thick, their lush branches crowning above the pair. "That'd be right after these once-razed granges were reclaimed by other Indies."

"How do you know that?" Sarah asked, not accusatory or menacing, but truly curious. They stopped thirty meters from the party. "I've lived here all my life, and yet you know more of our land's history than anyone I've ever met."

"My maps confirm it. Good old Marsco maps, yet it's only just now—since the Second Accord—that everyone's been given open access to those files." He wiggled his four blue-green implants. "Not a lefter."

"Like Devon."

"Right, like Lieutenant Colonel Chavez-Sherman," the cadet respectfully corrected. "Anyway, fifteen or twenty years ago, I'd have *never* gotten this intel. Today it's point-and-twitch!" He went back to his main point. "All sorts of old, stored info being made available again. Info openly available to everyone with a computer."

"If you have disks."

In the growing evening darkness, he reached for her right hand. She didn't resist. He turned her palm upward. A granger's daughter, her fingers were calloused from chores but without disks. "You can slip on finger mouse units now. *You*, Sarah Brunel. The Net's open to you as never before. Marsco *will* change the world, Sarah." He had whispered her name in a way that brought a sensation to her whole frame. "It *is* changing the whole solar system, Sarah."

Whipping her hand out of his, she replied, "I know all about computers and the Net. I finished my degree online last month."

They walked on, then stopped at the final tree before a torchlit lawn where four tables and a dozen other guests stood. The shrubbery down this lane hid them.

With a sheen in her eyes he'd never seen, Sarah softened her tone and asked, "But why would I want to do that? Use the Net now? I'm done with school."

"Your good cousin Devon tells me you're damned smart, that's why. Associate potential. The world is there for you, Sarah; grab it."

She looked directly into his eyes to defend her father's work at the Assembly. "But why be an associate? Feds are in charge now. Or will be soon." He nodded his agreement, lost in her looks. "Besides, I love New Grange," she snapped in her usual way of destroying a mood and cutting off those who suggested she look beyond her isolated granger circle. "Why do I want to leave?" She grew intense, replaying her standard replies to long-running arguments, ones she'd never even had with Kyle. "Why do others want me to leave?" The granger glared at the associate, all softness in her eyes gone. "Those maps of yours, are they telling you something we don't know, we aren't yet privy to?"

"Honestly, no. I promise you, no."

"Well, that's vague!" she shot.

Kyle laughed at himself. "Yes, I guess it is." He grew serious, tried to hold her hand to add emphasis to what he wanted to confide, but she refused. "My research is about the history of New Grange and this locale. Is that clear?" He drew a breath. "But, I don't know anything else. Hell, Sarah, I'm a cadet. HQ *may* have other plans, but I'm not privy to them. And, just look around. We both know that everything's changing. My world. Your world. It's all changing. We can't stop it. Marsco can't either."

Sarah didn't clearly understand his attempt at an explanation. But she knew enough to snap, "Can't it? Can't Marsco still control us all right now?"

He tried to laugh it off. "High wallahs up at Seattle HQ and I often discuss strategy and major policy decisions over a few beers now and again, but not about this." He grew serious in a nano, seeing hurt in her eyes. *Why joke with her at a time like this?* "Frankly, I'd be more concerned about the burning of granges. Who's behind that?" He almost began confiding about his fourteen-month tour with Security, what he'd seen, what he'd done. "I'd worry about *that* more than Marsco's ultimate plans."

He sounded like a loyal associate, confident in Marsco's promises through the Accords. "It's pulling back from local control. It's setting up new networks to run things at the local level. One hundred fifty-eight UIF members. Earth will not look the same as before. Won't be governed as before."

"I know," the young woman replied, reminding him. "My father's part of our provisional fed government."

"There you have it."

Change. Change was all around the young woman. Seasons change. Crops grow from seed to ripened grain. Calves become steers. All that change was natural and necessary. But all these other changes—she contemplated them with apprehension.

Without another word, Sarah bolted from the shadows to greet Hyacinth, who stood in a subdued knot of guests, a far smaller and more sedate crowd than had ever attended her delayed birthday before.

"Is there anything you're free to tell me, man-to-man, as my wife's cousin?" Trent and Devon stood on the highest grassy rise within the boundary of New Grange. Here was the family cemetery; a dozen graves were to the side, Darrows and several unknown PRIMS. Celine's stillborns. Others the granger once knew. The men had meandered their way up the rise from the main house, walking directly south, as though they wanted to put their back to all the troubles that had happened north of Brunel land. The quiet graveyard didn't bother them. The view here was excellent. Trent often came here to clear his mind.

Devon sensed the concern in the granger's voice. "Let me answer by saying that you're hearing what I'm hearing about the Millersville attack. There's an honesty with your security units. Probably because in two and a half years, with the implementation of the Fourth Accord, the rest of Security will answer to all these newly independent feds."

"I hope that Sac City has its shit together by then."

"You're part of the transitional team. Are you getting it together?" Devon asked.

"I think so but not without some bickering."

"You know, sausage making and politics are a good deal alike. If you like either, though, sometimes they're hard to watch."

"Yes, I know. I'm right in the mix. But, to answer your question, I think Sac City and West Con will be fine. We have good representation. Conscientious reps. Many will stand for official election. We'll select a good team."

"And you're fine being a part of the new West Con Federation?"

Trent nodded, "Yes, a no-brainer decision. A few—Richardson for one—wanted to opt out, to try and keep their Indie status. But the majority are in. We're starting to see evidence of rebuilding a fine infrastructure. We'll be stronger for it."

They looked west. Devon began again. "And soon Security control will be totally directed by *your* officials. At that point, there's no going back."

"Not after allowing half of the Six Accords to start," Trent added with a laugh. "But, for an associate, you sure speak like a believer in democracy. Like a fed."

"And why not? These new and truly independent federations will have the power to write their own constitutions, convene their own assembles, to enforce their own laws."

"That'll force all us Indies out here to cooperate all the more."

"And, West Con was a leader in pushing for the Accords negotiations in the first place. It'll take a prominent seat as a member in the new UIF."

Sitting on the western edge of the continent, the recently independent subsidiary, this newborn nation, stretched from the coast just south of Marsco's Seattle Sector to well below the Silicon Sector, from the ocean almost to the continental divide. It planned on its first parliamentary elections in 2156, even before all the Accords took effect. West Con wanted its autonomy that much. Trent had already agreed to run then. If he won, he'd remain in the Assembly as an elected member, no longer an appointed one.

"We'll soon see," the granger assured the associate, "how 'consent of the people' really works."

Devon needn't remind the granger it was a system that had worked for centuries until the Disenfranchise Movement, when many stopped voting or were prevented from voting. When many just stopped giving a damn, when the richest cut off their poorest citizens. All this was a known history that no one needed to be painfully reminded of, how fully functional democracies unraveled, fell apart.

"'Consent of the people,'" Devon said. "Sounds good."

"Old dogs must learn new tricks," Trent agreed. "Guess we can learn that."

"Have to."

From the small knobby hill, the pair surveyed the peaceful, sweeping scene that stretched for kilometers around. Richardson's spread looked bright and colorful, Hyacinth's party obviously in full swing regardless of last night's horrific events. Tillson's spread was without a light except for when a Security HFC swooped down to shine its spotlight on something in the dark, confirming it was one of his steers. The lights at the largest guesthouse, on another rise opposite, were in full blaze. Chase still hadn't come back from up there since last night when he left the party with his guests.

They listened to the summer wind picking up, crackling the dry grass at their feet, causing some settled birds near them to shriek, take off in a startled rush, and settle down farther off the hilltop from where the men stood.

"Well," Devon finally broke the silence between them, "as everything swirls and changes around here, I wish I knew for sure just what the hell Marsco was up to. I have to say, I don't know much for sure. When the push for negotiating the Six Accords started, I think everyone believed this was another Marsco dodge, a delaying tactic to keep the status quo. As in, 'We'll sit down with you, but we'll talk and talk and talk everything to death.'"

Trent gave a smirk. "Yes, Marsco did drag them out for thirty-three years."

Showing he still had pride in Marsco, the associate added, "To be fair, Marsco isn't alone in such tactics. And it's *not* the only empire Earth's ever known."

"Only one I've ever known," the granger answered with another smirk.

"I hear you. But, Trent, if this is to work, it is freedom for all or for none. We've no other choice."

"Strong words those. Strong words."

"I hope they are truthful words."

Trent drew a breath. "It's our job, as members of the Assembly, to make this a smooth transition. And you're right. There must be no attempt to punish those who were once in power. Any sign of blood retribution and the whole damn thing will collapse like a house of cards."

"Except, a house of cards falling doesn't cause a bloodbath."

The wind now brought the sound of splashing and swimming. For a moment, Trent thought Sarah had taken her friends up the rise opposite, to the guesthouse for a night swim. The evening was warm enough. But, lately with Columbus and his entourage ensconced there, his daughter stayed away.

"Do you think," Trent asked. "Do you think there's a connection between my son's guests and all these troubles? Any at all?"

"No evidence to suggest so. They were all present at the party, sulking about, Columbus and his half dozen malcontents," answered the associate. "Hardly seems possible they did anything that night, except maybe plan it. But is that likely?"

Anticipating the question, the granger explained, "I only tolerate them here because Chase asked me to." Noise from the guesthouse floated toward them once more, pushed by the increasing evening breeze. "Can you tell me something I can do with Chase, if it's not too late?"

Devon initially wanted to give an Academy suggestion. When cadets flunk out, often they are detached to a Security battalion as a common trooper. The discipline often works wonders. But Chase was a more delicate situation. Father might lose son entirely. "Can't really say. What do you think happened?"

"I don't know. Was I too hard on the boy? Too soft? I thought I was giving him everything."

"Perhaps that's the problem; he didn't have to earn it."

"In a way I didn't either. I married New Grange."

"Except with your hard work, you've doubled its size, increased its productivity." Proudly, the associate added, "Set in place ways to treat your PRIMS much better than Uncle Darrow ever did. But as for Chase, I gather from Celine, he gets pockets full of Darrow tokens."

"I begged the old man not to do that, set up that trust, but he was stubborn, my father-in-law. And Chase was his apple."

"And I am sure he thinks all this will just be handed to him." Devon swept his arm across the fields below them, tidy, verdant, thriving fields, almost all of them Trent's.

"Oh, he'll get his share. I can't bring myself to leave him high and dry with nothing, unless his new 'friends' really get their hooks into him. But if Sarah marries well, Chase will be surprised by what he gets—or doesn't get."

"Marries well?"

The granger laughed. "If I like the man. And if he loves my daughter. And wants dirt under his fingernails. Loves this abundant, fertile land."

"Any takers?"

"No, just a few crossed off the list. God love him, but it was never going to be Nate Richardson."

<hr>

The air was warm, the water temperature perfect. Chase dove a second time into Sarah's pool, the only taker for a night swim.

Columbus sat poolside with his feet cooling in the deep end.

"Tell me, child-son," the mystic called to the swimmer, "your sister has not been here lately. Why? I ask because she came here only once since I arrived."

Chase could care less about his sister, but the reminder of Hyacinth cut deep. He was sorry, wounded, for missing her party. Columbus wanted him to stay near in the guesthouse.

"Tell me, will she ever come back?" Columbus kicked some water at the young man who swam by, his head above water. "Perhaps I can speak with her, speak alone, convince her of our ways, ways that should be her ways."

"I don't know. It's funny—we live in the same house, but I don't speak ten words to her a day, not ten."

"Why is that?"

"Oh, she's so damn smart, for one. And such a suck-up to my folks, always the dutiful one."

"Duty to elders is prime in our ways. Especially from young girls as she is. Again, I say, let me speak with her. Bring her to me."

"Let her wait."

Columbus's eyes flashed with unrestrained fury. "*Wait?* Why must *I* wait? I am *telling* you. Bring her to me."

Chase seemed to wilt, having incensed so holy a man. "Yes, I'll get her for you, trust me."

"It's for her own good, as you know," he replied, forcing himself to hide his deepening rage and smoldering desire, his impatience for seeing the woman alone.

"I do, truly." Climbing out of the pool, he sat next to Columbus so their feet hung into the warm water, nearly touching. "Tell me, is there a way for me to reach Hyacinth?"

"She must come to know your will, child-son," he replied, calming himself, "and know that your will is the will that she must obey absolutely. Straightaway. With no hesitation. Tell her from your heart, the heart she must know and submit to. That is our way, our way of old."

"What if, what if I want her so, so much I might *ask* her—"

"It is not for you to be asking for what you deserve. What you desire. No man *asks*. We had our ways, our peoples of old, and our ways were the ways of leadership such the world only knew once. What we want, we grab. When we led, others followed, and in *devout silence*. Our wisdom was once so strong. Do you believe that?"

"Of course."

"Then so your woman must come to believe it, too, child-son. And obey fervently."

"Yes, yes, of course."

ELEVEN

NIGHT AND MORNING

(Richardson Spread and New Grange, June 2154)

"**H**ad enough, Lieutenant Kyle?" Hyacinth asked, giving the cadet a promotion. He had started the evening as a mere cadet, skipped warrant officer, and by midway through the small party, he was a lieutenant. "I've a nice breast here," she offered, leaning over him with a platter and low-cut top.

Besides plates heaped with food, Hy had served him sun tea cooled in old-style insulated jugs. Kyle was as giddy as when he had downed too much beer last night.

Who wouldn't be? the entertained associate rationalized.

Put out by this spectacle, Sarah had moved to sit between the Richardson grandparents at another table across from the cadet's where she could watch but not hear. Hyacinth had found Kyle as soon as he arrived, sat him down by her, and then tried to hold his attention the rest of the night. She rose now and again to attend to other guests but was back soon, glowing and doting.

"So, do you go to the Moon often?"

"Often enough, with field trips from the Academy and a spring-term project a while back."

"And you'll be a pilot, right? Wings on your chest and your cap set just so?" She pulled his off and ran her hand over his cadet-cut hair.

"No, actually, I want to work in hydroponics."

"*Hydro-what-ics?*" She laughed artfully, knowing exactly what the word meant. Space colonies relied heavily on domed gardens; even a granger's daughter was aware of that.

Kyle seemed to float into the charmer's deep brown eyes, even if the ditzy act was tedious. He went to classes with scores of bright, powerful women, worked side-by-side with them. Mia came to mind, but he dismissed her memory. Without meaning to, he looked up at Sarah over at the next table; she looked away purposely to avoid his glance. But this one, this coy one, caught his attention once more and held it for now.

"When will you leave New Grange? And then come again?"

"Is that an invitation?"

"Could be?" she smiled, her lips gleaming with the perfect shade of pink. Her light brown hair was fixed just so, her outfit hugging to its maximum benefit. Had her party been its usual size, this incandescent flame would have had a handful of transfixed moths, not just this one associate. But, radiant, she was pleased with her single catch. Chase would always be there; this associate may not.

"Well, the good lieutenant colonel's totally in control of my life right now; he may want to leave sooner or later. Can't tell." She made a pouting frown. "As for later in the summer, if invited back to New Grange, who knows? Classes begin 1 September; I'll have personal leave in August. And, I have reasons to return."

"Oh, Sarah, I guess," Hy returned with no emotion.

"Believe me, not in the equation." He cast a glance at her once more. She refused to acknowledge him, although she'd met his gaze a second time before turning away. She pretended to be engrossed with the elder Richardsons.

That seems clear enough, the fool, Hyacinth determined.

"I have a personal research project." He stated this rather formally, almost to create a barrier between them.

Not really believing his answer, Hy went on, "But August's so far away. Can't you stay longer now or come back sooner?" She added emphasis to her words by laying her hand on his right arm and leaning into him to whisper.

Patrice then came up to the self-occupied pair. Kyle jumped to his feet at her graceful approach. Hy made the introduction to her older sister. While the younger had light brown hair and brown eyes, the elder was blond with green eyes. Hy was moderate height, taking after her mother. Patrice was taller like her father. Kyle held out his hand to shake hers, his implants giving a slight tingle. "I've gotten used to that," Patrice responded, partly with a soft laugh, partly with a serious tone, as if remembering other tingles. Neither her sister nor Kyle understood.

"Any trouble getting down?" Hy asked.

"Not really," Patrice replied, "I hitched a ride with a Security squad coming here." She then added vaguely with a look toward their father, "Not sure I'd be welcome, though."

As Patrice turned away to greet Sarah sitting with her grandparents, Hy whispered, "Pop's still pissed at her. Says she up and ran away."

"Did she?"

"Did I what?" Patrice, returning, asked. "Run away?" She glared then softened. "I am almost finished with a nursing degree, that's all." Smiling again, the blond sister asked Kyle, "You must be bored having to mix with the likes of us."

"I'm happy to be here," the associate replied. "And a milestone, for sure."

Patrice laughed, then confided too candidly, "My eighteenth was the big one for my folks. Thought Chase and I should have become engaged then." She gave a deep sigh, feigning sadness over her lost opportunity. "They're stuck in some pretty traditional ways," she confided, sitting down on the associate's free side. "Well, Dad is. Mom's just pregnant mostly." She laughed silently, "You're safe. No land and you're an associate."

Without meaning to seem rude, Kyle's attention shifted to the older sister. She too was open, eager to command his attention.

"Do you ever visit Sac City?" she asked, her silken blond hair down her back, as pretty as she ever wore it.

"No cause to, unless ordered, of course. I have reason to visit New Grange, however." Both Richardsons shot a glance at Sarah, who kept her distance, ignoring the three of them. "It's about the history of this land. I have Truman ancestors; many of them lived around here before the PRIM Mutiny. I'd like to know their whole story. Why they left. What happened to their granges. Not that I want to reclaim any—don't get the wrong impression. I just want the historical record, that's all."

"They weren't pox-faced PRIMS, I hope," Hy blurt out. "They're all sick or carrying some disease or other."

Patrice shot her a silencing glance.

"No, in all likelihood, Indies like your family." Kyle also ignored Hyacinth's PRIM bias. At the Academy and his tour with Security, he'd worked with dozens of associates from PRIM stock. Turning to Patrice, her obvious intelligence a greater allure than Hy's affected girlishness, "But why do you ask of Sac City?"

Excitedly, because no Richardson believed she would succeed up in Sac City and actually graduate, Patrice explained in a confiding whisper. "I have a position at the hospital once I'm pinned in a year."

"You? Changing bedpans?" Hy scoffed, overhearing.

"Working in ICU, dear," her sister answered harshly.

"Could have used you last night," Kyle noted.

"So I heard." She quickly refocused her intense green eyes on Kyle's. "Well, if I'm there, will you visit sometime if you're in Sac City? I mean, if you're here, you can bring Sarah, too. I don't have many friends there. And Sarah will never leave New Grange, even to visit me. And it's really not far. I've been talking to her. She'll come if you take her."

That was news to Kyle.

"I could go, too, if our folks let me," Hyacinth volunteered. She had found dozens of reopened Net sites about college life during her idealized early twenty-first century: The parties, the beach cookouts, the hordes of sculptured men crowding around curvaceous girls not half as pretty as she. Back then, these old sites assured her, Hy could have taken her pick from dozens. What a life.

"That's fine, come visit," Patrice replied in a monotone to her sister. To Kyle, however, she stated with clear emotion, "You'll come, though, won't you? Please."

"Of course, maybe before classes I'll hop a lander down from Seattle, pick up Sarah. Easy enough." Easy only if Sarah genuinely wanted to visit; they both understood that.

Patrice rose to give her good nights to some other neighbors about to leave. "Don't forget now," she almost pleaded.

"I won't."

"Well, if you're in Sac City to see *her*, what about *me*?" Hy sulked.

"Can't I see you both?" the cadet asked with the assumed bravado that Indie women expected from associates. Finding this all so exciting, the young woman happily agreed.

——— • ———

Patrice stood at the edge of the party after her goodbyes to several neighbors and cousins. Then silently alone, she noticed two new guests approaching, Captain Andrews and a medic, DeShawn Cleveland. She especially watched him.

He seemed dark in the evening shade. Even with a Marsco Moon, the sky was hazy and dusty, still smoky.

"Just checking that everything's okay here," the captain explained, offering a lame excuse.

Patrice felt that the officer's remarks gave her an out, an explanation for her father why two former PRIMS were welcomed to his property.

An introduction to Lionel Richardson did not go well. He acknowledged the pair, shaking no hands but thanking them for keeping his spread safe, then backing away, eying his oldest daughter while she spoke in a too-captivated manner to the medical PRIM sipping lemonade. His daughter's spontaneous laughter and that PRIM's smile were nearly too much for any protective parent.

Kyle noticed this interaction as well. What struck him most was that it almost looked as though they knew each other already, Patrice and the medic.

Hy leaned in against the cadet as he concentrated on the whispering pair. "She won't talk to him long, that PRIM," she confided. "You watch."

——— • ———

Sarah broke up the whispering Hy and the patient Kyle by inviting the cadet to move over and speak with the Richardson grandparents. Why she had spent nearly thirty minutes repeating snatches of his information about this locale to them, she didn't know. But she'd asked them if any Trumans had once lived nearby and had gotten a longer answer than she imagined. And she had listened with more interest than she intended. Finally, she rose and brought Kyle back to her table and then helped the waiting elderly pair relax and speak openly to the associate, something they would never do on their own.

"Sure, Trumans lived out this way a time ago," Grandfather Richardson began hesitantly. "I knew some, but I wuz just boy. It wuz before those

185

damned rioting PRIMS chased so many off. Some away for good. My folks fled to Sac City, but it wuz half burned down in those troubles, too, by them damn PRIM bastards."

His wife gave her obligatory *shush*.

Ignoring her, he added, "Three or four years later it wuz, before we returned to pick up pieces. Trumans, though, not sure where they fled off to. Or why they never come back. Theirs wuz one grange total torn up and burnt down. Herd killed off or scattered. They wuz dairymen, mostly."

"Well, there was that one Truman dint escape," the grandmother explained.

"Oh, yeah, nearly forgot him. One wuz killed at a grange. Why," the grandfather turned to Sarah, "why, it wuz your grange, honey, what's become New Grange. I remember now. Kilt there. And buried there, too. By a damned associate later that same day. Strange times, them."

Sarah had never heard any of this before.

Sitting by the old man to listen, Kyle was amazed at the Indie's story. This granger's entire life had been spent working this land, resettling it, salvaging it from the rubble left after the C-Wars and later the mutiny. By the strength of PRIM and Indie hand labor, each parcel had become a flourishing grange.

"I had a sense of this, Mr. Richardson," Kyle answered, "my searching in old reports and posts tells the same but without any names. And my own granddad—he's a retired associate living on the Serengeti—he's told me stories."

"What's his name?"

"Aaron Truman."

"Knowed an Aaron Truman, oh, nearly sixty years ago. Bit older than me, as I recall. Left the area long ago. Never heard of him since. Had a brother more interested in the grange and their dairy herd; he's the one what loved animals."

"That younger man, was he Jeremy Truman, do you think?"

"Could be, could be." The old man looked up to the associate. "Say, y'know a lot of our lands."

"Trumans are part of my history, that's all."

The grandmother unexpectedly caught her husband's attention. "But, *that* young man dint die in the mutiny. Not the real one, the one that done so much damage and spread up to Sac City. He wuz long dead and buried before all that."

"Say, dear, you're right." Grandfather scratched his head. "Damnedest part. The only granges destroyed that one day at first wuz New Grange. But it weren't that name back then. And that Truman dairy place, too, and maybe one or two other spreads, too, tops. New Grange belonged to a real character. What wuz his—"

"You mean that Miller fella?" The grandmother interjected. "I wuz too young to know, really, but he wuz talked about for years 'n' year after. An associate hiding out down here, so they say."

"Yeah, and it wuz likes as if he wuz the real target, so the stories goes, but he'd skedaddled already. Died in space, so they say."

Kyle grew excited with all this information. Sarah sensed he knew only bits of this larger explanation, but now he was getting confirmation of what he'd only suspected. Pieces were falling into place for him. And some of them were connected to her.

"You know, geez, I haven't thought of the Trumans in years. The older brother did come back onest. Several months after the troubles had stopped. He wuz in Security then, that I know. Can't hide that uniform, no how." He eyed the two recently arrived troopers, one still commanding his granddaughter's attention. Different uniforms, being in khaki, but clearly Security personnel. He drank his lemonade, as concerned as his son, Patrice's father, that she was speaking so long to that dark PRIM.

"And it wuz after the real mutiny, he come back," the old man went on. "We wuz here restarting, because the real mutiny tore up all these places. That younger Truman boy died pretty much alone. Except with some dogs. There, at what wuz that Miller character's spread. Nice spread even then. A few other granges torched, like his pa's dairy place out by Tillson's spread now, but more like they wuz searching Miller's place particular. All just in that one day. Only then, months and months later, the real whopping mutiny cut a long swath of fire and killing. Lasted nearly three years, off and on."

"Happy to see Security then," the grandmother added.

"We wuz lucky to escape," the old man returned to repeat part of his story, his mind drifting. "Just around here at first; then later it all broke loose something fierce."

"And the Truman in Security?"

"Oh, yes, yes," grandfather refocused and continued. "He came with a squad of troopers to search for his brother's grave, if there wuz one." The old man turned to Sarah, who had been hanging on his every word in stunned silence. "He found the boy, nicely and properly buried, near what would be your main house, in those fine gardens of your mother's, Sarah. Used to be cisterns there. And he was there in the remains of the gardens, right where Miller's house stood, or the burnt down remains of it."

"What happened next?" Kyle asked.

"Reburied him, I'm sure. Probably on the property."

"And them dogs," the grandmother added.

"Oh, yeah, damnedest thing, that boy wuz found by his brother not alone but buried with two dogs with him. So, the brother kept them buried all together. This wuz at New Grange, in them nice gardens or what remained of them. Moved later on, I think."

Sarah should have said something to Kyle before. She should have taken him aside to speak with Celine. Her mother must know some of this. But, Sarah had decided not to like Kyle, not to answer any of his questions or give him any assistance. She felt a fool. An old grave did lie in the family cemetery, with no name. Her deceased ancestors had been placed there next to it because that single unknown grave already rested in so peaceful a spot. And it was rumored that the body of a boy lay there with two dogs. But maybe she had it wrong. Maybe this boy and dogs came later.

Even so, I should have told him, she chastised herself.

Their conversation was broken when Captain Andrews called for their attention. "Folks, just a reminder, it's nearly midnight. As we agreed with Richardson here, at midnight everyone needs to leave. Now, you folks going far, I'm authorized to send along an escort. You folks driving, stick to the roads and be assured our HFCs will keep an eye out for anything threatening."

———————

Kyle waited at the edge of the garden for Sarah. She was making sure that the oldest Richardsons were inside and comfortable—they were leaving at first light—and that Dot didn't need a hand. "You're a dear, Sarah," she replied in a cold tone, "but we've got it all under control. And you're with your fella." Nate could never challenge an associate; his mother realized that, another indication why New Grange had been lost to her son.

While the cadet waited, Patrice approached after saying her goodbyes to the medic. "Now remember, Kyle," she whispered with some warmth, kissing him on the cheek, "remember, you're bringing Sarah to see me." She held both his hands in hers, stepped back, and looked up at him. "You love history. Sac City's a place for that. End of the C-Wars and all."

Without hesitation, the blond vision kissed his cheek a second time and was gone.

Hy then joined him. "Oh, Captain Kyle," she teased, "you must come back to visit me, too. We've plenty of places to be alone." It wasn't a sandy beach with scores of buff hunks, but one was better than none, especially if Chase ever grew tiresome. She kissed him fully on the lips, deeply, more ardently than he expected.

"I'll be in touch if you promise to study up on hydroponics," he admonished playfully.

Catching his eye, she replied, "I'll do anything you ask, remember, *anything*."

———— • ————

As Sarah and Kyle drove silently toward New Grange, the young woman sat alone in her dizzying thoughts.

Halfway home, Kyle stopped the rover and got out, motioning her to join him. "Come look at this."

"This isn't some sort of trick?" she snapped, as tentative with him now as the first time they met. She ignored his outstretched hand.

"Sarah, would I—" His voice trailed off. In the dark, she was unable to see why, judge why.

Finally, stepping next to him, she whispered. "I'm sorry, Kyle. Granger's daughter, an Indie. We're all a bit stubborn." She let out a heavy sigh. "Still a bit suspicious of Marsco, too, even considering we have our Devon."

"No? Honestly?" he responded drily.

They stood at the edge of the road in almost total darkness. It stretched ahead, the dirt track contrasting with the pitch-black fields. Before these past few days, Sarah would have felt no hesitation to stand alone in the dark here. With those fires, not so. When she realized she was with someone who'd already protected her, she relaxed.

The night sky was ablaze with stars; the Marsco Moon with its trailing clouds had set. Kyle gazed at the canopy of infinity above, filled with awe. "What a sight," he whispered.

Sarah had not seen this side of him before.

"That's Mars," Kyle pointed at the reddish dot well above the eastern horizon. Sarah looked at him first, then the planet. "Wonderful gardens on Mars, at the Von Braun Center, its most important colony. Best example of planetary hydroponics anywhere." He confided. "I'm in Marsco for *that*, to get there." His voice had an apologetic tone, as if ashamed of the Security taint of his career.

"What's wrong with growing things Earth-side?" she finally asked softly, nudging him to look around at Brunel prosperity, the fertile lands. The main house shone; people were still up. The guesthouse, too, her future home, was lit.

Not really answering, he went on, "God, I'd love to see them. Live on the Red Planet, just once."

Finally, wanting to hear more, she asked, "What else is up there?"

"Jupiter, there," he pointed, placing his hand on her bare shoulder to move her to look. Her hair brushed against him unintentionally.

"Sorry," she whispered, gathering her hair away from him even as he silently drew in its clean, fresh fragrance.

"No need, honestly." He went on quickly, "It's the brightest visible object right now; it's facing us full-on. Brighter than Mars." He paused to make sure she saw, but he found her looking at him, smiling, then looking away. "Venus is the morning star at this time. Come morning, all the stars will be gone, but it'll be visible and bright all by itself."

"Night like this, if we had a telescope, we could see Galilean moons and some asteroids," she added. "Devon's shown me them before."

He was impressed.

They remained silent, and even though it was the Richardson daughters who'd kissed him, he wanted to pour out his heart and mind to Sarah. He wanted to speak with her in a kindly way, not gruffly as he had or weakly as though frightened of her. Maybe confide about Mia. Her promises made no sense at all. Hints of sustainability and Marsco recontroling everything. Talking about Mia to Sarah might help him sort it all out. But, no words came.

In the end, they walked back to the rover still in their separate worlds.

———•———

At the grange ten minutes later, he waited for her to say something. Anything.

Shadow was out in the garden as soon as they walked toward the house, greeting Sarah, protectively nudging Kyle away from his charge with a low growl. "Good dog," she petted him. "Good dog."

"Hey, pup," the associate stated to the hefty Lab, "S'up. I'm a friendly."

"He's not convinced," Sarah laughed sympathetically.

"Well," he said with abrupt finality, "I'll be off. I'm still five hundred meters away." In the distance due east, the pool house was now silent. In a more southerly direction, stood the smallest guesthouse he was sharing with Devon.

"You'll be fine," she said, trying to think of any way to keep him close for a moment more. She didn't know why, but she wanted him to stand beside her even if silently. "Do you want Shadow?"

"What? To protect me or attack me?"

"He's a good dog—aren't you a good dog?—always around, always a pal."

"You look like you need his company more than I do."

He walked along the vegetable garden path and once out of its beds, took his bearings to avoid walking into a cultivated field. Shadow followed. Sarah called the dog back. He returned to her but ran away a second time. "Stay!" she commanded, half thinking she meant Kyle as much as the dog.

Sarah walked to the last tree in the garden. She made out the associate's figure passing the far end of the raised vegetable beds and disappearing behind an auxiliary water condenser. As his route headed up a bit of an incline, she caught sight of him a second time, walking quickly, easily, confidently.

At the edge of the tree-lined garden, she sat on a bench and began to cry. Her perfect New Grange world shouldn't be one of burned-down villages and neighbors attacked. And strangers taking away her brother. And fear of walking alone on her father's land at night.

Half an hour later, entering the back of the house, Sarah was surprised to find her parents and Devon in the great room talking. She wiped her eyes, hoping no one could tell they were red.

"Is Kyle with you?" her father graciously called. "Come and have a brandy. Wish he'd have ducked in, too."

Her parents often welcomed her sit with them like this, even when the talk was serious. And theirs had been, she could tell. Her father handed her a glass with a generous measure of amber liquid.

"*Salut*," Trent toasted while their glasses touched all around.

As she sipped, she noticed her mother patiently waiting for Trent to sit back down. She sat on the arm of the largest leather chair so that when he did come back, she could place her arm across his strong shoulders. It dawned on Sarah how lovely her mother was: fresh even at this time of night. It also dawned on her that she looked that way because she was near the man she loved, a man who stood by her, honored her. Her whole posture implied how much she loved him.

Tears were in her eyes once more.

"Strong, isn't it," Devon kidded her.

Sarah smiled, sipped again; she'd never felt so grown up and childish at the same time.

"Damn," her father said under his breath, "wish that Kyle'd come in." He looked directly as his daughter with that and-I-want-the-truth look parents have. "I'd like to hear *your* side of his story, Sarah," he began softly. "I have the sense that yesterday afternoon you two ran into trouble, serious trouble. All over a few damn pineapples. Fifty-six confirmed, that's the latest count from Millersville. Fifty-six in what appears a well-planned attack."

"Mr. Watanabe, dear," Celine added, looking at Sarah. "After you and Kyle had just been there and he'd been so kind to us. And his son's still not conscious. We've spoken to the hospital up in Sac City."

Trent went on, "I'd hate to say it, but it was nearly *fifty-eight* if our young cadet isn't exaggerating."

"I doubt he is," Devon defended.

Trent nodded his agreement, yet still raised an eyebrow to signal it was Sarah's time to come clean.

"What did he say?" she answered hesitantly but quickly cut them off. "No, disregard that. Whatever he reported, I'm sure it's accurate. Isn't the term *Marsco precision*, Devon?"

"That the argot," the associate agreed.

"Well, you can tell a story without telling the whole truth," her father noted. "What he said was that a roadblock stopped you. You and the rover were a target of rocks. Some kids he thought. He fired a few rounds to scare them off. Removed the pile. Came home."

"What I'm sure he *didn't* report," Sarah finally let out, "was that I acted like an ass. Accusing him of being all bluster, just showing off. And me not realizing how serious the threat was. Really was. He knew how dangerous. Protected me, saved me. And put up with my arrogance in his face afterwards. They were after him, weren't they?" She looked at Devon.

"An Enfield's a valuable weapon to capture."

"I know that now. And they wouldn't have just left me alone. Not if they were prepared to kill fifty-six others."

Sarah began to shudder, thinking over the past two days. She looked at her parents then at her associate cousin for strength, at the flagstone floor, the brick walls, and the solid hearth for physical support. Late in the spring, Celine decorated this room simply with a large pot of flowers standing in front of the fireplace. No need for a blaze in June. In this room, like at New Grange itself, so many happy times had been celebrated, bountiful harvests, Christmases, birthdays.

Once more tears were in her eyes. To think that just beyond New Grange, fifty-six people died, one of them kindly Mr. Watanabe. His son still likely to die as well.

Her world seemed on the verge of shattering.

As Sarah's sobs deepened, she ran to her parents' chair and knelt.

Her father patted her hair as he had when she was a child. "There, now, Sarah," he whispered.

Across the way, Devon added, "The shock's finally hitting her. Typical response in some, this delayed reaction." She'd put up a brave face, but it was all dawning on her now.

"It's hit us all hard, dear," Celine said, her own eyes brimming with tears.

Trent kept soothing his daughter. "Honey, you were attacked by God knows who. Or why. Not a band of typical PRIMS, I'm sure, no matter what our neighbors might say. Hasn't happened around here for years, and it's never happened to you. But you're safe here."

"But I was so hateful, so insufferable to him. I'm sure they were after him, because he was an associate, off alone—I mean alone from his kind. And if they could kill such a sweet man as Watanabe, why not him? And me, too. And after all the insulting things I that I said, he'll loathe me. He does—he already does despise me. Not like Dot Richardson—silently, with her icy shoulder, still on about Nate—but he abhors me by being *kind* to me, like I was never despicable to him!"

"No one dislikes you, dear," her mother smoothed out her hair, which was a tangle.

"No one here, but everyone else. Patrice and Hy kissed him. They kissed him!"

"How is *that* hating *you*?" Devon asked with a sly lilt in his voice.

"Because I *won't* kiss him," she answered in a personal logic that made no sense to anyone. "I won't even tell him about that grave. I think it's a Truman grave and his relative, and I know there're two dogs with him, and" she waved off a fuller explanation, her tears choking her into silence.

Still teasing gently, her associate cousin, the most worldly wise one there, replied, "Sarah, dear, kiss him yourself. He'll love it."

But the young woman only cried deeply.

Devon rose silently, signaled his hosts good night, and slipped out of the great room. In her sobbing, Sarah didn't notice a rover starting and driving off to the smallest guesthouse.

That night, Sarah was not able to sleep deeply. Frustrated, before the first rays of dawn began to brighten New Grange, she dressed quickly.

Sarah loved the stillness before a bright summer day. No long shadows had yet appeared, but everything was gaining a measure of color. The bushes and grass nearest the house changed from gray to green. And Kyle'd been right. Venus hung bright against the starless pale sky.

With Shadow at her side, she reached the smallest guesthouse while the rim of the sun moved above the horizon.

———•———

Kyle heard something outside his room. Without another thought, he rose, primed his Enfield, and stood to the side of the French doors that were open onto a stone-paved patio. Clearly, soft footsteps were approaching, creeping outside.

Weapon at the ready, he lunged out through the doorway, keeping low to the ground as trained, whipping his laser designator at the intruder.

Shadow pounced. Thirty kilos of canine pack a wallop; the dog knocked the plunging man well off his intended course. Kyle smacked into the corner of the wall with a stone bench that surrounded the small patio outside his room. Coming to rest with Shadow holding him firmly down, Kyle waited for Sarah's response. The dog growled until Sarah silenced him.

The associate had held his fire the whole time, but the weapon's laser designator had run over the low wall, the guesthouse, a woman standing there, and the nearest tree before it stopped swinging wildly.

Sarah had just stared in shocked silence when she saw Kyle dive out initially and as she watched the red dot go to every target imaginable. Had Kyle fired his Enfield, its shells might have exploded anywhere.

"Why do you have to act so much like an associate *each* and *every* time?" She blasted him then cooed, "Are you okay, Shadow?"

"That may be because I *am* an associate," the cadet replied through locked teeth, wriggling out from under the frisky and unhurt dog.

Kyle then asked the fuming woman, "If you don't mind my obvious question, Sarah, just what the hell are you doing?"

"Would *that* have killed me?"

"Exceedingly well—so, go ahead, lecture me," he shot back at her, dizzy and sore and only now realizing he might have accidentally fired at her or Shadow if he were not so well trained. His shoulder thrummed with pain. The dog had pushed him into a sharp corner of the knee-high stone wall surrounding the patio.

"Is this how you get to Mars?"

"I get there by going where I'm ordered," he barked.

"Security needed there?"

"No, the Academy has the necessary degree. But, yes," he explained a second time, "I go where ordered."

After he released the Enfield's propellant pressure and stood up, he found blood on his fingertips when he felt his back. "Glad Shadow's fine," he groused. He found her sitting on a stone bench in tears.

Taking the place next to her, he put his arm around her gently, soothingly. At first, she turned away, then relented and dug her face into his shoulder, her head pressing into his neck. She was in such deep sobs, tears wetting her face.

"Am I *that* naive?" she managed to get out between heaves.

"I don't know what you mean."

"I *love* New Grange—"

"It's a fine place. Successful, flourishing. You *should* be proud of it." He drew an exasperated breath, "Hell, I've been here only a few days and I love it!"

"You do? Do you love it?"

"Of course I do."

"But, I've never seen anything threatening around here. All I've even seen here is life, new crops and cows calving. Kittens in the barn. *Damn*," she let slip, about the harshest remark she ever made. "What a bitch I am! And you, *you* having all this knowledge of *my* home. And so comfortable amid those PRIMS the other night and me so rude to you. And at the streambed, *where, when, you, you*—and last night, at the Richardson's. And before the way you were so kind to the PRIM Watanabe, and now he's dead!"

"I was afraid of that," he answered as considerately as he could. "Those attacks were well-coordinated, skillful." He drew a breath. "But for what it's worth, he was a sid. No PRIM-disk scar, notice?" He went on, "Never was a PRIM, for all the good that does him now."

His comforting arm stayed around her shoulders. Her sweater made her shape unmistakable. Sleeveless, it allowed him to feel her arm's soft skin. He had never imagined that in so short of time he would be sitting by her like this, especially since she reviled and derided him so. But he didn't resist. She didn't shy away.

Been falling for you from the first moment, he confided, a growing affection he vowed never to admit to her. Considering his passion for Mia, he hadn't been all that successful with women.

They sat for several minutes while her sobs slowly stopped. "Did I see blood?"

"Shadow's fine," Kyle joked, giving the dog at their feet a playful nudge. "Your blood!"

"I'll be fine."

She made him pull off his shirt, which was streaked with red. "Your wounds haven't reopened, just bleeding a bit." He had a first aid kit. "I'll clean and bandage them again before Nurse Patrice does," she let slip.

"So, I'll survive?"

"Definitely."

After finishing with his recent wounds, Sarah touched two other scars on his back. "Flak jacket saved me from much worse," he explained in a matter-of-fact-legionnaire way.

He sat back down silently, and she went on. "You asked me something the other day and I never gave you an answer." She drew a breath. "Actually, I ignored your request."

"What was that?"

"You asked me to take you around to meet some of the grangers and PRIMS in the area."

"Did I? I've forgotten with all that's gone down in the past forty-eight."

Feeling comfortable in his presence, Sarah smiled. "Yes, well, if it's safe, and if you still want to go with me, I'll take you, if you're staying a day or two longer."

"I'd like that. But, it's up to your cousin how long we stay. Oh, and I want to see that grave."

"Of course. And I should have mentioned it sooner. I'm sorry."

"I'd appreciate that, Sarah." His way of responding so simply and directly sounded like when he pointed out the planets to her last night, unexpected and intense.

It was full sun now. The patio was warming up, glowing in the dawn. "You're coming down to the main house for breakfast, right?" Her blue eyes caught the morning light. His own hazel eyes locked on hers, a view she held.

"You know something?" she whispered after their contented silence.

Kyle didn't know what, but he knew he wanted to hold her, to confide in her, to explain all he'd experienced.

"You would make a fantastic older brother," she explained, sure of the compliment she had just uttered.

"Oh," he responded with a start, pulling back. "Oh?"

"Sure!" She darted toward the main house. "Roxanne will have breakfast in thirty minutes. Don't be late."

Oh, my lovely Sarah, he thought watching her bound away, her ponytail and body swaying, Shadow at her heels, *it's not naivety you need to worry about. It's how you treat men.*

Later that morning, Captain Andrews made good on his invitation to West Con Security status. The cadet was ordered to Sac City for an officer's equivalency evaluation.

He went at noon and did not return.

Sarah remembered him remarking, *I go where I'm ordered.*

TWELVE

THE RETURN OF
THE EXPATRIATES

(Near Jupiter, June 2154)

Mei-Ling Shanghai worked the controls of the *Sirius Odyssey II* as the returning ship approached Jupiter. With just the right acceleration and correct partial orbit, in four days, the craft would fling around the giant and head toward the inner solar system.

"I wouldn't say, 'Mars dead ahead,' but we are on course for the VBC," the pilot reported. "And it's fluctuated again, Walter, number three engine," she added.

Walter Miller, at a side console behind the pilot, confirmed her remark. "Roger. See it." He twitched for more information. "Downward spike in power. This time, bottoms out at 21.6%."

Their three main ion engines had performed flawlessly throughout their abortive escape. But, with home so close at hand, number three was giving the crew fits.

"Isn't an underperforming engine better than one running hot?" Zot Grizotti asked. With the whole crew out of cryogenic stasis, the iceman had little to do. To give Tessa a rest—she had a touch of hibersickness—he sat at her usual console watching the data scrolling by. Ordinarily, every readout remained green. Zot could see number three going amber to red in a quick dip then sluggishly returning toward green status. His engineer wife understood the details; he was only reacting to the color-changing line.

"I need a better report of this data," Miller barked. "Get Tessa up here."

Her husband tried to protect his wife from her own father. "Walter, she's been sick again. She's resting."

Of the four crewmembers, only Tessa was queasy after their cryo. Although she had fully deiced a week ago, anytime she ate, she lost her meal. She kept down only dry crackers or sips of water. She had no fever and was fully conscious, by and large able to perform her duties. But give her a meal, and she immediately lost it. Often, she curled up on her cot and dozed.

"Except for her lack of fever," Zot explained, "I'd say she has a viral infection. If so, I expect we're all likely to get it."

"You more likely than me, Zot," Miller replied with a smile. *If Tess has a bug, Zot already has it. His symptoms will start any minute, I'm sure.*

Shanghai mentally confided, *Actually, I'm the one who feels like I caught it.* Her head ached and her back flared with pain, but she showed the men no signs of distress. Her role was too vital. *And, I haven't caught what Tessa has, you clueless guys.*

Whenever his daughter and son-in-law were together, Miller was pleased to observe, they were inseparable. Married on Mars just before their escape attempt, their honeymoon had been promptly interrupted by the Continental fleet's sortie toward Earth. They hadn't had much private time since. After the failed attack, the *Sirius II's* escape from the solar system began with its long stretches of cryogenic stasis, which kept the crew iced for years at a time.

Miller had no way of knowing for certain, but he suspected his daughter and son-in-law had deiced once or twice during their half-century-long escape attempt. While on their perilous journey home, he reasoned, why not share time together, given all the dangers? It might be their last chance.

With Tessa unable to keep anything down, Zot's uneasiness grew. "Dehydration's the principal concern," he explained, then added, "if she's not better soon, I'm going to start giving her an IV." Hibermen are the most medically trained of any member of the crew unless ship's company included a physician.

It was fortunate she'd been suspended at such a low metabolism; thus, her infection would run its course glacially. Her last ten-year stretch amounted to only a few weeks of getting older. Even so, Tessa had awakened mildly sick and unable to eat. *Now that she was up, it will pass quickly*, Zot reasoned. He saw no other possibility.

Walter stated bluntly, not bothering with rationale or excuses, "I still need a trained engineer—"

"I'm here, both of you," Tessa interrupted. Even without looking at her standing in the hatchway, the three on the flight deck heard her unwrapping a dozen saltine crackers. Her face was drawn from exhaustion. But they all were tired. They had come out of cryo into a burgeoning crisis with number three's spasmodic pulsing, first too strong, then too weak. No time to rest now.

As the old Hiber Service saw went, *No one wants to deice dead.*

"You okay?" her father asked, trying to smooth over his sharp remarks to his son-in-law.

"Yes, yes. I napped." She nudged Zot aside to look at engine readouts. "Definitely worsening with our third unit. And, Walter, look at the temps of each reactor core."

Their three propulsion units each needed an atomic reactor to excite plutonium ions for thrust. Number one and two were surface-of-the-sun hot but still within optimum range. Whatever was happening with number three, it was driving the reactor core higher than advisable. Still confined within a plasma field but super-hot.

"Hadn't noticed that," Walter admitted, suppressing a yawn, his mind on too many details to catch every last one. "Thus confirming I need an engineer sitting there."

"Okay, knock it off," Shanghai, as ship's commander, ordered. "I don't need my chief engineer and hiberman bickering." *When in command, command*, Shanghai thought. Tessa's sick, no doubt, the pilot knew. But the flier hid her own condition. That burning. And blood in the urine was never a good sign. "What the hell do I do, acceleration-wise?" The *Sirius* was passing within the orbits of Jupiter's outer moons. They needed a tight partial orbit around the giant planet to increase their speed. "Can I trust that engine?"

Zot wanted to say *Just jettison the bastard* but knew his opinion wouldn't be welcome.

"How long until home?" Walter asked.

"With our speed now and its projected increase with three viable ions, two months to Mars."

"And if we—" Zot began to ask but was cut off by a look from Tessa. Marsco Asteroid Service also had its own adages. *Icemen stay off the flight deck* was just one.

Appropriately, Tessa asked the question. "And if we shut down number three?"

"We'll have built up momentum," Shanghai explained, "but a third less power output during fling. Good guess is three months to Mars. Maybe a week more." The pilot paused. In her condition those weeks might as well be years in hell. "I'll have to run the numbers."

"Walter," Tessa asked, "if we are shutting it down, wouldn't it be better to just jettison it all together?"

Sound reasoning, even Zot knew that. The *Sirius* number four engine was a standard Herriff-Miller chemical rocket system, the MAS workhorse from decades before the *Sirius* escaped. And the ion-powered number three hung *below* their Herriff-Miller. Although the fuel tanks for the chem rocket were almost depleted, its partially filled tanks were still highly explosive.

In a split second, the fuel components—dimethylhydrazine and nitrogen tetroxide—might mix and instantly explode. Hyperbolic compounds react spontaneously without a catalyst when in contact with each other. If reactor three did rupture those pressurized fuel tanks, the *Sirius* would be a sudden, massive fireball.

The crew had no way to verify this hypothesis, but they were fairly certain something or someone had compromised the fuel storage on the *Akagi* in her final battle near Earth. Before their escape, they'd witnessed that attack carrier flash into a fireball. It was the most plausible explanation for what happened to Hawkins' fleet as it began launching its Lightning fighters against Marsco.

Zot took no comfort in knowing that either number one or number two might create the same scenario, the same explosion. But three was the only ion running hot.

"I want that reactor kept," Miller replied curtly.

"But why?" Tessa demanded, engineer-to-engineer.

"Once in Mars orbit, I want to know what failed. Get in there and figure it out."

The consummate techie, his daughter thought, *always learning, even if saving the body for his mechanical postmortem was filled with tremendous risk.*

"We're on countdown to our Jupiter fling," the pilot barked. "Can we wait on this discussion about that engine 'til after that?"

"Are you sure we're safe waiting that long?" Zot asked. Both engineers now shot him a silencing glance.

Their bickering and her own hectoring made Shanghai's headache that much more intense. Her iron will kept her hanging on.

———————•————————

Twelve hours later, Miller stood, stretched his neck, back, his arms. He had aged during their fifty-plus year ordeal but only a few weeks in actual physical change. That, and his hiber trips to and from Mars in the twenty-first century, kept him looking as though in his late forties. But this ordeal was taking a toll. Now, concern for his daughter added to his apprehension about the engines. Jovian moons, stray Trojan asteroids, the thin, almost invisible debris ring of this planet—anything might jeopardize a smooth, partial transit around the planet. It seemed as though he carried all these in the lines of his face.

He looks downright haggard, his son-in-law thought. "You okay, Walter?" Zot asked in his role as ship's medical officer. And this Miller wasn't his prime concern. "I think," the iceman confided, "our trek has been harder on us all than my preliminary research and initial experiments indicated. Everything on the *Gagarin* was all too pat, too controlled."

"And much shorter."

"Yes, and I stayed awake tending those in cryo-stasis during that whole four-year trek, checking everyone daily, thoroughly. Perhaps in planning this trip, we shouldn't have thought this was just an extension of that expedition, a ramped-up Jupiter run."

Zot and Tessa's concern for Walter kept them from asking about Shanghai, who continued to hide that she was growing worse. And she hadn't left the flight deck in days.

———————•————————

Shanghai drove herself, as they all did. The pilot stayed at her controls almost all four days before fling. Their preparations for the flyby continued even with number three reactor now offline. Mars was an extra five and a half weeks away.

Through the main view port, the largest planet filled most of the polymer pane that kept the habitable part of the ship safely pressurized. The red storm swirled on the surface, three times bigger than Earth. Usually, their view of space was packed with stars. Not now, with so much light reflecting back from the cloud-shrouded planet. Only a handful of moons were visible. Europa stood out against the cloudy surface. The largest moon, Ganymede, moved above the horizon. Others stayed visible, some against a black, starless backdrop of space; others hung above the stormy surface. Zot tried to find the research satellites the *Gagarin* had placed in orbit around each moon but couldn't.

Miller whispered in awe, "Just as Herriff had planned years ago when he circumvented our escape. We'll be home soon." Even with their diminished speed, the engineer knew they'd be nearing Mars in no time.

Too long for me, Shanghai admitted. Her intense back pain made sitting nearly intolerable.

Miller drew an exhausted breath. "Look," he said to her, "take a break for a few hours. You have to be at the helm fresh and ready as we finish gliding around the planet." The *Sirius* needed to move delicately between the orbits of the four Galilean moons. Not too close to Io or Europa but just right past Ganymede and Calisto. Not an easy maneuver for computer and finger disks, but the senior engineer trusted their pilot.

"You're the one who needs a break," the pilot replied, fighting the pressure to collapse. She was their only pilot. *Not yet*, she pleaded with her infirmed body. *Keep going! Not yet!* Her unbending will stayed strong.

"What?" Miller insisted. "I'm fine. Just need to figure out what went wrong with number three and if I can correct it."

She could have ordered him to stand down but didn't. And she stayed at her own post. Shanghai and Miller stood by their stations as the guidance computer did the rest. Still, the pilot's finger disks were at the ready, her tense hands waiting for any emergency.

———•———

Their Jovian flyby was flawless. Afterward, Zot was able to convince Tessa to rest.

On the flight deck, the gas giant behind them, Shanghai worked out their post-Jupiter alignment with Mars. She needed everything precisely programmed just in case her health failed. Their course would need adjustment as they sped over the asteroid belt and then on toward the Red Planet, but she planned to have all contingencies already handled. With each hour at the flight deck, she knew she was getting worse. Her condition was going to wallop her flat soon. Her will could keep it a bay only so long. Her headache ran from gnawing to throbbing. Pain shot through her back, emanating from her kidneys.

"I need to rest," she announced after what seemed like endless days at the controls.

"Do," Walter encouraged. "We'll lock down everything. Autopilot's running A-OK."

<hr>

While the men worked at the flight deck, Zot had Tessa meet Shanghai in her quarters. The pilot was resting uncomfortably.

"What is it?" the engineer asked.

"Pain in my lower back. Blood in my urine. I think icing threw off my cycle—"

"—mine, too."

"I don't have what you have, Tess. I can't stand it any longer; the pain is too much."

Looking deeply into each other's eyes, they considered the possibility of life beginning in Tessa while Mei-Ling could be perilously close to her own death.

"Zot said you may be best under ice until Mars."

"Not fighting him on this. I think the autopilot will—"

Tessa cut her off. "Don't worry. Your programs'll get us to Mars. The VBC will answer, and they'll guide us. No matter what, you've basically gotten us there."

Tessa was not sure the pilot heard; her fever had spiked. *God*, she thought, *my remark did seem rather ominous.*

<hr>

Even without a VBC med consultation—their com-link system was down anyway—Zot put Shanghai into hibernation. Her fever was high, but the process would control that. It wasn't the soundest treatment, but he didn't have access to a medical lab to run any tests. He'd be guessing at a diagnosis. At least hibernation he could control, and through it, keep her stable.

"Is that all you can do?" Miller asked, an edge in his voice, not only of concern but also of exhaustion.

"It's the best I can do under the circumstances." The hiberman felt no need to explain his actions. It had been his call, and he knew, if Tessa showed any other signs of illness, she was next.

———— • ————

Four days later, Tessa and Zot took a break together in the small galley. Zot was ravenous. "I *am* fine," Tessa insisted but still able to keep down only crackers and water.

"You should go rest," Zot implored, "especially since I don't want you spreading your virus around."

Tessa smiled broadly. "Oh, I think I'm past giving this to anyone, if I ever could. Besides, somehow I think *you* gave it to me."

"Me? I haven't been sick for fifty years," the iceman said, laughing.

To change the subject, Tessa asked, "How's Shanghai?"

"Comfortable and stable. Can't ask for more."

"And Walter?"

"He hasn't left the flight deck in several days as far as I can tell," Zot answered. "I'm sure he hasn't slept or even rested properly in two weeks. Maybe longer."

"He's a Miller. Stubborn." Tessa grinned.

"He's double-checking the autopilot whenever he thinks I'm not looking."

"Has he eaten today?"

"No. And probably not yesterday, either."

His daughter sighed. "We should take him something."

"It'd be better if he ate here, sat down here and rested, not grab-n-go, glued to his monitors."

Zot ate quietly then asked Tessa about that hot reactor again. "Is it that dangerous? Potentially?" They both knew that it was. He continued, "If we can get him to rest, get him off the flight deck, can't we just jettison it?"

"What, behind his back?"

"That puts it in a rather mean-spirited way."

Before they said any more, Miller entered the galley. "Not disturbing you, am I?"

"No, father, sit down. Make yourself at home. Eat something." She offered him some saltines.

The senior engineer was depleted. His eyes hung with heavy bags. He needed a shower and a shave. He lacked his usual healthy coloring. "You okay?"

"You okay yourself?" his daughter asked with real concern.

"Yes, yes, fine, bit hungry. Tired, of course."

Tessa smiled. "I am, too, but my appetite comes in waves."

"Well, don't overdo it," Zot cautioned. "As your medical officer, I forbid you from eating a third packet of crackers."

"It's funny," she laughed softly, "but what I'd love right now is ice cream." Neither man responded. "You remember, father, with mother in the old days before we first went to Mars, making ice cream with the hand crank? So creamy, remember? We'd use fresh peaches, raspberries, sometimes chocolate."

"Yes," Miller answered, "I remember. And the time at the grange with the Truman sons. Remember that?"

"Of course."

Zot only recalled finding Jeremy Truman dead, mutilated and floating in that cistern right after a PRIM rampage. That and burying him with Miller's dogs more than half a century ago.

They all ate, lost in memories.

After their silent meal, Miller stated bluntly. "You've got to get that com program running, stat, Zot."

"What? Are the com-links down, too?" Tessa shot. She had assumed everything was up and running normally, including their deep-space communications.

"Yes, but just a software problem. Cake to fix, really. Just part of my growing job description," Zot replied, peeved. He groused to himself, *They just look at engines; I get all the rest of it.*

Missing Zot's resentment, Miller went off on a new direction. "I hope to communicate with the VBC soon."

"Aren't you afraid they may choose to 'blow us out of the water,' metaphorically speaking?" the iceman responded. "Or clap us in irons for mutiny?"

"Heavy handed, yes, that's Marsco," Miller defended. "At least the Marsco of fifty years ago. What are they now, a bureaucracy that got out of control? Or something less sinister? I don't know. I doubt it's so malicious and unethical as to destroy us, no questions asked. What does it gain in that? Actually, I'm hoping we end up getting some low-ranking drudge when we liaise, a drone with no authority or power. We'll have the best chance of talking someone of that ilk into letting us dock at Mars. Someone with no authorization to order us to go directly to the Moon."

"Can they do that?"

"They can try."

Miller planned to put their craft right back in the same orbiting docking facility where she was constructed. The VBC had all the resources he needed to analyze their fluctuating unit. Then, he realized how changed that dock must be after fifty years. Was it even there?

To Zot, any additional weeks with that hot ion unit was going against the odds. But what did an iceman know of engines and reactors?

"So, communicating right now means what?" Tessa asked.

"We can ask for medical advice on Mei-Ling. And, you could use a checkup."

"I'm fine, believe me."

Walter added. "Well, you look exhausted."

The iceman agreed. "So, some serious medical advice on both your conditions."

"We need to get you healthy," her father added.

Laughing playfully, so much so the men felt she wasn't taking her condition seriously, she assured him, "No man-jack is going to catch what I've got." Growing solemn, she added, "What I've got I caught from Zot, and he's not contagious to the rest of you. We're all safe! Anyway, Zot can take care of the com-link. Get to bed, Walter."

"But—"

"No *buts*, Walter, just move along, and all four of us will be fine. I promise. *All* of us *are* fine. A little something like post-hiber spacesickness is normal. I'm fine and not at all contagious."

"Go ahead, iceman, fix this. And, iceman, do that," Zot fumed, nerves worn out. He'd been sitting at the sparks console for four hours before finally booting up the link. Like Miller and Tessa, his exhaustion prevented him from seeing the smallest mistakes that kept the system dead.

"So? Why can't you handle such a simple task?" Walter snapped, so dead tired he sounded much more critical than he intended. "It's only a crashed protocol, after all. A first-year could handle it."

The senior engineer heard himself, began to apologize, when Zot laughed out a reply. "An iceman, a theoretical engineer, an analytical engineer, and a flight deck jockey walk into a bar—"

"Okay, I get it."

"I mean, just look how stressed we all are. We're coming up to our second major flyby in a few weeks. Shanghai's iced. So, without her, we'll have to navigate that: shuttles coming and going, scores of asteroids—many unmarked—plus all those honed and aimed mining asteroids being sent to Mars or the Moon. Tessa's still weak. We all need to be sharp. You especially. Get some rest."

"Okay, I get it," the senior engineer insisted a second time. "How's our com-link?"

"Score," Zot smirked, twitching his last set of commands. "I've been able to upload their files." He waved his finger disks. "VBC records system still responds to my requests. I read her communication logs. We were hailed on November 12, 2146, from a ship identifying herself as the *Armstrong-Aldrin-Collins*. Then several times off and on by her for the next few months." The iceman pointed his head to the com-screen. "She's out of the VBC, on what appears to be the first mission since the *Gagarin* to Jupiter and beyond."

"Marsco must have gone to sleep all those years, not sending out another research ship for decades. When was the *Gagarin*?"

"In the early '90s," her former crewmember replied. "So, it took Marsco nearly sixty years to get beyond the belt and out to Jupiter a second time."

"Guess so."

"Hope it hasn't been as slow as that with reforms."

"Anything else we should know?"

"Only that Mei-Ling lined us up perfectly for home. We may still need some nuanced changes at the belt. We can handle them while keeping her iced."

But the pair knew they might need evasive action while crossing the asteroid belt, never an easy trajectory. Those objects aren't in cyberspace but real space, deadly space. They all needed to be alert.

"I've checked. Mars's in conjunction," Zot went on. "We'll be in orbit on or near October second. Those pre-Flight classes as a plebe paid off." The iceman then gave Walter a knowing look. "Can Marsco keep us from stopping at Mars? Or force us to dock at the belt?"

"Once we're inner-belt, it can do plenty of things. Who knows? After the Lost Fleet resurrected itself, asteroid shuttles may be armed; we simply don't know."

The men took an hour to review the communications between the *Armstrong-Aldrin-Collins* and their *Sirius II*. "Well," Walter finally concluded. "Starts routine enough. A hail that promises a friendly welcome if we're green men wanting to be taken to their leader."

"So, they didn't identify us?"

"Herriff disengaged our IFF, remember, to make it harder to track us when we left the solar system. We didn't want to risk anyone else's life chasing us."

"Glad we didn't risk anyone else's life," Zot quipped, knowing their own lives were as yet far from safe.

"After February 2147, the VBC took over trying to liaise with us. Wouldn't that suggest they know who we are?"

"Maybe, maybe not. It could be that they have the arrays for this type of communications and this *Armstrong-Aldrin-Collins* was done, gone into Mars orbit or even back toward Earth. Who knows?"

"Okay, so did the VBC push us up a rung, this knowledge of a reticent bogie, push this intel up to Marsco HQ, or keep it within Herriff's old fiefdom?" An open-ended question. Under Martin Herriff, the Van Braun Center ran as his own principality, at quite a distance from the direct auspices of the Seattle-based HQ. "Has that changed in all these years?"

"More to the point, all communication attempts seemed to have stopped once we were crossing the Uranus orbital path."

"Maybe they just grew tired of trying?"

"Once we swung by that gas giant, we were clearly headed for the inner solar system, no question. Shouldn't that make them *more* curious, not less?"

"Well, curious or no, what do we do now? Ring 'em up and say, 'Hello, here we are, back from our deep-space experience. We'd like a parade!' How's that sound?"

Miller chuckled. "I like the tenor."

"No, seriously, let's just say, 'Hey, guys, we're home. Sorry our com-links were dead.'"

Miller added with a snort, "Don't forget: 'Sorry about absconding with your spaceship.'"

"Boys, boys," Tessa clapped her hands like a schoolmarm. "I told *you* to go to bed," Tessa said behind the pair on the flight deck, nudging her father. She was growing into her incipient maternal role, seeing them as troublesome three-year-old twins. "And you," she nudged Zot, "I told *you* to make sure he got there."

"Tess, we're at a loss to begin this message."

"Just communicate with Mars, dammit." She no longer had any patience with either of them. "Just say something."

Zot looked directly at Tessa, "I know you're feeling somewhat better, but you're tried and terribly weak, too."

"I'm fine." She paused then shot, "And, don't you dare say 'bitchy,' iceman."

The hiber specialist drew an acquiescing breath. "Mei-Ling's stable. Her fever's down. I think she'll wake in the same condition as when I put her under. But, I'm beginning to think, re-icing is the best course of treatment for you, as well."

"How's that?"

"It'll freeze you *and* your infection, just like hers. Buy your body some time."

"I don't need to go under cryo—"

"It would be hiber this time, not cryo," the iceman answered knowingly.

"I don't want either, Zot."

"Do you think that wise?" Miller sighed, looking at the hiberman, filled with paternal frustration that he was unable to do anything to help his daughter.

"I don't really know what's best. That's the problem. Let her stay awake? Ice her? Flip a coin."

"What's best for all of us," Tessa smirked.

Their frustration and exhaustion sent them all into morose silence.

Finally, Zot roused himself and bent over the sparks program and twitched. "How's this: 'VBC Research Vessel *Sirius Odyssey II* to home base: returning to Mars but with spacesick crewmember. Need port docking coordinates and med assistance. Please advise. Walter C. Miller, commander.' That covers the direct and short message approach."

"It also lets them know we insist on stopping at Mars."

"Yes, I thought of that."

"Send it!" Miller ordered.

"Just to be sure," Tessa recommended, pointing her father's right hand, "you authorize it."

Miller held his ID disk over the pad and then looked at his daughter and son-in-law for final support. At their nod, he twitched the message away. "No doubt now. Marsco knows who we are for certain."

———————•••———————

Tessa escorted her father from the flight deck to his quarters like he was under house arrest. She finally got him to wash up, drink a sleeping concoction Zot knew would be efficacious, and lay down.

"How long since you slept?"

"I only need four or five hours—"

"That's not what I asked. How long?"

"A proper sleep on a cot? Probably two weeks. I needed to watch our new course and check on those autopilot programs. And, I kept trying to run engine failure scenarios. Damnable task. No pretty outcomes. Three ions were great. On two we're fine, just a bit slower."

Tessa replied, urging him along, "Okay, but rest now. We'll get VBC guidance. Mei-Ling's excellent; so's our autopilot. We're in her good disks even if she's not at the flight deck."

"I'm worried about her, iced like that. So sick."

"She'll be fine," Tessa defended her husband's decision.

Walter reached for Tessa's hand with both of his. His right and left disk arrays gave her hand a slight tingle. "You know, my dear, what I felt for Bethany, right?"

"Yes, now get to sleep."

"I will after I say one last thing."

"About how much you loved Bethany?"

"No, love you."

Tessa's blush of thankfulness was visible. "I've always known that, Father."

"No, listen, please. Okay, so my body's in its forties. No one lives forever. Promise me, promise Tess, at the end in about five, six decades from now or whatever, promise you'll make every effort to sit with me like this, at my gathering dark."

"Shhh, you'll never be alone."

"No, promise me," he implored.

"Yes, yes, Father, I promise—Zot, too—we'll do everything we can to be with you. But, you're talking decades from now." She kissed his forehead. "Now, you promise me something."

"Anything."

"Get some rest."

———— • ————

Alone on the flight deck, Zot looked out at stygian space. Countless stars were visible, the Milky Way thick with dots, here brighter, there dimmer.

What awaits us? Death? He loved and trusted Tessa and Walter, not so their finicky ion. *And after we dock successfully—if we manage to pull that off—what about that not-so-easily-overlooked fact that we stole this spacecraft from Marsco? How will Seattle greet its expatriates? Throwing us into the brig doesn't seem so far-fetched. Would twenty-second century Marsco court-martial us? Grant us clemency? Welcome their twenty-first century travelers with open arms? Will Marsco even exist after our half-century circular journey?*

The vast, silent universe made no reply.

———— • ————

"He's resting quietly," Tessa reported, herself drained. "He's really just shattered."

"That drink I gave him will knock him flat for twenty-four hours at least."

"He can sleep for the next few weeks as far as I'm concerned. He needs it."

Zot noted, "You were with him a long time; he okay?"

"Talking about his death like he was 110 and going fast."

"Well, he'd be over 125 if he'd have aged naturally."

Tess took her husband's hand. "He mentioned Bethany, that's all."

"He rarely does that. Were you okay listening to that? I mean—"

Tessa cut him off. "Both your parents died in the same Luddite attack when you were a child. But if one had survived the other, would you stand in their way of happiness later? God, he's been alone for all these years."

"I see what you mean. Your mother was a fine woman, a lovely woman. Wish I'd known her."

"He loved mom, no doubt, but she's been dead since 2080." She had to check the chronometer on the flight deck. "This is the last hours of July 31, 2154. It's time."

Zot stood, raised her up from her seat and held her. He grew contemplative. "I know Mei-Ling loves him. He loves her, too, but differently. I think he sees *you* in her, sees another daughter."

"Well, that's romantic."

"Look, you two women are scheming; I know it. Frankly, it's *you* who's matchmaking here. But, he's happy. He's fine. He doesn't have room in his mind for anything but his work. And I guess, you and his memories of Bethany. Let him be. If he changes his mind, fine, but you can't change it for him."

"And yet, you and I have such a wonderful—"

"Tess, he's fine. She'll be fine. Let it unfold, even if the outcome isn't what you want." Zot knew things of Shanghai. Remembered the night he first saw her after she'd blasted that rundown hotel lobby in Sac City. He wasn't protecting Miller, but he could understand some of Shanghai's reluctance. Maybe she didn't want to love, if it meant confiding that part of her history.

"I let Bethany go; he hasn't," Tessa went on. "And Mei-Ling, she'll love him in her own way, but she'll love him, if that makes any sense."

"Perfect sense." Zot paused, then added, "But, Tess, she's nearly your age."

The woman put on a false pout. "*Pleezzee!*" Tessa stressed. "She's *older* than I am! Besides hiber and cryo changes things, slows things. She and I, regardless of our real ages, our bodies are in our mid-thirties."

"And except for needing twenty-four hours of sleep, he looks forty-five."

She gave a broad smile. "Honestly, Zot, I don't need to remain an only child; a half-sib's fine with me, truly." She quickly did the math. If Walter overcame his reluctance, he might father a child younger than theirs. *A half-sib younger than my own kid.*

"There you go scheming again, Tess. Stop it."

She relented. "Now, did any belt colonies pick up our signals?"

"If they have, they're not responding."

"And Mars? The VBC?"

"Nothing yet."

"And autopilot's fine?"

"Affirmative. All our computer systems are on their game. We're golden. Still, I'd love to dump that piping-hot engine, but that's your call, you two wonks."

"Stop that. It's powered down, stable, and cooling down. Not all that different from what you did with Mei-Ling."

"I guess."

"Then come on then," she commanded, leading him away toward their quarters for what they needed more than sleep.

THIRTEEN

RETURN OF THE DEAD

(New Grange, August 2154)

"**Y**ou're going to have to repeat all that, sir," Lieutenant Colonel Devon Chavez-Sherman replied to his caller. After a yawn, he explained, "It's barely 0245 here, sir, and this's all too stunning to comprehend while half asleep." When his com-link woke him, Devon didn't at first catch the importance of the three-way call.

The most excited was the speaker at the Resnik Colony on the far side of the Moon. When the lunar lieutenant first received a startling message from Von Braun, she instantly got a ranking duty officer at Seattle HQ. Confused, that officer alerted Chesney's HQ. Those at the Bunker knew to have the full report go directly to Devon as well. Thus, this early morning call and this impromptu situation briefing between the Moon, the Bunker, and the Brunel grange.

"Yes, sir," gaining consciousness, Devon answered Chesney's officer, "A lander's coming for me here, not an HFC? Anyway, it'll be for *us*. I'll want Cadet Kyle Roncalli with me." He hastily explained Kyle's complicated situation. He mentioned further Security training but passed it off as routine and intentionally didn't mention him being at a West Con facility. "Locate him and your craft can pick him up before me," he went on with an assured tone that this was perfectly normal and totally A-OK. "Yes, he was at that briefing. Yes, sir, has clearance. We'll get to the Vandenberg Egress Port well before 0600 hours if you're sending us transport."

A counterargument ensued from the ranking wallah at the Bunker.

"I know he's *only* a cadet with third-year status," Devon replied, still hiding Kyle's recent transition into West Con Security. A quick check by

Marsco's Internal would expose Devon's purposeful oversight. "But he's received top clearance, as I said, and he knows most of the story. Why bring another source of potential leaks on board by giving me a new aide? We work well together. He has Security experience. And, yes, I totally trust him." *Even with my cousin's daughter, that's how much*, he added without speaking.

The Bunker official reluctantly agreed.

"Very good, sir. Yes, I'll be ready at 0445. Tell those jockeys to come in directly to my signal and not buzz the barnyards. I don't want some hot-shot dive-bombing the grange. Oh, plenty of landing clearance; I'm on the highest rise in an alfalfa field."

The dean of the academy was in no mood for this call. It was just after 0330. She had a few personal days with her sons and husband, a lander pilot home from his lunar tour, and nothing like this had ever been asked of her.

"Devon, professor or no, you're wanting the impossible at a pretty early hour."

"Well, I'm now on temp assignment with Security, space detail."

She took his remarks as matter-of-fact, not as Devon trying to use Security to maneuver her. "That complicates next term. Besides I hate those arrogant Security bastards."

"Joanna, I wouldn't let that slip out on this link. Let me deal with Security; you deal with staffing. Dean's purview, after all."

"And this?"

"I know I am pleading for a lander load at an insufferably early hour, but look, I need Kyle and he's only a cadet. And now he's technically under the auspices of West Con Security."

"That's no small technicality."

"Can't you arrange something?"

"I'm not sure what the commandant will say—"

"Actually, she said to speak with *you*."

What did they used to call this, 'passing the buck'? Joanna smirked to herself. "Why isn't Security doing this?"

"What makes you ask that? Who brought up Security?"

"Devon, *you* did. Your temp assignment and an aide. This aide will have to be in Security, *Marsco* Security, so let them handle this." She thought then added uncharacteristically, "Who authorized one of our cadets going to West Con Security?"

"All happening with the Accords anyway."

"That's not an answer."

"Look, Joanna, *they* want it black." Both understood *they* referred solely to Marsco Security. "If you authorize things, then it all seems normal."

Clandestine bastards, the dean thought but held her tongue this time. "None of this is normal. But, okay, what's he need?"

"Bless you. He needs a partial schedule for his first semester senior year. Nothing F2F; it's got to be all online. Then credit for his ADC work."

"Fine. It's a bit of a stretch, but that'll cover all his leadership theory classes. But, look, it'll mean missing his boards."

"Video conference them, then."

"Very well. Can do. Extenuating circumstances. If he's temporarily in Security, makes it easier."

"So, okay he's on a cyber-term?"

"Done. Registrar can do that—*later in the morning*." Devon could hear the dean repeating all this as she wrote notes with pencil and paper. She was one of the few associates he knew who still jotted herself reminders. Made sense, she was a fantastic administrator.

"Thank you, sir. And, he'll need a uniform befitting his status. His size will be in his file, I'm sure."

By this time, the dean was at her screen, reviewing Kyle's Q-7 service records. "Yes, well-above-average scholar, sits in the top twelve percent, wants colony work, not Flight. Highest leadership score in years. Already has one long hitch in Security. *Ours*. Then a semester of lunar independent studies under West Con Security auspices. Who authorized that?" she shot then caught herself when she saw her signature on that arrangement. *That* nonsense was purely educational; it made sense after a fashion. Gathering herself, she was back reading his file. "This summer detail with West Con. Now back to us. Technically, he's in his third hitch now. Devon, I can go with your request, especially since *our* Security's behind it. I'll twitch the orders as per your request."

"Thanks, Joanna."

"Boy, if Roncalli's career is any indication, we'll see many confused Q-7 files before the Accord transitions are over."

———— • ————

The cabin crew of Kyle's Security lander kept a careful eye on him during his short trip down from the former Marsco camp near Mount Lassen, where he was training with West Con. He sat quietly in his dress uniform, clean and not often worn. He'd been in the field with troopers for nearly six weeks, rarely polished up like this.

The ship, designed solely for Earth-side stealth, was hardly visible in the predawn gray. Kyle knew something extraordinary was up; a high-end Marsco lander doesn't often touch down at a West Con training facility, especially to pick up the likes of him. Obviously, West Con khakis and lieutenant bars—if these associates recognized the new insignia—weren't a routine occurrence for this crew.

Kyle unexpectedly remembered Mia in her unusual uniform but buried that thought.

The single passenger closed his eyes, hoping to sleep in the dark cabin he shared with fifteen empty seats. His past weeks were ethereal, uncharacteristic even in the Marsco world. Activated by West Con, damn near snatched like seamen off a merchant ship of yore, he'd ended up near Mount Lassen, where Marsco had once had its own training center. West Con considered that camp under its authority now.

Upon arrival, the training staff examined Kyle's records carefully. He was sure they were looking for where his loyalties lie as much as his experience. That experience, however, allowed him to move beyond basic and under warrant triangles, the new insignia for that rank. But he was quickly promoted to lieutenant when he began leading his platoon. He knew how to command troopers, keep them safe under fire, encourage the untrained but also discipline the malingerers.

By the end of the first two weeks, he was drilling a whole company and also instructing new warrants on their duties. Many of those Kyle worked with were raw recruits, eager to make sure West Con would become a truly independent federation. No question, many were also former troopers and Auxxies, but like the recruits, they were loyal to a sense of West Con and a world free of Marsco and full of sovereign feds. Their enthusiasm was contagious.

Kyle had always been less interested in Marsco and its Earth-side politics than its space colonies anyway. His devotion to Seattle rested on the notion that after the Six Accords were totally up and running, Marsco would be keeping the Von Braun Center and all Martian settlements. He never considered that those Martians might have their own ideas of independence. His tepid and somewhat jaundiced feelings sprang from his grandfather's own attitude toward the old Marsco as opposed to the new.

Additionally, the first independent-minded fed Kyle had ever met was Trent Brunel, a man like Devon, whom Kyle felt instinctively he could trust and follow. Trent was a strong factor in Kyle entertaining the thought of officially becoming a fed, a citizen of West Con. Plus, frankly, that particular fed's daughter didn't hurt this notion one bit.

Ignored by the cabin crew, the West Con lieutenant dozed but woke as he felt the lander shift in flight attitude. He began to make out the landscape below. The craft was small enough to maneuver and land like an HFC. And watching the ground as the craft lost altitude, Kyle soon realized they were approaching New Grange.

He easily made out the main house as the stealth craft went into her final landing glide. His eyes fixed on the darkened windows of Sarah's bedroom. Hers was in the middle of the southern wing, so it got strong morning sunlight all year. She'd explained that to him on one of their few and not-quite-friends walks. The lander coming in made a high-pitched whine. As the craft lost altitude and began to hover-glide, Kyle watched the grange. Nothing moved below except for Shadow, frightened by the nimble craft. It was the only time the cadet had seen the dog terrified.

Sweeping in from the north, the lander cleared the house and committed to a set-down near the small guesthouse.

———— • ————

After the lander's thruster blasts singed the alfalfa beneath its exhaust nozzles, the wind soon swayed the pasture grass as though nothing unusual had happened. The craft had hardly touched down when Devon entered.

Kyle stood but did not salute. As a member of West Con Security, the lieutenant had express instructions to wait for a Marsco Security officer, regardless of rank, to salute him first. This was West Con's show now, or so Sac City believed.

And all these chickenshit details get my ass to Mars, how? Kyle questioned himself.

Devon was not thinking of military courtesy when he entered. He shook Kyle's hand rather than saluted. The West Con officer was fine with that.

"Pretty posh," Devon noted as he sat across the aisle from Kyle. The craft, one of Marsco's newest, was designed for moving high wallahs in luxury, which, oddly, was how Devon felt. He'd expected a retrofitted lander used for inserting armed troops in hot arenas, not this.

"And just for us?"

"Affirmative."

As soon as the craft had altitude, the cabin crew fussed over the senior VIP. Breakfast trays appeared; coffee flowed. Their flight was a short jaunt to the coast and then down along it for another five hundred kilometers. All told, they had sixty minutes of airtime. Their craft never reached full speed.

Devon commanded the most attention from the cabin crew, all women and all smart in their Marsco uniforms. If they had been on their feet all night and into the morning, they didn't show it. One woman, who looked like Patrice—willowy, blond, smiling—approached Kyle.

"You have just enough time to change," she informed him, handing him a suit bag. Kyle didn't understand until he saw a pressed and ready-to-go Marsco uniform.

Devon stood next to him. "Get ready," he insisted. "We land in twenty minutes." To the former cadet's puzzled looks, he said only, "I'm now a full colonel, but I didn't get anything more than these." He pointed to new badges of rank he'd received. He also had emblems that signified a Security appointment, not an Academy post. The insignias showed Earth with a superimposed gloved fist holding an olive branch—Marsco bringing peace to the world via its Security forces. "I rate an ADC with officer status," he informed the former cadet, "but Marsco won't budge on your rank. You were made a warrant officer, however."

Kyle smirked, on the edge of insubordination. "Was a lieutenant in the other service, sir."

"I know that. I think Marsco's pissing on you to show up West Con."

Every military in human history has done that, the erstwhile lieutenant admitted.

"Under the circumstances," Devon went on, "this is the best I could do. All legit. And this isn't a temp promotion but the real deal. So, suit up smartly for the wallahs we're meeting."

Only when Kyle neatened his uniform a final time did he spot a Security emblem identical to Devon's. Back to square one.

———※———

Sarah woke to her bed shaking uncontrollably. She thought it all a dream, but it seemed to be continuously trembling, accompanied by a low whimpering. Draped across her feet stretched Shadow, panting, the source of the strange quaking. Her quivering dog blended into the bedroom darkness.

"What is it, boy?" she cooed, coaxing. "Come here," she pleaded. The once-courageous dog would have none of it; he burrowed himself under her covers for safety.

Voices in the house brought Sarah into the kitchen where Trent and Celine were discussing everything with Roxanne. For some reason known only to Devon, they speculated, he was gone almost as soon as he'd arrived. Before dawn, a lander had spirited their guest away, which at first didn't seem that extraordinary. "Had to leave," Celine added in a saddened tone. "Damn Marsco, always snatching that man from us. Can't let him have a rest for a few days."

Roxanne added for Sarah's sake, "Dint even give him time to say goodbye."

Staring hard, as though he could still see the lander moving away, Trent looked out the window toward the south and the rise with the smallest guesthouse now visible in the morning light. He wasn't sure, but he sensed the fleeting craft had left footprints where it momentarily rested on his land.

Hearing friendly voices, Shadow appeared, tail curled between his legs, his panting still labored and scared. The large dog nosed Sarah. "What is it, boy?" she asked, holding his head up to search his eyes. "He knows!" she blurted out. "Kyle was on that craft. I swear, he knows."

Her parents dismissed the claim. "How can that dog know when we don't know anything of what Marsco's doing?" Celine sighed. "We just know that Devon's gone."

"Besides," Trent added, "didn't Kyle leave last June to join *our* forces, West Con forces?"

"He would know," Roxanne supported Sarah, patting Shadow. "He knows, this one," she added, now patting Sarah.

The young woman disappeared to her room still not sure what exactly had happened earlier that morning.

———•———

When Sarah didn't appear for breakfast, her mother went to look for her. She found her daughter curled on her bed, mulling her summer's experiences with a faraway stare.

"There, Sarah, you've been in tears too much these past months," Celine admonished. "What is it now, hon?"

"I'm not crying, Mom," she replied, "and I haven't since last June when Kyle—I meant Devon—left." She then asked, "Are associate women pretty? Prettier than Patrice or Hy?"

Celine laughed softly. "Now what is this all about?"

"Associate women, that's all. What makes some men, *some associates*, prefer associate women?"

"And how's this related to the Richardson girls? They *aren't* associate women." *No arguing with a moping girl; let her sort it all out for herself,* Celine knew from experience.

"But, what are they like? Associate women?"

"Well, dear, the only one I really knew, Cindy, I knew through Devon."

Sarah perked up quickly. "*Really?*" The tenor of her voice was delighted excitement. "Devon? He had *a wife?*"

"He never speaks of her, dear, so we never do. Guess that's why you don't know. But not a wife, although they were engaged. Cynthia Maricourt. An officer like our Devon. A pilot. She was in and out of that Security business in those days like Devon but mostly did more work on the Moon, I believe." She waved her right hand to show she didn't understand any of Marsco's intricacies. "All this was close to twenty years ago now, so you were just a child. They came here together several times, always wanted that small guesthouse alone. Can't blame them, two powerful careers, so little time together."

"What was she like?"

"Very kind. Smart. They fit together, the way couples do. You'd never suspect she was Marsco, if you follow my logic. Never had that edge, and it was sharper then, twenty years ago, that edge."

"What happened?"

"She died, about when you were maybe three."

"That's why I don't remember."

"Yes, that, and the fact that Devon's never spoken a word of it. Not to us at the grange at any rate, never a word about her. He just confirmed she was dead. Then a few years after that, he went on that Jupiter trip of his, I think, to mend his heart. Away in space for years after Cindy's death."

"Do you know what happened?"

"No, not exactly. He doesn't talk of her, like I said. An attack of some kind, or so we heard. Nothing official but plenty of rumors. Always seems to be rumors in the Marsco world. Some sort of 'Luddite incident,' I think they called it. Something about sabotage to a spacecraft. Maybe your father knows for sure, if you can get him to talk about it. I really don't know, except her ship burnt up as it came back to Earth. Devon's Cindy was a pilot, that I know," she ended conclusively.

Clearly speaking of Kyle, the young woman let slip, "I'd rather lose him *that* way. It's final. I can get over that." She curled up again on her bed to brood.

"Hon, give him a chance, you really don't know what's going on. Marsco has its secret ways. Even grangers know that. Devon often gets called away. He comes here to rest, and they hardly let him be. Besides, they—Devon and Kyle—they both *say* he's a cadet, but that could be them just saying that. I mean look at how much he knew of our neighbors. Did they suspect something odd in this area?"

"*They?*"

"Marsco Security. Maybe Kyle was here to prevent those attacks? He sure knew what to do to protect you."

Wanting to continue to abhor him, Sarah shook her head. It was better if she loathed him, she rationalized. Easier to forget him. "I don't think so, Mom, since we talked about how cadets are sometimes taken out of the Academy and made officers in Security. He said it hadn't happened in years." She went silent remembering he'd vaguely referred to his own months on patrol, leading armed troopers. She'd seen his scars. And the way he guarded her on the road back from Millersville. His actions were too confident, clearly moves he'd made before. "But, that doesn't make sense, either."

"And we don't know where he is, really." Celine breathed out in frustration. "Your dog knowing." She shook her head in disbelief. "Oh, dear Roxanne," she sighed. "She still has such superstitious PRIM ways. He could get leave and be here today, if he's training. Who knows?"

"I sure I don't know; he's made no attempt to message me, send me some word."

"Give him patience, hon. You are young, only twenty-two soon. He's young. He may be under orders to do some duty we don't know, can't know about. And we all know that this Marsco world is changing so much, so rapidly. Although," the older woman caught herself, "he was taken away last June by us, by West Con."

Sarah gazed off through her window and stared pensively for a quiet moment. Rolling toward her mother, she added, "But Patrice and Hy, wanting to see him? They both have asked about him, even though Patty's up in Sac City."

Celine smirked, adding in a superior tone, "Those Richardson girls are always forward. Her belly will be swelling by summer's end, you mark my words. Either one would still love to get her hooks into our Chase."

"Have to stand in line," Sarah shot a glance at her mother, then the now-vacant guesthouse. "But not Patrice," she added, defending her friend. "Not anymore."

Soothing the girl, Celine brushed Sarah's long hair away from her face. "I think your father fell in love with me because of my hair. Mine was as shining and dark brown then as yours is now." As usual, hers was in a bun, but it was nearly as long as Sarah's. "That first time he kissed me, I'd loosened it and let it fall. Like you wear it."

"You were lovely then and still are." She kissed her mother's cheek.

"So are you, dear. And your Kyle—I get this sense, just you wait, he'll come around."

"He's not *my* Kyle, Mom, and even so, I hate him," Sarah blurted.

"Whatever, my dear. You *do* have a peculiar way of hating that man, that's for sure. But, he'll not just up and leave you, child: a Brunel, a Darrow, a Sherman!" she added smugly. "And Devon would *never* bring anyone here he didn't trust." She sighed. "And your father likes him, dear. You can tell."

"It's the not knowing that crushes me," the young woman whispered. "Not knowing if he'll come back. Not knowing if I'll ever—"

Yes, very peculiar form of hating. Her mother just smiled. "It's that Marsco world, hon," she tried to comfort.

"Well, Accords or no, it can't end soon enough for me."

After lowering the shades to darken the room, Celine left. Sarah stayed awake and drifted once more into moody silence, Shadow curled along her legs as comfort.

When she realized she was all alone, the young granger rose to dress. She had much to do with a cow ready to birth and at least one barn cat as well. Chores would keep his memory at bay. Besides, she could live without her odious Kyle if she had to.

Vandenberg Egress Port sprawled underneath the lander. Kyle spotted three enormous lunar-capable craft lined up along the southern edge. Around them, ground crew scurried, preparing each for off-planet flight. Along the north edge, Vandenberg served as an on-planet terminal with lander connections coming and going from around the globe. Even a mag-lev terminal was visible, its lines spreading north and south along the coast.

Their lander circled out over the bay and hovered at two thousand.

Kyle looked at his commander. "What's up?"

Devon wasn't sure. Usually, this was an easy set down.

The senior cabin attendant appeared. "Clearance verification. Twitch here." She held out an ID pad where the passengers each twitched their right index finger. "Security wants to know who is coming into their green zone."

All this made no sense to Kyle. He had seen the lander field, with dozens of landers an hour hovering, coming to rest, rising, heading out. *Did they check everyone?*

The lander banked and lost altitude steadily; Kyle managed to see a separate launch area through his bulkhead window. On it, a single craft set off by itself waited, space capable but only one-third the size of the three getting ready for their lunar run. Its black skin contrasted to the bright aluminum and white matte of a typical lander. Clearly a stealth ship, one designed for speed as well as concealment in outer space.

"Never set down here before," the youngest of the cabin staff remarked. "We're often called to perform VIP runs but never directly to the Security orbiter pad. You must be high wallahs!" she whispered, unguarded.

"I'm just the aide-de-camp, so point to him," Kyle stated, nodding to Devon.

As they exited the first lander, the pair went directly on board a second.

"May I ask when I'll know what's up, sir?"

"In about an hour, once we've cleared Earth orbit. HQ wants us at Resnik Colony stat. That's all I can say until we're briefed on board."

Resnik had wonderful hydroponics in its domes, Kyle remembered. He'd been that close to seeing them last time he was lunar-side. Spook elements of this mission aside, the thought of those domed gardens was enough to cheer up the future colonist.

In a few years, I'll be running Martian greenhouses, he assured himself.

Onboard the stealth Security lander *Hoover*, Devon and Kyle found three wallahs waiting: the head of Marsco Security along with his own ADC, plus the lunar Security chief, who had happened to be in Seattle when everything started going down.

"Colonel Chavez-Sherman," Captain Ndunda explained to her commander, Mateo Modena, "made the observations of this ion trail in—" As prepared as the ADC was for this briefing, she stumbled. She couldn't state the exact year.

"That's okay, Serena," her superior cut in. "During the *AAC* Jupiter mission, right?"

"Yes, sir. And it was June of '46 when we first tracked the enigma. We didn't first hail her until months later."

Devon's career had kept him in space or at the Academy for a dozen years since his time in Security. Nonetheless, he knew of Commander Modena's reputation as the longstanding Security director dedicated to guiding its forces to preserve the peace and make sure the Accords ran smoothly. Battalions of troopers and units of Auxiliary had already been assigned to appropriate federations in compliance with the Accords. Taking more upon himself, Modena had accelerated reassignment, moving numerous battalions and units before their mandatory changeover date, in some cases, years before. Not hastily but smoothly ahead of schedule. When that conversion was accomplished, Security as it existed today would cease to be.

Modena's build was compact but powerful. Rumor had it that on his rare off-duty times, he was a bon vivant. An invitation to one of his specially prepared meals was an incomparable event. He was famous for Med cooking, as his Euro heritage would suggest. His preparation of fresh fish—he lived in Seattle—was beyond compare.

Devon introduced his own ADC to the commander and to the lunar Security head, Katsura George Kiyomori.

Like Modena, Kiyomori had been born on Earth of associates with extended Marsco connections. He was lean, about the same age as Devon, but much more formal. His family had easily blended into Marsco generations before, but he still had the tendency to hide his distant PRIM ancestry. He asked to be called Kay-Gee to bridge his formality with approachableness. While Modena laughed and smiled, Kay-Gee kept a more reserved tenor.

But, a working pair, Kyle noted. *They have a synergy between them, even if both seem on edge.*

"Roncalli?" Modena repeated. "More Euro or SoAm, NoAm?"

"NoAm, sir," the warrant officer replied. Feeling comfortable, he added, "a degree of Indie in the distant past as well, although my grandfather was in Security during the PRIM Mutiny and long after."

"A Roncalli?"

"No, Aaron Truman, sir."

Captain Ndunda knew her boss. She clicked a pad to look up those records. He would want to interject some anecdote when the group had a relaxed meal together later.

As the *Hoover* made her last orbit and headed for the Moon, Modena gathered the passengers in a conference room. The three main players sat at the table while the pair of ADCs moved to places along the bulkhead. Kyle watched everything that Serena did, knowing he should be doing the same for Devon. She brought out a finger mouse notebook that she activated to record the proceedings. For his new duties, he had been given an identical unit with an exclusively linked thimble. Only he, using that dedicated wireless mouse tied to his own finger disks, could activate it.

Speaking to Devon and Kyle, the Security director explained that both now had access to various top-secret reports dating from 2099. They would have ample time to study them while on their way to Mars.

"Of particular note," Modena went on, "is an after-action report from the commander of a Space Rangers battalion. Serena can help you, Mr. Roncalli, to open those highly secure files." Kyle nodded. "After their actions of 2099," Modena explained, "these units were disbanded. But prior to this time, rumors that the Lost Fleet and Continental Forces were still iced somewhere in the asteroid belt kept Seattle from taking such a step."

The most important file covered every aspect of the last battle waged by the Rangers. It began with a summary of Security's discovery of the Lost Fleet as it left the belt even though disguised as an ore hauler bringing highly radioactive fuels to a lunar colony.

"Fallacious cover story that Security saw through in a nano," Kay-Gee added. Although this happened years before his time, it was his lunar unit that had initially recognized the deception.

Another report continued with an explanation of how those Rangers employed an override to deactivate all the Fleet's atomic weaponry as the attack formation maneuvered between the Moon and Earth, preparing to launch its squadrons of Lightning fighters.

"You know this history, right Devon?"

"Enough to follow along, sir. I know of the Lost Fleet. I know of the destruction wrought by a Lightning."

"Most of us born well after the C-Wars know those stories. It was an exceptionally lethal weapon. Add nukes to the mix and the C-Powers were ready to devastate Earth a second time."

"My only question is, how is this related to the ion trail and the mysterious message? Are you suggesting a Continental connection?"

"Far from it. Part F will fill you in more." Kyle quickly had that file open. It ran for dozens of screens. "Peruse it on your way to Mars. Section 16b lists the ships lost that day: the *Akagi*, the *Siryu*, and the *Hiryu* of the Continental Forces. These were the finest and last C-Powers attack carriers. Plus, their Lightning fighters: forty-eight in all. But note this additional point at 16c," Modena paused then went on, "Also destroyed was an experimental deep-space craft from the Von Braun Center, the *Sirius Odyssey II*.' Does this now make any sense to you, Devon?"

"No, sir, not really."

"The best way to explain it is this: At the time, the *Sirius Odyssey II* was a new ship of radical design. Martin Herriff of VBC fame was on board for her maiden voyage. We know he was accompanied by Walter C. Miller, the designer of the prototype propulsion units. His daughter was there, too, Tessa Palmer Miller, another engineer."

"Isn't there a wing of the engineering building named for her at the Academy?" Kyle interjected.

"She's the one," Captain Ndunda answered.

Modena continued, "The craft had a pilot whose background is totally sketchy, but her name was listed as Captain Ling Shanghai, MAS."

"Perhaps hiding PRIM background," Kay-Gee interjected. "Her records claim she was born in the Shanghai Subsidiary eight years before the C-Wars. However, few reliable records survived those times. Claimed she was an Academy grad, but we can find no record of her matriculation or graduation."

"Any other crew?"

"Yes, one other, Anthony Grizotti, who was operating an experimental cryogenic stasis system."

Serena added, "Grizotti was on the *Gagarin* for her one and only Jupiter run. And, he was the main designer of a cryogenic system the *Sirius II* used.

"So only five."

"Yes."

"And this ship, this *Sirius*, was destroyed in the fighting somehow?"

"Or so the Security records from that time maintain."

"I'm still at a loss, sir," Devon stated.

Modena nodded to Kay-Gee who added simply, "Recently, Marsco stations picked up this message sent from that ship, the *Sirius Odyssey II*. And I quote: 'VBC Research Vessel *Sirius Odyssey II* to home base: returning to Mars but with spacesick crewmember. Need port docking coordinates and med assistance. Please advise. Walter C. Miller, commander.'"

Devon and Kyle listened in silence.

"Those secure files Serena gave your ADC," Modena explained, "show the falsified cover stories and then the real course of the *Sirius*. She was supposed to be away for seven years to test the new propulsion system and the Grizotti cryogenic system. Only seven years."

"The 'official' records had been purged to hide that this ship *did* survive the last battle and *did* leave the solar system," Kay-Gee noted.

"Why do that?" Kyle blurted out, forgetting where he was.

"We're dealing with Marsco from over fifty years ago at this point. Can't really fathom why, but Security did it."

"So, what's that leave us with?"

"Your readings from the Moon, plus your initial ion readings from the *AAC* mission are as unique as a fingerprint repeated over and over. All are from the very same *Sirius*. Now, their message confirms it."

"So, they're coming back?" Devon was stunned. "They left our solar system and they're back," he murmured. "What a scientific feat!" Forgetting himself, he slapped his hands in triumph. "Imagine it. I've been to Jupiter, but they've gone through the Kuiper Belt beyond the Oort Cloud."

"Yes," Modena brought everyone back to the issue, "but don't forget the elephant in the room. They were on a seven-year mission. Not fifty-plus years. Out and back, not heading for another solar system, which is what they seemed to be doing before turning around."

"If we have this right by studying their trajectory before they reversed course," Serena explained, "they were heading for the Wolf system."

Kyle had paid attention during his colony habitation lectures; Wolf had the most likely exoplanet for habitable life. Liquid water. Earth-like atmosphere. Goldilocks Zone. Probability of life or conditions to support human life extremely high. His mind raced at all the possibilities. *Was it mutiny or piracy or just larceny, stealing a Marsco spaceship?*

"—but something happened. They reversed course and are heading home."

"And we have a problem with this?"

"No, *we* don't. *You* do!" Modena laughed slightly. "I'm ordering this mystery ship to dock at the VBC. I want you on Mars to ascertain what the hell is going on. I've a shuttle in lunar orbit waiting for you. You'll board from the Resnik Colony."

"Is there a potential issue with their return?"

"Not that I'm aware of, colonel, except that Marsco had a reason to hide this escape starting fifty-some years ago and I don't know why. And until I do—"

"You'll hide their return."

"Let's just say, with the Accords still unfolding, I want to bring this intel to the world in *a controlled fashion*. Not to mention that that ship might be highly radioactive. Plutonium is not exactly the most stable isotope. We don't want that craft anywhere near Earth or the Moon until the VBC gives its okay."

"We're guessing that might be why they had to return," Serena stated. "Fuel or engine problems."

"And where do you find a space port in an emergency out there?" Kay-Gee made the obligatory joke. "The universe is severely lacking a plethora of 'little green men' running service stations."

"But more to the point," Modena stated emphatically, "I don't want microbes from beyond the solar coming here. You know what happened to Earth during the pandemics of the twenty-first century. Plus, I don't know what *their* plans are. I only know Walter Miller is claiming to be on board that ship. At least his finger disks are there and still functioning."

"Miller?" Devon shook his head in sheer disbelief. "Miller? Someone from half a century ago."

"Affirmative. You'll have time to read his full and uncensored dossier before you reach Mars. All their dossiers. And you'll be on Mars in less than a month. Speed on your shuttle's so great, no need for icing. The planets are perfectly aligned. I want that returning crew treated with respect, of course, but escorted to Earth by you."

"Under arrest?" Kyle blurted.

"Essentially, yes, but more of a 'house arrest.'" Modena paused then reiterated, "Their ship, this *Sirius Odyssey II*, must remain orbiting Mars; is that clear?"

"Yes, sir," Devon answered before Kyle jumped in. "It was out of the Von Braun Center anyway; I suggest just leaving it in their charge."

"Fine. It's out of the question to risk that ship coming anywhere near the Earth. The VBC built her; let them decide how to safely decommission her."

Kyle's attention picked up whenever Von Braun was mentioned. The VBC housed the best examples of hydroponics in the whole network of Marsco colonies. Missing Sarah another several months was worth seeing those gardens. He'd communicate with her soon and let her know—if she cared enough to care.

"One last point," Modena added. "You two are now in total black. No one is to know anything about you except that you are alive and well. Serena will alert your next of kin to that fact. Only your next of kin. From you directly to anyone Earth-side—where you are, what you're doing—nothing. Total noncommunication status. You have just disappeared into the vacuum of space."

FOURTEEN

THE ASCENDANCY OF MARSCO

(Seattle HQ, August 2154)

"Have you read this?" vice-chair Chesney asked his shadowy assistant, Bobby-Tim Liddle.

He held up a pirated copy of *The Ascendancy of Marsco*, Walter Miller's compilation of stories, blogs, and statements about Marsco's rise to power nearly eighty-five years before.

Liddle gave a noiseless laugh then grinned his answer. "Well, yes, sir, I guess I've skimmed it. Nearly every man, boy, sid, and associate has by now, especially since the Net's opened after the Third Accord last year."

The pair sat overlooking Union Bay from a secluded balcony of the vice-chair's Bunker. A threat of thunder and rain hung in the air. Although north of the Bunker the Academy was on summer break, the rest of the HQ campus was its usual beehive of activity. Running a solar system was a 24/7 endeavor.

"I ask about the *Ascendancy*," Chesney went on, "because I've been thinking about the coincidence of it all. We have confirmation that our Rascal is the *Sirius Odyssey II*."

"Yes, my staff prepared your précis; you got it last week."

"Well, if Miller's on board, if he's healthy—"

"Oh, he's there and he's fine," Liddle interjected. "I've sent along all the status reports the VBC has about the condition of the ship and her crew. The med report for their pilot, Ling Shanghai, describes her condition. The ship's iceman put her into hibernation to stop any disease from spreading. Our folks here, reading her vitals, think she has severe and irreversible spleen damage, by infection or cancer, they can't tell yet."

"Now, when you say *irreversible*, you aren't implying that regeneration will not work, right?" Chesney tapped his chest above his successfully restored youthful heart.

"That's correct, with the proper techniques, her spleen can be restored. She can be brought back to full health. That is to say, such is *my* assessment. I'm not a physician."

"Well," the vice-chair stated, "keep that point in the back of your mind." He drew a thoughtful breath over his slanting grimace. "But, it's Miller I'm most concerned with at this moment."

"How so?"

"Open Net! Who's reading his *Ascendancy*?"

"Potentially, tens of millions, why?"

"And you're one of those millions," Chesney concluded, one corner of his mouth dropping lower, a sure sign he was pleased.

"Well, a part of one. My staff read it cover to cover. I glanced at their précis."

"Exactly. Then their conclusions are the ones you and I know."

Practically all I know, Liddle snidely noted, because he hadn't bothered to read anything directly in years. *Hey*, he concluded, *works for Oakes, and he's the boss.*

"What conclusion specifically did you have in mind, sir?"

Chesney paused his calculating once more. It took a moment for him to reach for the right words. "Miller stresses throughout his work that many associates *supported* Marsco before the C-Wars because *it* was the honorable alternative to the Continental Powers."

"I remember some mention of this in the summary."

"Well, what if he keeps speaking like that?"

"Like what?"

"Keeps speaking about this 'good Marsco' as an alternative to those old, dark, bullying Powers."

"The Powers are long gone, sir."

"Exactly! But glance at a map, Bobby-Tim, *a map*! The feds don't look all that different from the old Continental Powers. And I'm sure Rhores' PR machine can generate loads of Net chatter about this ethereal but worrisome similarity between 'the new feds' and the 'old, dark, bullying Powers,' if you catch."

Liddle's reptilian mind lit up. "Of course—prepare the public for the Accords being *suspended* because Marsco has always stood up against the horrendous factions that originally created the unincorporated zones, created the system of Disenfranchisement, created the world's lingering caste classification of PRIMS."

"Exactly! If we have the right sort of trouble—"

"—I've a report on that, sir—"

Chesney waved him off so he could finish his scheming, "*If* we have the right trouble that's just so, and *if* we can verify in Miller's very own words that the C-Powers were horrific and the source of all the world's troubles, then both the *new* troubles and Miller's view of the *old* troubles will assist us in pushing back the Accords. Millions will flock to Marsco—"

"—as they did in the '60s before the C-Wars."

"Exactly! Think of it, Liddle. Think of the ironic source of support *for* Marsco. Its chief critic. A man who tried, who risked not only his life but his daughter's life, his son-in-law's life, a man who risked everything to escape from the Marsco world; he's now its chief supporter. *Our* chief supporter."

"Sir, pardon me for being a fly in the ointment, but how do we win over Miller?"

"Every man has his price," Chesney retorted. He paused, watching Liddle's scheming mind churn before continuing. "And his price is—"

"I think I know, sir."

Not used to waiting, Chesney asked, "And?"

"Fame, sir."

The VC raised an eyebrow, confused but intrigued at the same time. His slanting grimace didn't change.

"*Fame!*" Liddle began explaining. "We've won over several officers to black-disk status because we've offered them power. I suspect that Miller's one of these perverse idealists who disdains power and all its trappings."

"Thank God not everyone wants it."

"Exactly, sir," Liddle sneered then went back to his central point. "But with Miller, he may have a weakness for fame. Imagine if the whole world wants to see him? Why write a book if you don't want fame? Imagine if we generate—and Rhores is the man for that—a sensation in Miller? 'Leader of an intrepid band of space explorers!' 'Thought long dead!' 'Returning safely from the void!' 'Visionary writer!'"

"And this'll work?"

"Fame is a close cousin to power, sir. And look at what we've achieved offering power and longevity to hundreds."

"Yes, the Black Brigade units are multiplying in size and scope." Chesney drummed his right array of finger disks on the mahogany arm of his deck chair. Looking across the bay at a horizon where a bridge once stood, he peered off toward Lake Marsco. "But suppose he won't cooperate? Isn't interested at all?" Chesney drew a breath. "He might just be one of those perverse types who truly believes in his own idealism."

Liddle grinned, "I think Rhores can create a sensation for the man and his mission *without* the good engineer's cooperation. We just need his face, his person on Earth, and a few carefully chosen passages from the *Ascendancy*." He reached across a table for the printed-off copy of Miller's tome and randomly flipped through it. "We have his words already, words we can use. Why risk him saying something we *don't* want to hear, words that we *don't* want others to hear? We'll just rely on what he's put in print, slanted for our benefit of course; that'll be enough."

"Cherry-picking. Worked with the Bible and the Koran and the Constitution for years."

<hr>

Adrian Lasher, MD, came as directed to a small dinner party at the Bunker. His chief researcher—and spouse—Penelope Kate Elion, PhD, came as well, because the invitation stated that Chesney was hosting an informal gathering of physicians and researchers to keep him abreast of the cutting edge of Marsco medicine. Both guests were suspicious.

Doctor Lasher was young looking, a wunderkind in the medical world. His hands guiding Marsco med-tech were famous. But, Doctor Elion's theories and practices in recombinant DNA regeneration techniques were second to none. Her applications, surgically put in place by her husband, Doctor Lasher, had reconstructed many a lost limb. Together they'd regrown and transplanted many an internal organ. And if tops in Marsco, then this medical couple were tops in the whole solar system. Even so, they carried themselves without any haughtiness or egotism. It never bothered the surgeon, Lasher, that in many ways, he was subordinate to the researcher and theoretician, Elion, as though he were her chief assistant. Their patients were their prime concern. Fame and its rewards were always a distant second.

Both were from associate stock but knew the limits of Seattle's reach as well as of science. They were dedicated practitioners who planned to steer through the murky waters and uncharted Marsco shoals that evening without incident or issue. And with the final Accords and their looming changes, the dedicated pair were biding their time until a state-of-the-art federation facility beckoned.

"Who else is coming?" Penelope asked under her breath as she and Adrian stood waiting to clear security outside the Bunker.

"Don't know," her husband whispered.

"Is Doctor Johns?"

"Possibly. Would make sense. Don't know," he answered a second time.

"Well, *do not* argue with him!" she cautioned as pointedly as she could in a whisper. "Not *here*, for heaven's sake! The VP thinks Johns walks on water."

"And pisses bubbling champagne," he smirked.

"Not here, dear." She smiled, loving the man for his sense of humor but worried about his self-control. *Pick your own battlefields*, she willed him.

"Besides," he went on, serious now, "it's the other way."

"What?"

"Johns thinks Chesney is the water-walker. Johns thinks he himself invented water." Penelope knew that these sorts of quips were exactly what would get them both in deep trouble, avoidable trouble.

The social gathering was indeed small. Just Chesney and Liddle joined by their spouses, plus Johns with his. Given the nature of the event, the more intimate dining room in the Bunker was decked out for them. The eight sat at the V-shaped table and thus all faced the waters of the Bay. Lasher and Elion thought such a social event should have been held at the vice-chair's residence, not his Bunker, ground zero of solar system control. They were tense, on guard.

The meal was served late in the evening. The lake before them glimmered with the setting sun. As it grew later, the sky and water darkened. With the deepening twilight, the shining lights of Seattle City Center stood out, the high-rises to the south standing tall and proud, ablaze with Marsco prosperity. Before them was the most flourishing locale on Earth with HQ ensconced there. The towers of steel and glass skyline, the restored Needle, the packed Herriff-Grid, they all proclaimed the majesty of Marsco.

For all this to function, Lasher and Elion both knew that many tentacles of power had to spread out from Chesney's Bunker.

Nothing untoward was spoken as they ate. The conversation stayed on safe subjects: the weather; vacations with children taken on the Moon; congratulations to Penelope, the newest mother, on the couple's second child; an obligatory reference to Oakes and his busy schedule, which had kept him from joining this friendly party.

"Would be an honor to meet him," Penelope stated sincerely. She wanted to add that she looked forward to raising their daughters as feds. Her federalist leanings were no secret. *Silence is my best defense right now*, she cautioned herself.

"Indeed," Chesney insisted, returning to Oakes, "a great man. Such unchanging—some would say, inflexible—leadership now in these times of *trouble*—or should I say, *transition*."

Liddle covered the gaffe with a low, "Hear! Hear!"

After their meal, the vice-chair rose to announce, "We'll have coffee and dessert on the deck. It's cool but out of any chilly wind."

As if on cue, his wife also announced in a shrill voice, "Come, my dears, I must show you a greenhouse I'm tending—so the men can talk—flowers and shrubs from around the world even here just outside the Bunker. Our dessert awaits us there."

Penelope shot Adrian a cautionary glance. He understood—by rights she should stay and he should go, if great minds were conversing. She was the prime mover in their scientific success. Willing his compliance and silence, she left the men knowing her husband's federalist mindset didn't need to shine forth. *Not here. Not now.* Tonight was a time to smile and nod and be silently crafty.

After a sip of coffee, Chesney asked politely, "So, Doctor Lasher, I understand from Johns here you are the leader in regeneration science for Marsco."

"I'm flattered, Mr. Chesney, for such a compliment, but Penelope and I work as a team, and I'm a cut and sew man really—"

"Ah, yes, Penelope. Also, a physician?"

"No, Penelope heads the research arm." He caught himself. "Pardon the unintentional pun." Her team and her lab grew what he merely transplanted. His hands running medical instruments—he rarely directly touched an actual scalpel—grafted or implanted what Penelope had grown and made ready for transfer to the patient.

"Is that difficult?" The vice-chair gave an embarrassed guffaw, "I mean, working so closely with a spouse, and at times you have to be the boss!"

The doctor laughed, knowing something was coming, but the chuckling hid his wariness. "I'm the boss only in the surgical theater. And I know when *not* to be boss—that's clear."

Liddle and Johns hung back, listening, but did not join in. Both thoroughly enjoyed the master taking on an idealistic knight errant who famously tilted so many windmills.

"Let me ask, hypothetically of course—"

"Of course."

"How difficult is it to restore an organ?"

"As, for instance, *a heart*?" Penelope had warned Adrian not to take the bait, but he disregarded her warning.

"Well, yes, or a spleen," Chesney said. "Yes, let's specifically speak of a spleen."

"As you wish, sir. I shouldn't speak for Dr. Elion, but it's as easy and as difficult as the patient's health makes it." Knowing he was speaking to a nonmedical man, Lasher made his remarks as vague and nontechnical as possible. "Of course, in a pinch, a patient can live without a spleen. Not so a heart. A human, beating heart, though we have plenty examples of metaphorical heartless humans."

He paused for effect and to mentally ask for forgiveness from his absent spouse. He was crossing a stopline here.

"If the patient's overall health is strong," the surgeon went on, "but the spleen is totally shot, then the process is complicated but not that much riskier. The spleen will be regrown in situ but more slowly since it has to essentially replace all the diseased and dead tissue." He drew a thoughtful breath, "Penelope can explain what tissue and graft additions she grows before I do my 'cut and paste.' I'm just the hands, really. She's the brains."

"I see."

"Now, if the spleen is partly damaged," Lasher continued, "but the rest of the body is unhealthy, all sorts of perils await. Our bodies are still pretty prickly about mucking with it. Complications abound. Slow regrowth with the overall lack of the body's ability to sustain this process, the possibility that secondary conditions may worsen as the spleen transforms. We're not debugging a computer here—we're tinkering with a human body, re-forming living tissue within a patient who is obviously so sick a vital organ is not functioning normally."

"Of course," Chesney added. He sipped his coffee for a moment, then began once more. "Now let me see, Doctor Johns here, he is experimenting with a process that may move beyond your regeneration—"

Lasher took the bait readily. This confrontation had been brewing for several years. "If his published results bear the scrutiny of his peers, Johns here is suggesting a method of not just regenerating a particular organ or a particular limb—yes, I've helped patients with lost limbs—but he is suggesting a self-perpetuating system of constant regeneration of *all* tissue."

Drawn into the conversation for the first time, Johns defended, "That's exactly what my papers show."

"Of course, doctor, your 'papers' are summaries of your work, descriptions of your work, not essays with data and longitudinal studies." Lasher was famous for his pauses for effect. "Not results anyone can follow or scientifically judge."

"I suppose you want me to publish in journals such as you and your wife use? These new fed journals."

"Yes, that's what I am suggesting. Peer review. A method that worked in the scientific and medical world for centuries. *Lancet* is publishing again after a hundred-year hiatus. As fine a journal as ever. Why not publish there? And the *New England Journal*."

"You trust these feds?"

"I believe with the Accords coming on, that's exactly what we are all expected to do, trust these feds."

"Well, perhaps the fed medical world is not ready for my processes and breakthroughs."

Looking squarely at Johns, Lasher pointedly continued, "*Sustainability*, I believe that's what you're calling this process, doctor, isn't that so?"

Johns nodded. "Yes, quite right. It's no secret, at least in the Marsco medical community." He knew he needed to shift focus and commence his attack, for attack was what he fully intended to do. "I believe that moving beyond your wife's established methods is only the next logical step. May I say, a step any scientist would want to take? Science is always about advancement."

Lasher bit his tongue, knowing a setup when he saw one. *Science* could advance as far as it liked, but *ethics* put limits on certain advancements. Penelope had recently had their second child. Would it have been right for them to Franken-select the exact child they wanted? Science in the disks of those like Johns allowed them to do so, while ethics allowed for only the roll of the dice. And they had a healthy, happy child in the natural way life had come to parents throughout all the past millennia.

"You know, of course, gentlemen," Lasher began, clearly noting that Marsco leadership of late tilted more and more toward a skewed, old-style gentlemen's club. Not a good sign for the future. "Doctor Elion, Penelope, should be the one here to discuss this. I sew, but she first regenerates what I sew in place."

"Yes, certainly, but obviously you can speak to this topic," said Chesney.

"I believe, Dr. Johns," Lasher continued, arguing clearly to a fellow medical practitioner, but to no one else at the table, "in your initial report to the board, you used an analogy of hibernation and cryogenic stasis. You said that hibernation is a six-month deep sleep. Cryo, on the other hand, is an actual process to freeze—thus suspend—all bodily function. In cryo-stasis, a patient is down—safely, now, remember that—is down indefinitely. I believe the record for Marsco is two years."

Liddle jumped in, adding the trivial note, "On the *Armstrong* mission, some crew members were down two years, seven months, and twelve days."

Lasher smiled. "But, isn't it a false analogy, a weak comparison for logic's sake but not really illustrative at all? You're merely relating time or duration. I'm comparing intent. The *intent* of hibernation and of cryo-stasis is the same: both safely allow crews to move through space without aging. My regeneration process allows for someone to regain health but live a normal life, a normal *lifespan* if you will."

"So, your patients don't live longer?" Johns interjected.

"They may live longer, perhaps, if what I replace is vital. Your spleen analogy, yes, they'll live longer with a healthy spleen and not a diseased one, because of their restored health via a regrown organ. However, the extension of life for the sake of extending life is not my object."

"I believe," Johns defended, "we're merely arguing semantics. If my process extends life longer than your process, what are we arguing?"

"*Intention*, doctor, as I said. I promise restored health by a focused change in the condition of my patient. Diseased spleen? We restore that spleen when possible. Weakened lungs, we keep them breathing easier, steadier. You seem to be promising longevity beyond natural boundaries and limits by using something like Penelope's practices to extend the life of *all* tissue indefinitely."

Doctor Johns listened without an emotion crossing his chiseled face. Seeing that, Lasher commented, trying to cut off the rising tension, "Well, I guess at heart, we're all treating patients as best we can." The banality of his remark ended their exchange. With that, the younger physician fell silent. His comments had already done great harm to his standing in Marsco, and he knew it.

A prearranged text exchange took place between Penelope and Adrian; their child needed attending, a bogus signal designed to get them out of this hotbed locale with limited exposure. "She's with my mother," Penelope explained, re-entering the Bunker, "and she's a trained nurse. But young ones won't settle down without their own mom."

With a round of good nights and thanks for the privilege of dining with the vice-chair, an honor to say the least, the couple was off. The Security escorts took them by hover platform to the HFC compound where they had left their four-seater.

———— • ————

For the remainder of the guests at the Bunker, the night was still young. Johns immediately began speaking with Chesney. "And you're feeling fine, sir? You look the perfection of health."

"Yes, fine. I feel like a new man."

Physician and patient gave a sly laugh. In so many ways, Chesney *was* a new man.

"I'd still like another diagnostic round of tests, just to make sure you're free of all nanobots and are stable after your transition."

"Of course, whenever you wish," the vice-chair readily agreed. But his own health was not what he wished to discuss. "Now, Lasher, he seems reluctant to assist you in any way. Is that a fair assessment?"

"Well, first, I hardly need his assistance," Johns retorted in a flat tone. "Before a patient comes to me, they need to be in peak health. Someone like a Lasher may have performed some tiding up of a patient, health-wise, some focused and pointed clinical restorations—"

"What he called *regeneration*."

"Exactly. As with yourself, restore the heart, then start the sustainability process with me. They are two totally separate procedures, except success for mine is incumbent upon success with the first. The better your health before sustainability, the better after."

Liddle had joined the pair at this moment and asked, "So, they're separate processes, but you can do regeneration without sustainability but not the other way around, right?"

"If I am to create sustainability in someone not fully healthy, yes," answered Johns, keeping the frustration from his face at having to answer such an elementary question. He hated dealing with those who didn't have a mind as quick as his. He felt like he was giving a lecture of the makeup of the stratosphere and having a plebe tell him water vapor is mostly really only H_2O. "However, I think Lasher fails to grasp, is totally blind to, the full potential of my sustainability."

"Marsco's Sustainability Project," Liddle corrected, softly but to the point.

"Why's that, do you think?" Chesney asked, ignoring the schoolboy tensions between the two other men.

Turning to the vice-chair, Johns' face lit up. When in *his* presence, the physician never felt anything but the rewarding sense of basking contentedly in strong sunlight. "Lasher is a realist. And worse yet, also an idealist who sees a limit to science."

"You mean the end of knowledge? That somehow humankind will reach a point where we cannot learn a speck more? That we have already fathomed absolutely everything there is?"

"Hardly that, sir. No, Lasher sees an ethical end to things. Has a distorted view that science has to reach an end simply because as humans, we cannot cross certain stoplines." Johns snorted. "Of course, these lines are his own personal and arbitrary ones, drawn here and there along old-regime fissures of no consequence."

Liddle nodded in agreement. His gut feeling about Lasher was the same, and his gut was never wrong. "Arrogant, too. With his perky wife teammate, that self-assured cockiness of a wunderkind."

"Oh, they're tops in that class, all right. For regeneration, none better."

"But, he fears sustainability, *your* sustainability process," Chesney commented. "Why do you think?"

"Professional jealousy, I'm sure." Johns drew a deep breath. "If I wasn't making waves in the recombinant DNA world, she would be. I've replaced her on her climb to the top of Marsco med science. Quite a steep hill. As Herriff was to the propulsion system, I am to DNA enhancement tech. My process outdoes theirs by far."

Liddle added, "Then the Millers came up with their plutonium system that outclassed anything Herriff ever did." No one paid any attention.

Confidently, the physician concluded, "Future generations will point to *me* as a gatekeeper who let science pass over to a new realm, an exciting realm. What Lasher and spouse do may impact medical treatments. What they're doing is stunning in its own small way; I'll give him that. But my process impacts humankind! We need no longer fear death! Think of that!"

Chesney did think of that. As did Liddle. Thousands of Immortals now existed. And the process was proprietary, an exclusive Marsco procedure much like disk implants at first many years ago. Chesney could authorize immortality as he chose. His godlike power didn't go unnoticed by himself or others.

And the key to reaching immortality, to receiving sustainability treatments, was not *regeneration*; the key was *loyalty*. And Marsco prided itself in its steadfast, dedicated associates. It thrived on fidelity to its dreams. Loyalty brought immortality. A simple equation, like $E = MC^2$.

Chesney drew a breath. And in his vision for Marsco, the Accords did not fit one byte.

An hour after their wives and Dr. Johns left, Chesney and Liddle were still at the Bunker. The VC had requested a follow-up report on some troubles to the south near Sac City.

Sitting in Chesney's private office, the pair scanned a Security summary.

"Interesting that the village is called 'Millersville,'" Liddle noted. "Any connection, do you think?"

"I shouldn't have to speculate. Get your staff on that. If named for whom we hope, that'll merely add weight to our raising him upwards."

"Yes, sir, on it!" He twitched himself a note on a small pad.

Chesney continued skimming the report and twitched over to a video summary of the damage. On a screen, he saw the smoking ruins of PRIM houses, some permanent, some temporary, set up in hopes of eventually building a solid dwelling later. The smoldering village, only three blocks long, was hardly arresting in its scope and carnage. Too few burnt structures, too few dead. Only sixty-odd PRIMS.

He twitched to the ramshackle granges. Before and after ops assessment showed the PRIM spreads not particularly noteworthy, "especially when compared to the two largest granges in the area: New Grange owned by Trent Brunel and a spread owned by Lionel Richardson," the Security report concluded.

Liddle snorted. "Rhores will have to work overtime to whip these attacks into something threatening the Accords. These are more like local rampages, not something threatening a whole sid."

"Well, let's stay politically accurate here—so as not to tip our disks—a new *federation*. This former subsidiary is now technically an independent federation. But you're right, local police action here. A few arrests of a gang of thugs. I imagine that if this were the old days, a few Auxxies, probably with non-leths, would soon have this under control."

The vice-chair rose from his desk and paced his large office. When the blueprints had been laid out for this Bunker, he had secretly measured the chair's office up at the massive HQ complex that sat in the public area of the campus. His office here was half a meter larger in width and length than the chair's. Moreover, it was much larger than his rarely used office at the HQ complex, an office he frequented on occasion just to be visible to the chair's inner staff. Jealousy kept the two staffs from working perfectly together, even if both Oakes and Chesney were openly devoted to erasing that tension.

A heavy shower pounded down soon midnight. The lowering clouds and sheets of rain made it impossible to see much from the solitary office window until a flash of lightning cut the sky. After a deep, silent contemplation, Chesney remarked to his only listener, "No, Bobby-Tim, we need a sensational upheaval. We need something brazen, bold, stunning in its ramification. A few PRIMS acting up in a subsidiary? Can't imagine all the old biases and longstanding fears and deep hatreds of PRIMS will evaporate overnight. A few federations in total turmoil *should* do the trick. Chaos works *for* us. There remains inherent, entrenched distrust of PRIMS out in our world. I'm sure most feds now harbor the same feelings for PRIMS they had just three, four years ago."

"Yes, sir. The changeover from PRIM status—removal of PRIM-disks, for instance—that all falls to fed administrators anyway. And, I've seen nothing on my screen to suggest these new independent feds are busting butt to get all that done." He paused as though rethinking his own assertion. "Well, I guess in the new Euro feds, yes, there, plenty is being done to eradicate PRIM status for the most part."

"So I've heard," Chesney concurred. "And on this continent, the midsection fed and the eastern seaboard fed—yes, PRIMS are gone. Places north of here. Absorbed in with little notice or effort. West Con is taking the lead, as usual. The South Fed—I can understand—a bit more reluctance."

"It's their tradition, after all. Being that slow."

"Certainly. They already knew how to keep pre-PRIMS in their place. It was their honored tradition, stepping on PRIMS."

Liddle looked at the timepiece behind the VC's desk. "Anything I can do to speed this along?"

"Speed? We need roadblocks," Chesney chortled, "but, no, nothing tonight."

"Well, I'll put it on my to-do list. 'Come up with a revolution.' How's that sound?"

"Fine." A smirk replaced the usual grimace that hung on Chesney's face. "Find me a nutcase, a paper tiger who wants to declare himself 'Messiah of the Solar System' and we're in business. The nuttier, the better. Easier to make sound-bites at first when he snarls and then easy to dispose of him and his ilk later."

"After we've gotten what we need from his messianic clamoring."

"Certainly," Chesney noted. "A disposable threat!"

"Just one?"

"That's all Mr. Oakes will need."

FIFTEEN

THE OLD IS NEW

(The Von Braun Center, Mars, October 2154)

"I'm afraid you are all under arrest," Major Gunnar Sturtevant informed the three members of the *Sirius Odyssey II* crew as they stepped through an airlock and onto a docked Security lander.

Safely orbiting Mars, the *Sirius* was tethered at the same platform where she had been first built. Their cover story, a seven-year shakedown cruise, no longer seemed plausible. The ship had been away more than fifty years. Arrest wasn't that surprising.

The Security officer stood as tall as Miller but with a ramrod for a backbone. His gloved hands suggested that both had extensive disk implants. He spoke with a slight Euro accent, but even back in the Marsco world of the late twenty-first century—the century the *Sirius* crew knew best—he did not seem out of place. Taking a close professional look, the returning hiberman concluded Sturtevant had some icing-delay in his aging. He looked late forties but was probably mid-fifties, old enough to be steeped in Marsco Security.

Miller took charge. He wore the most professional-looking outfit from his era, a blue blazer with a VBC patch on the left pocket. But he wore no gloves so that his lefter status was clearly visible.

Expecting some sort of hassle, the two other returnees—Shanghai was still iced—had dressed in their finest uniforms with prominent badges of rank. Lieutenant Anthony Grizotti stood in a MAS uniform with a VBC shoulder patch as befitted his last standing before leaving Mars. Captain Tessa Miller's uniform hid the secret she wanted confirmed before she told her husband. In her early stages of what she was sure was a normal pregnancy, her dress reds still fit her slim frame.

"Excuse me, Major," Miller asked, "but arrested for what?"

Because the charges against the *Sirius* crew were so extraordinary, the Mars-based security officer checked his pad to make sure he stated them correctly. "For one, you're utilizing a craft that cannot be serviced in space by a Marsco colony or docking port. Disregarding 'Twelve Thrusters' regs is a serious offense," the officer stated grimly. He'd never seen any of those regulations enforced; certainly, not this far out into the solar system. A few violations closer to Earth, maybe, but not here at the Red Planet. No spaceship in violation could actually *get* this far. "Plus," he went on, "it seems your fuel is 'nonregulation.'"

Zot was beside himself. "Non-reg? Dammit, the *Sirius* is an experimental craft designed and built right here. And we are at the Von Braun docking platform as we speak, the very station that fueled us to begin with."

"Affirmative, Captain Grizotti," came the reply, "but you are still in violation. And, you don't have a permit for that craft. Section 12B-104c mandates a variance clearance and prior approval to utilize any nonstandard craft within the belt ring."

"Major, we've been away fifty-plus years—" Zot pointed to a viewport facing the eternal blackness beyond Mars "—beyond our own solar system, and we still have a full tank of gas."

Tessa pulled Zot aside while Walter asked the bothersome officer, "What are our rights here?"

"Putting us in the slammer?" the iceman sneered.

"Security hardly needs to incarcerate you here," the major replied.

"Zot, back off," Tessa whispered. "Walter's got this. You're only making things worse."

"Major Sturtevant's making things worse," he whispered back. Then to his captor, he asked, "What's it to be? Bread and water? Solitary?"

"Very funny," Tessa hissed at him under her breath, not pleased with him or the major.

Miller cut to the important matters. "Look, one of our crewmembers is extremely sick. I don't care about us. Please get her to a hospital."

"We've had your messages. Help is standing by." The Martian officer nodded to a med team which immediately entered the *Sirius*.

"She's still in hiber," Zot reported in a neutral tone. "That was the safest way to control any infection."

"Fine. We've monitored Captain Shanghai since your first communications with us."

"Excellent," Zot answered cordially as though he hadn't been so abrasive only moments earlier. "May I accompany her? I can explain my methodology. Icing protocols have undoubtedly changed over the past fifty years."

"Certainly, Captain. And your *detention*, shall we say, is *house arrest*. You'll have the run of the VBC once we're on planet; just do not utilize any dirigibles, hovercraft, or surface suits."

"'Bubbled,'" Zot replied. They were to be kept in this pressurized locale and not allowed beyond the safety of colony life support.

"Exactly, although you'll find the Center much larger than when you left. Quite pleasant even if not Earth. It nearly doubled in size once Steerforth succeeded Herriff as director."

"Still in charge?" Miller asked, losing track of the intervening decades.

"No, retired more than thirty years ago. Passed away while living on Earth in '44."

"Well, I'd like to meet the current director. And I'm sure the Center will be interested in the reports from our trek."

"Director Yang-Murray does wish to meet with you once you're all settled."

As the lander pulled away from the docking platform, the three returning voyagers examined the planet below. They were on the night side at present, descending toward *Valles Marineris*. Hundreds of points of lights sparkled on the surface, each one a dome, each one a sign of human life spreading out just below the lifeless surface.

"More domes than before," Tessa stated to her father, shifting her face away from a viewport.

"Scores more," Miller replied at his own port. "Nothing existed on the *Utopia Planitia* before or the *Elysium Planitia*." He pointed down at the surface to locales presently in nighttime darkness. These dusty plains sat 180° from the *Valles Marineris*, home of the VBC. "Each locale now has half a dozen colonies at least."

"Just judging by the traffic," Zot added from the opposite side of the cabin, "the overall population's up." Landers rose from the dark side to join orbiting platforms where MAS shuttles prepared to leave either for Earth or the belt. Mining asteroids streaked toward smelter colonies; each shard left a hesitant trail of light and smoke due to the planet's low gee and minuscule atmospheric oxygen content.

"Well, fifty years." Tessa sighed philosophically. "Much can happen."

<hr />

Doctor Jenna Yang-Murray extended her hand to Walter. "This is a miracle. A lost ship—and so famous a ship—returning with most of her crew safe." The two met alone in the VIP suite, accommodations that had four bedrooms, along with plenty of work space and a galley kitchen even though they would be taking their meals with the senior staff at the Center's exec mess.

"Where are the rest?" Yang-Murray asked. She'd come directly from her office after a tense conversation with Seattle.

"My daughter is having her postflight physical. She was feeling nauseous, and Zot wanted her checked right way. Zot and I are up tomorrow morning."

"She's in the hands of some of the best physicians we have, thus the best on planet."

"Zot is with Captain Shanghai as the icing staff prepares to bring her out of hibernation."

"She's stable and all's under control," Zot stated, entering even as Yang-Murray was still standing in the entranceway to their suite. "She'll be coming out of ice in the morning."

"Captain Grizotti, I am sure," the director stated, taking his hand, creating a slight tingle, disk-to-disk. Just as Major Sturtevant had, Doctor Yang-Murray seemed to have given Zot a promotion. Like Miller, the iceman was still bewildered with the five decades of changes around him, but he liked this newly designated promotion, if true.

"Your chief hibernation officer has asked me to assist," he said.

"How is she?" Miller asked.

"Her illness seems to be confined to her spleen and not her kidneys as

I thought, but the whole process is affecting her eyes, too. Or so monitors say. Common enough in icing and generally not serious."

Overwhelmed by this historic moment, Yang-Murray gave a pleased sigh. She ushered her guests toward their sitting room, which had a basket of hothouse fruit and bottles of Earth water waiting for them. A touch of hospitality from Jenna. "I have to say," she began, proud of her Center, "that this is an event I thought could never happen. You four returning safely. The VBC could only be more elated if Doctor Herriff were here along with you. I'm sure you don't realize how important all of you are to Marsco."

"How so?" Walter asked, verging on naïveté, tasting the best water he'd had since leaving Earth.

"You have," she nodded at Miller, "a whole research wing named after you here. My husband's workstation is there. Herriff shall never be forgotten, but neither shall *your* contributions be overlooked. You know, your theories for improved performance of chemical engines are the basis of design that propels our shuttles today."

Miller had no idea.

Yang-Murray turned to Zot. "I'm afraid to say, hibernation is nearly a thing of the past, Captain Grizotti, but your cryo-stasis makes sure our crews can move safely when iced. Only during periods of planetary conjunction do shuttles use cryo between the Earth and Mars. Or when a trek to an asteroid colony dictates it."

"Why cryo and not hiber?" the iceman asked. "Cryo is so complicated."

"It's as easy to utilize now as hiber was in your day," she explained. "Steerforth made sure of that."

"And still, I presume, very little cryo is actually needed."

"Affirmative. That's due to the speed of a crossing, all those faster propulsion units." She nodded toward Miller. "But another Jupiter expedition is planned for 2157, in about three years if there are no more delays. Cryo-stasis will be part of that." Jenna then added about Tessa, "You should know that the absent Doctor Miller has a wing of the engineering building named for her at the Academy. The plaque will need to be changed. It does give the date of, well, her alleged passing."

"'Reports of our deaths,'" Zot shot cynically.

Dumbfounded by these changes, Miller noted, "'Alleged death' does take your breath away."

"Well," the VBC director explained, "much to comprehend. And I do admit Security was a bit heavy-handed today. After your physicals and some time to rest, I'll start the process of bringing you into the mid-twenty-second century."

"Anything pressing we should know immediately?" Miller asked. "Need to know?"

"I think the biggest change is in Marsco itself, if you haven't noticed."

Zot provided his customary smirk. "As a man under arrest, I'd say first off, it doesn't seem *that* changed."

Jenna smiled patiently. "Well, Captain, I'm afraid that's where you're wrong. Let's start with a quick overview of the Six Accords, shall we?"

<hr />

The following morning, the deicing ward was empty except for one patient, Shanghai, who was still hibering but stable. The vital sign screens around her looked far different from those of the icing bay on board the *Sirius*. Zot needed to ask a technician a few questions about the schematics and commands to understand this enhanced system; that much had changed in the past half a century. But, the principles were all the same, so Zot soon felt comfortable, competent. Miller was pleased at the skills of his son-in-law. "Knows his stuff," he confided to a technician. "No one can have more experience with cryo than Zot, that's for sure."

"She'll be fine. Captain Grizotti treated her correctly even if his diagnosis was inaccurate. Icing was the best course."

A nurse entered to adjust the insensible patient's warming cycle. "She'll start to have more color presently," she reported.

When the nurse stepped out of the ward with the iceman, Miller felt all he could do was hold Mei-Ling's hand, her left, because the other arm held a blood pressure monitor, a body-core thermometer probe, and an IV shunt. Alone, the engineer sat silently by the pilot until Zot re-entered the room.

"You know," Miller whispered "I don't know her whole and true history, but I wish her health. I've always suspected she was running from her past."

Zot didn't react.

"But, she deserves a future in this new world. Not in the Wolf system but back here. A future as open-ended and hope-filled as yours with Tessa."

Zot remained silent but wished the pilot the same.

As Shanghai's color started returning, her visitors were ushered away so the medical team could do its work. In the dim ward, nurses and doctors came and went. The staff was concerned about eye damage if their patient woke in too bright an environment.

Interns and cryo-stasis trainees asked to examine her because it was so rare to see someone who had undergone so much deep icing as well as her current hibernation. The doctor in charge reluctantly gave permission to a small group of personnel.

The still-sleeping woman didn't react to all the activity, the notoriety, around her. Although her face was showing signs of healthy color, an infection still coursed through her. It was going to be three days before she was fully awake and weeks after that for a full recovery, if at all.

That afternoon, Tessa was called back for a follow-up consultation with the chief physician, Claire Ross. She showed Tessa a viewing pad with all her test results. "Need help deciphering the med talk?"

"Some, I guess."

The doctor began a summary. Tessa's lab workup showed normal results, blood pressure, and internal organs all within routine range, the physician explained after a cursory glance at the data. "For someone born over ninety years ago, not bad."

"Hiber and then cryo help extend life."

"General equivalency age: 33.8." She looked her patient up and down. "You're fine, as healthy as anyone I've seen post-cryo."

"Thanks," she smiled.

"I ordered your ultrasound to check on an abnormality," she added softly. "You're definitely pregnant. But you're not surprised about that, are you?"

"I've suspected but couldn't check conclusively. Never suspected an 'abnormality.' That sounds ominous."

"I only use 'abnormality,' in the sense of 'very unusual,'" the physician explained. Doctor Ross had rarely hibernated, but like Tessa, she had those qualities that made older women look ageless—freckles, sandy straight hair, deep blue eyes. With most patients, to cover her youthful appearance, she maintained a firm professional demeanor that bordered on aloofness. The astro-OB-GYN had a child of her own, born here on Mars. Physician and patient quickly dispensed with formality. They were mother and mother-to-be with an unusual pregnancy to deal with. She smiled with Tessa to celebrate the great news. Kindred spirits.

"No, I'm not surprised," Tessa beamed. "I've suspected for weeks but haven't been able to confirm it."

"By *weeks* you mean?"

"Weeks while awake and not in cryo. My husband, our ship's iceman, wanted me to go under hiber like Shanghai for the last several weeks, because of my morning sickness, which he thought was a viral infection. I refused, unsure if it would be safer for our baby."

"So, he didn't suspect anything?"

"No. He's normally pretty astute, but we were running a touchy ion engine and trying to decide what to do next. The ongoing hot mess on the flight deck didn't help. Plus, he had to reboot our communications computer and deal with Captain Shanghai. He'd have figured it out quickly enough, given the chance."

"And you never gave him the chance, never let on."

"No. A wife's prerogative." She smiled.

"I see. Bart, my husband, can be like that when I sway him." She gave a rare non-professional smile, then back to business. "So, you weren't showing signs prior to your last hiber?"

"I had my suspicions, but at first I thought cryo may have just goofed up my cycle. It seemed to have Mei-Ling's, too, but for different reasons. I've made a note in our after-flight report to include PG test packs in the med stores of any future cryo adventures."

"Does Anthony know now?" she asked after looking at her chart. She hadn't met Zot yet.

"No. I wanted confirmation and a sense of how healthy *he* is."

"Your husband's results are in. He's perfectly fine, as is your father."

"No, *he* is *he*!" Tessa wrapped her arms maternally around her still-flat belly. "I've known I was carrying him, and I've known he's a he!"

"Take a deep breath," Claire stated in a detached manner that suggested a heavy blow was to come. She opened the file of Tessa's ultrasound, which the engineer hadn't yet seen.

Tessa didn't argue. "I'm very tired," she said, "but with pregnancy, that's to be expected, right?"

Her doctor nodded, adjusting the image.

"And I'd love some crackers," Tessa chattered nervously. "I feel much better nibbling them, that's all. Bit of space sickness and morning sickness, its queasiness."

Before the physician stated anything more, Tessa insisted, "I'm keeping him regardless. If I have a choice, that's my choice."

Smiling so she seemed less stern, Claire whispered. "First, relax. Second, we have determined the equivalency of your number one pregnancy thus far. It's about the same as twelve weeks give or take. There's a chance that the cryo slowed development but not harmed your babies."

All those words shot by Tessa without her reacting.

"In the past two decades, that part of your situation has become more common. The pregnancy and icing part. And many of these births, the vast majority, end up full term and normal."

Tessa nodded to show she understood, but she hadn't yet completely comprehended.

"More to the point with you, all seems to be going exceedingly well. All that cryo-stasis doesn't seem to have negatively affected your situation in the least, even if delaying them some."

Situation, Tessa mentally scoffed at the vocabulary but was nearly delirious with the fantastic news. "It's a boy, right? I hate to ask, but I've sensed from the beginning it's a boy."

"Would you be disappointed with a little girl?"

"No." She laughed. "I think Zot would love a girl. And Walter will spoil her only just slightly more than her father will."

"Well, Tessa, I want you on bed rest for a week. Really take it easy. Things may be tough later on."

The mother-to-be looked up, puzzled.

"You're carrying twins, Tessa, a boy and a girl. But not together. It's like you became pregnant twice. Separately. The boy is ahead of the girl by a few weeks' equivalency."

"I'm not sure I follow."

"I'm not sure I know how this happened. Cryo must have really goofed up your body. Never seen anything like it, although med records show it's possible. Even before hibernation, even before the C-Wars, although records from then are spotty, it has happened. Seems you got pregnant *twice*."

Tessa blushed slightly. All those weeks with Zot between their icings over the years while Walter and Shanghai were down.

"Cryo-stasis must have played a part. A body isn't right with all that icing. In your case, 'not right' but healthy enough to conceive normally. Then conceive normally *again* as though you weren't already pregnant." She gave a professional sigh. "Your name will be kept off all the articles that this will generate."

Tessa laid back on the exam cot dazed yet laughing, taking it all in. *Twice. Twins.*

Claire had prepared a chart showing the expected due dates. "They're twins only in so far as you are the mother and they have the same father, but they are developing along different timelines. One is twelve weeks, the boy. The girl about eight weeks. Twins slow the process sometimes anyway. And with their iced beginnings, I'm saying one in late March and one in late April, Earth dates. But both could be a week or so later." She gave a supportive laugh. "As you progress, we'll be able to assess your condition better, get some clarity on how many 'weeks' exactly."

"Birthing twice, a month apart? How's that going to work?"

"We'll cross that bridge later. Our job now is keeping all three of you healthy. Nature has a way. I'm not concerned." Claire gave another professional sigh. "And I won't start that medical article until we know how this plays out."

The news was beginning to sink in. *Initially, the confirmation, then the doubling of the population*, she mentally joked, giddy with the prospect of twins.

"Anything else?" Claire asked, ready to move on to seeing other women on the ward.

"Yes. Not a word to Zot—my husband—or Walter until I've told them. Promise."

"I'll add that on your chart. 'Status confidential until further notice.'

The rest will go through the usual channels of any returning crewmember, but you are the keeper of *this* secret until you're ready." Claire gave another knowing sigh. "Of course, in a colony, not sure how long your privacy will last."

———•———

Tessa was twenty-four hours in a ward then allowed back to her new quarters afterward so long as she agreed to rest. "Only move about for meals," Claire cautioned.

Zot chided her as they prepared for bed that first night. "I have to say, my doctor had a gray beard and has been here nearly twenty years. Where did you pick up the kid doctor? I don't mean she's a *pediatrician*; I mean she is a *kid*."

"Don't show your age, dear," Tessa smiled. "And, although a bit cool, she's a great OB-GYN."

"I won't need one of those," he answered, oblivious.

"Whatever, dear."

"I'll say this for Steerforth," Zot noted, his mind roving about with topics of his day, "he was predictably unpredictable."

"What did you find out now?"

"First off," he explained, "Security listed the *Sirius Odyssey II* as lost in 2099, right?"

"Yes, as you said, Jenna explained that when we arrived."

"Okay, so then, why do our disks still work?" He wriggled his right-only array.

"Affirm that. Those files should have been terminated."

"Exactly. And me a *captain*. My active records show a promotion to that rank in 2106 and list my assignment as Chief Hibernation Specialist onboard the *Sirius Odyssey II*." He looked deeply at his wife. Her face seemed radiant, her skin flawless. For all that hibersickness, the iceman concluded, she was aglow. "Never knew I was a captain on a ghost ship."

"Well," Tessa answered, "I can't explain it."

"I can," Zot concluded. "It has to be Steerforth. After we left, Steerforth was named acting director of the VBC. Then three years after the battle, permanent director. At that level, regardless of what Security or Seattle wanted, Von Braun was *his* fiefdom. It was within his purview to promote or assign anyone as he saw fit. And so, he kept us active."

"Makes sense, a case of the right disks not knowing what the left are doing. Always been the VBC's way of reacting to Seattle."

"How else could my promotion take place?"

"Beats me," Tessa whispered, waiting for a chance to speak of her secret.

"And, hon, look." He opened a screen that revealed his pay for fifty-five years of service on the *Sirius*. "Went batshit crazy when I saw this," he laughed. Due to a pre-war agreement—distorted and clouded over time—hibermen were paid essentially by the day when in space. When a crew was totally iced and the hiberman fully awake, the pay jumped up to a per diem based on the vessel commander's pay scale.

"My God, Zot, you were being paid for all those years we were iced?"

"Hey, if the bean counters at the MAS want to honor a contract made with the Icing Guild that goes back over a hundred years, who am I to refuse the coins of the Marsco realm?"

"Spoken like a true iceman. Your guild must be very proud."

He turned out the light but continued. "Well, here's the conclusion I draw. I'd say someone *really knew* we were alive or they would have terminated our disk-ops. Why keep a dead man active in a computer?"

"Or a dead woman?" Tessa needled then added, "Well, having a wing of the engineering building in my name is nice. Very thoughtful indeed," she noted drily, "after killing me off and all."

"Yes," Zot drew an exasperated breath but went back to Steerforth. "And not claiming *my* cryo-system for himself like he had tried to do before we left. So, are we wrong on him? Wasn't such a jerk after all. Especially since *he's* long dead, not us."

"I don't think so. The letch. But somehow, he seems to have tried to make amends. Who else but the director of the VBC was going to have that kind of clout? And that was Steerforth!"

"Yes, the bastard. Speaking of which, I wonder how many little bastards he left around the solar system."

"Zot, that's cruel; it's not the child's fault, being fathered by such a twit. Insulting and toothless, but a twit."

"Guess so."

"And maybe the mother *wanted* the child. I mean, if she had a choice that may have been hers. But, you're right about his randy ways. He made Mei-Ling and my skin crawl."

"You can be as cynical as me sometimes," Zot replied, fixing his pillow.

"And as secretive. But you're a mercenary, that's what you are. My personal mercenary. Look at that amount you raked in."

"Staggering, yes," Zot replied, "but have you thought what we are to do now that we're back? We're both young by the physical accounts of our bodies, but can you make up fifty years of science and engineering to re-enter a classroom?"

"Haven't given it a thought," she laughed. "I'll be plenty busy. You, too."

"No, hon, I'm serious. What are we to do?"

Flipping on a light so she was able to look directly in to his eyes, she took his hand in hers. "That is a gigantic *we*, as well, Zot. Or will be soon."

"How do you mean?" He sounded defensive, so he explained his own suspicion. "I wasn't excluding your father. I'd never dismiss Walter. Don't ever think I was implying *that*! He's youngish, too, but we'll take care of him, no question."

"I appreciate that. He will, too, but that's not whom I meant."

"Okay, now I'm really lost."

"What if we were responsible for two others?"

"I don't know *who*, but okay, *what if?*"

"I'm not being hypothetical here, my love." As she kissed him deeply, she moved his hand down to her belly. "You can't tell yet, but that's not a scenario down there. I'm carrying our twins."

───── ◦ ─────

When Yang-Murray was able to pull Walter Miller aside three days later, they had a long talk.

The director had been sitting at her office desk when Miller arrived, but she offered him a seat in a side parlor, where she joined him. The Martian sky he knew so well was ablaze with red hues. Her office was near the surface of the flat terrain north of the *Valles Marineris* rift and thus faced more skyward than down the endless canyon.

The director looked similar to Mei-Ling although twenty-five years older than the pilot. Jenna's Asian heritage predominated, but like Mei-

Ling, her Euro ancestry accented her delicate features. The director's hair was no longer completely black, but she styled it meticulously. On her desk and on the wall were digitals of her daughter and son-in-law and her two grandchildren.

"Like yourself," she noted, "I have only the one daughter. My husband works in fuels here. Still working to perfect *found fuels*, components in a frozen comet."

"Refueling in space still an issue," the engineer noted, "especially for a chem-fueled propulsion system."

Above them was a bubble of Plexiglas that showed a large swath of Martian sky and the gigantic valley in both directions. Along one wall of the parlor sat display models of VBC shuttles on separate shelves. The craft ranged from Herriff's first, actually designed while he worked from the Moon, up through several Herriff-Miller designs and ending with the latest.

"Not seen that," Miller commented, picking up a scale model, compared her to others on display. "It looks as if it would be nearly twice the size of anything I knew."

"That's the VBC-2. The -1 was a mock-up, never actually built. We hope to launch the -3 in '57. If there aren't more delays."

"Has to be faster."

"More than three times faster than the Herriff-Miller standards from the '90s."

"Tech advances, always stunning."

"And," Jenna went on, "I found this among the gear left behind by Director Steerforth. I mean to give it to your Captain Grizotti." She pointed to a sixty-five cm replica of the VBC *Gagarin* as the expedition ship was configured for the first-ever Jupiter run. "You know, between the Jupiter trek and your *Sirius* adventure, I think your Anthony has logged more time in space than any other human."

"I'm sure he'll be pleased to hear that. And by the way, he goes by *Zot*. However, more to the point, he's an extraordinary researcher concerning hibernation and cryogenic stasis."

"You don't need to convince me. Steerforth left extensive records crediting Captain Grizotti with discoveries often attributed to Steerforth. Quite generous of him since Grizotti wasn't here to defend himself."

"He'll be happy to know that. We left, well, under unusual circumstances," Miller said, grinning, "and several records may not be accurate about our departure."

"Like the fact that you intended never to return."

"Well, yes, that."

"Herriff left a message as such, addressed to the future director of the VBC to be opened on 1 January 2150. That would be me. He had no reason to lie, so I know the truth of the whole story."

Miller went blank. *Does Security? Seattle?*

"Fear not. I'd never give Sturtevant the satisfaction of knowing any of this. The Center works so much better without Security at every turn. He and his ilk trolling and lurking are relatively recent, dating from when Chesney, the VP of Marsco, ensconced in Seattle, began exerting his power. We're a wholly separate, wholly independent organization, but Security keeps shinning a light into our darkest corners. I don't like that." She shook her head in irritated disapproval.

Their small talk over, Jenna abruptly confided her concerns about the changing Marsco world. "The Six Accords are designed to move the world toward democracy, toward mutual cooperation as never before. It's unprecedented."

"But?" Miller asked then stated knowingly, "there's always a *but*, isn't there?"

"Either one of these two things could happen, or both. First, not everyone in the old Marsco bureaucracy—"

"The entrenched bureaucracy, I gather."

"Exactly. Not every boffin and high-end wallah *wants* this change. Or indeed sees the ultimate promise or appropriateness of this change. You'd be surprised how many associates want things the same simply because they know nothing different."

"And at present, they get all the cream and gravy exclusively."

"Exactly. At least many do."

"I grew up in the twenty-first century. Little astonishes me," Miller explained. "That's the era that brought the world *Disenfranchisement*. Countries simply cut their poor or sick or uneducated citizens loose. Created new 'countries' to house their most needy, most desperately poor, most vulnerable. I've seen abuses of power to rival nothing the Earth had ever witnessed before. And why? To 'cut taxes' and 'give tax breaks' to the wealthiest citizens? So much for the overall and general good of the commonwealth." He smirked. "So much for 'we hold these truths' and 'we pledge our sacred honor.'"

Miller shook his head to stop himself from waxing on about the major political blunders of the twenty-first century: allowing demagoguery to replace civil discourse and the passing of legislation that advanced the causes of an influential faction and not laws beneficial to the whole nation. Removing countless people from basic health care and education. Ending their right to vote.

"What do you expect," Yang-Murray added wryly, "when a nation places its highest trust in elected officials who were once actors or rape-wrestlers?" She gave a sly smile. "I read your *Ascendancy*—a clandestine read, mind you—but I downloaded it in its entirety."

"So, still online?"

"Yes. Our VBC IT folks make sure it stays available."

"Then," Miller drew his conclusion, "Marsco in the twenty-second century shouldn't surprise you. It is, I'm sure, very much like the Marsco of the twenty-first."

"Yes, yet, I'm concerned about some wallahs in power who might be reluctant to change," she went on, "but I am not naive. I'm just as concerned, if not more so, about those elements among the PRIMS—though not exclusively so—who want revenge, not release, not change. Don't get me wrong. Most PRIMS are overwhelmingly upright citizens, future voters, job holders, fine parents and guardians. But an element, a segment, wants our blood."

She caught herself. "You know, I'm stuck in old terminology. Technically, PRIMS no longer exist. They are all free citizens of federations."

Yang-Murray paused another moment then added, "I have two grandchildren on Earth, both at prep school. My daughter and her husband are based out of the Moon; they see them regularly. But even this school in a secure area of Europe, which hasn't had PRIM violence since the mutiny—"

The director could tell Miller wasn't following. "The PRIM Mutiny ended in '04, but riots and attacks had started as early as '97."

"Yes, I see. I do have much history to learn. But your point is?"

"Their school has associate children, sids, former PRIMS; it is very progressive. And it gets threats! Serious threats seeking to settle perceived old scores against Marsco."

"It's an ancient story," Miller reacted. "Attack the most vulnerable to claim a 'moral victory.' Sorry so little has changed, even though I'm excited about these Six Accords."

"Stay excited for them. I think they'll work. But at what price? After all, that small segment of PRIMS who rioted during the Mutiny weren't doing so for the franchise, weren't demanding better education; their carnage was solely for revenge. They wanted the blood of associates or even sids, if they got in the way. And yet, as it turned out, many PRIMS, many innocent PRIMS, were murdered at the hands of those rioting PRIMS."

"Any evidence of this happening now?"

"Besides a periodic threat to schoolchildren? No. I've heard of some random acts of violence; whether coordinated or not, I don't know. Yet, I don't hear much. Not out here on Mars."

"Won't that change with the Accords?"

"Certainly! Freedom of press is guaranteed. The basis of the Accords sets the old Bill of Rights and UN Charter of Human Rights as the cornerstones of every world constitution. With the First Accord, 158 nations were essentially created at a single go. By the Sixth, they'll be up and running, totally independent from Marsco. Even three Indie lunar colonies will be granted federation status in 2161, if all goes according to plan. But right now, what's really happening back on Earth? I'm not in the Security loop about that."

"If Gunnar Sturtevant is an example of a typical Security officer, I can understand why," Miller sneered.

"Oh, he's a bit officious, that's for sure. That reminds me," she moved back to her desk. "I have a message for you on that score. Gunnar tells me that a Security officer from Earth is arriving in seventy-two hours to take over you and your crew."

"And what does that mean?"

"Your guess is as good as mine, Walter." She paused, "But actually, I know and respect this new officer. He's an astro-researcher. Marsco Academy grad and professor. Graduated over twenty years ago, top in his class. Had a three-year stint in Security a way back but has been reactivated to Security recently. For a time, he was assigned here because the VBC coordinated his trip out to Jupiter. That's when I met him. He was on board the *Armstrong-Aldrin-Collins* exploratory vessel that made that trek."

"Like the *Gagarin* in my time."

"Affirmative."

"I'll check with Zot, but I think that's the ship that tried hailing us some years ago."

"Yes, it is. Then the Center tried."

"Well, to the point of our arrest, we'll just have to meet our new Security friend." Miller then added drily, "I'm sure we'll get along famously."

"You can trust him," the director stated firmly. After a pause, she added, "Here's a coincidence. I noticed this looking over your files. You and he both have a connection to Sac City. Ever hear of a Colonel Devon Chavez-Sherman?"

"When I lived there, it would have been his grandparents I was likely to know. But, negatory, I've never heard the name."

"He's coming along with one ADC, a warrant named Kyle Truman Roncalli."

"*Truman* is a name I knew near Sac City," Miller noted.

The engineer looked into the darkening Martian sky and thought back to his great room at his grange. All the talks he had there or on the patio just outside—with Allison, with Aaron and Jeremy Truman, Lieutenant Rivers, Tessa and Zot, and scores of others. Bethany's ashes were spread throughout his grange. He had first met Mei-Ling there before they bolted hastily for the VBC so many years ago.

"Yes, Sac City, of course," he finally broke his reverie. "I want to visit old haunts there once I get the chance."

SIXTEEN

MARTIAN MEETING

(The Von Braun Center, Mars, October 2154)

"**A**aron? My God, Zot, it's Aaron Truman!" The words were out of Tessa's mouth before she took note of the warrant officer's Security uniform. And his lighter hair. Regardless, she swore he was Miller's neighbor who lived near her father's grange south of Sac City.

The initial meeting between the Lunar Security detachment and the space travelers was held in the VBC director's office. Yang-Murray felt it would ease any potential tension if carried out in this private setting.

Tessa, Miller, and Zot all stared at the warrant officer who accompanied the entering Security colonel and thus paid no attention to the officer as he tried to explain their situation vis-à-vis Marsco HQ. Polite coughs didn't break the concentration the three pairs of eyes fixed on his aide. Because the two arriving officers had read every file given to them by Mateo Modena, they had no difficulty identifying the *Sirius* crew, especially with Major Sturtevant standing there looking officious. But that still didn't answer why the trio stared so hard at Kyle.

Feeling uncomfortable, young man stayed behind Devon, knowing he must not speak to anyone until the colonel introduced himself and stated their purpose.

Finally, the awkward gazing ended as Devon made his introduction.

"Pleasure to meet you all," he stated with calm formality. "Under different circumstances, your return would be hailed worldwide. What an event," he added warmly.

"I gather," Zot squeezed in a snide remark, "we're not exactly household names at present, kept incommunicado here on Mars." He shot a glance at Sturtevant.

"Do you know anyone on Earth we should tell of your return?" Devon asked pointedly but with a sly grin.

Tessa looked at Kyle once more. "Don't you remember us? We met at Walter's grange so often."

"Icing may have blocked his memory," the hiber specialist stated professionally, advancing his theory as to why the young man did not recognize them even though he had met with them so often years ago.

"I'm sorry," Devon interrupted, ushering Kyle forward. "This is my aide. Kyle Truman Roncalli."

"I believe," the young man apologized, "you're confusing me with my grandfather, Aaron Truman. They say I look a great deal like him, except the hair."

Miller gave a burst of self-deprecating laughter. "Our apologies to you, Mr. Roncalli. We're still time-warped here. Fifty-plus years on ice, then returning to all this," he gestured to the Security personnel around them, "caught us off guard."

"Or put us under guard," Zot smirked.

"But, yes," Tessa explained, smoothing over her husband's bitter tone, "you *do* look like him. Identical."

To put everyone at ease, Devon turned to Gunnar Sturtevant. "Major, we have this under control now. I'll take charge of your guests."

The Mars-based officer nodded. He'd been waiting nervously long enough for this prisoner transfer. "Very well, colonel. I just need you to twitch off." He held out a hand unit with authorization giving Devon complete control of the four returning adventurers. "They're officially Lunar Security responsibility now," the vexing officer announced, then left.

Alone with his new charges, Devon explained that he was indeed sorry that instructions may have been carried out through a Security officer who was a bit excessive concerning their detention. "Marsco HQ had ordered you detained here, not arrested. Lunar Security does not want the *Sirius* any closer to Earth, that's all."

"Does that mean we're free to go?" Zot was the first to question their changed status.

"Well, no, not exactly. I'm to escort you back to Earth as soon as possible."

"And that will be when?" the iceman continued.

"As soon as my shuttle's serviced. In forty-eight hours, perhaps sixty."

"Still under arrest?" Zot continued his string of questions.

Before Devon could answer, Jenna Yang-Murray entered her office after she'd seen Sturtevant exit. "Glad that's done," she said, sighing. Warmly acknowledging Devon, she reintroduced herself with the brazen pronouncement, "I hope you're still more a space explorer than Security wonk. They've been out of our solar system for more than fifty years; don't treat them like lepers."

"I have no intention of playing heavy-handed, if that's what you mean," Devon stated with a cool touch of authority.

He clicked a recorder hanging from his uniform belt. At that point, his voice shifted to an even more official tone. "I need only check two items before lessening any restrictions on these people. I've read your log while on my way here from lunar orbit. But I need to know, one, your health status: Have you come into contract with any alien microbes?" He looked at Miller.

Finding the Security officer not at all like a fellow space explorer, Miller answered calmly but far from pleasantly. "We never reached another planet, so, clearly no, we never left the *Sirius*."

"Didn't take any water or water components from an asteroid or comet?"

"You mean like oxygen and hydrogen?" Zot mocked.

"Exactly," Devon retorted, unperturbed.

"No on that score as well," Miller answered. "It's all in our log."

"I've read it, Dr. Miller; just clearing up a few open questions. Logs can be changed. Edited. Amended."

"If you have seen our log, then undoubtedly you've seen *why* we came back. Number three went south. Our overall power reduced to sixty-six percent." Miller hid the fact that Herriff had already reversed their course before the leak began.

The engineer added, "A design flaw. I should have seen it in the shakedown phase. I missed it. If we didn't turn back when we did, we would not have made our final destination or back home."

"There's precious little else out there," Tessa jumped in.

"So, no contamination from your reactors?" Devon asked, returning to his original course. "No radiation poisoning?"

"Our physicals prove we're in excellent health," Miller answered, "except for Shanghai, who's awake but weak. And not from radiation sickness."

"I'll accept all that," the Security officer noted, ignoring his knowledge of Herriff's final decision to return to Earth made without their consent and while they were under ice.

"We'd have been here sooner if we ran all engines at full," Miller explained. "I can show you our charts and our pilot's calculations."

"Does Herriff need to be mentioned at all?" Tessa asked, wanting to protect his reputation.

"He's already part of the preliminary report. Besides, his role as your leader, as clearly explained in a growing dossier, makes him look more and more like a loyal associate. To some in Seattle, however, he *did* seem to abscond with a VBC spaceship. But, the way I read it, you were all in a prearranged and extended experimental mission. Test those ions. Test your cryo."

Devon looked over at Jenna. "And the *Sirius* may remain here, right?"

"Affirmative," the director explained. "It's a prototype registered to the VBC." Not a stretch of the truth. "No need to move it yet, except that it's leaking radioactive fuel. My service personnel will patch her leaks, and then we'll chart a course inward toward the Sun—bypassing Earth—and remotely scuttle her. The Sun is a gigantic furnace; the *Sirius* will burn up in its photosphere with no harm to anyone."

"Very well," the Security colonel noted with aloof composure. "Welcome back from a successful mission," he concluded.

The shocked crew did not know how to respond. This officer seemed to be writing a fiction before their eyes.

Devon twitched off the recording device. "I presume your office's system caught all this as well, Jenna," he stated in a now-friendly tone. "If so, can you edit out what doesn't correspond to our new story? I'm not at my best playing the Security game, but I wanted the wallahs in Seattle to have a good show of it."

"Certainly," the VBC director complied, "easy enough to have an accident, say erasing a week or month. The larger the swath of missing intel, the easier to explain. No need to go for only eighteen minutes; I'll take the last six weeks."

He's planned this with the aplomb of someone accustomed to gaming the system, Zot mentally complimented the Security officer. The iceman was warming up him.

Turning toward the space travelers to offer a real welcome, Devon started his conversation with them all over again. "Let me say, for whatever reasons why you originally left, for whatever reasons brought you home, your trek there and back is an incredible scientific and technological accomplishment."

"And yet," Zot interjected, "we made it back by the skin of our teeth. Running with one totally shot unit is not advisable."

Tessa coughed. *Iceman, knock off the criticism of my engines*, her eyes demanded.

"But you're here, not adrift in the Oort Cloud."

"By the grace of God." Tessa sighed and added, praising the missing Shanghai, "Plus great piloting skills."

When Tessa and Kyle were alone in the director's office, she asked with an excited tone, "Tell me, have you met Aaron? Is he still alive?"

"Granddad? Very much so."

"I'd love to see him once we're on Earth."

"I'm sure he would, too. He lives in retirement on the Serengeti. He rarely speaks of you directly. Actually, he's reluctant to speak of his youth even though I've prodded him. Not sure why."

"So, you know nothing of Walter's, my father's, grange?" she asked with intense focus on the young man.

Tessa had an indescribable expression that reminded Kyle so much of Sarah. The women were quite different, of course, because Tessa had auburn hair kept shorter, a sprinkle of freckles, green eyes. Sarah's richly dark brown hair flowed down beyond her shoulders; her eyes were intense blue. The granger's daughter was deeply tanned. The passion in their eyes, however, was identical. When both women looked at a man, they looked as if seeing his soul. But, the fact remained that this woman was bonding with Kyle while Sarah still detested him. And yet, for the first time in all the excitement of traveling to Mars, working his online Academy classes, and reading up on the *Sirius* crew, Kyle had a moment to think solely of Sarah, to miss her. Not that missing a woman who abhorred you was a fantastic idea. For the first time, he felt homesick for New Grange.

The young man's face lit up. "Granddad Truman never mentions the grange, but I think I have actually been there," he explained.

Tessa was beside herself with anticipation for news. "Has it changed much?"

"Can't say on that score. Don't know exactly what it was like before. I've viewed only a rough layout of the old place. Sarah's family has made many changes." Kyle wished he hadn't mentioned her.

For the first time, Tessa's exuberant face dropped into a serious glance. "Have you been able to visit your great-uncle's grave? Zot knows that Jeremy, Aaron's younger brother, is buried there at the grange, not twenty meters from where he was murdered. Is his grave even marked, I wonder?"

The Truman descendant had recently heard bits of this story. But the reminders of murder at the grange only intensified his desire to know if Sarah was safe.

With no preamble or statement to give context, unguarded, Kyle let slip, "The family that owns the grange now, I'm worried about her—*them*." Tessa had a quality that gave instant comfort and deep confidence, so the young man didn't hesitate adding, "There's been trouble near them, deadly, horrific trouble. Then I was ordered to leave so hastily, off to West Con Security of all things—" he looked down on a Marsco Security uniform that actually hadn't changed much in the past fifty years "—I couldn't even say goodbye. To the whole family, not just the daughter," he faltered, "this one young woman."

As though his big sister, Tessa placed a hand on his shoulder. "Sounds like it's still a Marsco world." She then added thoughtfully, "But, it's silence that creates a void between people, not distance."

Kyle hadn't communicated with Sarah in more than three months.

The next morning, Kyle asked Tessa to give him a tour of the Palmer Domes, the hydroponics fruit and vegetable basket of the Von Braun Center. For an hour, the pair, joined by Zot, meandered among ranks of greenery. Even though the connection was to his grandfather, the returning explorers took to Kyle immediately.

"Miss this most of all," the iceman commented. "The *Sirius* adventure was one thing, but Earth-like life—can't beat it." All three breathed in the fecund and moist air. No spacecraft ever had air like this, air teaming with life and growth. Air that seemed as natural and clean as Earth air.

"All the water's from indigenous lakebeds, right?" Kyle asked.

"Affirmative," Tessa explained.

Under the dry, rocky floor of *Valles Marineris*, tens of thousands of hectares of ice waited to be mined. "Can we visit that ops?" Kyle pleaded.

"Off limits to us. Need pressure suits," Tessa explained with a hint of frustration. Although now technically Devon's responsibility, the Security officer hadn't reduced the restrictions given them when they were initially placed under house arrest by Sturtevant. "Besides, it's a working mine and not much to see except robotic harvesters cutting blocks of ice for pressurizing, melting, purifying."

"Sounds awesome," he replied. "That's my senior thesis topic, colony sustainability via water recovery and hydroponics."

Zot laughed, "You sound like an Indie, not an associate."

"How so?"

"Setting up an isolated asteroid colony with no outside connections."

"If you have the water, even from ice formations like those down in some mines, then the possibility of sustaining life out there exists. If so, with the right personnel, I guess you could live independent of Earth."

Zot grew serious. "It's dangerous down there in the mines. Nearly passed out in them once. God knows what would have happened if I had." He squeezed Tessa's hand remembering those tense times between them.

Kyle walked down a row of growing beds. At a glance, he saw hundreds of tomato plants on trellises with their fruit ripening under grow lamps. A separate bed had spinach and Romaine, green beans. "Colonists eat fresh, eat well," he concluded.

"Nothing but the best for Herriff's people," Tessa explained. "That's why he brought my mom here to begin with, to lessen the effects of strenuous life on this barren rock. He wanted isolation so his personnel would work hard, be totally dedicated to his projects. They had to be devoted to living here for years before rotating home. But he needed a way to keep his people happy. One solution was to give them those parts of home life he could replicate. Fresh food was one way."

A further dome housed an orchard so that apples, peaches, and nectarines ripened nearly year-round. Interspersed with the trees were rosebushes. "And her flowers," Kyle noted. "I've read that Dr. Palmer was famous for them on Mars."

"That's right; her blossoms were another sense of home."

"Small consolation," Zot groused, "the quartermaster boffins never got coffee right."

Kyle agreed. "I've heard that complaint even at the Academy. Drink good coffee on Earth; you'll never get it in space."

<hr>

At their noon meal, Zot found Devon the most cordial thus far. Miller was back on board the *Sirius* for the final handover and not likely to appear soon. Before Tessa and Kyle joined them, the two men sat alone in the far corner of the exec mess. Their nook was situated in a bubble along the cliff that looked over the vastness of the *Valles Marineris*. They were two-thirds of the way up the constantly shaded sheer face. A research dirigible drifted by a thousand meters in the distance, a sure sign that the winds in the canyon were calm today. Shadow and weak sunlight made the cliffs various hues of scarlet, orange, and yellow.

"It did seem puzzling to me," the icing specialist noted, "that on your trip to Jupiter, you used cryogenic stasis, not hibernation. I mean, the cryo process is so complicated and difficult to implement."

Devon gave a pleased laugh. "Steerforth *did* enhance the system quite a bit."

"Well, for the record," Zot noted professionally, "cryo is actually safer than hiber in the end." He then added as an afterthought, "Present crewmembers confirm that."

"But remember, the increased speed of the *Armstrong-Aldrin-Collins* substantially reduced the need for icing. None of the flight crew, for example, ever went under. Most of the science crew did, deicing only as we approached the outer Jovian moons. Saved many supply and life-support issues and kept them from total boredom."

Zot drew a breath. "I can't understand that, being bored in space. At times on the *Gagarin*, I was the only one upright. Even so, the marvels of the universe never diminished a bit after months of isolation."

"Must have been totally different on the *Sirius*."

Zot nodded. "Out there in the never-never, you begin to question: *What's out here? Who's out there? Out over there? Beyond those stars? Behind that fuzzy galaxy?* It's spiritual and existential and nihilistic all at once. I felt a presence of *something* besides myself—life, purpose, meaning—then I felt absolutely alone. Completely isolated. My wife iced, so close yet so distant, didn't help. And still, I sensed I was never truly alone, even though my three companions were down cold in the next bay." Zot drew a philosophical breath, "But, it's more than that. I'm not sure we belong out there like that, at least not as directionless as we were."

"I don't follow," Devon stated.

"We had scant evidence that we'd find life or a livable planet if we ever got to the Wolf system. I think we were just running away. We had the tech that allowed us to go, the hubris, but I'm not sure we weren't in the end just making a quixotic gesture. It was foolish to take Tessa. My God, our choices could have led to her death. Being totally secluded, thinking of all that, it got to me. I kept pondering our connection to Earth. And kept asking, 'Is it right to be so disconnected from it? To cut ourselves off from it so completely?'"

"I never sensed that on the *AAC* mission," Devon replied.

"Nor I on the *Gagarin*," Zot answered. "No, it was the forced separation that got to me on the *Sirius*. That abject sense of purposelessness and meaninglessness in our gesture. Steerforth warned us of that. And his voice echoing in my mind was the worst part of the isolation."

"You couldn't have been *totally* isolated and by yourself all the time, Zot," Devon replied with a wry smile. "Congratulations. I hear twins." Jenna had been right; on the colony, news traveled fast.

At that moment, Tessa came to the table with a tray heaped with twice the food of the men. "Eating for three, remember," she stated in a tone and with a look that preemptively silenced any remarks.

"And making up for your cracker diet," Zot quipped with a light kiss on her cheek.

Kyle also joined them but with hardly enough to sustain him. Sarah was on his mind, tying up his gut, keeping him from focusing on much else. Communication with her should be a cinch, if she cared to receive any word from him. After the Accords started, every method was open to her. But, express orders prevented him from attempting it.

"I hate to turn this into a staff meeting," Devon stated, "but we ought to talk." Getting their attention, he went on, "I'm concerned about Walter."

"Who isn't?" shot Tessa.

"Will he leave his ship?"

Tessa drew a breath. "You know, he's like a terrier. He's on a scent and wants to know about that leak and about the engines and their viability for another run."

"To Seattle, it looks like he's ready to bolt again. He's got to leave that damn ship."

"Our *Sirius* is hardly 'that damn ship,' sir," Zot defended.

"He's still an associate," Devon stated emphatically. "I'd hate to, but I can *order* him to leave Mars." After a pause, he added with no interest in using this, "Technically, of course, he's also still my prisoner."

"Is that such a good idea?" Tessa probed, "ordering him about?"

"No, not really. I can't foresee doing that, forcing him."

"Walter's a man of honor and commitment, colonel," Zot explained. "He's the leader of our mission. Explain it in those terms."

"Especially if he knows the end of the *Sirius* will be respectful."

"When will we be ready?" Zot asked.

"Twenty-four, perhaps thirty-six hours. I don't want to miss alignment. We can make the crossing in just over three weeks if we go soon. Then it grows longer by two days for each day we delay."

Planetary movements, the cadet concluded. *Give me a domed garden and ice lake any day.*

Director Jenna Yang-Murray sat at her desk with Kyle across from her, the young man a bit nervous at this meeting he had requested. *Admire your grit*, she noted, *tenaciously pushing your way in here.* He had only his duty uniform, nothing approaching a dress uniform, but he'd neatened it as though for a cadet inspection, shined what could be shined, and presented himself as fully spit-and-polish as possible.

"So," she began with the usual pleasantries, "Everything's set for your departure, right?"

"Yes, ma'am, in eighteen hours from now."

Anxiously, the young man finally got up his nerve. "I'll come to the point of my asking to see you, Madame Director," he began formally. "I'm completing my fourth year—"

"Online, I see," she interjected, looking over the resumé link he had provided.

"Yes, an Academy degree."

"Sure you'll finish this year? Graduate on time?"

They both looked at his uniform. Then Kyle began his plea, "Yes, I will, and you see, when done, I want to work here, at the VBC. Run your greenhouses, your water recovery units."

"Jumping out here straight from the Academy?"

"If possible," he mumbled out uneasily.

"You know, several unofficial policies are against you. Faster shuttle speeds aside, Martian life remains hard and lonely. Most colony positions go to seasoned associates, ones who have lived on the Moon for at least three years or have the equivalent time on shuttles plying back and forth across the void. Many bring their families for a five-year tour. I presume you did learn the number of AUs it is from here to home."

"Oh, yes, ma'am," he hesitantly answered, then went on. "So, are there never exceptions if a guy happens to apply who *has* been to Mars once, had lunar colony experience, and is really interested in Dr. Palmer's work, her legacy, her hydroponics gardens, and her domes?"

Jenna smiled matronly. "Is this guy, you?"

"Course."

"Been to the Herriff Ice Lake yet?"

"Yesterday. Spent the whole day down there. Even rode on one of the laser cutters mining ice diamonds." With little effort, pinpoints of intense light cut away blocks of water ice from the stretching bed of a buried lake. Martian water hadn't flowed on the surface for eons. Cut away from the ice face, these blocks, these diamonds, were placed into a pressurized system, melted, purified, and utilized. "It's nearly totally automated, but it was awesome to sit there and watch so close at hand."

"And that's your future life?"

"I'd like it to be, ma'am, although the dome garden part is my favorite."

"Well, Officer Roncalli," Jenna began her letdown as gently as possible. "I'll keep your resumé on file. And make sure you update it with next semester's grades. Let us know when you've actually graduated."

"Yes, ma'am," he answered jumping up, ramrod upright.

"No, please," she motioned him back to be seated. "Clearly, you're now in Security, right?" He nodded his affirmative answer while slumping a bit in his chair. "Are you sure that after graduation, your tour won't be extended?"

"Devon, that is, Colonel Chavez-Sherman, says no, that I'm his ADC, only temp, and he'll go back to his prof status and rank at the Academy very soon."

"Glad you trust *his* word; yet, it's *Security's* I would have misgivings about." She saw his instant anguish. "I hate to burst your bubble, but if you're in Security now, I'd be concerned about getting out soon. Traditionally, the usual Academy-to-Security hitch is five years."

"*Five years!*" the erstwhile cadet yelped, seemingly blaming the director for this harsh news. "Five years? I would've said *no* to that!"

"Not sure you could have," the director answered dryly. "Saying no to Security is a dreadfully difficult task, especially for a cadet. Especially in these times. Even with the Accords. Seattle is sending and implementing mixed messages, to be sure."

"I'll say," Kyle blurt out. "I've been in both Marsco's and West Con's Security over the past few years. West Con's only a few months ago. Makes me dizzy."

"Well, after you are totally out of whichever Security lets you go, you may apply here. We'll see about your status then."

<hr />

The Security Shuttle *Hoover* was nothing like any craft the passengers had ever seen. The seasoned *Sirius* crew marveled at her luxury. Each passenger had a separate stateroom but shared a common room for reading and relaxing. Even the toilets and showers, although not large, seemed Earth-like. The shuttle had ample water and ran at .95 gee, well above any MAS shuttle from before their escape.

Tessa was glad for the gravity. The closer to Earth's range, the better her chances of a "normal" abnormal pregnancy. She tapped her emerging baby bump. All was well so far.

Even with all these experienced space travelers on board, the flight crew did not extend an invitation for the explorers to see the flight deck or the propulsion system. It wasn't Devon's orders but someone above who'd prohibited it. Miller and Tessa were dying to see the engines. Although her weakness continued, Shanghai wanted to see the flight deck. And Kyle wanted to know if he might now send any messages. The flight crew sparks did not bother to answer his request. Lowest on the pecking order, what did he expect?

———— · ————

The *Hoover* fired her last burn and engaged in booster separation; she was perfectly oriented for a lunar rendezvous in two weeks, four days.

"You not feeling sleepy either?" Kyle asked Captain Shanghai, who sat quietly across from him in a darkened corner of the passenger common room eight days out from Mars orbit. Tessa and Zot had already drifted off. As had Miller, then Devon.

"No, just daydreaming, that's all," the pilot replied; her voice sounded worried. Besides back pain near her kidneys, her eyes still bothered her.

Sitting in a dark crook, the pilot spent her time watching Mars grow smaller. Under a bright reading lamp, Kyle sat opposite, hunched over a screen, applying himself to coursework. He had no idea what Devon had in mind after the shuttle deposited them all at an orbiting lunar platform. More Security—ordered by either Seattle or Sac City—was not inviting. Mia's scheme did enter his mind. Not as a temptation, although he admitted *she* was. He wasn't interested in her Security offer but was curious as to what it all meant. What was Marsco up to? And what was Mia's slice of it? And would West Con snatch him again?

"May I ask you something, Captain Shanghai?" the student said at last, his reverie broken and his studies commanding his full attention.

"Please Kyle, call me Mei-Ling. We're traveling together, not on a flight deck." She smiled cordially, softening her expression, which in her illness often looked harsh and severe.

"Okay, Mei-Ling," the cadet choked out. "'If a shuttle is oriented so that her engine nacelles are pointing away from Mars, but her orders call for leaving planetary orbit toward a specific colony in the belt, what is the best course of action for her pilot?'"

"Easy, use nitro jets to reverse angle of attack and establish a stable orbital pattern that aligns the ship correctly, then burn engines and boosters to maximum effect." She paused, "But why are you asking me this?"

"To pass the time," the studying cadet-turned-trooper replied. "Say, you sure you're okay?"

Mei-Ling had been rubbing her eyes as she tried to stare back toward Mars, now a reddish fist hanging in a black night sky. "I'm fine; just tired." Like the rest, she had no idea what awaited her on Earth. Unlike the rest, serious allegations just might await her.

"Is this reading lamp bothering you?" He was under intense light; she sat in the dark side of their shared space.

"No, I'm good."

"Great! Now, here's another question: 'Assume a mining asteroid is tumbling because one of its rocket pods burnt *all* the fuel available for the three engines—'"

"That's a design impossibility."

"Okay, assume it. This is all hypothetical. '—for the three engines. What is the best method for computing the tumble rate and the destabilized flux ratio of the asteroid if *not* orbiting a planet or the Moon?'"

"Easy," the pilot said, "any rotating body in space has an inertia force equivalent to its mass and speed around its axis computed by dividing by pi, so putting all that data in the computer first will give you a working equation to figure all these numbers out."

"It's a two-word answer."

"Then try, 'Gaul Principle.'"

"That seems right. Okay, one more. 'An air leak on a passenger module causes all twenty passengers to be evacuated into a second mod. Now, twice the number of passengers are in a standard mod designed for twenty. What is the best way to proceed safely?'"

The *Piazzi* flashed into the pilot's mind. She paused, her stare now on the bulkhead above the student's head. After a long silence, she brought her attention back to the question. "Say, is this your coursework?"

"Busted. But I don't want to fly; I want to operate a domed hydroponics garden. Why do I have to learn this crap?"

"*Crap?* Careful, plebe!" Her indulging smile charmed the young man from across the cabin. She did look like Mia, not that he thought for a second that he could have with the pilot what he had had with that other officer. "It's because you're at the Marsco Academy. Most of the graduates go to Flight afterwards." Even in the dark, she sat up straighter to show the wings on her tunic. "Why go to the Academy if not considering Flight?"

"Perhaps I want to be an engineer?"

"I'll give you that. Tessa's a fine example of that choice. But, you'll be working with these scenarios if in engineering."

"Water engineering," Kyle clarified.

"A farmer?"

"Well, yes, in a sense, but a farmer with a dome that uses mined water and is inconveniently situated a few AUs from Earth."

Mei-Ling gave a laugh. "Does Security know of this?"

Kyle tried to take her flippant remark as it was meant, as a humorous aside, not a direct assault against him.

"Can I ask you something serious," she finally stated, coming over to his side of the suite. "How did you end up in Security?" In the low cabin light, her face looked pale and drawn with ongoing worry. It was Kyle's turn to reply with a long silence. "So?" she asked, with a wry hint of wise older sister in her eyes that hadn't been there before.

It took about twenty minutes to explain, because New Grange, a few hints about Sarah, and Devon's internship on Resnik all had to be part of the explanation. He even added in the assault on Millersville and Patrice being so pleasant and Hyacinth fawning over him, although Sarah hadn't. He drew the line at throwing in Columbus and his suspicious but unproven connection to the murders of innocent fed grangers near the Brunel spread.

"Cross astro-cultivating off your list of professions," Mei-Ling teased, after Kyle finally drew a breath after his monologue. "I thought farmers were taciturn. You've spoken more to me in twenty minutes than in the past four days."

"I guess I can be chatty," Kyle admitted, "except around Sarah. Then I get so nervous I clam up."

Mei-Ling smiled. "That may be a good sign." She went back to the far side of their shared space and watched the Red Planet for a while longer. In time, she asked, "Ever been commanded to follow orders?" She then chided, "You *are* an associate, after all."

"I know. I go where I'm sent."

Shanghai softened her tone. "But if Mars, the VBC, or another asteroid colony, you don't need to go alone."

Kyle blushed; he always assumed he'd go back to Mars without Sarah.

SEVENTEEN

ENTICING MILLER; SEDUCING SHANGHAI

(Security Shuttle *Hoover*, Between Mars and Earth, October 2154)

"I realize I'm still an associate," Miller responded to the vice-chair's assistant, Mr. Liddle, "but technically I still work through the VBC, which gives me some options." The two spoke on a Security video link, Seattle-to-shuttle.

"I understand that, but Mr. Oakes, chair of the board—and in fact all the whole board—wants this *Sirius* feat known all over the world. The entire solar system." Liddle looked away from the cam, averting his eyes from Miller's intense gaze.

"I'm not sure this Security officer here would agree," Miller cautioned. "Even though an associate, I'm under arrest and escorted by one Colonel Devon Chavez-Sherman, so Security will need to nose into this issue as well." He drew an exasperated breath, "but Director Yang-Murray has the final say-so, as far as I'm concerned. If I still work for anybody, I work for her. Get the VBC on board, then *de facto* I'm on board."

"That will be fine. I'll get on to her ASAP and get back to you soon."

"Roger, Seattle, I look forward to your return call."

When the com-link went blank, Miller turned to Devon, sitting quietly off-camera. "I need a secure line to Jenna right now. And pray she's an engineer first and a publicity-seeking associate second."

Totally honest with Miller, even Devon couldn't explain what was going down.

Miller's link to Jenna came through instantly.

"I haven't much time," Miller explained to the VBC director. "Seattle's up to something."

"Reasons you think this?" the Mars-based engineer asked.

"Let's just say my usual Indie suspicion. They want me to make holographic messages from the *Hoover* about the *Sirius* to be broadcast around the world and around the solar system. Make them now, before we're even back on Earth."

"To what purpose?" the director asked.

"I thought you might know."

"I know nothing. What I suspect I wouldn't say even over this secure channel. I'll only say, trust your intuition and suspicions; have they ever served you wrong?"

"No, never."

"And your Security escort, not the young one but the one from the *Armstrong-Aldrin-Collins* mission. I have a high trust level for him."

"I'll take that under consideration."

"Yes. And now I've another call coming in. Seattle. A Mr. Liddle—"

"I just spoke with him. He's some sort of special assistant to the vice-chair."

"Oh, yes, Chesney, the power behind the throne." Jenna caught herself on a line that might be snooped. Exaggerating, she added the twist with a lilting, insincere voice, "His support moved the Accords talks along when they seemed stalled." She felt sure her comments were benign enough to pass a filter without causing suspicion.

"I catch your drift."

"Yes, watch my drift and how I must state this. Of course, releasing anything about the *Sirius* mission is not going to happen soon. She was on a black mission; her crew is resting and needs their privacy, even if Earth-bound. And the VBC does *not* make it a habit to discuss classified materials or disclose personal information about its staff."

"I like your rehearsal."

"Best if we all sing from the same karaoke program."

Miller's eyes locked on Devon's. "Why is Jenna so reluctant to speak? Aside from the obvious reasons."

"Look," Devon began, checking that his fuzzer was on, "Chesney's a forceful leader. Usually, highly influential toward Oakes. Also, a relentless supporter of Marsco, so what he wants, he usually does not stop pursuing until he gets it."

"So, 'proceed with caution.'"

"'Extreme caution.'"

"You're entirely right, Walter," Zot responded when the engineer finished explaining Seattle's request. "I can't see why blabbing about an escape attempt is in anyone's best interest, especially ours."

Tessa added her take, "Unless HQ intends to make it their interest. I mean, digitized records were distorted for years before the Continental Wars. Plenty of historical records were co-opted. Taking something out of context is not new to Marsco."

"Yes, some of it with 'good intentions,' but changing any historical record destroys credibility, betrays public trust. And since I don't trust this Liddle, I can't trust this whole bailiwick."

"Did you get a good look at him during your visual link?" Zot asked. "What's your take?"

"He has a sleazy side to him, that's for sure. Even on screen, he was reluctant to look me directly in the eye."

The next day, Miller sat with Tessa at a small table in the mess of the *Hoover*. Zot joined them with a tray and three coffees. None spoke.

As though playing a game with his daughter, the older engineer drew a design on a piece of scrap paper. When he elaborated, it was clear he depicted the Earth. Tessa picked up a red pen and drew a red triangle around the planet, the sign for danger and caution. Sipping their coffee, the three knew each other's minds without words or discernable notes.

Miller continued the game. He marked what looked like an engineering equation on the scrap: "$L < T?$"

Without missing a beat, Tessa took her red pen and turned the question mark into an exclamation mark: "$L < T!$" *Liddle does not equal trust*, she clearly implied.

Zot added, "2X!" to reinforce the idea and show he understood.

Miller began again: "$C\text{-}S \leq T?$"

Zot moved the paper so it faced him, thought a moment, and without giving any expression to his face since they were probably being digitized the whole time, changed the equation to "C-S = T?"

Tessa, probably the most intuitive of the lot, changed her husband's note to: "C-S = T!"

They sipped their coffee in silence then Zot finally noted aloud, "Java in space sucks! Can't wait for real Earth-side coffee!"

⸻ • ⸻

"How's Tessa?" her concerned father asked when she didn't appear for a meal.

"Bit nauseous each day still," Zot replied. "I'm glad we're moving at a good clip and there's no need for hiber—"

"It would be cryo," Devon corrected gently as he joined them.

"Point taken, but she's enjoying natural sleep. I'm guessing the first's about sixteen weeks along, equivalent weeks. The second's four weeks behind. Conception was fifteen years ago, after all." He then added, hiding a grin, "And ten years ago."

"So, one is fine, two is fine as well, but behind," Miller whispered.

"I'm married to a walking medical miracle."

The three men were alone in a small compartment off the main mess where an hour before the entire crew and all the passengers had eaten. From where they sat, the side viewport showed them Earth in the far distance. The Moon looked like a star, but the planet itself was nearly the size of a finger disk with a blue and white glow about it.

"Thought I'd never see this again," Zot noted. Looking at Devon, he added. "I understand you've gone a pretty far stretch from Earth, as well, colonel."

"Yes, indeed."

"So, why did it take Marsco so long to repeat the *Gagarin* mission?" Zot pointed out the viewport to an orange-hued dot, obviously Jupiter. Although its red spot was not discernable, the luminous sphere was clearly not a star, too big, too bright to be anything else but the planetary colossus.

"Ah, yes, Marsco and its decisions: HQ, MAS, VBC, makes a guy dizzy," the explorer-turned-Security-officer blew out an exasperated breath. "I can't see that things up in Seattle have changed that much in the past fifty, sixty years. You wouldn't have taken your *Sirius* jaunt if you thought things were going to change for the better. Why go when things are looking up?"

"Well," Miller responded, "I'm still not comfortable discussing the *Sirius* mission generally and for reasons I don't fully understand myself. The VBC's director considers our mission black. Until she makes a decision, I'm mum. I don't want to undermine whatever independence the Center now enjoys. I'm certainly not becoming a holographic image for Seattle to use, distort, trump up."

"Jenna supports you in your reluctance to be Seattle's—or Chesney's—poster boy. You can trust her," Devon stated softly. "Look, you can trust me, too. I have an inkling what those bastards are up to, but I can't fully put my disks around their true intentions. Whatever they are, I am wary. Oakes is like an icebreaker, not a subtle bone in his body. And Chesney, he's smoke. Distorting of your view, choking off your breath, signifying a fire somewhere even if you can't spot it, and giving off a distinctive odor."

Miller laughed. "I'd say the miasma comes from Liddle."

"That's very neat," Zot quipped moving back to Devon's point. "And so, *colonel of Security*, we're to trust *you* in this analogy?"

"I guess not," Devon replied, looking as though he was leaving since at least Zot was not budging an inch.

Miller rested his hand on his son-in-law's wrist. As the iceman backed down, Devon grew more relaxed himself. Finally, Miller stated, "Okay, cards on the table. Why would Seattle want to trump up the *Sirius* return?"

"I can't say exactly *why*, but I do suspect something underhanded."

"Well, we knew *that*, colonel," Zot shot.

"Just a minute," Miller told the hiberman, "I've had some time to read up on the Accords via the Marsco Net. They sound like Marsco's in the process of disappearing from Earth, keeping only a slice around Seattle and its solar system holdings."

"That's its claim, affirmative." Devon looked first at Zot then back to Miller. "But I'd be careful about what I found on the Marsco Wiki. It's supposed to be accurate, but its two prime editors, Erick Blair and Winston Smyth, are notorious for their unctuous support of the board. What we need is a reliable Net, a reliable set of sources for information that can get to the masses. Something accurate, fair, freestanding of Marsco."

"Had that once. It was called 'free press' but was co-opted long before the Wars. That's the Continental Wars, of course."

"'First casualty of war is the truth,'" Zot mused.

"Well, if the Accords do go through completely, we'll have 158 new constitutions around the globe. Each is mandated to begin with the old Bill of Rights and the UN Statement of Human Rights, if you remember those."

"You mean," Miller drew out the argument, "like, 'I can't be arrested without a warrant and probable cause'?"

"Yes, little minor, legal technicalities like habeas corpus, freedom of press, assembly, religion," Devon added to the list.

"Rights of women," Zot added. "No child labor." The iceman drew a proud breath, "Unions!"

"Basic human rights that were taken away mid-century, my century, the twenty-first," Miller stated.

"Yes," Zot went on, "fear of Luddite attacks started it all, *all* being the downfall of democracy. To 'protect' democracy, leaders abridged the rights of all citizens. It was an easy set of steps from there to Divestiture, to Disenfranchisement, to the unincorporated zones."

"To Marsco," Devon ended the logical equation.

Miller laughed. "You forget, Devon, I lived through those times, wrote a history of those times. Well, collected the stories. It's more of an anthology than a history."

"Yes, your *Ascendancy*. Still one of the few works put together without Marsco's finger disks all over it."

"Thanks," Miller replied. "But more to the point today. Do you really suspect that *not* honoring these Accords is actually the board's intention?"

"The board? The old board that drafted them? No. I know members from that board, of the negotiating team that drafted the Accords. Or should I call them *former members*, and they are all true federalists. Maria de Janeiro, Gwanda Bulawayo, Patrick Owen Mellon-Hart come to mind. But they were all summarily sacked as the Accords started to gain steam. And these former reps are now working for feds or are encouraging feds to push their independent status even harder."

Devon looked at both men who had been away from Earth for so long. *They may not be seeing the threats in all this political shifting.* "The former board pushed for changes in Marsco to grant more and more independence to the old subsidiaries. Even some board members wanted to settle back into their existing sids, as long as they were truly reborn nations. Oakes and Chesney first agreed and signed the Accords. But over time as the beginning of all these transformations to Marsco's power came online, they had a change of heart and sacked that board, even though the pair *had* signed the Accords *for* Marsco."

"Having second thoughts?" Zot posited.

"Affirmative. Big time," Devon continued. "I've seen some evidence: Vanovaras being prepared and placed in Moon orbit."

The pair of *Sirius* crewmembers froze at the mere mention of Vanovara weapons. Both Miller and Grizotti had lived through the Continental Wars of the 2060s, one as a man, one as a boy. The mere mention of such weaponry sent dread coursing through their veins. Mushroom clouds. City centers pulverized by one, vaporized by the other. Infrastructure destroyed wantonly. Most of it never rebuilt, so far as they knew. Dust clouds causing a long winter, a three-year chill that brought on another round of pandemics and privation worldwide. A nightmare that set Earth back at least a hundred years and stagnated the planet for the next seventy-five.

Devon finally went on, taking his explanation in another direction. "And, they're up to some process called, euphemistically, *sustainability.*"

Zot gave a laugh. "Sustainability? As in 'the sustainability factor of an asteroid colony'?"

"Exactly, as though the word was a cover. And Chesney's promising a nearly endless life to those who join them."

"You're sure on this?"

"As sure as I can be. And I have much evidence of Seattle amassing fresh troops, materiel. Utterly against the Accords, which call for all Security and Auxiliary personnel to revert to federation control." He paused, "Hence Kyle bouncing between two different Security HQs, Seattle and Sac City." He paused again, "I also think Seattle's deploying some sort of robotic weaponry to supplement their diminishing Security forces."

Miller let out a disgusted laugh. "Bot warriors? *Again?* Military minds and techno-boffins have tried that twice before, both times to the utter failure of the systems. Command and control to a bot is easy to crack, totally unreliable."

"I know," Devon responded. "I was placed into Security earlier in my career. From my little experience, I've drawn a few maxims about conflict. One, it comes down to the troopers in the field with the will to win, and two, an intelligent, flexible plan from above. Bots are too iffy, and looking at Chesney, I'm not sure he's thought out his plan thoroughly. But, I digress."

Miller rose to stand close to the viewport as though standing nearer would help him understand the universe better. "But this sustainability, as you called it, is anyone buying that?"

"Walter, you've had a fifty-five-year bump in your age via icing. Don't you think some associates are envious of you for that? And, what if Seattle offered someone those fifty years, one hundred years, or two, three? Without icing. Living each day fully awake. For all Marsco med-sci knows, maybe you're good for an indefinite number of years. Don't you think someone, scores of someones, would jump at the chance?"

"Yes, I guess: offer it to the right person under the right conditions," Miller agreed, "anyone can be tempted. Everyone has their price."

"Haven't most attempts at immortality failed?" Zot noted the obvious.

⎯⎯⎯ • ⎯⎯⎯

Mei-Ling did not feel any better during her first two weeks heading toward Earth. As such, when Chesney's assistant, Mr. Liddle, asked to speak with her on a visual com-link, she insisted on an audio-only discussion.

"Sorry you're not up to a full link," the assistant to the VP explained. "May I ask how you're feeling?"

"Still weak. It's just a long recovery time after cryo. I'm sure you know."

"Not personally. Never been in space."

Mei-Ling was struck by his honesty. The Marsco she knew was often run by pilots or engineers with space experience. They had a bottom-to-top understanding of Marsco: shuttles, colonies, philanthropy. Those leaders had met and exchanged ideas with the highest associate and to lowest sid. This connection seemed lacking in Liddle.

Well, away more than fifty years, the pilot concluded. *Must make allowances.*

"The board," Liddle explained, "wants to make a big splash about your return. About your exploration trek beyond our solar system, but Doctor Miller seems reluctant. Might I ask why?"

Shanghai felt her personal safety shield kicking in. This was the worst of old Marsco at play. "Have you asked him?" she replied evasively. "He's very direct; he'll tell you."

"Well, perhaps we'll try again. Even Mars—at the VBC—"

"Yes, we answer to them; we're still under their auspices. The director of Von Braun calls the shots." She gave a low laugh, held back by caution and her lingering illness. "And, speaking of 'still being under'—we're still officially under arrest. Can't Security back off at this point?"

"Well, we're working on that."

That's bogus, Mei-Ling concluded but didn't want to aid and abet him by saying so. *Continuing arrest won't put a bit of pressure on Walter to cooperate.*

The next day, Chesney himself was on the com-link to the *Hoover*.

"Flattered to have the vice-chair speak with me," the pilot responded in her weakened voice.

"I am sure I speak for Mr. Oakes, chair of the board, when I say how proud Marsco is of your scientific achievements."

"Thank you, sir."

"And the whole world! Proud! With the Accords coming online, we're just thinking now of the world as one, sort of like when Marsco first calmed the Earth after the Wars."

Nice take on history, the pilot concluded.

Mei-Ling was not on visual to Chesney, but he was visible to her. His slanted grimace didn't help her to trust him.

When Oakes was put through on the third day, her visual lockout was breached. *Knew I should have gone Ludd*, she admonished herself, *and put duct tape over the cam.*

On this day Security wonks had worked with a set of boffins to make sure Oakes and Chesney did see Shanghai. Her coloring was ashen, as they expected. What they hadn't counted on was just how attractive she was.

Even ailing, her looks were arresting. *Who wouldn't want to keep that for-ever*, the vice-chair silently concluded.

Oakes began. "On behalf of the board, let me again congratulate you and your crewmates on a successful scientific mission beyond the solar system."

"Yes, it was a crew effort, and we did lose one member, you know, Doctor Martin Herriff, who probably made it all possible."

"Oh, yes, Doctor Herriff," Oakes replied, totally at a loss. He had not been prepped on a mention of Herriff.

Had you been a shuttle pilot, you'd know about Herriff! the former MAS flier scoffed.

Oakes went on in his usual circles. "Well, your actions represent the true associate spirit of exploration, resilience, and independent scientific exploration, and resilience, so we thank you and praise you as one of our independent, resilient associates."

"Clearly spoken," Chesney, sitting behind the chair, breathed out in a slow huff.

"We here in Seattle have heard you're sick."

"Affirm that, sir."

"Well, you can trust us on the board, best med-sci Marsco has to offer is being made ready for you."

Chesney, behind still, nodded his agreement, easing up on his down-sliding smile.

"Regeneration," the chair continued, circling around his point, "a process of medical regeneration, is being made ready for you here in Seattle. When you're ready for this process, it'll be ready for you."

"Thank you, sir. I look forward to looking into it. But I should be fine by then. My prognosis suggests I should be."

———— • ————

"I am sorry," Dr. Johns informed his patient at the initial stage of their video conference less than three hours after Mei-Ling had spoken to Oakes, "but you must remove the duct tape from the lens, or else I cannot make a preliminary diagnosis."

Worn out from the constant barrage of calls from Earth, the pilot was still not ready to give in. Something about all this attention, the plethora of medical offers, something was just not right. She sensed it.

While Miller was having trouble sending messages to new federations seeking information about their scientific plans and universities, Seattle had no trouble communicating with her almost hourly.

"If need be," Johns went on as smoothly as he could while obviously frustrated with the woman, "I'll have Security order your escort to remove the tape."

Mei-Ling obeyed at that point, fearing her reluctance would compromise the others.

"There now," the physician noted, "not so painful." He gave orders for her to turn for a side view, to breathe deeply, to hook up a few medical monitors to her right arm. The whole time he kept making little remarks like "not so painful," and "that's a good patient" as though dealing with a child.

"Your readouts conclusively indicate it's mostly your spleen."

"Yes, been hearing that for weeks."

"Well, a spleen's an unusual organ. You can live without it in a pinch. But when it goes wrong, like now in you, it can stress your whole hemoglobin system, as it is now doing. Possibly giving you jaundice. In the old days, hey, just remove it."

"Is that a viable option now?"

"Hardly. This is the twenty-second century." He smiled, but Mei-Ling was not convinced his grin was sincere.

"We have now, medical science has now, a process called *regeneration*."

"I've heard something of this."

"Yes, simply put, your own DNA is recombined with a harvested batch of cells from your spleen to reconstitute healthy tissue. This process is at the micro level. Your own regrown tissue is reintroduced into your system, and this transplant repairs and replaces dying or dead tissue with renewed, healthy tissue. Naturally. In effect, your diseased spleen is rebuilt with healthy, new tissue of your own making. It's all based on your DNA—no tissue rejection, no need to readjust to outside elements—like a pig's artery as in the past."

"Or a PRIM transplant," the former dweller of the late twenty-first century noted.

"Oh, yes, of course, *that* process," Johns scurried away from the topic. "But this is a different one altogether. Much more ethical."

"I catch your drift."

"Now," the physician went on to openly explain, "regeneration is not experimental. It's standard. Done on a daily basis."

"Yes, that's clear."

"Well, let me just open the door to something a bit more cutting edge. Something a step beyond mere regeneration."

Mei-Ling thought a moment. How could something like the phenomenal regrowth of a dead organ be a *mere* process? Sounded pretty *miracle of modern medicine* to her. And much more socially, morally advanced than harvesting PRIM organs and tucking them into associates.

"Regeneration can be the first step in a process that locks the body into continued health on an ongoing basis."

"Let me ask you, Doctor Johns, isn't regeneration going to give me ongoing health? Why commit to a process if it's not to restore my health?"

"Of course, regeneration makes a patient well. But once stronger, this next step—of which I am the leading researcher—guarantees an even more prolonged string of healthy years."

"Now, you're less clear."

"I shouldn't say that much under these com conditions. You understand that."

"Yes, roger that."

"Just open your mind to the possibility of a long, and I stress *long*, healthy life. Open only to associates. *Select associates.* In your case, only possible after the spleen's up and ready. Only after the regen team has made sure all your tissue and organs are Marsco pink."

"Roger."

"But for the *right* associate, the one who sees with visionary eyes the benefits of my process, you can imagine the longevity, the health, the—and I say this modestly—the everlasting joy my process offers you. Think of the future Mr. Oakes and Mr. Chesney have to offer you!"

"I'll think about it, sir."

Growing more fragile rather than stronger, Mei-Ling knew it was a mistake for her to leave Mars so soon. She should be in a proper VBC med facility and not with her shuttle mates on the *Hoover*. In her impaired state, thoughts of death came to her. She felt isolated even on the same shuttle, unable to keep her bearing amid her declining health.

Kyle was a godsend.

He acted as a kind of mentor, explaining the new Marsco world to her, one that had so many trappings that seemed the same as her old Marsco world but was really quite different.

Nothing surprised her about his formal and matter-of-fact explanations about Marsco in 2154 until she brought up what Johns was hinting at.

Kyle froze when she described the doctor's vague description of his innovative process. "What does he mean? Any ideas?" she asked.

Mia flooded his memory. At first thoughts of initially falling in love with her, then thoughts of the complete termination of that love. What Johns described to Mei-Ling *had* to be the same process. Mia had been more elusive in describing it, but Johns had used the same obscure terms and nebulous promises as Mia had. The doctor seemed to convey the same formless golden promise. And both explanations stressed the absolute connection to a new Marsco to be a recipient of this miraculous procedure.

Mei-Ling might become Mia, snared in the same web. Kyle tried to explain to her what he feared without mentioning his destroyed affection and his deep concern for those who did move toward immortality. After all, he knew several others caught in this web via their shared Academy experience.

"If this process works," he cautioned, "I fear it robs you of your humanity." He gave a shudder. "I'm not sure we're meant to be perfect," he concluded with the authority of any philosopher confronted with an issue that has the scope of infinity.

"He may as well be in space still, never coming back," Mei-Ling whispered to herself as she sat alone. Like a dreaming tween, she sat curled up in a large viewport bubble. It was late, 0215, and as sick as she was, unable to sleep. Kyle and the others had crashed hours ago. But the pilot was restless. Thoughts of Julio Fuentes agitated her.

Because she often napped for hours, she was generally awake during the silent part of the night. And because the shuttle was somewhere between Mars and a lunar orbit, the endless night around her was deeper, darker, than when a ship was closer to Earth. In her past life, she had been in complete hiber during this stretch of a Mars-lunar crossing.

The isolation, the stygian view, her recurring fevers, all added to her depression.

At this point, Kyle's cautionary discussion of longevity worked to create the opposite effect. The pilot began thinking of the ramifications of restored health and then enjoying that vigor's ceaselessness.

Looking into the perpetual blackness, she rationalized she would be only joining the universe. It was perpetual and constant, why not humans? Wasn't it just the next logical scientific step? If humans were to voyage into the limitless beyond, to take even small steps across the never-never, why shouldn't they do it while prepared to live on and on and on? Cryo-stasis had given her a taste of this extended life, even if hers had malfunctioned. But just this negligible taste can become addicting.

The promise from Johns of this next step, the next logical scientific step, held out to her the same overall effect as cryo but without the hassles or fear of death, disease, or icing complications. *Why not have extended life but with fewer, if any, dangers?* she justified.

It was giving her her own life back from before the *Piazzi*. A clean slate. A total reset. With a fifty-five-year hiatus in her life already, starting anew was enticing.

Mei-Ling looked into the all-surrounding blackness and felt her soul stirring, yearning to become part of that alluring eternity all before her.

EIGHTEEN

THE GRANGERS MEET

(New Grange, early November 2154)

It was close to 2100 hours when Devon arrived at New Grange with Walter Miller, Tessa, and Zot. They had all been in Seattle for weeks. But finally, Devon commandeered a Security HFC and skimmed them down to Miller's former spread. Placing the nimble craft near his guesthouse, he made sure nothing was disturbed around the farm.

Walking down from the small rise toward the main house gave Miller time to get his bearings. The night was flooded with a bright Marsco Moon, but pockets of rising ground fog kept the light muted. "Yes," the senior engineer repeated several times as they moved closer to the center of the grange, "this was it."

Although looking like he was still in his mid-forties, his memory of this grange went back nearly three-quarters of a century. His remarks tumbled out like an expatriate returning to his home village after a lifetime in exile. Periodically, the former granger would stop to point out a particular memory-laden place, where a water condenser once stood or where a low wall previously ran.

"Is it easy to imagine everything as it was, Father?" Tessa asked.

"In many ways, it's so different, so vastly changed. The extent of their cultivation is enormous. In other ways, it's exactly the same. Like I've never been away."

Miller repeated that observation as they came up to the main house through the garden. The new orchard was triple the size of his, but in the PRIM riots that initially ravaged his grange, almost every tree nearest the house had been razed then replanted. Orchards, gardens, condenser units, all were redone on an impressive scale.

The former owner stood in the garden outside the kitchen and scrutinized the house. A cistern was no longer here. Fifty-year-old oaks surrounded a patio and lawn, giving shade in the summer. Once it was only a bit of latticework. While standing there, the current owners came out to meet their expected guests. "I've been waiting to make this introduction for weeks," Devon stated to his cousins Trent and Celine.

Touching the exterior wall of the great house, Miller stated, "It's all exactly the same, only somehow different."

Celine explained. "Grandfather Darrow used the layout of the former house and rebuilt it as close to its original shape as possible. That was forty-seven years ago."

"He's the one who brought down all the red brick from Sac City," Trent added. Miller saw no signs of his mismatched PRIM-salvaged bricks anywhere. "Used all new material," the granger went on, "actually, a Brunel cousin of mine was the supplier. Cast a wide enough net to catch a Brunel, and he's in construction of one kind or other."

Celine took Miller's arm cordially, "Welcome home. Come inside and see. We hope you like it."

"What's not to like," Zot whispered to Tessa, both overcome with memories and emotions of the house.

The current owners and their guests stepped out of the garden and into the inviting great room. "Original floor and hearth," Tessa stated with delight looking at the polished flagstones. The fireplace and mantel were exactly the same except lighter in tone. Its stonework had been sandblasted when reconstruction began to remove the soot from when the building burned down around it. Tessa had been an adult when her father had taken up his granger life here, but aspects of this place were still home to her. This room particularly meant so much. She took Zot's hand and squeezed.

People came back after I was last here, Zot noted, *came back and torched it completely.*

"We use this room for all our celebrations," Celine informed them.

"I try to never miss Christmas or the summer solstice," Devon added.

"We've plenty of room for you with us," Celine stated proudly. "I know

Devon wants his own guesthouse, our smallest, but you three must stay here."

"Kyle, my aid, should be here soon, too," Devon stated vaguely. "And we may also have another guest, Mei-Ling."

With the mention of Kyle, Sarah stepped from the shadows of a hallway leading down to the kitchen. Withdrawn and self-conscious around such an array of associates, the young woman had held back and stood gazing, awestruck while everyone entered.

"Oh," Trent stated, preparing to introduce his daughter.

Before her father spoke another word, Sarah lost all reserve and threw herself into Devon's arms. "You left without saying goodbye," she insisted but without any real anger or disappointment in her voice.

Devon laughed. "Now, was that meant for me or Kyle?"

Sarah blushed, but his teasing hit close to home.

"I'm Tessa," a woman stated, stepping forward.

Sarah glanced at the visitor as though she were a goddess. Tessa was the first associate woman the sheltered granger had actually ever met. And, to the young woman, the associate's hair and skin looked radiant; her demeanor pure happiness, contentment. She stood confident, yet comfortable. The granger remained speechless while eagerly reaching out for Tessa's hand. Their exchange gave her skin a slight tingle.

"Finger disks do that sometimes," the associate chuckled. "More of a shock because it's unexpected; it's not serious."

Zot stepped forward and also shook her hand with the same tingle. "Sarah, a pleasure." The young granger continued to blush. His dark features and hair, with a few gray strands, made him look an equal to Devon in her uninitiated eyes.

Tessa moved aside. "And this is my father, Walter."

"Welcome," Sarah whispered, overwhelmed with these visitors in her midst. Turning to Devon, she pouted and asked, "Why have you waited so long? Didn't you return to the Moon weeks ago?"

"Yes," Devon explained, "but HQ wanted our guests to stick around Seattle a bit. I finally pried these three away."

"Free at last," Tessa smiled.

"As free as a nebulous 'house arrest' ever is," Zot murmured.

Unsure what that all implied, Sarah said again, "Well, you are all most welcome to New Grange." Her eyes shot a glance at Devon that pleaded for a single word of Kyle, but none were forthcoming. *Just as well.*

"You must be hungry," Celine finally remarked. "I'm afraid all we have is what grangers call 'a little lunch' if you'd like to eat something." In true farming tradition, her little lunch was a spread of ham and beef sandwiches, her own canned pickles and watermelon rinds, preserved summer fruit from the orchard and berry patch in a light custard, milk, coffee, or tea and a chocolate layer cake Sarah had baked early that morning which somehow survived feeding all the hands.

Zot and Miller ushered Tessa forward. "I won't argue," she laughed. "Eating for three, you know."

Celine could tell—mothers have a way about them for that. Sarah stood puzzled for a moment until Tessa motioned the young granger to sit by her. "I'm somewhere along in my second trimester," she whispered. "My cryogenic beginnings slowed some development, but they're both right smack on track now. And loving the full-gee, rich oxygen environment of Earth."

"They?"

"I'm carrying our twins, Zot's and mine," she grinned with a thick ham sandwich in hand, ready to eat.

———————

Kyle did arrive four days later in the early afternoon. He came with Shanghai, whom he was technically guarding. She was still under arrest, like the others. The returning space travelers were to remain near Devon and his ADC at New Grange.

Sarah was in the kitchen helping prepare the field workers' meal when she looked up at an outline of a man standing in the door. "Ready in fifteen more minutes," she dutifully mentioned over her shoulder, thinking it was an eager hand come in early.

"Hello? Sarah?" It was Kyle's voice.

The granger stood motionless, tongue-tied.

"Well, say something," Roxanne urged her. "He's waiting."

"Hello," she tentatively spoke up. "Is that you? Finally?" An edge now in her voice.

Standing to the side, their cook saw her expression light up. With hand gestures, she told the granger's daughter to talk all she wanted. Serving the hands could go on without her.

Their conversation was two ten-minute bursts. Kyle described Mars, the Palmer Hydroponics Garden Domes, the Herriff Ice Lake, the shuttle trips to and from, and Mei-Ling as this awesome associate who was so helpful with his class on flight dynamics. "It's okay, though, she's *really old*; she looks thirty-five, however."

Sarah's news was less exciting but just as awkward and disjointed. Patrice had stayed in Sac City to continue school, but she wasn't to come home ever again anyway. No one wanted her here. "I mean, Mr. Richardson doesn't," she clarified a bit, but left that story. "And Chase is off and on here. He'll be away with Columbus and his characters for a week, two, then back. Dad's running out of patience with him and his new companions, since grain harvesting came and went and he was nowhere to be found."

"How's Shadow?" he asked.

"Lonely."

"How are you?"

She shrugged but really didn't answer back but asked, "Why so long in coming?"

"Well, that's because of mostly I'm escorting Captain Shanghai—"

"What kind of name is that?" the young woman questioned impolitely, contrary to her often-prissy granger manners.

"She came from China, or her family did. Mei-Ling was pretty sick. She has been iced, *asleep*, for more than fifty years. She was born long ago."

"Before the PRIM Mutiny?"

"Long before that. That ended early in *this* century. She's from the middle of *last* century."

Sarah shook her head in disbelief. "I have to meet this woman, if she's close to a hundred? And what do you need to do with the other woman? Mei-Ling, is it?"

"They're the same woman," Kyle answered with no emotion. To an associate, all this was possible. To the granger, not so.

"How does anyone her age still look thirty-five? It's just not possible." It never occurred to her to think of Tessa.

"Look, ask Zot, he'll explain; he's an iceman."

"Now you're really not making any sense, Kyle."

"It will, you'll see," he answered.

He didn't have the heart to tell her right off, he had nearly made up his mind to forego any time at New Grange and start working on the Moon at whatever domed gardens would take him. At least, that was today's plan before he stood in front of Sarah in the warm kitchen. Of course, Security might have other plans. If he stopped to think about it, *both* Securities might have other plans, Seattle's and Sac City's. He was still not released from either.

———————•———————

Mei-Ling found Walter and Zot. "You know, your personal guard is a welcome sight here," the iceman noted, "but his friend wasn't that ecstatic to speak with him."

"Well," she joked, "he's talked of little else: her or working at the Palmer domes."

Bethany Palmer's name hung in the air. Mei-Ling sensed that residual tug of a lost love, love cut off in its fullest bloom. She had no way of knowing Bethany's ashes had been spread here when Miller started his grange.

Zot, trying to ease the inadvertent tenseness, asked, "Can you stay long?"

"I'm partway through the first procedure for my spleen. With this young pair of doctors, Adrian Lasher and Penelope Elion. Already feeling better. Pain's eased. I guess a spleen's easy to tinker with. Cured my jaundice. My eyes are better, but I think that was just resting them."

"Glad to hear it."

She then added, "Devon's arranged for Kyle to return me to the Marsco Medical Center for my next treatment. He assured Seattle I'd add nothing to their intel by being debriefed up there indefinitely. I've already been filling out screens of questions, however."

"What sort?"

"All technical, about the navigation program, the paradigm adjustments to adapt our star charts for course alignments, that sort of bumf."

"Roger that."

Shanghai withheld all her talks with Dr. Johns. His invitation was still on the table, available after Lasher and Elion regenerated her spleen completely.

Sarah found the whole dinner conversation that first evening with Kyle back incomprehensible. The four explorers were together in a relaxed setting where they felt free of prying Security eyes, even if still detained. The four sensed that like Devon and Kyle, the Brunels were totally trustworthy. The two Security members were more akin to explorers like themselves than Seattle henchmen. And the grangers were devoted federalists; that reassured the returnees all the more.

Celine had set the table in the great room, so they ate feeling comfortably warm thanks to a roaring fire down at one end. Outside, welcome rain drummed the whole evening.

And still, as the meal went on, Sarah grew more and more frustrated. *Everyone*, she concluded, *everyone must be pulling my leg!* "Okay, okay," she waved her hands to get the table's attention. Devon sat near her while on the other side of her Miller was between his daughter and Shanghai, the lively but inconceivably old woman, who didn't even look to be thirty-five but was nearly one hundred. Farther down beyond her parents were Zot and Kyle. Tonight, it dawned on her that all these new visitors were near a hundred or older. It was beyond her.

"How can you just *live* without *aging*?" she demanded.

"Well," Zot started to give her a detailed answer, "there are two choices—hibernation or cryogenic stasis."

"Hibernation? You're not bears!" She snapped but in a good-humored way, bordering on flirting. Tessa didn't mind that the young granger showed a girlish crush on her husband. Zot basked in the attention as though from a kid sister.

The hiber specialist replied, "No interruptions from the peanut gallery or we'll have Professor Tessa here give you detention."

"She's not a plebe. I give her permission to harangue you anytime she likes," Tessa replied, refusing to defend him, although she did add, "within reason and decorum."

Kyle couldn't stand all this attention flowing down the table to Sarah and none of it coming from him. "Basically, hibernation," he started in with the best textbook answer an Academy cadet could muster, "is *elongated sleep*. Is that not right, Captain Grizotti?"

"Essentially. Your mind is controlled by meds and brainwave stimulators to convince your brain it is sleeping for ten to twelve hours under optimal conditions."

"But how long do you really sleep?" Sarah tentatively asked.

"Six-month duration max," the hiberman explained.

"But six months doesn't explain being almost one hundred and looking only thirty-five, if that old."

"And cryo," Kyle interjected, sure his answer explained it, hoping Sarah looked his way, "that's really freezing someone."

"Close enough," Zot responded. "Core body temp is reduced while the brain stays safe. Much longer duration." Growing serious amid all the frivolity of the table, Zot added, "We were all under cryo-stasis for fifteen-year stretches, Sarah, some of us for longer periods than that." The iceman shot a wry smile at Tessa. "Or shorter."

Tessa added proudly, pointing to Zot, "And you're looking at that system's inventor."

He corrected, "I enhanced a system, brought all the protocols up to standard Marsco schematics. That's all."

"All?" Kyle noted, amazed. He'd not heard this before.

"Yet, you haven't aged a bit," the young woman interjected, marveling at them still. And Kyle, who'd never iced, seemed to her part of this supernatural group.

"The change in our chronological age is hardly measurable, the infinitesimal amount we aged over those years," Zot concurred.

As the meal ended Tessa rose to help Roxanne and La'Shay with clearing up. "I won't have it, Tessa," Celine interjected, "in your condition, you stay seated. You too, Mei-Ling. You're our guests."

Sarah rose as expected, but the associate women urged her to stay. Both were taken with the granger: her freshness, her uncommon naïveté, her frankness. And they could see that Kyle was totally smitten but unable to say another word.

Trent brought out a bottle of his brandy. "Here," he insisted, "a little nightcap." In the warmth of the blazing fireside, Miller, Devon, and Mei-Ling, Tessa and Zot, and Sarah and Kyle spoke among themselves.

"More than a kid's sip, please, Daddy," Sarah whispered as he filled glasses.

The granger realized his daughter should have been helping somewhere. But no matter, he concluded, the joshing, the camaraderie, the after-dinner talk was too inviting. It was enjoyable to savor this time. Hard decisions lay ahead.

"What was your ship's name again?" Sarah asked.

"The *Sirius Odyssey II*," Tessa explained. "Named for the star Sirius, the Dog Star. Can't see it tonight but can't miss it either on a clear night. Brightest star in the winter sky."

"It's part of the Winter Triangle," Kyle noted.

"Very good, Lieutenant Roncalli," Zot laughed, giving the warrant officer a promotion. "MAS written all over him!"

In a jocular, mocking toast, the associates all raised their brandy to the coloring junior officer, "To *Captain* Roncalli, soon to command the MAS *Enterprise*!"

Sarah looked face to face, not understanding their in-jokes. As they laughed among themselves, she grew remarkably serious. "And you four were together out there," she pointed up, "sometimes *frozen*, sometimes *awake*—like me walking down to the Richardson spread for a half a kilo of butter—you were out there in the heavens for fifty years?"

"More like fifty-five," Tessa added.

"And lucky to be alive," Zot stated in a sober tone, tipping his glass to salute the health of their recovering pilot.

"She's so pretty," Sarah whispered to Tessa. "Will she get better soon?"

"That's our hope."

———◦———

The next morning, Zot entered the cold great room alone, his coffee steaming. It took only a moment to rekindle last evening's embers into a blaze at the hearth. The overnight chill would be gone soon. Outside, all around him was life: the flower garden blooming with autumnal colors, the swaying valley oaks, and the orchard holding end-of-season apples to harvest. Zot hoped a few late-opening roses were originally Bethany's. Two guesthouses were visible from his vantage point: Devon and Kyle at one, and Chase's mysterious cadre back at the other.

So much freshness after a rain, Zot thought, standing in the open door to the garden and drawing in a deep breath. *Life in space, even in a colony, can never replicate all this naturalness.*

Sarah joined the meditating Zot. She brought a carafe of coffee and cream on a tray. "Roxanne made the coffee so strong this morning," she noted.

"This is Seattle coffee, that's why. Bet you rarely get this fine a roast."

"Is that a perk of being an associate?" she asked with a raised eyebrow.

"Until you leave Earth. It's a great Marsco mystery: we can go to Mars, to Jupiter and beyond, but can't supply decent coffee to the colonies."

They stood in silence at the open great room door. Even though she witnessed this view every day of her life, Sarah had the same response as Zot to the loveliness of her family's expansive grange that morning: its near-winter crispness even in its bareness after harvest, its bounty, its promise.

In a moment, the young woman drew a serious breath. "Zot, did you always love Tessa?" Her blue eyes fixed on his brown; they almost pleaded with the associate's that their history would serve as a model for all her own confused feelings.

"Why do you ask?"

"Because, you know, I was twenty-two in August. And, his was then, too."

"*His?* Kyle?"

"Yes, our birthdays are a day apart. Coincidence. He was twenty-five. But, don't misunderstand, it's not like—" She sipped her warm coffee. "Isn't he *old* for the Academy?"

"I think he went to a Marsco Prep to get ready. A bit like me way back in my century, before all my hibernation and my sustained cryo-stasis." The granger looked puzzled; Marsco history and lore were still totally foreign to her. "I spent two years getting ready to enter the Academy. I passed all the entrance exams but needed to hone up on some academic skills. Got my first finger disks there." He raised his right hand. "Then, as now, Marsco wants the best; not to brag, but it seeks out future plebes with those characteristics."

"And Kyle? What of him?"

"I gather—just ask him, I'm sure he'll confirm this—that he needed the same sort of prep work. But that's not uncommon among associate ranks."

"Several years ago," the young woman went on, warming up to Zot as an older brother, "Devon wanted me to try it, try Marsco, and see if I liked it. Now he says, 'Get into that new university up in Sac City.'"

"I bet you'd sail through either, no question."

Sarah took comfort in the similarities between Zot, whom she was growing to admire more and more, and Kyle, whom she feared to love or even to like at all. He wasn't comfortable like Zot; plus, he was too determined to be so dissimilar to the ideal man she wanted to love. Disliking him kept her safe, safe here at New Grange.

After a sip of coffee, she asked, "Did you know right away, or when did you know you first loved Tessa?"

Zot gave a short laugh. "Oh, *I* knew instantly. But I was reluctant at first. We were in a study group together first term at the Academy. That helped. I saw her almost every day, and she saw me as a friend, a real person, not just someone in a crowd. Although I was a plebe, my folks were never associates. In fact, I was orphaned, raised by my grandparents, who ran a few restaurants in a subsidiary."

"Really?"

"Sure thing." He laughed. "All these ripe tomatoes, the last of your crop, I'd love to make my Nonna's sauce for you guys. I'm famous for it." He paused, then went back to his own life. "So, when I matriculated at the Academy, being a bit older than my class and being so new to the Marsco world with its hidden rules and pecking orders, I clammed up until I got my bearings. Tessa was already a rising star." Grizotti segued into a brief history of just how famous Walter Miller was at that time, his connection to the even more renowned Martin Herriff and their propulsion units speeding shuttles across stygian space to Mars and the belt colonies. "Imagine *me* shy," he snorted, "but I was around Tessa, who practically grew up in the center of Marsco's most celebrated research circle."

"A little like me," Sarah whispered. "Kyle knows things, and here I sit."

"This is a fine place to grow up. And your father. Aren't you in the midst of a political life beyond this grange? Just look. He's helping rebuild a country." Zot's voice lowered, "But do you love him?"

Sarah grew rigid. "I don't ever want to leave New Grange," she snapped, then sipped her coffee to prevent saying any more.

"That's not what I asked," the associate replied softly.

"You sound just like Devon sometimes." Sarah pouted at him; that was the best compliment she knew.

Tessa joined them. Sarah glanced at her with such appreciation. She looked so contented. The granger knew that Dot Richardson had a dourness when expecting. And she seemed always pregnant. Tessa's whole body celebrated giving life.

"Maybe you'll answer some questions, Tess," Zot said. "Sarah's interested in our history."

The young granger's eyes filled with wonder. "You must have had it so easy. Here we are in so undisturbed a spot, and a day or two after we first met in June, there's an attack against neighboring PRIMS and their peaceful village."

Picking up that Sarah didn't want to talk about that, Tessa chided, "And *we* had it easy? Guess Zot didn't get to *that* part of our story. Let me just give the abbreviated summary: we were married on Mars, then had a seventy-two-hour honeymoon that was interrupted by an attack against Earth by a madman armed with dozens of atomic weapons."

"And through all that, you risked getting married?"

"It's a Marsco world," Zot replied, thinking that cleared up everything.

Shadow appeared before Kyle did, but the associate was not far behind. "Let me get you a cup," Sarah said, rising. She soon returned with hot muffins, a plate of Richardson butter, more coffee and cream. Roxanne was right behind her to set a full breakfast on the sideboard: bacon, eggs, potatoes, the works.

"I'm game," Tessa acknowledged. Soon, the great room was again alive with table talk and fine food. Kyle, though, remained quiet with just his coffee.

Finally, Zot asked, "Isn't that where a pool once stood, Tes?" He pointed outside.

"Yes, the one converted to a cistern," she acknowledged.

Sarah gave the story of the drowned Sherman girl so many years before, "when Devon was only one; she was his older cousin. My mom's, too. The pool was removed after that tragedy. The garden just outside took its place."

"So, that makes two," Zot explained, trying not to be gruesome. "I found Jeremy floating there."

"Jeremy Truman?" Kyle asked, speaking for the first time that morning. "Is this where he died? He drowned? Do you know how?"

"He was dead before being thrown into the water," Zot stated flatly, a way to show he was not giving the grisly details, not here, not in front of Sarah and Tessa.

"I buried Jeremy right near here," Zot went back to his story by pointing through a large window overlooking the garden.

"Well," Sarah added, "I've heard over the years that a body was found buried here when they reworked this area into these gardens. It was reburied up near where all the Darrows are." She pointed off toward the south, beyond Devon's guesthouse. "Those remains were with two dogs. That's always part of the story."

Zot stayed silent.

"Will you show me?" Kyle asked. He was finally devouring a cadet-size helping of Roxanne's fare. Sarah was pleased; he'd lost weight.

"I'd be interested in that, too," Zot added, coming out of his reverie, starting to rise as though this walk was beginning in that instance. Tessa kicked him under the table. "Well, perhaps I'll have another cup of coffee instead," the rebuked iceman remarked.

───※───

Sarah and Kyle walked slowly up the hill toward the smallest guesthouse. Once on the downslope from Kyle's digs, the rest of New Grange faded away behind them. They were heading south, toward a hill and grove of trees at the farthest edge of Brunel property. Beyond its border sat a series of granges and a small village, one untouched in the recent pillaging.

They walked mostly in uncomfortable silence. After a moment, Kyle reached for Sarah's hand. Reluctantly she took it.

"Is this the Lovers' Hallow?" Kyle asked as they approached a thick grove.

"It's *Haunted* Hallow," Sarah corrected but growing serious added, "but lovers have used it." They moved under a large stand of oak and sycamore, intermixed with nonnative trees that clearly suggested this grove once surrounded a massive house from a century and a half ago.

"Part of the outward migration from cities at the beginning of the twenty-first century," Kyle explained. "Undoubtedly, those with the resources started abandoning cities, living on their own."

"Sounds like today," Sarah acknowledged.

"In a way, yes, but your grange is a working spread. These homes— these 'starter castles' as I've seen them referred to—were a means to escape connection from the decay and violence of the cities."

"Was it *that* terrible back then?"

"If things weren't that horrific, I doubt we'd have had Divestiture and then the Disenfranchise Movement."

Ahead of them stood the obvious ruins of another starter castle. Three chimneys rose, two broken off above blackened hearths. Basement walls were visible, but their rooms were almost completely filled with rubble. They walked around the ruin's edge, mounds of grass that suggested the foundation of the long-gone structure. "It's double your place's size," Kyle concluded.

"Clearly," Sarah agreed. "I can't imagine who'd need so much space."

"Hard to say."

Hand in hand, Sarah led him down the small knoll and across a strip of pavement that was once a hovercraft pad, then onto a shaded lane beyond.

Out here all alone, Kyle wished he had brought his Enfield. He had been issued a Security 9 mm, but since arriving here at New Grange, some-how strapping it on made little sense.

"Well, here's the cemetery," Sarah stated as they paused.

The graves sat atop the tallest rise of the Brunel spread. The two dozen Darrow graves faced north: Sarah's grandparents, their children who died young, other extended family members, the Sherman girl. The tall trees lower down the slope blocked most of the view back toward the north. Through the autumn-bare branches, Sarah pointed out the smallest guest-house; seeing anything more of New Grange was impossible.

"The story goes, some graves were already here when my grandfather Darrow staked out New Grange in the first place." Sarah brought Kyle to a polished stone with the man's name and dates. "The founder of our way of life," she whispered with pride. "He started all this the year before my mother was born."

Other Darrow graves showed that Celine had lost two brothers in childhood and that her mother preceded her father here by a few years.

"She had no living sibs," Sarah explained, "so when father married her, they got New Grange."

"I've pieced that together," Kyle added. "Brunels were doing fine with plumbing and building supplies up in Sac City at the time."

"Exactly."

"But no land."

"Not until New Grange."

Kyle found himself at a loss for any other words, until he asked, "What's up there?" He wanted to move behind some trees and into some privacy with her. Every direction but north was treeless and so they stood exposed from three sides.

"More graves. C'mon, I'll show you the one I think you want."

At the far end of the plots were twenty-some graves in three crooked rows, showing hasty burial. Each plot was marked simply with a stone crudely carved with only the notation "PRIM Summer 2102."

Kyle explained. "There were riots and pillaging raids in '97, well before the PRIM Mutiny but a sort of precursor to it. That's when Uncle Jeremy was killed, January 2097."

The last stone in this line had the note, "PRIM, unknown date, reburied here, 2116. With dogs." Jeremy Truman for sure.

"My great-uncle was a sid, an independent sid, much like your family," Kyle set the record straight. "Trumans never were PRIMS."

The associate drew a labored breath, touch more deeply than he'd imagined. This was no longer a research project; it was family. Here lay his kin, his ancestry buried in New Grange soil. "You are part of the land; it's part of you when your own are deep within it," he whispered.

"Did you know all this before you came to New Grange your first time?"

The associate shook his head. "Mostly speculation. I've learned much since I began coming here. Zot cleared up a great deal. The Richardson grandfather, too. On the whole, however, I only knew in general terms that he died somewhere around here. And not on his own place." He threw a point off toward where believed the Truman spread once stood. "In the January '97 rampaging. The rumors were always that it was during the PRIM Mutiny, but now I know it was before then. My granddad was reluctant to tell me any other details."

Sarah knelt next to the grave and picked away clumps of weeds growing around the headstone's edge. "I haven't been up here in years," Sarah began, hoping this explained her muddled feelings. "I mean, alone with a man."

Kyle looked puzzled. He took a knee next to her.

"I brought Nate Richardson up here once."

"Sarah, you don't have to explain. I've been with—"

She put her hand to his lips. "I need to. I was only sixteen. Not yet really interested in such things. I didn't know what it really meant. Lucky, just lucky I didn't swell up like Dot Richardson. I was so naive. I let him. He didn't force me. I was just sure it was for love *of me*. Then, within days, I realized that Nate's love was for New Grange, not me. His folks want Chase to marry a daughter—any will do—and me, Nate. Father won't have it, unless Chase really loves either Patrice or Hy."

Kyle drew a breath, "And you never loved him?"

"God, no. Not like you," she let slip. "But let's not talk of him," Sarah said, rising and holding the man tightly in her arms. In a moment, she whispered, "Kyle, I'm just not ready yet. Is that okay?"

"Yes, of course. I understand. I thought I loved someone, too. And she was there to lure me into Security."

"Aren't you *in* Security?"

"A different kind. An unending kind." Kyle kissed her gently. "Sarah, I've loved you since I first saw you." He kissed her a second time. "I know it sounds so silly."

Sarah embraced him willingly. She held him in a snug grip but kept asking herself, *Oh, Kyle—are you leaving again? Going back to Seattle? Staying an associate?* It never crossed her mind to wonder about distant Mars.

"Look over here," she finally said, pulling away. She walked him out to a rising point along the ridge. They stopped where the crest dropped steeply down. From the ridge's highest point, nothing blocked the eastward view. "That's Tillson's spread," she pointed.

"Was the Truman place," Kyle went on about his history once again. "An Indie dairy farm. I know of the two boys who lived there. One is my grandfather; the other's buried back there."

"I want to tell you something no one knows, not even Patrice," Sarah confided, pointing to the dry and desiccated Tillson property. "I want that land one day. I want my husband and I to farm that land, make it prosper."

Kyle gave a gentle sigh of gratitude for her being so trusting to share her dreams with him. "And so you shall," he promised. "Couple of condenser units, solars and windmills for power, plow up that dead grass, plant decent alfalfa—"

"With you?"

He balked. The land he wanted to cultivate was under a red and dusty sky, within a pressurized dome and utilizing recovered planetary water.

"No promises yet, Sarah," he whispered before kissing her.

"I don't need your promise today. We have time. Please give *me* time."

They stood arm in arm looking at Tillson's in the distance. From this spot, it was the only spread they could see. Both imagined that dilapidated land now a prospering rival to New Grange. Due north, a grove blocked their view of the irrigated fields of New Grange, but they knew that sight well. Another nearby grove blocked the Richardson spread, a second example of cultivation and a measure of Indie success.

Facing due south should show them emerging granges started after the First Accord and a thriving new village, but today, the pair witnessed a different story.

In the growing dark, the early evening wind swirling around them started bringing dust and bits of ash. The air smelt burnt. In the distance, four hazy kilometers from the border of New Grange, thick smoke circled from an Indie grange and that new village situated near it. Both burned fiercely.

Kyle slapped his hip where an Enfield holster should be hanging. "Damn," he swore hoarsely. "Last time I'll go without it."

Menacing inky smoke curled into the gray sky. Another brazen attack had gone down.

NINETEEN

AT THE MASTER'S COMMANDS

(New Grange, November 2154)

"**Y**ou can ask my parents' guests," Chase explained without a care, "that Asian woman and her companions. They saw me coming in late last night."

"They confirm meeting you at 2220 hours," the Security officer noted.

Chase Brunel and Colonel D'Metrus Summars spoke alone in a small room off the kitchen. Both had the sense that Roxanne was hovering about, trying to pick up what she could, in her protective way. *Know her impulse well*, the officer noted, *so like my own mama*. The back of his left hand had a scar that clearly showed his PRIM-disk removal twenty-five years ago when he first upped to the Auxiliary from a mid-continent zone.

"Whatever time you say," Chase answered curtly. "The next day—the day of these attacks—I was in the work shed the whole time, morning 'til night, with our PRIM gang. Working on cleaning and storing irrigation equipment. Ask Tomas, my dad's foreman. We were there most of that day."

"Yes, we can confirm that."

"In fact, I got there after only a cup of coffee from Roxanne for breakfast." He motioned toward the sound of a broom sweeping the kitchen flagstones just outside the closed door.

The Security officer had that in his files as well. Chase's whereabouts were narrowed to only a few hours' gap, the time he said he was sleeping in his bedroom. *If so, first time in months*, the officer snidely noted.

"And you say your guests up there," the officer pointed out a small window and up the rise to the largest guesthouse, "they never leave those grounds. Ever?"

"Well, not *ever*. We were away off and on over the summer and fall." The Security colonel checked his notes. The way Sarah explained it, Chase and his guests were away anytime work was to be done. "But I didn't know I had to be accountable for all my friends' actions," the granger shot. "But, yes, my guest and his followers—"

"The one called Columbus?"

"Yes," Chase added, then pausing, he thought out his next words carefully. "They're prayerful, meditative men. When the evening comes, they pray, meditate; Columbus teaches a lesson. Roxanne arranges our evening meal to be sent up there. We have no reason to leave the guesthouse."

"*We?* But you said the night in question you left around 2200 hours."

"If that is ten o'clock, then yes, the other night I came down here to the main house—I still live here, after all—at ten-ish and haven't been back there. But now we've come around to everything I've already explained. Do we have to go around and 'round?"

The Security officer found Trent and Devon waiting in the grange's great room. With them was another officer just come down from Sac City.

"Captain Kati Singh," she introduced herself. "Liaison officer for the provisional Sac City authorities." Her khaki uniform contrasted with Summars' traditional Marsco Security grays. "Since this area falls under our auspices soon, West Con thought we should be involved in any investigation from the outset."

Trent offered everyone a cup of coffee. Perhaps when Miller owned this house, its great room had such visitors. Looking at the pair (Asian ancestry and African ancestry) the granger had to marvel at the Marsco world even as it was dissolving. With a touch of smugness, he concluded, *Not see the likes of this at the Richardsons'.*

"I hope my son's not in any trouble by association," the granger finally said, as he seated himself close to the massive hearth. "He's a good boy at heart, bit troubled at the moment, but what kid his age isn't at times?" Trent took a sip of steaming coffee. "And, I guess I should have put my foot down earlier about his guests." He grew deeply serious as his lowered voice indicated. "You got kids, Colonel? Would you risk severing ties with them when there's tension between you and them? I think you see the delicate position I'm in."

"Yes, I've two sons and a daughter."

"My daughter's the steady one," the granger stated, then grinned at Devon. "Except she's head over heels for an associate at the moment. But, that's fine with me."

The four shared a pleasant laugh.

Summars put his coffee down, back to business. "I wasn't here earlier this summer, but I read the reports. No trace was ever found linking your guests—"

"*Chase's* guests," Trent corrected.

"Yes, pardon me, your son's guests with those attacks. Security in the old days," he drew a convincing breath, "would of brought in a lander and packed everyone off. I mean every single one of those 'guests'; not you grangers or your PRIMS. But those days are long gone."

"Now, we'd like a thorough investigation before anything goes down," Captain Singh added. "Is that not so, colonel? 'Rule of law.'"

"Precisely." The Marsco officer agreed, "Besides, my job is disappearing as the federations come online."

"As I am well aware. I have a seat in the provisional Assembly," Trent noted as he rose, "but I also have fields that need attending. You are, of course, welcome to go anywhere and ask anyone anything."

"We thank you for your cooperation," Captain Singh replied, showing in this subtle gesture that the new Sac City authority held sway down here now, not Marsco.

Colonel Summars nodded his agreement, acting as though he had already faded into the background.

When the three officers were alone, Devon asked, "And what will your next step be?"

"I've requested a meeting with this Columbus and his entourage," the Security colonel noted, "but they've put me off."

"Can you force this meeting?" Devon went on. "Send them a subpoena or something archaic like that?"

"Wish we could," Singh answered for the colonel. "Those powers don't come into being until a later Accord. Technically, we're still acting under guidelines Marsco put out in 2070, as the C-Wars ended, emergency powers it used to rule for the past eighty-something years."

Colonel Summars winced. Security had a fine tradition he was proud to share in, but parts of that tradition were not always the easiest to defend. What happens next, he didn't know, couldn't say, but at present he was bound by implicit instructions to cooperate fully with these grangers and especially the West Con captain. She represented the future, Marsco's replacement. "Since I have already asked Mr. Columbus up there to meet with me, let's proceed on that, if I may suggest it?"

"You may," Singh acquiesced.

Checking his palm unit, the Security officer stated, "He says he has a teaching session slated for tomorrow night; thus, he is not free until after that. That would be Friday morning. Will that work?"

"Not ideal, but it'll have to do," the captain responded.

"Anyway, I have an HFC at the ready. If you two would, I'd like you to tour the attacked areas with me."

"Certainly," the West Con officer answered.

"You want me as well?" Devon asked.

"Affirmative," the colonel replied. "I'm leaving a group of Auxxies down here after my investigation is complete. You'll be their ranking officer. I'd like you in the know and quite visible, if you don't mind. I don't know what's up, but I want things to run smoothly between us." He pointed to Singh.

"As we all do," the Sac City liaison added.

"And I'd like your ADC to be seen as part of this as well."

"Warrant Officer Roncalli? He was specially assigned to me for a single off-planet mission. I really don't see him as part of Security. Nor myself, for that matter."

"Sorry, you're here; he's here. By all accounts, you *are* in Security. And you both have Security clearance and experience."

"So, he's to remain here, as well?"

"For the present, affirmative."

"Kyle, please," Sarah said pulling back from his embrace, "I've got work to do. You do, too, right?" The grange's root cellar gave them ample privacy even if only 12.5° C all year. Kyle's screen was glowing off to the side. Sarah was making an inventory of all the jars left from last season's canning and preserving. Roxanne and Celine were sharing a portion of the grange's bounty with those neighbors who'd lost everything in the recent attack. No one near New Grange would be left wanting.

"It's just my online classes," Kyle offered as an excuse for not working but caressing her from behind, kissing her neck.

"I did all my studies online," she responded with feigned irritation. "*Online* doesn't mean you can blow it off."

Kyle drew serious. "Sarah, what if I *didn't* need to finish that way?"

She whipped around. Her blue eyes bore down on his hazel ones. "What do you mean by that? C'mon, you've more on your mind. Spill it!" she commanded, jamming a box with a dozen jars of plum jelly into his chest for emphasis.

He was not able to resist her when she looked deeply into him like that, glimpsed into his soul. "Well," he put down the jars and took her hands, "I don't need to finish my degree *online* if—"

"You're *not* staying in Security, are you? I'll scream at Devon if he thinks—"

"It has nothing *directly* to do with him and nothing *at all* to do with Security," he reassured her, even though he did have his Enfield's webbed belt draped over a chair. "It has more to do with me. And you, Sarah."

"Me?"

"Yes, I want to return to the Academy."

"Way up in Seattle? Can't you stay right here and just finish off—"

"Not really an option for me. Technically, as you say, I am *in* Security." He tapped his holster as if that added all the evidence he needed. "I'm not just a lowly warrant to be ordered about at Security's whim. If released, I'm still a cadet on temporary assignment away from the Academy. Either way, Marsco still calls the tunes. I can't just *stay* here."

"Well, why not try?" She wasn't pleading but reassuring him that compelling reasons existed for him to stay near her. "You were in West Con Security last summer. Stay with them. Or arrange to remain at New Grange with me, do an independent study on soils or something," she whispered before kissing him.

"Wish it was that easy. But my future soils are all *extra*terrestrial, remember. Red Martian dirt made fertile by melting frozen Martian ice."

Devon found them at this point. "Roxanne said you two were here. Kyle, hate to break this up, but you're needed."

"Yes, sir," he responded smartly, snatching his holster and leaving Sarah's embrace without another gesture toward her.

Leave me today to help Devon, fine. Leave me tomorrow to go to Mars, and we're done.

"You sure pulled the short straw," Colonel Summars smirked to Kyle as the Security HFC settled down near the burned-out PRIM village. "You've witnessed the signs of more attacks."

"Lucky me, to keep being an eyewitness from a distance," Kyle responded too snidely to such a senior officer. Summars was career Security, not someone like Devon who took his role much less solemnly.

The cadet thought better of his attitude and added, "Sir, I did fire at a group of attackers early on that first day, sir."

Summars hid a laugh. *Security has again intimidated another associate. We've a long, ignoble tradition of doing that.*

An Auxiliary squad had patrolled the area while the village was still smoldering. It then returned to bury the dead. Kyle was saved the gruesome sight of forty-two charred bodies: women, children, old men. "Most of the working-age men and women were away when this attack started," Singh conjectured, "which probably explains why the attackers had so easy a time leveling the village with no resistance."

"That," Devon added, "and the fact that up until a few months ago, nothing had happened in this locale since the '30s."

"I told them nothing, Magus," Chase insisted, having rejoined his guests for an afternoon awakening. "Nothing they didn't already know."

"You did well, my child-son. They come to see us tomorrow."

The eminent Columbus sat in his corner while six of his most worthy personal attendants filled in a circle at his feet. Patchouli filled the air, too stifling to be pleasing to the granger. All light was blocked from the room, aided by the lowering gray November skies.

Columbus fell into his trance while his acolytes waited patiently for the sign that he had reached a spiritual realm unachievable by them.

Chase chided himself for thinking this might all be show with little substance.

One acolyte rose to burn more cloying incense. In unison with this teacher, Chase breathed in deeply, held his breath, breathed out slowly, aware of only his innermost thoughts. The whole room grew hushed except for the sound of air coming and going into expanded lungs, expanded consciousness.

"Let your mind receive insight," Columbus whispered hoarsely. "Breathe in our enlightenment. What wants you is calling to you. Receive that call."

I'm sure this is not right, the granger chastised himself, because at once Hyacinth filled his entire mind. The lithe woman haunted the young man, her smile, her features, her body that he ached to possess. He might have her the way his father and mother were, but Columbus's way showed him clear dominance. Clear supremacy. Never give, only take.

And yet, in the recesses of his mind, Chase knew Trent's way was best. Straightforward. Committed to her. Guarding and protecting her. Make her a partner in his dreams.

Relentlessly, Columbus' voice told him differently.

The teacher's declarations resonated in a tone that made it sound distant and detached from earthly form, "Imagine what the dream has given you. What has come is that which you deserve, what the universe wants you to possess, to control."

Chase breathed in unison with the rest of the men in the room. Slowly, heavily scented air went into his lungs, but with his mind fixed on Hy, the air seemed to assure him that his vision was more real than his comrades around him. She was *not* imaginary; rather, the others had become illusionary.

Columbus's droning dictates grew more insistent, "You must discern to possess what you see. It is your right to seize it, to dominate it." The room breathed out, in, out, in. Chase kept his eyes too tight for relaxing; his breath seemed to be racing as he imagined Hy waiting for him, wanting him. The neighbor down the lane, the girl next door, the younger sister of his first love: she had grown into quite a beauty, a faithful companion who fixed her hold on his affection.

"Tell us what you desire, Alexie," commanded Columbus.

"I see an Enfield," the follower confided with eyes closed. He had to gulp down air and run his tongue around his lips to continue speaking; he was that animated. "I hold my own Enfield."

"Yes, Alexie, it shall be yours to command, not our enemy's to destroy us. If you envision it, that means it is calling you, calling you to own it, possess it, use it as we see fittest for our purpose."

"I see flames," a second acolyte offered without bidding. "I see more villages becoming embers when their PRIMS resist us, resist our ways."

"Hold those thoughts of rage. Retribution is calling on you to seek and commit yourself to bloody revenge. Savor those visions; one day soon, you'll act on them. Our past injuries mean their future blood."

Chase remained motionless except for his breathing. In, out, in, out. Hyacinth remained on his mind, in his mind, in his whole being.

The rest spoke softly of what they beheld: weapons, the dead ones who'd first tried resisting, the tortured who'd futilely pleaded for mercy.

"They really want this. They are commanding us to give them what they really want. We have to control them as they call us. It's what they want."

In, out, in, out went the room's single breath. Chase treasured inhaling, because each breath seemed to make Hy more alive before him, more solid and tactile than the very room where he sat. In, out, in, out. He held her hand and they walked across New Grange. Lush, green springtime New Grange. He had never loved his family's land so much. It was like she was giving him his own, what was his, but from her, he took it and loved it, cherished it. As he would cherish her.

"And you, our child-son, what do you see?"

"I cannot say." The granger's son shied away from sharing his desires.

"Cannot or will not!" flashed the teacher, his instantaneous anger unrestrained. "Tell us or leave us. For you *must* know that *we* must know." His voice almost broke, but he forced a pleasant request at the last, "*I* must know, my child-son, to guide you."

"Please forgive me," the young man whispered, shamed, caught between the exhilaration of the moment with his imaginary Hyacinth on the fertile land he so unexpectedly loved and this pronounced anger of his mentor. "It is hard to know."

"Know? What to say or what you see?"

Fearful of losing touch with the holy one, Chase caved with little effort on the sage's part. "I see," he hesitantly began, "clearly I see—"

"Yes, my child-son," the mystic cajoled, with sharp impatience slipping into his tone with each word, "what do you see?"

"A girl."

"Any special girl?"

"A neighbor girl."

"Does she come here to swim?"

"She has, with my sister, Sarah."

At the name of that young woman, Columbus moved out of his trance like a stalking animal, prowling, moving so slightly as the last rays of sun dropped and all the world became pitch black. The listener moved slightly closer, opening an eye.

"Tell me," the mystic continued, "what is her visage? Her face like?"

"She has light brown hair and eyes, not dark hair like Sarah's." Chase drew a breath, not in rhythm but in desire to hold that woman.

"And why do you bring her to you like this, my son?"

"I don't know. When I was asked to fix on an object I desired, she came to mind." He knew he must refuse to speak of New Grange to them.

"Then, she is wanting you to have her. Do not resist her call. Seize her, possess her, as with the others as I have commanded. Take her at your will; bend her to your will. A mere child-girl!" He derided. "She is there but to be commanded. She is calling you to command her. Whatever you desire of her, it is really her calling you to do so."

"Yes, as you wish."

"Not as *I* wish. But as *she* wills!" he sneered. "It's thus in our old ways. But, do you also speak of your sister? Is she in your mind as well? Calling you to bring her to us to hear us?"

"My sister would not come here again," Chase replied, too honestly.

"*Why not?*" Columbus demanded before controlling himself. "But it is her will to be here, too. I feel it. She draws us to her because she wants us."

I don't think so, Chase heard himself answer. He did not share that thought.

"You need to bring them both here, your sister and her friend, bring them to meet us, let us know their rightness for our Elect. Women must come to us, else how can we continue? So we call them to be here as we bid them. For women are dear to us."

"So then, with Hy, with this girl who calls to me, how do I proceed?"

"Demand her obedience," the master replied in his ethereal voice. "She wants only to be commanded by you, a man, commanded and bested by your strength to help her weakness. Else she wouldn't be calling to you."

"Y-yes," Chase agreed hesitantly.

"But, she's chosen well. You are a wise choice for her, but bring her to me, first, so I can judge her fitness for you."

"Yes," he answered clumsily.

"And your sister. She must know what we have to offer her as well."

"Yes," Chase responded, assured of the master's powers.

———————◆———————

"I'm ordered to leave sixteen Auxxies here," Colonel Summars explained to the other three officers. Their impromptu meeting took place in the New Grange great room. "These two squads will bivouac in this locale, one at this grange and one to the west."

"That'd be the Richardson spread," Kyle noted. The warrant stood by patiently, sure none of this affected him. He had inexplicably received recent orders from Seattle that detached him from Chavez-Sherman and then a readmitted him to the Academy for a final semester starting January. It was that close to happening. Even if it was the fifth change in his orders over the past few days.

"Have you cleared it with everyone?" Devon asked. "I mean, these are Indies, grangers who may *not* want Marsco help."

"These Auxxies fall under my auspices, actually," Captain Singh noted.

"That's fine, Kati, but still, placing them on someone's land. Under the Accords, the housing of troopers—"

"They aren't Marsco's Auxxies, but ours," she noted firmly. "These units answer to the new Sac City authority."

"*Provisional* authority. But they will still likely be perceived as Security troopers by local Indies, I'm sure."

"But, clearly, a locally controlled Auxiliary squad is not a Marsco Security unit."

"A fine distinction easy for *us* to grasp. Maybe not so for a granger, especially since the Accords covering all this haven't yet been fully implemented." Devon looked through a window at the Auxxies milling around. Each carried an Enfield sidearm along with its shoulder-fired big brother. *Originally, they carried only non-leths*, the experienced associate noted. *Except for khaki, they sure look like Security troopers.*

"I'll make sure to speak with—" Captain Singh turned to Kyle, "Richards is it?"

"Richardson."

"Come with, if you don't mind, Roncalli. You seem to know this area."

"He does indeed," answered Devon.

"That's extremely important," Summars noted. "As we're speaking of such, the situation calls for another member of Security of at least warrant rank to be stationed with these Auxxies. I'll be reassigning Roncalli here to stay with them as my liaison."

What the hell? Kyle thought but dared not voice. His experiences in both Security units had taught him that much.

"What the hell?" Devon shot. Decades as an officer allowed him to fume aloud. "It's my understanding that *his* Security status was tied to *mine*. He's *my* ADC. I'm to be released from Security duties in time to start teaching spring semester at the Academy. It's all been arranged over the past few days. Plus he's to resume his studies then, too, so he graduates next May. Our new orders just came down."

"Emergency contingency plans. I need another officer."

"But he's untrained."

"Trained enough," the Security officer noted. "One fourteen-month Security hitch already. And training with West Con last summer. He's actually in his third hitch now."

Singh interjected. "I've arranged a three-week crash course, not far, up at the campus in Sac City where our new Academy is temporarily housed. Perfect place for a liaison to train right there amid the very troopers he's to motivate and command. He'll finish soon enough, in the next few weeks."

Great, Kyle smirked inwardly, *I'm being fought over by two officers, two command structures. Damned by both sides.*

"I want him out of Security," Devon steamed, colonel to captain.

"He's free to appeal this decision, but that process takes at least six months."

Singh thought she was saving the day. "He'll probably be done here soon after Christmas, in time to start next January up in Seattle." Trying to appease the young warrant, the federation officer added, "I'll do my best to get you promoted to lieutenant right away, a fed commission. No need for you to graduate."

That will just muddy the waters more, Kyle noted, pissed at the entire situation. But then, with a sidelong sly glance, he imagined a silver bar on his shoulder rather than the bronze triangle warrant emblem. *Well at least I'll reach commissioned status permanently,* he rationalized. *Hell of a way to do it, but an honor anyway I cut it.*

Sarah never crossed his mind.

⸺ ✦ ⸺

"This is my land. I'll protect it myself." Richardson would have none of any federation personnel on his property. He barked at Kyle and Captain Singh on his gravel drive running down from his small house, his large frame barring the visitors from entering his property.

The captain stayed patient with the fuming granger. "Surely, you must understand, sir, we're concerned for your safety and that of the other granges. As a new federation, we need to bolster all our local constabulary during this transition."

"I'll protect my own," the Indie growled. "I'll do it my own way and the old way."

Kyle drew up short at his remark. It sounded so like something Chase had been saying, all that confused gibberish from Columbus. Returning to old ways made no sense in these evolving times.

"Mr. Richardson," Singh continued, "if you're not part of a trained federation team, you cannot be armed, at least with a shoulder-fired Enfield. It's for your safety and ours. Trent, I'm sure—"

"Brunel can be damned as well, trying to take my Enfields."

"Not take," the officer countered, "make sure you are trained, that they are stored safely. And making sure in an emergency that you are assigned as part of a team, following orders—"

"What? To save his ass and lands, but not mine?"

"He'll help you and you'll help him. It's that simple."

"Simple is this. My land. My Enfield. My own defense." The tall granger stood his full height and bore down on the woman. "Get off my land! Or be carried off!"

Trent shook his head knowingly. "That's Richardson. Independent to a fault. Headstrong. And dead wrong." The granger, Captain Singh, and Kyle spoke back at New Grange.

"It's the *dead* I'm worried about," replied Captain Singh. "How many dead will be laid at his feet?" She paused. "Threatening me like that, I could have him arrested."

"I'd ask you not to do that," Trent implored. "He's a cranky bastard, yes, but I think he'll stay within the law, as far as that goes. A few granges burning down closer to his, he'll change his mind."

"Meanwhile, what do you suggest?"

Kyle spoke up. "The Tillson spread will do just as well."

"Your family's old place?" Trent questioned. "Yes, why not. It's to the east, but not far really. You'll need a better water supply. Tillson land is pretty dry."

"I don't have time to speak with him," Singh explained.

"Let Sarah take Kyle," Trent suggested. "He's cantankerous as all hell but more likely to throw cow chips at you than fire an Enfield wildly. He's fond of Sarah."

"And you'll be able to keep the water condenser they're bringing," Kyle explained to Mr. Tillson, as instructed, "and you'll be paid a per diem for every day the squad is quartered on your land."

The grizzled granger listened with his head turned to one side slightly, making up for poor hearing. His eyes were rheumy and drooping. A ragged cap was pushed back so far on his head it looked like it might fall off.

And yet, Kyle found Old Man Tillson more cordial than anticipated.

He knew Sarah, and he enjoyed her company. Had a soft spot for her, no doubt. He urged them to stay for dinner, pointing to a simmering stock pot of pork-seasoned beans and a heaping salad. As dry as his land was, he managed to keep a thriving kitchen garden. He was more provided for than Sarah had thought.

"I don't bother irrigatin' a pasture," he explained. "Can't afford no PRIMS to work a larger herd, and I'm fine with my garden and such out back." They had no doubt what was out back. The pungent smell of his hog pen rode the air at times. "I can make a wicked sausage when it comes to it. Hard to stuff casings alone, so I just make up patties. Fry 'em up and keep 'em in their own grease as I go, in stone jars," a centuries-old preservation method.

Greens and savory beans, some cheese. He actually provided them a fine meal.

"Alone too much, y'know," he confided. "Three sons. Oldest out there—" he pointed to the family plot, "And two off doin' God knows what."

"Associates?" Kyle asked.

The old granger nodded. "One up in space. An Indie. Comes by now and again. The other just in Sac City doin' this or that. Thought he'd do for this lass, at one time that is, but guess not." Sarah blushed. "Mechanical work, wirin' up buildings. The place is goin' guns, up there, goin' great guns."

As it grew dark, the young pair tried to leave, but the old host produced a bottle of brandy. "I hear Patrice's got herself a man up there, too," he started. "Hitched to him, too, real legal, not just shackin' up."

"How'd you hear that?" Sarah asked as gently as possible while hiding her shock. If true, it explained why Patrice's father ordered her to never return to his spread again.

"Oh, this and that. Here and there." He sipped his brandy and stared off in the direction of Chase's guests. "Them are trouble, no doubt, Sarah, my lass."

She nodded agreement.

"Your poppa oughta sent them packin' months ago."

She nodded again. She knew her father's fear, that driving them off would be pushing Chase away for good as well.

"They tried snatchin' one of my piglets. She was squealin' like 'twas a fox took her away."

"How'd you stop them?" Kyle asked.

"Hit 'em with wet cow shit, how else? Tol' 'em rock salt was comin' at their thievin' asses next. They lit outta here damn quick then." He gulped at his brandy. "A heifer was mutilated dead the next night and one of my pig shelters torn down, too. Bastards—" He glanced at Sarah over his tumbler brandy. "Sorry, lass."

Tillson now looked at Kyle. "Them troopers will keep their filching hands off my livestock, right?"

"They'll only take what you sell them. They'll not pillage, if that's what you mean."

"That's exactly what I mean. I know y'think I'm dotty, but I read a great deal." He motioned to a darkened room he had not shared with them. It was lined with books. "History. Armies. Armies encamped somewhere— Napoleon. Lee's in Pennsylvania. Y'think I don't know."

"These men and women will be under strict command and will not be pillaging."

"She seems to believe you, lad," Tillson replied, pointing first to Sarah then to Kyle. "If she does, I do."

———— • ————

"What was he doing at your spread?" Chase demanded of Hyacinth as he brought his four-wheel ATV to a stop. They were just at the hedges below the guesthouse. It had grown dark, and Chase was doing as instructed.

Filled with feelings for the woman but also filled with Columbus's lessons, once in shadows close to the house, he stopped and pivoted to Hy, looking her in the face.

Rage burned. He knew he was losing New Grange. He knew somewhere in the recesses of his mind that he was going to have to share this woman. He knew he loved her as well and should be protecting her. That he should run down the hill with her now and stay safely at New Grange. Bring her to New Grange as his guest, not a conquest. All these thoughts jolted him. He knew too much, but the commanding words of the teacher took control of him. In his pulsing uncertainty, he decided he would have her first, then demand her exclusively. Those others be damned.

All this rage and bewilderment lodged in his face.

"Don't look like *that* to me!" Hy ordered when his face filled with all this desire and conflict. He glared down at her, confused, stirred up, enraged.

For her part, Hy felt that in many ways, Chase was easy to control. Glare all he wanted, she'd have him begging for her, for it, as harmless as a puppy. Patrice had wasted her chance at winning New Grange. She wasn't wasting hers.

"If you want me, come on," she whispered. She took the lead and ushered him down to the secluded spot they'd used before.

In the grove, she backed herself to a tree so she could balance with a knee cocked. Her pose had the immediate effect on him.

Chase kissed her neck first, and as she sighed, he next leaned onto her supple body. "Oh, Hy, you're mine, right?"

"Could be, if I knew why you think so."

"Because I sense you wanting me to have you."

She seemed to purr with that, fingering his neck, rubbing down his back.

"Columbus says you really want me, you're really longing for me, even when playing at your game of *not* saying so."

"Is this *not* wanting you?" she teased, her hands moving farther down his back, around to the front of his legs. "What's the best way for us?"

"You'll be mine!" he insisted, leaning harder, breathing harder. "Columbus says so, that I must take what I want! It's the old ways he believes in."

In that moment, she stopped him. She *did* want his passion, especially now that she had him, but she wanted him for himself. She was damn tired of hearing of Columbus, as well. Her teasing and invitations stopped once that vile old man entered their discussion.

"No, Chase," she whispered at first, believing her longtime friend and neighbor would respect her definite wishes. When he kept on, his hands all over her, shoving aside her own resisting hands, tugging at her jeans, Hy had to jerk him hard and slap him once to make him back off. "*Stop!* Stop yourself, *you must!*"

"No!" he yelled, knowing Columbus would approve, attacking with renewed strength. He was the man. She was his to be taken, especially because she really was wanting this all the whole time, putting him up to this.

"Chase," she hit at him once more, a glancing blow that only made him irate.

When he struck her back hard across the face, she crumpled to the ground. As much as she didn't want to, she broke into tears. If she sensed he really liked her, if she sensed he wanted her just to please himself, she would have complied, eagerly. But *this*, this was not what she wanted. He stood over her, threatening.

Hyacinth had never seen this before, this mix of lust and violence. And she had never been confronted with failure to make anyone like her and want her on the terms she set and totally controlled. She had never been wanted merely to be used up and then cast aside later.

"Damn!" Chase shouted, more at himself than her. "Hy, I'm sorry. I'm so sorry." He crouched down to help her, acting gently now, Columbus's spell broken. "God help me, I'm so sorry." He was breathing hard, dizzy. Bewildered. Did he really want her like this? Violently? With no real feelings but his own power and lust?

They needed to escape. Now. He knew. It was time to run from Columbus.

Before he could make another move, rough hands pulled him away.

Hy screamed, but her voice was cut off by a hand over her face. Columbus's acolytes were on her. What Chase had only started, they aimed to finish.

Crying, she pushed the first away, got to her feet, her clothes torn. But, too many hands, too many men were there, on her, singly, while others leered or held her against the tree. One, two, three, she lost count. None gentle.

Not content to take her, as she cried out and bit and scratched, they hit her, hard, across the face. Once. Twice. Again. Again. Then on her once more.

Columbus held Chase back. "She wants this, my son. This is her urging us on. She wants this, like the old ways."

The acolytes left the sobbing heap and walked off, pleased with their actions. Columbus turned to Chase. "Come with us, or you'll be blamed for her. By her. She'll lie about this and blame you. They always do, those that wanted it anyway and drew us to them. She'll lie about this and about you."

The magus was pleased with his followers. They'd been thorough.

The young man hesitated. Could he console her somehow now? Or even face her? Fearing being left alone with the beaten, bleeding woman, fearing facing his father, he abruptly followed his spiritual leader in confusion and guilt, leaving the moaning woman.

———•———

Driving back to the main part of New Grange, Kyle and Sarah found her. The headlights of the rover illuminated a balled up human form alongside the road. Sarah recognized Hy's hair before anything else. She had passed out, but her swollen face and shredded clothes made it clear what had happened.

Back at New Grange, Celine, Roxanne, and Sarah cleaned her and got her to bed. Hy hardly knew where she was or what really had happened. She had tried retreating from Kyle in the rover and later from Zot when he came to administer medication to help her sleep.

Before she drifted off, she murmured over and over, "Chase, make them stop. Chase, stop them."

Everyone at New Grange knew what she meant.

———•———

Sarah was out in the kitchen garden when Kyle found her. "You okay?" Hy was finally quiet and resting in one of New Grange's spare rooms. The night had grown darker, with a thin, high fog that hid the sky but not the outbuildings and guesthouses.

The woman collapsed into his arms. "Tell me this is a nightmare. Tell me I'll wake up."

"I wish I could."

"I've known her all my life. I thought she'd become my sister."

Kyle didn't know how to respond. Finally, Sarah asked, "You're leaving again, right? Sooner than we thought."

"How'd you guess?"

"Devon set me up with some clues. But not to the Academy, right?"

"Affirmative."

"Damn," she swore, one of the first times he heard her utter anything like that. "I hate it when you talk like you're in Security."

"Sarah, I *am* in Security. Cadet or not, I *am* still a member of Security. I answer to commands. Once in Marsco's. Now back to West Con's."

They stood at the edge of the garden. Even for all her love of him, Sarah felt: *take me and my life here or take your damn Enfield and leave me alone.*

Kyle got in his words first. "Sarah, I have to leave. My status is now permanent, but it's all a blur. As far as I can tell, I'm somehow in a federation unit—your federation."

"Here?"

"Damn, I really don't know."

Shocked, she stepped to him and put her hands on his shoulders to reassure herself as much as him. "Why would Devon do that?"

"It's not him. He was square with me going back to the Academy with him in January. But that's not my orders. They're from West Con. He can't change them."

Sarah didn't want to hear any of this, but what she did hear seemed more serious.

"As I understand it, I'm to be away three weeks, then be assigned right back here."

"That's rich isn't it? By 'right back here,' you mean New Grange?"

"Yes, here or Tillson's."

She nodded and let him continue.

"The problem is, Sarah, I'm not sure what's ahead for me or Marsco. Dammit, for the federation. Especially once I'm promoted a lieutenant and trained. When shifted back into Security last summer, I was tied to Devon."

"He'd never harm you, assign you to anything dangerous."

"We don't know that. Can't know that. It's not Devon, anyway, but this is Captain Singh. God knows. She's the one in West Con. Jumping the gun a bit—do you follow?"

Sarah's looks showed she didn't understand. Instead of replying, she held him tight. "But you'll be here, you'll be safe and here in a few weeks, right? Promise me that."

"I'll do my best, Sarah, to be here, be here by you, to protect you and this grange."

"Unless there's a war."

Kyle froze but managed to ask, "What makes you say that?"

"I've heard dad and Devon talking. And they've talked with mom and me present. It's possible, right? A war with Marsco? West Con and Marsco, right? And you on both sides, right?"

Before the soon-to-be lieutenant answered, commotion broke out noisily down in the Auxxie tents that were staked out under the shelter of the closest grove. Personnel there were saddling up their body armor and grabbing their weapons. Their squad leader shouted orders, and they were responding smartly.

"What's this?" Sarah asked, unsure of what was going on but catching the fierce tenor of the action.

"Oh, hell," Kyle spat. In the distance, New Grange's largest guesthouse was ablaze. Orange flames leaped above the tall hedge, the windbreak surrounding Sarah's swimming pool. No doubt, those dancing flames fully consumed the dwelling hidden behind.

Kyle nudged Sarah toward safety. "Get inside," he yelled. She didn't move, so Kyle ordered her. "Get inside, now. You stay inside!"

Turning away from her, he ran toward the hustling squad, where he knew he belonged.

TWENTY

AS AUTUMN FADES

(New Grange, November 2154)

"It wasn't *him*, ma, it wasn't." Hyacinth insisted, although Dot Richardson wasn't listening. Her daughter's protests made her fume the way life had taught her, in a barely visible rage felt by others but never expressed. Her long walk from her spread to New Grange in her condition didn't help either.

"If not that damn associate, then who? Father says he came to take our land and his Enfields. Why not take our child, as well?" The woman looked over her daughter's freshly bruised face, several deep cuts held closed by butterfly stiches. Dot had seen wounds like that on her children before. Had her own. She wouldn't let disloyalty allow her to cry, but she felt like she might. But, not here, not at New Grange, where a Brunel might see such betrayal and her weakness.

It was best to blame it on outsiders, as she always dutifully did.

"My Lord, I'm sorry this happened, Hyacinth, my darling," she hoarsely whispered and then held her gently for the first time since she was a child, tenderly but awkwardly, her swollen belly making any embrace difficult. She was due soon.

Ever calculating, the woman wondered, hoping no Brunel or one of their shameless PRIMS overheard, "You can stay here, right? I mean, Chase may come around, come see you—"

"Oh, ma, listen. It's over. It'll never happen again. *And* it wasn't men we knew; it wasn't." The daughter paused, strengthening herself, "And as far as Chase goes, that's over, too."

"Have you seen him?" Dot Richardson asked softly, thinking her daughter still held a chance for a future Brunel alliance. Only Hyacinth's shock after this attack, her mother knew, kept the victim from seeing this as an opportunity. "I've heard crazy stories that Chase has run off with that strange man and them peculiar boys. But who'd run away from you, sweetest?" The granger's wife looked off over her shoulder. "Why Trent put up with that gang of PRIMS for so long is beyond me. Put up with their antics. But Chase will come 'round right, you watch. He'll own this spread, hon, and with you—"

Her eyes brimming with tears, Hyacinth turned to look directly at her mother.

"*He* did this!" Dot Richardson spat, furiously blaming Chase. "Knowing his old man, knowing how high and mighty these folks all are. I just don't know—" She gulped hard to suppress what she might say that was best unsaid here.

"Don't know what, ma?"

"Curse their boy and his land. Richardsons don't need no land from the likes of them. If he's gone and hit you—"

"Ma, we're fine without Brunel land and their son," Hy proclaimed, holding her mother tightly as a child does when trying to reconcile with an enraged parent. "And it wasn't him, ma, it wasn't. I promise it wasn't."

Her mother ceased returning any affectionate grip, her cajoling over.

"He's so unsure of himself," the mother went on, "when you think of it. First, he hounded our Patrice, then you." She caught herself before undercutting her own schemes to attach a child to New Grange. "But he'll come 'round."

It was Hyacinth's turn to swallow hard to keep from admitting more than she ever wanted her parents to know. She'd had a hand in breaking up Chase and Patrice in order to win him for herself. A devoted Richardson then, she'd figured if Patrice had failed, she'd be sure to win. She'd set her trap but then caught the wrong prey. And if no one in her family suspected, if no one drew that conclusion, she wasn't about to confess schemes against her own sister.

"We need each other now, Hy," Dot Richardson admitted, once again holding her daughter.

It was one of the most compassionate moments Hy had ever experienced with her mother. And yet, she realized it still was about her marrying. And her marrying land. And her marrying this land. The Richardson way. And she had to have children soon, legit children, not bastards.

But, in that second Hy also knew she needed to find an excuse, any excuse, not to return home. She needed to find a way to stay here at New Grange. Not to catch Chase but to escape being a Richardson. Like Patrice, she must find her own way and never go home.

The young woman stated firmly, "Sarah says I can stay as long as I want, ma, so I'm staying here."

"No, hon," Dot Richardson changed her own mind once more. "I'm due any day now," she went on, her voice showing vulnerability. "Patrice's gone, probably for good. I warned your father not to be so harsh with her, but, well. All these changes with the way the world runs. More attacks." Her mind settled on a better scheme. "You come home, and when your bruises are gone, Chase'll see you again. That's all it will take—"

Her grown child cut her off. "Trust me, ma," Hyacinth whispered, "I'm standing on my own now. I'll figure it out. I'll be steady, you watch—"

"Of course, babe. Have to be if we want to keep this land. We'll all have to be steady. Curse Marsco. Between them heathens and what all's going on up in Sac City, and these attacks and all!" She lowered her voice remembering where she was, "Makes Brunel's head swell more, him being so often at the capitol. Still, your father will protect us. Protect you. You watch, he'll—"

"No, ma, I'll be steady, but not back there." She motioned with her head toward the family spread. "Like Patrice but not back there," she whispered again. "Never there."

Dot Richardson glared at her defiant child. "Now you sound like that willful Sarah Brunel," she snapped and rose coldly. "If that's what you want, child, you stay here," she shot, balancing herself carefully. "And you don't come home again never, neither."

"That's how poppa put it to Patrice," Hy whispered, but her mother didn't want to hear another word from this disrespectful, brazen mongrel.

"It's out of the question imagining Chase had something to do with Hy's attack," Trent stated firmly, even while knowing he was not being truthful to himself and the others seated around the table. "I know my son." He hardly ate, a sure sign of his guts in knots. And his self-deception wasn't landing as believable to his guests. He could tell that.

Zot, Tessa, Shanghai, and Trent's family spoke among themselves at dinner four nights after Dot Richardson's visit. Hy stayed in her room with only periodic contact with Sarah and Roxanne. Kyle had already gone. No one else dared bring up Chase and his friends, who'd disappeared from the area as the guesthouse burnt down.

"Hy says that straight out," Zot confirmed. As an iceman, he knew a great deal about medical procedures. The victim had finally relaxed enough around him to let him examine her every morning and administer a sleeping aid each evening. She needed rest, and his medicine helped.

After Dot Richardson stormed out the only day she'd looked in on her daughter, the iceman and his charge began having long, serious talks.

"She's a nice kid," Zot spoke of his patient. "Seems sophisticated at first but then very naive. Bit confused about men, how to act toward them. Not because of the attack, but before, how to attract them." The women at the table shot him a look. "I'm not suggesting she's at fault. Not at all. She was attacked, no question."

Being more honest than necessary, Mei-Ling noted that Hy wasn't the first to ever use this tactic. "She's pretty and probably got her way for a long time by harmlessly flirting and teasing. Only takes one angry guy to change the rules." They all knew it had been more than one.

Sarah sat at the end of the table hearing all this but focused on the suggestion that Chase may have had something to do with beating and raping Hyacinth. She thought of her absent Kyle. *Would he ever raise a hand against a woman? Against me?* She knew instinctively that Kyle, like Zot, would never harm her in anger.

"Zot," Sarah finally had the courage to speak up, "when she's better, when Hy's better, will you take us to Sac City?" All eyes around the table whipped around to her. "To see Patrice," she hastily added.

"How'd you know he was heading up there?" Tessa asked.

Sarah explained he'd said something about visiting the campus. The hiberman had contacted the university about possibly working there. He was leaving tomorrow morning early by light rail from one of the newly reopened stations.

Feeling like no one believed her motives, Sarah added nothing more.

The whole table, however, knew she wanted to see Kyle more than Patrice. "We'll wait until Hy's better, though. Not this soon."

<hr />

Captain Grizotti had a 10 o'clock appointment at the library on campus. Arriving early, he walked for thirty minutes, plagued by demons. It was here, fifty-seven years ago. This quad, its water tower gone. Any signs of the murder of the young girl and the boy pushed from the so-called watchtower and Allison with her bleeding forehead, all signs of those were gone except in Zot's mind.

From the quad, it was a short walk to the new pedestrian bridge. At this locale, Lieutenant Rivers had crash-landed Miller's HFC with a jerry-rigged bridge atop to allow armed Bradley vehicles into the complex. Rivers and his troopers stormed in, expecting a firefight, rumors of armed resistance that proved to be false, exactly as Zot had insisted to Rivers before Marsco's attack.

As the iceman walked along, he found every sight plaguing him with memories of that deadly morning so many years ago.

It's a miracle I'm alive and with Tessa, he realized. The passing students and professors seemed to be looking ahead. Zot was looking behind. *This was once a thriving campus*, he realized, *before it was squandered and ruined by neglect. When too many citizens forgot how important all this was for an expanding society. Before internal forces shattered the republic that had been such a promise, a beacon of hope. All ideals can die, can fade by neglect and greed.*

The former Security officer took a few slow steps. *This new federation, all these new feds*, Zot vowed, *they have to survive. Or all they're doing is setting up another oligarchy, another Marsco. The next tyranny may have a different name, but it'll probably be worse. And once more darkness will return to this planet if these feds fail.*

<hr />

Zot spent the rest of the morning in an interview for an intriguing position. With the expansion of the university came the expansion of its library. But more than a century of intellectual carnage had left a stain. Which works were legitimate, which falsifications? Digitally, anything could be altered; plunging into any wiki site today showed that.

Professor Sandra Falls, the head librarian, had held a similar position at the Academy, before moving south to Sac City to take on the project of restarting a top-notch library on this emerging campus. It was her idea to bring Zot in as a sort of historical detective, since he was smart, honest, and had coincidentally lived through a good slice of the events in question. The university wanted to hire someone of his stature. A journey to Jupiter. A fifty-year journey into stygian space.

"I expect this library to boast of an accurate collection," she insisted with a mix of associate pride and stubborn federation determination. "I don't want just any schlock to sit on my shelves, in our computer banks. Nothing that smacks of truthiness, nothing post-truth."

"I'll keep the crap out," Zot promised.

⬤

The university at Sac City had been reopened for ten years when Kyle arrived to start his classroom training. With the Accords coming smoothly over the past several years, however, the activity and sense of renewed purpose were in full swing here. Dorms overflowed. Buildings that had been vacant for years were now completely renovated or replaced altogether. Labs and the library brimmed with new equipment and resources. The newest quads boasted replanted lawns shaded by recently added saplings, all signs that the school intended to grow as the newly instituted federation stretched the boundaries of its complete independence from Marsco.

Has that brand-new quality, Kyle admitted to himself, glancing at a classroom building that wouldn't be finished before the start of January term. *In time, it'll rival any university.*

The newly reinstated West Con lieutenant knew he had to move fast that morning. Patrice had classes all that afternoon, and he needed to report back to his own barracks before 1330.

Intense training doesn't give anyone much time, he concluded when he reached the medical student dorm. He rationalized that he was too busy to send Sarah a message.

"Strict rules. They say it's like Marsco," Patrice explained about her res hall as she greeted Kyle. "We're in six-student suites—two doubles and two singles." One dorm wing was for women, the other for men: nursing students, premeds, even a few pre-dental and pre-vet. Both wings were off-limits to visitors. "Old-fashioned, I know," she pointed out again. "They do that at the Academy?"

"More so," Kyle responded, explaining twenty-bed dorms and gang showers for the first two years. Drawing an exasperated breath, he added, "And sorry I only have time for a quick bite. I'm heading north later today."

"What? Aren't you in training here? Then back to New Grange?"

"Senior officers changing their minds; it's their prerogative. And I have more experience in this—" He paused. He didn't want to explain his first hitch in Marsco Security and what all he'd learned then. "I've had much previous training and don't need any more classroom time, that's all."

"I can't understand all this," she insisted as they headed out across campus, "all this training going on around here."

I can, Kyle admitted. This federation wanted its independence from Marsco. *It will fight to protect it if the Accords inexplicably don't go as smoothly as promised.* And he was caught with a foot in each camp. Nothing was settled yet.

The paths on this side of campus were mostly unpaved, so their walk was dusty. Nonetheless, Patrice looked radiant. Her short skirt wasn't one her stringent folks were likely to approve of. Her top was flowing and relaxed, colors such as her family spread had never seen. She'd have to change into her nursing-student whites before class, but she had time. She also wore her hair up in a stylish swirl, not at all suggestive of her granger background. "Fits under my cap this way," she explained, beaming.

"Looks Euro," the lieutenant complimented.

"I found it online. The site said it's a Swedish style. Do you like it?"

"Looks great."

Her step and gait were relaxed, and like her sister Hyacinth, she had an affectionate way about her that made her immediately take his arm in hers so they walked along as though a serious couple. Kyle enjoyed the glances of others passing by. His smart khakis, this beautiful woman he was escorting, it came to him: *How retro!* He had a sense of campus life before Divestiture, before Disenfranchisement, before the Continental Wars.

Patrice remarked, "Imagine how wonderful this campus—*my* campus— will look in a few years, perhaps in only ten or fifteen, when the quads are lush grass, the trees grown tall and shady, all the buildings finished." She sighed. "The paths paved finally. Just imagine."

On the eastern edge of campus bordering the river, a newly opened footbridge stretched to a locale once again thrumming with activity. "This area is all done up to look like the 2050s," she explained, "like the last years the campus was open before the C-Wars." Cafés, two bookstores (new and used), coffee shops, a grocery store, a bike shop. An attempt to restart campus normalcy.

"Can you imagine the rules we have?" Patrice asked as they started crossing the campus end of the bridge.

Kyle saw a sign: *Walk all bikes.* "What? That you can't *ride* across?"

"Not that," she laughed lightly, "we cannot be off campus after ten on school nights, Sunday to Thursday, after midnight on Friday and Saturday. I have to check into my dorm, too, so they know I'm in for the night."

"Well, they've got you intimidated; you've memorized the rules."

"Is that wrong? Wanting to succeed?"

"No," Kyle laughed. "Why should it be?"

"You see," she grew solemn for the first time on their walk, "I've broken the rules. Serious rules." She blushed deeply and looked down at the shallow river below the bridge.

Without another word, they continued on to a café just beyond the opposite levee.

After ordering, they sat at by a front window. To the left, they could see a park with a number of shaded tables.

When their meals came, Kyle twitched off the bill. "Perk of working for West Con Security. The pay's better than my cadet stipend."

Patrice smiled, but looking up, abruptly asked, "Can we go outside?" She seemed agitated.

As if planned, as they sat down in the warm autumn sun, a khaki-clad trooper came over to the table. He was tall, bronze, and clearly expecting to meet Patrice here. He had his own rations and wasn't free for more than a few minutes.

"Kyle, do you remember trooper DeShawn Cleveland from last summer?"

He did remember. "The medic with that squad. After those first attacks." In the intervening months, DeShawn had seen action. He had a small scar over his left cheekbone and a more recent burn healing on his wrist. He wasn't in training. He was in action. New Grange wasn't the only locale with hostiles raising hell.

The medic sat next to Patrice, and they naturally held hands under the table.

"Kyle, DeShawn's my husband," Patrice whispered. "We'll be in our own place soon."

"Not yet authorized by my commander, but we're legit." DeShawn explained hastily, pride in his brown eyes.

Patrice looked around and went on in an even quieter voice. "But, no one must know," she paused, "we're going to make this work."

DeShawn added. "Got your back, hon. Just a couple of more weeks."

After leaving the library, Zot met Professor Jordan Watson of the math department to speak of Tessa's possible role there. Watson, on campus for the past five years, was his guide for a lunch and a tour. The department chair brought Zot to a pizza shop so that the iceman might get a flavor for the growing campus and its environs. "Not that different, in its way, from the Marsco world," the instructor insisted.

The iceman wasn't so sure of that; this world seemed less divided from sids, less separated away from PRIMS. Zot hadn't seen the Marsco world in more than half a century—*his*, the world he knew—but this one didn't seem anything like that old one. This one seemed alive, open, growing, prospering.

"Like pizza?"

"Certainly, but I'm quite a severe critic. My family owned several pizzerias in the Chicago subsidiary once," Zot remarked.

"Now, you're thinking old-school, pre-Accords," Watson laughed. "There are *no*, underscore that, *no* subsidiaries any longer. The Accords, remember?"

"Hardly. All that went on while I was in cryo."

After biting into his first piece of dry-crusted pizza in sixty years, Zot asked, "So, you're married." Zot had noted Watson's wedding ring. "Does your wife teach as well?"

"She's still in Marsco. Landers. She supervises servicing them at three lunar docks. Her monthly rotations keep her based at a near-side colony." The professor explained that she was close to a partial retirement after she hit fifteen years of service. Then she'd work for the West Con Federation. To keep this new fed stable, *everything*—the domestic lander service, the trains, the utilities—was to be run centrally before possible privatization ten years after complete independence. "If you're following all these economic decisions," he concluded.

"I think I do. The provisional government wants to avoid a land grab of services."

"Exactly. Underscore that. And any way you slice it, West Con needs a lander service, so she's aiming to keep at them over the next few years. Meanwhile, she's got a plum Marsco assignment, a month away doing lunar work, a week home. After nine rotations on the Moon, eight weeks totally off. Do you have family, Zot?"

"No, but twins on the way."

"Well, besides being an expectant mother your wife's an engineer, I understand."

"Yes, but fifty years out of date."

"Well, when Professor Falls said you'd be on her staff, she asked what— *Teresa*, is it?"

"Tessa."

"She asked what classes Tessa might be able to teach over here in math. Sure we can find some pre-calc or maybe something remedial," he explained.

"I'm sure she'll be fine."

"Well, have her contact me and I'll see, underscore that, *see* what can be done." He handed over a business card.

Checking the time, the math prof declared he had to leave. "Did you like their pizza?"

"Not Grizotti's finest, but good nonetheless. *'Make our house, your house,'*" he mimicked an ad for his family's business that had long since ceased to air.

Watson laughed. "You're a real historian all right. Know all the minutia, underscore that, all that's useless. All of it."

Zot laughed as well but not a sincere one. *Glad I'll be far away from these comments and ensconced in that new library. Tessa may have to deal with you, but I'm sure she'll handle you. And she'll run you in circles with her math skills.*

It was a dream come true for Sarah and Hyacinth, made possible only because a week later Zot was making the trip back up to the Sac City campus. Neither mother would have allowed her daughter on a light rail and onto the university by herself, even at their ages. Dot Richardson had no say in the matter now, even if Sarah's mother still took some convincing.

"The two of you going up there alone?" Celine shot at Sarah. "Do you think I've lost all sense of decency?"

"You've lost nothing, Mother, except your trust in me."

"Do you know how wild, *absolutely wild*, students are?"

"That was in the past, for heaven's sake. Patrice says things are incredibly strict and very quiet now. She says if they get into *any* trouble, they lose their scholarship."

"*They* can say anything they want to calm *their mothers*," the granger insisted, "but they can't change history and nature."

Sarah hadn't a clue what she meant, but her mother wasn't about to plant ideas in her daughter's head by talking of debauched, all-night parties and unfortunate girls, or so Celine imagined college life. She had seen some old films like that and even read a book or two in her younger years that supported her dim view of college-aged men.

When it was clear that a respectable married man, Zot, was heading there, Celine conceded to her daughter. Hyacinth was allowed to go as well.

"Two can make more than twice the trouble of one," Celine cautioned. Turning to Zot, she added, "Bless you for doing this."

On the light rail, a ride lasting forty minutes, Hyacinth kept her eyes unfocused, hardly noticing any passing scene. She was present but not totally there. Zot read an actual book he'd checked out from the library where he'd soon be working. Sarah prayed over and over: "Dear God, help my mother join the twenty-second century, the twenty-second century."

Once off the light rail platform at the south end of campus, Zot quickly walked the pair of grangers to the library on the main quad. Pointing off into the distance, he showed them an adjoining quad where Patrice's dorm sat.

"Plenty of folks about. If you get lost, just ask someone. They'll direct you."

Crossing campus, Sarah expected Hyacinth to make a point of stopping every young man even though the way to the med dorm was clearly marked. But that impulsive Hy was gone. She walked soberly and focused only on looking for her sister. In less than five minutes the pair reached Patrice's hall.

"Imagine living here," Sarah said, taken aback with the lack of mature greenery and the dusty nature of her unfinished quad. The med dorm wasn't far from the library, about the same as from the main house to the smallest guesthouse, but the granger's daughter was exhausted from the walk. Too many faces, too many new sights, too much activity; they all drove her to distraction yet fascinated her.

So, this is university life, she thought, almost voicing the words aloud. *It's so perplexing yet somehow intriguing and so right.*

The scores of people, the motion, the knots of students and profs speaking with one another; it seemed ethereal, unreal, but achievable.

I could do this, the granger knew.

Patrice ran into her sister's arms as soon as she came down the short flight of stairs at the main entrance to her dormitory. She hadn't seen Hyacinth for nearly five months and was taken aback at her own emotion at their reunion. The older sister had never imagined missing home so much and Hy in particular. She gingerly touched the scars of so changed a young woman.

Almost without emotion, Hy asked, "How did you hear?"

"I've had lunch a few times with Kyle." Sarah perked up. Patrice stayed vague.

"Well, at least I'm not like ma," Hy forced a smile and patted her still-flat stomach. Patrice gave her another hug. Hy stayed as listless this time as last.

Reaching out, the nurse brought Sarah into the embrace. "I've missed you, too. Missed you both. Even missed Shadow jumping up and scratching my legs." The neighbors cried, laughed, then cried again. "I've so much planned," she whispered, still overcome. "First lunch, my treat, then a walk around campus. Oh, it's so good to see you both." She laughed, then grew serious. "There's someone you have to meet."

"He said he wouldn't be gone long, promised me that the day he left. And he saw Patrice a few times. I know that," Sarah explained to Tessa the morning after her escorted campus visit. "But, he's *not* to be reassigned down here."

The two women walked around fog-shrouded New Grange. The expectant mother had been advised by her physician, a former associate with a practice in Sac City, to cease from jogging for exercise. That cut out her early morning runs with Zot; he would hear of nothing that jeopardized her dual pregnancy. Walking was fine.

When Tessa next planned to go up to her OB-GYN, she offered to have Sarah come along, but the granger refused. Something had happened during her visit that still bothered her, the associate assumed, something she was reluctant to discuss. Yet, the associate also knew it was only a matter of time before the whole story came out.

"I'm so glad walking's permitted," Tessa remarked. "My doc's very insistent; nothing too strenuous and nothing pounding."

As she said this, the pair were nearing the blackened hedges that surrounded the burnt-out guesthouse and stagnant pool. Around the ruins, the now-dormant fields stretched out. Chase hadn't reappeared. With Trent often up in Sac City for meetings, taking Miller with him to assist, Sarah and Celine had shouldered the burden of running New Grange. As the end of the year approached, much still needed to be completed.

"Any word?"

"Of my brother?" Sarah asked the obvious. "No, nothing. Gone like the rest in the dead of this night." She motioned to the charred ruins.

Tessa asked, "You okay?"

"Just thinking," Sarah answered, distracted as she had been for the past few days.

"Sarah, you know we can talk about anything. I won't force your confidence, but I'll never break it, either."

"Not even to your husband?"

Tessa laughed. "Well, that doesn't count. Couples often divulge things to each other, *secrets*, but they'll be safe with me and him."

"He does seem trustworthy."

"More than that, let me tell you."

Sarah perked up, grinning at the thought of hearing some of their intimate mysteries. But none were forthcoming. In the end, she stopped at the ruins and stood close to her fellow walker. "It was hard visiting that campus," she confided. "Very difficult."

"Why?"

"Lots of reasons. The first was—and it got worse later, lots worse—was I realized all day long that my cousin, Devon, was right. He always pushed me to try to go to the Academy or to that university. Walking up there, seeing all those students, I saw that I could have made it."

"Honest point to admit."

"Not that I'm wishing I was an associate or anything foolish." Tessa touched her arm to signify that *not* being one was perfectly fine. "But," Sarah continued, "what do I have to look forward to by staying right here? I realized that there's a bigger world than New Grange." She stopped herself. "Is that okay, Tessa? Can I think like this?"

"I think what you're asking is, 'Will my father and mother still love me if I move away?'" Sarah nodded her agreement. "Well, Walter and I had our disagreements once." She laughed and added, "About six decades ago. But, we got over them and in a lot less time than sixty years."

"Your father's a fine man. So is Mei-Ling—oh." Sarah shot a glance away from Tessa.

"It's okay. I know what you're thinking. But, they're not. He loved Bethany, my mom. And even though she's been dead for more than seventy years, I just don't see him wanting anyone. He's restless for another project, for work. Walter was true and devoted, especially at the end when she was so sick and dying. But, his work drives him. He's pitched in with all kinds of enthusiasm helping your father and this federation. He's thrown himself into several projects. We're still entangled with Marsco, after all. Mei-Ling is a wonderful person as well. And she owes her life to him, and *we* all owe our lives to *her*. But some things don't come off like we expect, that's all."

Sarah hoped that wasn't an indirect remark about her and Kyle.

"See, all you associates, you have reasons to do things. I just watch alfalfa grow and Shadow growl at visitors." She gave a sly smile remembering her black Lab and Kyle when dog and man first met.

"You know that's not true," Tessa replied gently. "You've plenty of reasons. You're helping to run this grange, for one. Helping those neighbors right now, rebuilding their village, restarting their school," the associate pointed off south. "You've helped Hy immeasurably."

Sarah grew deeply serious and took their talk in a different direction. "I got some unexpected, disturbing news yesterday."

"About Kyle's transfer?"

"Yes. I haven't seen him since he left." Sarah turned to face the associate, her intense blue eyes looking deeply into Tessa's calm green eyes. The young woman felt like she was looking into pure trust, so she continued, "Patrice is married," Sarah whispered. "Secretly. To a PRIM. Well, a man who's PRIM stock. And they'll be able to have their own place after Christmas."

"So they're apart now?" Tessa shot. "What gives?"

"She didn't have time for all the details, but he's—her husband, DeShawn—he was in Marsco Security once but moved over to our federation forces. Seems all his files are balled up and he can't move his status without his commander's permission. But, which one? He's in a muddle, don't you see? It's so like Kyle. Who's he really answering to? And where is he?"

Sarah grew silent; she'd confided much of a secret she swore to keep.

Tessa caught her tension. "Patrice's secret is safe with me. Don't worry. But, surely she'll tell her folks when she's home for Christmas."

"Can you imagine telling Old Man Richardson *that!*" Sarah burst out. "'I married a PRIM without your approval. *A PRIM!*'" Sarah then whispered, "I don't mean any disrespect, but you know I'm right. That's partly why Hy is still here, to avoid her father. And he's another reason I didn't accept Nate back in the day. Either he'll end up *like* his father, or just as bad, I'd end up like Dot, my future mother-in-law. Really, with Nate, I'd be expected to be just like her."

"Oh, Sarah," Tessa said, putting her hand on her arm gently, "as you grow up, some things hit you hard, and sometimes you don't know how to respond. All I can say is, be true to yourself and to those you love. It works out, mostly. It does work out. For all the pain, the hard times, life sorts itself out when you're honest with yourself."

Sarah managed to speak all her churning feelings without sobbing. She didn't want to any more tears; she'd already cried she share over the past summer alone in her room when it all hit her about Kyle.

Finally, she asked, growing stronger in her voice and demeanor, "Do you want to know something good?"

"Good would be nice," Tessa responded.

"Kyle's birthday is the day after mine. And they passed us by last August. We were going to celebrate them together, but it never happened."

"A forgotten birthday," Tessa responded. "That sucks."

"Well, if he's back for Christmas—which is what he promised me once—we'll be able to celebrate them together like we planned, even if months late. I was twenty-two, him twenty-five." The young granger held onto that promise made before one Security or another—maybe both—got involved.

Still so young, Tessa thought. *God, so young.*

"I'm holding onto that: seeing him and celebrating together, belatedly."

"Hold onto that," Tessa encouraged. "The whole world, your whole world, is changing around you, but I don't think *love* ever changes. In fact, I've seen love stop wars," the associate said, convinced that Julio Fuentes had destroyed the C-Powers' fleet rather than let it attack Mei-Ling. His self-sacrifice surely saved the *Sirius* and possibly the whole Earth. It was all conjecture, but it was the only scenario that made sense.

The morning walk had grown long. Both were now ravenous. Tessa especially so. The kitchen was buzzing with activity and gossip when the walkers entered.

Columbus and his coterie had returned, had turned up *welcomed* at the Richardson spread.

Chase was with them.

TWENTY-ONE

MANEUVERS

(Remote training camp near Mount Rainier, December 2154)

"A lieutenant? *You?*" Cassy Tomas-Higgens, a Security lieutenant herself, didn't believe it. "You should still be a cadet!"

The cadet in question was in his physical training kit, standing next to thirty-two trainees, dripping wet with perspiration and drizzle but clearly of officer status. He was leading a West Con Security platoon on a 5K morning run.

"You?" she repeated, still in disbelief.

"Yes, as you see," Kyle replied, standing next to his trainees, the lot gasping for breath from their interrupted exercise, "although junior grade to you, obviously."

"*Sir!*"

"Sir."

"That's right. I *graduated* from the Academy last May," Tomas-Higgens said. "You're a year behind me. So, how'd you—"

"Was switched into Security on an emergency basis, sir," Kyle answered the half-asked question. He wasn't about to fill her in on all that had happened over the past several months.

"But these are clearly troopers from one fed or another."

"Yes, sir, West Con. Here for training. This *is* West Con territory, sir."

"*Will be*, Lieutenant, *will be*." Her tone had a sense of *we'll see about that*.

Cassy had no time to debate the issue and no time to dress down her subordinate for letting his unit trot by her without properly saluting. The offended officer was on her way to a meeting, and this offending lieutenant would never forget to have his platoon deliver a proper salute to a superior.

As this confrontation broke up, Kyle ordered his unit to stand at attention and deliver the crispest salute Lieutenant Tomas-Higgens ever received in her life.

Bitch! Kyle mouthed as his unit picked up the pace. They were under no obligation to acknowledge her, given where they were when she passed them. By his calculations, she was nearly behind his squads when she recognized who he was. That's what this was all about. *Let her raise a stink*, he mentally challenged. The West Con officer took secret delight in the fact that while at the Academy with Cassy, he had outperformed her in every class they took together, every time. *Too focused on Elkton*, he concluded.

During the final two kilometers over a beaten track surrounding their camp, while his troopers pushed themselves to keep to his pace, Kyle thought about his early Academy years. *Before Security, before the Moon and Mars. Before Devon. Before New Grange. With Mia.* He shook his head; he wasn't going there. Sweat and rain ran down his face and neck. So much had changed in such a short time.

"Platoon! Keep it up! Let's beat our best time!"

"Whu-rah!" they answered.

But that group, Kyle went back to his Academy days, *Elkton and his Cassy, Mia, Clarke and Crosley, the others—they all wanted to join Security. Wanted to! Probably the only ones graduating the Academy in decades that did.* "Keep it up, half a pace faster now!" he shouted after spinning on his heels to run backward so that he faced his four squads. "Platoon, step it up! Lopez, Zimmer, no lagging. KayBolt, KayBolt, you can do this, KayBolt."

Kyle trotted in place until the lagging runner joined him. "We're not falling behind, KayBolt. We are *not* falling behind, any farther behind," Kyle huffed out. "*They* depend on you. *I* depend on you. We're a team." The pair moved up a slight hill, but they were falling farther behind. "Don't let them down," the platoon leader exhorted. "They won't let you down. No quitting on them, KayBolt."

Now, the trooper's squad mates dropped back and surrounded the lagging runner to encourage him, nudging Kyle, their officer, aside. They had this under control. They worked the pace up a bit at a time so finally, the lagging member picked up his own pace. This whole squad caught up with the remaining platoon and continued in rank step-by-step.

The lieutenant, now behind his platoon, leaned forward and paced himself to catch up. His lungs strained in the thin atmosphere. Their camp sat at more than a thousand meters of elevation. *C'mon, push yourself or they'll leave you behind, dammit!* He refused to let that happen, so he set his mind on his pace, one step, a second, natural gait, easy but steady. He allowed no further thoughts of Cassy or Elkton or Mia. He was soon at the head of his platoon. But, now, they focused on pushing him to his limits, showing him they could outpace him to a trooper.

He never allowed himself any thoughts of Sarah. Only thoughts of this platoon.

"Still hard to believe it. Roncalli—here!" Captain Roland Elkton looked first at Cassy Tomas-Higgens, then out the window of a squat office block. Each officer had a platoon as well, but they let their leading trooper take them for a morning run. While Kyle was out in the drizzle and mud, they sat dry and warm.

Their offices stood in the center of the largest Security and Auxiliary training facility in the Seattle Sector. Although West Con was to become the authority over most of this region, Marsco was keeping control over Seattle proper, plus a large swath inland from the Puget Sound all the way to well below Mount Rainier. No matter what happened to the rest of the Marsco world with the Six Accords, this locale was to be Marsco's last bastion.

This training camp was in question. Marsco and West Con disagreed over which one should control the camp, one of the thousands of sticking points in the Accord transitions. West Con's main argument was that because the federations alone would have all responsibility and authority over Security units, they alone needed this training facility. And this particular one sat amid West Con, thus, belonged to them. Marsco was surrendering all Security units. It had no counterargument for keeping this or any such camp.

"Can he be part of a sustainability team?" Harold Crosley asked.

"Not likely, Hap," Elkton answered. "Mia says he wasn't all that interested." *As hard as it was to believe any man not being interested in her.*

"Besides, we've the list of officers we can trust. He's been taken off it."

"And hanging around that Chavez-Sherman didn't help."

"Too star-struck. Wants a colony assignment more than anything."

"Then he should have become a pilot."

Didn't we all want to be in space once? Weren't we all pre-Flight? Cassy wistfully asked herself. *But who can pass up immortality?* All of them had commenced their bio-recombinant process. They each knew the promise held out to them by Chesney: perpetual youth, unlimited authority, unceasing power at their finger disks enhanced by their single black disk on their left palm. They were immortal for all intents and purposes. Or were to be soon. Marsco meant to make it so.

"Perhaps I should go have a chat with him," Hap suggested. "You know, feel out the situation, *his* situation. He might just confide in me."

"Negatory," Elkton answered. "Too obvious. Let's send Mia again. He was always interested in her."

Crosley clarified, "More like the other way around. Does Wicks know?"

"He'd be a fool not to notice, but yes, let's send Mia," Elkton remarked with the voice of command.

Cassy was sitting next to their leader, Elkton. She smiled up at him. "You always know what's best."

Two days later, Kyle and his platoon finished staking down their tents in light flurries, which abruptly changed to drizzle, ice, then back to large, floating flakes. The wind didn't help. At least self-heating meal packs gave them a warm lunch; that did help. But, this winter exercise was straining his leadership and the limits of his troopers' endurance.

We'll nail it, the lieutenant assured himself, *they'll nail it.*

"I want Second Squad," Kyle ordered. It was KayBolt's. To train his weaker members, Kyle demanded they do increasingly more difficult tasks. And always led them. He wasn't being overbearing. He was showing them his confidence in their skills. KayBolt would have his own platoon one day, Kyle was sure.

In the weak afternoon light, Kyle left orders for the remaining squads to have night watch positions set. They were guarding themselves as though surrounded by hostiles. At present, they were surrounded by old-growth pines and outcroppings of lava from eons ago. Moss and lichen colored the black rock, softened the edges, and encouraged deer to rummage here, but the forest was dark and formidable. Unexpectedly, the troopers actually enjoyed their maneuvers out here. Kyle kept them busy, kept pushing them, but they'd accomplished so much. Each trooper carried an Enfield; that alone kept their collective experience from being a retro-Scout camping excursion. One day, they might need to use that weapon to defend West Con.

"I'll be back before dark, I hope," Kyle told the lead sergeant.

The rest of the platoon watched their fellow trainees head up the slope northward. No doubt where they were headed. Mountain mist soon engulfed them. In their gear, the squad was almost invisible. The forest and motionless ground fog aided in their concealment, but these were by now well-trained troopers, adept at stealth.

"Found them, sir," KayBolt reported.

"Fresh?"

"Seem to be."

"'Big Foot' again," Lopez added. The pair were twenty meters ahead of the rest of Kyle's patrol, deep in the woods an hour from their base camp.

Almost by accident, on one of their first hikes last month, Kyle's troopers had stumbled upon large footprints. Larger than any man's. In the mud and snow, it was difficult to measure an exact size, but these were easily fifty centimeters. And the gait showed a long stride. Whoever or whatever made them had to stand at least 225 cm tall. The depth of the impression suggested at least a thousand kilos in weight. And judging from the evidence around the trail left by these prints, the creature was strong. Unstoppable. Toppled saplings. Broken branches. Large displaced rocks.

The squad quickly named the unseen creature *Big Foot*.

Kyle joined Lopez and KayBolt. "Good work," he whispered, then checked the direction of the tracks. No matter where they found them, the tracks usually pointed to a higher elevation, one marked as off limits to Kyle's training exercises.

"Look here," KayBolt noted, "they were single file at first, but one went lower down there then rejoined. Those single tracks will give us the best intel."

Kyle broke his squad into three teams, each to examine a different section of the single Big Foot as it moved alone. The evidence was clear. Something on two legs. A creature well over two meters tall, making long strides, stomping at will.

"And mechanical," Lopez confirmed. He found a broken bolt laying near one of the foot prints. A glob of lubrication grease.

"Could it walk on a broken foot?" Kyle wondered.

"I've got blisters, sir, and I'm here." KayBolt grinned.

The wind whipped up. What had been a gentle fall of snowflakes now turned to an icy rain. "Okay, pack up. Back to camp."

Third time he'd found the tracks. Third time Kyle debated mentally about reporting them. It was a training exercise, more to build endurance and unit integrity than a true recon patrol. So, in good faith, he could again refrain from reporting it.

Silently, his squad made their way down the slope. Even when one trooper slipped, others braced and guided the straggler. They were a tight team. Kyle was proud of that.

He wished he could tell Sarah.

Her memory brought about Devon's memory. *He got me into this mess.* Kyle laughed. *Maybe I should drop this crap in his lap.*

———— ⋅ ————

Overnight, the clouds lowered so that the platoon's camp was shrouded in a thick, gray mist that deadened any sound and made visual contact nearly impossible. A few large snowflakes dropped slowly, but nothing else seemed to move. A tree limb cracked in the dark like an Enfield shot, but its distance from their camp was impossible to tell.

Trooper Zimmer put her head under the tent flap where Kyle slept. Without a sound and without emitting a light, she woke him. "Bogie, sir," was all she said in his ear. The pair moved noiselessly to a second tent housing the command unit of their infiltration tech. KayBolt had night duty along with Zimmer.

Anti-infiltration sensors fifty meters out picked up something coming nearer. That tree limb cracking might have been part of its movement. "Something that big can't just glide along," Kyle whispered to Zimmer. "I'd love a look at it."

"Sir, if we see it, it sees us," Zimmer noted.

KayBolt added, "It's trying to damper our IR sensors, sir." The creature was a sophisticated intruder.

"Okay, let it." The two troopers monitoring the infiltration system understood. They knew where the beast was; they wanted to give it as little return information as possible. They cut power to their systems. "It'll think we're blind," Kyle added before realizing that was superfluous. His people understood their job perfectly.

Outside the command tent, the three crouched down and looked into the dense forest where Big Foot must be standing in the distance. They saw nothing. Whiffs of mist, trees, a few snowflakes, and the dark kept them from seeing more than a few paces. The creature probably stood fifty meters away.

"If it's where I think," Zimmer whispered, "we can slip through the trees behind and get closer to it. Have a look-see."

"We'll go," KayBolt stated, as if he were giving the orders.

"You have to be quiet," Kyle warned.

KayBolt grinned. "Being slow has its advantages." As his two troopers disappeared into the night, Kyle had second thoughts. They were armed with Enfields but with harmless blanks, not live projectiles. They were, in effect, unarmed. If this creature wasn't just some piece of equipment run rogue on a training exercise but something with actual hostile intent, his people were defenseless.

Using a joined pair of trees as cover, Zimmer and KayBolt moved to within twelve meters of their target, around its left side. They had yet to see anything, hear anything. This close, something that big would hardly be able to move without some noise. Sure enough, they began making out faint whirling and power-driven noises in the fog as the beast moved. Their mechanical Big Foot. Its skin gave a sheen in the moonlight that came and went in the hillside mist. Design flaw, Zimmer noted. Skin should be matte black.

KayBolt tapped Zimmer and motioned. Her eyes swept the horizon following his hand. Then his thump pointed up a tree. Big Foot was intensely scanning the horizon, especially in the area where the camp sat. It wasn't scanning *up*, as far as they could tell, and it wasn't whirling its head, which must contain its sensor pack. Every weapon had its strengths and weaknesses. Like a human, this one seemed to see only where it looked.

Zimmer held up two fingers: *Both of us up there?*

KayBolt lowered her hand. His thump hit his chest and pointed up. He was going up alone.

———————•———————

Twenty-five minutes of silence without a word from KayBolt or Zimmer nearly killed Kyle. He'd alerted his troopers but ordered them to keep off anything electronic; Big Foot was surely monitoring the camp.

Kyle was about to order First Squad forward when two cracks and a thump broke the tension. More thumps of footsteps, coming closer. Big Foot was stomping toward the camp. *Now what?*

Before he could order any response, the forest in the creature's direction lit up with a blinding flash and then another just as intense. No explosions, just concentrated radiance.

A flare, Kyle realized. Then a second. Distance and the stands of trees cut the light, but in the thick forest, something glowed brilliant white in the surrounding blackness. Big Foot was bathed in intense light. As it turned away, the light dimmed. Those flares had attached themselves to the creature.

The oncoming thumping and cracking stopped and then retreated quickly. Big Foot was on the run, away from the camp, taking the light with it.

———————•———————

KayBolt was so excited his report was a jumble, but Kyle made out the gist of it. Big Foot didn't notice him up there in his perch, but then the creature started toward the camp. And Zimmer was right there in the way, nearer to the machine than safe. All KayBolt had by way of a weapon was a pair of signal flares that fired from a RPG launcher. Having nothing else, he shot them at the creature.

"I didn't figure they'd stick like that, but they did. And they're so damn bright. Blinded me momentarily. Well, they must have blinded its IR and visual or whatever optics it has. I landed them both on or near its head. They stuck there glowing and showering sparks."

"Must be its optics housing, sir," Zimmer added. "Where you'd expect it."

"Hard to say. But just like us, it seemed blinded instantly. Like when we're in the dark and the sun peeps through, so it spun and spun twice, like trying to get its bearings."

"Then it figured out where home was and shot off," Zimmer added. "I was no more than three meters from it. Mechanical for sure, only with black metallic skin. Too shiny to hide. Bad design on that."

"'Big Foot' is an apt name for it." KayBolt paused then added, "Two legs, long arms, head and torso. Arms and legs can bend, excellent balance. Like a man."

"Or a woman," Zimmer added, reminding her comrade that their platoon was nearly 50/50 women and men.

"Yes, yes," her fellow trooper added, "But could have been armed, and with all the housings it has, could carry plenty of muscle if it wanted —"

Kyle calmed everyone down and then sent off two patrols to make sure the creature was gone.

No one slept the rest of the mist-shrouded night. The smell of burnt phosphorus hung in the air. KayBolt's pair of flares was their total arsenal; the platoon had nothing else for defense if Big Foot turned back.

———————— • ————————

It was only 1900 hours, but Kyle was exhausted; training was constant hustling. But, his platoon was home, back in solid and warm huts. He had made sure they had showers, hot meals, and some personal time. Even though lights-out was an hour away, he was prepared to crash. A five-K run awaited him the next morning, but no more out-of-camp overnights scheduled for the next several days.

"Zimmer, KayBolt, tops," he muttered, his mind racing. "And Lopez, a few others, they're all getting too good." He wouldn't sleep until he decided whom to promote as squad leaders and assistant platoon commanders. Only twenty-five, but Kyle was speaking like an old sweat, someone in battle harness for years, rather than the short time he'd been an officer.

"And mine isn't a liaison position at all," he commented with finality, flipping off his lamp. "It's looking more and more like I'll be commanding these grunts for good." At least it seemed settled, that he was under the full authority of West Con.

The vacant bunk across the room signaled that Lieutenant Carlson wouldn't be in until later. *Probably calling his girl.* A new officer like Kyle, he wasn't having trouble adjusting to the rigors of training, but he'd never left home before. *Going to the Academy cured me of missing people,* Kyle rationalized. Then he concluded in a half murmur alone in his hut, "So many cadets were pilots in training," And then he remembered seeing Cassy the week before. *Still makes no sense, that whole clique joining Security voluntarily. From pre-Flight to this.*

Someone knocked loudly at the door and entered the darkened room. "Kyle? You here?"

It was Devon Chavez-Sherman.

When Kyle raised a light, he immediately saw that his visitor, although still a colonel, was no longer in Security. He had been officially posted back to the Academy.

"Sorry, did I wake you?"

"That's okay, sir, please come in." Kyle jumped up and slipped on his jogging shorts and a dry sweatshirt. "Please, have a seat, colonel," the lieutenant invited formally.

As Devon did so, he noted how much the cadet had filled out, grown stronger with all his Security training.

"I'll only stay a moment," Devon explained, then pulled what looked like a twentieth-century travel clock from his pocket. It was a fogger, a powerful unit given its size. "We need to talk," the Academy colonel stated.

"This *has* to be serious if you're packing *that*, sir."

"It's not that I don't trust you, believe me," Devon explained. "Look, there are few I *should* trust; probably fewer I *do* trust. I count you in the group I can. But, I need to know first, have you seen any exact orders for a final transfer? Seen anything from Commander Modena yet?" Devon hesitated. "West Con wanted you, grabbed you, but has Marsco complied? It's all a muddle right now, and nothing *is* official. So, you could be jerked back to Marsco in a shot."

The lieutenant refrained from snidely adding that being jerked around was becoming all too familiar. "But I am in Security, sir," Kyle offered timidly. "West Con Security. Besides," he went on, "the Accords strip Marsco of all Security forces." He sounded like a fed officer. Devon was pleased.

With the Accords in full operation a few years hence, Marsco was keeping only its space branch. It was to relinquish everything else. Outside of a slice around Seattle metro and a few various pieces of other sectors worldwide, it was out of the ruling-the-Earth business. That's what Kyle held on to, a vague and counterintuitive sense he'd get back to Marsco, specifically at its Martian colony, the VBC.

"That's what Seattle says," the colonel added.

The lieutenant caught himself. "Wait a second, sir. You aren't trying to suggest that something or someone will cease implementing the Accords, are you? This is '54, sir. Almost '55. The first three have already come online." He wiggled his finger disks to show his blue-green implants to suggest that they were virtually obsolete. Among other things, the Third Accord guaranteed total open access to computers. And the Third Accord had come and gone smoothly in 2153, nearly two years ago already. *And the world still spins on its axis.*

Devon got up and pulled down a window blind, then made sure his chair wasn't in the same spot when he sat back down. Kyle knew why, to cut off a head shot and a digital recording of his moving mouth to analyze this conversation. *He's being cautious, very cautious.*

"Okay, lieutenant, act dumb and uninformed to anyone, *anyone*, who brings this up to you another time. For your own protection, you have heard *none* of this."

"So, 'If I told you, I'd have to kill you,' right?"

"If it weren't so serious, yes."

Devon wasn't a comedian. Kyle's gut tightened. This warning was somber, grave. The room was warm, but he felt himself growing colder. Instead of mistrusting Devon—who'd gotten the former cadet pulled into Security in the first place—the lieutenant knew he should trust him. Must trust him. Nothing Devon did or said suggested otherwise.

"The Marsco Sustainability Project is larger than you and Mia Wang," he began. Kyle knew Devon had spoken to Mellon-Hart. *What else did he know? How?* "It aims to select a group of associates totally committed to the current admin, especially the board's chair and vice-chair. *Loyalty* is the key. Blind allegiance. Total devotion."

"Seems logical. Not all that far from Marsco of old."

"Nice way to put it, 'Marsco of old.' Sounds so benign. Oh, the board couches itself in that rhetoric, claiming, like the Old Marsco that 'it only wants to stabilize the Earth before relinquishing its power' and that 'all subsidiaries *really* are independent and will be more so in the future.' Copy?"

"Yes, I know the drill, sir."

"Well, what if that's a mask?"

"Then, fall in line. Marsco's been offering that dodge for years. So what's new?"

"These Six Accords are new. You can't be granting real and true freedom on the one hand while secretly scheming to hold onto power with the other."

Kyle smirked. "Heavy accusations, Colonel, but the board's gone too far this time, implementing *three* of *six* Accords. Half, dammit! Can't renege now. To break its, the board's, promises of change *now*, impossible." Kyle drew a breath, "But, how does this tie in with Marsco's Sustainability Project? You're suggesting a tie-in, so what gives?"

"What if the MSP included a system of eugenics via cloning?"

"Now, you've really thrown me for a loop. What does Marsco gain by having clones? Perfect associates in the future? Copies of one perfected human?"

"What if that is exactly *not* what this process offers?"

"Then what is it offering?"

"Suppose you were offered a chance to remain the same tomorrow as you are today? Or, if I were offered a chance to be thirty all over again? Or Sarah could remain fresh and young and innocent forever?"

"But *a copy*, right?" Kyle was surprisingly defensive about the prospect of anything happening to his Sarah. "Some sort of so-called *perfected copy* other than her *real* self; some*one*, or a better analogy, some*thing* wholly different based on her DNA!"

"No, that's *not* it. It's more of a temptation than that. More insidious. They're not looking to make copies. It's recombinant DNA but with *your own* perfected DNA. I'll spare you the scientific details, but it's *you*, living on and on, self-restoring as you go along. What they're offering is your own, unique, but perfected life and near immortality."

Kyle remembered Mia's lovemaking and misguided message.

"Not a machine-like, robotic clone," Devon went on, "but *you* made permanent and perfect. The way you are *now*, to remain unchanged, unaltered, indefinitely."

Just such a promise was once dangled before him in pretty attractive wrappings. "Mia and me. Why me?"

"You're a great officer, Kyle. Imagine if your loyalty were to Seattle and not West Con."

The lieutenant remembered Sarah. She trusted her cousin, Devon. Her father, Trent, he trusted him as well. And Trent was part of the West Con provisional oversight team, the forerunner of an elected body to govern the new federation. Even Roxanne, a PRIM—or more exactly, a former PRIM—trusted Devon. That says something. But it wasn't love of Sarah alone that made Kyle trust West Con. What it offered was the future, a clearer and better future than Seattle's, unless at the VBC on Mars.

It then clicked for the lieutenant. "Immortals? Why risk a high-value asset? An Enfield would still tear through your flesh."

Both men sat silently for a moment until Kyle began at last, dropping his military courtesy and speaking to the space explorer as a friend and confidant. "You should know about this, Devon. I've found something, something odd. My troopers and I. Up the hill toward the north." Out came the specs and digitals of the mysterious footsteps and trails, its estimated size and agility.

Devon looked at the new evidence, intrigued but not surprised.

"These creatures seem strong. Able to dislodge large rocks. Uproot trees if necessary." Devon nodded, encouraging Kyle to go on. "I didn't put this in my report because I'm not sure who's reading it. But, one of these mechanical creatures tried to enter our camp the other night—" he motioned to show it was well away from this barrack area. "Or at least, get close enough to have a good recce of us. One of my troopers chased it off with two phosphorus flares. The light seemed to blind it; then it seemed to panic once it appeared to lose com-link with its handler."

"Typical of bot weapons. Handlers safe in the distance while the bot does their bidding."

"Glad it didn't come back. We only had those two flares we expended. Our RPG training is with flares, not explosives—no live ammo for any weapon yet. And we found evidence of at least three bots up there working together. Only one tried entering our camp, fortunately."

Devon waited to make sure Kyle had finished, then added, "I've had other intel of robotic warriors that fit your specs."

Intel? Who did Devon really answer to? Kyle regretted having this conversation. Mars and the VBC domed gardens seemed beyond the Oort Cloud now.

Perplexed, Kyle had to ask. "Who are your sources? Devon, trust me or get out. I'm between so many command structures and *this*, *you*, it doesn't seem like I'm really party to this."

"Trust Modena. That's all I can say."

"All?"

"Well, and trust me." The colonel paused then added vaguely. "All those trips to New Grange weren't just to visit family."

As Kyle pondered that, Devon now produced a set of digitals of footprints in a muddy path. The lieutenant-turned-sleuth remarked, "These look remarkably like what my troopers found up the slope. And these bots are agile and quick, as I said."

"Well, I'm convinced that Marsco is making walking robotic warriors."

"And Immortals to operate them remotely," Kyle assumed, hanging his head. Mars was now light-years away.

"They asked you to join them as an Immortal," Devon stated that as fact, not a question.

Kyle nodded.

"Can you get them to ask again?"

"I don't think so. Most of the ones I suspect are in on this don't particularly like me. Nor I them. They'll trust me even less now." He pointed to his khaki uniform hanging to the side of his cot.

"But, *if* they make a pitch again—"

"You want me to follow it." Kyle was not shocked but also not eager to do as asked, either. "Devon, I'm a space farmer. Now a lieutenant training a platoon. And now—"

"A spy, I know." Devon drew a breath. "But, Modena will act soon. I can promise you that. His actions will clarify your position. And that'll end your spy business."

"But still in Security."

"Yes, but West Con Security."

No fool, Kyle realized if he followed Devon all the way as this was unfolding, he could lose both Mars *and* Sarah.

TWENTY-TWO

NIGHT AT THE NEEDLE

(Seattle, December 2154)

An expanded version of the old Seattle landmark, the Marsco Space Needle, housed the Eagle's Nest Bistro. From its perch, the club slowly rotated, giving its patrons a lofty, breathtaking panoramic view. For the past thirty years, it boasted of refined interiors reminiscent of the 1920s.

Mei-Ling had insisted on bringing Walter Miller here. "It's the most retro place in the Marsco World, so they say," she justified. She loved the posh elegance of the early twentieth century and the slow-moving perspective.

Miller, sounding too professorial, added, "The old Needle had just been destroyed by Luddites when I arrived here to matriculate at the Academy." Once seated at a secluded table lit by candlelight, the pair watched Marsco's expansive city slowly rotate by. Every direction sparkled. In time, the campus came into view below their perch, its quads and buildings unmistakable. Chesney's lair wasn't visible in the winter darkness.

The *Sirius* pair were to meet Devon here. Shanghai had reasons to keep the men from talking Marsco exclusively; it was her night to celebrate. To avoid talking Marsco exclusively, she wore an evening gown which didn't seem out of place in the Eagle's Nest. She shimmered in metallic blue that accentuated her slim form. More men than her escort noticed her iridescence. Miller was in a dark suit from his prewar world. They looked well matched. But clearly, she planned to be Miller's and Devon's focus.

Periodic cryogenic stasis had prolonged the returned escapees' lifespans well past every patron in the club. In Miller's case, his protracted life was healthy and hale. Mei-Ling was totally over the recurring bouts of exhaustion and listlessness thanks to her regeneration treatments. Her spleen was on the mend. She was beginning to feel like her old self.

The medical couple of Penelope Elion and Adrian Lasher had worked wonders. The pilot's prognosis suggested no more surgery. Her microscopically and precisely inserted tissue was re-growing steadily, replacing the unhealthy with the healthy. In a matter of days after her initial treatments, she was much better. All indications were that her spleen would, in the course of the next four weeks, be as normal and fully functional as that of any healthy thirty-five-year-old associate.

She tried to think only of what her doctors had confirmed this morning after the latest round of tests. And she tried not to think of history and what this city spreading below them must mean to Walter, because of Bethany's final years here.

Mei-Ling suspected she'd made a poor choice of locale. Walter seemed not to notice. At least, he didn't wear his inner feelings on his face.

And she refused to think of Julio on the *Piazzi*. Or of Bryce and her tribunal, which had taken place in this city, the heart of Marsco. She thought only of her restored health and the future it would bring.

And that other choice laid before her.

Their table attendant suggested a light Pinot Grigio with its delicate, fresh taste from the Yakama Valley. Mei-Ling was hungry, so they ordered a smoked salmon hors d'oeuvre. A prewar evening.

"Excellent choice," the fawning attendant assured his guests before leaving them alone.

In the candlelight as Seattle slid by, Mei-Ling saw that Miller was distracted, not totally with her. "Is this wrong, meeting here like this?"

"Why should it be? He wants to speak privately. Sitting here shows we've nothing to hide."

That wasn't at all what she meant.

Devon came to their table from the bar. He wore an officer's uniform from the Academy, one without a Security emblem. To those able to pick up on his subtlety, the colonel was not hiding Marsco, but he wasn't leaning toward the board, either.

With two hundred other guests rotating in the Needle and with Devon's fogger placed unobtrusively on the table, it became easy for the three to converse, unnoticed in plain sight.

"I wanted to talk to you in confidence," the colonel began, "because I fear the board is moving more quickly than anyone expected."

The waiter interrupted and fussed over uncorking their bottle and arranging their plates. As soon as he was gone and after the obligatory first sip of wine, Miller turned to Devon. "You were saying?"

"I won't go into a long preamble why I'm asking, so I'll get right to the point. Captain Shanghai, in your procedures with Lasher and Elion, did another doctor's name come up? Did they mention a Doctor Johns? Did he perhaps visit you? Or possibly did Mr. Liddle speak to you?"

Mei-Ling had always felt conflicted with Devon. He reminded her of the best of Julio, but an air of mystery hung over this explorer. His former Security rank hadn't helped. She looked at Miller for guidance. He spoke up, "Why are you asking?"

Devon sipped his wine. "You are aware of the ramifications of the Accords," he paused, making sure the space travelers understood. He went on, "I fear their full implementation is increasingly in jeopardy."

"How's that possible at this point?" Miller asked. He always wanted evidence for any claims.

"One means of upsetting them is to tempt officers like yourselves with the Marsco Sustainability Project." Devon sipped again, knowing his direct reference would take a moment to settle in. "Essentially, loyal associates are being offered what amounts to immortality."

Mei-Ling's eyes danced. She had been severely ill and now wasn't. Lasher and Elion had successfully saved her. She asked if that's what Devon implied.

"It's more than that," he explained. "Your procedure was the natural and logical step of recumbent DNA therapy. It's regeneration of diseased tissue, nothing more. From a diseased to a healthy organ using your own body."

"So, what's the issue?" Miller asked, sounding like a father defending a daughter.

"The issue," Devon went on, "is that much more than regeneration is being offered to select officers. Doctor Johns, acting under Chesney's direct auspices, is promising more than health."

"What does the board have to do with my, or any, medical treatment?" Mei-Ling whispered.

"Because Chesney—via Johns—is offering *sustainability*, not *regeneration*."

"I don't see the difference. I'm feeling stronger. I have a healthy spleen. Modern Marsco medicine. What's the issue?"

"The issue is that sustainability is much more than it appears, and it comes with a price. A steep price. And many have been tempted."

Mei-Ling gave a laugh reminiscent of her life before the *Piazzi*, when she might employ guile to slip in and out of any situation. "I'm a little far along that road to worry about temptation." Devon was stuck by her charms, no doubt. But, she stopped herself from being that kind of scheming woman. She went on, up front, without anything coy except her natural grace. "I'm still not sure I understand."

"Chesney is offering selected associates a chance to live practically indefinitely."

Before Miller cut in, Devon assured the engineer that he had ample proof. He then returned to Shanghai, who in the candlelight continued to shimmer. Tonight was the first time he'd seen her healthy. She was aware that his gaze lingered on her and was inexplicably pleased. "I'm sure that if you'd bitten the bait, they'd be more specific. From what I've learned, that's how they operate. But, nothing said to you? No offers?"

"I'm not sure how this concerns you, Colonel," she replied softly even with a fogger near at hand. Actually, she had heard of all this. Exactly as explained by Devon. Exact same players and promises. And it was intriguing, tempting. She had to admit, part of the lure of the *Sirius* was an extension of her life, no doubt. That, and Miller, but she was clear to herself that he was no longer an issue. As wonderful a man as he was, he was content to see her as a second Tessa, not another Bethany.

Johns, however, had explained precisely what a life, a sustained life, would mean to her. What it would give her. For her, it promised restarting her life from before the *Piazzi*.

She had said nothing of this to Miller. She said nothing of it to the colonel now. It was her decision to make. Hers alone.

———— ❖ ————

Only when a hush fell upon the room did the three realize the shifting nature of the crowded nightclub.

Part of the irresistible ambiance of the Eagle's Nest was the chance to catch a glimpse of Marsco dignitaries. Tonight was no exception. A low buzz followed the arrival of the chair, Mr. Oakes, with his chief advisor, the vice-chair Chesney. They had come from the HFC platform at the top of the club, moving down a spiral staircase that provided every patron a chance to gaze at the party of eight.

The objects of attention had hardly disappeared into a private suite across the club when one of Chesney's aides was at Miller's side.

"Mr. Oakes requests that your party join him, Doctor Miller."

Walter was amazed he was recognized.

"Should anything surprise you these days?" Devon asked.

The three were even more dumbfounded when polite applause accompanied their movement to the Chair's suite. It was as though the other patrons needed Marsco approval to acknowledge the space travelers. They had been recognized from the start, but obviously, the board was welcoming them with open arms. That changed everything.

As the trio walked along, hands reached to shake Miller's, offering congratulations for their triumphant spaceflight. "Monumental achievement," one shuttle pilot mouthed. Women rose to embrace Mei-Ling with kisses on each cheek and sisterly hugs for her part in the *Sirius* triumph. One pulled back to admire her slim form. "You look fine after your ordeal, my dear," she assured the flier as though longstanding intimates.

"Do they know," the pilot leaned into the engineer, "that we were hoping to escape?"

"Let's not spoil it for them." Walter winked.

"Well done, well done indeed!" The board chair pumped Miller's hand, their finger disks giving each man a slight electrical tingle. "Quite a feat! Please," he motioned to the seven standing, admiring guests, "we've so looked forward to meeting you again, like this, informally." He glanced up at Devon. "And you, Colonel, another space explorer extraordinaire. Always a pleasure to see you."

Miller and Mei-Ling immediately stole the limelight of notoriety. All admired the illustrious pair. Chesney was there. The chair's entourage included other dignitaries and the ex officio head of Earth-side Security,

Jackson Roberts, who stood faceless at the dark fringes of shadow down beyond the end of the long table. Modena, the actual head of Security, was not present. It was a social gathering, not a working meal.

"We're glad to know you're better, Mei-Ling," Chesney greeted her. "Spacesickness of this kind necessitates a long convalescence," he explained but not from experience. Except for a few obligatory trips to the Moon, he had never left Earth. "But I see you're remarkably better." He stood back to admire her. "Perhaps we can offer assistance to guarantee your full recovery," he added vaguely.

Once everyone was seated, Chesney described Mei-Ling's medical condition in detail: her fluctuating low red count, her periodically high platelet count, her bout with jaundice. "Poor hemoglobin is never a sign of good health," the vice-chair noted. "I know from experience." He tapped his chest as his own regenerated heart beat steadily.

"Thank you for your concern," the pilot replied, holding back her shock at his knowledge of her. *So much for patient/doctor confidentiality*, she sadly thought.

"It's the fibrosis of your bone marrow and your enlarged spleen that had us most worried," he went on, trying to seem concerned while purposely letting the pair know he had the ability to find out anything he wanted about them.

"Guess there are no secrets left," Miller shot defensively, protecting her.

Chesney turned the snub into a compliment. "Of course, associates of such fame, we want to foster your care and well-being as much as possible."

"Will you join us for a drink to that health, Doctor Miller?" the board chair asked formally. The table rose at once to salute Miller and Mei-Ling.

The engineer ended up at the right of Oakes, while the pilot sat across from them but next to Chesney. Devon sat farther down, next to Jackson Roberts, who wore no badge of rank. His dark suit was something like Miller's.

"Isn't Commander Mateo Modena in charge of Security?" the space explorer asked.

"Certainly," Roberts replied, "my actions are simply observatory. I'm actually a glorified ADC. A gopher more than anything. I oversee and guide when necessary, when the board thinks it necessary."

"Necessary to what? Stop or derail the Accords?" Devon dug deep.

He was sure *that* would be in Chesney's evening brief. People he hoped he could trust—Kyle, Miller, Mei-Ling—were all being tempted. And officers in charge of smoothly moving the Accords were being co-opted or countermanded. That explained Modena's absence. Marsco's control remained tight and inflexible.

Devon wasn't so much concerned for his own safety as that of the new federations. The board was making its intensions increasingly clear. Out in the field, maybe not. Trent wasn't seeing this. Not yet. But to those near the thrumming board and its manipulations, it was obvious. This board intended to keep itself in power. To stall. To sidetrack. To consolidate all the more.

As soon as the guests broke into quiet conversations among themselves, Chesney leaned toward the pilot, "You must persuade Walter, you know, you must, to work with us. His fame, his knowledge of the prewar world. Everyone's read *The Ascendancy*, even I have, after a fashion."

"He'll be pleased to know," she replied cautiously. "All writers long for an enthusiastic and growing readership."

"But, we'd love him speaking *for* Marsco and sharing *our* concerns as these transitions take place. I know we're halfway home, but we fear trouble, more serious than just outside where you're staying, New Grange, his former spread."

"I see," she replied in a noncommittal tone.

"Yes, with him making our appeal for calm, strong reassuring statements supporting our approach to all these issues in flux—well, things will go smoother." His steely eyes bore into her brown. "There's been other issues worldwide, larger than the latest ones at New Grange, Captain. In some places, even more disruptions than a few villages sacked."

Although seated far down the table, the shadowy Roberts added, "Been forced to increase, not decrease, the number of Security battalions and Auxiliary units under training." With that officer sitting at such a distance, Mei-Ling hadn't suspected he was listening.

Devon, on his left, asked, "But, aren't all Security forces supposed to report to their federations? Wasn't that part of the Second Accord that went into effect years ago?"

"Oh," Chesney retorted, "the academic with his pinprick remarks." He sighed. "All in good time."

Devon withheld his response, *Now seems like as good time as any.* "Good time? You signed the very Accords that gave over those battalions to the feds. Why the delay?"

"You see?" Chesney smiled one of his crooked sneers at the pilot. One end of his cockeyed mouth seemed to grin arrogantly, and the other end drooped into a scowl. "What a help to us if Doctor Miller cooperates."

"I'm sure he understands, sir," Mei-Ling whispered.

"And you, your own well-being. Take a lesson from me." He gestured by placing his right hand over his chest. "My own heart, revitalized and made perfectly wholesome, like your spleen. Like a teen's. All with my own DNA—no rejection, nothing artificial. As robust as a cadet jogging around campus." He looked side to side then whispered, "But, you know, that's only the beginning. Imagine, this health nearly forever."

Leaning closer still, he said, "And for Miller. You've both tasted extended life. We offer you that. Not for everyone—sids and PRIMS are out for sure. Not for every associate, either. Just *loyal* associates. But think of your prolonged lives and being healthy and awake for the whole time, enjoying every nano second of them."

"I have thought a great deal of our unique situation, sir."

"Well, our 'unique situation' is yours for the taking with just a byte of trust and support from you both."

"Or either one of us."

"Well, yes, we'd like a pair, but we'll take one."

"We ask so little," added the Security head, even if his position at the table relative to Mei-Ling implied he was not part of her private conversation.

A bug? The pilot wondered.

"It's not every associate who's offered the ceaseless benefits of our Sustainability Project, my dear," the vice-chair assured her through his menacing, off-kilter leer.

"We'll keep that in mind, sir," she reassured him.

———————————◆◆———————————

Kyle's epiphany came as he rode the Space Needle elevator up to the Eagle's

Nest with Mia Wang. Devon's operative realized the professor wasn't all that a great spymaster. The lieutenant was asked to verify the wrong intel. The colonel's directions made no sense. Kyle needn't corroborate what he already knew, that the woman at his side had been swayed by Chesney's sustainability promise.

It was those bot warriors. They were the unknown, the clear and present danger. Kyle was a field hand, a platoon leader. If his troopers again met three of those stomping robotic knights, what could his people expect? How were they to protect themselves in the future? Two lucky flares had chased one monster away. But, next time?

Kyle was pleased when two large glasses of beer and two of wine appeared at their table. "Forty-eight hours of leave, like that," he snapped his fingers, the pop made louder because of his disks. "Amid all that training, I get leave, not my platoon. Just me, nobody but me. Imagine that."

"Yes, imagine," Roland Elkton smirked. It'd been easy enough for him, with his deep connections at HQ, to arrange the leave, even for a West Con officer. He left it to Mia to invite Kyle up to Seattle. Two couples, Elkton and Cassy—oozing cordiality, on her best behavior—Kyle and Mia, on the town.

Few more beers, he'll be singing any tune I want, the Marsco officer noted.

Elkton's method was foolproof; he gloated in self-congratulations. He had set the trap. Mia was the bait.

"Oakes and Chesney are here tonight," Cassy noted. "The Eagle's Nest certainly draws them."

Kyle lifted his head. "You know them? Our bosses?" He paused, "Well, *your* bosses. I'm under West Con now." His khakis attested to this. Although Elkton was clearly in Marsco Security, Kyle showed off a new uniform indicative of an independent federation.

"In a way, yes, but we answer to Roberts, the head of Security, first."

Puzzled, Kyle asked, "What happened to Modena? I thought he ran *your* Security?"

"He essentially answers to Roberts now, that's all."

The foursome drank and joked, told stories about their Academy days until the room erupted in polite applause for Doctor Miller and Captain

Shanghai as they moved across the room to the private chambers of the chair. Devon was with them. He and Kyle exchanged glances.

"You know," Kyle said turning at Mia, "you look a lot like Mei-Ling, a younger version. Although she hardly looks old."

"Mei-Ling?" she shot, confused at the comparison.

"Captain Mei-Ling Shanghai," Kyle motioned as the trio of space explorers disappeared in the executive suite.

"You know her?" Elkton demanded. "She and Miller are famous. Returning from nowhere to home." His eyes flickered with distrust. "How could *you* know her?"

Cassy tried to calm him so that he didn't totally betray his generally low opinion of Kyle.

"It's black," Kyle replied, pushing away his half-finished beer. Things around the table were growing serious; he didn't need to complicate his situation. He looked at Mia. "Black," he reiterated.

"*You*, on a *black* mission?" Elkton continued to grow irate with envy and disbelief. That khaki uniform spoke against that possibility.

Unintentionally sprinkling salt into a raw wound, Kyle tapped his lieutenant bars. "Before these, I was ordered to report to *your* Security. And that's all I'm at liberty to say."

"How does that explain your West Con status?" Elkton challenged.

"C'mon, let's take in the view," Mia stated, breaking the growing tension.

———————

The top of the Needle had an enclosed, wraparound viewing area protected by polymer panels. With Seattle spreading before them, the couple had the space virtually to themselves.

Mia knew her role, took Kyle's hand, pleased and conflicted to be alone with her target. "Roland gets hot-headed," she began, trying to set herself apart from him, make herself seem more trustworthy. "Gets that way when it seems that others are moving ahead of him in rank."

Although protected from the wind, the viewing area swayed in the December night sky. That brought the pair even closer. She gripped him tight, snuggling into him. "Can I ask a personal question?"

"Certainly," he answered, holding her as though this evening was a long campus walk years ago.

"Did last summer mean anything to you? It was pretty intense. And then you just disappeared." A wind gust pushed the needle noticeably, giving Mia another excuse to edge in closer.

"Are you trying to restart our past?"

"That's not what I asked."

Soothing, Kyle replied, "And if I did want to take up your offer?"

Silently, they let the wind sway them. The buffeting aided her embrace. It began to feel like the years had melted away. Kyle wondered if it were possible to restart everything on a new footing. All indications were there.

"So, you really did meet that pilot? The one who went to Oakes's private suite?"

"I've no reason to deny that."

Mia wore her hair down just as Sarah usually did. Because they were coming to a chic nightclub, she wore a tailored black dress; its design kept one shoulder bare. Their viewing perch was heated, but the December gusts chilled her, so he held her to keep her warm.

She was petite, about the height of Hyacinth, with fine porcelain skin and sparkling deep brown eyes that looked black in the low light. Kyle remembered why he had fallen for her so long ago. *Not so now*, he cautioned himself. *Sarah or no, not so now*. And still, it was difficult, nearly impossible, to stop gazing at her.

"Look, this is awkward," she started, then pulled him to a secluded bench, one of dozens that surrounded the viewing area. Sitting down, they realized several other benches were filled with couples too intent on themselves to notice any newcomers. No wait staff would bother them; orders were made electronically. Neither had any interest in another drink. Their private perch afforded a slowly changing view of the imposing city if they cared to pay any attention. She whispered, "Roland's not eager to share any of this, but I think you should know."

"What?"

"That project I alluded to last summer. It's set in place," she began hesitantly, "the one that promises elite associates vastly improved lives. But you have to act now. Commit now."

"And doesn't just being *an ordinary* associate give us that automatically?" he asked. "Granted, with the Accords, the gap between a well-off fed citizen and an associate is closing, but we're still pretty well set. Pampered in many cases."

"This alteration will more than pamper us, this will—"

Kyle felt himself tense up. Mia slid closer to speak in a lower tone but also to coax him, sway him by her inviting presence.

"Have you ever thought of an endless life?" Her dark eyes begged that he listen with an open mind and total trust.

"Except for what you suggested last summer, can't say I have. Do you mean hibering? Or using cryo-stasis?"

"Don't play coy with me," she shot, then controlled herself. "Child's play to this." She paused, fearful she was overstepping what Chesney wanted, but seeing real trust in Kyle's eyes, she went on, "I mean holding onto life as it is right now, or better than, and keeping that life indefinitely. Ever give it any thought after last summer? Ever suspect such a thing possible?"

"How could I not?"

She entwined her hand in his. "We need loyal associates, Kyle. Headquarters asks you to join Security out of your proven loyalty. Your true fidelity."

To cover his lie, he answered, "I think my devotion to my duties, black duties, proves my loyalty, not the other way around." His uniform spoke against his assertion.

She raised an eyebrow, not buying his vague answer.

"I was given special assignments," he went on, "and I've performed them. Very well, I hasten to add modestly."

"Well then, you are certainly exactly what HQ wants."

Kyle felt she was on the verge of admitting to the very project Devon warned him about, but he'd known all this since last summer. And he'd suspected something was up with Elkton and his followers even back at their shared Academy days. A clique like that—one plotting to snatch as much power as they could—stands out. And that cohort had a clear link all the way back to Chesney.

"I hope my job performance is what it should be," he lied with every word. "Am excited about my lengthening career in Security. Life on a colony is fine, but—" he motioned to the sweeping vista of Marsco benevolence and bounty all around him. No stars or planets were visible, not even the Moon. "—but, living on the top of the world would be nice, too."

"Yes, those willing to accept will be at the top," Mia added, trusting him more. "Kyle, this project gives you nearly endless life, perfected life. It's a matter of unquestioning devotion, that's all. And you seem to have it."

The West Con officer sat silently. To hide his deep fear of detection, that his expression might betray his disgust of her offer, he swept this created woman into his arms and kissed her passionately. It was the only way he knew to deflect any thought of his ever rejecting her—and Chesney's— offer. Kissing deeply, he was unsure of all the dangers that lurked.

"Mia, you are all beyond belief," he whispered, "but trust me. I'm only temporarily in West Con now. Can't shake that." He hoped that answer was enough to take him out of their crosshairs.

He drew a breath, playing along to protect his troopers now. "But, I'll let you in on something. My platoon, we found something startling on a routine hike." Mia's eyes tensed. "We found evidence of a robotic creature. Stands well over two meters. Long strides. AI functionality, we're—*I'm* convinced. Body armor won't protect any trooper from *that*." He gave a smirk. "We dubbed it Big Foot." He was giving away nothing more. Why tell her that his trooper blinded it with flares? Their side's after-action reports should have figured that out.

Mia sensed him shifting away from her. He'd been playing her. She'd failed once before with charms and hints. And now she'd failed again. This man was independent to a fault. She was sure he considered himself so damned noble. That uniform hung well on him; he seemed to be believing in all that federation nonsense, not her promises.

"I'd like some specs on that beast," he went on, sure he'd gained a measure of her trust. "Weapon capability. Range. Type of com-link—"

The Marsco associate bolted upright in her seat, distancing herself from him. She was to win *him*, and yet, here he was pumping *her* for classified intel. "Why do you think I'd divulge anything restricted to a mere West Con trooper?" His bars indicated a different rank.

"Well—"

"I'll tell you this, *trooper*. Our bots are awesome. Unstoppable." She spit out, hurt and triumphant both.

"Mia, for heaven's sake, don't stay with them. You know better." He reached for her hand.

"Oh, do I? How would I?"

"Humanity teaches you that." His hold on her was strong yet tender and earnest.

Pulling her hand away, the Security officer resorted to what had been so successful in the past, a show of Marsco power. She went on, ignoring him, ignoring their past. "Those creatures, our Big Foot. Damn impressive! And why not? Marsco needs to maintain control."

"It's only controlling a bit of Seattle and its colonies."

"Why so little?" she shot. "It's done so well for nearly eighty-five years. Why cease functioning? Why accept so little?"

"It signed the Accords. Made promises."

"It's making new promises now, better promises. And we'll be right there to carry out—"

"Don't be a fool. The feds will resist."

"With what?"

You're so right, Kyle mentally answered. *With what?*

His communicator buzzed, alerting him to a priority message, an unmistakable chime. All officers carried their com-links, even when off duty. Against standing orders, Mia had left hers behind at Elkton's table. Certainly, Elkton and the others were right then reading their screens.

"You know anything of this?" Kyle asked, showing her the glowing device. "'All temporary transfers to federations to be considered permanent. All Marsco Security forces henceforth to answer to local fed control exclusively. No Security forces exist that are answerable to Marsco HQ. All forces answer to an appropriate federation command. Mateo Modena, Marsco Security Commander.'"

No one, and least of all these two officers, knew how this order was going down worldwide. Kyle read his screen carefully a second time. When he looked up, Mia was gone.

TWENTY-THREE

FEASTING

(The Tillson Spread, December 2154)

"**W**hoever taught you troopers to line up tents?" a young, half-trained sergeant shouted as he pulled up six pegs and collapsed three tents on the east side of a grove at Tillson's spread. "Now, line these up straight so you show these grangers you know what a camp is supposed to look like."

Eight troopers complied with lackluster effort.

Lieutenant Roncalli, returning from a morning patrol, witnessed the exercise in futility.

"Sergeant Parks, a word," he motioned toward the tent he shared with his second in command, a man who really should still be in training, not here. West Con felt that pressed. The best trained and equipped troopers were up in Sac City now.

In the empty tent, the officer made sure he privately dressed down his subordinate, Derrick Parks. "I think we can dispense with the chickenshit, okay? I'm more concerned with them having a warm and dry tent than a straight one."

"But this mud, sir." Inside the tent was as muddy as outside.

"Mr. Brunel has floor planking. Get your men to use it. Winter's here, and it's wet. Do you want your men to sleep in the mud?"

"No, sir."

"Sac City's paying for it, top price. Just to keep you dry."

A patrol was scheduled to leave in thirty minutes. Kyle checked his Enfield sidearm, one of the few in camp, and looked at his disheveled unit.

To his mind, the weakest needed the most work. He looked at Parks; that was true of him, too. "I'll lead First Squad on this one."

"Even if you just came back?" He paused, thought, then added, "Sir."

"You feel ready to take them, Derrick?" Kyle asked without threatening the young leader who stiffened, reluctant. Lining up tents in camp was easier than in-the-field command.

Kyle nodded. "Have Second set up flooring by the time I return." The sergeant nodded. "There're two tents in the gear I brought down from Sac City. One tent for me and the other to act as our platoon office. Make sure they get up as well." He added softly, "We'll no longer be roommates. Gives you some breathing space."

"Yes, sir," snapped the second in command, "promise I'll get it done."

"Lead from up front," Kyle urged him. "Don't bark so much as show them."

"I'll try, honestly," Derrick took the instructions well.

"And, some sappers are coming down to set up a firing range."

"For what, sir?"

Few weapons had been distributed to the four squads, two here at Tillson's and two at New Grange. Kyle went on, "Our troopers are supplying the backs to do the work. Make sure that range is as far away as possible from anything we don't want to hit. It'll need a hut and a storage bunker for live Enfield rounds close by it. Those sappers will have the plans and layout."

"Yes, sir." Derrick hesitated. "But, troopers don't like so much work, sir. Can't those sappers do it?"

Pleading with me doesn't help, Kyle thought. *He's tougher to train than young KayBolt.* The officer went on with his orders, "Another storage bunker needs to go here, near our men."

"But, sir," Kyle's subordinate pointed out before leaving the tent, "you can't hit anything without a weapon, sir."

Tillson, who happened upon this dressing down, observed how much Kyle seemed an officer and no longer a cadet. A note of dejection came with his observation. *He's changed so much*, the granger realized. *They'll all be changing so much.* He caught Kyle's attention. "I thought this was an Auxiliary unit." Their bivouac was in a grove three hundred meters from his house and barn. He'd come down to offer his tractor to help with any construction.

"Sir," Kyle responded, "acting under directives from West Con Security Central, all Auxiliary units are moved to full Security status and are to be armed and trained accordingly."

"Shit's getting real," Tillson whispered.

"It is, indeed, sir."

"Will your people be okay?"

"Help if I could arm and train them."

"*He* be okay?" the granger pointed with his head to the sergeant who held tenuous control over the squad.

"I would have picked someone else," Kyle confided to Old Man Tillson, "but, I'll work with him. Have to."

Besides clearing up the two camps at New Grange and the Tillson spread, over the first three days since reporting here, Kyle made sure that two patrols went out daily to scour the area. Just what they were looking for, the officer wasn't sure. After the last attacks and the burning of the guest-house, nothing had happened. But since harvest had been completed, these grangers and their hands had more time to fret. Seeing the patrols morning and late afternoon reassured the locals that *something* was being done to protect them. It gave them that much less to worry about, even if more to complain about.

The Richardson situation cast a pall over the calm. No patrols crossed his land, but troopers carefully watched that granger and his guests as they skirted around it. These patrols gave Kyle a chance to train his people better. Weapons or no, they needed unit discipline and team savviness when out in the field.

As soon as Kyle settled in, a liaison sent by Singh, now a major, arrived to make sure all connections to federation HQ went smoothly. Captain Anderson Jecky's principal job was to ensure cooperation between the new bureaucracy and the former Marsco Security units in place. Old allegiances die hard, and the fledgling federation wanted to make sure this transition to its command-and-control ran without a hitch. Like Kyle, Jecky was trained by Marsco but had been in West Con since the first Accord. Most of that time he was without rank; now that the fed had official forces, he was commissioned.

"Part of my job is superfluous," he explained, "since technically, all these Auxxie units answered to Sac City all along anyway. At least under old Marsco guidelines. At present, it's a matter of clarifying the lines of authority. Flowchart adjustments, really. Not just down here but throughout West Con."

"Explain that to Seattle," Kyle smirked. "But, they're our troopers now."

"I know, hard to keep track of all the changes."

"Well, when orders come, I hope there's no confusion. A uniform doesn't make allegiance." Kyle'd stated that before he realized his own words applied to himself as well. Many in West Con still looked at him askance, regardless of his khakis.

"I'm sure you're aware that Marsco's put a considerable amount of time and effort into training some of these units. Maybe not yours, but others."

"Yes, sir. Mine are pretty green."

"No one up at Sac City is convinced that Seattle won't in the end want its troopers back. Demand them back or try ordering them directly. And some may comply."

Kyle remembered the Security battalions being trained at Mount Rainier and those he'd seen on the move months ago. "You're right, sir. Not as simple as a new diagram." He hated the thought of being jerked around yet again, as much as he feared any serious confrontations. And the continued distrust.

Mars colony gardens seemed light-years away.

———— • ————

Coming back from patrol late the next afternoon, Kyle found his camp already lit by portable lanterns. Thick tulle fog shrouded everything. He could do nothing about the location at Tillson's, which sat close to the river, where the fog was thickest. After patrolling for four hours and finding no signs of any impending trouble, he and his squad returned soaking wet and bone tired.

Captain Jecky was again waiting for him with that look of disturbing news. "Still no word on resupply," the liaison reported.

Kyle smirked. "Food I've got. And my people are relatively dry." He stamped the newly installed planking with his boot. "But, they're supposed to be issued Enfields. Both types. They'll need training on them, sir."

"Another delay. Marsco held up our shipment—"

"Marsco is supposed to be going out of that business. Can't our Assembly rattle Seattle's cage?"

As Jecky left, Kyle returned to getting into something dry. Peeling off saturated gear, he shivered even in his heated tent, when he heard voices just outside the closed flap. "Yes, ma'am, the 'tenant's returned, ma'am. Which is I'll ask if he's receiving visitations, ma'am."

"Which is," his orderly's head, sticking in through the tent flap, reported, "a pair of young stunners, locals, to call upon you, if you will. Or will you be wanting 'em to stand out in this pissin' drizzle outside this here tent or come in out of it?"

Kyle told his orderly, Jonathan Chico, to show them into the adjacent platoon tent while he dried off and hastily dressed. Jonathan had served forty years with the Auxiliary, never venturing farther than Sac City and its neighboring areas. For the past fifteen years, with no family or connection to any particular locale, he stayed as a sort of ADC to whatever officer he took a shine to. Kyle had been so chosen.

Kyle's visitors had walked down from New Grange. As Sarah and Hyacinth entered the platoon tent, several voices from the camp erupted in catcalls and suggestions. A smaller—but equally loud—number of voices from the women troopers answered.

Hearing all this, the lieutenant ordered, "Jonathan, have the camp put a lid on it, if they don't mind."

"Which is right that they ain't callin' like that."

Turning, Kyle greeted his guests. "Haven't much in the way of comforts," he hastened to add. A wooden door over two solid equipment boxes served as his desk. The tent had little else besides two canvas chairs. Kyle seated the grangers, then pulled a stool from a corner for himself.

Hy hung back, a husk of her former self. Her face was no longer bruised, yet she lacked her spunky confidence. Her friendship for Sarah had brought her, not a desire to be out or see Kyle. Sarah looked serious, churning under the surface at all this marshaling gear and training in her world, which had known only bounty and serenity.

"I've nothing but cold morning coffee to offer."

"Thank you, no," Sarah began formally. "I came with Hyacinth because I expected *that* kind of greeting—" she motioned outside. "It was worse until you came back, but it's still pretty disgusting the way they call and shout and leer."

"Mr. Brunel's had to threaten a few out of the kitchen, and Roxanne thinks they've been stealing eggs," Hyacinth added in a monotone. "The ones down at New Grange."

"Father's come out here twice as well. One time after some of yours chased a Tillson calf back to our camp. Yours at New Grange. They were preparing to butcher her when he arrived. Good thing it was him and not Tillson. He'd come with an old shotgun loaded with rock salt."

"Yes, I see," Kyle responded to their information, promising to put an end to these issues and outbursts. "Jonathan, yo, there!"

The orderly stuck his head in the flap, "Which is your calling me?"

"Of course I am. And is that a way to address an officer?"

"Which is your calling me, young sir and ladies?" To the old PRIM long past his razor-sharp Auxiliary service, the two women may as well have been officers; they demanded that much of his respect.

"Bring up my rover. I need to take these young ladies home."

"Yes, all you sirs," he answered with a sort of salute. "Your driver, too?"

"I'll take them myself." Shaking his head, the old Auxxie left. "I promise," Kyle said, "I'll look in to all these complaints and make sure everything's set in order." The sergeant at New Grange was more seasoned than here; that would make it easier for the lieutenant to exert control.

Ordering the rover was not what Sarah wanted to hear. She'd rather walk home with Hyacinth to make sure she wouldn't be beholden to the officer. "We can get back okay ourselves, thank you," Sarah insisted. "We don't want to bother you."

Jonathan returned with a meal portion for Kyle. "Which I forgot. Evening rations. Will they be wishing any chow?"

Sarah laughed. "Thanks for the offer, but no, we'll not be staying to dine," she laughed again, loving the old man for his forced manners and fondness for Kyle. *If nothing else, at least he has this old codger.* She appreciated the devoted Auxxie all the more.

Kyle was insistent, so they approached his rover. Sarah wanted Hyacinth to sit up front next to Kyle, but the other woman climbed in behind the driver first, to force Sarah sit next to him. It was a quick drive to New Grange. Quick, but quiet. When they got to the main house, both women bolted to the great room door, but then Sarah returned and climbed back into the vehicle.

"Can we talk a bit?" She suggested they drive off to a secluded part of the grange.

"Affirm—I mean, of course, Sarah, I want to, too."

Down the road away from all the central buildings and past the grove with its trooper encampment, Kyle pulled the rover under an old oak. In the fog, the evening was totally dark. He lit a dash light, which outlined more than illuminated them. The young woman pressed her point immediately. "Devon's been down a few times and is coming for a week tomorrow."

Kyle only nodded.

"He says he's seen you a few times up near Seattle."

"Yes, true."

"Are you seeing anyone else, up there?" She was direct and blunt. "Mei-Ling says she saw you with another officer."

"Sarah, believe me. You have to: nothing happened. I can't tell you *why* I was with Mia, but in part, it was self-protection."

The granger gave a snort. "Oh, spare me. I'm not an idiot." In the dim light, her eyes bore down on his. "You take me for a fool? Some country girl yokel?" He shook his head. "You don't communicate. Answer my messages."

"I didn't get them," he replied, pleased that she'd at least tried. "But, let's go back to Devon a second," Kyle defended. "Do you trust him?"

"Of course. Besides being a cousin, he's a truly honorable man."

"Does he tell you anything?"

"I don't understand."

"*Can* he tell you anything, about his job, about Marsco? About me?"

"No, no, I suppose not. But what's that got—"

He held up his hand to silence her. "Devon got me into all this crap. I've been put in a position of trusting him without question. He tipped me off about something, which I cannot tell you but which *is* serious. Life or death serious. With implications to the future of this federation. All the newly created feds. To protect myself, not give myself away, I needed to pretend to love this woman."

"Oh, that's rich. What I'd expect from an associate."

Kyle shrugged, stung. He was an associate once, no doubt. "But, everything changed in a nano," he explained vaguely. "And I was out of there before anything, *anything*, happened. I'm sure it made her handlers' heads spin."

"What's a *handler*?"

"Spy talk."

"Spy? It's *that* serious?"

"It was. Underscore, *was*."

"And I'm to believe this, this barn muck?"

He switched off the lamp and started the rover. The surrounding darkness was made deeper by the closed-in ground fog. He could no longer see her face. "You know the answer to that," he replied, silently heading back toward the main house. *This is how we end*, he was sure, *with bull shit*.

Parking near the great room, Kyle was around to her side to walk her to the door.

He turned away before she stepped inside, thinking her stern reserve explained everything.

As he restarted the rover, however, she was back. "I saw your rations earlier. Let me at least offer you a decent meal." Her invitation came with an extended hand.

If the war's not over, certainly a cease-fire is in place, the officer concluded.

"How's Old Man Tillson treating you?" she asked when they were seated alone in the great room, close to a roaring fire.

Not exactly like old times, but a damn sight better than fifteen minutes ago, Kyle realized. "Being the great-grandson of a previous granger on his place helps his attitude," he explained.

Sarah heaped Roxanne's ham in mac and cheese onto a plate. "I've watched his spread for years, never knew he made such excellent cheese. The meat's his, too."

"Do you think," Kyle conjectured, "that having such a lovely woman pay attention to him might have melted the cagy bugger a tad?"

"Possibly." She smiled and buttered some bread for him. "You look like you've lost weight."

"I probably did. I ran 5K nearly every day. Up and out on some serious winter maneuvers."

"*With* or *chasing* that other woman?"

Kyle didn't know where to go with that, so he just put his fork down and glared. She stopped as well, since his glance was at first angry then amused. "*Trust!* Remember? And *Devon*. Blame him. I'd be at the Academy at this very moment safe and sound if he hadn't gotten my scrawny ass into a Security uniform to begin with."

"Which one?"

"Take your pick, gray or khaki."

"And are you ever going to get your tush out of it?"

Kyle wasn't at all sure how she meant that, although he was positive, she meant it innocently. Believing that to be the case, he went on, "No telling when, Sarah. Literally, *no telling!* Look, I can't say a word about what I know, what I suspect, what I'm doing. Nor should I tell you what I think is going down with Marsco, except to warn you. I think the final Accords are going to be implemented *after* a rougher time than these past few quiet years indicate."

"Quiet? Millersville? The guesthouse in flames."

"Tip of the spear."

"That's what Father thinks, too." Sarah looked intense. "That Marsco may not give way."

"Not without a fight. At least from *some* of Marsco. There're plenty of associates like Devon who believe *in* the Accords. How typical is he? Can't say. To protect you from being implicated in any 'plot against Marsco,' if things go down poorly, I won't say more. You now know nothing of what *I* know or suspect; I'm keeping it that way on purpose."

"Ignorance isn't bliss," Sarah chided. "But, I want to hear. And from you," she stated firmly, no argument. She then gathered herself to demonstrate her mettle. "I'm Trent Brunel's daughter. That ought to count *against* me in plenty of Marsco circles."

Kyle didn't respond but loved her grit, her political savvy.

Alone with him in the great room, Sarah dropped her demands to urge him to eat, as any granger would. "I baked the bread," she cooed. "Roxanne's recipe, but my kneading."

When finished, the dark and silent great room provided ample opportunity to make up for the past four months. Sarah rekindled the fire in the hearth, inviting him over to a thick rug before the stones. It was a feast of kissing only, but Kyle had no complaints. She was truly his; he sensed that. Nothing like Mia.

"I'm sorry I missed your birthday," he said, coming up for air.

"Me, too. Both our birthdays."

After a long embrace, Sarah looked deeply into his eyes in that way she had of melting his resolve. "I'm the daughter of an Indie," she reminded him. "We're fiercely proud and free. Father has served for a couple of years now on the first West Con transitional Assembly. It's provisional until actual elections take place in two years."

"He's gotten busy, right?"

"Yes," she whispered then added, "I promise not to tell Father, unless I need to. Since I have to trust you, you have to trust me. Kyle, I want to know, if you have something weighing on you—"

He kissed her, not to stop her but because he was overwhelmed at her courage. "Look, Sarah, there are plans afoot in an element of Marsco. High elements, powerful elements, to stop the Accords." He knew he had to continue. New Grange may seem like a backwater, but it might not be. She should know. All West Con citizens should know. "I've seen the muscle it's training. The materiel Seattle's massing, here and in Europe. Probably all around the world. Not to help ease the transition, but to agitate it, make it impossible."

He took her hand. "Do you know some of the history of those times before the Wars?"

"As well as any, I guess."

"Back then, well over one hundred years ago, there were troublemakers in the masses; Luddites they were called. But call them what you want: antidemocratic factions, militant anarchists, frenzied religious groups, malcontents, people looking for a cause, *any* cause, which stipulated that violence and murder and mayhem were the best and only answer. None of these groups in league with another so much, each with a separate agenda.

Some just had the attitude of 'Burn a coffee shop for peace' or 'Keep *them* away from *me.*' That sort of element."

"Now you lost me."

"Look, when enough anarchy is loosed upon the world, then the average Joe and Jane just wants stability. Get a few violent mobs, a few riots, a few marketplace bombs, almost everyone else says, 'Oh hell, crack down on all the bastards, and let's go back to the way things were.' Follow?"

"Burn a few innocent villages and Indie granges," Sarah added.

"You got it."

She sighed. "Doesn't take much to destroy confidence in democracy."

"Not much at all. And, give some faction the power to crack down, and they rarely put things back the way things were. In all likelihood, rather, they seize total power for themselves."

Again, she nodded to show her understanding.

"Back in the '60s, right before the C-Wars, there was enough political and civil turmoil that millions of well-meaning folk thought, gee, since everything was going to hell in a handbasket, let's just have Marsco run the show. Those Marsco folks looked fine, upright, honest. And Marsco took care of PRIMS. *Marsco philanthropy*, it was called. But, Seattle was a sleeping tiger that didn't change its stripes. Once in control, and without any checks or balances, it quickly became what all monolithic organizations become."

"'Yesterday's revolutionary is tomorrow's tyrant,'" Sarah interjected, showing she was following his tight logic.

"Exactly. And think of this: what if today some group that *wants* power, what if it simply agitates or has others agitate for them. Then that first group can stand back, wring its hands, and say, 'Oh my, isn't that awful, Sarah and Kyle and Devon are rioting.' Only, they've *helped* Sarah and Kyle and Devon riot to begin with, knowing they had the power to crack down on us anytime. And more than us. They get society's blessing to crack our heads and say to themselves, 'Well, let's crack Hy's and Roxanne's and Jonathan's asses, too, while we're at it.'"

"Yes, I see your point, Kyle." She kissed his hands, fearing they would have blood on them one day.

"Whoever's attacking grangers around here, with or without direct permission from those in Seattle wanting to stop the Accords—*with or with-*

out—this local violent faction is playing right into the finger disks of those who *want* the Accords to fail and fail miserably."

"Just like when Marsco seized power initially," Sarah added, nailing the point perfectly. She was a better historian than he realized. Trent trained her well. Knowing Miller helped.

"Exactly. The world looks calm with the Accords going online, but it's really a powder keg, and any number of folks—together and separately, in conjunction or accidentally simultaneously—are playing with matches."

"And gasoline," she sighed. "Thanks for telling me. And now, I'm going to make you a pledge. No matter what, Kyle, I'll trust you completely."

"I'll never betray you either, Sarah. Never."

"You've got to get back," she finally stated. It was late and they both had long days tomorrow. "But, can I ask one more thing?"

"Sure."

"This spy? Was she cute?"

"She looks like a younger Mei-Ling, Captain Shanghai. Bit shorter."

"Stiff competition, especially if a bit shorter," Sarah acknowledged playfully, standing to her full height.

"Not really. She no longer smiles. She's cold as ice, and I knew she was just digging for intel I wouldn't divulge. Terrible kisser. And in many ways, really no longer truly and fully human."

"Don't tell me anything more," Sarah switched to a sharp tone.

"There's nothing else *to* tell. Trust me, remember. Besides, *looking* like Mei-Ling does not make her *act* like Mei-Ling."

"She's growing stronger, you know. Seems completely recovered from her cryo-stasis and jaundice." Sarah paused and looked deeply into his eyes. "You know, I never said exactly why I paid you a visit, besides the egg filching."

"To sass my ass, I figured."

"Not that you didn't deserve it, but no, my folks are hosting Christmas dinner next week. I came to invite you. Hy was my protection. Two safer than one. You can see why."

Kyle nodded, remembering the scene. "*Christmas?* Is that a granger event?"

"Was a celebration long before Marsco took over. We celebrate a bountiful harvest. And this year, it celebrates the Accords and peaceful times ahead."

"Let us hope."

<hr />

Celine outdid herself heaping the great room table with mounds of New Grange bounty. She had a turkey basted to golden perfection, an enormous roast beef, bowls of potatoes in pools of melting butter, warm bread, steaming winter vegetables. Trent offered their guests two varieties of wine.

Kyle had never seen the likes outside of Marsco. He was forced to order his own subordinates not to attend, because he felt not all his squad leaders should be away from their posts at once. In the spirit of the celebration, however, he suspended all patrols and afternoon details except guard duty. In keeping with tradition, Celine and Roxanne sent ample food to the troopers down at Tillson's and here at New Grange.

Sarah sat with Kyle while Tessa was on his other side. The granger's daughter felt a little nudge by a married woman might help her cause. *See how happy she is*, Sarah willed Kyle to comprehend by osmosis. *We can be that happy right here at New Grange.*

Beside these three, along one side of the table sat the rest of the *Sirius* crew and Devon.

On the other side of the table sat newly-promoted Major Kati Singh and Captain Anderson Jecky, the two Sac City liaisons who frequented New Grange regularly. Hyacinth insisted on helping in the kitchen; she refused to sit at the table.

The meal was delightful as they ate their fill. No one in the Brunel family put their head in the sand, but Celine was adamant that the evening would hold no politics. Their hosts guided the guests to speak of space and other places they'd traveled. Kyle spoke of Mars, seeing the Palmer greenhouses. Miller added stories of their first years of operation.

Tessa laughed. "You know, as the only child at Von Braun at first, I felt sibling rivalry toward those gardens." She told other stories of a girlhood on the Red Planet. To Kyle, they added to his conviction that he was absolutely going to farm on Mars one day. And raise his family there, too. Sarah was miffed. Tessa was supposed to show him Earth-side marital bliss, not entice him with evidence that his pipedream about Mars may be possible.

Celine kept the table on these lines of conversation with laughter, stories, and feasting. Trent's wine helped. Storms might be brewing over the horizon, but this long winter night was one of merriment.

Sarah finally stated that she wished her brother were here. Celine started to object, but Trent held her hand to urge her to remain silent. Chase was indeed missed.

The meal broke up and Trent gathered his guests in his study for brandy. All except Zot, who stayed to help and keep an eye on Tessa, who refused to sit still while the other women cleaned up.

Also, Kyle was absent. He'd said a quiet goodnight to Sarah at the great room door. He then returned to his duties as any good commander would.

"Damn, I thought he'd join us," Trent held up the bottle of brandy to show he had plenty.

"I'm sure he's off with Sarah." Miller smiled. The young pair did remind the former granger of Tessa and Zot when they first were falling in love.

"You do approve, don't you?" Devon asked.

"He's a fine man," Trent replied. "I like him." He took a deep sip of brandy. "I'm very pleased to see him in *our* uniform, that's for sure."

"And not behind a metaphorical plow?" Miller asked.

"I'll take him there if that's what he truly wants. You can't force anyone but a fool to love farming."

"I only wish the times were more certain," Devon added. "Three Accords down, three to go. Let's hope Marsco's as good as its word."

"Ominous coming from you, Devon," Trent responded, "ominous."

TWENTY-FOUR

CONFRONTATION

(New Grange, late December 2154)

Three evenings later, Hyacinth was alone in the small Brunel milking barn. New Grange kept only six cows, four Holsteins and two smaller, younger Jerseys. Hy's father had a much larger herd, but they were not this well cared for nor loved. And his barn had no electricity. Trent's solar panels, even in this fog, gave enough power for milking machines, separators, and refrigeration. Devon had helped secure the latest Marsco-issue panels; Tessa had tweaked them recently. A gray blanket from horizon to horizon dimmed the days and brought on full darkness early, but the barn hummed nonetheless.

Hyacinth was often here. She knew her way around animals and enjoyed their faithful company. They were safer than men. They accepted her, even when sweaty and dirty, especially the youngest Jersey, one still a bit skittish during this, her first winter of milking. "Still just a bit uptight, right, kiddo?" Hy cooed to the gentle animal, whose deep brown eyes comforted the young woman as much as knowing Sarah and Tessa.

Then Chase entered the barn. Hy tensed up, ready to bolt.

"Big do here the other day," he noted. In the past he might have invited her to such an event. Or her older sister. Hy knew she had to forget all that now.

"Yeah," she responded as coldly as possible, in a single word with none of the confidence her voice once had. Tonight was the first time she'd seen him since the hedges near the guesthouse.

"You alone?"

Without answering, she kept her distance, looking for an exit. She was struggling to pull down a straw bale when Chase handled it and easily dumped it where needed.

"You know," he noted, "if this area ever gets an electrical grid up and running, your dad can streamline his barn."

Chase tried bringing out a naturalness between them, like what they had once enjoyed. He wanted that. To return to a time when Columbus didn't exist. When he had his own room here at New Grange and Hy was an easy walk down the lane. They had time and privacy in the lofts, here or in the Richardsons' larger barn.

Chase almost forgot why he was there. He was on a mission to bring the girl back to her home. Columbus wanted this girl. Chase still felt he must obey.

But as he thought about it, a knot tied up his stomach. Why must Columbus want *this* girl? *I want this girl*, Chase repeated to himself. *And I've screwed up any chance of ever letting her know how much I do.*

Hy pitched straw into a stall, keeping the large bale between herself and Chase.

"You must be getting callused," he whispered, taking the pitchfork from her. "Rest up, I'll get this." Chase had almost forgotten what it was to work hard, lifting heavy bales, taking care of the family's livestock, taking care that their workers never felt scorned. He moved smoothly, actually enjoying himself.

Suspicious, the young woman stood back on guard. When he wanted, he could be an unflagging laborer at any task and could be tender, too. Then she remembered her bruised face—and how she got it—and stiffened. He'd hit her first. The others beat her, took her, but he'd hit her first.

"Why are you here?" she demanded.

"To see you."

"That's flattering," she scoffed, pushing back her dirty hair, smudging her face. "Always at my best mucking a barn." A cow finished her pie as if to underscore the moment.

Chase inexplicably became terse. "Look, kid, no matter what, you stay away from Columbus, okay? Promise me."

"You don't need to tell me *that*, so why say it?" she asked after quickly washing up.

"Look, I'm going to be in trouble for this, but you stay away from Columbus. Your father. Both."

"Don't worry, I won't go near either. Or you. This is your folks' land, or I'd tell you to go away. I can at least say, 'Stay away from me.'"

"Why?" He moved closer to her. She stepped back. "If I don't, you going to clobber me again?"

"*Me* hit *you*?" She stood firm, unafraid of him. "You hit me once. Hard. And then let them take me. Why? Why did you?" She saw the pained look in his eyes at her blunt truthfulness.

"I did it because, because—" he had no real answer except to say grangers often hauled off and smacked their women. Chase knew Hy's father had, although Trent never did.

"And you thought you needed to force me? Why? And those men. You got me there. You allowed them. I will never trust you again." She exploded with more explanation than was needed, then caught herself.

"Now that's part of the old ways," he stammered, feeling foolish, defensive. "I said so, I acted so, because Columbus told me that I was to be in total control of every situation, any situation with you. 'The old ways are the best. We men are in charge.' That's all."

Another cow cut loose. "She has the best answer," Hy smirked, cocking her head at the splattering. But fierce and angry. Not forgiving. Never forgetting.

He didn't believe all of Columbus's chatter now. He wanted to tell her that, but words didn't come. He wanted to say he now believed in something that had consequences that the mystic never imagined. Chase knew *he* was the one who mattered, that now he was never going to share this girl with anyone, especially not one of them. He drew a stopline around her. In his mind, he was sure he could put back their lives to the way they were after he'd stopped seeing Patrice.

"If I only knew what to say to you now, Hy," he began softly, thinking this helped, "I'd say it so diff. I'd act so diff. You know that."

"I don't want to hear any of that crap from you." Her tone was sharp and clear. "Please go."

"Hy, I want you so bad—"

"That's not the same. Get away from me. Stay away. Now." She pulled up defensive. Tense.

"Oh, Hy, with Patrice, she'd stop me before anything. I mean, *nothing* we ever did could get her, that's to say, with you, you stand up. I like that."

"Did you ever force her?"

"No! And, I would never have forced you, or tried, if Columbus hadn't pumped me up so."

"That's no excuse."

"I know."

"Did you ever hit my sister? Or anyone else?"

"No! No one."

"Except me?"

"Yes, and I didn't know what I was doing."

"That's rich! And it's all Columbus's fault."

"Hy, if I could hold you again."

"You never will," she shot. "No one will. Never touch me with a fist or backhand or a kiss or their prick."

Stepping closer to him, Chase thought she was ready to forgive. Then, Hyacinth slapped him. Once. Twice. Again. He took her powerful hits silently, then left her alone.

———— • ————

Two of Columbus's followers found Sarah by herself in the great room. They'd lurked outside in the darkness until Kyle had embraced the granger a last goodnight. Shadow went with him; the dog often walked him home then came back to Sarah. The spying pair were silent and patient, experts at prowling and stalking. A moment after she stepped back inside alone, they slipped into Chase's former home.

Sarah froze. Kyle was gone, but Roxanne was in the kitchen if needed. That thought kept her from shouting right away. Help was near. And maybe she'd learn about Chase.

The young woman stood conflicted, wanting to ask about her brother, wanting this pair to leave her home. If Chase were there, not these two, she'd hug him, welcome him home. She would want to squeal about her love for Kyle and tell her prodigal brother all the love she had for him too. Her lost sheep. And she would demand the truth of Hyacinth that night. She still wanted answers.

But Chase wasn't there. Just two other dirty followers, gazing around the room in wonder. Perplexed, she hesitated, unsettled. They stood there emotionless, unapologetic, brazen enough to walk in like this.

In the light, they looked pathetic. Grimy. Famished. The comfort of the room intimidated them. They'd rarely seen the like.

"What do you want?" Sarah finally demanded, hoping the concern in her voice carried down to the kitchen.

The taller acolyte spoke up. "Your brother has brought his woman down to us. She, they, want you, too."

"Down at Richardsons'?"

Not knowing the actual name, the other follower stated, "Yes, where our sage is now."

The first added, "Our new host is seeing the truth. Discovering the old ways."

"He needs no help there," Sarah shot.

"That girl is already there," the second one lied. "She is begging our master, Columbus, to instruct her."

The mention of that impostor made Sarah's flesh crawl, but the thought of Hy back at her father's, going there alone, brought out that fierceness in her that she had bragged about to Kyle. *How? Why?*

Without a moment's hesitation, she left her chores unfinished and headed up the path to the neighbors' spread.

<hr />

Hurrying down to the Richardsons' alone gave Sarah time to think. Hy wouldn't leave New Grange at night without mentioning it to someone. *And why would these two come in to speak with me?* They seemed furtive. She knew she could never trust them.

This was a trap, Sarah realized, turning back several paces to look for Kyle. But, he was at Tillson's by now, all the way across her father's land and beyond. And if this wasn't a trick, Hy would be that much longer all alone, in the clutches of Columbus.

Sarah stopped. Even in the foggy darkness, she knew exactly where she was. And she was pretty sure she wasn't being followed. And yet, the two acolytes might be near. She looked around, seeing nothing, hearing no one. The risk to Hyacinth was too great to head to Tillson's first. She turned around once more to rescue her vulnerable friend.

"Where is she?" Sarah demanded to whomever it was in the dark corner of the Richardson house. "Where's Hy?" She'd burst in the closest door which lead to a room much like her great room only smaller. She was sure that her friend wouldn't be that difficult to find.

"So, *you* are with us at last," replied a voice from the room's icy gloom. "You knew you wanted to come here; showing feigned resistance only excites our interest. But you really wanted to be here." The voice grew a body in the far corner.

"Cut it, Mr. Columbus," she seethed, but not surrendering her granger politeness. "So many of you want to make sure *we* think like you *say* we are thinking." She tapped her skull, "I think for myself. So, where is she?"

"If she is here, she came because she wanted to."

"Oh, you guys always spew that. I saw her after you finished with her. She never wanted that!" She was incensed, but her anger gave her strength. "You guys think you can wrap your lies in mysticism and call it spiritual, but it's just the same as before."

"Yes, we call it our *old ways*."

With grunts and short breath, Columbus rose from his pillows to approach her. Sarah sensed someone else was moving in the dark room. She heard the door behind her closing as quietly as possible. The two who'd tipped her off? Others? She froze, trapped. Escape blocked.

"It's okay that you want to know our truth and experience our deepest love. You've seen our truth and have called to us even as you tried to convince yourself otherwise. We offer you so much. We'll show you how a woman behaves around us, faithful and obedient—"

With a whoosh and a thud, the door flew open behind them. Someone abruptly yelped in pain.

Mei-Ling Shanghai was outlined in the frame. "Sarah?" the associate shouted. The kicked-in door had cracked the arm of an ethereal attendant who agonized in pain. A fortunate, unplanned takedown. "Out here, Sarah, just step back to me. Fat ass over there's going to play nice, or he's so much wasted meat."

Just that veiled threat was enough to make him retreat into a corner. The woman seemed unarmed, but with an associate, one never knew.

When the writhing attendant by the door tried to rise, the associate gave his broken arm a swift kick. That kept him helpless, whimpering, squirming all the more.

The granger's daughter had never heard the other woman speak with such an edge. Never seen her with such decisiveness. Growing up in the tumultuous era of early Marsco had given Shanghai that. Sarah had never known the like.

The granger took a few paces out the door. Mei-Ling slammed it, and the pair took off running along the gravel drive toward the far gate. It was a long way to New Grange, but they weren't stopping.

"No use sticking around until they figure out I'm not packing," the associate explained. Thinking back to her younger self years before, if she had had an Enfield, this room might come to resemble a hotel lobby in Sac City. She was relieved; she knew the carnage she might have wrought in that dark room.

Sarah abruptly stopped and started to turn back to the Richardson spread. "But, where's Hyacinth?"

"Hy? At New Grange, where else? I saw her before I followed you."

Reassured, Sarah picked up their pace.

Almost at New Grange, Shanghai gave a groan and clutched her side. "Damn my gut." The pain caused her to contort, unable to continue.

Sarah bent over her. "Come on," she urged, "I've got you. We're nearly home."

Both women were gasping for breath. But Sarah was strong, able to support the still-infirmed woman. Wrapping the associate's arm around her shoulder, the granger moved the pair at a walking but steady pace toward safety. "It's okay. I've got you," Sarah kept repeating. "I don't hear anyone, and we're nearly there." She prayed they'd run into one of Kyle's patrols, but no one was in the darkness.

"I saw you leave alone," Mei-Ling huffed out to explain. "Saw two furtive bogies, too. Figured out who *they* were. That's why I followed." She gasped. "I knew Kyle and Shadow had gone the other way. And I saw you heading this way alone. Made no sense. But you got ahead of me. I had to catch my breath," she huffed, "and I had to let my pain ease before I could come to you."

"You did great."

"I think I snapped his arm."

"You're safe, Mei-Ling, we're both safe. So's Hy."

"I've never been a snitch," the pilot assured her, "but your friend with those troopers is hearing about this."

⸻ • ⸻

Chase was glad for all the commotion when he reached the Richardson spread. He'd spent more than two hours pacing the land lost to him, his whole way of thinking about Columbus shifting. The granger didn't know what the mystic would do or say next, but he knew he had to escape.

He wished it was as easy as just walking down to his bedroom at the main house. Clean sheets. Hot showers. Roxanne fussing over him.

When he entered the uproar, Columbus fumed. "Where have you been?" Not allowing time for an answer, he shot, "Your family's guest has attacked one of my attendants, broken his arm."

Columbus was livid. The woman who rescued the boy's sister was formidable. Possibly armed.

Tougher measures needed to be taken with the neighboring grange.

⸻ • ⸻

After Sarah's escape, it was time for a stronger confrontation of Richardson and his guests. Trent knew that Captain Jecky had yet to get any real cooperation from Columbus's cadre. Many unanswered questions led to lingering suspicions about the cult. Trent decided to conduct his own interrogation. And so, the granger, Devon, and Miller went down to Richardsons' without Kyle early the next morning.

Trent didn't state it, but the underlying reason was the vain hope that the granger would understand how he lost his son. How the young man had slipped under the spell of that malicious charlatan. Getting his prodigal back was still the main desire, but if the father only gained a clearer perception of his son, so be it.

⸻ • ⸻

Under the best of circumstances, Richardson was likely to lose his temper and fire off a three-burst at visitors, but this group felt sure he'd control himself. Bringing Kyle, Trent had reasoned rightly, would be showing too much force. This was to be a talk, man-to-man, neighbor-to-neighbor, nothing more.

Their welcome was cold and took place outside on the spread's drive. As soon as the New Grange visitors stepped out of Trent's rover, Richardson swooped, confronting them with his usual scowl. The neighboring granger didn't offer to have them come in. Richardson demanded his daughter's return, but Trent pushed his request aside. "She's of age and a friend of my daughter's. Thus, she's at my home as a guest. When and if she wishes to return here, she's free to do so."

The rebuff didn't help the situation.

Standing on the gravel drive beside his rover, Trent felt the tension rise. Behind Richardson, the cadre appeared.

Columbus began pontificating about the cause of his peoples' long suffering, a tangent unrelated to anything anyone had said. "Marsco still suspects us of wrongdoing but without any cause," he insisted. "We are only seeking what is justly ours, since PRIMS were created when Marsco destroyed our peoples and our old ways."

Miller cut him off. "Interesting misguided point," he shot, still standing on the gravel.

The mystic was taken aback. His world was not one of an exchange of ideas. It was a world of his pronouncements and his minions agreeing without hesitation. A world of his vengeance, of his iron will, and his craving for gore fulfilled. "We lost *all* to Marsco. Our peoples roamed free two hundred years ago. We followed our lives as we saw fit."

"Just curious," Miller asked, "but wasn't there already a great nation here two hundred years ago?"

"Why do you ask? Of course, it was *our* nation. We were free and did as we wanted. And all obeyed."

Suppressed snickers came from Brunel and Devon. Miller just grinned. Columbus was in no mood for any such mockery. No one wanted to pick a fight here over such a wrongheaded and dangerous theory, but Columbus's twists on history were ludicrous.

Miller, the only one standing there who could make the claim of being an historian, continued to challenge the mystic. "You say you're a leader of a countless host, that you have scores and scores at your command. May I ask: Where are they?"

"Where I know they are," Columbus responded as though an ethereal response added truth to its meaninglessness.

Miller scoffed. He knew a minor player when he saw one, an annoyance making boasts while others, the *real* power of the world, held sway over countless lives. Here he was, Miller knew, a self-proclaimed leader of legions but really the head of a ragged mob of famished stragglers, malcontents, lost souls.

"Let me say," the engineer went on, "I knew of a Leader once. He made boasts and claims like you. But that Leader really *did* have power. Dark, horrible, dangerous power. Did command thousands upon thousands of devoted followers willing to die for him. And die for him they did. This Leader nearly brought on a renewed war that would have surpassed the Continental Wars in its ferocity and meaningless death." He paused, then added, "But those deaths would *not* have been meaningless to him, to that Leader. They would have proven to him—the poor, little-minded bastard—that he was a great leader, if you catch his convoluted logic."

"You have so little faith," Columbus responded. "And your eyes are without a window to your withered soul."

"I'll ask you to keep your greasy fingers off my soul, thank you very much. Besides, my soul and my fingers are not smeared with the blood of others, blood spilled simply to make *me* feel big and powerful."

Columbus was incensed with barely constrained rage, a common-enough sight at the Richardson spread.

Miller had him and knew it. Pull away the mystical and opaque covering of a conman—any conman—and often you find an angry, hollow person making bold claims to mesmerize the simpleminded. It was a story often repeated in history. A story whose second chapter frequently played out with all these devoted followers becoming maniacal killers for some farcical cause or other.

Trent might have stopped this confrontation between Miller and Columbus, but the granger had waited many months to see the sage humiliated for what he had done to Chase.

At that point, however, Richardson stepped in, insisting that Trent and the others leave his land and not return.

—— • ——

Driving back to New Grange, Miller apologized, "I'm sorry I got so carried away chiding our "Big 'Little Man.'""

"Don't apologize for putting that fake in his place," Trent insisted.

"I guess I should have been more circumspect."

"Not a bit. He's a bloodsucking tick sunk deep into my ass. And you were actually pretty self-controlled. He's been playing this gig for years, so I'm told, so undoubtedly you're not the first to scoff at him."

Miller sighed. "He is the type that derives his meaning only by lording what little power he really has over other little people. And I've seen real artists at this. Real players. He's nothing compared to experts who can call upon millions to seek out and destroy what they hate. Alaric before the Continental Wars comes to mind as an example. The Leader of the Nexus after the C-Wars was another."

Devon added that these charlatans always seem to have a willingness to cover over sexual attacks committed at their behest. Hy had been violently assaulted. Sarah almost as well. This wasn't calling armies into being to strike troopers; this was victimizing the vulnerable and the undefended.

"He may be a little guy by comparison, but around here, he's still a parasitical tick buried deep in my ass."

———•———

Only after the tense confrontation ended did sheepish Chase appear that morning. Before dawn, as he had most of last night, he walked his father's land in troubled restlessness. He hadn't slept.

As soon as he returned to the Richardson spread, Columbus was in his face. "Where have you been?" Not allowing time for an answer, he fumed, "Your family's guests have threatened me once more with insults right here in front of our most sincere host."

Chase had had enough. He was gathering his strength to desert this cadre when Columbus gave him a direct order. "We're leaving tonight. Burn New Grange!"

"What?" the granger screamed.

"How dare you question a command from *me*!"

"It's not that, Master, far from it." His voice fell to trembling. Indecision made him waiver, but somewhere deep inside he found new strength. "I fear for your safety, that's all. Armed troopers are sitting down there right now, spoiling for a fight. Why attack them at their strongest? That Kyle, I've heard him vow to kill you, kill us all. Why provoke him?"

Columbus, roiling, listened silently but quickly recognized the postulate's astuteness. "You're right, Child-Son," he stroked his wavering novice, but the sage's words and voice no longer blinded him. "We've always waited patiently, sprung our trap just so. That Watanabe, how we waited until he was least prepared, remember?"

At long last, Chase had confirmation of what everyone at New Grange suspected. But bolting was dangerous, absolutely impossible. He was stuck in their midst, in deep, over his head with little chance of successful escape.

Rediscovering his love for this land—his land, his ancestors' land—he clenched his teeth. "We'll burn down that damn grange in good time, Master," Chase began, hoping his deception worked. "Leave it to me. I'll burn that damn place to the ground." He swallowed hard. "But, when the stars are with us," he threw in.

"We'll see it done yet," the mystic promised his wayward postulate.

The next morning, another foggy, still day, Columbus and his cadre were gone, Chase with them.

TWENTY-FIVE

CELEBRATING THE ACCORDS

(Seattle and Sac City, January 2155)

"They say it's like during the Great Mutiny all over again. Back in January '02, when they last locked down the Academy," Devon stated, his pronouncement putting a damper on what had been a pleasant flight thus far.

Mei-Ling and Devon sat in the pilot and copilot seats of an otherwise empty eight-seat hovercraft the university professor had secured for their trip from Sac City to Seattle. Short visit. They were both expected to be back at New Grange in a few days.

The pilot remarked with no emotion, "I was under ice in '02. We think that's around the time Herriff rewrote our trajectory, out and back to Earth."

Devon didn't say it, but he was glad that Herriff had.

Shanghai was a natural with the controls, even if the HFC practically flew itself. They kept steady at five hundred meters, the ceiling of such a craft. Below them the land was brown except where, obviously, irrigation and water reclamation, like Trent's system, made farming possible.

"I miss this," Shanghai stated under her breath. She ran a graceful hand along the flight controls as her other hand settled lightly on the joystick. "Years of training. Years of being a third officer, then a copilot. Then command snatched from me." She cut herself off. She almost returned to the *Piazzi*, not the escape ship where she *did* command. "Of course, I miss the *Sirius*, a real spacecraft."

If I live on as promised, how much of it would be here, in this seat? Or in space at all? Johns promised longevity. But, Chesney demanded loyalty. The brewing trouble, as she saw it, would demand officers for Security, not space travel.

It was her choice. Tomorrow in Seattle, Doctors Lasher and Elion were seeing her for the final time. When they released her, Johns was waiting.

She longed for a life that would be under her total control. She'd lost that. Lost Julio. Lost it in that hotel lobby. Hid her past. But for Miller, she realized. Walter—whom she'd been devoted to, had loved—returned only paternal affection. It wasn't a lover's snub. It wasn't really even unrequited love. Walter caring for her as a daughter was wonderful. He'd trusted her. Saved her life. But, she'd known ardent love, true love—Julio before their hiber on the *Piazzi*. Was she wrong to miss that intimacy, that warmth of love?

Would her new life find such tenderness? Chesney's stern and unmoving grimace came to mind. No affection there, even for all her potential loyalty.

Devon looked up from the pad he was reading. "I want to tie up some research before they shut the campus totally." He shook his head in disbelief. "The Academy hasn't been ordered to suspend all activities like this since the middle of the Great—" He stopped. Uncharacteristically, he was repeating himself.

Now, even as the Accords unfolded, that move seemed to shred the peace surrounding them. Marsco was doubting. Tensions increasing. With the Accords, Marsco wasn't staying Marsco. Yet Seattle was hesitating, backing off, threatening what was already in place. But the federations weren't having it. So, closing the Academy meant only one possibility. Marsco wanted officers for units it was supposedly releasing back to the feds.

"You know," the pilot finally stated, "I'm not sure I'll be able to return with you. Can you handle this?"

"An HFC? I'm not a shuttle pilot, but yes, I can get back to New Grange no problem. I hope in three days. Sure that won't work for you?"

"Can't tell yet." Her life would swing one way or another in three days' time. *Can I, do I, trust Chesney? Or, Devon as much as Walter?*

Devon's mind was just as unsettled. If all went perfectly as spelled out in the Accords, a second *AAC* mission might still be possible, but that trek was still clearly a few years away. Marsco, the enlightened Marsco of the Accords, might be relinquishing all political power, but it was holding onto its space endeavors. And he was expecting there to be another deep-space expedition. That's where his life was best spent. He was an explorer. A scientist. And like Kyle, he imagined that meant some sort of connection to Marsco, the *new* Marsco, not the old, and certainly not Chesney's nightmare.

I'd still be in Marsco, but I'm no flier, the explorer mused. He'd asked Miller and Tessa and Zot about their pilot. They agreed. Shanghai was tops. "Would you," Devon began tentatively, "would you ever consider another deep-space voyage? I mean, after this, after all this?"

The colonel's manner wasn't the only awkwardness. The pilot listened, pleased to be asked. But with her health and these times, what could she say? Everyone's future was uncertain in this transitioning world. Almost as cautious as the colonel had been, Shanghai replied, "Devon, I appreciate—" But, she had nothing more to say. The *Piazzi* loomed too large in her memory. And Fuentes.

Devon's meeting with Mateo Modena was shorter than he expected; the Security Director had nothing new to add. Modena had taken it upon himself to accelerate the movement of Security personnel from Marsco control—technically, under his auspices—to the feds. His move hadn't gone over well with Chesney and Jackson Roberts.

His orders made it clear that Auxiliary and Security units were now to be totally commanded by federations. "The feds love it," the Security director noted. Any ambiguity with the earlier Accords and the future Fourth Accord was crystal clear. Feds were now in charge of every unit of Marsco's former armed forces.

"You do have confirmation that feds are making this work?" Devon asked. Trent's assurances that all was going smoothly with West Con was one thing, but what about the other 150-plus federations?

"Gwanda Bulawayo isn't too worried about her fed or those around hers even if she has no guarantees. But Mellon-Hart's concerned about the stockpiles at Harrogate. Are those battalions moving over to local fed command or not? Where's their loyalty?" Modena drew a breath. "It seems that the closer to Seattle, the surer the trouble."

"Would you expect anything less?" Devon asked. "Chesney's right here. His strength is right here." The space explorer paused, "But, Chesney is surrounded by West Con."

"Surrounded doesn't mean he'll simply let go of that much power without a fight." Modena looked out over the distant mountains. "I've a retirement villa on the Med. Quiet. Secluded. I'll do some consulting with some feds on transitional matters. Training programs. Command-and-control issues." He laughed lightly. "Some fishing. A dig here or there—archeology."

"I want to be back in space."

"Not a university position?"

"No, not yet."

Modena held out his hand. Shaking Devon's, he said, "Here's to both our long-term plans reaching fruition."

"Yes, after this transition."

"That's the hitch, isn't it? Transition."

"Is this the way an empire ends, with a bang or a whimper?"

———•———

Penelope Elion and Adrian Lasher couldn't be happier with Shanghai's total recovery. "As good as expected and better," Elion noted. "You were in great health generally anyway, so your spleen didn't compromise other organs. Your blood work is normal. You're fine."

Lasher remarked to her as their patient was preparing to leave, "We needn't see you again. And we're off to Sac City ourselves. We might meet down there."

Shanghai stood up straight. "Sac City? Why? What's there?"

"New med center. We're resigning from Marsco. It's official next week. The fed is now far enough along to welcome us as part of their medical staff."

The pilot sat back down. "Oh."

Lasher asked if she needed anything.

"A moment alone," the pilot replied softly. Neither observer had ever seen her so crestfallen. Elion motioned for her husband to step out of the examination room.

"Do you want to talk about it?" She sat close to the pilot, letting her know she'd listen. Shanghai shook her head *no*. In the sterile exam room, the young doctor brought warmth and understanding. "I wasn't going to mention it, Mei-Ling, but your file says you're scheduled to see Johns in a few days."

When the patient didn't respond, the physician rose. "I sincerely hope we do see you in Sac City sometime, not as a patient, but as co-residents." Her remark was clear enough.

Shanghai remained alone in the bright room. The immensity of the step she was taking loomed darker than she'd imagined.

———◆·◆———

Evening meals at New Grange settled into a familiar time for the Brunel family and their guests. Kyle was there about one in four nights. When he wasn't able to slip away, one of his subordinates often joined in. Miller, Tessa, and Zot were there. Other guests now and again who needed to be down from Sac City to consult with Trent sat around the table. Hy was still at the Brunels'. Tonight was the first time she'd joined everyone at their evening meal. She'd become a part of the family even if still reticent and withdrawn. She was a hard worker. Trent and Celine treated her as their own.

This night was a particularly festive night.

The First Accord had gone into effect a decade ago, and the federations worldwide were throwing massive celebrations at the milestone. Ten years prior, on January 15, they had all officially begun. One-hundred fifty-eight federations with the same birthday. The day was marked everywhere with parades, festivities, and pageantry.

"Imagine the celebration in two years," Sarah gushed, "when the Fourth comes up." She sighed. "And then when we have all six in place." Trent loved his daughter's optimism and knowledge of politics. A strong offshoot of his beliefs.

"It's like the old days in July, before the Wars and before Marsco's rise," Miller noted.

Practical Roxanne added as an aside, "Weather's better in July. Be more fun then."

Trent was leaving early in the morning to be part of the contingent on the platform during the speech by the of current prime minister of West Con. Everything was excitement in Sac City, so Celine agreed to let Sarah and Hy skim up there for the gala celebrations. The fed had heard rumors of trouble, but none had surfaced.

Because so many from New Grange would be in Sac City the next day, the Brunels held their own small feast the evening before. Devon had arrived back from Seattle alone—Shanghai's absence the only constraint on the night's lightheartedness. He felt concern that the pilot wasn't there, but like the rest, he was bursting with enthusiasm for the future.

As they ate, Zot announced his plans for the spring. His position at the university was working out beyond his wildest dreams. It had gone from part- to full time. Instead of taking the train up two times a week as at first anticipated, now it would be every day, five days a week. "I've gotten an old HFC that Tessa and I will be restoring this spring."

"Whenever the pair are down for a nap," the engineer grinned, knowing her limits, patting her swollen belly. "What did they call us back in the twentieth century? *Super moms?*" Carrying an unusual set of babies—they were due a month apart—she was anxious for any signs of delivery. When the first came, and if the second was healthy enough, both were to be delivered.

"Our first guy's due in about six weeks with no signs yet of early labor," she explained. "And our 'Stowaway Missy,'" as the younger one was known, "is coming on his heels, one way or the other." The pampering Roxanne assured her all was fine.

Miller laughed at Zot's suggestion of restoring an old but skim-worthy HFC. "That's not mine, is it?"

Zot answered without emotion, "I'm sure it's not."

Nothing could surprise Miller at this time. He drew a breath. "God, I hope that old robotic warrior I once had doesn't resurface, as well."

Kyle and Devon shot cautious glances at each other.

The expecting couple also had their eye on a small spread north of Millersville that needed a great deal of work; it had been abandoned in the '30s trouble. Several Indies had tried taking it over since, but none had succeeded. "But I've plenty of MMUs saved, and we can get a new house up there very quickly."

Trent smiled, "Stay here as long as you need." The *Sirius* crew was still living at New Grange because they really had no other place to call home and because the Brunels wouldn't hear of them moving.

"No grandkids yet," Celine beamed. "I'll just use yours, Tessa, until such a time."

It was hard to say if Kyle or Sarah blushed more.

Besides Hy, another Richardson attended this small party, Patrice. It was her first visit down from Sac City in several months. It didn't go well. "Mom cried when I showed up," she explained. She wore a simple wedding band. She was warmly welcomed at New Grange, not her family's home.

"She'll get over it, after the shock," Hy stated. She then added bitterly, "They always expected us to be married and continuously pregnant anyway." The remark chilled the table. Hy suspected if she had swelled up after being raped, they'd have been happy for her having a child. Especially her father.

As the others went back to eating quietly, she stared at her plate.

"So, you're going back tomorrow?" Sarah asked Patrice, breaking the uneasy silence.

"Yes, sooner than I planned, but DeShawn is there, of course," Patrice replied. She hadn't intended on keeping her parents at a distance but knew her father was happier the less he saw of the daughter he'd disowned and who'd wed a former PRIM.

Hy smirked. "Good luck on ever bringing *him* home for supper."

It was after Devon's remarks about the Academy suspending classes that the evening took its bleakest turn.

"What are they doing with the students?" Miller asked.

Devon gave a laugh and pointed at Kyle. "You're way ahead of the curve, lieutenant. Everyone below third year is getting warrant rank. The rest, lieutenant rank. They're all being posted to Security."

"Security? All?" Miller shot, "That seems a tall order."

"I don't think so. I've seen the fresh battalions being trained," Kyle added.

Sarah reached for his hand. "Will this change your status *here*?"

"No. I was transferred to West Con. And I'm staying put."

"All Security forces are already under fed control," Devon reminded everyone. The Fourth Accord, the crucial "Internal Security Abatement Accord," was set for implementation in January 2157, two years away. It was to formalize all this transferring to federation control. The feds, however, felt that *de facto* this had already happened.

"That's the critical one, certainly," Trent went on. "Marsco can say what it wants about relinquishing its stranglehold on subsidiaries, and if it has the muscle to dictate terms, the Union of Independent Federations is sunk. DOA before all of the Six Accords are brought fully online."

"Yes, but Modena accelerated that transfer. So far it's stuck." Devon pointed to Kyle as an example of that early transfer of power. Modena's action undercut any attempt by Marsco to hide units and keep them under Seattle's auspices. It's done. All units are answerable to one fed or another now. "I hope what's happening with the Academy is not indicative of what Marsco's really thinking. Why beef up Security, disrupt all those lives, if it's truly turning Security battalions over to the federations?"

"Marsco has one helluva way of goofing up lives," Kyle noted bitterly.

Between Devon's connections and Kyle's authority in Security, the revelers from New Grange had the use of an HFC for the day. Kyle was on duty, but the rest headed up to Sac City before noon. Hy and Sarah sat in the back, with Sarah talking excitedly the whole time, in part to cover over that Kyle wasn't there. Tessa and Patrice whispered about pregnancy issues, expectant mother to fledgling nurse. Zot, Miller, and Devon soaked in the excitement of the times. This day was momentous, worth celebrating.

Even in winter, the weather cooperated, with a mild West Coast day. A few days back, the valley had been shrouded with ground fog and drizzle, but today the sun was bright and the temps almost springlike.

From New Grange, Devon first skimmed over to the abandoned grange Zot and Tessa were planning to buy. Although the house and a barn had been burned down, a cistern was still operational. It had a small, overgrown orchard. Enough land for a flourishing garden.

"Only six acres," Zot noted, "but by skim, fairly close to campus."

"A fine start," Patrice noted, impressed. Couples could make a new life in this post-Marsco world.

Devon next took the hovercraft to its maximum altitude. The land directly beneath them was a patchwork of granges and small villages. The earth itself was dark brown from the few centimeters of rain that had fallen. Not enough to run a grange, so Zot having a cistern on his future spread was reassuring.

"Can I show you all my school next?" Patrice eagerly asked.

By this time, their HFC was approaching the river flowing next to the campus.

Patrice, her eyes glued to a viewport, expected the campus to be abuzz with activity. Classes were over for the fall term, and spring wouldn't start until after the Fifteenth festivities, but students were planning to celebrate here nonetheless. Their future held so much promise because of the Accords.

And yet, nothing was happening down below. The quads, the walkways, all were deserted.

The Security craft entered campus airspace without any trouble. It went into a landing glide with its skids extended. Other HFCs were turned away; six Security runabouts buzzed them and cut them off from landing.

Zot, at an opposite viewport, was reminded of the other time he had come here in a Security HFC. For him, it might have been that winter day in '97 replaying itself. He was unsure for a moment if it was his memory playing tricks or if he actually did see several black Brads moving through his campus tearing up new lawns and knocking saplings flat.

Returning to New Grange from Seattle, Shanghai felt an urge to tell Miller right away. She should have confirmed her decision with him first, but still she wanted to speak to him. Let him know. She had a communicator, but felt he should hear it from her personally. She felt she owned him that. He'd be crushed if he weren't among the first to hear her news or got it via a text.

A Security captain threw open the side hatch of the just-landed HFC, expecting to find reinforcements. Instead he found seven revelers.

"What the f—" the officer began.

As Devon rose up from the pilot's seat and stood in front of the captain, he pointedly noted, "I'm *Colonel* Chavez-Sherman. May I ask what's up?"

"Wouldn't have let you land if we knew this," the captain barked. "Closed campus. Closed until further notice."

"On whose authority?"

The captain snorted, letting that be his answer. *His* Security was accountable to only one HQ—Seattle. Confusion and power struggles may exist the world, but not in this Security officer's purview.

"I won't detain you folks, but get this craft up and skimming away, pronto," he ordered, not caring a bit for the colonel's rank. He was assigned to the Academy. The captain wondered why this colonel hadn't been reassigned to Security along with all his students.

"I'll try City Center," Devon responded as he took the command seat and lifted the HFC off the ground.

"What's that all about?" Zot asked. Tessa squeezed his hand and tapped her belly. "I knew you should have stayed home."

"Nonsense."

"What if you break your water?"

"Don't jump the gun, Zot. I've got six weeks yet." Tessa laughed as she reassured her anxious husband. "Women have given birth for eons. I'm fine. No contractions, no false labor. I can walk for a bit—it'll do me good. Them, too." She ran her hands around her swollen belly. "Then find me food, I'll be fine. Promise. They'll be fine."

Patrice was in silent tears after seeing her campus like that. She turned away from the view panel to weep into Tessa's shoulder. Why was it so hard in their time to make a life? She didn't know where her husband was.

If the campus was closed, City Center was a beehive of festive activity. Food booths festooned with balloons and streamers; West Con and UIF flags lined the streets for blocks near the Capitol. Hordes of excited children happily separated themselves from parents but under one watchful eye or another as whole families moved about in celebration. Beaming lovers seemed to skip hand in hand, in love with freedom as much as each other. The ecstatic crowds swelled as the ceremony approached.

After the HFC was down and everyone from New Grange was walking around, they caught the spirit of the reveling. Sac City Central was active, delirious, thrumming with exhilaration and potential.

Clusters of revelers carried streamers of scarlet and deep blue, the colors of West Con. The jubilant horde moved in unison, clad for the cold sunlight but hungry for freedom. A few older boys with bright, infectious smiles walked along, sporting bare chests painted with scarlet and blue chevrons. The joyous mass surged along with laughter, banners, songs, embraces. These feds wanted their total freedom. They had tasted some; they wanted more. Wanted it all.

The main part of the celebrations was on the steps of the old Capitol building, a historical landmark preserved over the years since it had been the final seat of the last Continental Powers standing up to Marsco so many years ago. It was here as well, under the partially destroyed rotunda, that the last of all civil authority vested in the remnants of the C-Powers surrendered to Marsco in 2070.

Because of its significance, it made sense that, after thirty-three years of interminable negotiations, the Six Accords had been inked here, a sign that legitimate governing bodies were being restored in a timely, measured way.

Behind the partially destroyed Capitol, a new building rose up where the gathering bureaucracy of the Western Constitutional Federation would actually sit. Known as "the Hex" for its modern hexagonal shape, this brand-new glass and polished marble structure was completed but not yet officially opened.

"Ribbon-cutting at two," Zot informed them. If anyone among them kept a close eye on a chronometer, it was he.

"Possibility is in the air," Tessa noted, breathing freedom in deeply. "If our twins live amid this joy, oh Zot, think of it. Have you ever seen crowds like this?"

Sids and former PRIMS, who had been liberated with the Second Accord six years ago, embraced, sang old songs, walked arm in arm as though eighty-five years of Marsco hadn't happened. Streams of people. A river of ecstatic revelers.

"Possibility," Tessa cheered once more. "Reconciliation."

"And promise," Patrice added, linking her arm to Tessa's free arm. She had stopped sobbing when confronted with the rejoicing multitude. "What a world for all our children and future children." She nudged Sarah. "It's too bad Kyle's not here."

"Ah," Tessa yelped in discomfort. "Wow, that's a pretty hard kick from the little ones," she explained, with Zot balancing her.

"We should leave," he insisted.

"Are you kidding? They want to party." Tessa's pain passed, the gleeful crowds grew, and the tenor of the merriment heightened and reached an unbelievable, triumphant pitch.

Devon enjoyed one woman after another kissing him. Whether they recognized him as a famous Jupiter explorer or simply were embracing every man in sight, no one knew. They certainly weren't concerned about his Academy uniform. Zot and Miller weren't overlooked in this celebrating, although each was steadily growing concerned about Tessa in this crush. As if on cue, she experienced another pang of strong discomfort.

"I want to hear the speeches, see Dad," Sarah announced, having to shout above the throng. "But only if Tessa's well." The crush nearer the steps and platform intensified.

"I'm A-OK, really."

Zot shot her a glance. "Truly?"

"I'm sure we can hear if we stand at the far side," Tessa appealed. The flood of euphoria was taxing to her, but she refused to leave. Experiencing all this meant too much. "An old world reborn anew." The crush was nearly overwhelming, even if it were all joy and celebration. Young men and women looking like Kyle and his khaki troopers patrolled the area, but even they smiled and embraced and kissed the exuberant citizens mobbing them. Those passing the troopers hung flowers on their kit.

"Come this way," Devon instructed in what came out as too much a command, but no one argued. Because they were in front of the old capitol building, they all needed to wade through the mass of revelers to the side to avoid the worst of the jubilant swarm. He snaked them through the packed bodies and found a less crammed spot thirty meters from large speakers and a projection screen. "See *and* hear." He got them water and food from a vendor who was having a field day in the endless stream of humanity.

"Can *I* get closer?" Sarah pleaded like an excited teenager, wanting to see her father better.

"I'll go with," Hy added with little enthusiasm but longstanding friendship.

Devon handed his cousin a com-link. "You good with this?"

"Fine."

"I'll give you a shout if we need to leave. You'll find us *here*—repeat, right here no prob." Sounding like the officer he was and not the benevolent relative she knew, he added, "And if I give a call, you come, stat."

"Yes, sir," she mocked until she saw he wasn't amused. "Of course." She added to Tessa, "We won't do anything to delay you. Thanks." She kissed Devon's cheek where smeared lipstick remained from a dozen previous celebratory gestures. The youngest two of the New Grange party, arm in arm, were enveloped in the horde. Sarah, as delirious as the crowd, tugged along Hyacinth, who was trying to let her old self reemerge—their new world was all before them.

———·———

The gathering host watched several large screens. The revelers stretched beyond the Hex's park and gardens into the adjoining street. On the screens, celebrations were broadcast from around the globe: London. Rome. Paris. Sidney. Tokyo. Taipei. Cairo. Johannesburg. No part of the world overlooked this significant day to acknowledge Marsco shifting in power, diminishing. The world was partway there; it wanted no delays or unexplained changes in direction.

All the fed capitals worldwide were dancing in merriment but willing to roll up sleeves and accept the awesome responsibility of self-governance. Half the Accords done. Ten years into the whole process. The Marsco chrysalis was breaking apart, and newly born nations were awaiting their opportunity and their duty to rule themselves and their people justly.

———·———

The provisional prime minister of West Con was an appointee from Marsco but also a nationalist who stood as independent of Seattle as he dared during this tenuous transitional period. It was no secret he was running for a House seat in a left-central party, one with a strong self-determining and sovereignty-minded agenda.

He had a thin brown beard flaked with some gray but was actually young, only in his mid-thirties. His youth and vigor, however, were an asset. His ideas were fresh and free from previous exchanges with Marsco. Beside him stood his smiling wife and their two young children. Like Tessa, she was obviously pregnant, due later in the spring. Birth—another propitious sign of renewal in this former subsidiary.

Trent was also there, looking proud, soaking in the view from the platform. The granger sat amid three rows of officials like himself, twenty-four in all, who represented the whole provisional Assembly. As far as he could see, the cheering crowd stretched, imploring these fledging officials to make their new government something all could share in and be proud of.

In that moment, the prime minster began. "What has happened over these past dark years," his speech rang out, "must not be forgotten. No, we will never forget that past, but we will strive—giving our blood, sweat, toil, and tears—to live under a new government *of* the people, *by* the people, *for* the people. Now, Marsco is granting us political powers, slowly, it is true, but we must pick up those powers with all their awesome responsibility. We must rule ourselves *well!* No West Con citizen will be left behind or marginalized."

Applause interrupted him several times, as he spoke of a new beginning, a renewed sense of hope and purpose, of a unified federation that would separate out none of its citizens as the Disenfranchise Movement had. "Our purpose, as *your* government, is to make the people—all the people—*the* government of this federation. A government answerable to all, not to a few, a government serving all, not just a select faction."

More applause stopped the prime minister, who barely constrained himself. The energy and affection of the crowd were infectious. The whole platform party felt the adoration.

Trent sat there proudly. Other representatives from granges and cities, from small towns and large, listened and applauded. Owners of businesses and workers. Several in uniform. This was unity, a unity Marsco had kept at bay for years to stay in power, playing one against the other. Now, everyone wanted the full freedom and liberty to pursue their lives as never before.

"And of Marsco—we must bind up the wounds that have cost us so dearly. But without retribution. I know a very few among you feel that retribution *must be* sought. That Marsco *must be* punished. But, if we seek to attack it, blame it, we are merely seeking the blood of associates who did not perpetrate this world, only inherited it. We must not seek innocent blood of the children to simply satisfy one small faction's anger and a lust for revenge against others," he declared. "We must move forward *with* Marsco, or we'll fall backward because Marsco becomes a stumbling block."

Applause again stopped the speaker. He raised his hands, a gesture that thanked his supporters and begged them to let him finish.

"We must be the example to the world. We are going forward in peace to all other federations and to Marsco. We citizens of the whole planet have learned a terrible lesson—settling old scores with blood and violence only brings on new scores to settle. It only makes hatred a policy. We stand for going forward in peace, *not* for repeating the past in anger and distain, *not* for seeking revenge—"

Instead of applause interrupting the prime minster, this time a set of loud drum beats brought the speech to an abrupt end.

Several men had cut the leads to the speakers and projection screen a few meters ahead of Devon's group. A drum at the back pounded loudly because it no longer competed with the prime minister's amplified voice over the hushed crowd. The respectful silence of the listening throng allowed the drum's thumping and a roar of malice to fill the air.

"Marsco must pay with its blood! Marsco must pay with its blood!" chanted a group of no more than thirty protesters. Their actions were so abrupt, so unexpected, that the crowd of several thousand listening peacefully to the prime minister stood in silent awe.

"What do we want?"

"*Marsco's blood!*"

"When do we want it?"

"*Now!*"

"What do we want?"

"*Stop the Accords!*"

"Why?"

"*Marsco goes unpunished!*"

The miniscule crowd by comparison to the throng seemed farcical. A few placards danced above the gaggle of anti-Accordists. "Your hands drip with Marsco blood! The PM is its puppet! Kill all associates! Kill all associates!"

A company of Auxiliary, who numbered three times the amount of the protesters, allowed the naysayers their march, but their officers had been instructed to keep the dissenters well away from the PM and the platform.

Yet in trying to do so, the Auxiliary escort inadvertently let the demonstrators mix in with the peaceful crowd. And once amid the celebrating listeners, the protesters made straight for the prime minister's platform. The aggressive pack never had a chance to reach those dignitaries. The prime minister had been whisked away by his bodyguards, the ceremonial ribbon-cutting disrupted.

"Oh, shit," Zot shouted. He pointed at the front of the crowd where Auxxies were unsuccessfully trying to divert the direction of the antidemocratic protesters. As the malcontents gave way a bit, moving slightly to the right, those from New Grange saw what Zot was referring to. At the front marched Columbus, and at his right not far behind, Chase, unmistakable even if partially buried amid the remaining followers.

From the start, Columbus was actually seeking a way to get at the New Grange party. Having made his feint toward the platform, the mystic had one more issue to settle. He let the Auxxies believe he was diverting away from the PM, back away from the platform, but in reality, he was aiming his handful of loyalists directly at Miller. The sage knew where his nemesis stood. And what he stood for.

Scuffling between the protesters and a portion of the jubilant crowd broke out. The Auxxies, attempting to herd the rowdy cadre, found it easier to push away the closing-in democratic crowd. This made it possible for the anarchists to head toward Miller even faster. Amid the confusion and jeering, the pushing and shoving, Columbus' band came at the engineer.

Zot grabbed his father-in-law and tried to shield him from the blind, raving pack bearing down on them. No doubt, Miller was the target. The iceman felt as though he was in a frantic, mindless herd, even if only a score of protesters surrounded them. The violent group reached Zot first. Fists and signs came at him. Miller was ripped from his side. Grizotti himself was hit several times, punches flying from all directions.

Tessa screamed across from the angry, flailing crowd. "Zot!" he heard a different woman's shout. In the melee, he thought it was Shanghai screaming. They must be together—Tessa and Shanghai—the iceman assumed, but how? Two more punches landed on his face and ear. He fought back to protect himself. And tried to find Miller but couldn't in the roiling of blows and punches.

Struggling to free himself, the iceman knew he had no chance to reach Miller or Tessa. Besides, Miller was being dragged ahead by a small, irate pair of thugs who were throwing punches, kicking, hitting with the handles of their signs.

Axe handles, Zot realized after a glancing blow across the forehead. The demonstrators used heavy axe handles for their light cardboard posters. An easy way to disguise their weapons. The mob attacked anyone in the crowd; the aggressors didn't seem that particular whom they struck. Blood ran down the iceman's face.

Reinforcements of Auxxies poured in. A voice of authority came over the rebooted loudspeakers and urged everyone to remain calm. Most listeners complied.

A dozen rioters broke and ran, a few were caught. Columbus vanished into the mayhem and was gone without the Auxiliary apprehending him.

Zot never got a clear view of those beating him. Blood ran down his face; he had trouble seeing. Across the mayhem, as the crowded pulled back, he saw a woman huddling over Tessa, who was down on the ground. Patrice, too, was down. A young man stood over them with an axe handle, but he was swinging it to keep two rioters at bay. When four Auxxies grabbed that pair, the single man dropped his axe handle and fled.

It had been Chase Brunel protecting the women from his own ilk. But in a nano, he was gone, as insubstantial as his mystic master.

Zot staggered forward, trying to run to Tessa, but his feet weren't answering. Blows to his head had made him partly blind. The swirling crowd dispersing around him made him dizzy.

Across the way, both Patrice and Tessa were still on the ground, with a woman now standing over them frantically pointing behind him, pointing wildly to something behind him. *Mei-Ling?* It was Mei-Ling. *Where had she come from? How had she found them?* Zot had no time to answer these questions.

The pilot looked to the two women on the ground as Zot staggered their way, but then she rose and kept pointing behind Zot. Her gestures implored him to turn around, turn around, turn around to look behind.

Complying, Zot turned and staggered back toward Devon, who like Zot, was bleeding from cuts around his head. The explorer was standing over a crumpled mass made darker by its own fresh blood.

Zot finally looked down at Devon's feet, where Walter Miller lay beaten to death.

TWENTY-SIX

DEATH AND REBIRTH

(New Grange, January 2155)

"**Y**ou'll be near your grandmother, Bethany Palmer, who's every-where in this soil," Zot whispered to a motionless bundle he held across his chest. In the New Grange great room, the fire crackled. Alone with his still child, Zot rocked and sobbed. "That's where you got part of your name, Maria—that's my mom's name—and Bethany is your mom's mom's name. Follow all this, my little Maria Bethany?"

He rocked the bundle back and forth to the rhythms of his sobs.

"And your grandfather, Walter," Zot went on, not holding back, "he'll be there, too. You'll never be alone."

Slowly, the new father rocked his daughter, dead at birth, and explained everything to her.

"Your brother, and mom, and I, we'll come visit. Trent and Celine want you here at New Grange, and we'll be here a bit longer sorting things out."

"Zot," Sarah called softly from behind. "Zot, it's time." Her gentle voice guided him.

"Just a sec longer," the father pleaded.

"Zot, you've a son and Tessa to visit later today." Without sounding cruel, she added, "The living need you now."

Hearing that, he surrendered Maria Bethany to Roxanne, who finished preparing her for burial.

Pulling out his handkerchief, he wiped his eyes. "Thanks. I needed that last time with her."

Two days before, Devon and Hy had brought Miller, wrapped in a blanket, home to his former place. Everyone from New Grange, except

Sarah and Hyacinth, needed medical attention. Tessa was still in Sac City with her newborn son, the surviving twin. Moments after her attack, Tessa's birth pangs came on in earnest. Zot and Sarah stayed with the laboring woman, trying to relax her, but between the shock of her beating and the anguish of losing her father, her labor grew excruciating and protracted. Her son, who was farthest along, came but survived. Her daughter didn't.

Although traumatized, Walter Anthony was resting in natal care and doing well. Maria Bethany never drew a breath.

"Even at Marsco's finest maternity ward," the attending physician explained to Zot, "I doubt we'd have saved her."

"You did your best," Zot assured her.

"Your son's stable, doing well. He was further along developmentally than we thought; that helped."

"And Tessa?"

"Weak. She's suffered two tremendous losses. I gather she was close to her father."

"Extremely. He was a remarkable man. They were very close."

<hr />

At the funeral for Miller and his granddaughter, the anguish around New Grange was insurmountable. Hy had gone up to Sac City to be with Tessa and baby Walter, but everyone else from the grange was present.

On the cemetery hill at the southern edge of the Brunel spread, two open graves waited. One for Walter Miller, one for his granddaughter, Maria Bethany.

Winter held everyone in its grip that raw, cold, damp morning. Unlike those celebratory days with so much sunshine and promise, this day was thick with heavy mist. A wind was whipping up, which to the granger Brunel suggested actual rain was on the way, not just drizzle. No one seemed to remember that winter inevitably ends with spring, a ray of hope. A child is lost, a child lives. A father dies, his daughter recuperates. Any glimmer of promise seemed as dreary as the sky to everyone standing graveside.

Sarah stood next to Kyle. Devon inexplicably felt connected to this loss. Trent and Celine surrounded Zot as though he were their own son. In the back of the knot of mourners, Roxanne and La'Shay cried. What little dealings they had had with Miller, he'd always treated them with respect, like Trent and Celine did. They knew instinctively this was a great man. Tillman came. A few of Trent's hands stood in the midst of the mourners. Even six of Kyle's troopers, including Sergeant Parks, stood at attention.

Devon looked around and found Mei-Ling on her own at the back.

Trent wished he could explain it to Sarah, Kyle, himself. The death of one whose promise of life was snapped shut. And the senseless murder of a man who had lived through wars and a harrowing space voyage. Who first broke up the abandoned building foundations and removed pavement of this very spot to create farmland that grew into his own thriving grange. He found no explanation.

After the bodies were lowered into their graves, each mourner stepped to the edge and let fall a handful of dirt, the rich New Grange soil.

Zot nearly broke down completely when it was time to begin covering Maria. But he gripped his emotions, thought of Tessa and little Walter up in Sac City, and moved away from his daughter's yawning pit.

As the others drifted away, Sarah, who hadn't cried graveside, thought of her brother. Only later, alone in her room, did she cry for the first time since she'd stopped crying over Kyle last summer. Hearing of Chase's actions, his sister took some comfort in the fact that he probably saved Patrice's and Tessa's lives. But, where was he? What was he to do next? What danger was he now in?

Mei-Ling remained while Trent's workers filled in the graves completely. She added no dirt to their efforts, whispered no final words.

——— • ———

It rained heavily for the next three days. Each morning, Trent went to the cemetery first thing to make sure the ground was settling evenly over the fresh graves. Coming down the hill, he had to admit, the rain was beneficial for his land. "My land, and yours, Walter," he offered up as a prayer. "We both poured our sweat and blood into this soil."

While Trent went each morning, Shanghai roamed up there in the dark of night.

She suffered deeply. She tried to be stoic, tried dispelling her grief, but instead withdrew from helping around the grange. Devon tried explaining his own loss so many years before and how he'd dealt with it, but she put him off. Restless, directionless, torn, she grieved separately from the others, inconsolable.

Worse yet, she felt she really had nowhere else to go, that she was totally outside of place and time. At the gravesite, as each night closed in on her, she couldn't see the sky to get any bearings. She yearned for the eternal blackness of space.

———•———

After the rains came and stopped, a cold winter sun shone, low on the horizon, shrouded by gray clouds and haze.

Zot visited Tessa every day up in Sac City. When the three were together, mother, father, and child, Tessa brightened. After ten days in an oxygen-rich incubator, his parents were free to hold him. "I'll always keep Maria in my heart," she explained to her nursing child. "But I love you so much." Looking up, she said to Zot. "Walter will always have his place, Zot, but I love you so much."

Her strength was returning with each day.

As close as the pilot had grown to the engineer over the years, Shanghai never visited.

———•———

Life continued on.

The winter gray lingered near Sac City and New Grange. It was wetter and colder in Seattle when Devon ventured north seeking clarity about the next *Armstrong-Aldrin-Collins* mission. The world seemed to hold its breath waiting for clear signs from Marsco about what lay ahead, strides forward or steps backward.

A clear indication would be Marsco's commitment to renewing solar system exploration. Was Marsco true to its stated goal to become solely a space-orientated corporation, or was it holding fast to its worldwide control?

Devon aimed to find out. Thus, to Seattle for answers, straight to the Marsco Asteroid Service office.

"I have experience with deep space on the first—and only—*Armstrong* mission, for heaven's sake," Devon explained across the desk of the head of the MAS. "That has to count for something."

Putting Devon off, the head justified himself, "Until Security has finished with reassigning officers, plans can't go forward for naming a crew."

"I'm not really affiliated with Security at all. I'm an explorer and professor." Devon thought that was explanation enough.

"But," the head replied, "you had enough affiliation to be sent to Mars to guard the *Sirius* crew back to Earth."

"That's a little different than heading a Security battalion."

"Security will have to be the judge of that." Adjusting his glasses, the head left-twitched more of the colonel's record.

Devon noted that he had never seen a living associate with spectacles on. Only in old digitals of Martin Herriff had he seen anyone in Marsco wearing them. *Bit of an affectation, really*, he concluded. Like the famous glasses-wearing Herriff, the head had been at the VBC early in his career. Unlike that famous engineer, this officer hadn't delved into R&D but instead swiftly passed through that colony to do everything in his power to rise from a plum job on Mars to the highest position at the MAS in Seattle. He'd reached the summit. Currently, every Marsco craft from Earth orbit out to the asteroid belt fell under his auspices. His control even reached beyond Jupiter if and when it came to that.

"You know," the head went on, "Security's combing the whole of Marsco looking for officers at this point. What's up, I don't know. Most Earthside wallahs may not even know."

"Or may not say."

"Whatever." That was the head's indirect way of saying, *my finger disks are tied*.

"Look, that's all fine," Devon offered. "I understand Security HQ sensing its need to switch me—and scores other officers—to their branch. I think I understand their logic to attach me to Security along with all those Academy students." Devon drew a breath, hoping the worst speculation wasn't coming to pass. "But I have invaluable experience from the first *AAC* expedition. I've been at the Academy most of my non-Flight career and only a few recent months last year on a black Security mission. Any real Security training was nearly two decades ago."

"Yes, seems like your career has been mainly at the Academy or in space," the head confirmed after a cursory glance at dozens of screens of Devon's file. "But, you were again in Security recently."

"I know, but that was a temp stint to escort Miller and his party back to Earth. I was actually more of a liaison, not really an operational Security officer."

Devon sensed movement on the other end. "If Roberts leaves you alone, I'll see about duty rosters as soon as we expect another expedition. We've a mission beyond the belt scheduled, that's true, but it's still at its planning stage. And while not *officially* delayed, how can I begin to name a crew and backup with so much turmoil here in Seattle and at various feds? We'll need pilots, experienced pilots, for that trip. And a cryo specialist. Researchers like yourself, certainly. But, given all the present uncertainty, who can say if it'll go forward at all?"

"Fine, I can wait for a decision," Devon replied. With the campus closed, he would return to New Grange and *not* report to anything remotely Security until those wallahs had definitely clarified his status.

The professor sensed new orders reassigning him to a lunar research colony to start the *AAC II* ops might arrive at any time.

"You know them all, right? The *Sirius* crew," the MAS head asked before the pair's meeting broke up.

"Yes, obviously."

"Pilot—this Captain Shanghai, if her health is truly better," in the age-old Marsco fashion, the head knew a great deal about Mei-Ling's constitution and recuperation, "and Grizotti—you'll be in cryo a long time. Their experience can't be matched."

Don't you love indirectness? Devon vented mentally. *Am I to make them part of this crew? Feel them out? Or ask them to sit on their finger disks like I am?*

———◆———

It all had too much of a ring of familiarity about it, the place where Mei-Ling Shanghai walked. She paced aimlessly around the ruins of the deserted Sac City capitol building, then off around where Miller had been fatally beaten. Grounds crews had cleaned his blood, but the pilot found the spot. And where Tessa had fallen. And then where Patrice lay injured.

It was a cold, somber winter day with an early darkness closing in. Ancient oak trees that had survived drought and war, neglect and wind, were mere outlines in the growing dark. Other walkers, moving quickly and with purpose, came and went through the mist.

Where Mei-Ling Shanghai now walked, Mei-Ling Chen had walked once as well, years and years before. Lifetimes ago. On that morning, after Benny had bounced his unreliable HFC hard to the ground—Miller's craft it turned out, stolen weeks earlier—she had eagerly stepped over to him, to what she thought was freedom.

Chen never came back. Shanghai did, dragged back, brought back by Benny.

I could find where I killed him if I had to. But she sensed no need for that. *Walter trusted me in spite of all the unanswered questions I came with,* she shuddered. *I never told him, yet, I think he knew. Knew I had a hidden past, not one of torrid indiscretions but much worse, much worse.*

Walking a large circuit around Capitol Park, past the ruined rotunda, in front of the new Hex, across the winter-dormant gardens, memories flooded her mind. Wilkes. Fuentes. She wiggled her finger disks: that doctor who helped with these whose name escaped her. That toad, Steerforth. Miller. Zot and Tessa. The daughter guarding her father from the pilot, distrustful at first, then opening up. Sharing her father in such a unique way. Zot rescued in outer space yet dying in that escape pod Fuentes had jammed him into. But, she thought of Miller mostly. Not as her father. Not as her lover. And now gone.

While others dealt with the death of a child and a father, it was easy for the rest of the grange to overlook her loss. Walter had been a guide and mentor. She missed his steadiness, his gentleness and kindness. And the pilot had so few ways to express her enormous grief. Her desolation left her directionless. So, she walked. A whole gray afternoon into early evening, solitary, in the concealing fog. Aimless.

She had come back that day from Seattle to confide in Miller. She had wanted to tell them all but especially him. Tell him how she had decided at first to go forward with Johns' sustainability. How she'd made up her mind to do it, convinced that it would bring her back to space. Give her a pre-*Piazzi* life. She knew she had to tell Walter, but to add to her confusion, she felt she owed it to Devon to explain it all to him as well. That perplexed her. Miller pained her. Devon muddled her thinking.

The pilot hadn't told the explorer any of this.

She had gone to her appointment with Doctor Johns in Seattle a few days before Walter's death. She was totally surprised when, after arriving at the med center, she was whisked off to HQ and ushered directly into Chesney's personal branch of the bureaucracy. Soon, she stood there in his presence. Plush carpets. Dark oak walls. A view of Seattle at its best from the center of the Marsco world. As a good officer, she remained standing. He never offered a seat or asked her to stand at ease.

Chesney ordered that Captain Shanghai of the MAS and the VBC report to him before commencing her DNA replenishment treatment.

"Spleen only," she insisted, now trying to backpedal. That comment was superfluous. Lasher and Elion had made sure of that. Any further treatment was sustainability, not regeneration.

The vice-chair began with a sneer. "In my case, it started with my weak ticker," he touched his chest above the heart, "but soon developed into a total body makeover. I look and feel fine, even though I'm well past seventy. And when I'm past one hundred, I'll still look and feel as healthy as I am today."

He smirked his notorious slanted frown. With a wave, as his smugly self-satisfied grin implied, *I can dispatch you at will.* "I'm afraid it's a total treatment, or 'it's all or nothing.' That the only way I'll authorize it."

She stood there knowing instantly it was *not* the path to take. She knew she had to speak with Walter. The choice was obvious: one, an unrequited lover but kind father; the other, a distant smug master, for master Chesney would be.

Glowering, the vice-chair hailed his assistant from the next room. "Set up a round of sustainability treatments for the captain," he ordered.

Nearing the Hex for a third time, Shanghai stepped past where Miller was struck down. She imagined Zot, bloody and dizzy, staggering. She imagined Tessa down, moaning. How Shanghai had found them in the crowd was a miracle. And when she pushed one attacker away, she felt sure Tessa was dying. It never crossed her mind that fifteen meters away, Miller already lay dead.

Then, she recalled looking up to see another attacker but this one straddling the downed Patrice. His axe handle swinging. His grim determination. He appeared so like one of the many attackers. In that melee, with Chase swinging his wooden weapon, had she been armed, she'd have taken him down. Later she realized he'd kept others, those real attackers, at bay, protected Patrice and Tessa from the same brutal fate as Walter's. He'd scattered their assailants, defended both downed women.

The fourth time that she walked by the location of the bloody attacks, she remembered them more clearly, more intensely. She had less confusion of what had transpired that afternoon but had more acute pain. Her sorrow wasn't going away soon.

Two new figures loomed to her left, coming out the gray, silent and barely visible. She turned away, unconcerned about them but cautious, once more wishing she were armed. The pair, with guilty and furtive movements, seemed to be examining the old capitol building. Seeing they were watched, the two men slipped back into the gray veil that surrounded everyone.

Shanghai was certain that one of them was Columbus.

———— • ————

Celine had done up a suite of rooms as a nursery and bedroom for the new family back at New Grange; the main house was that big. The granger made sure they had space and privacy. The Brunels were delighted to have them.

"You going to be a happy baby?" Tessa asked the day she and Walter came home. "Or gloomy like your dad?"

"Thanks a lot, Tess, poisoning the mind of my son."

"Our son," she beamed.

The banter delighted Zot; it was the first time in weeks that Tessa seemed her old self. As her strength returned, young Walter took much of her time. Nursing, bathing, changing, rocking him to sleep became the natural pattern of a new mother's life, and it lifted much of her suffering.

Even Zot went three days without visiting his daughter's grave. He too was entering into a new equilibrium.

"Tess," Zot broached the subject. "February's ending. What are we to do?"

"No word from the campus?"

"Their website continues to say, 'Closed until further notice.'" He groaned. "Even Trent can't get a straight answer, dammit!" Young Walter fussed. "Sorry," Zot whispered and continued softly, "his Assembly meetings scheduled to begin this week are off indefinitely as well."

Feeling stronger, Tessa rose with the child and handed him over to his father to walk and burp. While Maria had thick black hair and dark eyes like Zot, young Walter had Tessa's auburn hair and green eyes. Fathers and daughters. Mothers and sons. "We'll make it through, Zot. I know we will. The Brunels have been more than kind, yet even so, I know we can't stay here forever."

"I've been helping around the grange a bit, but I'm not a farmer and it's winter. Not much need for another set of hands or disks at this point," he noted once more. "You know, I'm *still* an associate." To reinforce his idea, he wiggled his right-only finger disks. "There ought to be something I can do."

"Geez, Zot, they're apt to slap you into Security gray."

"Again? Not likely."

"You did have a short hitch with them."

"Fifty-six years ago."

"But Marsco never forgets," she replied in a flat tone.

"No, but there must be something I *can* do. Something Earth-side or something lunar. Something close at hand."

"And not Security," Tessa noted. "Stay clear of that."

———— • ————

Eventually, Devon's new orders came through, officially assigning him to the Saturn mission as vehicle assembly coordinator. He had been away to both Seattle and the Moon at the Herschel Deep-Space Research Colony with wallahs and boffins from the MAS. When he returned, he quickly sought out Zot. "You interested in a few lunar-based projects?" With March had come spring with heavy showers and warm drying winds.

"Depends, I guess, what they are. Not connected to Security?"

"No, far from it," Devon assured the iceman. "you'll look at the schematics for our cryogenic system, *now*, while they're still at the design phase, before the hardware is installed onboard the *Armstrong-Aldrin-Collins II*."

While the VBC worked on the propulsion components of this new expedition vessel, the crew modules and cryo bays were being fabricated at a lunar orbiting platform before being transported to Mars. "Now's the optimum time to take a look. We're going from computer graphics straight to the real thing with no mock-up in between."

"I'd be glad to, if Tessa's game."

"How do you mean?"

"Will I be in-colony long? Can I take her? Is she up to space travel, even just a lander ride to the lunar surface? How kid-friendly is this place, if that's an option?"

"I'd forgotten," Devon laughed at himself. "I'm asking you for a decision that impacts three, not one. Life as a bachelor! Been at this alone too long."

"If you rig up the computer ops, I'll take a look from here right away."

It felt exhilarating for the hiberman to be putting into practice his years of experience. Work filled his time and mind with something besides a dull ache. Mucking around the milking barn had given him some satisfaction, but putting his mind to a technical problem that advanced science kept his attention.

Zot felt absolutely giddy. For the first time since the January deaths, he really cheered up.

Viewing the first download to get a sense of the total project, it didn't take the cryo-expert long to realize that much had changed since the *Sirius Odyssey II*.

"It'd be hours of butt time at a console," Zot concluded to Tessa after his first day. "And I'll need some time based on the Moon, too."

Tessa was pleased. "I've got plenty of help here, Sarah and the rest. Gone for a week or ten days? It's not like they'll whisk you off to Mars."

"Or Saturn and Neptune," he teased.

"Or into Security." Her comment was deadly serious.

———— • ————

"If you're up for it, Mei-Ling, I have a research project at a lunar colony, a science hub on the near side," Devon explained. "I'll be away about three weeks on the Moon once more next month. Then back to Seattle then off again to the Herschel lunar station. The issue is, would you like to come? You can assist with trajectory planning. And there's also a spot for you on the crew if that's an interest. We're taking a total of three pilots plus a flight commander." He added, "I'll eventually be leading the science crew."

Mei-Ling showed reluctance. Without any real occupation, with no other place to live, she'd stayed as invisible and reticent as possible here at

New Grange. She ate alone thanks to Roxanne providing her meals in the kitchen corner when all was quiet there. She knew she had to move on but didn't know where to. Besides, her life now kept her close to Walter, whom she still visited each night.

"Look," Devon went on, "a break may do you some good. Just work at Herschel Colony as we assemble our vessel."

"I can appreciate that, but—" She hesitated, reluctant to explain fully.

"As I've been saying, Saturn and then Neptune. The pair of giants will be aligned just right for the *AAC II* to cross Uranus's orbit and skip any flyby of the seventh planet."

"When is departure?"

"Not for at least another thirty-six months. The launch window is then open for about six months after that, so that'll give you a time frame. But right now, we need prelaunch trajectory and guidance evaluation. Who better?"

"Yes, a fifty-year course, bang on target, suggests something, doesn't it?" The *Sirius* pilot didn't say that to brag; her voice was too deadened for that. And yet, a slight smile did slip out. Devon noticed.

"We depart from Mars, although most preliminary work is presently lunar-based."

"Duration?"

"Of the whole mission? Close to six and a half years."

"Truly, Devon, thanks." She held out her hand and shook his. Their finger disks tingled for a second. "I need renewed purpose in my life, that's for sure. And I've seen Zot smiling again. I need something." If she agreed, at least the next several years of her life would have direction. And it would be surrounded by the eternal void of space that matched the emptiness of her soul.

"Well, please give it some thought."

"That's asking a lot, considering Seattle and all. You know many, Chesney in particular, seem to be creating an endless life for themselves." Overcoming Miller's death was taking its toll, but the associate was not immune to the shifts in Marsco. What was next from Seattle?

The woman drew a tense breath. The temptation of immortality had been nearly insurmountable, using the recombinant science as a Franken-life, not medicine. But, she'd stepped away from it and toward Walter, only to have him crushed and thrown out of reach.

Yet, given all before her, Mei-Ling declined the invitation to join Devon's *AAC* crew. She felt she had nothing left to offer anyone.

Needing to catch an immediate lander to Seattle, Devon left the perplexed and perplexing woman to herself. What he'd offered in its own small way might begin the healing of such a bottomless, aching loss. He well remembered how space had aided him after his devastation over Cindy's death.

To accept, she would have to trust again, in herself, in another, in a space-based Marsco. Such trust might possibly lift her burden; she knew that. It was working for Zot. And yet, such trust was asking a great deal of transitioning Marsco.

⸻ • ⸻

Moonlight came through the sparse clouds above the cemetery. A solitary figure stood next to Miller's grave, as it had done so often, unnoticed. For the first time, the figure scooped up a handful of damp, fertile earth and stood over the grave. The pilot whispered, "Dear Walter, you gave me back my life, my purpose." She paused, then releasing the black soil slowly, a gesture she hadn't yet been able to do before, she asked, "My love, what should I do next?"

TWENTY-SEVEN

BETWEEN THE CRACKS

(Near Sac City, April 2155)

"**H**e may no longer be trustworthy, but his presence protects us," Columbus assured Lightwind, his chief acolyte, recently returned to the group. He had been well south of New Grange and brought with him a dozen new followers. Columbus's devoted ones, however, remained at thirty.

"How so, if you have misgivings?"

"He is a local granger, one of their own. His father is prominent. If he's visible beside us, they'll not hurt or even attempt to harm us."

The subordinate nodded at this wisdom. In all ways, the sage was superior to anyone.

Columbus and his second in command walked down a long gravel road through the center of an orchard about to bloom, the one lumbering, moving side to side to get ahead. The other much younger but wizen and rail-thin, with distrustful eyes that darted rather than fixed on anyone or anything. It was early in the season. They ambled amid almond trees, the first to show signs of spring. It wouldn't be that long before the surrounding acres of trees here were white and pink: almonds, walnuts, cherries, peaches, pears.

Their new host, a granger, reluctantly tolerated Columbus and his cadre's stay; ostensibly in exchange for work, but so far, no work had been done. They huddled in much less luxurious lodgings than the largest guesthouse at New Grange. Here, the disciples only had six old tents, a rundown cabin, and a single outhouse downwind from their camp.

"We'll need more space soon," Columbus assured Lightwind with a labored breath. "More supporters will be gathering; I sense it. Soon they'll number more than enough." He pointed skyward. "They'll be coming like spring rain. Once we've amassed them, right under the nose of Marsco and their new jackals in Sac City, we'll once more let them know who has the power of the people."

"Well spoken," Lightwind agreed, in his clipped way.

"How can they govern if we take their place? And our presence shall be a beacon to rally all our own, all those truly hungering to follow me."

"A matter of pure truth."

"Our propitious moment will arrive soon. We'll strike now as the iron is cooling."

Each morning, each evening, Lightwind walked down the long dirt path to where it met a recently paved road. "A sure sign that these sycophants of Marsco have little to do but fawn," the devoted follower concluded as he paced the stretching roadway into a thriving village and beyond. On each side, the granges showed signs of renewed promise and prosperity. Several flew the West Con flag proudly, its blue and scarlet border around an image of fertile fields, renewed manufacturing, and a healthy, happy populous.

"Coerced, I'm sure," he snorted.

Each day, the walk ended the same. No new followers appeared.

"We wait not in vain," Columbus assured his ragged followers. "We will be brimming under the canopy of this orchard come high spring. You watch. Safe here in this garden, we'll strike when our numbers are beyond counting."

The next morning, the next evening, Lightwind walked out to the new road, saw the industrious grangers preparing their lands and orchards. Lately, the foundation for a school had been laid out. A city park sat next to it, then a planned library. This federation was keeping its promise of total restoration shared by all.

Each day, Lightwind strong-armed no new followers to join their cadre and attack Marsco and West Con for their evil and pernicious ways.

Each morning, each evening, New Grange greeted the upcoming spring with renewed promise. Tessa and Zot grew optimistic, stayed busy. Their two winter deaths still cast dark shadows over them, but they grew stronger together watching young Walter grow into a happy, healthy child. Six weeks, then seven, the time passed quickly.

Sarah helped both Tessa and around the kitchen as the size of the spread's work crew grew with the approaching spring. Hyacinth threw herself into New Grange, much more than she'd ever had at her father's. She spent yet another night with a second birthing cow. Hy then took her turn when the power shorted—a failed coupling Tessa fixed in the morning—and the small Brunel herd needed hand milking. Without complaint. Without any sullenness. Without flirting with the hands or wishing her life otherwise. She felt free to stay or go, to labor or not, and so she chose to stay and to work, and work hard.

One day, it seemed, the fruit trees nearest the kitchen were barren of leaves and buds, looking as though they might never flower. The next day, their limbs showed signs of new growth. When new blossoms opened, bees hummed their ceaseless labors.

The cycle was repeating as it had for eons: spring, at first a season of mud, bleak as ever, then a season of rebirth.

With the changing seasons, Devon made fewer appearances. And, Zot was away for days at a time, going out to the Herschel Lunar Center to boot up the cryo-stasis schematics for the forthcoming Saturn mission.

Only Mei-Ling continued hopelessly lost in grief. She had stayed living on at New Grange in the guesthouse vacated by Devon and Kyle. She walked alone and rarely spoke with anyone, even Sarah. Eventually, she began visiting Tessa and holding Walter but didn't stay long. It was as though they hadn't been on a perilous mission together beyond the solar system, as though the pilot hadn't loved the young mother's deceased father.

Tessa reflected with sadness at her friend's continued listlessness. *Grief is robbing her of her vivacity, of her next chance.*

Mei-Ling grew sallow, lethargic. The pilot started believing her totally healed spleen still caused her pain and discomfort. Everything seemed to be conspiring against her. She watched her life slipping away right before her eyes.

When Devon reappeared, he made it a point to invite her once more to join his expedition, but he got nowhere.

"It's as though she's decided to let herself die," the explorer confided to Trent and Celine.

"And amid so much renewed life." Celine shook her head. A gentle spring rain saturated the ground; in the morning all of New Grange looked refreshed and alive for the first time in months.

———•———

"Your father's a miracle worker," Kyle stated to Sarah one Saturday evening. He had been at the main house for dinner, a festive occasion since Devon and Zot had returned. Even Mei-Ling came down from her self-imposed hermitage to join them.

"What's his astonishing deed this time?" Sarah smiled, confident that her father could indeed work miracles.

The pair sat alone in the great room. The large oak table used for Celine's special dinners had been stripped. With Kyle here, Sarah was forbidden to enter the kitchen to wash up. "Roxanne wants to be alone with her La'Shay, she says."

"You fighting that?"

"No." She kissed him.

They sat near the glowing hearth. Because he was on duty at 2400 hours, he had come down in his uniform, hanging his holster behind the door of the great room. He only had a half hour more before getting back.

"Sarah," he began slowly, "your dad's miracle affects me, me personally and professionally."

"Whatever do you mean?"

"Look." He produced a palm unit and twitched its screen to show the exact document. "These are my new orders."

She glanced at them but caught only the words *promoted* and *report to Sac City*. They seemed ominous.

Kyle laughed and kissed her cheek. "Let me read this to you carefully." He cleared his throat: "'Lieutenant Second Class Kyle Truman Roncalli is forthwith promoted to Lieutenant First Class in the Western Constitutional Federation Security Forces. Lt. Roncalli will report to Sac City for immediate assignment.'" He kissed her again. "Sarah, it's totally settled. I'm in West Con forces. I answer to Sac City now, officially."

"You're *out* of Marsco?"

"Out of Marsco *Security*, that's the germane point here."

Sarah saw their lives together as an unbroken road with him always right here at her side. That was her dream come true.

He went on to explain, "You do know this means I'm leaving New Grange."

She nodded.

"But, my transfer is only up to Sac City. I'll be based out of a former Security Cantonment, transforming it into a West Con post, not one of Marsco's." Foolishly, he added, "Exciting work."

"*Exciting?* Leaving me here and you going there? You call that exciting?"

"Well, I meant professionally, not personally."

"*Professionally?* Is being an officer now your profession? I thought you wanted to farm? Farm here?"

"Sarah, in all fairness, I want to farm *on Mars*. There's a big diff between New Grange and Mars."

"I'll say. And one humongous diff is that I'll *never* set foot on that desolate dusty ball."

Kyle reached out to hold her. She melted into his arms, a sure sign they weren't actually fighting. "It's the unknown that makes you—" he caught himself, "makes *us* testy. I was pulled into Security on a temp basis. But, isn't better that I answer to West Con rather than to Seattle?"

"Of course."

"I do want to farm, but where is up for grabs."

"Well, if you want me—"

"Is there any doubt of that?"

Her blue eyes scanned his face. "No, no doubt you love me," she admitted. "So, can we talk about things long range?"

"How do you want to begin?" the officer asked lightheartedly. "How about those *without* finger disks have to go first."

She hit his shoulder, forgetting under his khaki uniform was body armor. "Dang, that hurts."

"Offers some protection."

"Okay, Tin Man, I'll go first."

"Kevlar, but no matter."

"All I want is to stay here. You've been up there—" she pointed toward the distant cemetery. "We both have family in the earth up there. And friends. We should stay here, Ky, *here*, where we both have deep roots."

"I hear you; I do. But, we're young. The solar system's out there. Marsco's not changing its planetary rule. Imagine the excitement, the challenges, the once-in-a-lifetime opportunity. I'm not suggesting going like Devon into the vast endless unknown, trekking out to Saturn and Neptune. A colony's all I want. And life at the Von Braun Center. Aside from the pressurized domes and buried chambers, aside from the artificial-gee giving us roughly 80% of Earth's pull, aside from never going outside except in a safety suit, it'll be like home. We'll make it our home." He held her hand tenderly even though his finger disks gave her skin a slight tingle.

She kissed him.

"Sarah," he began, "I don't need an answer, but I've a question for you."

Her heart pounded.

"Sarah, marry me? Marry me this summer, please?"

She took a deep breath. She had wanted this question for months, but now with so many changes afoot, she wasn't so sure. "I have such a conflicted answer. I hope you understand."

"What? Is it *yes* or *no*?" His look was pained and confused.

"It's closer to, 'I need to wait a bit more.' And it's a lot of 'Don't stop loving me now.' Ky, I need to have more of a view ahead before—"

"What more do you want? We can work this Mars crap out, for heaven's sake."

"It's *not* Mars. It's Marsco. It's what's happening now. The Accords are only half done." She surprised herself at her own reluctance. Only days before if he'd asked, her answer would have been an enthusiastic and immediate *yes*.

His com-link beeped. He'd asked Jonathan to remind him as 2400 hours approached. "Which it is in about twenty minutes, Kyle, Lieutenant Kyle, sir." The orderly barked so loudly Sarah heard his hoarse voice.

"I have to go. I'll be getting settled in Sac City over the next few weeks. I'll say goodbye in the morning before I move on. And I'll be back down as soon as I can. Promise."

With that, he left her. The next day, he was gone from Tillson's without any time for a proper goodbye.

"What the hell?" Zot fumed. Working with Devon, Zot'd taken the risk of Marsco finding him, checking his record, and deciding he was suitable as a Security officer. Maternity kept Tessa safe, but Zot was in the crosshairs of Marsco. Then this.

"Security calling you up?" Tessa asked, anxious. Young Walter felt her tension and began fussing.

"Yes, Security all right. Get this—*West Con Security*. I've essentially been drafted." He mumbled reading his new orders. "Report to Sac City Security HQ on—*that's only in two days*—for induction into West Con Medical Corps."

"Med Corps," Tessa put on a brave face. "Hibernation specialist and all. Makes some sense. And your fifty years as a MAS captain."

Zot saw through it in a moment. "If I'm in a West Con unit, Marsco will have trouble snatching me. Some good in that. And I'm sure those at the Hex are concerned that Seattle's power isn't dissolving as it should."

"Trouble?"

"Can you imagine there *not* being trouble?"

Tessa tensed up. Walter cried. Zot put his arms around them both. "Dad's going to be fine, kid. Promise."

"Zot, don't go."

"Tess, you know I can't refuse. I'm solidly back in Marsco now via Devon's lunar work. Damn, if I refuse this, it'll be *Seattle* calling me next. And then what? Report to that faction wanting to ignore its own Accords?"

Tessa held him. Walter stopped fussing.

"Damn," the iceman whispered. "Those folks at the Hex are smart. It's like chess. Their move blocks Marsco from taking me."

"You're not a pawn, are you?"

Zot laughed. "No, actually, they're offering me captain's rank, as I have in Marsco." The calculating iceman's mind couldn't help but wonder how much a West Con medical officer with two dependents earned.

Shanghai's call-up was as curt as Zot's. Report to Sac City HQ for assignment as a training officer making sure incoming personnel knew how to handle HFCs. With all her flight experience, it made sense. Her rank, as with Zot's, remained captain. As quickly as Zot had put it together, the pilot realized the strategy behind the Hex's move. Yet another potential Marsco officer placed firmly under West Con auspices.

If she wanted to stay here, in this fed, she needed to cooperate. She'd already seen the alternative, handed to her with that slanting sneer. She knew what she needed to do. It meant no space travel for the immediate future, but it also meant a degree of freedom. Her choice.

———— • ————

Devon received his directives, too. He was ordered to Sac City, for a commission in the new fed as a liaison officer standing between the civilians in the Hex and its own fledgling military.

Worldwide, feds were preparing for the worst from Marsco. And West Con needed steady hands communicating with its own armed services. If it came to escalating tensions, Sac City wanted to stay in control as it warded off Marsco.

The spring had brought renewed hope and a delicate balancing act as this sovereign nation demonstrated to Seattle that it was truly independent.

———— • ————

"Kids? Boys and girls! Look at them!" Chase fumed in disbelief.

Lightwind had a dozen dirty children in tow one evening after his long walk down the orchard's dirt path. This collection ranged in ages from six to twelve. Emaciated, filthy. Their clothes in shreds. Half were barefoot. These castoffs represented the total number of new recruits Lightwind was able to muster since coming north. Not an adult in the bunch. Worse yet for Columbus, a few of the longstanding older followers had slipped away, vanishing into the night.

Chase was both baffled and bitterly amused at this ragtag band. "If you're planning to take over the Hex," he sneered, "you'll need more than twelve scrawny kids."

"It matters not what we look like. Our hearts are pure. We will prevail."

Chase could tell Columbus was seething at him once more. *Was a time I could do no wrong. But, that was at New Grange, milk and honey flowing from my family. All's totally changed.*

441

Columbus turned to the granger. "Never speak of our plans in front of newcomers. Our plans are *our* plans, not yet *their* plans. We must nurture them first."

***

As April drew to an end, Columbus's cadre had been ensconced for weeks in the orchard well west of Millersville. Juan Mendez and his wife, Rosa, the owners of the grange, happened upon the procession of waifs and followed them to the camp. Mendez had had it with this treacherous collection of idlers—as he called them—taking up residence in his orchard. They had promised work but had yet to do any. Their camp was filthy. Some of the clan had broken branches of his fruit trees, presumably for firewood.

"You don't burn green wood," the granger cautioned, but the damage was done. "And you have been tramping down my spring wheat." He pointed to a field nearest their small camp. "And two calves are gone, butchered I'm sure by one of yours."

Already enraged by Chase, Columbus was livid that the grangers wanted to dismiss him. "I'll call down a plague of locust on your fields if you don't let us stay here in peace," he threatened.

Rosa scoffed. "*You're* the locusts. This is our land, so clear off—"

"I'll have none of that," Columbus warned. "We're here until we move along of our own choice, so do not menace me again."

"Damn you and damn Marsco, but I'd rather have them here than you. Get going or I'll call for troopers to move you out."

His wife nodded her head to show her support. They had farmed this grange since the '30s PRIM unrest ended but had never been troubled with workers or trespassers until now. For years their families had been without PRIM-disks. Their roots went deep here. They weren't surrendering their land to squatters willingly.

Columbus turned away, then looked back at the infuriated grangers. He bowed formally. "It is just as you say. We'll have all this settled by morning."

***

A Fed Security Force HFC came in through the low clouds to set down in the Mendez barnyard. Twenty pigs were squealing in their sty but not from fear of the hovercraft. They were out of water and hadn't been fed in three days.

"Pigs are pretty particular," one of the troopers, a granger originally from nearby, explained. "They like to see the farmer morning and night. Want fresh water, plenty of feed. You mess their schedule, a hog'll let you know pretty quick."

Strolling casually over to the pen, the former granger expected to find just an unhappy herd waiting for some water. Instead he found a roiling mass of pink and spotted bodies, some rooting in the dirt. Several looked at him, blood running down their raw snouts from thrusting their heads into the dry soil. No water in days. They were frantic.

In the next sty empty of pigs, two bodies were sprawled face down in the dirt. The remains of Mendez and his wife, partially buried in the muck. Flies were thick over the murdered pair.

"Shit, Lieutenant," the trooper called. "Shit!"

"Com-link protocol, dammit, Howard," his officer answered back.

"Shit, Lieutenant, come see this. Oh, shit." The callow trooper, running behind the barn, vomited. The shock was too much; he'd yet to be in any real action.

Although calloused by duty, the lieutenant had trouble holding down his own nausea as he ordered the dead properly buried and sent teams out to search the scene for evidence of what happened.

In half an hour, troopers discovered an abandoned camp.

"Just as sickening," the officer noted to his subordinate. Deep in the orchard, the camp showed signs of a hasty departure. It had been empty at least three days, the length of time the murdered bodies had been in the sty. A boy and a girl—stiff and cold—swayed in the light morning breeze, dangling from a sturdy limb.

"Why the hell?" the commander tried to understand.

"Someone wanted cooperation from the witnesses of this execution," a savvy, old legionnaire suggested. "It's the oldest method of any cult, sir, getting motivated teamwork out of the unwilling by punishing a few of the reluctant."

A West Con Security HFC came to rest on its skids outside the main house at New Grange. The insignia was newly painted over the Marsco Auxiliary emblem. Whether a smooth transition or no, West Con was flexing muscle throughout its territory.

The transport was taking all three new officers away.

It was a short, silent skim from New Grange to Sac City. As the three officers left the craft upon their arrival, Shanghai called to Zot and hugged him. "I'm going to miss you and Tessa and young Walter," she whispered. The pair had been through so much, seen so much. Shanghai was surprised how strongly she felt at their parting.

"Take care with those newbie fliers," Zot replied, tightening his brotherly embrace.

The pilot stood next to Devon and beckoned him. "Probably not the way it's done in West Con, colonel, but there you are," she stated then gave him a hug. Before she let him go, she added, "When you go on another deep-space mission, if you go, I'm in if you'll still have me." Before he replied, she added, kissing his cheek, "If we get a tomorrow."

— • —

An abandoned warehouse served as the next base for Columbus and his followers. It dripped, being so close to the river and no longer having a complete roof. The ten remaining ragged children sobbed and shivered but not too loudly for fear of the rope. The exposed beams above their heads would serve better than any tree branch. The children had come hungry and without adequate clothing, believing Lightwind when he had promised them both. They hadn't seen much food, and they wore what they had come with, not a stitch more.

"Can't we do better?" Chase asked, himself shaking from cold. In the back of his mind he remembered the great room with a blazing fire. *What would it be like to sit there laughing with Hyacinth?*

Lightwind began instructing the children. "Marsco is getting off free for all its sins, my children," he insisted. "It took your parents' and your parents' parents' lands and all their livelihoods, but it lives on. It hasn't been punished. We must punish it and each one of its blind followers. And to do so, we must stop this changeover, stop it in order to rebuke every last associate."

When he finished his harangue, the children curled up to sleep, colder, more fearful, less sure of their world. They hadn't understood every word from Lightwind, but they heard his fear, anger, and desire for bloody revenge.

———— • ————

The cadre's new lair sat several blocks away from the old capitol building with its ruined rotunda. Behind that abandoned building stood the new seat of power, the Hex. There, the Western Constitutional Federation showed signs of renewed status. Lights burned late as the emerging bureaucracy laid plans for restarting the Herriff-Grid above the city to handle the growing HFC traffic, staffing schools and the new med center. With civil and controlled tempers, negotiations were underway to reopen the university campus that Marsco had closed.

"And without proper authority to do so," Trent Brunel reminded his colleagues in the Assembly chambers. "We need a functioning educational system if we're to rebuild and prosper. Our children and their children have that right."

———— • ————

Kyle found his HQ in a former Marsco Cantonment block. Hastily fashioned West Con Security signs hung over faded Marsco emblems. No time yet for permanent replacements. The neighboring area was thriving with activity. Businesses and shops were reopening. The citizens nodded with broad smiles when they saw shoulder patches on khaki signifying West Con units were patrolling their streets, not Marsco troopers. Local police were present as well, not to make the people fear but to help them where they could.

At the blockhouse, Marsco Security had packed up whatever it wanted. "Seems the only criterion was whether or not the materiel had been tied down," Kyle's senior warrant noted when the lieutenant arrived. "If it could be moved, Marsco Security's grabbed it."

Of a more ominous note, Kyle learned, Marsco hadn't abandoned all its bases within West Con as stipulated, keeping several active posts just beyond the capital city. "Are they leaving or redeploying?" he asked his superiors.

"Time will tell; that's for sure. In the meantime, get your hands on as much of *our* materiel—once *theirs*—as you can. Rovers. Communications equipment. Enfields."

———— • • ————

"*Security!*" Chase yelled, the whine of the gliding HFC making his shouts nearly impossible to hear.

"Hardly that, my child-son," Columbus insisted, standing in plain sight outside their warehouse.

"Get down! Security shoots first and takes body counts after."

Columbus only scoffed.

For all his bluster, not long after arriving at this empty warehouse, the head of the cadre had made good on one point. The HFC settled on its skids and soon off-loaded a crate of Enfields: shoulder-fired models, outdated but still serviceable. The cadre also received shells and propellant cylinders, plus four 9 mm sidearms. Fortunately for the children, the shipment included food, water, and blankets.

Tokens changed hands. These were not sent by other members of this confederacy but bought on the black market. Odds and ends. And obsolete.

"Not enough for our whole ragtag collection of warriors," Chase snorted, "but we shouldn't arm the children anyway."

"We'll do what we need to do," Columbus erupted, his temper so close to the surface even as his grand plan was nearly operational.

Chase was disappointed that the hovercraft hadn't brought Security down on their heads; capture was better than this continued charade. He had too much blood already on his hands. *None of it directly*, the granger rationalized. Lightwind was too eager for vengeance to force Chase to participate in any violence. The top aide enjoyed killing and hated to share. But Chase was a guilty witness to all his senseless brutality.

The old ways? the granger scoffed. Marsco was heavy-handed but rarely as mindlessly merciless as this. If he could escape, he would, but no opportunity had as yet presented itself. *Given the chance*, he reassured himself, *I'm gone and safe.*

———— • • ————

Just before dawn, an acolyte woke Chase and beckoned him to follow.

Gray light seeped into the abandoned warehouse as the pair crept through the debris-strewn storage area to a metal staircase that wound to a perch on the roof. In former days, a crane supervisor sat in a small hut here to oversee ops in the now-empty loading docks for barge traffic along the river.

Columbus and Lightwind were waiting, looking eastward from this perch. In the distance stood the dome of the former Capitol. Out of sight beyond it sat the Hex.

"Soon, we'll make our way there," Columbus gloated. He had scoped this unwatched entrance weeks before in the dead of winter. "Once inside, it's only a matter of declaring to all the world that true believers have arrived to take control. Others will rally to us without hesitation, knowing their true blood and true calling to return to our cherished old ways."

"And the children?" Chase asked. "What of them?"

"They'll be with us. Further protection from any Security onslaught. Troopers do seem weak about children at times."

"Is it Marsco we need to fear?" Chase asked. "This is West Con's capital."

"A mere puppet. We aim to destroy whoever speaks for our sworn archenemy. Fools, thinking they can stand in the way of our rightful destiny."

Chase wasn't convinced. He thought hard, trying to avoid getting the ten remaining children involved. First, he argued the trouble they presented. Tired, whiny at times, not quick to move when directed. "Why not leave them behind? We'll travel faster without."

"We are all going," Columbus insisted.

"Or," Chase winced, "what if they create a diversion? Make a scene, get Security looking for something that's no longer here."

Lightwind was about to cut the granger off when Columbus raised a thoughtful hand, stopping his subordinate. "Go on."

"If we leave them here and have them burn down this empty warehouse, the fire and these children will make the Hex suspicious but also confuse them. Security will be busy *here*, not looking for us *there*." He pointed east. Chase's plan was vague but intriguing enough to capture Columbus' imagination.

Distrustful of the mystic's nod, Chase nonetheless had gained control of the children.

A southpaw, Chase took a 9 mm Enfield and adjusted the holster so it sat snug on his hip. But for all the sense of power the weapon gave him, he knew it was all wrong. His father had a pair of handhelds like this one, only more advanced. The son had fired such a weapon at New Grange. But against live targets? That was something he'd never done.

As the day brightened, Columbus took the older followers to one end of the warehouse to pack up what they needed for their takeover. He left Chase with the listless children. The followers had packed all the food, leaving the children hungry again. Except for Chase's Enfield, the adults had also grabbed all the weapons.

"Look, kids," Chase explained in a whisper, hiding them from the others. "We're going to play a game. But when it's dark, so not yet. After this game, you'll all be safe and warm."

"Will we get food?"

"Oh, yes, plenty. We must wait until dark, and then I'll show you how to play."

Chase took no chances with them. He kept the waifs secluded at the far end of the warehouse, especially far from Lightwind. The granger feared the chief acolyte might devise a new way to abuse them or use them as human shields or have them carry IEDs strapped to their emaciated bodies.

Chase's plan for a diversion was simple. Promise Columbus a conflagration but spirit the children away to anywhere the granger could get them. The farther away he and the children were, the better; Chase knew that for sure.

But they wouldn't have to go far. A few blocks south of the warehouse was a Security blockhouse manned now by locally controlled personnel, not Marsco troopers. *There*, he planned, *get there and we're all safe*. He drew a confident breath. *And with me guiding them, I'll be safe, too.*

Chase called aside the two oldest, a boy and a girl, both preteens. The girl was the taller, gangly, quick. So far safe but eyed by the acolytes. The boy was lean and wiry. Both streetwise, cold, hungry.

"Look," Chase began, "you two will have to learn what to do in case, in case—" he thought quickly, "Yes, I'm making you colonels, okay? Like my cousin." It was the only rank he could think of on the fly. "In case I get sick or fall behind." He imagined a trigger-happy trooper eagerly waiting a chance to blast away at someone.

The two dirty-faced neophyte officers nodded. They understood but showed no alarm that Chase might not continue to be at their head.

"No matter what happens," the granger's mind raced at all possibilities, "no matter what, even if I'm taken away or called away, you get to that blockhouse. Don't be afraid."

They nodded again, too emaciated and strained to argue. Having lived by their wits, they showed no emotion, even while terror gripped them.

"Now, this is just our little secret. Just ours alone. No matter what, don't tell Columbus or Lightwind. They'll spoil our secret; got that?" He had a confident tone that invited acceptance, almost as though leading a troop of Scouts in a bygone era; the group trusted him immediately, completely.

"Everything you need—food, it's a warm, dry place—it's right there. Now, as colonels, make sure every one of your charges, every last one of the remaining eight kids, make sure each one gets there safe."

More nodding.

"We'll wait until after dark and the others down over there have gone. Then, we'll push off."

Evening shadows gave way to total darkness. Chase at his end of the warehouse prepared to disappear with the children as soon as Columbus and his cadre left at the other end.

At the last moment, Lightwind and a pair of followers appeared. "You're coming with us, Columbus says."

"*What?* What about these children? And starting a raging fire? Our diversion?"

"They're strong in our old ways. They are cunning and brave. They'll be courageous with their new duties."

The attendants looked as though they intended to take command of Chase's children. The granger stepped forward. "Look, they're ready, they know what to do without me or you." He pointed at the oldest two. "Actually, you may confuse them; I've got them that prepped." Chase's colonels showed confidence, often the best bluff.

The acolytes looked first at Chase, then Lightwind. Finally, the top aide gave in, and the four adults moved away from the children, whose big eyes watched their backs disappear into the shadows of the large, empty warehouse.

In a moment, Chase returned. Calling aside his officers, he handed them a letter. "You know the extra secret plan, right? I know you can do this without me, and please, do this for me." The girl tucked the letter into her pocket.

They nodded. He was the only one of this clan who ever treated them with kindness.

"Now, I'll watch, and you start."

One by one the children moved out of the cold warehouse into the colder night. The back alley was cluttered and hard to navigate quietly without any light, but the two oldest waifs had the others moving away and into the blackness smoothly, noiselessly.

When he saw no more movement, Chase rejoined the adults.

"Ready?" Columbus demanded of the granger.

"Yes, sir, of course."

"Then lead the way—" Columbus pushed Chase up front, "first to the old rotunda. It is there we'll find our way to the Hex."

Like the children, the armed group left the relative safety of the abandoned warehouse and moved through a cluttered street heading east. *They'll be there about now*, Chase thought with each step. *At least they'll be protected.*

It took more than two hours for the clandestine group to make its way only a few blocks. They were hauling weapons and food, but they needed to fade into the shadows for fear of discovery; they got lost once by turning down a dead-end alley. Finally, they stood at the replanted and restored corner of what had been a famous park surrounding the longstanding capital seat.

Intent on reaching the rotunda, neither Columbus or Lightwind looked back to see if their warehouse was blazing as Chase had elusively promised. No flames shot into the sky lighting the night; Chase's alternate plan seemed to be working.

The granger believed the children had to be totally safe by now.

"Under the front steps," Columbus whispered. As with the weapons delivery, this part of his wild scheme had been well planned. A flight of marble steps rising one and a half stories stood at the west side of the Capitol. To the left at the back side of these steps, a small stairwell went into the building below the grand front entry.

In a matter of moments, Chase and the remaining followers were down a flight of metal steps and in the unguarded and unwatched subbasement, an abandoned and unlit route no one in Hex security imagined ever being found much less utilized. It was just a matter of moving along a dank passageway to the true locus of sovereign power for the new Western Constitutional Federation, the Hexagon.

As his ardent followers inched toward their goal, Columbus's senseless and irrational conspiracy was thus far working out.

TWENTY-EIGHT

COLUMBUS MAKES HIS MOVE

(New Grange and Sac City, May 2155)

"**W**ho's there?" Sarah woke with a start. At the foot of her bed, the ghostly outline of two children silently stood. Shadow, more alert than Sarah, only glared; kids were no threat. "Who are you?" the waking young woman demanded, not frightened so much as bewildered at these apparitions, a girl and a boy in the dim light cascading down from a full Marsco Moon.

"They came with a letter for you, Missy," Roxanne explained, raising the light. Sarah hadn't seen such scruffy waifs in years. The pair looked a fright. Stringy, dirty hair. Open sores from poor hygiene. Rags for clothes. West Con took better care of its myriad street children than this.

"For me? From Kyle?"

"No, Missy Sarah," the former PRIM explained, holding out a yellow sheet of folded paper.

"It's addressed to me," she noted, looking at the outside of the doubled-over note, "and it looks like Chase's handwriting."

Unfolding the smeared paper, Sarah read softly, mumbling her way through the hasty scribble. "'Sis, first off, you have every right to hate me for what I pulled a few months back. I didn't know what I was doing. Please don't stay pissed at me forever. If I try to escape, I'm doomed. I'm still safe, but they may be on to me. I helped these kids get away, but they don't know what's going on—I hadn't time to explain. Tell Mom and Dad I love them. If I ever get back to New Grange, I'll never, ever leave. Promise. Once more, I beg your forgiveness. Your former bro, Chase.'"

Looking at the children, Sarah asked, "What does this mean? Where did you get this letter?"

Reluctantly, the children began to explain with overlapping voices and confused comments. From the mesh, Sarah and Roxanne figured out the story. The ragged pair had followed Chase's instructions to leave the others at a Security station, then find New Grange. They ran off, following a crude map Chase'd drawn them. Streetwise urchins, they worked out how to get here, no problem. But they were tired and hungry, shivering. They needed comforting more than an inquisition.

"And you say there're others?"

"Yes, Missy," the girl replied, trembling still, but picking up Roxanne's formality. "Eight more. Yur'ta keep'n help us all, so he goes." Sarah had no doubt who *he* was.

"Let me get them warm," Roxanne insisted.

"What time is it?"

"Close to four, nearly dawn."

"Get them to the kitchen and feed them. I'll be down in a minute. We must contact Kyle."

———— •·•———

A rat running across his arm woke Chase. He had been asleep for nearly two hours, cold, wet, hiding in a dripping, dark tunnel that ran from under the former capitol building toward the subbasement of the Hex.

No one else moved in the small band of followers. He checked his chronometer. It was 0510. They'd entered the old Capitol around midnight and waited for other devoted followers that never showed. Finally, impatient, Columbus had them work their way through this service tunnel to be in position to rush the Hex's main chambers. Their surprise attack would net scores of important hostages to ensure the cadre's safety as they took over the bureaucracy of the federation.

By Columbus' reckoning, at noon today he would be in total control of this foundering former subsidiary. It was all that simple.

Everything was working like clockwork, minus the reinforcements and the fact that this unused access tunnel was sealed at the far end closest to the service basement of the Hex. The intruders either had to break through the crossed rebar obstructing their way or retreat to find a new route to make their attack.

While Columbus and Lightwind debated their options, Chase slept until the rat ran over him.

"Still in the same fix," he groused.

Lightwind approached the crisscrossed bars as he had done when they first encountered them. He put his shoulder against them and tried moving the bars aside by throwing his weight at the barrier. With such a wizened body, he hadn't enough heft to manage it.

"Too new," Chase explained as the chief acolyte repeated his farcical attempt of brute strength over steel. "Too new." The bars, the granger noted, had been recently installed; they hadn't been weakened by rust and age. He ran his finger along them. "Besides, they're pretty thick and cemented in. Someone'd blocked this entry. I'd say about two, three months ago."

"It's impossible for us to come this far and be stopped by mere iron." Columbus fumed.

"You know what I've already suggested," Chase stated. When they first reached this barrier, he had proposed tying a half dozen exploding Enfield shells in a bundle where the bars were cemented into the walls. "I've seen my father blow out stumps on our grange many times like that. Hit the bundle with one shell, and they all explode. It'll pack quite a wallop." But, Enfield shells were in short supply.

"If we had the children, they could slip through," Lightwind complained. He was against leaving them behind and now used their absence to indirectly accuse Chase of not being a loyal follower.

Well, got that right, the granger concluded, *but I'll be no party to the deaths of any more children.* "Look," he said, "if we wait any longer, the building may be so full of people they'll hear us. We need to act now or leave. What's it to be?"

Columbus nodded assent, and the young man set about unloading his sidearm. He placed six shells in a bandana and tied it at the best spot to blow away the barrier. "Everyone needs to get back, way back," he ordered. At New Grange, a few shells sent a deeply rooted stump sailing skyward. In the confines of this tunnel with half a dozen shells exploding at once, anything might happen.

Chase walked back from the barrier where the tunnel turned right.

Finding a backpack full of food—he made sure no more shells were jammed into the nylon bag—he held it in front of his face, a small measure of protection. He laid down safely around a corner but in a puddle of slime. His Enfield's laser designator wasn't functional, but he figured out how to align his aim.

Without regard for his safety, he fired, placing his detonating shot perfectly.

In a blinding flash, the reverberating explosion blasted away the bars and part of the concrete walls holding them in place. Unexpectedly, it also punctured a steam pipe that ran along the ceiling. Dirt and steam made it impossible to see what was happening. The blistering cloud also made it impossible to move forward.

"Shit!" Chase screamed after assessing this deteriorating situation. The way seemed clear, except that a scalding jet of white-hot steam shot into the passage.

"Well, there's good and bad news, Columbus," he smirked. "The good news is the way's open. The bad news is the way's blocked."

Lieutenant Roncalli's days were filled with amassing materiel left behind from Marsco Security's abandonment of its strongpoints within Sac City proper. His troopers found five working rovers, two Bradleys with serviceable engines, crates of up-to-date Enfields, and dozens of pieces of communication headsets.

The last thing he expected was to have eight waifs on his doorstep one predawn morning. Two guards at their post saw them in the distance. Night vision glasses exposed their movement, at first actually away from the checkpoint. Then they seemed to be ushered back toward the blockhouse.

Regardless, Kyle had them now. Cold, hungry. Filthy. Making no sense.

"Get them fed and dry," he ordered. Food and blankets, he had. Cots, not so much, but he had them down in the infirmary as soon as possible.

"Wherever they came from, they're frightened of us," his medic explained. She'd examined them all and found the usuals. Head lice, open sores from lack of hygiene. "Anywhere we can get them that's safe? People who'll look after them?"

"Not until I get a chance to talk with them," Kyle ordered, acting too much like an officer. "Has to be some sort of explanation we should know about." New Grange and Sarah crossed his mind—the perfect place and person to help these children—but he couldn't solve this situation yet.

Kyle was still pondering interrogating kids when his senior warrant handed him a com-link. The incoming message changed Kyle's priorities. "Emergency report, sir," a flat voice reported in monotone. "Explosion in the Hex's Service Tunnel Two."

"Any cause? Accident? Device?"

"We think a detonation of some type started it. Alarms are for a steam explosion. Loss of pressure in that service tunnel's main line."

The voice on the com-link next explained that his cameras down under the Hex also showed what looked like intruders. "Either that or we've got humongo rats in that tunnel. We got nothing before the explosions, but as soon as things started to rock 'n' roll, we thought we saw bogies moving. The steam's cutting our view." The trained and steady voice might have been explaining paint drying.

"Roger, copy that," Kyle muted his link and thought a moment. He had only recently taken on the responsibility for the Capitol grounds and the Hex. Protocols weren't yet fully developed. "Is there anyone *in* the building right now, I mean who's *supposed* to be there? About twenty? Well, get them all out, stat. Treat this as an intruder scenario and get all friendlies out. Seal off the building. No one in or out. We're on our way."

"Roger."

"Can you keep that steam up? It may block off those bogies."

"Negatory. We had to cut the steam already, sir, or we'll blow a boiler when the water drains too low. It's a closed, looped system, but it ain't getting no return pressure. What's still escaping is what was in the line. But, the pressure will end soon."

"Fine. Have to live with that. I'll be there in less than ten minutes. Keep me posted on those phantom intruders."

"Roger that, sir."

Kyle walked in a circle around his quarters, trying to juggle steam, possible intruders, and eight waifs.

"Another call for you, sir," his warrant reported, handing him a second com-link, one tied to the whole area, not just the City Center.

"Which it is young Master Kyle, ain't it?" Jonathan yelled in the officer's ear.

"Jonathan? Yes, dammit, and this better be important!"

"Lieutenant Roncalli? Lieutenant Kyle?" Sarah's voice spoke softly, "Kyle, it *is* important! It's about Chase!"

"Sarah? I thought you were Jonathan yanking my chain."

"Okay, let's skip that part of this mess. Listen," she spoke in bursts but with more confidence as she read her brother's letter. "And the two children who delivered it, they say they were in Sac City, near a river, when Chase sent them away to come here. And they—my two—left eight others somewhere. I don't know the city well, but I think they were held near where you are."

"Sarah, no need."

"What? He's my brother. I thought if you loved me—"

"Sarah, I think those kids're already here. I have them under my authority."

"My kids," she went on to explain, "seem to know where Chase is. Some abandoned warehouse down by the river in Sac City. If you talk to them, you can find Chase."

"Sarah, two rivers meet in this city. And do you know how many abandoned warehouses are near here?"

"Well, how many can there be?"

"I haven't counted them all, but since the Wars and the Mutiny, I'd venture to say fully half of them fit the bill." His voice rang with impatience. With something up at the Hex, he hadn't time to discuss her runaway brother. If the officer found the lost sibling, he'd grab him, but what's up at the Hex took precedence. He softened. "I'll have a chat with those two; that may help," he suggested to get her to back off.

"What? What does that mean?"

"I've got the eight restrained here already—probably those you mean. I thought it best to restrict them to this locale—"

"What? Arrested?"

"Only detained." That didn't land well, Kyle knew.

"Well, my two are here and the others may seem to be prisoners to you, but—"

Shifting, Kyle offered this to console her. "I'll send down an HFC to pick up those kids. Have them ready in thirty minutes. Once I interrogate them—"

"*Interrogate?* My God, they're little kids, not criminals. Why say that?"

"Force of habit. Look, we'll get them here, have a chat. They may take us to that warehouse. We'll track Chase from there; it's our only lead. If I have time and if possible. But now I must be off."

———————

As the steam pressure and heat dropped, Chase stood up and shouted, "It's our only chance! Let's go!" The granger's reluctance was gone. He had no choice but to move ahead or, he was sure, the cadre behind would cut him down. Besides, he was inexplicably filled with a rush at the sheer audacity of Columbus's plan. This foolish, death-wish plan. With his children safe by now, the granger wanted to make sure any others weren't hurt as well. The best way for that was to keep the group moving. If they stopped, trouble might erupt. Escape for him would come, might come, later. For right now, he acted the part of a devoted follower.

First chance, he smirked, *I'm surrendering to Security*. Louder, he yelled to the followers, "C'mon, let's go!"

Columbus and Lightwind followed, as did most of their band, except those who used the confusion to slip off, away to safety.

At the first turning, Lightwind saw a cam housing that he covered with slime from the walls. "No use us being watched." It was too late.

"C'mon," Chase shouted to the rest lagging behind in the shadowy passageway, "we'll miss our chance." He urged them forward from their tunnel into a wide service corridor. It was recently built, dry, and well-lit. They had to be in the subbasement of the Hex by now. Where the passage ended was a single elevator and an archway opening to a stairwell.

"Don't use the elevator," Chase ordered. "Might get locked in the car. Climb, let's go!" He was first up the two flights of stairs, but the pounding of feet behind him wasn't encouraging. It didn't sound like a host of followers at all. How many remained behind, he wasn't sure.

Please let there be Security up top. Let me surrender right away before anyone gets hurt.

At a landing, the service door opened next to an elevator bank. Only one car had access to the subbasement, but four cars were available to take bureaucrats to any of the eight floors above. "Where to?" Chase yelled to Columbus. "Where are the Assembly chambers?"

Columbus was dumbfounded. He never imagined he would be here, right in the middle of the Hex, with followers behind and no opposition to his break-in ahead.

Chase had to find the way. He read info signs on the walls. And, partly by scouting ahead alone, partly by returning to the group to force them to move on, he got them up two more flights and around to the south side of the building.

In several minutes, after urging on those lagging behind, Chase stood outside the visitors' gallery. The whole collection of Columbus's intruders, down to only twelve, collapsed against the oak panel walls and gasped for breath. Excitement drained their strength. They were covered with ooze and muck from the disused tunnel under the old Capitol, hot and breathless from running. And yet, here they were, unopposed, ready to take over the whole Provisional Assembly of the West Con Federation.

"Remarkable," Chase signed.

"You lack faith, child-son," Columbus chided with a breathless huff.

"You telling me this luck-out of yours was planned?"

"Precisely. And in moments, I'll rule here," Columbus insisted, rising unsteadily to his feet, proudly throwing out his gut, and then pushing open the tall, heavy visitors' doors with a flourish. He strutted down the short aisle of eight rows of empty seats around the walls and down into the chambers. Here was the center of this fed's heart and soul. His daring and boldness had brought him to the verge of controlling more power than he'd ever known. Ever imagined. Caesar and Napoleon knew this feeling, this feeling of sheer audacity coming to fruition. Few other mere mortals ever had felt this way. Now, Columbus luxuriated in it.

Not a soul was to be found. It was now nearly 0800. The Assembly started its day's business at 1000, but the whole building appeared to be totally empty.

"Hostages! Find hostages!" Lightwind ordered the remaining followers. Doors closest to the Assembly chambers were kicked in, even if unlocked. But search as they might, no one was around.

"How many?"

"We count twelve inside, sir," a cam operator in the Building Security office reported over his shoulder to Lieutenant Roncalli. "Three stayed in the basement and three others tried to slip off, but we got 'em all."

"All twelve in the Assembly chambers?"

"Affirmative."

Drones scoured all eight floors. No one was left behind. No other bogies lurked.

"Any IDs?" Kyle asked the group of troopers in another part of the Hex who had access to the whole building's computer system and the fastest links to the federation's network. Six troopers manned screens, digging for information.

"FRM has only one so far," the warrant in charge of the Hex's system reported. "We're hunting through files for the rest." A few twitches with a finger mouse opened a dossier on Columbus in the Face Recognition Memory program. In a moment, all that Marsco Security ever knew about this face was available online. "One name of many, sir, is *Columbus*," the trooper shared the intel with Kyle, who remained in the command center closer to the Assembly chambers. "Never a PRIM. Born in the Cincy Sid. A sid all his life, as a matter of fact. Raised in a rundown subsidiary near Hollister." The trooper gave a whistle. "Then went to a Marsco prep and was accepted into the Academy until he flunked the PSP."

All the warrant and troopers in the command center except Kyle snickered. None of them, all former associates, had failed Marsco's standard Psychological Stability Profile. If they had, they might be the ones waving Enfields around a vacated Assembly chambers instead of sitting at a console watching the brazen antics of a dozen reckless men.

"And the other honcho," Kyle asked the face recognition operator back in the computer center. "What of him?"

"Here's his rap sheet. *Lightwind*—a recent addition to his many names, it appears—but real name Juan Lupé Carlos James."

"Anything else of note?"

"Yeah, looks like he got religion once and tried out some sort of sid seminary." The trooper skimming the intel scan laughed. "Seems he grew more interested in preteens than spiritual life."

"Hell, what stopped him from being ordained?" another trooper at a separate screen smirked.

"Knock that off," Kyle barked. At this crucial time, he wanted accurate info and focused attentions, not crude jokes. "And," he demanded, "it's definite, they have *no* hostages? None?"

"Roger, sir," a trooper next to the officer replied. "We evac'd the building when we initially detected an unknown occurrence in the passage. We left these intruders with no targets to detain."

"So," Kyle assessed the standoff, "no hostages, no way to escape, no muscle behind them. It's their dozen to our platoon, plus we've established their Enfields are what, twenty-year-old models?"

"Blow you to hell just the same, sir."

"Roger," the lieutenant went on, "but we've the situation pretty well in hand. Very good work to you all. Let's keep them confined and work to arrest them. And com-systems," Kyle called down to the computer control room, "make sure they *don't* have any outside access. They can talk away all they want but let no one else hear them."

"Roger."

"At this point," Kyle said to the troopers nearest him, "taking them down is out, repeat, *out* of the question. The federation wants this absolutely bloodless, if feasible."

Kyle walked to the bank of monitors focused on the Assembly floor. Nanobots inserted into air ducts allowed at least one cam lens to focus on each fugitive at all times. Assassin bots were also on the way, robotic micro snipers easily and stealthily placed to take down the unsuspecting bandits.

"You'd think they would flood the place with a fogger," the first trooper on cam-ops muttered loudly to no one in particular. "I think they don't know or understand our capacity here. They should be blinding us right now, flooding our eyes and ears with crackling static and e-disruptions. And they're not!"

"This is *our* backyard," a second remarked, peeved that someone this ill-equipped would try this sort of break-in on his watch.

"Assassin bots ready in thirty," the first reported.

"Too soon for that," Kyle, as the officer in charge, ordered. "We are *not* authorized to use those bots yet, so don't even think about it." He then tapped a screen. He was positive it was the young man who might one day become his brother-in-law. "Focus on that one, the young lefty. Get me a face scan and run it through your files."

Because he was an unknown, it took two minutes. The report came back empty. No file. "Means he has *zilch* record, nothing at all. Never been in Marsco or anything related to this federation."

"Roger."

"Never in trouble."

"Affirmative, sir. He's in our system now, but no priors."

"Blow up his face scan." Chase Brunel filled the screen in front of Kyle. "So, he's never been in trouble, which makes sense since he's an Indie, a granger from near here."

"Doesn't explain much, sir."

Leaving this ops room, Kyle walked down to Hex Central Security to report directly to Sac City Security HQ. No backup was available. HQ confirmed that he was the officer totally in charge at the Hex.

"How can that be?" the lieutenant thundered. "I have hardly enough troopers, and I'm only a junior officer."

"Marsco's churning up stuff, so we're keeping all available units on standby in case we need to shift forces elsewhere." The voice on the line paused as if deciding to confide anymore. "We're in negotiations to have them pull back, leave our territory outright. We're trying to de-escalate any potential flashpoints."

"Well, at least I have this situation well in hand," Kyle answered.

"Affirmative, but Marsco is muscling down pretty damn hard on Fed Security. We're on Red Alert because Seattle's acting like it's still calling all the shots, still thinking it's in control here. So, tag, you're *it* at the Hex, Roncalli."

The lieutenant shook his head at West Con nobly trying peace before shooting. Will their diplomacy work? But, his orders clarified, albeit completely unsatisfactorily, Kyle reentered the ops center. "Look, I've been given complete control of this standoff. I want only monitoring at this point unless they try leaving the chambers or attack someone. Once again, nothing goes down in there without *my* express orders."

No one argued—he had the one bar on his shoulder—but a trooper asked, "If they try to break out?"

"If they do, let everyone defend themselves, of course. But no heavy-handed cowboy antics on our part *first*, clear?"

"But why, sir? We have them dead to rights! Why so particular about these damn whacked-out intruders? I say dust the two leaders for sure. Hell, dust all the bastards."

"Will you explain it to *him* if we do knock off that lefty?"

"Explain what to who, sir?"

"Representative Brunel. That's his son down there, that young south-paw." The ops room went silent. "So, no action without my orders."

"Affirmative. We're on 'watch and wait' status."

"Don't even lock and load those assassin bots yet either."

Another trooper from the system monitoring room was on the com-link with everyone and asked, "Is he there willingly or not?"

Kyle sighed. "Looks willing. He has an Enfield." The lieutenant reiterated, "Monitor only."

For an hour, Kyle and his troopers watched and waited. The intruders in a vacant building frantically tried to open outside lines.

"Have you locked down the elevators?"

"Roger. All intruders stuck on the second floor, south side. We can cut the ventilation if you like. Cut all electric."

"I want to communicate with them eventually, not scare them." The officer watched the fugitives on the scores of screens that lined one wall of the Security Center. "Have they eaten? Do they have water?"

"Fountains are working. Near their locale, they've discovered a food trolley that was serviced before the evac. So, they have access to breakfast snacks, some coffee, juice. Same like we're being supplied with." He held up an orange juice as evidence.

Kyle had an operator zoom in on screen three. "What are they up to?"

Columbus and Lightwind were behind a wooden partition well to the left of the Assembly's central podium. That control panel managed all broadcasts from the chambers. All sessions were to be streamed live. In stark contrast to Marsco, this fed was to be totally open about what went on here.

A second trooper remotely moved a cam-bot up behind the pair, who were hunched over the consoles trying to boot up the central broadcasting system.

"Can they run that console system from there?"

"Not a chance now, sir. That pair of pongos have hit every command willy-nilly, and most still take some sort of disk command. What they've essentially done is over-program the system."

Kyle watched silently for another moment. "Can we help them?"

"*HELP?*"

"Certainly. Can we run their broadcast from here?" Kyle asked.

"Affirmative. We can do it either way, make it look like they're doing it or just do it our way."

Kyle gave a delighted laugh. "You got that control? Can you let them think *their* poking and pounding on the console has allowed them onto the airwaves?"

After closing and locking the connections from the abused console in the Assembly chambers, an operator slowly booted a camera and lit up a monitor screen next to the speaker's podium. "All they need to do is stand at the podium. They'll see themselves on the monitor. I assume they'll know things are uploading."

Columbus and Lightwind, banging away on the control panel off to the side, paid no attention to the activated system at the front podium.

"Let me try this," the trooper operator snickered. He pinged the camera so that it gave a repeated low chime; the tone caught Chase's attention. It was the granger who first stood in the camera's view and noticed himself on a screen.

"This is it!" Chase shouted. "If you want to be on the air, you're in!"

Lightwind, as spokesperson for Columbus's cadre, prepared to address the cam; once more, Kyle's team made sure he wasn't on a live uplink, just a loop back to the screen in front of him and to the control room.

"I've heard their leader speak before," the lieutenant noted to his subordinates grouped around monitors. "He'll make as much sense as whip cream covering a shit pile."

It was then that he was interrupted by his senior warrant. "I've just returned with the children, sir," the warrant began his report.

"The *two* women, well *three*, they all—none of them—wouldn't give in," the warrant's words came out in a rapid defensive string. "Those *two* needed a bath—so I was told—and clean, dry clothes, and the *one*, the younger one—she says she knows you, sir—she would not, repeat, *would not* hand over the children to me alone. She insisted on coming along." The warrant gasped for breath. "Sir!"

None of this made sense to Kyle, who was trying to make sure that Lightwind got a screen crawl, assuring the speaker he was going out to the whole world when he actually wasn't.

Failing to explain anything, or even get his lieutenant's full attention, the warrant left the ops room and returned with the two children Chase had sent to New Grange. Behind the clean and freshly dressed boy and girl, Sarah stood as well.

Like she had with the warrant, she started in immediately with Kyle. "I wasn't letting them be carted off like prisoners. Besides, they're children and were dirty and cold and hungry. Roxanne had already drawn them a bath and Mother made sure they had breakfast—"

Pulling her out of the room, Kyle silenced her by putting his finger to her lips. He used his left hand so no disk tingle startled her. Calling over his shoulder, he got a warrant at his side. "Take those children to our block-house. Keep them safe. No hassling them. Have the medic look after them. Do anything so they're not frightened."

Kyle laughed, looking at the tall, muscular warrant whose torso was clad in body armor. The lieutenant then saw his youngest trooper, a lad not much older or taller than these kids. West Con was that pressed. "*You!*" the officer pointed to the callow trooper who jumped. "You, yes you! You take them. Keep them safe. Play with them. Cards, checkers. Launch them onto Marsco Civ 15." Looking at Sarah, he explained, "It's safe. The other kids are there now. I won't let them get distressed."

"But, they'll led us to Chase, I'm sure of it."

At that, the ops room called. "Lieutenant, sir, he's on."

Taking Sarah's hand, Kyle brought her in front of the wall of monitors.

Half the screens were filled with the same shot of Lightwind's thin, drawn face. His hair was long and dirty. Crawling through mucky passage-ways hadn't helped, but he never thought to try cleaning up even a little before his broadcast.

An operator from the control board informed Kyle, "I've just sent him confirmation that he has 159 live connects, sir. He'll think he's going out to all the feds and Marsco, Earth-side only. Or so I've told him. I left it doubtful if he's being rebooted out to the Solar. Thought that gave it some air of authenticity."

Showing he was inexperienced using the tech system before him, Lightwind blew hard into the mic and tapped it several times, both actions creating feedback that the control room eliminated.

"I come here today," he began in a chirping way, believing he spoke confidently in a deep voice. He went on, sure that everyone listening world-wide was in agreement, "come here to explain why *we* have taken over this federation. *We* represent the true ways of you, our peoples. We are the ones who brought you so much in years past, because we are the true peoples of this continent, the solely pure people from before Marsco."

"That won't go over well in Seattle," someone smirked, "if they could hear it."

"Not only are we now in control," Lightwind droned.

"Bold twit, ain't he, insisting on that," another voice smirked. "He controls about fifty square meters of this fed, and *he's taken over!*"

"And so," Lightwind continued, "as I know you'll agree, in reestablishing ourselves as your rightful spiritual leaders to rule you as we should and as you should be ruled, here are our demands: *Give us finger disks!*" he shouted while pounding the podium before him. His boney fist came down hard; his head seemed to shake on his thin neck. "Marsco has had finger disks for centuries and centuries, even though we, *we!* the free peoples of this land, invented them!" he insisted with another podium pounding.

Even Sarah, an Indie's daughter, knew that everything he was saying was inaccurate, but the manner of his delivery was terrifying yet riveting for all its utterly false nature. Confident men, pounding a podium, seemed to utter the truth even when entirely false. The way of history.

"Marsco has had them for so long, too long. We want disks, implants. And soon any former associate who still wears them will be punished! They have had them long enough! It's our turn to run the disk program! As your new chosen leaders, we will make sure no associate ever uses finger disks again! It is only fair! We will have them, solely, exclusively! As *Marsco* in the past, so *us* in the future, your new beloved leaders. We will have this, and we will make sure Marsco never does again!"

One of the troopers behind Kyle and Sarah gave a blunt assessment. "He's asking to simply replace Marsco—the Marsco of old—which handed out disks only to its own adherents, and that was it."

Sarah whispered in Kyle's ear, "Didn't the last Accord essentially end Marsco's monopoly of disk tech, anyway?"

"Affirmative," he answered. "He's asking for revenge first off and then for an impossible solution to a problem that has already ended."

"Is he insane?"

"Yes. Irate *and* totally nuts. And threatening to all around him. His outburst has lasted only a few minutes, but fortunately, his delusional message was heard by no one beyond the Hex."

Sarah couldn't stand viewing the petulant face any longer. She was relieved her brother was in some warehouse and far from here. She knew Kyle would find him soon. The shouting zealot's disgusting and misguided words made her shift her glance.

When she looked at a different control monitor, however, one that gave a wider view of the nearly empty chambers, she screamed.

There, sitting off to the side was her brother, Chase, wearing an Enfield, but to his sister, looking as lost and frightened as the little boy he'd sent down to her at New Grange.

TWENTY-NINE

THE RESURGENCE OF MARSCO

(Seattle, May 2155)

"'As Marsco in the past, so *us* in the future, your new beloved leaders. Our path will become your way. And we will make sure Marsco never has power again!'"

Vice-chair Raymond Jon Chesney watched the clandestine recording of this ranting with delight. The glee on his lips slanted downward, yet his dour happiness did little to lighten the gloom in the Bunker. "Proves we were right. These new so-called federations, they're really old subsidiaries. And they're not at all ready for self-determination and self-rule."

Chair Barston Oakes, always in the habit of agreeing with his subordinate, nodded. "Yes," Chesney went on, "if one goes, all will go. These feds, either they're still complying with Seattle's wishes—*our wishes*—or anarchy prevails. It's as simple as that." The vice-chair gave a self-satisfied, listing smile.

"So," Chesney made his point clear, "you see this serious, emerging threat. The tip of a swelling movement, not an isolated case of a few armed, crazed men?"

"What's Security's assessment?" Oakes asked, more out of politeness to the newly Chesney-appointed Security chief, Jackson Roberts, than real interest.

Chesney, acting the buffer, referred the chair to dozens of screens of internal intel, knowing his chief hated to wade through so much bumf. "Allow me, Mr. Chair. A verbal précis. This main doc is twenty-seven screens, and that's merely the preamble and summary statement. Mostly about the mental instability of these leaders and their lack of followers.

This was Modena's team's work before he was removed. Always too lenient toward PRIMS, that Modena."

The next eighty-nine screens, however, were devoted to thorough analysis. "A bit overdramatic for a report, I believe, stating that aside from a few isolated attacks on grangers, this vicious group under this so-called, self-stylized organizer, this Columbus, is of *no real threat* at all. Wants us to treat him as a homicidal lunatic, not a political genius."

Grunts greeted the vice-chair from his top aides and Jackson Roberts seated near him. As Chesney leaned, so leaned the Bunker.

"Moreover, Modena suggested letting the fed deal with him *locally* because his brutal crimes are all within West Con. Look at this nonsense," the vice-chair stated as he twitched through screens to read a few passing cherry-picked highlights, "'he has no reach beyond Sac City and its environs; thus he remains a local issue.' Once these wonks—our own analysis wonks—even referred to this cancerous cell as 'solitary malcontents armed with outmoded ideas and obsolete Enfields.' Dangerous stuff that, disregarding Seattle's safety. Can't have that. It generates instability."

"So right you are," the chair agreed. "Stability's what Marsco seeks. Everything must be stable to step aside from our role of country-builder in these new feds."

"But, Mr. Chair, look at *this* remark in a sub-para on the last page. Another remark by Modena's incompetent team, before Roberts here officially took over his duties as Security chief. And I quote, "'strongly suggest this group be moved to an amber status since violence is a pronounced tendency.' And later, 'strongly suggest Security watch this group closely for connections to previous Luddite movements.'"

Chesney drew a deep breath of triumph. "See, Mr. Chair. Our previous Security boffins drew some weak, misguided conclusions, whether or not this group indeed does pose a deep and severe threat to the good order of Sac City and its fed, and thus by extension, the whole of the other newly created feds."

"Oh," Mr. Oakes began working up his own assessment, "but this seems pretty vague. This group isn't particularly large, as Security notes. Only twenty, thirty followers, tops." Chesney looked sternly at his boss, the way a parent glares at a recalcitrant child. Oakes saw and retracted. "Of course, this is only *their* assessment. Can't you have your office draw up a new assessment—"

"At hand, Mr. Chair," Chesney reported. A few twitches and he furnished a one-screen, Roberts-generated file that recast everything the restrained Modena had put forth. "But, you'll see, Roberts adjusted that imbalanced attitude. See how detailed his new report is on the violence capability and destabilization factor of this group. His new team's *unbiased* assessment is that if we don't act immediately—preempt this cell—then Sac City will be paralyzed by this takeover and thus a main federation will be reduced to chaos. Once one fed gets bogged down in these internal squabbles, all the rest will follow suit. It's like an untreated cancer."

"Yes, I see," Oakes replied after only skimming the bullet points presented by Chesney. Reading it carefully was not necessary if it came from Chesney's office; any gloss he received would be thorough and to the point. Finally looking up, the chair asked, "And so what should I do?"

"Oh, Mr. Oakes, I *cannot* suggest what to do. I am *only* the vice-chair. You lead, sir, I follow," he insisted.

"Of course," the chair laughed then snorted, pleased. "If I'm in charge, then we'll show how *in charge* I am."

"Rightly proclaimed, Mr. Oakes."

"What do you suggest?"

"Well, since you ask, Mr. Chair, I have taken the opportunity to preposition several Security battalions near Sac City in case you ordered them there."

"Of course, that's what I want to do."

"Yes, sir, I just need you to twitch this authorization; then they are there under your direct command and not my temporary orders."

"Of course, my command."

"And since, I'm the subordinate commander in chief, these domestic squabbles will fall under my purview."

"Of course, a chief can't get caught up in minutia and day-to-day details; they give that over to subordinates!"

"That would be me," Chesney noted.

Grinning his approval, Oakes pointed his right fingertip with its red command-and-control disk onto a reader. "Didn't the Accords limit the use of these?" he asked, wiggling his finger, as though he was not a signatory of the Six Accords.

"Yes, Mr. Chair. But was that wise? Think of it. We *are* devoted to protecting Marsco. And Marsco has brought stability on this planet, to the Moon, the Red Planet, the asteroid belt, partly through its complete and absolute control of finger disks and the computers they operate. Why do we want to eliminate ourselves from running things so successfully as we have?"

"For eighty-five years, right?"

"Of course, right, sir."

"Long time. Shame to see Marsco, our world, just end."

"Well, as long as you hate to see Marsco and our rule of the Earth just end, remember, it's *your* name history will actually see on those Accord documents. Remember, the PRIMS and subsidiary officials forced us to use pen and ink. And they actually insisted that those docs be handwritten on parchment, not just a cyber-form and a point-and-twitch e-doc. One-hundred sixty identical parchments really do exist. That's one-fifty-eight for the new feds worldwide, one copy at the HQ of the UIF in Switzerland, and one here with us in Seattle."

"One-sixty. I remember signing all those. Long day. Writer's cramp."

"Well, just twitch a few supplemental docs now, sir, and you'll erase portions of those Accords that are detrimental to Marsco and its rule. These supplementals," he held up a palm unit with its cyber documents, "only make sure we—you and I—keep a measure of power over what was almost entirely lost by the Accords. Keep a measure of power during our transitional period."

"Well, I suppose I should. How many?"

"I have twenty here, sir."

"*Twenty times one-sixty?* I'll be here until my grand-kids make me a great-grandfather!" he shrieked.

"No, sir, you misunderstand, these need not have any duplicates. They're black and secret, these exempting docs. We only need them as a *record* that we are *off-record* as not agreeing with all the Accords that are *on record* with all the feds."

"Clear as ever, Chesney. Clear as ever." Pressing duties, and a mid-afternoon tee-time at a coastal Marsco resort, made the chair rise. "I've got to clear my desk," he noted to his subordinate as though Chesney were taking note of what work was or was not completed by the chair.

———•———

"Are you ready for the Chavez-Sherman report?" Bobby-Tim Liddle asked Chesney after Mr. Oakes left. Along with Liddle and Rhores, Roberts was now part of Chesney's closest advisory group. The two longstanding aides wore comfortable sport coats. One loosened his tie. Roberts was in a black suit that bordered on a military uniform but without insignia or badge of rank. Even his cap, left outside the office, seemed of a military style.

"Yes, of course. What's our good explorer been up to?" Chesney asked with little real interest.

"Not joining us, I fear," Liddle answered.

"What?"

"He did return to Earth from the Moon, where he's prepping for the Saturn-Neptune run," Liddle went on. "But then he headed straight to Sac City, even though we ordered him here."

"Sac City, that hotbed of insurgency," Rhores noted.

Roberts nodded. "Trouble there from both sides. We have this piss-ass group making a nuisance of themselves at the Hex. And, we have the fed leadership proclaiming total independence as though all Six Accords have already gone into effect."

"Stick to Chavez-Sherman," Chesney brought the meeting back under control.

"He didn't report here at first, ostensibly to see old friends and relatives near Sac City," Liddle stated.

"Was he deserting his post?" Roberts asked.

"Technically, no," Liddle answered curtly.

"Well, if Sac City is nearly in flames as we claim—" Roberts continued.

"Merely *the potentiality* of such," Rhores stated, siding with Liddle.

"Do we still want him?" Liddle asked. "He just might have too much of an Accordist leaning. We have to be careful about that, don't want our senior men actually *wanting* the Accords to succeed."

"I understand," Chesney snickered with his usual sneer. "I may have signed 'em, but I sure hate 'em."

"Exactly, sir," all three listeners responded.

Rhores added, "And, he's close to this Brunel."

But Roberts countered, "But, I think we have the goods on him. Brunel's son, only son, is part of *that* takeover." He motioned to the screen on the left wall. "I can show you the video evidence, if need be."

"You have it all, right?" Chesney asked about the Hex takeover.

"Yes, sir, Security's been able to insert surveillance methods in every fed chamber worldwide," Roberts reported. "And we're using that capability, even if the former head, Modena, didn't want to. Thought it unethical and beneath us. And yes, in Sac City, we have all those fanatics' speeches. Blocked at the source so it isn't going anywhere else at the moment, but we have them. I can make them live with one twitch." He showed his black disk on his left hand. Marsco's long tradition of overriding any security system continued.

"Okay, let's think on that a bit. Advantages and such. But, meanwhile, Chavez-Sherman, he's out. Not in *our* Security but now an officer with West Con, am I reading your report correctly, Roberts? The good space explorer has gone over?"

"Affirmative, sir."

"Okay, then onto this iceman character."

Roberts explained how in Grizotti's case, archivists had to dig deeply into his files to find his Security time under Lieutenant Peter Rivers in Sac City way back at the end of the last century. "But, now, he's a captain in the West Con Med Corps. His hibernation training makes that a natural fit."

Liddle commented, "I forget how old they are, this Grizotti and his wife, and Miller."

"Well, Miller's dead, thanks to those fanatics." Once again, Roberts pointed to the wall unit broadcasting from Sac City. "But, yes, cryo-stasis changed his lifespan."

Chesney smacked the edge of his desk. "I don't give a damn about that sulking iceman who might have been a Security lieutenant at one time."

"Yeah, I guess icemen are pretty useless," Rhores noted.

"Now Miller, there was a catch. But, he's dead." The VP shook his head in frustration. "What about that last one, that pilot?" he finally asked.

The mention of the woman brought Liddle back into the conversation. He'd met her several times while trying to interest her in the MSP. Exotic, striking. Few men were *not* interested in the mention of her.

"Captain Shanghai completed her spleen regrowth. Doctor Johns was to handle her next step, but when his team was ready to start her treatments, she bolted."

Roberts added drily, "And, it should be of no surprise, she's now a captain in the West Con forces."

"Damn," Chesney snorted, with a second slap on the corner of his desk. His plan was in tatters, his notion gone of using the *Sirius II* crew to aid in assuring the world that Marsco supported law and order while it kept the old Continental Powers at bay. And by analogy, these new federations were really just the old C-Powers come back to haunt Earth. "Okay, that prime minister down there—" he didn't even want to mention the location— "he's done enough. He's brought in officers to *his* forces that *we* should have mobilized. And he's setting a pace for the Accords that's energized the whole world."

"They say he's masterful at chess, sir," Liddle offered his point with a self-satisfied grin. Stroking his boss was his mainstay.

"Screw the damn game," Roberts chided. "He's masterful at statecraft."

"Okay," Chesney resumed control, "let's deal with all this. We have an internal group—"

"A throbbing boil on someone's ass," Roberts pointed out.

"Not even," Liddle countered the new Security chief once more. "A pimple."

Chesney silenced the squabbling with a light slap on his desk. "Here's the situation. One, *an irritation* via this Columbus and his dozen armed followers. Additionally, a serious situation with a *single* fed, one that could make it a *leading* fed, one to set the tone worldwide. They're accelerating the Accords; they're taking leadership to develop a viable economy, parliamentary rule, education, the works."

"Educated citizens wanting self-determination—can't have that," Liddle breathed.

"So, two things. *One*, let those irritants have their rant worldwide. Get it on the air, everywhere, 24/7, with no comments from West Con. Let 'em rant like everyone is listening and cheering—"

"But no one *is*."

"No one *will*."

"Immaterial. Marsco has it out there that *this is* happening. And then *two*, we retake Sac City."

"Sir?"

"Get me Elkton. I have just the role for his Black Knights." Roberts explained he had taken it upon himself to have Elkton at the ready. "Well, get him in here so we can send him down to Sac City to 'restore order.'"

Waiting in an anteroom deep in the Bunker, Elkton sat with Harold Crosley, his second in command. They were watching Lightwind's rant as it now went out to the whole Earth-side system.

Both were dressed in a uniform that looked like Roberts' suit but with insignias and badges of rank. Even with years of Security and Internal Security holding sway over the Earth—each with a distinct uniform—their black garb was new to the Marsco world. They wore it proudly with a dash of swagger.

Once inside Chesney's private office, the conversation turned to the young officers' reactions to that telling broadcast.

"To what purpose do you suppose this Lightwood—or Lightwind—is speaking?" Chesney asked.

"I gather," Elkton began with Hap standing silently at his side, "he really, truly thinks *everyone* in the West Con will follow him. He feels that his message is that compelling, that his words resonate with that many discontented former sids and PRIMS—who are all citizens of a new fed now—that he can gather the masses to him and his insane cause."

"Will they?"

Elkton gave a stiff laugh, one of noise with forced mirth. "Most West Con citizens follow such a madman? God, no! The residents of Sac City, of the West Con Fed, they generally have more sense. They're enjoying their independence too much, and they want to chart their own course. If they're devoted to a cause, it's to the Six Accords, I fear."

"But, that's not in our best interest, is it?"

"No, sir, it's not," replied Elkton. Hap remained silent.

"Well then," Chesney drew a tense breath, "we ought to do something to help these idealists, this Lightwind and Columbus."

"Help them, sir? I don't follow." No one in the room followed the convoluted logic of the vice-chair at first.

"If we," Chesney began deliberately, "if we help these malcontents, not only by rebroadcasting their messages worldwide but by implying their growing popularity, that they *are* a rallying point for discontent, then West Con looks weak. And by extension, every other fed looks weak."

"And," Roberts got it, "many in those weak feds will look to Marsco for stability, like a moderating voice, a calming balm on troubled waters."

"Ready to control the situation," Chesney resumed, "as it has for nearly the entire past century."

"Sir, if I may," Elkton began hesitantly, "are we sure that's how this will be received? I listened to only a portion, and the speaker seems to be a spit-ranting maniac, sir, with due respect." Hap nodded, enough to agree but not enough to need to defend his belief if he felt compelled to change his mind later.

"But," Chesney interjected, "we believe that this takeover *will* have negative effects on the whole *subsidiary*—"

"Excuse me, sir," Rhores spoke up, "it is technically a federation now, an independent governmental entity separate from Marsco altogether."

"So right you are," Liddle added, "and thus we must make absolutely sure it stays stable."

"We are doing them—the residents of West Con, be they sids or PRIMS or so-called feds—we'd be doing them all a favor, bringing them all the promise of stability."

"I'm sure West Con Security is well aware of this group," Elkton pointed out. "It has to be; they've got them surrounded. And so, I ask again, who can truly be threatened by the ravings of a single madman?" Elkton looked directly at the vice-chair's deadened eyes. Those staring eyes were intent on *him* following *their* suggestion without question.

"Let me put it like this, sir," the Security officer went on, "Sac City has to deal with this *in its own fashion*, to show the world it can rule peacefully, if nothing else. No more running back to Mama Marsco like an insecure child, or it looks like this new fed *is* still a subsidiary, if you follow my logic explaining their logic, sir."

"Marsco would *never* think of interfering, Mr. Elkton, but we are prudent here in Seattle." Chesney spoke as he booted up a file on a screen and projected it behind them on a wall-size monitor. "Take a look at the map."

The projection showed the disposition of six Marsco Security battalions plus twelve Auxiliary units around Sac City. Those Auxxies were now nearly identical to troopers in weaponry and training. Except without Black Knights. "We aim to keep the whole area secure."

"And as you do, the fed looks weak, sir."

Chesney nodded slightly.

Elkton took a different tact. "And this affects us how, Lieutenant Crosley and myself?"

"You're being immediately sent to Sac City to take charge of one of those Security battalions. Your rank, Elkton, is now major. Yours, captain," he nodded to the taciturn Hap Crosley.

Roberts added, "When the sid's leadership doesn't lead, it's time to look elsewhere."

"Where else but Marsco," Elkton stated, beginning to see the wisdom in the vice-chair's plan.

Neither Elkton nor Hap felt it wise to reiterate to these senior officials they were dealing with a fed that considered itself totally free of Marsco and not a subsidiary any longer. These officers and their battalions would be occupiers, not liberators.

"One last thing," Roberts added. "We've gleaned intel about who is in this West Con's Security Forces, people you might know. Professor Devon Chavez-Sherman, for one. He's some sort of liaison, so he may end up trying to communicate directly with you. Carries a rank of colonel."

"Understood, sir, but not a problem."

"And we understand that Kyle Roncalli is the Fed Security officer in charge of the standoff. He was a classmate of yours at one time, right?"

"Yes, sir, but he was a year or two behind us at the Academy. Again, not a problem."

Hap, who had been standing by in silence, spoke up. "May affect Lieutenant Wang, sir, but I doubt it." None of the senior officials caught the mean-spirited intention of this remark.

Roberts went on. "I've seen Roncalli's file. He's a strong leader. If controlling this standoff is in his hands, then it appears the situation is in competent finger disks, although he seems pretty young to have such responsibilities."

No one seemed to question the age and total lack of experience of the two Young Turks standing before them.

Also, no one in the room felt they should point out the fact that Marsco *had* already relaxed its presence and that this current standoff was best handled by the new, legitimate government of the West Con Federation. Anything or anyone weighing in from Seattle looked like a resurgence of Marsco domination.

Finally, the taciturn Hap added a twist to this dance. "They played into your plans perfectly, didn't they?"

"Who's *they*?" Elkton asked, trying to keep his subordinate from gumming the works.

"Those renegades sitting in the Assembly chambers. They're quite a whipping boy, aren't they?"

Chesney let the vague words pass, but Hap seemed less and less trustworthy. "Those thugs won't get away with this, in the long run. No one seems bothered by them. Our own Intel reports Sac City's running West Con like usual except that the Assembly chambers themselves are out of service at this time."

"Yes," Roberts added, "the Assembly members are meeting in a ballroom of a hotel barely half a klick from the Hex."

"Well, get down to Sac City as ordered," Chesney stated, then added, "it might even be all over by the time you arrive."

Elkton rose and saluted. "If not, I'll make sure things go in the best direction for all involved: Marsco, the new fed, their Security folks." Ambiguity was a wonderful cover, the new major noted.

"There's a lander to Sac City for you at the ready," Roberts informed his junior officers. "She'll be direct and quick."

"Even if push comes to shove," Chesney noted, "I have no doubt you can handle a collection of dissidents armed with light weapons. Ragtag at best." Neither Elkton or Hap understood which group the vice-chair meant, the agitators or the feds.

"Excuse me, sir," Hap added without hesitation, "but ragtag armies, historically, have a way of defeating their enemies."

"Prove history wrong."

THIRTY

STANDOFF

(Sac City, May 2155)

"Another day, another broadcast," Kyle smirked when Lightwind started his nightly harangue, as he had every evening for the past week.

"PRIMS and sids of this subsidiary!" the insurgent brayed from the nearly empty Assembly chambers through an open channel and out to the world. Kyle and his team were unable to block his tirade going live. Marsco's reach was still that strong.

"Don't he know we're *free* citizens of a *new* fed? Ain't he got that yet?" The trooper who disparaged the bellowing speaker had him in the crosshairs of a bot sniper. One twitch and the rebel's head was so much blood and brain matter blasted all over the podium.

"Patience," Kyle reminded everyone, even though his own was wearing thin. Waiting them out was a great strategy to show that the new fed believed in the rule of law but it played hell on his nerves. And his team's. "No one take any provocative actions," the lieutenant cautioned his frayed troopers.

"PRIMS and sids of this subsidiary! We, who now control this allegedly free federation, call out to you and the world. Rally with us to punish Marsco for its actions against our long dead. For 150 years, nay, 200 years, oh, how Marsco made our peoples suffer so! Now is the time to seek a vengeance that's gone unheeded, unheard, unrectified. For if we don't, Marsco gets away with murder! We must slaughter associates to make sure the sons of murderers, the grandsons, the great-grandsons of the so-called innocent descendants of Marsco *today*, make sure they *suffer* as our peoples once did in a past so far gone we can hardly imagine it now. Our long dead call to us to make sure we keep alive their thirst for revenge."

One of Kyle's troopers snickered. "Why don't we just kill off the whole damn human race? Everyone's ancestors popped off somebody else's ancestor at one time or another. It's history."

"And part of human madness," her comrade added.

"Knock of the snide remarks," Kyle tensely ordered. He began to shake. He was tired, under too much pressure. A solid week of this standoff was more than enough.

The lieutenant felt this stalemate to a greater degree than the rest of his team; he was sure of that. And for the past five days, these insane broadcasts had been streaming worldwide.

But why am I out on this limb? On my own? He asked himself those questions dozens of times a day. As much as West Con wanted to *look* competent, internally it seemed frozen, unable to sort out who really should handle this drawn-out standoff. And what would be the best response to Marsco provocations north and east of central Sac City? Military or political? The lieutenant could only imagine the pressure the prime minister and government felt.

And, he gathered, Marsco's interference was increasing. But he knew this federation had to stand strong or essentially give back all its freedoms to Seattle.

"So, here I sit," Kyle muttered to himself while he watched Lightwind implore the masses of displaced peoples on every continent to rally around Columbus. "Come to us, and let men rule again as in the old days. Let our women also heed our call and obey. Be commanded by us. Shoulder your burdens, our women, as we now destroy the dregs of Marsco. Be freed from Marsco and the props of your independence, you women of ours, be ruled by us as we attack Marsco. The more we shed of its blood, the better! How sweet and just it is to slaughter the allegedly innocent descendants of those responsible! Their mere ancestry makes them guilty of past crimes committed by others!"

Two women at monitors tensed. One snickered, "My mom was an associate, my dad a PRIM. Do I kill myself?"

Kyle stood near them to calm the situation. "He's all bluster," the officer whispered. He didn't want their bots taking down anyone just yet.

No one anywhere seemed to pay Lightwind any attention. No new followers flocked to him, even though nightly he claimed their ranks were swelling, a point Seattle kept stressing as well, without any evidence. If anything, his own followers were deserting their cause. The night before, two more slipped off—they weren't the first—leaving only eight men total in the Assembly chambers.

Kyle's private com-link buzzed. *Damn*, he breathed. Sarah was on the line. Kyle had sent her back to New Grange with all the rescued children as soon as she recognized her brother, Chase, as one of the conspirators holed up in the Hex.

"What's going to happen?" she demanded over the link.

"I haven't the foggiest idea," he replied vaguely then added, "but the next move is up to them." He shouldn't have confided that, yet he did.

Torn between brother and the man she loved, Sarah pleaded. "Kyle, don't hurt him, please."

"I'll try not to."

"Only try?"

It was impossible to explain. If Chase, who still carried his Enfield, leveled that weapon on one of Kyle's own, he would have no choice. But how to explain that to Chase's distraught sister?

The woman grew pensive, then sharp. "If you *do* hurt him, I'll, I'll—"

Her sobs broke her voice, but Kyle knew what she was about to threaten. *I shouldn't have answered this damn thing*, he realized, blaming the handheld link.

"I'll never forgive you," the weeping woman choked out. "He's my brother. My only brother. He didn't mean to fall under their spell."

Foolishly, the officer tried laying out the tense scenario he faced. "I'll have to decide, maybe in a split second, what's going down. I can't help it if he draws—"

"I hate you, Kyle! I'll hate you forever!" She clicked her link off with a defiant crack in his ear.

The second call came in from Trent twenty minutes later. "You okay, son?" He, too, was down at New Grange, a quick trip home before returning to the temporary chambers where the fed's Assembly was meeting.

Since his call sounded official, Kyle answered positively.

"Can I have an assessment?"

"Yes, sir, we're holding them confined as we have for a week now."

"Can I ask if you have definite plans to storm the place?"

"I'm really not at liberty to discuss operational and tactical details, Representative Brunel. I'm sure you appreciate that, sir."

"Yes, son, I do. And it's Trent. Always will be." He cleared his throat to give himself the courage to say what he intended to say all along. "Kyle, you do what you have to. Chase put himself in there. You didn't force him. No one did. No one put an Enfield to his head; he walked in there of his own accord. Stormed in there, as a matter of fact. You do what you're called to do, son, got that?"

"Yes, sir. I'll do what I need to do without playing the cowboy."

"Thanks, I assumed that, too."

"No buckaroo tactics from our end, sir."

"And son, half the time Sarah cries for her brother, the other half for you. Don't pay her threats any mind. Just do your duty."

"Yes, sir. If she'll listen, give her my love."

As deeply as he felt for Sarah, as soon as Trent signed off, Kyle mentally exploded. *Bitch! Keep your hands off this detail. You think I love this, standing here ready to blast your brother and half a dozen other hapless loonies?* He then let fly against his own fed. *Why no help? I'm a damned lewy, a lieutenant at the bottom of the heap. Why am I still in charge here?*

"Shit!" he swore. Calling his senior warrant, he ordered, "Try contacting Colonel Chavez-Sherman again."

———— • ————

The next night, not long after Lightwind's two-hour berating tirade ended, Lieutenant Roncalli and a warrant left the Hexagon Command Center, where they seemed to live night and day. Kyle was exhausted from the continuing strain and ready to eat anything besides an MRE. He had rotated his troopers out of the Hex on a regular basis to give them a break, a good meal, a chance to clean up some. This was his first time outside since the standoff began.

Over the past few days, West Con had moved a battalion into the center of Sac City. The unit began using the capitol grounds and park for a mobile field hospital and com-center. They cleared a large section for landing HFCs. Kyle was surprised by all the activity around the Hex. Fresh troops bivouacked near him were encouraging even if none of the armed troopers were under Kyle's command.

Kyle and his warrant walked through the activity then directly toward a small restaurant just beyond Capitol Park on a thrumming thoroughfare north of the Hex. Here peace was evident, even as troopers dug in only a few blocks away.

They soon reached a Szechwan place that had survived Divestiture, the C-Wars, and Marsco's iron fist holding down Sac City. The restaurant stretched from curbside into a vast interior of small rooms, booths, and dim corners. Customers came and went, a sure sign this federation, this city, was thriving once more. Freedom brought people out, confident of their future.

"Bet plenty of surreptitious nightlong dinners were held here once, arranging government affairs over the decades," Kyle surmised.

"Yes, sir, that's probably the case," the warrant replied, as pleased as Kyle to be outside and removed from the direct strain of the standoff and the hum of the new encampment.

"And you know you are to eat alone," he reminded the warrant. "I just want you as muscle but stay cool. Watch my back." Devon had arranged this meeting here, but with all the provocations outside city center from Security—*Marsco* Security—Kyle wasn't exactly sure they'd converse without interference. "I am concerned about other rabbits showing up and poking their heads in my dugout."

"Roger, sir. I'll eat, have a beer."

"Hands off the tarts, too. I don't need you with HH GAS any time soon."

"My hands are like altar boys' when it comes to such babes, sir."

Kyle didn't believe him on that score but knew the warrant would keep an eye open while on duty.

The slender, quick-thinking head waiter was expecting Kyle. Artfully, he sat the warrant at a table where the armed trooper had a view of the front door and then walked the lieutenant down a long, dimly lit aisle that threaded between several booths. Off-duty officers were at it with whomever they found for the night. Kyle paid no attention. Coupling of personnel while on their downtime was their own business. Mia crossed his mind first, then Sarah. *Damn*, he fumed, *damn Marsco and Columbus and his ilk and all this shit.*

"No one comes through our kitchen unless we know," the waiter stated before motioning toward the swinging half-doors down the hall.

If Kyle didn't trust the waiter completely, he'd have been more careful entering the private room. Even so, he pushed the door slowly so as not to surprise anyone inside. Whoever waited was armed, as he was, and it wasn't wise startling anyone packing.

"Kyle!" Shanghai yelped. The pilot was on her feet and embracing the lieutenant as a brother. "What gives?" she asked, not wasting a moment. While in her embrace, Kyle felt a strong slap on his shoulder. Zot was there as well. Both fellow officers wore khaki uniforms with different insignias. Zot's was for the medical corps. Shanghai wore wings.

Kyle nodded to Mei-Ling, who appeared fully healthy, her strength as obvious as her returning looks. He stood with her at arm's length; the similarity between her and Mia Wang was all the more striking now that the pilot had fully recuperated.

Mia moved through his memory like a stormy cloud, and then Sarah came on again but in a sunnier aspect. *Two different women, two different lifetimes ago*, he groused to himself as he sat down.

Mei-Ling discreetly made sure two foggers were operational. "Devon thought it would be less conspicuous if we came and he didn't."

"I understand. Cloak-and-dagger." Kyle paused. "Damn him, *again!*"

"Affirmative. I'm running Zot down to see Tessa once we've eaten, so that his trip there masks this sortie here."

"More cloak-and-dagger," the iceman added.

"Regardless, eating sounds fine," Kyle stated, "I'm starved."

"I ordered," the iceman replied. It never dawned on Kyle that Devon wanted Zot to use his medical expertise to evaluate how the lieutenant was holding up under the strain.

A knock brought the waiter with several platters of steaming food. Also, three bottles of cold beer. "Bless you," Kyle grinned, "but I'm on duty."

"So, it won't the first time you've broken a regulation," Mei-Ling laughed, tempting him with a frosty bottle.

"Okay, what gives?" Kyle asked after a long swallow.

"As you know," Mei-Ling began, "Devon acts as a liaison for the civilians in charge and us." She motioned to their three uniforms. "He wanted an evaluation of the standoff, without the formality of a direct meeting."

That was easy to supply. A week and a day and counting. No end in sight. Marsco allowing the broadcasts out no matter how hard West Con tried blocking them.

"No surprise there, right?" Zot reminded them. "Marsco's a master at snooping." He pointed to their foggers, hoping they were up to the task of blocking any prying now.

"No one's joined them," Kyle added. "And a few more have slipped off. We have just eight cornered now. Chase, Columbus, Lightwind and five others."

Talking and eating turned into a situation report about the fed generally. Mei-Ling had been acting as Devon's—and periodically the PM's—pilot, so she was privy to what they knew. "Does appear that Marsco intends to move in and recontrol Sac City," she explained. "Seattle may use this standoff as an example of how the Accords are failing worldwide."

"That's a stretch," Kyle began, "but that means this standoff—"

Zot cut him off, "—yes, gives Marsco a pretext for recontroling this whole fed. A bogus cover. Reneging on the Accords here and probably around the globe next."

"Damn," Kyle swore. "And I thought eight skinnies were a problem." No wonder, he realized, he was left on his own. The meager forces of West Con were needed elsewhere.

Mei-Ling continued. "Hard to say exactly what Marsco intends, but that's Devon's estimate. Security, *West Con Security*, is keeping Marsco away from your locale, but that's hardly reassuring. Six battalions of troopers practically inside Sac City right now. No hot and live confrontations yet but tense. More terrifying than your standoff. West Con is trying to end this standoff peacefully."

Zot added with a cynical laugh, "Seattle's pissing off the PM and his cabinet, to say the least. That many troopers wield plenty of power."

"And several additional Auxxie battalions, armed with Enfields, are parked outside the city as well."

"Dozens of Brads, all heavily armed. None of those old-fashioned crowd-control non-leths as before. Marsco isn't planning a Sunday picnic if it moves on the city."

Kyle nodded as it became clearer to him. "If Seattle keeps broadcasting Lightwind worldwide, then it can claim that retaking Sac City is necessary to keep the peace."

"Affirmative," Zot added. "That's the assessment from HQ. Seattle is drumming this up as smoke and mirrors to its real intensions, totally reneging on the Accords."

"Explains why I—*damn*, I'm *only* a lieutenant—why I'm given so much authority and no, *none*, no goddamn backup."

Shanghai suggested that keeping these renegades trapped with so small a unit shows the world how insignificant they are. "You look more like police than troopers."

Kyle wasn't sure that's what his Enfield and body armor conveyed.

"And remember, Marsco wants you to fail," Zot concluded, his off-handed manner not giving offense. Being so direct was refreshing to Kyle.

"What help do you need?" Mei-Ling asked as the waiter arrived with another round of beers.

"I guess I don't need any help with the standoff. My troopers are still sharp. My skinnies are down to eight players. We've kept the ventilation on, the power, but even so they're getting restless. I let them get to the jakes. I've even ordered them cleaned daily. I send them food and water. I'd rather keep them comfortable than so angry they start blasting. The Hex is decorated so nicely." He snorted, "if nothing else, I want to preserve the décor."

His listeners laughed but understood. It was a new symbol for self-determination. No one wanted it despoiled by vandals or exploding Enfield shells.

"What," the fed lieutenant went on, "what I need to know most is if Marsco acts—will *all* the battalions come? Are we talking about a real incursion or just a few renegade officers loyal to Chesney who're willing to disregard the Accords?"

"Hard to say," the pilot explained. "Devon's been locking down battalions, committing them to fed control all over the world, and meeting with officers he taught back at the Academy from other units. He's trying to establish who's down with the Accords—truly—and who's rogue. Chesney's rogue. He's having some success convincing officers here and there to stand down if ordered by dubious means to step in. Modena is nowhere to be found. Feared dead. This new draconian head, Jackson Roberts, seems to be issuing orders like he's running Security—Marsco Security—of old. Many battalions are with him, while others are openly questioning their deployment in these newly independent feds."

"How many?" Kyle asked. "Is he finding some who will act against us?"

"Devon said you'd understand. 'Plenty of Young Turks are in key positions,' that's how he said to explain it."

"Yes, I understand. They're the ones offered sustainability."

Captain Shanghai paused a moment then added, "Sustainability's a pretty strong temptation: ceaseless, changeless health, life."

"Do these names mean anything?" Zot had them memorized so they weren't in a palm unit or in a cyber doc somewhere. "R. Roland Elkton? He seems to be the *de facto* leader."

"Is Cassy or Catherine Tomas-Higgens with?"

"Affirmative."

"Makes sense."

"Another is Mia Wang."

"Makes sense as well," Kyle acknowledged coolly and professionally. "She's taken the sustainability treatments; she's what's called 'an Immortal' now. We can't just marginalize her," he went on, trying to convince himself, "we can't disregard her as a serious threat." He added, "I feel for her. She's a good kid, serious student, a great shuttle service career ahead of her then sucked into this mess." Kyle pointed to Shanghai's wings. Both his listeners could hear and see Kyle's regret as he explained.

Brushing that aside, he asked, "Who else?"

The rest of the officers were ones Kyle would suspect to be on Zot's list: Altina Clarke, Cole Darby, Harold Crosley, Arthur Wicks.

"Hap Crosley may be a doubter," his former classmate responded, "but Wicks has the nickname 'Cutter.' That has to tell you something."

As their meeting broke up, Zot asked, "Any message for Sarah?"

Dozens of emotions coursed through Kyle's mind, not the least of which was a confused set of feelings for Mia, whom he had not thought about for weeks. What love he had felt for her, her subsequent betrayal, his manipulation of her—he wished he was able to separate those emotions from what he might have to do later. His attachment to her went all the way back their early years at the Academy, naive as it was. *Was I really ever there? How long now since I left? And Sarah. What does this all mean? My body armor, this Enfield, her brother in my crosshairs?*

In the end, Kyle replied softly, "Tell Sarah I said, 'Chase remains safe.' Say it just like that. I think she'll understand. I hope she does." He paused. "Oh, tell her thanks for taking care of our children."

The iceman and pilot exchanged glances. Zot looked at the man in the throes of emotional pain and felt for him. "Got it. I'll fill her in."

After handshakes, wishes of good luck, and a kiss on the cheek from Mei-Ling, the pair retreated out the kitchen with the waiter's help. Kyle met his warrant at the bar.

"Buy you a beer, sir?" the warrant asked, not wishing to leave.

"No time. We need to get back."

"Hard to believe what's going down, or *not* going down, just a few blocks away." Kyle's warrant commented as they walked from the restaurant to the Hex and its standoff. In this lively district, shop lights blazed, crowds of friends and intimate couples—some in uniform, most in civvies—entered clubs and diners. This fed and its capital city wanted to believe that freedom was here, that Marsco was disappearing rapidly. Peacefully. Lawfully.

Above, HFCs came and went smoothly. A Fed Security hovercraft was amid the stream in the Herriff-Grid, but the patrol craft didn't need to arm its weaponry. Seattle wasn't utilizing any HFCs like Kyle assumed it would. The skies remained West Con's.

The crowd smiled at Kyle and his warrant when the passersby saw the pair, even if they looked like they were on patrol. But patrol or not, they were clearly federation Security, part of their very own local forces. The citizens gladly moved aside, a gesture once made in fear if the pair had been Marsco Security or its grim Auxiliary members brought in from another continent like occupiers from a distant, conquering empire.

We've got to keep this place independent of Marsco, the officer was adamant.

The bright lights along the streets, the celebrating people: all these made it difficult for the officer to imagine the continuing tension at the Hex. It wasn't that these people didn't care—Kyle was sure that they *did*—but they viewed the promise of the Fourth Accord, the Fifth, the Six in such a positive light. And they agreed with the PM about the acceleration of the remaining Accords. None of these citizens believed they needed to be tethered to Marsco any longer. Also, none saw the sinister past that Lightwind harkened to. None wanted to put on that malcontent's hair shirt of guilt and rage and vengeance. They saw possibility in a future with their own hands helping to fashion it.

None of us, the crowd seemed to say, *none listen to that madman with any openness to his slogans and hatred. We're committed to our futures, not his loathing and thirst for blind revenge. Let the dead bury the dead. By seeking revenge for those now long gone, you're only restarting the senseless blood-letting that we sensible humans deplore.*

"They're looking ahead, not behind," Kyle commented.

"Pardon, sir?"

Kyle's com-link buzzed. The warrant left in charge at the Hex gave a routine report, assuring the absent lieutenant all was quiet.

"C'mon, pick a club," Kyle urged his companion, "I'll buy you that beer."

Two more tense nights passed and more tirades streamed out. The Assembly chambers were beginning to show signs of abandonment as the eight remaining insurgents slept wherever they wanted, clutter and trash tossed everywhere.

If I had clear orders, this would be over in an instant, Kyle had thought several times. *Begin at 0300 hours; done by 0310, no question.* He was that sure; his troopers were that well trained.

But yet, the wait continued. He was still alone in the Hex.

On the third afternoon since meeting with Mei-Ling and Zot, Kyle received a call from the iceman on the command link. "Sarah needs to speak with you. She sent word via Tessa to me."

"That's straightforward."

"She's afraid if she called you directly, you'd cut her off again."

Kyle shrugged. *Why try to explain that it was exactly the opposite last time?* "I'll give her a call when I can."

When he reached her hours later, it was midnight. With no comment to him, she blurted out, "Nate Richardson's been murdered! And two of his sisters. The pair younger than Patrice and Hy." Sarah was trying to deliver the message without tears, but her voice cracked. She knew all the dead; she'd grown up with them. They were older teens, sixteen and seventeen, just beginning their lives. "All happened at the Richardson place," Sarah explained.

"But why?"

"We tried talking to Dot. She's in hysterics. During the rampage, she was holding their infant son. That saved her, I think. One of the youngest survivors, a girl, only seven, ran down frantically to look for Hy here. When they went back, Hy discovered the dead. Found Dot alive but incoherent."

From Sarah's cryptic explanation, Kyle pieced together the story. Old Man Richardson was determined to join this takeover. While Columbus lived on his spread, the granger had come to believe even more deeply in his old ways. He saw a connection with his own cherished, stern convictions and this messiah. Richardson ordered Nate to come with him. He was also bringing his now-dead daughters.

"When Nate and the girls refused, so Dot sobbed while telling Hy, he just starting shooting."

"He who?"

"Lionel, Lionel Richardson."

From the very first night, Chase had chosen this particular representative's desk to settle in at. It had a firm high-back chair, a monitor, supplies of pens and paper as though the Assembly were meeting in 1955 and not 2155. It also had a brass plate with the name Representative Trent Brunel printed in classic lettering, bold and strong like the man himself.

Chase took comfort sitting here, sleeping in the black leather chair with his legs propped up on his father's large desk.

It was small comfort, since even from that first night, the smell of his clothes was overpowering. The tunnel they'd used getting in had been long and dank. He was filthy from their various camps anyway. Nowhere he'd stayed with Columbus was as clean and well-kept as the largest guesthouse at New Grange.

It crossed his mind this abject comparison between the representatives who had once sat in this chamber and this ragged group who now occupied it. Certainly, the first Assembly was appointed and provisional, as the new federation drew itself together. The reps, however, came from all over the fed, men and women, old and young, educated and self-taught like Trent. Former associates, those who had been in space, some born here, others on the Moon, even one from Mars, a good number PRIM-born. It didn't matter. They were here to bring forth a government that would answer to all the members of this fed, answer in a way that actually took the will of those governed into account.

Chase looked at himself, grubby and wearing a torn shirt and boots still caked with the scum and slime of the passageways. *Should we govern? Those of us from the ooze and muck?*

He looked at Columbus, whom he now saw as a hollow, posing charlatan, pretending to be spiritual but really mouthing age-old adages that boiled down to "those in control must simply exert power to stay there." *Power, dominance*—and if men started by dominating women, that seemed to satisfy Columbus and Lightwind. *I would have never hit my Hyacinth but for them. What was I thinking? I never saw Trent raise a hand against Mom, Sarah, or even Roxanne. Never to me.*

"How could I be so blind?" he murmured, not caring if any of the others heard him.

He looked across the aisle at Columbus sitting a few rows back. His large belly showed through his stained shirt. *If he knows one true event in history, I'll shit. He's just another blustering, shallow, self-satisfied bastard. Out to get what he can by whatever means he can.*

He held his head in his hands. His weeping solved nothing; he'd made such a mess of so many lives he couldn't fix. *Why did I let them take Hy without fighting to protect her? Fighting for her? I should have died trying to protect her. I'd be better dead now anyway.*

After staring at the debris-strewn floor, he jerked his head up and wiped away his tears. An image of New Grange filled his mind: peaceful and calm, cool in the morning before the summer heat, bountiful under the sure guidance of Trent. His mom and Roxanne in the kitchen. Sarah and Kyle together, happy. Hy down the road, coming to the grange's great room for supper.

I should walk out of these chambers right now and into the arms of Security. Several others have since our takeover. Why not me, too?

Chase shook his head remembering the last gentle couple that Columbus forced to host them, that helpless pair Lightwind had butchered. And the two children Columbus had his attendants hang. These charlatans had enjoyed that.

Wish it was that easy. To just walk away.

While he sat in his father's chair, rocking slowly, almost like a child in a grownup's seat that was slightly too big, a light blinked next to the com-link. Chase hadn't realized all the systems were still live.

At first, he ignored the blinking light, but when the unit beeped softly, he reached for the link.

"Chase? This is Sarah. Listen to me, please." His sister had asked their father to make this call possible. She was still at New Grange, but she had Chase on the line.

"Yes," he answered softly, "I will."

"Are you okay?"

"Fine, well, as good as can be expected, given." He gulped and sniffed. "Truthfully, I need a shower."

"I won't say much," Sarah tried to explain. "Just this. Come home. Get up. Walk out of the chambers. Don't stay there."

Kyle had approved the call, although Sarah didn't know that. One of his troopers was recording the conversation. She also had a finger disk as the ready to twitch off the link should either begin to say anything best left unsaid. The lieutenant listened and prayed that Chase would walk down the aisle toward the rear of the Assembly and simply disappear. Others had, why not him?

Columbus and Lightwind stood in the shadows and overheard Chase's part of the conversation. Nothing being said pleased them.

"And, Chase, are you there? Listen, get out. We want you home. Mom. Roxanne." When the granger didn't respond, Sarah asked, "Are you still there?"

"Yes."

Columbus then snatched the link from his follower and demanded, "Who is this? What are your plans? *You* come in here and I'll kill *him*, you hear me? Just try it, and *I'll kill him!*"

Kyle gave the cut-throat sign to his sparks and the link went dead. "Damn, I hope she didn't hear his threats!" Taking out his own link, he ordered the nearest warrant to place two calls, one to Devon and other to their own Security HQ.

"Sarah, did you hear that madman? Don't worry, that's all I can say." His men watched his expression change. "I can't say that and certainly won't say. I'll do whatever I can, but—" She cut him off before he could finish.

Putting the unit away, he swore, "Damn. Can't I just run this my way?"

Devon was on line one. "Look, sir, I've got to go in. They're threatening Chase." He listened and explained, "Tonight. I'm going in. I have no other choice."

When fed HQ came on line two, Kyle simply reported, "All's set. We're taking them down at 0115, in about an hour."

Cutting the link, he ordered his sparks, "Don't answer any outside lines." He knew the routine: easier to ask forgiveness than permission.

To a warrant near at hand he snapped, "Get your people ready. We're taking them down."

The forceful command, "Halt," was answered with Enfield fire.

In the north corridor of the Hex, down from the command center and farther still from the main doors to the Assembly, Enfield fire erupted. Two distinct weapons. One firing, one answering.

"Who's shooting without my orders?" Kyle thundered.

He ran with his weapon at the ready until he reached a checkpoint where a dead trooper lay sprawled over a temporary barricade thrown up to keep anyone from approaching the danger of the chambers unknowingly. No one had expected trouble here at this side door.

A second wounded trooper was seated on the floor, tended to by a medic. His head was bleeding where he'd taken a blow down across his face.

"Was on us before we knew it," he muttered to his lieutenant. "He hit me with a broken table leg—he's a big man—then just started firing." That three-burst had cut down the other trooper. "I returned fire, but he was already entering the chambers by the time I did." The door, designed to withstand Enfield blasts, showed where the shells had hit.

Back in the command center, Kyle got the clarification he sought.

"New skinny burst in," an operator reported from her monitor. "Him, that tall one."

"Face recognition?"

"Negatory. Nothing in the system. Unknown bogie."

But even as he was asking for a tech answer to identify this intruder, Kyle knew the name of the wild-eyed man standing next to Columbus and holding an ancient Enfield. Lionel Richardson.

"Damn!" Kyle swore and then ordered, "Stay alert, everyone. But wait my further orders. He changes everything."

The young officer with so much resting on his decisions needed a moment to size up this deadly new predicament.

THIRTY-ONE

COLUMBUS'S ASSEMBLY

(Sac City, May 2155)

"**L**adies and Gentlemen of this Assembly," Trent Brunel spoke in a controlled but forceful tone, "if we do not assert our independence *now*, we may as well go home in abject shame."

Several listeners in the Assembly scoffed. Getting home *once* before midnight during this takeover crisis appealed to them. Brunel taking the floor, however, meant another speech, even though some reluctant members of this chamber still believed in letting the Accords and this standoff move along at their own pace.

Yet tonight, Brunel's words woke up long-dormant feelings. More of his fellow representatives leaned forward to listen and take note. "Lazy-boy patriots will shrink from making hard decisions about the fate of this federation. But, look at this continent's history. True men and women of vision stood fast, first in revolution, then in civil war, and eventually in international wars. Our greatest forbearers made the hardest decisions."

Nods and agreement came from the Assembly and the scattered listeners at the edge of the temporary Assembly hall. Men and women. Young and old. Some of Marsco background. Some of sid and PRIM ancestry. Now, all members of this free federation.

"When did that mettle weaken and disappear?" Brunel went on. "When did too many of our self-satisfied ancestors decide to stop caring for *all* our citizens? Decide to stop funding schools, hospitals, roads, science, and our own citizens in need? They gave their narrow-mindedness fancy titles. *Divestiture* or *Disenfranchisement*, fuzzy words used to disguise the abandonment of their responsibility to their own society and its future.

Weren't those fancy terms just guises for simply *not* standing firm, *not* holding fast? Law, debate, precedent, and the will of the people: some of our ancestors—free but misguided ancestors—sacrificed those virtues by cutting up a once-glorious nation into factions and pieces, 'You go there; we'll stay here!'"

A round of applause. Brunel's audience was stirring, listening, moved by his words.

"But by cutting themselves apart, those cowards allowed the worst of rulers to rise among the people who were now powerless to stop this dismemberment. They allowed rulers who promised renewed greatness to take over, leaders who actually lined their own pockets or their family's pockets or their friends' pockets. The average citizen suffered and was shunted off to a life without a future. Things fell apart. First came gridlock and anarchy and then the Continental Powers promising that diminishing and cutting up that once-great nation all the more would make all the pieces even better off. Then later still, Marsco came promising to restore order. And Seattle promised. And promised. Today, we live with all the signs of the carnage brought on by allowing two such bodies—the Continental Powers and Marsco—to rule us, the people of this continent, the people of the world, *without our consent.*"

Reluctantly, the Madame Speaker of the Assembly let another member of the body demand of the representative from rural Sac City, "And how does all this relate to our matter at hand?"

Brunel had anticipated this delaying tactic. "We have waited ten days while our real Assembly chambers remained occupied. We have watched Marsco amass its battalions, without our consent, around this city, waiting to reoccupy us. Seattle HQ has acted on the pretext that we *cannot* or we *will not* put our own house in order. The whole world watches and asks, are we a true nation able to run ourselves? Or, do we return to the false luxury of inactivity, of not standing firm to the beliefs we say we hold dear?"

"Easy words to say," another naysayer baited Brunel, "And they translate into what?"

"We have declared our sovereignty already. Now we must be sovereign. Totally. And insist that Marsco turn *all* its forces over to our control or remove them from inside our borders. This capital city must remain free from Marsco intervention."

A large number of other reps cheered Brunel on.

"We have earnestly and repeatedly tried to avoid the clash and consequential suffering a war with Marsco brings. We have tried by using the very Accords Marsco signed. Throughout their protracted negotiations, our representatives let it be known to Seattle that we want to govern ourselves—reasonably, lawfully, peacefully. Marsco agreed, and thus fourteen years ago the Six Accords were signed. Once signed, these agreements set up 158 free and independent federations worldwide. Ten years ago, this federation—along with 157 others—came into being: reasonably, lawfully, peacefully. It was ten years ago in 2145, that the First Accord took effect and with it the UIF was born; the Union of Independent Federations, a body that allows these new feds to discuss their differences reasonably, lawfully, peacefully."

"Is this a debate or a civics lesson?"

Brunel's supporters quieted the solitary heckler.

"If these Accords mean anything," the granger went on, "they mean Marsco must continue to comply with the documents it signed. It has no right, using a thin pretense as a guise, to base dozens of battalions near this city. It has no right to wait in the wings for the chance to reoccupy our capital."

"A weakness Marsco fosters," one of Brunel's many supporters stated.

Seeing that his audience was electrified, another one of the granger's chief supporters rose. "Representative Brunel, may I ask for a plan here? What's to be done?"

"What? No man or woman with a child at their side says, 'Let trouble avoid me that my children may suffer it!'"

"No, never!" several shouted in agreement.

"The strong leader," Trent continued, "the independent citizen, merchant, parent, grandparent, says, 'If trouble is to ravage my lands, let it be in *my* day, that my children may have peace!'"

Low murmurs swept the chambers but ones of consensus.

"Then, Madame Speaker, I propose we authorize our Security forces, *ours*, not Marsco's, step in and cleanse *our*, not Marsco's, our Assembly chambers. They are not this Columbus's Assembly. They are ours. We must assert that fact. We must show we have a legal right to rule ourselves by law and consent."

"Motion?"

The grindings of the Assembly sped up as a motion was restated, seconded, passed unanimously by voice vote. The small naysayer gaggle didn't raise their few frail voices against the obvious sentiment of self-determination. Delay they may want, but they wanted freedom more, as much as any Brunel follower.

"I will be seated now," the exhausted granger declared at last, "my fellow citizens, you make me proud to be a member of this august Assembly."

"May we live to see a peaceful resolution to this crisis," the Speaker replied.

"Except for a few madmen," the granger added. "Why not? Does Marsco want war? All of Marsco? I think not. I cannot believe for a moment that *all* of Seattle is willing to risk standing up to 158 determined federations."

"But perhaps there are a few madmen left in Seattle with finger disks at the ready?" The Speaker shrugged.

One final question came from the Assembly. "Madame Speaker, point of clarification before we adjourn."

"Certainly, Mr. Kenney."

"A question for Mr. Brunel." The fatigued granger rose to field the question. "Is it true your son is presently part of the group occupying our Assembly?"

"Sadly, it is true, our only son."

"And you spoke tonight so eloquently about restoring order. Does that not put your son in danger?"

"'What we obtain cheaply, we esteem too lightly,'" he answered with a sad hitch to his voice. "If he were in our Security forces, his life would be at risk. Would I hesitate from putting him in danger then? No. In fact, the officer in charge at the Hex may become my son-in-law. I do not hesitate from asking him to risk his life and possibly end the life of my own son. Would that our ideals made for easy and simple choices."

<hr />

Frantic activity was thrumming around Kyle as he attended to last-minute details. Enough flash grenades, a med team at the ready, every trooper wearing a blast vest, every Enfield charged. Everyone with ear protectors. For the second time in two days, he readied his troopers to storm the chambers.

"Number?"

"Still at eight. One in, one out. An old-timer slipped out earlier. Bagged him in the south corridor."

"P-S weaponry ready?" Kyle demanded.

"Affirmative. Charged and ready." This pulse-sound weapon was a throwback to the days of non-lethal crowd-control systems. The high-decibel tone immobilizes anyone without ear protection.

"All bots in place?" the lieutenant asked, continuing his preparations.

"We've got two cams on each skinny. And one assassin bot."

Kyle cautioned his ops team, "Those killer bots are last resort only, remember. Backup only. No twitch-slips and then someone getting plastered for nothing. The PM wants a trial for these criminals, not a takedown."

His private com-link vibrated. In the frenetic prep for this mission, he had forgotten he was still carrying it. *Best leave it behind*, he noted, wanting to just toss it on a desk when he saw the call was from a warrant who stood by with the Assembly in case they changed Kyle's order.

"He's on his way," a young woman's voice explained.

"What? Can you be clearer?"

"Mr. Brunel is coming down your way," Kyle's aide reported.

"Coming here?"

"Affirm that, sir," the WO acknowledged before Kyle clicked her off.

"Damn! Now what?" The officer had another com-link thrust at him, a command line. "Roncalli here."

Devon came on. "We're not sure who else *is* or *isn't* on this line."

"Roger, sir."

"I'm pretty sure we've locked down most unwanted campers around the city but not all. Your friends, Elkton, Hap, Cutter. They're all aiming at you."

"Will it hit the fan?"

"Has hit. Skirmishes east of you where you and Zot and Patrice have roamed." Devon drew a breath. "Kyle, sorry to say, I expect a large and coordinated situation from there. Seattle's just looking for an excuse. Worse yet, no confirmation on the movement of our drifting friends above the Moon awhile back. Seattle may hit us *after* it rocks us."

"Like in the C-Wars?"

"Affirmative. I spoke to Miller about that as we were coming in from Mars. He was none too pleased to hear that I had actually seen dozens of 'accessory units' as harmless as cows."

Kyle sighed. *Guess that would be chilling. Miller'd lived on Mars during the initial rain of these weapons, but he'd seen their aftermath firsthand.* "Thanks for that assessment."

"And Kyle. I hope no man dies tonight." That vague *no man* really meant *one man*, Chase Brunel. Both Devon and Kyle knew it.

"Best to end it sooner rather than later," the colonel added philosophically. "Sometimes forcing the issue precipitates an ending to a larger crisis." Over the com-link, Devon could hear the clatter of troopers preparing. Like Marsco of old, this new federation was playing for keeps. A smattering of madmen weren't going to take the rule of law from them.

"Well, let's hope we don't end up with shards of asteroids in our lap."

As soon as Devon ended his call, two orders reached his command center. From Seattle, the colonel received orders to reoccupy a quadrant of Sac City as though the fed officer still answered to *that* HQ and hadn't left Marsco to answer to West Con at all. The units Seattle presumed he commanded were in the southern neighborhoods, near an old airport turned into a lander and HFC field. With that base, troopers would seal off the southern part of the city from any interference. Other battalions were heading west from the university campus toward the Hex. Yet a third group was coming down from the main lander field north of City Center.

South, East, North—Security's circling the city, Devon realized.

But, the colonel knew, these orders were Bunker orders from delusional men, just as insane as those occupiers of the Hex. Seattle was shouting orders and moving units that didn't exist anywhere except on some Marsco HQ map. Only a few units appeared to be answering Seattle's call. Those units, controlled by officers who had gone through sustainability, stood firm with Chesney. These officers commanded scores of robotic knights. All other units seemed to be standing down or had openly joined West Con. For the most part, Seattle was sending bogus orders to phantom units. But, the remnants of its power were still lethal, especially if backed by V-weapons.

A second command came from the West Con Assembly to any and all Marsco Security units within its borders. "Cease and desist any attempts to move into Sac City proper. Consider yourself under orders from this federation only. Do not take any actions that will be deemed by this body or its armed services to be aggressive or provocative."

Two orders. Devon hoped most units would follow that second one, the one that would keep most fighting from ever beginning. But would those knights' battalions obey?

Devon called to a warrant officer. "Find Captains Grizotti and Shanghai."

———

As warned, Kyle found Trent at his side in the frenzy of the control room. Unarmed. Without a blast vest or helmet, demanding to enter the Assembly to persuade Columbus to surrender. More than likely, to reason with his son one more time.

The granger noticed the strain visible on the young officer. The tension of this standoff lined his face. But he was poised. Ready.

"Sir, I have no authorization to let you begin negotiations in there."

"I'm going in, Kyle. Let me in. I have to speak with my son and that senseless conman."

———

Late into the night, Columbus and Lightwind discussed their obvious dead-end situation. The chambers were calm while the storm of preparation surrounded them. "We had it once, the total control of this former subsidiary."

"Yes, but it's been wrested away from you," Lightwind offered.

"Yes, usurped! But really, so few actually *wanted* us," Columbus lamented bitterly. "I blame the people who were not strong enough for the old ways I offered them. A weak people don't deserve a strong leader."

It was easier, Lightwind realized, when they came at night, threatened unprepared PRIMS a few at a time, taking down those bold enough to oppose them, offing the innocent and unsuspecting.

"Yes, the light of day and facing large groups to argue and discuss and disagree, those ways are not the old ways. Better as we did it—threatening, burning, killing those who spoke up against us." The chief acolyte paused. "So, they will come soon?" He motioned to the main door where they expected an attack.

"I fear so, but do not fear the end," Columbus answered. "Are you ready, my old friend?" Both brought out their Enfield sidearms. "That mongrel son of a granger should be removed from our sight first."

"As you wish," Lightwind replied, delighted for the opportunity. "We should have done this sooner." The more blood they drew, the acolyte reasoned, the better the people loved them. Or at least feared them, obeyed them. True, devoted disciples pine for compelling leaders who promise to avenge their wrongs, old and new, real or imagined.

Columbus reached out and touched his acolyte's hand before he began another two-hour harangue on the all the wrongs ever perpetrated against their peoples, wrongs he devoted his life to avenge.

Silently, Lightwind rose, his charged Enfield in hand.

Chase sat a few paces away, his head in his hands, his back to the pair of mystic guides. It was a pose he'd taken for a few days on end. "Perfect shot," Lightwind whispered, seeing the broad shoulders and crown of the unsuspecting man clearly. Stealthily and from behind, it was an effective way to silence a reluctant follower.

The main doors of the chambers thundered open without warning, stopping Lightwind abruptly. The acolyte, close behind Chase, watched as Trent Brunel marched toward him down the center aisle. As though this unarmed man were dangerous, Lightwind raised his Enfield at this intruder. The granger stopped halfway to the podium, only five meters from Chase, who sat slightly to his right.

Not knowing how else to protect him, Kyle followed. His troopers all remained outside, waiting clear orders, anxious.

All eyes focused on the granger—those in the chambers, those at monitors.

"You, sir," Trent shouted, pointing to Lightwind, "lower that weapon. We must resolve this without violence."

The father made a more tempting target than Chase. With no one noticing, all Columbus needed was to raise his weapon. The mystic lurked in shadows to the left of Lightwind but with a clear line of fire at both Brunels. With everyone focused on Trent, Columbus moved closer to both grangers.

Trent tried to control his nerves, sure everyone could tell how he shook. Speaking to an Assembly was one thing; this was quite another. At least the Assembly was unarmed and might take his words kindly enough. He glanced at Kyle, who stood firmly at his right side.

Kyle admired Trent's steadfast determination. The officer hoped he was half as courageous as the unarmed, defenseless granger. And hoped his own jitters weren't noticeable.

Everyone in the Assembly stood frozen, unsure of what to do or say next. The granger finally implored, "C'mon, son. Let's go home."

"Father," Chase yelped then rose. Columbus, having now stepped from the shadows to stand behind Chase, struck the younger granger with the grip of his weapon, knocking him down.

"Should we go? Go in, sir?" Through his helmet's com-link, Kyle heard his troopers yell. "They're getting ready to finish the job."

The lieutenant kept his teams outside two side entrances of the Assembly chamber, at the ready to finish off anyone resisting, the PS weapon set for use. Kyle withheld his command.

"Father!" Chase yelped again, from the floor at the feet of his former leader. When he tried to rise, Columbus pushed him back down between a row of desks.

From the shadows on the right of the chambers, Richardson shouted. "Brunel, it comes to this."

Still searching for a peaceful resolution, Trent looked over at his neighbor. "Same applies to you, Lionel. Let's talk." He hadn't expected Richardson to be part of this.

Richardson's old Enfield hissed as it slowly charged, an ancient weapon, one more likely to misfire than send a three-burst at its target accurately. The incensed man felt no fear; the hand of his wrathful god held him steady. If he needed to kill in the almighty's name, so be it. He felt the same as when he condemned his oldest son and two daughters to perdition after they'd openly defied him. Uncompromising righteousness was enough reason for the granger-servant to do his god's unyielding will. If his god wanted his son's blood, his daughters' blood, so be it. Blood sacrifice.

"What's to talk about?" Richardson began rambling, his Enfield waving about. "You kept your whelp of a son away from my two oldest daughters. Could have married either one. Been part of my family then—"

Kyle, frozen in this standoff, smirked. "Marrying for New Grange, you mean."

Richardson answered by swinging his temperamental Enfield at the lieutenant, then back to his neighbor.

"Stay out of this, Kyle," Trent insisted.

"You kept your daughter from my son, too," the wild man with his Enfield rambled on, "even though she committed herself to him. He told me *that*. She obeyed him. She spread for him. Gave of herself. He humped her good, like a man ought to own a woman. Then like a harlot, she backed off. Either you or your wife or that bitch PRIM of yours talked her out of it." Richardson's eyes were wild with the loss of Brunel's thriving grange. His own increasing family, his small spread, the lush and larger New Grange right next door. It wasn't right that his progeny didn't marry his neighbor's spread. "High and mighty, you all are."

Kyle was slowly raising his Enfield. This had gone on long enough.

Before the lieutenant was ready, Richardson fired a three-burst at his unarmed neighbor. Trent crashed back against a large desk, held upright by it, gasping his last. Only one shell hit home, but it was enough.

Kyle reacted, pivoted, and cut down the shooter with three perfect shots. Then he pivoted back to level his recharged Enfield at Columbus who pointed his own weapon to fire at Chase, rising from on the floor in front of him.

The next seconds were a blur, without exactness in Kyle's mind as events swirled.

Fury surged in the sage who'd made a life of proclaiming that his wrath was the only way. Venom filled his already poisoned mind. To take one last life at the cusp of his own death bestowed unfathomable satisfaction. And to take the life of a betrayer, one he had tried to mold into his image of hatred and abhorrence for all—one who then rejected that boon of loathing—it seemed most fitting.

"Drop—" the lieutenant started to shout when the disgruntled sage fired wildly. In rushing to get to his father, Chase blocked Kyle's aim; the lieutenant held his fire for an instance. Columbus's first shell caught Chase's right arm solidly, exploding it above the elbow. The other two shots missed both the granger and the lieutenant.

With the wounded man now knocked down and out of the way by the Enfield's impact, Kyle fired. Without body armor, without a clue of the real power of an Enfield, Columbus hadn't a chance. Three exploding shells ripped his chest. The three-burst blew apart his bloated body. The officer had aimed true. His shells effortlessly tore through the sage's heartless chest.

He died instantly in a way he never suspected, a madman cut down by legal authority.

In that split second, the Command Center blared the pulse-sound weapon. Everyone without ear protection in the Assembly chambers held their heads and crumbled to the ground. The piercing sound rendered them immobile. Kyle wished he hadn't been stopped from deploying that weapon days ago. "Stay down, down, everyone down," he ordered, his Enfield motioning to add to his insistence. His troopers swarmed into the Chambers, in no mood for reluctance.

The surviving occupiers complied to the gestures ordering them to lay flat and not move even as the blare seemingly split their heads with a wedge.

When the pulsing tones ceased, Lightwind received the most attention. He had his Enfield drawn, and as Kyle's unit rushed him, he raised to fire. A sniper bot ended his attempt, a single, clean head shot.

Out of the corner of his eye, Kyle saw what he feared most, Chase, wounded, stunned, his right arm blasted off, leaving him bleeding to death after slapping him down hard at his father's feet.

Rushing to him, Kyle whispered, "Med team's on the way." Kneeling in a pool of blood, the officer started a tourniquet on the wet stump.

"Thank you for saving my life," Chase moaned hoarsely, looking over the pulpy shambles of his right arm. "I'm alive at least long enough to say I'm sorry. Tell them all back at New Grange how truly sorry I am."

"Will do, Chase, will do," Kyle replied, tightening the bandage, calling again over his com-link for that med team. "But no need, you'll say it yourself. You'll be fine." He lied.

"Can I get to father?"

"If you move, you'll bleed to death," Kyle held him down. Chase's blood covered his body armor. The tourniquet just barely stopped his bleeding; he passed out from loss of so much blood.

As the wounded man fell into shock, the medics arrived.

———•———

At his HQ, Devon monitored the situation. The second firing broke out in the Hex, com-links came alive with reports; his plot board lit up. Several attacking battalions immediately advanced.

"At least it's the ones we expected," Mei-Ling noted as she looked over the large monitor that kept the Sac City situation up to date. The capitol building was at the center of the map. All paths led there.

"They're leaving the campus all right," Zot pointed out. "Heading west."

"I think we can hold them down south," Devon answered, having worked out a blocking strategy well in advance. "Any word from the other Marsco battalions?"

"None, sir," a warrant sitting at the master console, answered. "Several have broken communications with us, however."

"Of course," Zot smirked, "no fraternization with the enemy."

"Well," Devon groused, "are they in, on our side, or sitting on their finger disks?"

No one knew.

"Anything from Herschel? From Resnik?" The feds had eyes at the Moon colonies to watch the Vanovara that floated there in synchronous orbit, keeping the lunar sphere between the weapons and Earth. "Any movement there?"

"Negatory, no word. Their com-link just went abruptly down."

"I hate putting you in harm's way, Captain Shanghai," Devon sighed, "but I need you at the controls of my lander."

"Ready, sir."

———•———

For fifteen minutes within the Assembly hall at the Hexagon, all continued to be a riot of noise and shouting as personnel rushed in to carry away the four dead and the one wounded survivor. Other teams were instantly at work assessing the damage to the chamber's infrastructure. The absent provisional Assembly wanted to meet in that very spot as soon as feasible to show the world that a legitimate government was again in control of the West Con capital.

One unit brought in portable fans to clear the air; several unwashed men living in the same room for so long left a stench. Another highly trained group came to look for evidence, any scrap of paper, any file left behind on a computer, anything that might lead investigators to more of the master's clan. Little was found. For all his boasts, it appeared Columbus commanded no other followers besides the few remaining fanatics apprehended right here.

"Get him into the operating tent," the head surgeon ordered as two medics rushed in a single wounded man. "I'll have a look."

As she began stabilizing her one patient, the first medic explained, "He's it, doc. Only one we've got. Over faster than anyone expected."

"This an Enfield blast?" the surgeon asked. It was her first experience with this type of wound.

"Affirmative. He'z a mess, ain't he?" the second medic answered. "No effin' arm left, lost lotz'a blood."

The surgeon shouted orders—plasma, pain meds. "And get me a scalpel kit. And a bone saw. I'll need to smooth out the torn and blasted flesh, trim that jagged bone."

The field hospital was nestled under old oaks and sycamores in the south corner of Capitol Park, the oldest part of the grounds near the deserted and abandoned rotunda. With the fighting inside the Hex over so quickly and casualties so light, the doctor sensed she was witnessing a lull before a major battle. Given what excited chatter was coming over the com-links, she knew she'd be busy later today.

Taking a moment, Kyle found a spot outside the Hex to his liking, a private and quiet spot in a garden untouched by the violence inside. Once alone, he breathed in the cold predawn air deeply. He needed to clear his mind before being called back to action. Sitting in the silence of a vacant garden, the officer heard his weapon hiss to full recharge. He pulled it from his holster to shut it down.

Holding it in his hand, he was forced to confront the fact that he had just killed two men outright. And, certainly he had held a doomed third one as his life slipped away.

"Four, maybe five, dead in there out of eight, nine?" the officer muttered. "And how many more if Marsco hits this city with V-weapons and dozens of battalions?" he asked to no one in particular. "And they're coming on with robotic warriors, don't forget that," he said. Lumbering, independent killing machines with no regard for human life.

Looking up, Kyle saw a command lander was hovering, ready to land, vectoring jets slowing its descent. Next to the craft, a nimble four-seat fed HFC was coming down as well, its skids extended.

He replaced his Enfield into its holster and moved to the edge of lawn as the two craft settled down.

Devon and Zot found Kyle. "All done in here?" The colonel asked.

"Yes, sir, locked down in only minutes." Kyle wanted to give a more thorough report, especially about the death of Devon's cousin, but Zot cut him off.

"Any of that blood yours?" the iceman demanded.

"No, it's—"

"Get some clean gear," the colonel ordered, "and as many troopers as you can gather. There's trouble, and we need every available fed."

"What's up?"

"Security units—with an attitude—are ignoring our orders to stay put, and some're pushing this way."

"Shit—clear the hall of rats only to have the jackals want to take it right back."

"Not that we weren't warned," Devon added. "Or prepared."

Zot smirked. "We might still have a chance to stop them, if they stay with ground troops only." None of the officers mentioned the threat of Vanovaras; that thought was too heinous to contemplate with an oncoming battle soon to envelop the city. Last century this city had seen those mushroom clouds blossom; no one wanted to witness them now.

Kyle took Devon by the shoulders so the lieutenant knew the colonel would listen. "Trent's dead. I was right there. Couldn't prevent it."

Devon just looked away, down.

Kyle jostled him enough to command his attention again. "Chase's badly wounded. I think he's bought it."

"Where is he?"

"He's in our med tent." Kyle thought of Sarah but had no time for any feelings or softness. No time to send word to New Grange about her father and brother.

"Was he the only wounded?" Zot asked.

"Yes."

Before Kyle could answer, the colonel demanded, "Was it you?"

"No," he responded bluntly. "And like with his father, I was just a sec too late to stop it. To save either of them. All my fault. I should have acted faster, should have saved them both. Shit, gone in there days before. But tonight, I failed. Might as well have been me, killing Chase, killing Trent. Sarah will believe that, won't she? That I essentially killed them both."

Then ignoring it all, Kyle started giving orders to organize his troopers milling around. Devon had no time to argue with him, shake him out of such a misguided belief.

The eastern horizon glowed a bit earlier than anyone expected.

<hr />

When a nurse leaned over Chase, the wounded man couldn't believe his eyes. Patrice. He was powerless to speak, although his vision cleared and his former neighbor was right there, no question. She was the only calm one surrounding him; the rest were frenetic but professional in prepping him.

Chase felt sure they would just let him die; he had made such a mess of all their lives these past months. *It's okay if I die here*, he thought, *except I want to see them again, Sarah and Hy and my folks.* He'd already forgotten about Trent, dead in the Assembly chambers. He willed Patrice to understand him. *You'll tell them all for me. Ask their forgiveness, especially Hy. I hurt Hyacinth so much.*

An IV bag hung next to Chase. Patrice slipped a needle into his left arm, gently and effortlessly. Another nurse standing at his head where he couldn't see put a mask over his mouth and nose; before two deep breaths he was out cold.

While the surgeon cut away ribbons of muscle and trimmed the bone before closing the man's wounds, a medic bent to her ear. "A colonel outside wants your prognosis. What do I say?"

"If he survives the shock and loss of blood—"

All of the monitors promptly flatlined, their low rhythmic hum replaced by a single shrill note. "No, tell him I'll speak with him in a moment, if he can wait." *That was quicker than I thought*, she chided herself, finding greater damage and blood loss than her initial diagnosis suggested. The surgeon had heard stories about the effectiveness of an Enfield. Here was proof.

Removing her mask, a nurse next to the doctor whispered, "I can do that, sir." After tenderly covering Chase's face, she added, "I know his family."

Outside the one tent, two other temporary surgery bays were going up. If Marsco was coming, this locale was going to be the fed's last stand, right here in the shadow of the rotunda, right near the new Hexagon with its promise of independence. All around Patrice, other med teams were prepping for the upcoming battle. She went to find Devon.

———•◦•———

Fifteen minutes later, Devon was heading back to the campus in his command lander. That appeared to be the center of Marsco's strength. "Well, some good news," Zot reported. He was monitoring the com-links behind the flight deck of the lander. "Marsco's units coming in from the north have stopped approaching the City Center on the far side of the river. Just stopped in their tracks. No attempts to cross over from there."

"And they're closest to the Hex," Shanghai noted. "Any reason given?"

"Can't say if they're regrouping or confused or just quitting."

"Well, just standing there is fine with me." Devon sighed. He hadn't sufficient troops to stop a three-pronged attack. In a moment, the colonel confided, "I worked with those units. I know some of their officers from their cadet days. I tried to reason with them *not* to join in Seattle's plans. But I think I failed."

"Time will tell," his pilot replied. Shanghai tried to reassure him he may be wrong, that those battalions might be sitting tight.

"No," the colonel responded, "no, they're coming. I think waiting to coordinate a drive to the city center and the Hex."

As Shanghai did a slow circle above the campus to recce the battle below, Devon fumed. "And here's another thing. It's no wonder Marsco made the fed shut down the college. Seattle planned to use this locale for a staging area all along. The folks at the Hex trusted too much in Marsco really upholding the Accords. Or believed that a coup up there might stop this, this Chesney nonsense. Once Modena was out, we should have known better."

The colonel shook his head. He had three battalions of former Marsco troopers and one fed battalion at his disposal inside Sac City to stop several loyal Marsco units coming at him. Three possibly unreliable units and his one definitely loyal—albeit, only partially trained—unit. He'd hoped more of Marsco's troopers would stand down, but Seattle's reliable units were already in neighborhoods beyond the campus and heading toward the Hexagon. The colonel's numbers weren't good. And he had little to use against them.

And who's going to remain loyal to whom? he wondered. *The Accords are a theory, an ideal. Do my troopers die for an ideal? Will former Marsco units stand firm for a federation they have no connection to?*

Sitting behind the pilot, Zot looked down at the campus where only a few months ago he'd begun to work. "I've seen it like this once before," he murmured to the officers seated in front of him.

"Seen what?" Devon asked over his shoulder from the copilot seat.

"Seen this campus covered with troopers and Marsco spoiling for a fight."

He concentrated on the scene for a few seconds as Shanghai prepared to land. Several Bradley vehicles were ablaze. The fighting had ebbed and flowed. Fierce, at close quarters. Whose losses burned below the command lander, the officers couldn't tell. Perhaps from both sides. Lines of ants went forward into battle; were those troopers under Marsco or federation control? No one knew for sure.

Everywhere the Marsco battalions went, buildings burst into flames. Two buildings were alight on campus already, one in which Zot had worked. That seemed to be Marsco's tactic, to burn as much of the city as they advanced behind robotic warriors followed by troopers in protected armored vehicles.

"See any knights?" Devon asked as he scoured the glowing scene below. Smoke and dust even distorted his use of night scope.

"There!" Zot pointed. "Six have just crossed the river on the footbridge. Looks like nothing will stop them." Fortunately, the number of bot warriors wasn't that great, and they were having trouble navigating the battle-littered roads beyond campus. Citizens had cut trees, put up barricades, started their own fires across streets, anything to disrupt the easy and direct route to the capitol.

"If we can cut off those bot knights," Devon shot, "we may have a chance."

"It looks to me," Zot gave his assessment, "that only the units *with* knights are staying in the fight."

As he spoke, two more robotic warriors appeared. The river wasn't stopping them. The blockaded streets were slowing them down only temporarily. They marched on burning relentlessly, mechanically advancing toward the heart of Sac City.

THIRTY-TWO

MONSTERS AND MEDICS

(Sac City and New Grange, June 2155)

Patrice Richardson moved from patient to patient in the field hospital, careful where she stepped. Gingerly, she moved over and between dozens of casualties, some on cots, others just on the ground using a blanket as a mat. Most were women and children. Many showed signs of shock or abject terror. This corner of Capitol Park overflowed with the collateral damage of the great battle encircling them. Patrice made them comfortable, gave them water and a little food, administered medicine. Nearly surrounded, this temporary hospital had to keep its wounded as the fighting raged. It had no other safe place to send them.

Far cry from working with kids, she thought. Her future life as a pediatric nurse had taken a sharp turn.

She untied her long blond hair and retied it behind her head. She hadn't washed it in days. She remembered how vain she had been once, curling her tresses for an hour before Chase visited, back when she listened to her father, urged on to love a young man for his land. Her green eyes sparkled as he would approach. And before her own marriage to DeShawn Cleveland, she'd fixed her hair as well but not the way she had for her young neighbor. A world gone. Her eyes were bloodshot from lack of sleep. Covering her hair with a clean surgical cap, she went back to her patients.

As soon as the real fighting started, Devon had taken control of the defenses of the city. Under his command, federation battalions quickly stabilized the two fronts, east and south of the City Center. Marsco, however, was feeding in fresh troops while this Fed had limited reserves. The colonel's forces felt constant pressure as Marsco probed and advanced, probed and advanced.

And, to the north along the river, Marsco battalions threatened to encircle Devon's defenses. The enemy kept its pressure from three sides, from the east and south fiercely, from the north in a strategic blocking position, if Patrice understood the military terms correctly. But as yet, those units just across the river showed no signs of advancing.

DeShawn had tried to explain it to her twenty-four or thirty-six hours ago. She couldn't get the past few days straight. Even looking skyward was little help, since day was nearly as black as night. Uncontrolled fires continued throughout the city. DeShawn appeared at irregular intervals with more wounded, skimming in via an HFC sometimes piloted by Captain Shanghai. He caught Patrice between patients for a moment then was away. From him, she gathered that "the issue was still in doubt." The nurse wasn't totally versed in military jargon, but she gathered the indirect sentiment of this euphemism.

When Marsco forces advanced, they burnt as they went, DeShawn told her. This explained her casualties. Mostly burn victims. Mostly civilians. Slightly wounded troopers were patched up at forward aid stations, but then put back on the line.

"Small arms against monsters," her husband had explained.

One of her patients was restless in her pain. Patrice tried to calm her so that everyone else in the overcrowded ward could rest. "On, on they come," this seriously injured sergeant, one likely to die, moaned, "crushing, burning."

"Any pain meds?" Patrice asked.

"I'll fetch some," another nurse answered.

Both nurses had heard DeShawn explain about these much-feared bot knights. Standing 2.5 meters, with a swift, strong gait, these black robotic warriors were equipped with a weapon that incinerated whatever its ray touched. "They look man-like, two arms, two legs, a head that must be a housing for guidance."

"But heartless, it appears," the other nurse reacted.

"How are you fighting them?" Patrice asked.

"Me? I'm not. I'm a medic. But with guts, Enfields, and something, anything to block its head. That's the key, it appears. If its head is disoriented, then their operators behind the battlefield can't remotely run the machine. It's blind."

"Is that working?"

He grinned, "We've taken down a few." His expression grew serious, "More by accident than plan, and they keep coming."

The nurses shook their heads.

"Trying to get close enough," the medic continued, "that's the hard part. They're always in pairs or groups of four or six. They cover each other tight. And Brads with platoons of troopers guard their backs."

"Be safe," Patrice implored, kissing him, not knowing if for the last time.

"You're safe here," he whispered during their short embrace. "Don't think they'll attack a hospital."

After bringing in a dozen wounded, DeShawn was off again to the front with supplies and water.

Kyle looked up from the situation monitor that had the whole of the city before him. He was in Devon's headquarters with Zot as the battles raged. The issue always had been dealing with these metallic creatures that were impervious to anything the fed had in their arsenal.

"Look," the lieutenant explained, "when my training platoon confronted one of these up near Rainier, purely by accident, we hit one with a pair of flares. Phosphorus. Brighter than hell."

"That won't stop it," Zot admonished.

"No, but it blinded it, I'm sure. My trooper put two flares on it. One stuck near its head. That's its infrared housing. And must also contain its antenna for communicating with its handler. Without it, the bot's remote operator off somewhere in the distance behind can't see. That's its one weak spot."

"But how to get that close every time?"

"I bagged one the other day. Hit it with phos flares. When it staggered and lost connection with is minder, I knocked it silly with RPGs from behind."

Rocket-propelled grenades—a twentieth-century weapon forced into service for a twenty-second century battle—was the heaviest weapon of the fed. West Con hadn't had time to develop any artillery. And over the years since Marsco's takeover, its Security hadn't deployed more than troopers with Enfields and armament mounted on a Brad. Stunners and ooze weapons mainly for crowd control. A 30 mm Enfield was the only real muscle on those armored vehicles. Victory disease. Marsco never imagined fighting another army again with tanks and armed drones, weaponry resembling the early twenty-first century. Without heavy armor or artillery, the robotic warriors were it. But those knights were vulnerable to attackers with courage, stealth, and RPGs.

"This is why Marsco relies on Vanovaras," Zot reminded them. And those horrific weapons were out there somewhere, menacing them still.

Kyle wouldn't be deterred. "Look, the knights march ahead. They burn and march. But, the Brads behind with troopers, they need to let the fires cool a bit before catching up. Debris clogs the roads. The Brads have to move carefully. A gap develops between the leading bot knights and their support."

"And?" Devon asked, having noted the same thing but unable to figure out how to exploit it.

"We own the sky. We let them come on, we set hunter-killer squads down behind the bots. That's the key, *behind* them. Flares blind them. RPGs kill them."

Devon put his foot down. "You'd be setting down a thinly protected HFC between two highly armored groups. Then, letting our troopers, protected only by light Kevlar body armor, attack metal-encased machines. I won't send out suicide squads."

"I'm volunteering."

"No."

"Wait a sec, colonel," Zot stated, "Kyle's got a point."

Within days, Kyle was an expert bot killer. And word went out to all federations. But, the ploy was costly and dangerous. No cakewalk, no sure bet.

After Patrice had witnessed Chase die in surgery, she'd hardly rested. That was more than two weeks back, when she had spoken with Devon and Zot. The night she learned that her own father was dead. And that Kyle had killed him and why.

Chase. Trent Brunel. Her own father and older brother. Two younger sisters. Neighbors. Grangers. People she knew. And how many more besides had died out there under the thick, smoky blanket that hung above Sac City?

This federation better be worth the sacrifice, she thought, then shook off that notion.

It was, she knew. She breathed free. She'd married the man she loved, even with his PRIM heritage. And her father's warped beliefs no longer mattered, no longer swayed her life. Nor did Marsco's. It was worth it. And better fighting for this future than acquiescing to what her father had unfortunately believed in. Columbus only reinforced all those twisted views. That was the only reason, she realized, when she heard the whole story of the slaughter back at her girlhood home, why the granger was drawn to that deranged hypocrite.

When the fighting restarted, the clashes must have been horrific, especially the one in the east near her campus. Fighting had raged for three days, but for the past two, relatively quiet there. And in the south, Marsco seemed to be gathering its forces for a strong push northward. The lull in that sector was not comforting.

Amid the wounded and injured, amid exhausted nurses, doctors, and orderlies, she heard whispers. "If they get on this side of the river up north, coming down at us, we're surrounded."

Two rivers met in Sac City to the north of the capitol grounds where the hospital tents stood. One river flowed several blocks from here. The university campus was on another branch upstream from where the rivers converged. Clearly, the biggest threat was in the north. "If they cross the river there, what does it matter?" the grumblings went. "Once across, they can spit and hit the Hex."

The nurse didn't understand the strategy, but she understood the danger and the dread.

Of other clashes and skirmishes, she knew nothing else. What was happening in Portland, a location of another great battle, she didn't know. And worldwide? Places she'd only heard about: Paris, London, Tokyo. Were they battling there as well? Patrice believed so.

Later that afternoon, on her way to pick up supplies, she walked by a command tent jammed with communications equipment and overheard officers at consoles in deep conversation. "All links are totally blocked. We don't know if Silicon has been taken, sir; we're that cut off. Rest of the world might as well have gone to hell!"

"Hell," another answered, "we don't even know if Marsco units have reached our City Center or not."

Most of the time, she had no idea where DeShawn was. And all the others. She knew so many in this battle. Sarah's Kyle, of course. Zot she'd seen. Like her husband, he brought casualties here. And Shanghai, she often piloted a large hovercraft with the wounded, looking for supplies. The nurse saw them here and gone, one or two days ago. Maybe a week. Time was that blurred. And even if she'd just seen them, by now, they might all be dead.

She shuddered for her husband.

She assumed Sarah and Hyacinth and the rest were safe at New Grange, but she wasn't sure of that either. Or whether a battle had stormed near them as this carnage spread. The granges she knew as a girl were well below the southern front. Was Marsco swarming over their fields? Using her family home as its own aid station? A command center? She just didn't know. The smoky and cloudy view of war surrounded her.

A doctor hurried past. "Nurse, I need plasma!"

"Yes, sir, of course."

———— ◆ ————

"Try Herschel and Resnik both again," Devon ordered from the first days of the great battle. Two, three times a day, whenever his mind wasn't fixed with the immediacy of this raging fight, he checked on the status of those Vanovaras floating above the two lunar colonies.

"Com-links are still blocked, colonel," his sparks reported for days on end.

"Anything on our scans of lunar orbit?"

"HQ reports they're blocked, too," the sparks replied, disappointment in her voice.

"So," the colonel groused in a flat tone, "we're blind and we don't know what else is coming down at us."

"That expresses it quite well."

"And Silicon, Portland?"

"No word on them, either, sir. Fighting there, not sure how it's going."

"Any other news from somewhere, anywhere?"

"Nothing, sir."

Then on the last morning of the second week, Resnik did get through. "Vanovaras departed, 0230 local time." That was it.

Amid the third week of the battle, as exhausted as he was, Devon was alert enough to know that if Marsco's weaponry had left lunar orbit, they were very likely circling the Earth right now. Ready for an accurate placement. What was already horrific was going to grow worse at any moment.

In the course of the fighting, Kyle remained at HQ, his troopers ostensibly to act as guards but really to be Devon's special hunter-killer platoon, sent out when needed most. Already, they'd been out and back eight times in two weeks, each time with fewer troopers, but the lieutenant had whipped them into an effective, determined force. Eighteen kills to their credit. They feared no bot.

Kyle smirked at the old military adage, *Don't be too good at a task, or you're stuck with it.*

Since the beginning of the fighting, Sarah had seen Jonathan, Kyle's former aide, nearly every day. He came over from Tillson's, sometimes with the granger, sometimes with a medic. Tillson's became a hub of fed forces, scarce as they were in this area. A few units had moved up from the Central Valley, where Marsco had made no effort to reestablish control.

"Missy," Jonathan explained early in the fighting, "we're getting folks coming down from where Marsco's burned them out. Which it is, we beg you to take some, about a dozen or so."

"No need to beg," Sarah replied, eager to help. The pristine fields of New Grange had the space. Without consulting her mother, she took charge. The children Chase had sent—and Sarah had argued over with Kyle until he relented—were adjusting nicely to warmth and regular meals. Taking more was imperative.

Jonathan had tents and cots for a temporary camp. Room for forty-eight, max, he assured her. The first dozen refugees helped set up the few tents. Under Tessa's directions, they dug a latrine system. Set up a makeshift bathhouse. The field was thick with clover as a cover crop anyway. The main house's kitchen, often feeding a large work crew, handled the meals. Celine, Tessa, and Hy all helped. Even a few refugees pitched in, glad to be of use. Her family's land was soon a burgeoning camp. Those left behind at New Grange became part of the ceaseless sideshow of this war.

As the first weeks of June passed, New Grange was the temporary home to a hundred. Each day, another handful arrived. Sarah never woke to a day without a trickle of six or a dozen more.

Letup and then renewed fighting, nights of fire, days of smoke and haze. Sounds of distant Sac City battles wafting over her fields. A tense silence, on the verge of more clashes. And clusters of refugees making it there, either via Tillson's first or directly to New Grange as news of her camp spread.

When the battle sounds up north, closer to Sac City, ceased, Sarah could hear distinct firing from Tillson's. Regular and rhythmic Enfield fire, clearly practice. Fresh troops were gathering there, but they lacked training. Even to the granger, newly-arrived troopers were obviously receiving weapon instructions.

Soon HFCs started arriving. Squat Brads and agile rovers as well. Auxiliary vehicles now hastily rearmed like Security's, with Enfield weapons. Each one had a clear West Con insignia. Tillson's began to look like a staging area.

The worst day wasn't one with additional refugees or muffled training on the wind but one with hard decisions and the cruel realities of war. Jonathan appeared with an officer in khaki whom Sarah had never met.

"We need to address your guests," the major began. Even in the midst of battle, his uniform was neat and spotless. He didn't appear much older than Kyle. At first Sarah wanted to ask if he knew him, had gone to the Academy with him. It never occurred to ask if they'd served together in Security a few years back.

Without an introduction, the major stood on his rover's roof and addressed the five hundred refugees now encamped at New Grange. They were cleaner and better fed than when they'd arrived. And attentive to the officer.

"I need volunteers," he implored. "Anyone with any training, even Auxxie training, we need you. Can you drive? Help with transport? If you're strong and can walk, we can use you, if only to hump equipment."

"What's up?" Sarah asked Jonathan, angry that her place of shelter was now being scoured for troops.

"Which it is that he means to say, missy," explained the old Auxxie, "is that there's a chance to hit 'em from our sector. They're focused *north*, don't you see, headin' directly towards Sac City, a second time, and ain't looking for us from this direction. Us out here in the boondocks. They ain't using no recon drones. Even I knowed that—look around. Always look around. They're eyeless, blind cocky bastards." He paused, almost too excited to explain Marsco's vulnerability. "Which it is, a soft underbelly, waitin' our gleamin' knife. Wide open to hit 'em now, with everything we got."

"But if *everything* is children and refugees—" Sarah searched for words.

The major done, he joined the pair. "Piece of cake, miss, Marsco's asleep at the switch, so focused north, if you understand their strategy and ours."

Even before spending time with Kyle, Sarah understood. She'd read enough history. Hit your enemies at their weakest, where they least expect it. But these were boys and girls with no training. That she didn't understand.

"They don't want no Marsco in their face no more," Jonathan assured the granger. Scores of volunteers from New Grange moved off to join the fed forces gathering at Tillson's. The old aide's gleaming knife.

———— • ————

As busy as she was, Patrice hardly noticed that DeShawn was back. It was more than seventy-two hours since his last trip. She was dead on her feet. So was he.

He came with a warrant officer, an old Auxxie who wore a bandage over a head wound. The pair, ragged and dirty from their close quarters with the fighting, cornered the head surgeon between patients.

"We've come, hen sent here, fur anyone what can walk," the aged warrant garbled a message while motioning to the large HFC hauler they came in. The head wound had knocked the old-timer pretty hard.

"Walking wounded," DeShawn explained to the doctor, showing orders from Devon. "They're to draw weapons, and we've a lander to move them up." The medic stopped to swallow some water, his first clean drink in a day. "Oh, I'm to bring up a nurse to act as a medic, too."

The doctor asked, "Aren't you a medic?"

"Was. I'm to draw weapons now."

"I'll go," Patrice blurted out, standing at the side of their conversation.

"Makes sense," the doctor noted, "you're the fittest of the lot. Your farming background."

"You can't go, Patrice. It's dangerous up there."

The doctor, who held a major's rank, looked at the medic. "Draw weapons as ordered, trooper, and give her your first aid satchel." He'd earned med school by serving time in Marsco Security; he knew how to give and take orders.

As they stood there, tension mounting, Patrice noticed the doctor's left hand. Clearly it had a PRIM-disk scar.

He noticed she saw it. "All that's past now," he shot, then drew a calming breath. In every direction signs of the raging battles were visible, some distant, some so near they heard it as constant a low rumble. "Can't let PRIM-ification happen again. That's why I'm here." He pointed to their fed uniforms. "We have to win this. Have to."

With that, DeShawn went forward to battle, Patrice following behind, filling his role as a medic.

Sarah sensed that the hastily assembled units over at Tillson's were gone. A stillness in the air, the altered sounds just before dawn alerted her.

Then growing tension all day, a long, nearly silent early summer day. At nightfall, the northern sky was flashes and thumps from terrifying weaponry she could scarcely imagine. She feared her children and the major's troopers were dying.

Toward midnight, the lights and sounds intensified, then lasted another whole day and night.

"I was a girl on Mars during the C-Wars," Tessa explained, "but it must have been like this." She paused. "At least no V-weapons, yet, as far as Zot knows."

A lull finally came near morning after two violent days and nights when out of that smoky gray dawn HFCs went to and from Tillson's, the wounded going to the inadequate aid station over there.

It was noon before New Grange received a fresh wave of refugees.

None of those first volunteers who'd gone off from Sarah's returned. They were either dead, wounded at Tillson's, or still on the line.

No one at New Grange was immune from the intensity of this war.

That night, no flashes crossed the horizon up north. For the first time in the weeks, this lull seemed different, steady, sure of its own continuance.

"He pulled it off, that young major," old Tillson reported to her. "Things should stabilize now. Marsco's got real bloodied up and ain't likely to advance either down towards us or up towards Sac City. Caught with their backs to us and their drawers pulled down to their knees." The granger drew a breath, "Ol' Marsco never imagined that a ragtag bunch would put up this much fight, but we did."

Jonathan jumped in while Tillson paused. "That major bought it, missy. Leadin' a charge to stop this here robotic creature a-goin' after them kids of yours."

"Bought it," was that how it was? Sarah asked herself. She'd heard about her father and brother. But had Devon, Zot, Shanghai, Patrice, had they bought it? Even Kyle, whom she still blamed for so many deaths, where was he now? Besides Tessa and Hy and the others at New Grange, she felt as though almost everyone she knew was in Sac City. *Have they all bought it?*

A day into the continuing lull in the southern fighting, Sarah and Tessa visited Tillson's. New Grange was filled with more than seven hundred refugees and growing but no medical station to serve them. And after the fighting erupted toward Sac City, many refugees were coming in wounded.

The chief fed doctor at Tillson's promised to do what she could, but she was stretched to the limit herself. Ever since fighting started, Tillson's had the only medical facility for all of the fed forces in this sector. And it wasn't much. After the recent battle, it grew overcrowded and frenetic.

In one corner of Tillson's easternmost field, the pair from New Grange saw a large enclosure surrounded by barbed wire and a handful of walking-wounded guards. "What's that for?" the engineer asked. Hundreds of men and women milled around, dressed in Marsco Security gray, uninjured so far as Sarah could tell, if dazed and frightened.

Jonathan explained. "Prisoners. Many of them units we hit up north were Auxxies." Marsco had kept them from returning home as promised.

"No stomach for a fight," the former legionnaire explained. "Surrendered in droves."

"Any with medical training?" Tessa wondered.

"Don't know."

"Let's ask and take them to New Grange," Sarah suggested to the nodding Tessa.

"No way to guard 'em if released to you two misses," Jonathan explained.

A fed sergeant watching the enclosure came over, his left arm in a sling. "Look, if you ask who's a medic in there, half these pongos will say yes. And I can't spare no one to secure them over your way."

"I'll take the risk." Sarah was determined.

"I'll check them," Tessa answered, her voice a commanding officer's voice. Marsco training left an impression and a rarely tapped aptitude.

For two hours, the women walked throughout the prisoner enclosure and spoke with scores of men and women who answered about their skills. Tessa looked each in the eyes and took those who appeared trustworthy. Eight seemed most likely, a doctor, a PA, and six nurses. A dozen more were eager to be orderlies.

Back at New Grange, Sarah explained to the newly found med personnel, "We have no way to guard you." As she spoke, her confidence in her decision rose. "You're safe here. You'll be fed, given places to sleep comfortably. But, if you cause trouble, I can't help you or protect you." They all understood. A few had language disks, and all had PRIM-disks still, although the Accords had ended them several years before.

In an hour, a medical tent was up and functioning. With the prisoner med personnel completely immersed in the spread's bustle, the whole camp settled into its new routine.

At that point, Sarah breathed a sigh of relief. She'd trusted them and it seemed to be working. Word got out. More refugees arrived.

The last week of June was another time of stalemate. "Still not moving down from the north," Devon reported. He had Zot and Kyle with him at his latest command center closer to the Capitol and the Hex than he'd like. If pushed again, he'd be back at the locale he was ostensibly defending. Marsco was that close to breaking through from the east.

"I can't understand this," the colonel went on, "it's not deploying any drones."

"Affirmative, we own the skies," Zot answered.

"And, for the life of me," Devon continued, "I can't understand why they aren't moving troops around us with HFCs or landers. Mobility is such an asset; why not use it?"

Zot had been south after the battle to give his assessment. Meager but spirited West Con units coming up behind Marsco's southern thrust had stopped them cold but at a high cost. Marsco was stopped dead in its tracks. "They were moving toward us here in Sac City without the benefit of any recon surveillance. Ahead or behind. Why? What army does that?"

Marsco was fighting like it was being led by those who didn't understand the modern—or ancient—battlefield. Even Caesar and Napoleon sent out cavalry to scout ahead, to reconnoiter their flanks, to guard them. Marsco didn't bother with any drones or HFCs.

"And bridges," Zot added. "They move their knights across the rivers only via bridges."

Kyle, probably the most militarily trained of any of the other officers closest to Devon, shook his head. *If I were in charge, I'd be dropping units behind us, like we're doing to them.*

"Does this make any sense?" Devon asked, half philosophically, half searching to understand the situation map that looked too neat, too much like an old-style, kid's strategy game instead of a fluid battlefield with loose ends and unsure skirmish lines.

"The only explanation," Kyle suggested, "is that Chesney and his advisors are running this under such tight control that they aren't letting anyone else have a say."

Devon noted, "When Modena sent Security units to the federations, many of the best officers went over with them."

"And if Chesney doesn't trust his officers' corps any longer," Zot was quick to point out, "he'll rely less and less on the remaining ones, the trained ones."

Kyle added, "Precedents exist, after all. Stalin gutting his officer corps. Hitler not trusting his own generals. Other modern examples from early last century when madmen thought they were martial geniuses and sent orders that made no sense militarily."

Nods of agreement. "More and more," Kyle thought out loud, "Chesney is relying on a limited team of officers. Those who've gone through Sustainability."

"Thank God for small mercies," Zot replied softly.

An orderly came from the com center with an update. "They've started coming south, that northern group. They're on the move." Devon glanced at his officers. He looked at the situation map. Four bots with Brads as follow-up. A full battalion at least. Using an old railroad trestle to cross. Hitting where the feds stood the weakest.

Devon hadn't wanted to commit all his reserves in case Marsco came on again from near the university, so the colonel had no other choices. Kyle had to make do with the remnants of his platoon, now down to a squad in strength, and whomever he could scratch together, to block a whole battalion led by robotic warriors.

The river was wide, swift, and black.

The trestle spanning it was still standing firm, a testament to early twentieth-century engineering. The railroad bed had no safety railing; it was nothing but two sets of tracks with a narrow catwalk on one side. No train had crossed this two-kilometer span in a century, but it easily supported four bots striding south toward the far riverbank and Sac City proper.

The black metallic creatures moved along with ease, their 2.5-meter height giving them a long stride, their mechanical innards giving them an easy gait. They marched along, impervious to attack, unconcerned about any enemy.

Their follow-up Brads started to creep along the trestle, which was only wide enough for a single file line of menacing vehicles. The heavy Brads had to move slowly, tentatively on the span. Hundreds of troopers advancing behind the screen of Brad became bunched up, their movement now stalled.

The fed side of the river was lightly defended. During the recent battles all around Sac City, Devon had thinned out his ranks here to shore up the two hot zones in the east and then south of the city center. This much

Marsco muscle hitting this weak spot might easily collapse fed resistance and quickly strike the Hex.

Not for the first time, everyone at HQ wondered by the feds hadn't blown this trestle. Oversight? Over confidence? Sheer confusion? The fog of war.

The long, straight span offered no cover. That night, Shanghai set her large hovercraft gingerly down near the north side, balancing it on the wide trestle. Feds were now between the advancing bots and the cautious Brads. The hauler disgorged troopers, three teams jumping out. Kyle's hunter squad headed off south, festooned with flares and RPGs, running along the span to catch up with the bots striding forward. At least they were already coming on the mechanical warriors from behind. The HFC was far enough away from those knights that they didn't notice or care. A team of sappers prepared to blow a gap in the trestle to block the follow-up Brads and lines of troopers. A third squad provided covering fire with Enfields and rocket grenades to distract the oncoming enemy.

Speed and audacity were the feds' main weapons. Hope for using darkness as cover evaporated when the northern flank lit up the night sky with flares, putting the whole scene in a yellow light, almost as bright as dawn. The feds all stood out clearly.

In the initial chaos, Shanghai was off the fight deck and firing her handheld at the outlines down the span. Whether she hit anything or not, she felt her firing did some good as the combat engineers wired explosives while other troopers launched RPGs. The yellow-lit air zinged with streams of Enfield fire.

"If those Brads find our range," she muttered, watching the sappers work, "we're toast."

Shells streaked over their heads. One trooper, caught in an Enfield blast, was down in the river and gone before anyone could react.

"Quick, quick," Shanghai urged the sappers on. As she returned to the pilot seat, she felt a few hits on the side of her craft. "Tell me again why," she shouted over the noise of battle, "no one ordered this effing span destroyed weeks ago?"

The remaining handful of sappers were done, back in the HFC's bay. "Fire team'll blast the hole once we're all clear," a lieutenant reported to Shanghai. The craft lifted, caught more Enfield fire, then skimmed toward the fed side. As the fire team ran along the span, they'd turn, return fire, then run toward Kyle's hunter team. Each time they ran, fewer moved. They made well-defined targets. Another trooper fell into the black water.

When clear of the blast zone, they detonated the sappers' work.

A fireball filled the night. Debris flew, and smoke blocked any view of the oncoming Brads, now stopped by the yawning, twenty-five-meter gap blown in the trestle. Vehicles and troopers were not crossing this river here.

But their fire didn't stop. The HFC was hit again. The craft jerked as Shanghai struggled to keep it straight and level. Safety was ahead, over and beyond the striding bot knights and closer toward fed own lines—if she kept her bucking craft airborne long enough.

"I'll get us close to our people," Shanghai coolly reported to the surviving sappers in the passenger compartment. Their raid wasn't going smoothly.

<hr />

Kyle's squad and the following fire team watched the HFC as it scooted forward, sparks showering behind, the unstable craft just barely clearing the levee ahead. One bot gave a burst of ray weaponry as it passed. The fed troopers couldn't tell if the craft was hit by that ray or not.

Behind them, along the stretching trestle, light from the explosion dimmed. The Brads on the north shore raked the flat trestle with fire. The span was so long that the troopers heading south weren't clear of it yet. Enfield fire took down two more. A third was knocked off the trestle by a near miss and fell five meters into bushes and boulders along the riverbank where this end of the span met dry land. Her khaki body landing in the rocky shadows didn't move.

The levee loomed in front of Kyle. But his squad was going to be sitting ducks outlined against the sky when they crossed over it. If the bots on the other side were waiting, his troopers would stand out as clear targets. And to the distant Brads, the same. Kyle had to risk it. All the fed troopers wore IR jamming vests, but they were still visible moving along the top of the levee.

"Crawl, crawl over," he ordered. "Down on your bellies, crawl."

Kyle was over first. Then a second trooper made it safely. A third stood up too soon and was cut down. *Any more?* the lieutenant wondered when two crawling figures slipped over the top to his side of the levee. Cutting off the knights from their rear had been costly. Kyle had three troopers with him. He had expected two-squad strength at least, sixteen or more troopers. And he still had four robotic warriors to deal with.

"We're in luck," DeShawn whispered to Kyle as they caught their breath. The medic-turned-trooper pointed ahead fifty meters. The four knights were dividing up, three searching for Kyle and his team closest to the levee, the last one scouring the terrain ahead, looking for the crashed HFC.

"Some luck."

This side of the levee was grassy, with periodic trees and low shrubs. The metallic black skin of the bots shone in the light produced by the skirmishing and streaking shells. No mistaking them, no hiding them.

A warrant found Kyle. "Sir," she reported, "I have only one trooper but plenty of flares and grenades."

Quickly, Kyle devised a plan. "Look, I'll go back over the levee, down thirty-five meters, then over again. I'll be situated exactly right to annoy those looking for you three. I'll draw fire. When the bots turn to face me, you hit them."

The warrant would have none of it. "Sir, you're in command. I'll go. But with all them rockets and flares, I'll need a loader." She motioned to the fourth trooper. The other side of the levee was still catching sporadic Brad fire from the far bank. Their movement into position was not a certainty.

The lowly trooper mumbled but loaded up with what they needed. "Let's go muck up some tin men."

The pair got over the top without drawing any additional fire. Soon they were on their own, out of sight. What intermittent Enfield blasts hit the far side of the levee from across the river seemed random and ineffective. *Just may work*, Kyle thought.

"What if those three bots split up and some hunt *us*?" DeShawn whispered.

"I'll improvise."

The forward platoon Patrice was attached to held positions where park-lands stretched from the levee's edge toward the main city. Four squads watched an HFC skim from the river and then make a forced landing just ahead, beyond their defensive pillboxes. They lost sight of it in the trees.

From their position, troopers had also spotted four robotic knights stride over the levee. In the eerie light of the flares and Enfield fire, it was impossible to miss the striding bots; they stood that tall. And their metallic skin glimmered too glossily to be mistaken. At first their intentions and directions weren't certain. Then the platoon's recce drone gave a clear picture. The bots had split into two groups, one warrior heading toward the HFC, three staying near the levee, hunting.

With so much fighting going on for weeks east and well south of these positions, this area had seen most of its troops repositioned away. This one platoon with its thirty-two troopers created a blocking point, close to where the unused trestle reached the riverbank. They had dozens of RPGs but little else to stop any incursion. They expected probing patrols by troopers, not a full-on thrust by bots with Brads. A well-placed grenade hit may stop a Brad, but never a knight warrior, not from the front.

The commander could spare only a squad to search for that downed craft. "Has to be ours," she noted. "Marsco's not using anything that flies."

"Helluva way to get reinforcements," someone grumbled.

"C'mon," the squad leader barked, "let's get to our people before the bot finds them."

Patrice grabbed her med kit and lined up at the back of the troopers.

The commander tried to stop her, but the new medic insisted. Downed craft, bound to have wounded on board. As the night darkened with a lull in the firing near the levee, they were off.

———— • ————

Improvise Kyle did. One knight now stalked him and DeShawn. The other two stomped back toward the levee and the two troopers there. The fourth continued moving in the direction of the downed HFC. Three bots against two hunting pairs of troopers. And Kyle and DeShawn were face-on to their own knight, the worst way to attack it. They needed to hit this oncoming bot from the rear. Then quickly light up one or two of the others before it was too late.

"Can we get over, you think?" DeShawn pointed back to the levee.

Kyle got a flare ready, anchoring it in the ground so it would stay right where he planted it. "Go straight," he ordered as the flame's plume erupted. "Keep the light between you and the bot." Military logic dictated zigzagging, but the creature's IR scopes had trouble once bathed in the bright flare. "Just might block its vision." The radiance and heat, placed between bot and men, distorted any infrared scans. The troopers' IR suppressing gear helped as well.

As the flare's plume grew brighter, the two troopers scrambled up the levee. Fortunately, this side had thick groundcover, so between the brilliant burst of light and the spread of rambling bushes, the bot had difficulty making out any clear targets. Fed low-tech outdoing Marsco high-tech.

The pair was up and over silently, swiftly. In only seconds, they were back on the Brad-side of the levee, but the vehicles across the river remained unresponsive.

The troopers scampered along the riverside, then up again to the crown of the levee. When they looked over the top, the rear of their bot was twenty meters away.

Kyle raised two fingers. DeShawn handed him a pair of flares. In quick succession, the lieutenant launched them. The first bounded off, but the second stuck right below the back of the creature's head. The phosphorus-fed light blinded the machine's IR scopes. Its optics housing whirled. Its whole body staggered.

The troopers had no trouble aiming at the backside of the momentarily disoriented metallic creature. They each fired two RPGs. One misfired, but three hits pierced the thin back shielding. At least one grenade exploded in the very innards of the human-shaped torso, burning and blasting circuitry and whirling cogs. The machine stopped, still standing but a smoldering wreck.

"What was that?" Kyle whispered, listening to the sizzling and cracking of the burning bot knight.

"It sounds like an animal yowling." DeShawn whispered. "Something in the bushes caught up in our fire."

The horrific wail soon ended, but the stench of burning wiring and flesh lingered in the air.

In that instant, to their right, a set of flares and explosions lit up the darkness. Kyle's second team attacked the remaining pair of knights down the levee. But something was wrong. A single bot knight exploded like Kyle's just had, but then a burst of ray fire set off explosions that rocked the levee where his team must be. Cornered, that team had hit one bot, but the hounding unharmed warrior had slaughtered those attacking troopers, caught them with its ray. What flares and grenades the pair carried exploded in the weapon's heat.

DeShawn and Kyle still faced two menacing bots. The one that just torched two troopers down the way and one closing in on the crashed HFC. The knight looking for the lieutenant and the former medic stopped, waited for orders from its handler, then moved off away from the levee, striding to catch up to its partner nearing the HFC.

———— • ————

The damaged flight craft had hit hard, skidded in a clearing Shanghai fortunately found, and stopped before tossing the sappers around inside too roughly. All were shaken but safe, except the pilot, whose leg was pinned under the collapsed control panel of the flight deck. She knew she was bleeding, not heavily, but enough to make it impossible, if freed, to run to safety. She feared shock from loss of blood.

The threat monitor on the flight deck went to red. A bot was striding toward her. The downed craft had settled on a rise. The knight was below, leaving a tree line and crossing up the grassy incline straight up toward her.

"Out, get out, fan out," the sappers' commander ordered. "This way. We'll circle around," he shouted. Five troopers disappeared into the night, this handful was all that had escaped in the craft from the touch-and-go fighting on the trestle.

As Shanghai tried to free herself, she heard the troopers dashing out into the surrounding blackness. Heard orders for them to move off, hunt down that incoming bot before the squad became the hunted.

The sapper commander was back, looking in on the flight deck. "I'll come get you once we dust off our friend." He had no time to check the pilot's bleeding or free her leg. "Sit tight," he whispered, unintentionally logical. Shanghai was pinned in place, wounded, vulnerable. She heard more sounds in the darkness, mechanical thumping and the scampering of determined troopers.

Warily, the pilot felt down her thigh and found where she was bleeding. An exposed piece of metal under the flight deck had cut her above the knee, but it was like a blade across her muscle, only a slice, not a sword tip deep in her flesh. If she could lift up the console a bit, shift it just a fraction, she was free. But impossible to do from her position. The bleeding wasn't from the femoral artery—she'd have been dead by now if that—but muscle tissue. Her wound was painful, the spreading blood warm. And, she remained immovable.

Her com-link came alive. "Christ, two of these SOBs," someone shouted. "Where?"

"Check to the right. See it, another one in striding up. Fifty meters away." A gleaming movement in the trees showed the second approaching one's position.

"We're caught between the pair."

"Shit!"

"Hit the one closest to our HFC." Enfield fire and flares erupted, lighting up the darkness in the distance but to no effect. On strode the metallic beast closest to the trapped pilot, boldly heading where it was ordered.

***

Patrice found Shanghai as her squad reached the downed HFC. The nurse began tending the pilot as the recently arriving troopers slipped off into the dark to tangle with the first of the two stalking bots. "It's superficial," the medic reported calmly, aware speed was essentially for their safety.

Throwing her helmet off and using the surgical cap she wore to keep her hair up, Patrice pulled up the blade; the cap served as padding to keep her own hand safe from any slicing. Shanghai's leg was at once free. The nurse examined the wound. With quick, sure movements she stopped the bleeding with butterfly stitches, jerking her head now and again to keep her long hair off Shanghai's leg.

The wound closed, Patrice got Shanghai out of the flight deck and leaned her against the fuselage of the downed craft.

The whole time, weaponry flashed and exploded not thirty meters from the two women. They were momentarily safe, even with a firestorm so nearby. Then it pivoted.

The com-link was active again. "One's heading back to us."

"We need it to turn."

Patrice wrapped the wound with clean bandages to allow Shanghai to limp back toward her platoon's original position, back toward relative safety.

"They need our help, those troopers," the pilot insisted, refusing to leave a battle that raged, one now moving closer to them.

"What can *I* do?"

"We can distract it."

In the dark, the pair heard the knight stomp toward the HFC, on the move toward Patrice's lightly armed troopers. The massive humanoid figure was only fifteen meters away, its back to them. The metallic skin gave a sheen; it was easy to follow in the darkness even as it stepped between trees and behind clumps of low bushes.

The beast's ray weapon lit the ground to its right. Two troopers approaching the beast in the shadows were caught in the heat and burst into flames. Whether sappers from the HFC or members of Patrice's squad, the women didn't know.

"Damn, we have to do something," the pilot swore, trying to get to her feet, charging her 9 mm Enfield.

"If you move quickly like that, you risk opening your wound, bleeding to death." Patrice ordered her to stay where she was.

"Our troopers are dying." Another ray blast lit up a clump of shrubbery, but any troopers behind it were already gone.

The knight was no longer interested in the crashed hovercraft but started going back down the slight gradient away from the pilot and nurse. It was now twenty meters down the slope, one free of any trees or shrubs. Its back and shoulders were square to the pilot. It had found fresh targets and was closing in for the kill, hunting in tandem with the other oncoming bot.

Shanghai let fly a three-burst, then another, another until her weapon's clip was empty. Exploding shell after shell hit the metallic back of the humanoid monster, but the hits did nothing. The shells cut through body armor on a man. They cut a woman in half. Shanghai remembered the hotel lobby—torn up flesh and burning wood. She knew what a three-burst was capable of, but tonight her shells hit reinforced metal made to withstand just such a weapon.

The bot didn't bother to turn or respond to the gnat-like hits.

"Damn, you have a weapon, use it," the pilot shouted at her nurse.

Patrice did have a holster but had never fired an Enfield. Withdrawing the sidearm, she handed it to Shanghai. "Here, you use it."

The wounded woman now had two weapons, the first one reloaded, both charged. Patrice rose and stood to the side. The flier, leaning back awkwardly against her HFC, let fly a three-burst from her right weapon, and one from her left, back to her right. Again and again, the metallic creature was hit, but once more nothing really happened.

The bot raised its right arm, the housing of the ray weapon, and let another burst of energy fly at the troopers in the dark. All was confusion. For a moment, the night was lit by weaponry. After a moment, dark once more. Orders and catcalls came out of the obsidian gloom. Still these two giants moved at will, striding closer to each other, threatening troopers, nurse, pilot alike.

While Shanghai was reloading her pair of weapons, Patrice seized her chance. Shanghai saw clear determination, intensity in her eyes. This nurse was a free fed citizen. She wasn't living under the tyranny of her father or anyone who thought like him. Or Seattle. She and her husband were going to make a life here, a free life. It was a fed worth fighting for, dying for. Patrice knew it. Felt it.

In a few strides down the rise, Patrice stood at the back of machine that towered over her. She could smell the Enfield shells that smoldered on the undamaged metal of the creature.

She found a fist-sized rock at her feet and used it to pound on the creature. "Damn you, face me, you coward." Nothing happened. "You bastard! You piece of soulless, heartless metal, face me." She banged away on its metallic skin once more.

She seemed wild in the night, lit up by the smoldering of the Enfield shells and the fires started by the creature's ray. Her hair blew back in the wind. It was unmistakable that this was a young, unarmed woman trying to beat an alloy-clad monster until it listened to her.

The creature side-stepped and turned fully around. It now stood to the right of Patrice, but not far enough that Shanghai could risk another series of three-bursts.

But, the creature had enough of someone blasting its back. It began striding up toward the flier once more.

Patrice cut it off. She was quick and her speed brought her in front of the wounded pilot before the creature reached Shanghai, who still stood leaning against the downed craft.

The pilot yelled, "Get out of my way. Let me fire." But the nurse ignored her.

Waving her arms, the medic caught the creature's attention again, making it stop. A ray blast this close to the fuselage would incinerate the metal warrior as well as its targets. The creature stood motionless while its handler off somewhere in the distance—and safe from any hazard that night—analyzed his choices.

"You, soulless, heartless, tin man. YOU LEAVE HER ALONE. YOU LEAVE US—"

Patrice's voice was cut short as the creature's left metallic claw seized her by the throat. It took no effort at all to lift the nurse half a meter and shake her by the neck, its snap a loud crack.

"No!" Shanghai yelled, struggling to move so she had a clearer shot at the creature's head. "You murdered her!" The pilot shouted as she fired at the head. "Damn you, you bastard!" She fired again and again, her Enfield hits not impairing the beast.

At that instance, two grenades hit its back. Then a third. Patrice and Shanghai had distracted it so well, the troopers didn't need to fire any flares. The blasts ripped the back open in a way no Enfield sidearm could ever do, innards and circuitry instantly in flames.

———•———

Drone intel had informed Kyle what he faced. The downed HFC. A squad fanned out after reaching the hovercraft. A bot there. A band of sappers who'd been onboard the crashed HFC. The closest knight once again pivoting and drawing near Kyle and DeShawn as they followed behind. Alerted to the pair, this monster once more began hunting down the officer and medic.

Then in the blackness and silence of the night, Enfield fire, explosions, confusion.

The drone reported the bot nearest to the HFC was on fire.

But the remaining knight was bearing down on them, face-on, coming with killer intent.

———•———

The back panel of the mortally wounded knight near Shanghai blew open, the innards exposed. Internal guidance kept the standing beast upright, but something moved inside, screamed and struggled to get out of the fiery torso. Something alive was in there, something now on fire and squirming to get out of the metal beast, falling to the ground but bringing the flames of the innards with it.

On the ground, it writhed and tried to drop and roll to smother the fire it carried, but in seconds, it stopped, exhausted and then dead.

None of the troopers who approached knew it, but Arthur "Cutter" Wicks lay lifeless at their feet. At the front of the flaming remains of the tall robotic warrior, in its left claw, the body of Patrice still hung. No handler had remotely operated this creature. The feds had assumed that the monsters' operators were well away from the fighting and safe. Instead, each had a soldier inside, an Immortal, encased in Kevlar and steel for protection. Unbeknownst to the feds, each bot was an armored exoskeleton housing a human being.

———•———

Something distracted the last attacking bot as it came on toward Kyle and DeShawn. Its ray weapon was poised, but something from behind stopped it. A call? A signal? An order from the knight's hidden, distant handler? Kyle assumed that.

The massive, striding beast was nearly on top of the pair of hunting troopers. Abruptly, it stopped, turned, as if gazing off toward the downed HFC, as if wondering what was happening, confused, all too human-like. The creature exposed its undefended back to Kyle and DeShawn in that instant.

The pair had heard the explosions across the field, didn't know what was happening there, but knew they couldn't miss this shot. Both men fired two grenades each. All four hits rocked the soulless creature. It exploded. It staggered.

Like Wicks' exoskeleton, the back panel flew open. To the utter surprise of both attackers, the innards were full of movement, human movement. Some*thing*—some*one*—was struggling to dismount from within the fiery alloy body. Like Wicks, this form blossomed in flames, a petite form compared to the larger man.

A thought crossed Kyle's mind, but he didn't want to believe it.

Then the control helmet of the flaming, black-clad form flew off. Even in flickering light, she was unmistakable. And like Wicks, dead.

Mia Wang fell from the burning knight's torso to the feet of Kyle. He rolled her to put out the fire then knelt down to cradle her remains, but his classmate was already beyond him.

<hr />

In pain, Shanghai rose to limp over to the lifeless Patrice. The exoskeleton's arm still clasped her neck. In the gentle breeze and all the firelight, her blond hair glistened, as pretty as the day she wed. A young, brave woman, one small part of the cost of this fight.

"Oh, my God," the pilot cried, her tears and the smoldering warrior blinding her. "My God."

Troopers and then DeShawn were next to her. It took only a moment to get the nurse down and lay her in her husband's arms.

Somehow, this night's fighting had brought them all together, the quick and his dead beloved, the quick and his former lover.

THIRTY-THREE

COUP DE GRÂCE

(Sac City, early July 2155)

Days of respite from battle stretched into a week. Time for fed patrols in all directions to make sure Marsco was sitting tight. Seattle's Security made no attempt to cross the river again near the blown trestle. Four destroyed knights smoldering on the fed side of the levee seemed to be enough. Nearer the university, the same. Knocked-out bot hulls stood in mute testimony to the fierce fighting. Marsco pulled back over and beyond the river eastward, far from the campus, and waited. In the south, the same silence.

Raging fires slowly burned themselves out. Calm returned, but vigilance did not slacken. Colonel Devon Chavez-Sherman didn't trust this stalemate. Sac City was quiet, to be sure—no casualties in days—but Marsco was up to something.

Although he wanted to move his HQ forward to the campus, he kept his staff back from areas where fighting might break out at any moment. With Vanovara weapons, however, no place was really secure. Devon guarded himself against a false sense of serenity. Given the stakes, West Con thought Chesney had more fight left.

Lieutenant Kyle Truman Roncalli reported to HQ as the sun rose on the tenth day of the lull. The morning promised to be a sunny summer day.

"You're shivering," Devon noted. "Want coffee?" Between Kyle and Devon an easy relationship had always existed, even when the lieutenant slipped into military formality.

"Yes, on both accounts, sir," the officer replied. An orderly brought him coffee and a dry blanket. "I needed to swim back."

As Kyle sipped his coffee and adjusted the blanket, Devon tried to remember the callow cadet he'd asked to assist him with some deep-space observations. *Was that only a year ago? Who could have imagined this?* Kyle appeared aged, tempered by battle, death, loss.

"Floated over okay and dry," Kyle began his report. The lieutenant had been ordered to send a patrol across the river where he had helped bring down four bots. True to form, he led the mission himself. A dinghy, three troopers with him, cover of darkness. On the far shore, he went farther from the riverbank than planned. And by himself. His troopers followed his express orders and crossed back over to their own lines without him. "Swam it, sir, but stayed near the trestle pilings so if I did drift, I had something to grab."

"And you found?"

"Not much. Encamped Security, that's for sure. But no sign of any bots. No signs of any imminent movement." He sipped his coffee to hide his shivering. "They seemed settled in, not prepping for another sortie."

"Confirms all our drone data and com-intercepts." A worried looked crossed Devon's brow. "They're just sitting tight."

"That's good, isn't it, sir? Them hunkered down, not advancing?"

Devon handed the young officer a pad. Kyle read the dispatch on the screen aloud, "'Confirmation: Vanovaras in launch position, polar orbit.' Damn," he grunted. *Will this never end?*

"Now," the colonel asked, "why pull back and sit tight?"

"So as not to be collateral damage when that shit hits the fan." Kyle examined the dispatch again, hoping it was in error.

"Exactly."

"Damn," the lieutenant swore once more. "Just like last time." He, too, had read Miller's *Ascendancy*.

"Good morning, Lieutenant," Captain Grizotti said, entering with a meal tray. "The good colonel said you'll want this."

"My troopers fed?" he asked, his mouth filled with half a bacon sandwich.

"Yes. Same as you, exactly," the iceman replied.

"Zot's taken over for Mei-Ling," Devon explained. "I've ordered her out of the area, actually down to New Grange. Zot's running her there."

Kyle thought, *Wife and kid for a visit; do him a world of good.*

"How are your hovercraft skills, lieutenant?"

"As good as any with an Academy degree, sir."

"Well, with Mei-Ling out of action, and while Zot's away, you'll be here. Temp only, mind you. I need you back on the line." The colonel didn't bother to explain why he still needed tactical leaders in the field.

Kyle understood instinctively. The colonel's voice gave no possibility of *If I need you on the line* but only *When I need you*. It was coming down to this; guts might soon be the most important factor.

"Can you name your replacement?"

"DeShawn Cleveland would be the best, even though he's really a medic. But given the circumstances, I don't think he'd be the wisest choice."

"Yes, I read your report."

"Warrant Cairo would be next. She wants to return to her home sid—I mean, federation—when this is over. But, she's loyal. Smart. Any chance for some brass?"

"Sure. I'll bump her in rank to lieutenant." Devon made a note. "And, you, too. You're my ADC now, *Captain* Roncalli. Rank's permanent. The duties aren't."

"I'll just get cleaned up then, sir."

Devon held him back so that the pair might talk, almost father to son. "I also read in your report about the operators of two of those bots, Wicks and Wang. Any ID on the others?"

"We couldn't identify the remains, sir, too badly burned. But, I probably knew them. You, too, from your times at the Academy. Chesney picked officers loyal to him. Many from my class or around it. I am sure we both know most of the Immortals we faced here."

Knew, Devon wanted to correct. The bot knights had been cornered and knocked out around the world with ruthless dispatch. "It surprised everyone that they were actually manned."

"Caught us all off guard when burning bodies began—" The young officer could say no more. Failure of their own intelligence ops, both officers realized.

"And we now know the price they paid for their longevity, loyalty to Chesney."

That they both already knew. The new captain just nodded.

"You knew Wang well." Kyle nodded. Devon added. "I taught her just one term."

Kyle hesitated. With Trent's death, Devon might one day become something like a father-in-law to him; the older man was that close to Sarah. He caught himself. That was a dream now, no longer a possibility. "Frankly," he began, "well, yes. We—Mia and I—dated, seriously dated but before Immortality entered. But we were drifting apart well before then. Had drifted apart. Of course, I'm what they call an Accordist or a federalist now. She decided on Chesney. That sealed it."

"And, you were the one who—"

"DeShawn and I both let fly at her bot, sir. I have to think of it that way. We both fired."

———•———

Two hours later, dry and dressed in a clean uniform with captain's badges, Kyle reported to Devon.

"First, sir, Captain Grizotti reports all are safe down at New Grange."

Devon looked at the message. They'd arrived okay and found everyone fine.

At least Sarah was safe, Kyle realized, even if she might never speak to him again. He'd failed to save her father and brother. *That* ended it for them, he reminded himself.

"And this," the ADC went on. "We picked it up from the head of lunar Security, Katsura George Kiyomori. It's broadcast worldwide but on a Marsco Security channel. Our Intel are convinced Marsco's got it and understands it."

Devon read, "'46.852. -121.760.'" The colonel drew a breath.

Kyle explained, "These are coordinates for Mount Rainier. This peak's significance to Marsco, if any, escapes our intel at the moment. And why Kay-Gee would want Seattle to know that? Know it ahead?" The captain asked then bitched, "Hell, why do anything like this at all?"

"Shows Marsco that Resnik now controls those weapons and is willing to use them. They want this over with Seattle. And it's clear they now have the muscle to do it, force an end."

———•———

Messages continued from the lunar colony.

Kiyomori repeated this one for another twenty-four hours, every hour on the hour, regular as clockwork. Set to Seattle time. No mistaking whom it was for.

And soon Kiyomori sent a different message, declaring that all the lunar colonies—Indie and Marsco—now considered themselves to be four new feds. They asked to join the UIF, the Union of Independent Federations. Like many Earth-side feds, these colonists weren't waiting for the final three Accords to take effect.

The message ended with a cryptic: "'46.852. -121.760. Wednesday next, 2359 hours, Marsco Standard Time." In five days. "Chesney step down!"

"But why are they so heavy-handed with those V-weapons?" Devon asked.

———— • ————

Those at New Grange received a different message altogether. Anyone with a communication device even remotely connected to federalist activities received it.

Tessa got hers from Doctor Claire Ross, the physician who tended her on Mars. The doctor was leaving the Moon, on her way to Seattle. Shanghai got hers from pilots she'd met. Even Sarah received it, shared to her from other students she knew from her online classes. An open web of interconnectedness was reemerging in the world as Marsco receded.

Zot felt he must return right away with a new crisis brewing.

As Tessa held him, he whispered, "I don't want you to risk it. They're asking too much." They'd talked most of the night about Tessa's cryptic message from Claire. Tessa had responded with no hesitation. Shanghai, healing leg and limp, was in. Sarah, too.

"Walter will be here. Celine and Roxanne will watch him."

Zot laughed. "If Devon has his way, we might be in Seattle, too." The *we* was West Con Security.

"Then, I'll be waiting for you there. But our way works better than Resnik's."

Both ways, theirs and the lunar fed's, were fraught with danger. But Chesney had to go.

After Zot left New Grange, Tessa received a follow-up from Claire, "All need to be there soon, before everything starts popping."

Chesney had yet to respond.

⸻ ◦ ⸻

Tessa, Shanghai, and Sarah stood in the kitchen garden outside the great room. The Moon was a waning crescent, but even in partial light, the Vanovaras orbiting were clearly visible. Those in Sac City hadn't seen this sight yet because of the battle fires, but New Grange had been watching nightly. At first confused over who controlled the orbiting weapons, it was now clear that Resnik did. Even so, their use was totally unacceptable. This had to end another way. A better way than using Marsco's own weapons against Seattle to force a capitulation.

The tight formation of reflected lights like a dozen satellites or a phalanx of unarmed space shuttles passed early in the evening. Then again nearer to midnight.

To the pilot and the engineer, long associated with Marsco, the lights were unmistakable. When Sarah had first seen them a week ago, the granger dismissed them as high-flying landers or HFCs in formation. The trained eyes of the two other women taught her the difference.

The former associates worked out the details of trajectory and delivery. The weapons passed in a higher orbit than V-weapons of the Continental Wars. Tessa groused, "They seem to be launched from orbit without a weapon platform to guide them." She paused, sounding too much the cynical Zot, "'That's one small step—.'" She ended her imitation with a sigh.

"A phenomenal scientific advancement indeed," Sarah added, a rare snide remark from the granger.

"We can't let them be used," Tessa declared. "Not now. Not so near the end."

Old Man Tillson joined them. They'd seen his rover coming down from his spread but thought nothing of it. "I heard you were all going."

Sarah laughed. "No secrets among thieves or grangers."

"Got the same message," he explained. "One son's up and volunteered to our fed, so he's under orders and can't go. The other's going. He'll meet me there."

"I thought this was just for women?" Shanghai asked.

"It's for feds who want Marsco out. *All* feds," Tillson returned. "How you going?"

"We're working on it."

"I have a way, but I get a seat."

The three women looked at the neighboring granger, one always filled with surprises. "Those pongos your man left here, Sarah—" the young granger began to blush, "—they have an HFC that'll get us all to Seattle. You two—" he pointed to the two officers, "—you go down in your uniforms, brass polished, all bars and attitude, you can just *borrow* it. I'm sure Kyle won't mind."

Tessa, always the one to negotiate any Marsco dealings the best, thanked him. She still had her Academy uniform. To a fed guarding that HFC, she'd look legit, impressive, some mucky-muck with her pilot. Shanghai with her Fed Security uniform and captain's rank to escort her, they'd make an imposing sight.

"Always bluff your strength," the Old Man shared tactics with a wink. "But, I mean it. I'm going, too."

So it began. From Sac City. Portland. Silicon. Even neighboring feds that got the message. In groups small and large, just one and two at times, sometimes dozens, they started moving north, west, south. All heading to one spot.

The determined crowd wanted Chesney out. This war over. But not the way Resnik wanted. They were forcing both belligerents' hands, Seattle's and Resnik's.

———— ◦ ————

The next night, Devon and Zot were able to see the Marsco-created weaponry clearly for the first time. Sensors had tracked them, but as the smoke above Sac City dispersed, the pair stood and watched.

"I count twelve," Zot said drily, wishing he were wrong.

"That's what my report stated." Devon acknowledged then asked, "And we're clear Resnik's controlling them, not Seattle, right?"

"Affirmative," Zot answered and mumbled, "'Hoisted on their own petard.'"

———— ◦ ————

Early Wednesday evening Zot reported to Devon, "Southern hemisphere stations report the separation of one unit."

"Will we see it?"

"Takes an orbit to align the ordnance. All our calculations are for it to hit exactly on time."

At 2042 hours, the skies were dark enough to see the dozen Vanovaras moving across the heavens, south to north, a pack of eleven with one stray still with them but no longer part of a tight formation. That separate one was coming down.

At 2357, in the darkest part of the night, the remaining eleven weapons drifted by, still in their tight formation, visible in their high orbit well above the atmosphere.

The stray weapon took three minutes to catch up. It had drifted downward, been caught by gravity, burning in the lower atmosphere. As it came, it filled the Sac City sky with dazzling light, a long tail.

The head was more brilliant than any mere flare used to distract bot knights. It brightened the sky as golden as the sun's first light, but its flyover was quick, here and gone. It was so dazzling it was impossible to miss. Sonic booms trailed in its wake.

Only those alive in the '90s remembered the sight. Then, Marsco Security had decimated Luddite strongholds; the total number of weapon placement sites went uncounted, but rumor held the total at a hundred. Today, only one.

No one alive, except the few crewmembers of the *Sirius Odyssey II*, had seen such weaponry as a daily, nightly event, stretching on for months at the end of the C-Wars. Zot had witnessed them as a boy back in the Chicago subsidiary nearly a century before. When he watched near the Hex that night, he knew the streak was not hitting nearby, but he knew what it could do at ground zero.

Hell of a thing to know. He shook his head.

Down it streaked, its vivid tail lengthening, its head growing brighter. This descent was planned as a demonstration, so its trajectory was flatter to burn off most of its mass, the tail longer, so millions could witness it crossing the night sky. As it streaked by, heading almost perfectly due north, it created sonic boom after boom in its wake. The trumpet blast at the end of the world.

Devon had his com-link open. Fed forces were near the planned target area; he wanted to know the moment there was a strike.

Seattle would know. Every fed would. *Is it back to this?* He was born after their last use, but he'd heard enough stories of them growing up.

Zot had arranged to watch the peak via monitors, so Devon and his staff gathered around a screen and waited. In the background, professional voices counted down the seconds, clarified that the trajectory was accurate.

"On time, on target," came a report.

"Thirty seconds."

"Fifteen"

"Ten, nine, eight…"

Was Marsco watching as well? Devon wondered. The fed officer could only hope.

"Six, five…"

Zot prayed for Tessa, now in Seattle. And for Sarah, who was like his kid sister. And Shanghai, whom he'd trusted with his life more than once over the years.

The monitor flared with the bright blast as the diminishing asteroid head went home, on target 0.35 seconds early.

A flash on the monitor—they were picking up no sound—then a rising mushroom cloud visible to IR cameras. This weapon, a V-2 of old, was a solid, honed metal shard. It pinpoint-landed where the lunar colony—now a federation—wanted it. Close enough to Seattle to make an impression, far enough away from everyone to be harmless. This time. The blast left the Rainier peak smoldering.

Is it back to this?

Tillson had been a young Auxxie back in the '90s when he saw these falling last time, hitting a Luddite bastion in the Amazon. He shuddered at the thought.

Tessa was a girl on Mars during the C-Wars so hadn't seen anything like this. Shanghai, then Mei-Ling Chen, remembered them. But those gathering, those standing at the Marsco Academy and Marsco Institute of Technology campuses, felt only a slight tremor. They saw the blinding flash in the distance and an eruption of clouds, the blast 95 kilometers to the south.

But the gathering crowd felt it innately. Knew its import. Many held mobiles, so the crowd knew the news instantly.

After that first blast in the distance, the growing crowd moved toward the center of campus. It grew all night. Women, men. Shanghai wore her fed uniform. Dressed as an Indie—Tessa thought it best to change out of her Marsco uniform—the engineer might be mistaken for a granger. Sarah was hesitant but as committed. When she saw a rare trooper, she hoped it was Kyle come to join them. Old and young. Three generations. Another trio represented four; the youngest stood with her belly swelling with new life, showing the way fearlessly.

They moved amid all the buildings of the Academy and MIT. Intrepid. Sids and PRIMS—but now fed citizens. Associates, both active and discharged, men and women. They came to be here at this gathering as well. No stopping them.

The aftershock of this isolated hit reinforced their commitment. If the feds wanted Chesney, this burgeoning crowd's way was the best way. The only way, really. Not with rocks slamming into the planet. He must come out. Surrender and face trial.

They moved in unison. Their single objective allowed them to grow in strength.

And still silence from the Bunker.

———•———

Not long after the first hit, the eleven remaining Vanovaras drifted overhead during the still-dark hours before dawn. The absent twelfth one was a reminder to Marsco of this weapon's power. And its placement was a warning of the intention to release the more of the same, dead on target.

Even before the dust settled on Mount Rainier, Kiyomori sent another message. "'47.653. -122.291.' Friday, 1200 hours."

Zot figured out the coordinates. Devon glanced at the iceman's calculations.

Many in the gathering crowd figured it out. Associates, MAS pilots, women and men who had been to the Moon, Mars, the asteroids, anyone who knew celestial navigation figured it out. Those who could pilot a lander worldwide knew. This was *terra firma*. Earth. Their home. Yet still they stayed.

Ground zero in less than thirty-six hours, at a locale just beyond the campus. None of the witnesses knew that was where Chesney's secret Bunker sat.

"Get me eyes on Seattle 24/7," the PM ordered Devon. It was time for civilian control of the situation. When this ended, rule of law was going to prevail, not chaos or military control. "And get me Resnik. Who the hell's controlling those damn weapons?"

Zot was standing transfixed at the monitor that was showing the replay of Mount Rainier. The streak. The hit. The flash.

"Tessa's there," he whispered. "She's in Seattle."

"Zot," Devon tried getting his attention for the impatient PM. "ZOT! Get mobile medical teams ready and on standby. One of those things hits Seattle, we'll have a crisis on our hands."

"Of course, sir."

"We'll need a security corridor around the blast zone. The PM wants personnel in the wings to take command of Seattle after it hits. And get Kyle up there. I want a team ready to get into Chesney's Bunker."

Zot looked up. "Sarah's there, too. And Mei-Ling."

Damn, Devon thought, *when did unarmed women change places with us, the trained men and women prepared to go into harm's way?*

Harm's way or not, they gathered. Women mostly, but men, too. And some with their children. They brought dogs and blankets. Food to share. Some had tents. They came, seemingly endlessly. They filled the quads of the former state university, now Marsco's Academy. Then overflowed onto the Marsco Institute of Technology quads. Then the restored parklands and dry dunes over Chesney's hidden Bunker.

Drones kept them under surveillance. West Con's, not Marsco's. Resnik inserted a geosynchronous orbital platform that watched, they had that much tech. No one on Earth had imagined their skills, not Marsco, not West Con.

And with each pass of the remaining V-weapons, each report, a larger and larger crowd. A swelling crowd.

The first estimates, 50,000 when the single V-weapon hit Rainier. By the time Devon had the eyes on them, more than 150,000. It soon swelled to 250,000.

And still they came. From the East Coast. Japan sent hundreds, landers bringing women mostly, some men, their children. Africa was represented. London, Old Mexico City, Rome, Moscow. No fed wanted to be left out. No one who yearned to be free wanted to be left out. On they came. Rio, Sidney, Istanbul.

They gathered, greeted each other, then waited patiently to be witnesses. They were stand-ins for the millions who couldn't come. The hundreds of millions worldwide who wanted federations and peace and a modest livelihood for their families.

Devon's people estimated more than 400,000 before noon on that Thursday. By nightfall that number more than doubled.

Other drones broadcast the sight worldwide. Just as Lightwind's tirade had gone out, imploring everyone to hate, calling everyone flock to the Hex for blood and vengeance—a call ignored by all but a few—these pictures were a resounding call for more witnesses. More gathered here to take part in a peaceful vigil as testament to this way, this better way, to end Marsco. No place on Earth, the Moon, Mars, the asteroid belt missed these images.

Columbus and Lightwind had broadcast their call out of revenge and blood-lust. No one listened or came. These witnesses stood resolute; more and more flocked to them.

Chesney didn't acknowledge the first V-hit.

He didn't acknowledge the hundreds of thousands standing outside his isolated fortress.

But the chair, Mr. Oakes, made a statement from Marsco HQ a few kilometers away from the Academy. All forces under his command in the Seattle cantonment were to cooperate with West Con authorities. "Direct traffic and make sure they have water." Miraculously, portable johns appeared. Supplies of meals and diapers for the youngest in the group.

Oakes had started out his long Marsco career in supply distribution. He understood the needs of personnel.

And still, it was Chesney who wouldn't respond to that first V-hit, or acknowledge the crowd surrounding him, or relinquish power.

That night, Thursday leading to Friday, as it grew dark, the V-weapons crossed the sky, still a tight formation of eleven glimmering objects. Any cloud-free locale on their north/south axis showed them, a phalanx of honed asteroids. No one doubted that those who had ordered them to Earth knew what they were doing, intended to use them. Scientific observation confirmed that these were as well-made as Marsco's best from eighty-five years ago.

Devon's staff estimated almost two million people were swelling Seattle by midnight.

And still they came.

And still they stood, unarmed, undeterred, forcefully demanding the rule of law.

The stream of landers from the two feds of old China was nearly continuous. Taiwan came. The Philippine Fed. Europe, Asia, Africa, the Americas. None of the newly created worldwide federations wanted to miss this call for peacefully ending Chesney and his Marsco.

On the ground, because Tessa and Shanghai were essentially from an earlier century, they knew few who gathered. But Sarah was surprised how many online classmates she recognized. She knew others from granger meetings her father had organized.

But the crowd hadn't gathered to socialize.

Tessa, Shanghai, and Sarah, among the first in Seattle, reached the restored wetlands that acted as innocuous cover for Chesney's malicious lair. The three stood atop the small rise and looked back at the massive, burgeoning crowd.

In their excitement, none of the witnesses noticed uplinks and obvious signs of many buried bunkers throughout what was allegedly a restored wildlife area. None knew Chesney was ensconced only meters below their feet. He remained silent even though he had to know he was ground zero. Resnik was making that clear.

———————●————————

Seattle could take no more witnesses. So, along the restored lakeside in Chicago, supporters of those in Seattle stood. Outside Sac City's Hex, more stood.

They wanted the world to know. Marsco to know. Chesney and his Immortals to know. They wanted a better world. They were standing with the Seattle witnesses in spirit.

Japan stopped sending landers, but her parks soon overflowed as witnesses gathered in Tokyo and Hiroshima and Nagasaki.

Paris, the same. London. New York. St. Peter's Square. Even Red Square. Tiananmen Square. Tahrir Square. Where in other historic epochs innocent blood was shed, now peacefully, witnesses for a better way stood. All of them with ground zero in spirit. All these crowds grew in size.

Everywhere gatherings grew. Even in small towns and on granges. The citizens of every fed worldwide wanted Marsco ended in this peaceful way, not by a rain of fire.

———————●————————

As noon approached on that Friday, Celine and Roxanne, La'Shay and Hyacinth stood in the kitchen garden at New Grange. Shadow joined them. Young Walter was asleep in Celine's arms. Hy offered to hold him. She whispered to the sleeping infant, "Your mom's coming back. And your dad."

And my own daughter, Celine prayed, angry Sarah went off like this but proud she went off like this. *So like her father.*

"Kyle's coming back, too. Devon'll make sure of that," Roxanne assured them.

It would be over soon. The time was approaching. It was the least they could do, to stand and pray.

———————●————————

"'They also serve who stand and wait,'" Sarah whispered as noon approached.

"Milton?" Tessa whispered back.

"What was that?" Shanghai asked.

"An old poem. Seems appropriate. 'They also serve who stand and wait.'"

———————◦◦◦———————

Once more, a few in the Seattle gathering knew, from handhelds and mobiles, from messages sent by family and friends, from direct reading of federation transmissions.

"On time and on target."

This better way waited silent now and still at ground zero, everyone looking skyward, Seattle possibly drawing its final collective breath.

London, Chicago, Moscow, Beijing—over a million each—all waited. But, only Seattle was ground zero. The world watched Seattle. *Ground zero* was never a more ominous term.

———————◦◦◦———————

"Dammit, Resnik, you can't do this," the PM implored the lunar colony over a clear channel. "Two million civilians are standing there in your target area. You're not even sure Chesney *is* under them?"

"Eight minutes," a professional voice noted from a console. The operator wished she were with them, even as they faced this.

"Will they see this one?" an aide to the PM asked Zot. She knew of his connection to Marsco from last century.

"It's coming in steeper and straighter down at this target than Rainier," the iceman tried to report without choking up. "She'll see it."

She? his interrogator wanted to ask.

Tessa would be right there, Zot knew. She knew the campus. Knew navigation. Knew how to translate those numbers.

"What's 'the point of no return' here?" Devon asked. Again, Zot the logical choice to query.

"During the last minute before hitting, it'll be too late to change its course significantly."

With five minutes to go, Devon ordered a four-minute countdown.

———————◦◦◦———————

Between them, Tessa and Shanghai figured out the same calculations— Marsco training. The trajectory must turn away during the next three minutes, or it would be too late.

Old Man Tillson had found his youngest son. They stood together without speaking, as men do. He reached out to include Sarah, placing his young neighbor between the two solid men. "It'll be fine, lass," he assured her. "We'll shelter you." He'd seen a V-weapon take off the top of a mountain in Brazil when he was a young-buck Auxxie. He hoped his lie wouldn't be discovered in the next few moments.

Waiting Seattle drew its breath.

Worldwide, the kindred witnesses drew their breath.

At the Hex, the civil authorities who would have to deal with the aftermath of this catastrophic political blunder, drew their breath.

"Two minutes to PNR," Someone reported at Devon's HQ. Zot smirked, *Point of no return, as though a shuttle leaving the belt.* "Touchdown in three."

Zot had programed his screen to give him updates at five-second intervals. He had a red line aiming for Chesney and a countless throng of innocent witnesses, then a black line of actual descent. Black covering red. The two lines were one after the latest five-second change of screen. Then a gap seemed to appear.

It took another five-second upgrade before he felt sure. Then another.

"Changing trajectory."

"Was it enough?" Devon demanded. *Damn, Shanghai'd have this figured out.*

"Look, a dragon, mommy," a child perched high on his dad's shoulders shouted with glee, pointing skyward. As told in his favorite book, a point of light emerged in the perfectly clear, blue sky, a fiery dragon descending. The boy giggled. The adults on the Academy lawn so near ground zero watched in horror.

It would end soon.

Tessa's engineering mind wanted to know the exactness of this. An algebraic thought crossed her mind. *The math, the science, to get this rock all this way from the Moon and hit us exactly.* The human mind could do so much with knowledge. Unfortunately, even propel a shard through space and hit a target precisely. She caught herself and silenced that part of her mind. She thought only of Zot and both young and old Walter.

Shanghai knew that since it was falling, plus being pulled by gravity, it soon would be uncontrollable. By then, it was too late.

As adults counted the final seconds, the giddy boy chattered to his mom and dad, "Isn't it a pretty dragon? I've seen my dragon."

The dragon grew larger, brighter even against a sunlit sky, casting shadows. Even in the noon sun, the silent gatherers saw it looming like a mythical Angel of Death come to announce the end of the world.

———————◆———————

Thirty seconds of readings were enough for Zot to yelp. "*It's altering course! Turn, you bastard, keep turning!*"

Streams of data on three other monitors confirmed his declaration.

Devon leaned in at the flat screen. Two lines—the plot of what the feds expected to happen, the plot of what was actually happening—diverged. Separated.

"Where will it hit?"

———————◆———————

"We shouldn't see a tail," Shanghai noted to Tessa, the pilot's own skills as analytical as the engineer's.

"Only see it if it's turning because of axial differential and trajectory variance—"

But the streaking dragon, looming larger as it approached the ground, didn't give them time. High above, safely above, the tempest of fire and molten metal flattened its trajectory, giving a lightshow in the noon sunshine no witness would ever forget. But, only for two seconds, its speed was that tremendous, and then the colossal dragon flung itself past Seattle and over and out toward the northwestern horizon.

"Where's my dragon going?" the boy shouted, crying not because he was scared, but because his winged fire-breather was gone that quickly. His father had a mobile and enough space travel experience, like Tessa and Shanghai, to do the math.

"Gulf of Alaska. Harmless," he shouted. "Harmless!" he let out again.

Only then did the dragon thunder, its speed outrunning its sound. Boom, boom, it blasted innocuously.

A final sonic boom shook the campus, then silence returned. And, after the creature had streaked away, a chant began. "Harmless. Alaska. Harmless. Alaska. Harmless."

The circling drones beheld celebration and relief.

———— o ————

"Where?" Devon barked.

"Over Victoria, but at thirty-thousand meters."

"And it'll hit—"

"Gulf of Alaska. Almost due west of Sitka. In thirty-five seconds."

Devon sat down. Exhausted. He felt like he'd been on his feet for months. But when the prime minster called, he stood at attention. "Yes, sir. At once."

Finishing with the call from the Hex, the colonel ordered Zot, "Tell Kyle to land on top of that Bunker. Have him locate and arrest Chesney."

THIRTY-FOUR

RETURN TO NEW GRANGE

(New Grange, November 2155)

The weeks slipped by after the final demonstration in Seattle. After the final earth-bound V-weapon streaked over the millions waiting there and those watching around the world, hitting ocean waters clear of any land. After Chesney's Bunker was breached, Kyle leading the way.

At New Grange, the passing time meant another harvest. Much smaller than usual, given the past spring and summer, but work kept minds occupied so sorrow didn't overwhelm everyone. The small flower garden near the kitchen once more blossomed with vibrant, late-season colors. Bees came a final time and filled the quiet air with their promising hum. The laden apple trees were picked; all the surrounding granges were in the midst of chores. The dead were buried, the wounded recovering, refugees returning to their homes. The federation was stable and thriving, but a steep price had been paid here.

Months passed, and New Grange felt its losses.

"You miss Kyle," Tessa stated to Sarah with concern as the pair watched Walter.

"Of course." Trent, her father, gone. Chase, her brother, as well. Patrice, her best friend. Grieving them was difficult enough, but with Kyle, for Kyle, his absence from her life was harder to accept or ever understand. Four months. Four silent months.

As was her way, Sarah deflected any further questions. "You must miss Zot."

"Yes, but he'll have leave soon."

Captain Grizotti remained on Chavez-Sherman's staff, supervising the demobilization of Marsco forces still in West Con territory. They even assisted in other feds. Getting Auxiliary units transported to their newly independent federations was generally straightforward. Auxxies usually came from a single locale even if stationed worldwide. Security battalions were trickier with their mixed-up personnel; individual legionnaires and centurions needed to find a permanent place to call home after years of service.

As the former world power dissolved itself into the background of international politics—a process spelled out in the Six Accords, all now fully in force—tens of thousands of associates of all stripes moved near and far, to join federations they intended to make their own.

But, the transition was going smoothly.

Even the smallest aspects of change grew visible. Tessa had her left finger disks surgically removed months ago. After those fingers healed, she had her right hand done as well. With no implants, she slipped on fitted gloves holding all the disk-power she needed. Computer networks ran solely with ops gloves. Even voice command came back. The need for tight Marsco control over networks vanished. No one held up a hand to show off their disks, thus their importance in the Marsco world. Or their imprisonment by it.

What remained of Marsco itself ran a space transport enterprise, landers and shuttles. It controlled no earthly locales. It held no colonies in the solar system. Its Twelve Thrusters' Policy was no longer enforced. Nothing in Seattle proper was exclusively Marsco's, not in the old sense. Its headquarters, which coordinated its space fleet, worked out of a leased office building.

Sarah confided to Tessa, cooing with Walter as an aunt might, "Celine loves that you're living here."

"I know," Tessa replied. "But just until our grange is ready." With all the rebuilding, that might be a few years yet.

Shanghai joined the three. The dedication coming up at the Hex, the first of many commemorations, neared. Everyone connected to the Brunels was gathering here first. Mei-Ling was now family; they had Devon to thank for that. Weeks ago, Celine had whispered to Sarah that she'd not seen her cousin so happy since he'd periodically visited with Cyndi Maricourt, years and years ago.

Sarah turned to the pilot, once more blocking out any questions addressed to her. "And you're in lunar service, right?"

"Yes," the pilot answered. Like Tessa's, her right-only finger disks had been removed. "I'm part the UIF oversight delegation witnessing the destruction of the scores of Vanovaras that Marsco had marshaled there." She paused then added, "And the Resnik fed thought it needed to use against Seattle."

"Must be exciting," the granger stated, her blue eyes wide but not with their usual eagerness. Both former associates saw the lingering dejection in the young woman's drawn looks. She put up a brave face, but she still missed her father and brother, as troubling as his choices had been. And Kyle.

The older women sensed it, having both faced this kind of loss, Sarah's sorrow made worse by not knowing the whole story, not hearing any word, not fully knowing why, not being able to bring closure to such a yawning, open wound.

The flier continued, "I command lunar-based landers a great deal, moving personnel up to the Vanovara fields. Crews cut these weapons down to shard size for surface placement. We're salvaging the comet nuclei for fuel, of course."

Sarah understood some of the pilot's lingo and tasks but felt too listless to ask for any clarification.

"Science," Mei-Ling added, "can have a good side and a bad. Can do wonderful things, can be abused." She went on without sounding defensive. "I wasn't abusing it, not by utilizing bio-tech that regrew my diseased spleen." She needn't list any obvious abuses.

<hr />

Later that week, Hyacinth, Sarah, and Celine attended the dedication of Trent's cenotaph in the recently laid out memorial park near the Hexagon. Trent's remains were in the family plot at New Grange, but his life was being honored by a monument in Sac City memorializing the sacrifices paid by so many. Countless lives had been lost to free the Western Constitutional Federation from Marsco domination. The monument sought to make sure none of her citizens ever forgot that. Like the man himself, the granite monument was simple, with a plain tribute: "'The mind once enlightened cannot again become dark.' Thomas Paine."

For all her grief, Sarah couldn't have been any prouder. For the ceremonies, she wore a simply cut navy blue wool dress with a scarf in the fed's blue and red. Her hair was pulled up to give her a sophisticated look, an older look, in keeping with the solemnity of the event. Even so, she turned heads. Hyacinth was almost her former self, as elegant as Sarah but in a subdued sienna. Neither woman basked in the attention; their losses remained that tender.

"He'd have liked that quote," Devon said to his cousin, who stood at his side. Zot came with him. Many of the main figures of those times were here in fact or in spirit. Those in the West Con forces—Devon, Zot, Mei-Ling; those lost in the fighting; those who went to Seattle to stand silently as witnesses.

Kyle was especially missed.

After the award ceremony where Devon, Shanghai, and Zot received their medals, Sarah walked alone amid the graves and gardens. It was a brisk autumn afternoon; the best everyone could hope for, given the time of year. In the far corner of the old park, the ground was outlined where the field hospital had once stood. A temporary sign listed each medical team that assisted with the living and the dying. In time, the sign would be replaced by a permanent brass plaque. Sarah found Patrice's name there. A surge of pride and then grief coursed through the granger. Her neighbor had stood firm and paid the ultimate price.

Other markers explained which fed units had fought in those final battles. A prospectus of the memorial gardens gave a rendering of what the park would look like when finished. A printout provided the names of those who'd died. One day, all those names would be carved in a marble wall along the park's southern edge. Patrice was on that list as well.

As Sarah read through the names, she remembered many of them, some refugees at New Grange and others she had known growing up. It had been a tremendous conflict. Tens of thousands had died. Hundreds of thousands were connected to the dead, the wounded, the recuperating, the missing. Like her, many survivors still saw their faces, heard their screams. Like her, still loved someone who hadn't come back. Peace resided now, but her own inner peace would be a long time in coming.

Drying her eyes, Sarah turned to rejoin her group when she saw her mother embracing an elderly man whose back was to her. Approaching the pair, the gentleman turned around. Even though much older, he had a look like Kyle's in his demeanor and the sparkle in his hazel eyes.

Coming toward the pair from the opposite direction, Tessa shrieked. "Aaron, oh my God, Aaron Truman!" She ran to embrace him, Walter on her hip.

It took Aaron a moment to work everything out mentally. Tessa looked only few years older than when he'd last seen her, but that was nearly sixty years ago. He was then approaching twenty. She looked wonderful, lively, and as lovely as he remembered when both he and his brother, Jeremy, had boyhood crushes on the womanly associate. All those years ago at Walter Miller's grange.

Tessa ushered Sarah forward to meet Aaron. "This is Kyle's grandfather. Retired now on Madagascar."

"Well, on the Serengeti," he corrected. He shook the young granger's hand.

Same strong grip, she noted. *Same look in the eye.*

It had been years since Aaron had worn his uniform, but he was proud of his service. He felt no shame in displaying a sign of Marsco's former days. "I worked mostly with food and medical distribution," he explained. "After the PRIM Mutiny, never served in *that* part of Marsco again." Sorting out the history of Marsco would take several generations. Nothing is ever totally black and white in an accurate history which examines with nuance and subtly.

"Shame Kyle's not here," Tessa said.

"I thought the same," Aaron whispered, choked up. But he quickly beamed. "So, Miss Sarah Brunel, I've heard of you."

"Me? I don't know how." She blushed.

"Well, our Kyle of course, whenever he'd call me. He did as often as he could. Nearly every week up until the real fighting. He certainly didn't describe you as this pretty, though. He liked your eyes and iron-willed spirit. He'd met you then went into space with that colonel cousin of yours—"

"Devon Chavez-Sherman," she said softly.

"That's the one. Got a medal today."

"Yes."

"Remarkable times that first summer with you," Aaron went on. "Kyle visited my father's grange, his great-grandfather's, where I grew up."

"Tillson's spread."

"Yes, with you. And visited my brother's grave where it had been moved up the rise."

Sarah nodded. One of the many times she'd not given Kyle a chance.

"Of course, that time wasn't anything like this past winter and spring." His eyes teared a bit.

Their uneasiness was broken when Celine finally asked her daughter, "Did you find Patrice's name?"

"Yes, hers will be on two sets of plaques." Sarah couldn't get out a clear explanation that it was for her hospital work and for the battle. Her friend had been so brave. "A temporary display explains where." She pointed off toward the incomplete park restoration.

"Hyacinth wants to see her sister's name."

"Should I show her?"

"No, dear, stay here with Mr. Truman."

Their self-conscious silence returned until Aaron spoke up delicately. "He was silent a good deal, our Kyle, but then he'd be chatty all of a sudden. Had no father or mother—" Sarah tried to remember, had he explained that he grew up with his grandparents? "And I did my best, you see, so we talked a good bit when we talked with each other. Talked all about you and your Shadow that first visit. Damnedest time figuring out Shadow was your dog."

Sarah brightened but grew morose at the same time. "Shadow loved him."

"We all loved him. He loved you, too, Miss Sarah, believe me."

"I do. I didn't know really how much until, well, not hearing from him after all this fighting and after our silent witnessing up in Seattle. At the Bunker. Then knowing he'd gone down into it." She held back renewed tears.

"Yes, I've heard."

"And he loved those he led," she added. "I mean, I realize now, he'd have done anything to protect his people."

"Sign of a great leader."

Sarah realized painfully once more that she hadn't give him a chance at first. And then later. And now she would never be given that chance again.

"Look, Miss Sarah, let him have time," Kyle's grandfather confided softly to her. "That's all I can say as an old trooper." Sarah understood where Kyle's surprising gentleness came from, underneath his tough exterior. "Look, you see things in the field, a trooper does. You must do things that you can't explain to just anyone. And sometimes it's, well, it's just that for those of *you*—you others *not* part of it all—it just takes time from *you* to understand *us*. And listening, just listening."

Sarah wanted to say, *He's not even giving me that chance*, but couldn't find the courage to admit it. She'd pushed him out of her life; she was responsible for that.

Devon came up. Sarah introduced her cousin to Mr. Truman. "Congratulations, colonel." The long-ago trooper snapped a smart salute.

"Many deserved this, not just me."

"Our Kyle spoke of you, too, Colonel. Spoke highly of you. He'd have followed you to hell, sir, our Kyle."

"He went wherever I ordered him," Devon replied.

"Comes from a long line of troopers, that boy. Only one at the Academy. My career was sidetracked with the Great Mutiny. Got his brains somewhere else, but his guts were Truman."

"I haven't seen the Assembly hall yet," Sarah suggested, hoping she didn't seem rude.

"If it's not too painful," Devon said.

Aaron understood the significance of this visit and assured them he'd see them again afterward.

The cousins slowly made their way around to the front of the Hexagon. They walked amid rows of evenly laid-out graves set down between plots of flowers. The memorial committee wanted to preserve both aspects of these grounds, the original historic gardens here for centuries and the recent graves of those who made the current federation possible.

"He's almost done," Devon finally revealed to her.

"But he should have sent some word, any word."

"I know. That, that I can't explain."

"Will he be changed?"

"We're all changed."

Sarah sighed, "Yes, I guess so. All of us."

◆

The Hex still wore signs of the battle. Its marble on the south side was clean, the scaffolding having just come down. Inside, the Assembly chambers were open for tours, but many scars remained, silent reminders of the standoff here.

"Have you been inside since?" Sarah asked.

"No, as you saw, our ceremony this morning was in an adjacent auditorium." Like Zot's and Mei-Ling's, Devon's chest sparkled with his new medal. "Until now, I hadn't actually been inside here since the fighting."

"Too painful?"

"I don't think so, but it might be tough on you."

The young woman was reluctant to answer, knowing she had to face this scene sooner or later.

Dignitaries at the front of the chambers listened while a docent explained the takeover and how the night Columbus's ill-conceived rebellion ended, the night the real war started. His voice had already taken on the impassioned saccharine tone of someone retelling ancient history, someone thinking he needed to add superfluous drama to embellish an already harrowing tale. Mid-sentence, he looked up, did a double take, checked his palm unit's screen.

"Well, bless my soul, ladies and gentlemen, it is, am I not right, Colonel Chavez-Sherman?"

"Yes, sir," the officer replied, downplaying his significance.

With that, the group had their digitals out, clicking and flashing, stepping closer, angling to include Sarah as well as Devon's medals in the shots and selfies.

A bit surprised at all the fuss, Devon calmly stated, "If you give me fifteen minutes alone," he reached for Sarah's hand to let her know *alone* meant *with her only*, "I'll gladly speak with you all then."

Turning to her, without a preamble, Devon began about that night. "Trent burst in before Kyle was totally prepared to act. And Richardson was here, inside, already."

"Yes, and I know what he'd just done down at his spread, although I'll never fully understand why," Sarah whispered.

"Kyle entered right after your father. He wanted to safeguard your brother and offer Trent some protection." He paused. "Without authorization. He knew he didn't have time for direct orders."

Sarah gave a slight laugh. "He always said, 'Easier to ask for forgiveness than permission.'" She hesitated then added, "And I understand now that he was trying to save them."

Devon walked her down the aisle describing that night. "Trent here. Kyle beside him. Columbus over there, aiming at Chase. That Richardson off there in the shadows." Behind that spot, the wall was still under repairs. Its damage gave Sarah an inkling of what an Enfield did. "Richardson fired first," Devon went on. His voice fell, his mind saturated by the full realization of what it meant to describe to Sarah how her father died at the hands of his own neighbor. A madman to be sure but a neighbor nonetheless.

Devon pointed, "That's your father's desk. Chase was there."

"I think I understand. Was it sudden?" Sarah was finally able to ask.

"Yes, this all happened in a matter of seconds. No one that night, not Kyle, not his troopers rushing in—none had an easy decision. Then it was all over in a blink."

"He tried to save *his* life," she admitted. "Certainly, in hitting Columbus."

"Yes, then Kyle got Chase stabilized and out to a med tent, but—"

"I know. Patrice got word to us. He died there."

"Kyle had a nano to make a decision. Quick, all so quick. I've witnessed what an Enfield can do; your father, your brother, neither really stood a chance."

"Yes." Searching for anything to break this conversation, Sarah pointed after taking a few steps amid the rows of desks and finding the one she was looking for. "So, this was my dad's."

Devon nodded. He would have been here only for one plenary meeting and a few of the early sessions before Columbus and Lightwind's actions forced the Assembly to meet in a nearby hotel. But this had been his.

Sarah tapped the oak lightly with her knuckle.

The cleanup crew had replaced the leather chair, bloody with Chase's carnage, and removed any stains from the desktop.

Sarah sat down, moved the chair forward to a working position, and imagined her father here. She felt his arms go around her, felt Chase holding her as well.

"He was a good man, a courageous man," Devon added. "Kyle did his best to save them both." The colonel drew a labored breath. "And afterwards in the real fighting, Sarah, I asked him to do so much above and beyond. He's a fine officer. A true leader. I needed him to attack those bot knights, almost with nothing."

"That's when Patrice died." Sarah paused, then ventured, "And the Bunker, up in Seattle?"

"We trusted no one more."

"And after that?"

"Yes," Devon answered but added nothing else.

"Still can't understand his silence."

"Nor can I," the officer admitted. "His no-com status was lifted months ago."

In the deepening quiet between them, Sarah saw the small crowd off to the side waiting patiently for Devon. "You promised to speak with all of them, remember."

Retaking her father's seat, Sarah watched Devon field questions about that night and the ensuing battles around Sac City. She was proud of her cousin, knowing he acted without malice, knowing he did the best he could under circumstances wildly beyond his control. Kyle would hold no spite toward the man; nor would she.

And she was as proud of these chambers as any citizen of West Con could be. *I can sit here*, she assured herself. *I will sit here one day.* She was young, but she knew she'd be back to take a rightful seat here in the not-so-distant future, take the same oath to serve the Western Constitutional Federation that her father had. Listen, understand, speak when it was appropriate, be a leader.

⎯⎯⎯ • ⎯⎯⎯

Over the next few weeks, the Marsco trials began. Oakes, for all his help near the end, still had to answer to his complicity in letting Chesney gain that much power.

Scores of Immortals survived as well. All were prosecuted.

At their trial, it came out that the immortality Doctor Johns had promised wasn't a sure bet medically. The world was not facing convicting criminals who would live for five centuries. Natural aging would set in, albeit somewhat delayed, but by only a few years tops, not centuries. The Marsco Sustainability Project that so many officers had embraced, accepted, killed for, and died for, ended up being illusionary.

And still no word from Kyle, who had been detailed to escort Marsco's most notorious and loyal followers to their tribunals.

—————•—————

Those ongoing, sensational trials and Kyle's continued silence cast the Christmas Eve celebration at New Grange in somber light.

But Celine wanted Walter's first Christmas to be special. Wanted New Grange celebrating again, a not so subtle hint she wanted some grandkids of her own to help lift the gloom.

Wearing a forced smile but with renewed energy, Sarah set up the long table in the great room. Logs were laid out in the stone hearth for a fire later, after the table was moved aside. A decorated tree dominated one corner. Everyone connected to New Grange was coming.

Roxanne thought turkey best this season. Celine was far from arguing, as long as a roast was served as well, Trent's desired menu each winter holiday.

On one score, Sarah put her foot down. For all intents and purposes, New Grange was hers now, and she wanted a new tradition. "No servants' table in the kitchen," she told both her mother and Roxanne. "We'll all eat here, every last one of us, *here* at the long table."

"But, we'll be crowded," Celine objected, counting sixteen total, with all the *Sirius* folks, Tillson and a son, and Hyacinth.

"I'll have to jump up," Roxanne stated.

Sarah squelched such talk with a determined look she'd discovered when she galvanized New Grange into a welcoming and well-organized refugee camp. A firmness she discovered when she stood atop that mound above the Bunker. When she wasn't sure if she was going to be incinerated or not, but knew she was right. Same now. "We need to add more to the table, that's all. We're all feds now." Their bickering ended. All New Grange was eating together.

—————•—————

In the Brunel great room on a dark and fog-shrouded Christmas Eve, Zot dodged suggestions that he go back to space *without* Tessa and Walter.

Although Devon and the iceman were still in the midst of demobilizing Marsco forces, the end was in sight. And, West Con was seriously speaking with other feds about launching the *AAC II* but through an international science consortium. To be sure, the world was rebuilding after the years of neglect under Marsco, but science needed to be fostered as well. As he would have been with Marsco in charge, Devon was commander of the research team with Shanghai on the flight crew.

"Oh, c'mon, Zot" the pilot teased. "You'll only be away *six* years." Devon nudged her to egg on the iceman. The colonel sat with his arm over the top of her chair. Celine saw. Sarah saw. They exchanged delighted glances.

Zot was taking all their kidding seriously. "Look, away six years? *Six? Away?* It's just that, that—I can't, I can't—"

"Oh, c'mon, you're an iceman. Do what hibermen have always done, make stuff up, improvise, and muddle along," Shanghai baited and smiled.

"You're a natural for the *Armstrong-Aldrin-Collins II* maiden voyage." Devon pointed like they were back in the command center, "I want *you* on board operating her cryo bay."

Tessa knew they were teasing. But Zot had a way of sometimes missing the obvious, getting sucked in. That only encouraged her. "Yes," she needled, straining to keep a straight face, "away six years, I'm down with that, dear. Honestly." Her husband could tease with the best of them, but it was with pronounced delight that she strung him along for a change. Fair play. And then she also ribbed Mei-Ling. "Six years. Coming back with twins or triplets?"

As Zot grew more serious while the others feigned heightened interest in his counterarguments, "Look, Mei-Ling, your piloting skills are for a spaceship initially designed by Herriff's team over seventy-five years ago."

"I'm not that old," Mei-Ling protested. "Besides, I'm going as a navigator."

"No, I meant the *Sirius II*—"

"Careful," Tessa joined in, not missing a second chance to have a go at her rarely-gullible husband. "I helped design that ship, and I'm not that old, either."

With Tessa ganging up on him, the light went on. "None of you are serious, are you?" The table went silent, staring him down, laboring to hold in their collective laughter.

Sarah loved the man like a brother, yet even she couldn't resist one last jab, "No shit, Sherlock."

The table erupted. Chuckling at himself, Zot leaned over to Sarah— she was sitting between him and Devon—and planted a fraternal kiss on her cheek.

The table roared once more, almost like old times. But, Sarah was taken up short. She blushed. "My God," she let out before she could stop herself, "the last man who kissed me was Kyle."

Her comment dampened the mirth of the table. No one knew how to respond, which made her feel even more uneasy. "No, no," she waved her hand, "I'm fine. I'll be fine." She wanted to jump up, wanted to bolt from the room, but knew that would make everyone feel worse.

Sipping wine, she tried thinking of something to say, when Shadow was at her feet whimpering. "What is it, boy?" she asked looking down at his penetrating eyes under the table.

"He knows something," Roxanne pointed out. "Never knowed that dog *not* to know something's up."

The lab tugged at his owner, insistent. "What, boy, what?"

When Sarah finally stood up, the dog shot to the door, jumping at it, trying to get outside. But with an unusual, frantic edge. He knew something or someone was prowling.

"Should we go check this out?" Zot gave Devon a serious look. Still vigilant, their holsters hung from pegs beside that door. They did periodically encounter armed legionnaires and centurions roaming about aimlessly.

"No, you two stay here. I'm fine," Sarah insisted with Shadow not stopping his agitated prance at the door. Coat on and flashlight in hand, she fled outside.

Roxanne understood. "Let her go. Shadow wouldn't lead her to no harm."

As is often the case in late December, the night was foggy and close. Shadow, as black as his name, was nearly impossible to see. And the flashlight hardly cut the thick tulle fog.

"Where are you, boy?" Sarah heard him bark in the distance. She knew her way; his bark was partly along the trail toward her family's cemetery.

———•———

Tessa would have none of this. "Zot, you go, or I'm going." She motioned to Devon, too. "You two don't know who's out there." Mei-Ling added that she'd go with Tessa if the men wouldn't.

The engineer's goading forced the officers to gather their coats and strap on their holsters.

Once outside, they charged both Enfields for the first time since the fighting against Marsco had ended.

They could make out Sarah's flashlight beam partly along the rising trail. They followed without hesitation.

———•———

Shadow had run way ahead of Sarah but came back excitedly, urging her not to quit. The rise wasn't steep, but it was slippery with mud. The dog was agitated like a puppy, jumping and whimpering to hasten her on. Sarah instinctively knew to fear nothing. Fear no one.

The officers weren't far behind, but when Sarah approached the graves—some old and a few new—they picked up their pace. In the closed-in misty gloom, they weren't sure, but it appeared that someone was sitting on a bench just inside the fence.

They watched Shadow go up to the seated figure and back to Sarah, once, twice, as the young woman, still outside the cemetery, stood looking from the open gate. The officers were also sure the figure sitting there all alone was a man.

Zot held Devon back. Unseen, they heard Sarah whispered, "Kyle?"

The figure looked around, suspicious of the sound. Shadow acknowledged him, barking wildly once more.

As the figure looked directly toward her, Sarah now shouted, "Kyle!" He didn't answer but rose.

"Kyle, where have you been? Why haven't you come home?" She was walking slowly toward him, fearful he'd evaporate into the obscuring mist, fearful this apparition wasn't him at all but her own tears and imagination playing tricks.

He stood stationary as she stepped closer. He made no move to greet her or to slip away.

Devon and Zot turned and moved down the hill silently. This wasn't a scene they needed witness, but they smiled at each other. "Maybe he's shaken off his demons," the iceman whispered.

"We can only hope."

Sarah stood as near as she dared. Shadow made being closer impossible as he planted his thirty kilos between them, begging to be petted, licking Kyle's free hand.

Kyle's other hand touched her face. "Your hand's cold," Sarah whispered.

Her own hand went to his face. "Yours is warm," he replied softly. Neither knew what to do: shake, embrace, kiss. They stood there ill at ease for a moment, for too long a moment.

"Why?" Sarah began, not pleading, but reassuring him she'd accept any answer, "why didn't you contact me? Why didn't you come back? Are you okay?" She was instantly infuriated with Devon. "Were you wounded and my cousin didn't tell me?"

"No, nothing like that." He smiled his old smile. He was thinner, but he still had that instant grin. "Devon insisted I say something to let you know, but I wasn't ready—"

"Not ready to send a message telling me that you were alive?"

Kyle ignored her remark and kept going on, "and I was busy guarding them—Oakes, Rhores, and Roberts. Other Immortals who survived and surrendered."

"What? Some cousin! He knew! Half the time I thought you were dead," she shrieked out, but the thick fog muffled her voice. "The other half, I thought you no longer cared."

"No, not dead in that sense. Just needed time."

Sarah felt every emotion: pissed off at both Kyle and Devon, relief, resentment, eagerness to hear more, frustration. And cold. She shivered. He put his arm around her; she slid into his grasp. They sat down on the graveyard bench together in a clumsy embrace.

In a moment, he asked, "Is that your father's?" He pointed to the closest headstone, the largest and newest, wet with the fog and only dimly outlined, too dark to read.

"Yes." Sarah shined her flashlight toward the recently erected monument.

"I tried, but I couldn't save him, Sarah." Kyle's voice sounded funny, it hitched, a tone Sarah had never heard before. "And is that Chase next to him?"

"Yes."

"That's why you despise me so, right? Because I couldn't save him, them." He curled and twisted away from her. "I tried. I did try."

"I don't despise you, Kyle," she whispered, shocked he felt that way. *Well, I gave him a plenty of threats that I would.* "I'll never hate you." In all honesty, she knew she should have added *again*, but refrained.

Forcing himself to speak, he went on, "And the other new ones?"

"Nate and his sisters. Dot Richardson didn't want them on her land. Mom took them in."

"You Brunels have a way of taking in people." He then added drily, his only attempt at anything funny, "Richardsons were always trying to get some piece New Grange land."

Caught off guard, Sarah laughed lightly. "Well, in a way, I guess they finally did."

"Is *he* here?" They both knew who *he* was.

"No. He's somewhere else. Dot wanted an unmarked grave. Somewhere," she waved vaguely, off toward the gray vapors in the distance.

"Damn," Kyle muttered, but Sarah was having trouble understanding his voice. He'd slumped forward, his head down to his knees, his chest heaving. "Damn, Goddamn," he kept saying and heaving. He took in a labored breath, his voice not clear. "I killed him, Sarah, that night. My Enfield practically cut him in half."

More heaving and labored breathing, his head down. Sarah realized as he sat bent over toward his knees that he was crying silently, deeply, like men cry, with chest-shuddering sobs.

She leaned herself over his back and they rocked to his heaving, a minute, two minutes—how many, it was impossible to tell. "I couldn't save your father. Your brother." He stopped to catch his breath and then heaved again, but still bent double, not at all trying to look at her directly or talk distinctly. "I know you despise me for all that." He went into another silent round of deep sobs. "And did I ever tell you of Mia?"

"No, Kyle, but it's okay." *Another lover? With* her *now? Maybe she could, maybe she would understand him?* This Mia couldn't love him more than Sarah did, but maybe as a trooper she understood him better. Maybe that's what Grandfather Truman was trying to tell her last month at the dedications. Well, if so, Sarah knew, she would let him go, if it was best for him. She'd let him go. The granger loved him so, but if this Mia could support him now, comfort him more, so be it. "You don't need to tell me anything, explain anyone—"

"No, Sarah, you need to hear."

"Okay, Ky, tell me. Do you love her, your Mia?"

And so, it all came out, between his sobs and gasps. The Academy. Their immature love, tender at first, but not like how he loved her, *Sarah*, now. Kyle made sure he told her that over and over. He repeated that as clearly as he could, given his tears and downturned head. Three times, four, he repeated, "Not like you, Sarah, not like I love you now."

Then, he explained everything else in such a rush, so quickly and muddled, that it confused Sarah. Chesney and the black disks and bot knights at a trestle.

Most of his cascade of words Sarah didn't understand at all, but she listened to his streaming. Holding him, just listening. Rocking as he sobbed, laying her head onto his left shoulder.

"And that night," he rambled on, his head close to his knees. He was talking to his feet more than to her. Awkwardly, he held both her hands near his knees, tears and dribble covering them. "Dark like tonight," he started in once more, "but no fog, warmer. That's when I lost most of my troopers on that trestle. One we should have blown weeks before those bots used it. Damn," he paused, "damn, all told, that night, twenty good troopers and then some, down in half an hour, then it was just DeShawn and me, and he was married to Patrice, did you know that?"

Sarah's head pressing into his slumping shoulder answered. He felt her movement and knew she understood, knew she was listening to his incoherence. But, he had to continue now that he'd started.

"And then we hit that last bot knight the way troopers should, hit it in the back with rocket grenades, knocked it silly with four—dammit, *four*—

and we didn't know before then that they were manned." He stopped to repeat so it was clear, "Actually *manned*, an operator inside. Alive until our RPGs slammed into it. Although we'd heard all that screaming earlier, we didn't know what that was, never suspected that the bot's guts were living flesh, and then abruptly she fell out on fire and dying. Mia dead at my feet."

Sarah didn't understand it all, but she caught enough of the pieces to have a clearer picture. Mia was dead; he blamed himself for that, too.

The granger's hands were in his tight grip, wet with tears as he stumbled along. She understood so little of what he explained next—tactics and flares and RPGs from the backside—but that didn't matter. He was here. She listened and let him ramble and get it all out. Her love for him kept her listening and rocking with him. She would love him no matter what. He was home and he was going to know she loved him so.

"Then DeShawn," he went on slowly, distinctly, "found her hanging from that metallic claw. Just hanging. Dead."

That Sarah knew. The body was Patrice's, who now lay not far from their bench.

Then he was ordered up to Seattle to take that Bunker. At first, she could follow his explanation, but soon she didn't understand that a 9 mm Enfield shell—an unexplored shell—needed so many meters to charge. And that at close range, it really was like an old-style solid metal bullet. And what that solid shell does to the brain. "I was the one," he explained, "I was the one who discovered Chesney, the back of his head gone, the Enfield still in his hand, slumped over at his desk, his brains splattered on his office wall behind. And so many others in that Bunker dead or cowering, pleading for mercy. Liddle dead. Roberts whimpering. Rhores all bloody, unsuccessful at killing himself."

Sarah continued to lean on him to show she understood even if she didn't fully.

"I told Devon, 'I need a break.'" He sighed after a long silence, "and he'd have let me have it, except the PM ordered *him* to order *me* to guard them all."

"Could you have said no?"

Kyle stopped and reflected a moment. "You know, I'm not sure. I just went as ordered. Did as ordered."

"Your grandfather said you would."

"I'm an officer, Sarah. A captain now." He stated with pride then returned to his history, "An Arctic camp in old Canada, well away from everyone. Was there until just three weeks ago." His sobbing had ceased and he was calmer now, clearer, explaining that he guarded the prisoners, ensuring it was impossible for anyone to get at them. He made perfect sense. "The UIF and our PM feared another Columbus lurked out there, someone wanting blood for blood. Some unstable demagogue who'd try to restart the whole mess by getting at those prisoners. A lynching or worse."

"Yes, I understand."

"A trial by law, that's what they're getting. No one stood against a wall and shot and strung up by their heels."

"By law," she repeated.

"Yes, law. That's what we fought for."

"And these last weeks?"

"Sarah, I just needed some silence."

"I thought you were dead and that Devon was afraid to tell me." Rage and disgust toward her cousin rose in her once more but then her increasing devotion for Kyle stopped her outburst. "Does your grandfather know you're here now, safe here now?"

"Why do you ask?"

"I met him last month at the Hex. Then he spent a few days with Mr. Tillson. I thought your granddad knew you were already dead but wasn't letting on." Hastily she added, "He's a dear. He loves you so. And I love him. And you, too." Sarah blushed, her own words racing out almost as fast as Kyle's had earlier.

"I'll speak to him tonight. Almost dawn there. If I can use someone's com-link at New Grange. Mine's gone dead."

"Of course." Sarah was afraid this might scare him off, yet she whispered, "They're all there tonight, Kyle. It's Christmas Eve. We're all there, teasing Zot."

"That's okay about the others. I don't mind. I'm better now. Good to see them all." He sat up and leaned his head against hers. "I'm done with my tears, promise." He paused, then asked, "Is young Walter there?"

"Of course."

"Is it okay if I don't have a present for him?"

"He's not yet a year old. He'll forgive you." She paused, "And Devon's there."

"I thought so. Has he proposed to Mei-Ling yet?"

"How did you know that?"

"You ever seen him look at her? And her him?"

She smiled. "I left them all down in the great room."

As if just now realizing they were sitting the damp and cold, he asked, "Fire roaring?"

"No, not yet, because we have the long table set up."

"If I come down, and after I talk to my Grandfather, Sarah, will you sit with me by the fire?" He caught himself, "*When* I come down."

"Of course."

"But, I don't have a place to stay if Devon and Mei-Ling—" He paused. "And I need a shower."

"I have room. You're staying with me," Sarah stated firmly. No discussion.

It was the first time Kyle had heard her newfound determination, but he wasn't fighting it. It suited her, them. "Promise?"

"Promise."

"I'm done running. I'm done crying. I had to cry over this. Over Mia." He looked deeply into Sarah's blue eyes. In the dark they looked black, almost like Mia's. "I wanted you to know. It meant something once but not like us." He kissed her hands. "Man, wet." He withdrew a blue bandana and dried her hands, talking the whole time but sensibly, coming back to himself. "We were kids, really. We met as cadets, and we had broken up. I shouldn't have had to—who knew a former girlfriend—and it was pitch black like this."

"No one's blaming you."

He drew a breath. "Fog of war. But, it was over long before that night."

Now Sarah was holding back her tears. "I know."

"And I'm not going to Mars, either. I thought of that. Running away there. But, you'd not go with me, would you?"

"I'll go anywhere you want me to, Kyle. I'll go to Mars with you, yes. You know that, right? If I knew you were going into that Bunker, I'd have followed you. I was right there."

"I know. I saw you in the chaos when our hovercraft came down on top of Chesney."

She reached up to pull his face close, and they kissed, a salty, teary kiss.

"But, Mars," he whispered at last, her hands still holding his head close to hers, "I don't want to go there anymore. I want to stay here with you. Is that okay?" He paused, grew serious. "I'm *not* marrying New Grange. I'm marrying *you*."

"Yes, that's fine. That what I expected. That's what we both want, isn't it?"

"Yes, more than anything." He paused. "And dinner. Soldiers travel on their stomach."

"So, are we now engaged?" asked the practical granger's daughter. She wondered if they were to shake on it like selling cattle.

"I think so. I hope so. *Yes, we are!* But who asked who?"

"Does it matter?"

"No, actually, it doesn't."

She kissed him once more. "Oh, my God, I love you, Kyle."

Rising, Sarah took Kyle by the hand to bring him home. Shadow danced at their feet, his excitement reflecting their own. The evening sky stayed a blanket of thick, starless cover, but they felt a slight breezing stirring.

The morning just might be a bright dawn; they felt it coming, that bright dawn. A fresh wind would drive off this clinging ground fog.

They stepped down the trail toward the main house, visible as yellow light smudged by the obscuring mist. But warmth awaited them in there. And fellowship, the camaraderie of those who'd faced danger together and had come through it all. Scarred but surviving. Wounded but healing.

Sarah had purged Kyle of his tears. He no longer felt any need for them or rambling on or mulling over the past. He only felt the need to love her, to have her in his life totally. And when those foreboding memories came back, if they came back some nightmarish time, she would be there with him to hold off their terrors. From now on, they'd face everything together.

The pair entered the welcoming light of the great room, to be greeted by affection and kindness, a place—as with every other place around the Earth and throughout the solar system—a place no longer ensnared and buffeted by Marsco.

The Six Accords Notes

Fifty-Year Timeline

The **Six Accords:** an agreement between Marsco and the subsidiaries that outlined how Marsco would withdraw peacefully and completely from its position of world dominance. At first, these negotiations were without PRIM representation.

The Accords consisted of six steps (thus Six Accords) to be taken over a twenty-year period so that each step could be fully implemented and evaluated before the next was undertaken.

Marsco felt it tantamount to avoid violence and to avoid creating a power vacuum that would allow in other dominating and illegitimate ruling parties.

2108: The start of Six Accords negotiations. Marsco began these negotiations, partly in reaction to the Great PRIM Mutiny of 2101–2104. At the table were Marsco and representatives from leading subsidiaries. Not all subsidiaries were seated at the initial talks, nor were any PRIM representatives. At first, only one topic was under consideration, more freedom for select subsidiaries. Over time, the discussions broadened into the six major changes in Marsco's rule.

2109: The arrest of Mandela Transkie-man, the nonviolent PRIM leader who had rallied PRIMS worldwide for a say in the single Accord talks. Cofounder of the PRIM Freedom Movement, the PFM. He was given a seven-year prison sentence.

2110: Fifteen months after Transkie-man's arrest was the arrest of Javâher Panditji, the other cofounder of PFM. He was also given a seven-year prison sentence, in early 2111.

2116: Transkie-man was released from prison.

2118: Javâher Panditji was released from prison. At this time, Marsco granted PFM legitimate status. Sids agreed to have PRIMS at the table of the Accord talks. It would still be twenty-three more years before the settlement of this three-way agreement.

2124-25: Sporatic PRIM violence in NoAm and Euro areas mainly. Locally intense. Mostly confined to metropolitan riots with occasional attacks in more remote areas. Some granges near Sac City burned out. New Grange spared but well aware of the danger. Not as devastating as either the Great PRIM Mutiny or the 2139-41 rebellion to follow. At this time, these talks grew into a discussion of the Six Accords.

2135: As Transkie-man and Panditji aged and became too ill to continue, Gwanda Bulawayo joined the negotiations as one of the PRIM representatives.

2139–2141: The last PRIM rebellion raged, nearly as serious and as widespread as the Great PRIM Mutiny. Many in Marsco were angered that the PRIMS had rebelled while the Six Accords were under negotiations.

2140: The election of Barston Oakes as chair and Raymond Jon Chesney as vice-chair of the Marsco Board of Directors. They are considered by many around the table as liberal-minded associates who back the Accords. Also, at this time, a cease-fire brokered by the PFM begins. This PRIM rebellion had been intensifying during recent years. The cease-fire allowed for the signing of the Six Accords. Even as the Accords were being negotiated, Chesney restarted the Marsco Sustainability Project.

2141: After thirty-three years of protracted talks, the Six Accords are agreed to, ratified, and signed. Delays in settlement were caused principally by the bottlenecks stemming from allowing PRIMS at the table, expanding the talks to include all Six Accords, and deciding what to do with PRIMS and the Unincorporated Zones, where most PRIMS had been forced to relocate and live. The Union of Independent Federations (UIF) was formed. Based on the US Bill of Rights and the UN Charter for Human Rights, the UIF Charter allowed each subsidiary to develop any one of several democratic models for internal governance. Parliamentary rule with a prime minister became the most popular form. A bicameral legislature with a separately elected president became the second most.

2145: The First Accord was the Marsco Power Sharing Accord. Marsco was to begin sharing power with subsidiaries, now newly created and free federations, so that they became truly sovereign for the first time since the end of the Continental Wars in 2070. All federations were listed under the UIF Charter; each was given equal status to Marsco. This Accord set the stage for free and democratic elections in each fed. For the time being, federation assemblies were made up of Marsco-appointed officials. Many federations chafed at this. Although none of the original federations were in space, lunar and Martian colonies immediately began seeking to be recognized as federations as well.

2149: The Second Accord was the Subsidiary Parity Accord. This Accord ended PRIM status as Unincorporated Zones were taken over by federations; consequently, PRIMS essentially ceased to exist. The distinction of PRIM status legally disappeared. Marsco backed away from control of subsidiaries even more as Auxiliary Forces fell under direct control of their respective federations. Federations began taking control of elements of Marsco's Security forces as well. Stoplines ended where feasible.

2153: The Third Accord was the Finger Mouse and Finger Disk Accord. This accord virtually ended the distinction between finger mouse and finger disk technology and capacity. It allowed anyone the use of a computer by dropping the last prohibitions against computer use by PRIMS. The monopoly of the Net and computers use by those with implanted disks ended. An associate could elect to have and/or keep implants, but the necessity of them was totally removed. Computers were to run equally as well with finger mouse thimbles as with finger disk implants. The accord also ended the Marsco monopoly on computer networking. Mobile technology and communications reemerged.

2157: The Fourth Accord was the Internal Security Abatement Accord. This accord was to end Internal Security's control over the use and content of the Net. Anyone would be free to post whatever they wished, except for pornography (broadly defined) and sexual predator material or any links to illegal drugs and weapons sales. With the assistance of Internal Security, the UIF was to ensure no former PRIMS were bought or sold via the Net. All transfers of Security forces to federation control were to be finalized at this time, thus completely ending any Marsco Security operations.

2161: The Fifth Accord was the Consortium and Free Enterprise Accord. With the Fifth Accord, Marsco was to relinquish control of the Food Consortium, the Transportation Consortium (Earth-side), and all similar business ventures under its control. The UIF dollar, modeled on the MMU, was to become the standard monetary unit worldwide under the control of an independent central bank. The UIF would begin supervising world trade policies, while internal trade programs would be left up to each individual federation. Additionally, with this Accord, Marsco's "Twelve Thrusters Policy" would cease; this effectively gave any federation space agency permission to enter space however it felt. Marsco was to retain only its space-based businesses and colonies.

2165: The Sixth Accord was The New Marsco Accord. With this Accord, Marsco would cease to be a world power and would devote itself entirely to space travel, space exploration, and solar system colony development. More important, with this last Accord, the UIF agreed never to pursue Marsco for "damages" or "criminal retribution," essentially freeing Marsco associates from prosecution for any past acts under any new federation laws. The single exception was for associates who delay, interfere with, or ignore the implementation of the Six Accords as they became law.

Abbreviated Glossary for The Marsco Sustainability Project

A complete glossary of the whole Marsco world
found at the end of both

The Marsco Dissident and *Marsco Triumphant.*

Accords or **The Accords** or **The Six Accords**: See **The Six Accords Appendix**.

Black disk: The Third Accord, the Finger Mouse and Finger Disk Accord (2153), essentially ended Marsco's control of computers via finger disks. Black disks are illegal, left-hand implants that allow selected associates to manage secret and separate Marsco systems in order to maintain the level of computer control and surveillance that Marsco enjoyed before the Accords.

Black knights: See **robotic warriors**. Generally, the term *black knights* refers both to the officers in charge of the robotic warriors and to the robots themselves.

Bot or bots: See **robotic warriors**.

Fed: 1) Abbreviation for **federation**. 2) A citizen of a federation.

Federation: Independent nations created by the Accords. With the signing of the First Accord in 2145, 158 federations were recognized.

Great PRIM Mutiny: Devastating, worldwide PRIM rebellion spanning several years, roughly from 2101 until 2104. Exact dates vary. Some historians give the dates as 2100 to 2104. Note: the troubles around Walter Miller's grange in 2097 clearly happened *before* this rebellion.

Immortals: Marsco officers who have gone through sustainability treatments and thus have artificially lengthened their lifespans. They are committed to Chesney and preserving Marsco as it was before the Accords.

Immortal battalions: Those Marsco Security Battalions led by Immortal Officers. They are the only battalions to have robotic warriors under the direct command of Immortals. No one else in these battalions has had sustainability treatments.

The last PRIM rebellion, 2139–2141: worldwide PRIM rebellion that started, in part, because of the impasses at the Accords negotiation table. The **PFM** disavows itself from this violence and calls for peaceful negotiations to resume. This insurrection nearly as severe or widespread as **The Great PRIM Mutiny**.

PRIM Freedom Movement, the **PFM:** Founded by Mandela Transkieman and Javâher Panditji, this organization worked for PRIM rights. At first unrecognized by Marsco, the PFM eventually gained seats at the Accords negotiation table to represent PRIM concerns.

Ray weaponry: The right arm of each robotic warrior has a heat ray weapon of immense power.

Regeneration: Medical treatment that allows a patient to regrow diseased or otherwise unhealthy tissue through a recombinant DNA process using the patient's own DNA.

Robotic warriors, also **robotic knights:** Robots that stand 2.5 meters. These are the main weapon of the Marsco forces trying to retain control even as the Accords are surrendering Marsco's authority. Human-shaped, they appear to be controlled by remote handlers using communications housed in the head of the robot. The left arm has a claw. The right arm is a ray weapon. The metallic skin of these warriors is black; also, it takes a black disk to operate them, hence **black knights**.

Rocket-propelled grenade (RPG): Shoulder-fired rocket launcher from the late-twentieth century. The weapon is utilized by federation forces because feds had no time to redevelop armor and artillery. It is the heaviest weapon fed troopers carry.

Sustainability: Euphemism for a series of medical procedures that enables the body to sustain itself indefinitely. In theory, someone who has gone through sustainability may live five hundred years. Reserved only for associates loyal to Chesney.

Union of Independent Federations (UIF): International body formed with the signing of the Accords, based loosely on the United Nations but with stronger and clearer governing power.